# 編者的話

親愛的讀者：

　　今天，我的好朋友，兩岸達人，鍾藏政董事長，傳來好消息，我在「抖音」的粉絲，已經超過10萬人，並且在急速成長中。我是一個很會把握機會的人，一個月前，北京「101名師工廠」董事長Alex邀請我時，立即無條件答應，能夠一次上課有百萬人聽到，能夠把自己的「好方法」和人分享，是人生最大的幸福！

　　看了梵谷的傳記，他一生窮困潦倒，生前的畫打破傳統，被排斥，他氣得把畫當柴火燒，死後100多年，竟然被別人標售「向日葵」一億美金。所以，我從來沒有預期，在我有生之年，我這種「革命性」的發明，會被大家接受。

　　我的方法：學習外語，應該先從「說」開始。音標、字母，都先不要學，而且要學就學「有教養的英語」，一次背三個「極短的句子」，並且要「馬上能夠用得到」。例如：Thank you. I appreciate it. You're very kind. 這三句話，不是天天都可以用得到嗎？學了要馬上能夠使用，才有成就感，要使用，才不會忘記，只有不忘記，才能累積，否則背到後面，忘記前面，太划不來了！背一句會忘記，三個句子一起，說起來熱情，又不容易忘記。

　　「啞巴英語」危害人類兩百多年，大家浪費時間，就是浪費生命苦學英文的人，方法不對，到最後都「絕望」收尾，吃虧太大了！

# 每天說三句，英文不進步都難

　　昨天，和美國老師Edward逛街，他說：I know this place. I've been here before. 我們想不出第三句，沒有想到，小芝突然冒出一句：I remember now. 這三句話合在一起，說出來多棒。

　　晚上，我們在「康迎鼎」用餐，巧遇Vie Show老闆翁明顯一家人在自家用餐，又造了三句優美的英文：This place is excellent. I highly recommend it. I give it two thumbs up. 我們把restaurant說成place，這三句話便可天天使用了。

# 發音是原罪，經過苦練的英文最美

我有一位朋友，台灣大學外文系畢業，當了助教，最後升到教授退休，他是好學生、好老師，一路上走來都是名人。他寫了一封英文信給我，看起來很棒，但是，給美國老師一看，錯誤百出，慘不忍睹。這是傳統英語學習的典型結果，也就是說，用傳統方法，自行造句，到美國留學，和美國人結婚，無論多麼努力，英文永遠沒有學好的一天。

我發明的方法：背「現成的句子」，以三句為一組，先學會說，不要管發音，很多英文老師喜歡糾正發音，反而害了小孩，讓他們失去信心，終生不敢說英文。我強烈建議英文老師：Encourage students. Don't discourage them. Don't correct pronunciation. 發音是「原罪」，有我們中國口音，經過苦練的英文最美。The most beautiful English comes from hard work. 我的英文都是「背」的，我說出來自然有信心。

有人問我文法要不要學？當然要，美國人寫的文法書，很膚淺，把美國人害死了，很多美國人，不敢寫文章。我們國、高中文法書，還使用清朝的文法術語，文言文，把學生害死了！基本文法，一定要學，只要會做「極簡高中文法1000題」，便知道句子正確與否。需要這些資料，可以找長沙新航綫黃芬老師。現在，大家只要看「快手」和「抖音」我發表的免費「作品」即可。

# 「進步」讓我每天快樂！

　　我的同學告訴我：「你已經75歲，一隻腳已經踏進墳墓，不要再工作了！」其實，我從來沒有感覺自己是個老人，我覺得我還是「小孩」，每天在成長，「進步」讓我每天快樂。

　　很多人在網路上說：「我們是中國人，為什麼要學英文？」這是心理學上的酸葡萄作用，非常正常。傳統學「國際音標」、「漢語拼音」，文言文的文法術語像「賓語」、「狀語」，害大家失去學英文的信心。美國小孩是會說話後，才學閱讀和語法、背單字。學習是件快快樂樂的事，你試試看，不要拿課本，直接和外國老師聊天，你就在進步！

　　我不願意回到30歲，因為那時沒錢，什麼也不懂，一位大陸朋友都沒有；不願回到上個月，因為我還沒有在「快手」教英文。現在，通訊進步太快，手機是最好的老師，裡面有無數人的智慧。我希望能夠在短時間內，讓大家學會英文。「擊敗啞巴英語」是我一生的心願！

劉毅

# 不會説英文，反倒是好事

　　百年來，人類爲了學習英語，花了太大的功夫，發明了英文文法，把英文歸納成五大基本句型，歸納了很多的文法規則，認爲只要學了文法，就會造句，英文就能學好。事實上，沒有人眞正學好文法，因爲文法有無數的規則，又有無數的例外，今天學了這個，明天忘了那個，總是有不懂的地方。例如，在本書中，Bags go in the trunk.（行李要放在後車廂。）爲什麼 Bags 前面不加 The 呢？或 Are you tired at all?（你累不累啊？）**at all** 是什麼意思呢？這類疑惑，我們都有詳細的解釋。像這些問題，在傳統的文法書中，都沒有説明。

　　自從「一口氣背會話」發明後，學習英文變得很簡單。只要背，立刻會説；只要背爛，就能變成直覺，就可以累積。從前有很多人背 900 英文句型，有誰背得下來？現在編者已經背完「一口氣背會話」，都不會忘記，方法就是，背給別人聽。每一本只要背到 2 分鐘，中英文一起背，就永遠不會忘記。一回接一回地背下去，愈背愈快樂，愈背愈有成就感，身體也無形中變得更好。

沒想到，不會說英文，反倒是好事，可以藉著這個機會，訓練我們的口才，講一些別人喜歡聽，又體貼的話。例如，叫別人不要遲到，與其說：Don't be late.（不要遲到。）不如說：I'll be there on time.（我會準時到那裡。）講這句話既有禮貌，也暗示對方不要遲到。這種句子在「一口氣背會話」中很多。再例如，聽不懂別人講的話的時候，你就可以一口氣說出：I beg your pardon?  I didn't catch that.  What did you say? 等九句；有了這九句話在腦海中，你可以今天說：I beg your pardon? 明天說：I don't get it. 後天說：Could you speak up? 大家都會認為你的英文很好，怎麼會說那麼多不同的句子？

　　美國人常說的 *Why the hurry?*（為什麼要這麼匆忙？）*Why the gift?*（為什麼要送我禮物？）像這些句子，文法書上找不到、一般會話書中不敢寫的，我們都有徹底說明。看「一口氣背會話」，不僅可把會話學好，也能了解美國人平常真正怎麼說話。英文老師研讀過「一口氣背會話」，那上課就精彩了。

　　「一口氣背會話」一定要中英文一起背，中文反倒是說英文的助力，而不是干擾。

劉　毅

# BOOK 7 帶外國人逛街

▶7-1 下班後，你和你的朋友說：

Let's hit the road.
Let's get moving.
Let's hustle out of here.

▶7-2 走到ATM(自動提款機)前，你可以跟你朋友說：

Oops!
Hold it a second.
I almost forgot.

I need to hit an ATM.

▶7-3 你從提款機回來，跟你的朋友說：

Thanks for waiting.
Sorry about that.
Sorry I took so long.

▶7-4 你手指著天空，和朋友談天氣：

How about this weather?
We really lucked out.
What a beautiful day!

▶7-5 要過十字路口時，你和你朋友說：

We need to cross.
Let's cross the street.
Let's get to the other side.

▶7-6 不管你的朋友有沒有闖紅燈，你都可以跟他說：

Don't jaywalk.
Don't go against the light.
You'll get hit by a car.

▶7-7 走到公園，你和朋友說：

> Here's a favorite park.
> It's a popular spot.
> It's a super place to unwind.

▶7-8 走到夜市，你和朋友說：

> Here's a great market.
> It's pretty famous.
> It's noted for its bargains.

▶7-9 走到一家名牌店，你和你的朋友說：

> This store is number one.
> It's the top place to shop.
> It's the hottest store in town.

▶7-10 走到路邊的椅子，你和朋友說：

> Let's hang out.
> Let's stick around.
> Let's stay here for a while.

▶7-11 晚上看到車水馬龍的街道，你和朋友說：

> This city is dynamic.
> It's a mix of East and West.
> It's a combination of old and new.

▶7-12 回家路上，你和你朋友說：

> You're a fun person.
> You're great to be with.
> I like being around you.

# 1.　Let's hit the road.

| | |
|---|---|
| *Let's* hit the road. | 我們走吧。 |
| *Let's* get moving. | 我們走吧。 |
| *Let's* hustle out of here. | 讓我們趕快離開這裡吧。 |
| | |
| *Do you* like to walk? | 你喜歡走路嗎？ |
| *Do you* mind walking? | 你介意走路嗎？ |
| We'll see more on foot. | 我們走路可以看得比較多。 |
| | |
| *I*'m a big walker. | 我常走路。 |
| *I* walk to stay in shape. | 我走路是爲了保持健康。 |
| Are your shoes suitable for walking? | 你的鞋子適合走路嗎？ |

\*\*

*hit the road* 出發；動身
move〔muv〕*v.* 移動；走動；離去；出發
*get moving* 動身　　hustle〔'hʌsl̩〕*v.* 趕快；急速行進
mind〔maɪnd〕*v.* 介意　　*on foot* 步行
walker〔'wɔkɚ〕*n.* 步行者；常散步的人
stay〔ste〕*v.* 保持
shape〔ʃep〕*n.*（健康等的）狀態；情況
*in shape* 健康的　　shoes〔ʃuz〕*n. pl.* 鞋子
suitable〔'sutəbl̩〕*adj.* 適合的

## 【背景説明】

　　當你想要邀請朋友一起走的時候，你就可以連續説這九句話。

1. **Let's hit the road.**

　　hit〔hɪt〕v. 打；打擊；到達（某地）

　　**hit the road** 出發；動身

> 　　hit 的主要意思是作「打擊」解，這句話字面的意思是「讓我們打路吧。」引申爲「我們走吧。」

> 【比較】 **Let's hit the road.**（我們走吧。）
> 　　　　【較常用，坐車、走路都可以用】
> 　　Let's hit the street.（我們上街吧。）
> 　　　【常用，只是提議別人走路，而不是坐車】

　　Let's hit the street. 等於 Let's go to the street. 這種用法和 Let's hit the mall.（我們去購物中心吧。）Let's hit the ATM （我們去自動提款機提款吧。）用法相同。而 **Let's hit the road.** 不一定是走到路上，只是表示「出發」。hit 的解釋，詳見 p.605-606。

　　下面都是美國人常説的話：

> **Let's hit the road.**（我們走吧。）【第三常用】
> ＝Let's leave.（我們走吧。）【第二常用】
> ＝Let's go.（走吧。）【第一常用】

BOOK 7

= Let's rock. ( 走吧。)【第八常用】

= Let's roll. ( 走吧。)【第七常用】

= Let's rock and roll. ( 我們走吧。)【第九常用】

= Let's move. ( 走吧。)【第六常用】

= Let's get moving. ( 走吧。)【第四常用】

= Let's get a move on. ( 我們走吧。)【第五常用】

　　Let's rock.　Let's roll.　Let's rock and roll.
這三句話源自從前在搖滾舞會中，表示「我們開始
跳舞吧。」現在引申爲「開始吧。」或「走吧。」

　　get a move on 除了表示「走」以外，還表示
「趕快」。Let's get a move on. 是慣用句，不能說
成 *Let's get a move*. ( 誤 )

2. ***Let's get moving***.

move〔muv〕*v.* 移動；走動；離去；出發

　　move 的主要意思是「移動」，在此作「出發」
解。這句話等於 Let's get going. 表示「我們走
吧。」也可表示「我們趕快走吧。」要看說話者的
語氣，決定是哪一種意思。

【比較1】　***Let's get moving***.【常用】

　　　　　　*Let's be moving*.【誤，唯有黑人用】

　　美國人雖然不說 *Let's be moving*. 但他們說
We should be moving. ( 我們該走了。) 或 We
ought to be moving. ( 我們該走了。)

BOOK 7

【比較2】 ***Let's get moving.*** 【常用】

= Let's move. 【常用】

這兩句話意思完全相同，使用頻率也相同。

【比較3】 ***Let's get moving.*** （①走吧。②趕快走。）

Let's hit the road. （我們走吧。）

3. ***Let's hustle out of here.***

hustle〔ˈhʌsḷ〕*v.* 趕快；急速行進

hustle 的主要意思是「趕快」，等於 hurry。

這句話的意思是「我們趕快離開這裡吧。」

【比較】 下面兩句話，意思不同：

***Let's hustle out of here.***

（我們趕快離開這裡吧。）

Let's get out of here.

（我們離開這裡吧。）

下面各句意思相同：

***Let's hustle out of here.*** 【第二常用】

（我們趕快離開這裡吧。）

= Let's hustle on out of here. 【第四常用】

= Let's hurry out of here. 【第一常用】

= Let's hurry on out of here. 【第五常用】

= Let's leave here quickly. 【第三常用】

上面各句使用頻率很接近，只有 Let's hurry on out of here. 較不常用。

【比較 1 】　***Let's hustle out of here.***【正】

Let's hurry out of here.【正】

上面兩句話使用頻率相同。

【比較 2 】　***Let's hustle up out of here.***【誤】

Let's hurry up out of here.【正】

（ 我們趕快離開這裡吧。）

hurry 可説成 hurry up 或 hurry on，但是，

hustle 只能説成 hustle on，不能用 *hustle up*。

## 4. *Do you like to walk?*

這句話有兩個意思：① 你喜不喜歡走路？② 你要不要走路？（ = *Would you like to walk?*）到底是哪一個意思，要看實際情況或前後句意而定。

下面是美國人常説的話，我們按照使用頻率排列：

① ***Do you like to walk?***【第一常用】

（你要不要走路？）

② Do you want to walk?【第二常用】

（你要不要走路？）

③ Would you like to walk?【第三常用】

（你要不要走路？）

④ Would you care to walk?
（你想不想走路？）

⑤ Do you enjoy walking?
（你喜不喜歡走路？）

⑥ Do you care for walking?
（你喜不喜歡走路？）

【第一、五、六句的基本意思都是問「你喜不喜歡
走路？」也可暗示「你要不要走路？」】

「**care to** + 原形動詞」表示「想要」，「**care
for** + **V-ing**」表示「喜歡」。第六句不能說成：
*Would you care for walking?*（誤）但是可以說
成：Would you care for a walk?（你喜不喜歡
散步？）語言就是這麼複雜，永遠研究不完。最
簡單的方法，就是背「一口氣背會話」，一次解
決，永遠不忘，說的對，寫的也正確。

5. *Do you mind walking?*
mind〔maɪnd〕v. 介意

這句話的意思是「你介不介意走路？」也可以
說成：Would you mind walking? 也有美國人
說：Is it OK if we walk?（我們走路可以嗎？）

6. ***We'll see more on foot.***

   ***on foot*** 步行

   這句話的意思是「我們走路可以看得比較多。」
也有美國人説成：

   > We'll see more if we walk.
   > （如果我們走路，我們會看得比較多。）
   > We can look around while we walk.
   > （當我們走路的時候，可以四處看看。）
   > If we walk, we can see more.
   > （如果我們走路，我們可以看得比較多。）
   > 【***look around*** 環顧四周】

7. ***I'm a big walker.***

   walker〔ˈwɔkɚ〕*n.* 步行者；常散步的人

   這句話字面的意思是「我是一個大的步行者。」
引申為「我常走路。」( = *I walk a lot.* ) 也可能含
有「我喜歡走路。」或「我很能走路。」的意思。

   下面是類似常用的句子，字典上都沒有，但
美國人常説：

   > ***I'm a big walker.*** ( 我常走路。)
   > I'm a ***big eater.*** ( 我胃口很大。)
   > I'm a ***big drinker.*** ( 我很能喝酒。)
   >
   > I'm a ***big smoker.*** ( 我常抽煙。)
   > I'm a ***big jogger.*** ( 我常常慢跑。)
   > I'm a ***big traveler.*** ( 我經常旅行。)

> I'm a *big swimmer*. ( 我常游泳。)
> I'm a *big dancer*. ( 我常跳舞。)
> I'm a *big reader*. ( 我常看書。)

似乎所有「動詞 + er」的名詞前，都可以加上
big，但是有些並不常用，有些則有兩個意思，如：
He is a *big talker*. 可能表示「他常說個不停。」
或「他常說大話。」而 He is a *big singer*. 可能表
示「他是有名的歌手。」或表示「他常常唱歌。」

8. ***I walk to stay in shape***.
stay〔ste〕v. 保持
shape〔ʃep〕n. (健康等的) 狀態；情況　　***in shape*** 健康的

這句話有兩個意思：

I ***walk*** to stay in shape.
= ① I walk in order to stay in shape.
　　( 我走路是爲了保持健康。)
　② I walk so that I can stay in shape.
　　( 我走路，所以我能保持健康。)

不定詞片語修飾動詞，可表示「目的」、「結果」、「條
件」等。在這裡，可以看出是表示「目的」和「結果」。

下面是美國人常說的句子：

***I walk to stay in shape***. 【第一常用】
( 我走路是爲了保持健康。)
I walk to keep in shape. 【第二常用】
( 我走路是爲了保持健康。)
I walk to keep fit. 【第三常用】
( 我走路是爲了保持健康。)【fit〔fɪt〕*adj.* 健康的】

9. *Are your shoes suitable for walking?*

shoes〔ʃuz〕*n. pl.* 鞋子

suitable〔'sutəbḷ〕*adj.* 適合的

這句話的意思是「你的鞋子適不適合走路？」
下面各句意思相同，我們按照使用頻率排列：

① *Are your shoes suitable for walking?*
【第一常用】

② Are those shoes suitable for walking?
（那雙鞋子適不適合走路？）【第二常用】

③ Are those good walking shoes?
（那雙鞋子好不好走？）【第三常用】
【字面意思是「那雙鞋子是不是好的散步鞋？」】

④ How are those shoes for walking?
（那雙鞋子適合走路嗎？）

⑤ How do those shoes feel?
（穿那雙鞋子你感覺怎樣？）

⑥ How do those shoes treat you?
（穿那雙鞋子你感覺怎樣？）

【feel 在這裡作「有…感覺」解。treat 的主要意思是「對待」，在這裡 treat you 的意思是 make you feel。】

上面只有第一句話合乎中國人的思想，其他句子用 those shoes 和我們中國人的思想格格不入，唯有背下來，才會使用。

## 【對話練習】

1. A：**Let's hit the road.**

   B：Good idea.
   
   Just give me a minute.
   
   Okay, I'm ready.

   A：我們走吧。
   
   B：好主意。
   
   等我一下。
   
   好了，我準備好了。

2. A：**Let's get moving.**

   B：Yes, it's time to go.
   
   Lead the way.
   
   I'm right behind you.
   
   【*lead the way* 率先而行；領路】

   A：我們走吧。
   
   B：好，是該走了。
   
   你先走。
   
   我就在你後面。

3. A：**Let's hustle out of here.**

   B：What's the rush?
   
   Take it easy.
   
   There's no hurry.
   
   【rush〔rʌʃ〕*n.* 匆忙（= *hurry*）】

   A：我們趕快離開這裡吧。
   
   B：急什麼？
   
   慢慢來。
   
   不用急。

4. A：**Do you like to walk?**

   B：Sure, I love to walk.
   
   I often walk.
   
   It's the best way to get around.
   
   【*get around* 到四處】

   A：你喜歡走路嗎？
   
   B：當然，我很喜歡走路。
   
   我常常走路。
   
   要去任何地方，走路是最好的方式。

5. A： **Do you mind walking?**

　B： Not at all.

　　　A walk sounds nice.

　　　I think I'd enjoy that.

A：你介意走路嗎？

B：一點也不。

　　走路聽起來不錯。

　　我想我會喜歡走路。

6. A： **We'll see more on foot.**

　B： I agree.

　　　It'll give us a chance to

　　　look around.

　　　And there's a lot to see in

　　　this neighborhood.

　　　〔'nebɚ‚hʊd 〕 *n.* 鄰近地區

A：我們走路可以看得比較多。

B：我同意。

　　走路可以給我們四處看看

　　的機會。

　　而且這附近有很多東西可

　　以看。

7. A： **I'm a big walker.**

　B： So am I.

　　　I really enjoy it.

　　　I can't get enough of it.

　　　【*can't…enough*　無論…都不夠】

A：我常走路。

B：我也是。

　　我眞的很喜歡走路。

　　我非常喜歡走路。【字面意

　　思是「我怎麼走都不夠。」】

8. A： **I walk to stay in shape.**

　B： Me too.

　　　It's great exercise.

　　　It really keeps me fit.

A：我走路是爲了保持健康。

B：我也是。

　　它是一種很棒的運動。

　　它眞的能使我保持健康。

9. A： **Are your shoes suitable**

　　　**for walking?**

　B： Yes, they are.

　　　They're very comfortable.

　　　I can walk all day in these

　　　shoes.

A：你的鞋子適合走路嗎？

B：是的，很適合。

　　這雙鞋子很舒服。

　　我可以穿這雙鞋子走一整

　　天。

# 2. *Hold it a second.*

| | |
|---|---|
| Oops! | 哎喲！ |
| Hold it a second. | 等一下。 |
| I almost forgot. | 我差點忘記了。 |
| | |
| *I*'m short of cash. | 我缺少現金。 |
| *I* need some bucks. | 我需要一些錢。 |
| *I* need to hit an ATM. | 我必須去提款機提款。 |
| | |
| *You can* join me. | 你可以和我一起去。 |
| *You can* wait here. | 你可以在這裡等。 |
| It's up to you. | 由你決定。 |

** ———————————— · ——

oops〔ups〕*interj.* 噢；哎喲　　*hold it* 等一下
second〔'sɛkənd〕*n.* 秒　　*a second* 一會兒；片刻
short〔ʃɔrt〕*adj.* 缺乏的；不足的　　*be short of* 缺少
cash〔kæʃ〕*n.* 現金　　buck〔bʌk〕*n.* 美元
hit〔hɪt〕*v.* 到達 ( = *go to* )
*ATM* 自動櫃員機；自動提款機
　　( = *automatic-teller machine* )
join〔dʒɔɪn〕*v.* 加入；和…作伴；和…一起做同樣的事
*be up to sb.* 由某人決定

BOOK 7

## 【背景説明】

　　當你和朋友在一起，你突然想到要去提款機
提款，你就可以跟朋友講這幾句話，請他等一等，
或和你一起去。

1. **Oops!**

oops〔ups〕*interj.* 噢；哎喲

　　當你忘了某件事，或是不小心
把東西掉在地上，或是不小心做錯
什麼事，或是你不小心碰撞到某人，
你都可以説 "**Oops!**"（哎喲！）。

**Oops**, sorry.（哎喲！對不起。）
　【不小心碰撞到某人時，就可説這句話】
**Oops**, I forgot my umbrella.
　（哎喲！我忘了我的雨傘。）
**Oops**, I spilled my drink.
　（哎喲！我把飲料灑出去了。）
　【spill〔spɪl〕*v.* 灑出】

**Oops**, we are running late.
　（哎喲！我們快遲到了。）
　【run〔rʌn〕*v.* 成爲（某種狀態）；變成】
**Oops**, I lost your pen.
　（哎呀！我把你的筆弄丟了。）
**Oops**, I'm sorry.  I forgot your name.
　（哎呀！對不起。我忘了你的名字。）

一般小事情，用 Oops!，大事情則用 Oh, no!。

*Oh, no!* I left my wallet on the bus.

（糟了！我把皮夾忘在公車上。）

【leave〔liv〕v. 遺留　wallet〔'wɑlɪt〕n. 皮夾】

*Oh, no!* We're late for class.

（糟了！我們上課遲到了。）

【說這句話時，在教室外面，進了教室，則說：
　　Sorry, we're late.（抱歉，我們遲到了。）】

2. ***Hold it a second.***

***hold it*** 等一下

second〔'sɛkənd〕n. 秒　***a second*** 一會兒；片刻

　　這句話的字面意思是「抓住它一秒鐘。」引申
爲「等一下。」可能源自古時騎馬的時候，會抓住
繮繩，當騎馬的人要讓馬停的時候，就會把繮繩往
上拉（hold it up），人類語言會慢慢簡化，就變成
hold it，或 hold up，都引申爲「等一下」。

　　美國人叫別人「等一下」，說法很多，下面各
句使用頻率非常接近，都非常常用：

> ***Hold it a second.***（等一下。）【第一常用】
> = Hold it.【第二常用】
> = Hold up.【第三常用】

Hold it a second. 中的 a second，可用 a sec,
a moment 或 a minute 取代，都很常用。

$\left\{\begin{array}{l}\end{array}\right.$
= Wait a sec. 【第四常用】
= Wait a second. 【第一常用】
= Wait a moment. 【第三常用】
= Wait a minute. 【第二常用】

sec〔sεk〕*n.* 一會兒；片刻 ( = *second* )
moment〔'momənt〕*n.* 片刻
minute〔'mınıt〕*n.* 分鐘；片刻

$\left\{\begin{array}{l}\end{array}\right.$
= Hang on. 【第三常用】
= Hang on a sec. 【第一常用】
= Hang on a second. 【第一常用】
= Hang on a minute. 【第二常用】

***hang on***　等待片刻

$\left\{\begin{array}{l}\end{array}\right.$
= Just a sec. 【第一常用】
= Just a second. 【第一常用】
= Just a minute. 【第二常用】
= Just a moment. 【第三常用】

美國人光說「等一下」，就這麼多，如果不歸
納起來背，東學一句、西學一句，永遠學不好。

### 3. *I almost forgot.*

這句話的字面意思是「我幾乎忘記了。」也就是
「我差點忘記了。」美國人常說的有：

***I almost forgot.*** 【第一常用】
I almost completely forgot. 【第三常用】
（我幾乎完全忘記了。）

I just remembered.【第二常用】

（我剛剛想起來了。）

I just recalled.（我剛剛想起來了。）【第四常用】

It almost slipped my mind.【第五常用】

（我幾乎忘記了。）

It just crossed my mind.【第五常用】

（我剛剛才想起來。）

recall〔rɪ'kɔl〕v. 想起

*slip one's mind* 被某人遺忘

*cross one's mind* （事情）湧上心頭；掠過腦海

4. *I'm short of cash.*

short〔ʃɔrt〕*adj.* 缺乏的；不足的

*be short of* 缺少　　cash〔kæʃ〕*n.* 現金

這句話的意思是「我缺少現金。」

以下都是美國人常說的話，有些使用頻率相同：

*I'm short of cash.*【第一常用】

I'm hard up for cash.（我缺少現金。）【第四常用】

I'm hurting for cash.【第四常用】

（我非常需要現金。）

【*be hard up for* 缺乏　　*be hurting for* 拼命想要】

I'm broke.（我身無分文。）【第一常用】

I'm almost broke.【第三常用】

（我幾乎身無分文。）

I'm almost out of money.【第三常用】

（我幾乎沒有錢。）

【broke〔brok〕*adj.* 沒錢的　　*be out of* 用完】

BOOK 7

I'm low on cash. ( 我現金快用完了。)【第二常用】
I'm low on money. ( 我錢快用完了。)【第二常用】
I don't have enough money. 【第四常用】
( 我沒有足夠的錢。)
【low〔lo〕*adj.* 不足的；短缺的　*be low on* ～快用完了】

【比較】 ***I'm short of cash****. ( 我缺少現金。)
I'm broke. ( 我身無分文。)
【broke 是形容詞，不能説成 *broken*。】

## 5. *I need some bucks.*
buck〔bʌk〕*n.* 美元

這句話字面的意思是「我需要一些美元。」引
申爲「我需要一些錢。」雖然 bucks 等於 dollars，
但美國人不說 *I need some dollars.* ( 誤 )

【比較1】 I need twenty bucks. 【正，常用】
= I need twenty dollars. 【正，常用】
( 我需要二十元。)

【比較2】 下面三句話，使用頻率相同，一樣常用：

***I need some bucks****. ( 我需要一些錢。)
= I need some money. ( 我需要一些錢。)
= I need some cash. ( 我需要一些現金。)

【比較3】 ***I need some bucks****.
【正，這句話是固定用法，不可改變。】
*I need bucks.*【誤】
I need money. ( 我需要錢。)【正，常用】
I need cash. ( 我需要現金。)【正，常用】

6. ***I need to hit an ATM.***

hit〔hɪt〕*v.* 敲打；到達（= *go to*）

***ATM*** 自動提款機（= *automatic-teller machine*）

美國年輕人和中年人，常喜歡用 hit，來代替 go to。（詳見 p.605-606）這句話的字面意思是「我需要去敲打提款機。」引申為「我必須去提款機提款。」ATM 也可說成 cash machine 或 bank machine。

【比較1】 ***I need to hit an ATM.***【正，第一常用】
I need to hit a cash machine.【正，第二常用】
I need to hit a bank machine.【正，第三常用】

【比較2】 ***I need to hit an ATM.***【第一常用】
I need an ATM.【第二常用】
I've got to get to an ATM.【第三常用】
I need to get to an ATM.【第四常用】
I need to go to an ATM.【第五常用】
【***have got to*** 必須（= *have to*） ***get to*** 到達】

【比較3】 下面五句都很常用，我們按照使用頻率排列：

① ***I need to hit an ATM.***【第一常用】
② I need to get some money.【第二常用】
（我需要領一些錢。）
③ I need to take out some cash.【第三常用】
（我需要提一些現金出來。）
④ I need to take out some money.
（我需要提一些錢出來。）
⑤ I need to withdraw some money.
（我需要提一些錢。）【withdraw〔wɪθ'drɔ〕*v.* 提取】

BOOK 7

7. ***You can join me***

join〔dʒɔɪn〕*v.* 加入；和…作伴；和…一起做同樣的事

這句話字面的意思是「你可以加入我。」在這裡引申爲「你可以和我一起去。」

美國人常說：

> ***You can join me.***【第一常用】
> You can come with me.【第二常用】
> （你可以和我一起去。）
> You can come, too.【第二常用】
> （你也可以去。）

> You can come along.【第二常用】
> （你可以一起去。）【*come along* 跟著來】
> You can come along with me.【第二常用】
> （你可以和我一起去。）
> 【*come along with* 和～一起來】
> You can come if you want.【第一常用】
> （你如果想去也可以。）
> 【這句話也可說成…if you want to.】

中國人說「你可以和我一起去。」美國人可以說：You can come with me. 或 You can go with me. 用 come 代替 go，較爲親切，因爲 come with me 是指來我這邊，一起去。

8. ***You can wait here***

這句話的意思是「你可以在這裡等。」也可以說成：You can stay here.（你可以留在這裡。）

BOOK 7

9. ***It's up to you***.

  ***be up to*** *sb*. 由某人決定

這句話的意思是「由你決定。」這種說法很多：

> ***It's up to you***.【第一常用】
> = It's your choice. ( 由你來選擇。)【第二常用】
> = It's your call. ( 由你決定。)【第三常用】
> 【choice〔tʃɔɪs〕*n.* 選擇　***be one's call*** 由某人決定】

> = Depends on you. ( 由你決定。)【第四常用】
> 【省略主詞 It】
> = It depends on you. ( 由你決定。)【第五常用】
> = It's your decision. ( 由你決定。)【第六常用】
> 【***depend on*** 視～而定】

> = You choose. ( 由你選擇。)【第七常用】
> = You decide. ( 你決定。)【第八常用】
> = Do what you want. ( 做你想做的。)【第九常用】

> = Whatever. ( 隨你的便。)【第十常用】
> = Whatever you want.【第十一常用】
> ( 隨便你想怎樣都可以。)
> = Whatever you decide.【第十二常用】
> ( 無論你怎麼決定都可以。)

> = Whatever you want is fine.【第十三常用】
> ( 無論你想怎樣都可以。)
> = Whatever you like is OK.【第十四常用】
> ( 無論你想怎樣都可以。)
> = Do whatever you like.【第十五常用】
> ( 你想怎麼做都可以。)

## 【對話練習】

1. A：**Oops!**

   B：What happened?
      What's wrong?
      Are you okay?

   A：哎喲！

   B：發生什麼事？
      怎麼了？
      你還好吧？

2. A：**Hold it a second**.

   B：What's up?
      Did you forget something?
      Take your time.

   A：等一下。

   B：什麼事？
      你忘記什麼東西嗎？
      慢慢來。

3. A：**I almost forgot**.

   B：What?
      Is it something important?
      Can I help?

   A：我差點忘記了。

   B：什麼？
      是重要的事情嗎？
      我可以幫忙嗎？

4. A：**I'm short of cash**.

   B：Don't worry.  I've got money.
      I could lend you some.
      How much do you need?
      【*have got* 有】

   A：我缺少現金。

   B：別擔心，我有錢。
      我可以借你一些。
      你需要多少錢？

5. A：**I need some bucks**.

   B：Sorry, but I'm a bit short
      myself.
      I wish I could help you out.
      There must be another way.
      【*a bit* 有點　*help sb. out* 幫助某人解決困難】

   A：我需要一些錢。

   B：抱歉，但是我自己也
      有點缺錢。
      我希望我可以幫你。
      一定有其他的方法。

BOOK 7

6. A：**I need to hit an ATM**.

　B：That's a good idea.
　　 There's one across the
　　 street.
　　 How convenient!

A：我必須去提款機提款。

B：那是個好主意。
　　對街就有一台。

　　真方便！

7. A：**You can join me**.

　B：Thanks, I'll do that.
　　 I'll keep you company.
　　 It won't take long.
　　【*keep sb. company* 陪伴某人
　　　take〔tek〕*v.* 花費（時間）】

A：你可以和我一起去。

B：謝謝，我會和你一起去。
　　我會陪你。
　　不會花太久時間。

8. A：**You can wait here**.

　B：All right.
　　 Take your time.
　　 I'll be fine.

A：你可以在這裡等。

B：好的。
　　慢慢來。
　　我沒問題。

9. A：**It's up to you**.

　B：OK. Then let's have pizza.
　　 I know a good place in
　　 the neighborhood.
　　 They make the best pizza
　　 in town.

A：由你決定。

B：好的，那我們就吃披薩吧。
　　我知道附近有一家很好的
　　餐廳。
　　他們會做城裡最好吃的披
　　薩。

BOOK 7

# 3.  *Thanks for waiting*.

| | |
|---|---|
| Thanks for waiting. | 謝謝你等我。 |
| *Sorry* about that. | 很抱歉。 |
| *Sorry* I took so long. | 抱歉，我花費那麼長的時間。 |
| | |
| The line was long. | 排隊排很長。 |
| *It was* slower than slow. | 非常慢。 |
| *It was* the line from hell. | 排隊排得很長。 |
| | |
| *I almost* lost it. | 我差點要生氣。 |
| *I almost* blew a fuse. | 我幾乎要大發脾氣。 |
| *I* was ready to explode. | 我快要大發脾氣。 |

\*\*————————

take〔tek〕*v.* 花費（時間）    line〔laɪn〕*n.* 行列

hell〔hɛl〕*n.* 地獄

blow〔blo〕*v.* （保險絲）使燒斷

fuse〔fjuz〕*n.* 保險絲

*blow a fuse* 燒斷保險絲；大發雷霆

*be ready to* 快要；就要    explode〔ɪk'splod〕*v.* 爆發

BOOK 7

## 【背景説明】

凡是你去提款機提款，或去買電影票等，讓你的朋友久等了，你就可以説這九句話。

1. **Thanks for waiting**.

　　這句話的意思是「謝謝你等我。」

【比較1】 **Thanks for waiting.**【正，較常用】
*Thanks for waiting me.*
【誤，wait 是不及物動詞】
Thanks for waiting for me.【正，常用】

【比較2】 **Thanks for waiting.**【語氣輕鬆】
Thank you for waiting.【語氣較正式】

> 如果表示鄭重地道謝，就可説：
>
> I appreciate your waiting.
> （我很感激你的等待。）
> I appreciate your waiting for me.
> （我很感激你等我。）
> 【appreciate〔ə'priʃɪˌet〕v. 感激】

2. **Sorry about that**.

　　這句話是 I'm sorry about that. 的省略，字面意思是「對那件事情，我很抱歉。」引申為「很抱歉。」

> 　　人難免犯錯，道歉是一種美德，要常説 **"Sorry about that."** 通常是先講為什麼事抱歉，再説 **Sorry about that.**

BOOK 7

【例】 Oh, I totally forgot! *Sorry about that*.

（噢，我完全忘了！很抱歉。）

【totally〔'totḷɪ〕*adv.* 完全地】

I forgot to call you last night. *Sorry about that*.

（我昨天晚上忘了打電話給你。很抱歉。）

I'll do better next time. *Sorry about that*.（我下次會做得更好。很抱歉。）

3. ***Sorry I took so long***.

take〔tek〕*v.* 花費

　　這句話源自：I'm sorry I took so long to get here.（抱歉，我花了那麼長的時間才到這裡。）

【比較】 ***Sorry I took so long***.【最常用】
= Sorry it took so long.【常用】

　　Sorry it took so long. 源自 Sorry, it took so long to get here. 一般懂一點文法的人，以爲 take 只能用「非人」當主詞，事實上，「人」也可以當主詞，像 *I took so long*. 這句話就很常用。也有很多美國人說：Sorry I was so long. 意思都是「抱歉，我花費那麼長的時間。」源自 I'm sorry that I was so long in getting here.

（我很抱歉，我花費那麼長的時間才到這裡。）

【*be long* (*in*) + *V-ing*　～費時很久】

4. **The line was long.**

line〔laɪn〕n. 行列

這句話字面的意思是「隊伍很長。」引申爲「排隊排很長。」美國人常説：

**The line was long.**【第一常用】

The line was huge. ( 隊伍很長。)【第四常用】
〔hjudʒ〕adj. 巨大的

The line was awful. ( 隊伍長得嚇人。)【第二常用】
〔'ɔful〕adj. 嚇人的】

The line went on forever.【第三常用】
( 隊伍很長。)【**go on** 繼續】

The line was unbelievable.【第五常用】
( 隊伍長得令人不敢相信。)

The line was ridiculous.【第六常用】
( 隊伍長得很不可思議。)

unbelievable〔͵ʌnbə'livəbḷ〕adj. 令人難以相信的
ridiculous〔rɪ'dɪkjələs〕adj. 荒謬的

5. **It was slower than slow.**

這句話字面的意思是「它比慢還要再慢。」引申爲「非常慢。」**It was slower than slow.** 可以用在排了很長的隊，或交通阻塞的時候説。也可以説成：
**It was longer than long.** ( 隊伍很長。)

當天氣很熱的時候，你可以説：
**It was hotter than hot.** ( 天氣太熱了。)
當天氣太冷的時候，你可以説：
**It was colder than cold.** ( 天氣太冷了。)

當你看到一個人做一件事情做得很快，

你就可以説：

*He was faster than fast.*（他動作很快。）

當你看到一個人很聰明，你就可以對他説：

*You're smarter than smart.*（你很聰明。）

6. *It was the line from hell.*

hell〔hɛl〕*n.* 地獄

這句話的字面意思是「這隊伍是地獄來的。」

引申爲「排隊排得很長。」美國人常説：

*It was the line from hell.*【第一常用】

It was the worst line.【第二常用】

（排隊排得很長。）

It was the worst line I've ever seen.

（這隊伍是我看過最長的。）【第三常用】

It was the worst line I've ever

been in.（這是我排過最長的隊。）【第四常用】

It was an awful line.【第五常用】

（排隊排得很長。）

It was a terrible line.【第六常用】

（排隊排得很長。）

【第五、第六常用，使用頻率很接近。】

7. *I almost lost it.*

　　這句話字面的意思是「我幾乎失去它。」這是慣用句,意思是「我差點要生氣。」it 是指 temper〔'tɛmpɚ〕*n.* 脾氣,或 patience〔'peʃəns〕*n.* 耐心。

　　*I almost lost it.*【第一常用】
= I almost lost my temper.【第二常用】
　　(我差點要發脾氣。)
= I almost lost my patience.【第六常用】
　　(我差點失去耐心。)

= I almost lost control.【第三常用】
　　(我差點失去控制。)【不可說成 *my control*】
= I almost lost my cool.【第四常用】
　　(我差點失去冷靜。)【*lose one's cool* 失去冷靜】
= I almost lost my mind.【第五常用】
　　(我差點失去理智。)【*lose one's mind* 發瘋】

【比較】　*I almost lost it.*【較常用】
　　　　= I nearly lost it.【常用】
　　　　【nearly〔'nɪrlɪ〕*adv.* 幾乎】

8. *I almost blew a fuse.*
blow〔blo〕*v.* 使(保險絲)燒斷　　fuse〔fjuz〕*n.* 保險絲
*blow a fuse* 燒斷保險絲;勃然大怒;大發雷霆

　　這句話字面的意思是「我幾乎燒斷保險絲。」引申為「我幾乎要大發脾氣。」美國人容易生氣,所以光是「生氣」的成語,就有三十幾個,唯有歸納起來,才容易記住。以下我們歸納與動詞 blow 有關的成語:

***I almost blew a fuse.***

= I almost blew a gasket.

（我幾乎要大發脾氣。）

【gasket〔'gæskɪt〕*n.* 墊片（在引擎中，防止汽油外洩的襯墊）】

= I almost blew my top.

（我幾乎要火冒三丈。）

= I almost blew my cork.

（我幾乎要大發雷霆。）

= I almost blew my stack.

（我幾乎要大發脾氣。）

top〔tɑp〕*n.* 頭頂（= *top of one's head*）
cork〔kɔrk〕*n.* 軟木塞　　stack〔stæk〕*n.* 大煙囪

你看，美國人說話多麼幽默，把保險絲（fuse）燒斷；把引擎中的墊片（gasket）燒斷，讓汽油外洩；把一個人的頭頂（top）吹掉；把香檳酒的軟木塞（cork）衝開；把工廠的大煙囪（stack）燒掉，都表示「很生氣」。

9. ***I was ready to explode.***

***be ready to*** 快要；就要
explode〔ɪk'splod〕*v.* 爆炸；爆發

　　這句話的字面意思是「我快要爆炸了。」引申為「我快要大發脾氣了。」美國人也常說：***I was ready to kill someone.*** 或 ***I was ready to go crazy.*** 都表示「我快要大發脾氣了。」就像我們中文常說的：「我快要殺人了。」、「我快要發瘋了。」一樣。

BOOK 7

## 【對話練習】

1. A: **Thanks for waiting**.
   B: Don't worry about it.
   I didn't mind.
   You weren't that long.

   A: 謝謝你等我。
   B: 別擔心。
   我不介意。
   你沒有那麼久。

2. A: **Sorry about that**.
   B: That's all right.
   It's not a problem.
   Don't be sorry.

   A: 很抱歉。
   B: 沒關係。
   那不是問題。
   不用抱歉。

3. A: **Sorry I took so long**.
   B: It wasn't your fault.
   It couldn't be helped.
   Besides, I didn't mind.
   【fault〔fɔlt〕n. 過錯
   help〔hɛlp〕v. 避免；防止
   besides〔bɪˈsaɪdz〕adv. 此外；而且】

   A: 抱歉，我花費那麼長
   的時間。
   B: 那不是你的錯。
   那是無法避免的。
   而且，我並不介意。

4. A: **The line was long**.
   B: It's busy today.
   A lot of people had the same
   idea.
   That's always the way when
   you're in a hurry.
   【busy〔ˈbɪzɪ〕adj. 熱鬧的；繁忙的】

   A: 排隊排很長。
   B: 今天真是熱鬧。
   很多人都有相同的想
   法。
   當你很急的時候，總
   是這樣。

BOOK 7

5. A：**It was slower than slow**.

  B：You must have been bored.

     I know it's hard to wait.

     You must have a lot of patience.

     【hard〔hɑrd〕*adj.* 辛苦的

      patience〔'peʃəns〕*n.* 耐心】

A：非常慢。

B：你一定覺得很無聊。

   我知道等待很辛苦。

   你必須要很有耐心。

6. A：**It was the line from hell**.

  B：It wasn't that bad.

     I've seen worse.

     Just be glad it's over.

A：排隊排得很長。

B：沒有那麼糟。

   我看過更糟的。

   高興點，快要完了。

7. A：**I almost lost it**.

  B：I'm not surprised.

     I would have, too.

     I hate to wait.

A：我差點要生氣。

B：我並不驚訝。

   要是我也一樣。

   我討厭等。

8. A：**I almost blew a fuse**.

  B：Good thing you didn't.

     It's no use getting angry.

     Try to relax now.

     【*It's no use* + *V-ing*　~是沒有用的】

A：我幾乎要大發脾氣。

B：還好你沒有。

   生氣是沒有用的。

   現在試著放輕鬆。

9. A：**I was ready to explode**.

  B：I don't blame you.

     I would have been angry, too.

     What he did was wrong.

A：我快要大發脾氣。

B：我不怪你。

   要是我，我也會生氣。

   他所做的事是錯的。

# 4. How about this weather?

| | |
|---|---|
| How about this weather? | 你覺得這個天氣怎麼樣？ |
| We really lucked out. | 我們真幸運。 |
| What a beautiful day! | 多麼好的天氣！ |
| | |
| *It's* not too hot. | 不會太熱。 |
| *It's* not too cold. | 不會太冷。 |
| *It's* just right. | 天氣剛剛好。 |
| | |
| I hope it holds up. | 我希望天氣能保持良好。 |
| *Let's* cross our fingers. | 希望我們有好運氣。 |
| *Let's* enjoy it while we can. | 在我們能夠的時候，享受這個好天氣吧。 |

**

weather〔ˈwɛðɚ〕 *n.* 天氣
luck〔lʌk〕 *v.* 逢凶化吉；靠運氣　　*luck out* 運氣好
*just right* 剛好　　*hold up* 維持；保持良好
cross〔krɔs〕 *v.* 使交叉
*cross one's fingers* 祈求好運

BOOK 7

## 【背景説明】

這九句話使用的機會太多了，只要天氣好，就可以講這九句話。美國人在一起，爲了打破僵局，往往會談到天氣。

1. *How about this weather?*

　*How about* ~?　~怎麼樣？；對於~你有何想法？

　weather〔'wɛðə〕*n.* 天氣

　　這句話源自：How *do you feel* about this weather? 意思是「你覺得這個天氣怎麼樣？」

　美國人常説：

　　*How about this weather?* 【第一常用】

　　How do you like this weather? 【第五常用】
　　（你覺得這個天氣如何？）

　　How do you like the weather? 【第四常用】
　　（你覺得天氣如何？）

　　What do you think of this weather?
　　（你覺得這個天氣如何？）【第三常用】

　　What do you think of the weather?
　　（你覺得天氣如何？）【第六常用】

　　Great weather, huh? 【第二常用】
　　（天氣很好，不是嗎？）

　　【huh〔hʌ〕*interj.* 哼；哈】

BOOK 7

雖然文法書上說，How about～? 是 How do you feel about～? 的省略，What about～? 是 What do you think about～? 的省略，但是美國人不說 *How do you feel about this weather?* 和 *What do you think about this weather?* 文法是由語言歸納出規則，常有例外，用文法造句很容易出錯。

2. ***We really lucked out***.

luck〔lʌk〕*v.* 逢凶化吉；靠運氣
***luck out*** 運氣好；走運 ( *= get lucky* )

這句話的意思是「我們真幸運。」這種說法有：

***We really lucked out.***【第一常用】
= We were really lucky.【第三常用】
（我們真幸運。）
= We were really fortunate.【第六常用】
（我們真幸運。）

【fortunate〔'fɔrtʃənɪt〕*adj.* 幸運的】

= We got lucky.（我們很幸運。）【第二常用】
= We got a lucky break.【第五常用】
（我們很幸運。）
= We got a break.【第四常用】
（我們很幸運。）

get〔gɛt〕*v.* 變得；獲得
break〔brek〕*n.* 運氣；幸運　***a lucky break*** 幸運

3. **What a beautiful day!**

beautiful 的主要意思是「美麗的」，在此作「天氣十分晴朗的」解。這句話的意思是「多麼好的天氣！」

【比較】**What a beautiful day!**【正，常用】

**What a beautiful day it is!**

【文法對，但美國人不說】

這類的說法有：

**What a beautiful day!**【第一常用】

What a nice day! ( 天氣眞好！)【第五常用】

What a wonderful day! ( 天氣眞棒！)【第六常用】

What a great day! ( 天氣眞好！)【第四常用】

What a perfect day! ( 天氣眞好！)【第八常用】

What a terrific day! ( 天氣眞棒！)【第九常用】

【terrific〔tə'rıfık〕*adj.* 很棒的】

What a marvelous day! ( 天氣眞棒！)【第十常用】

What a fantastic day! ( 天氣眞棒！)【第十一常用】

What a super day! ( 天氣眞好！)【第七常用】

marvelous〔'mɑrvḷəs〕*adj.* 很棒的
fantastic〔fæn'tæstık〕*adj.* 很棒的
super〔'supɚ〕*adj.* 極好的；超級的

BOOK 7

What a day! ( 天氣眞好！)【第二常用】
What an awesome day! ( 天氣眞棒！)【第三常用】
Gorgeous day, isn't it?【第十二常用】
( 天氣眞好，不是嗎？)

awesome〔'ɔsəm〕adj. 令人嘆爲觀止的；很棒的
gorgeous〔'gɔrdʒəs〕adj. 很美的；非常好的

4. *It's not too hot.*
   *It's not too cold.*
   *It's just right.*
   *just right* 剛好

這三句話的意思是「天氣不冷也不熱，剛好。」
這三句話可當作會話公式來看待，當你看到一個人
身材很好，你就可以說：

You're not too fat. ( 你不會太胖。)
You're not too thin. ( 你不會太瘦。)
You're just right. ( 你的身材剛好。)

當你吃到合你胃口的食物，你就可以說：

It's not too sweet. ( 不會太甜。)
It's not too bland. ( 不會太淡。)
It's just the way I like it. ( 正合我的口味。)
【bland〔blænd〕adj. 淡而無味的】

當你試穿衣服的時候，衣服適合你，就可說：

It's not too big. ( 不會太大。)
It's not too small. ( 不會太小。)
It's just right. ( 剛剛好。)

BOOK 7

5. *I hope it holds up.*

*hold up*　維持；保持良好 ( = *stay stable* ; *remain the same* )

　　　　hold 的主要意思是「抓住；抱住」，up 是「向
上」，hold up 的字面意思是「抱住使它向上」，就
像柱子維持住整個建築物的屋頂。所以，hold up
引申為「維持」。

【例】 I hope this weather holds up.
　　　 ( 我希望這種天氣能夠維持。)
　　　 I hope this economy holds up.
　　　 ( 我希望這種經濟能夠維持。)
　　　 【economy〔ɪ'kɑnəmɪ〕*n.* 經濟】
　　　 I hope his health holds up.
　　　 ( 我希望他的健康能夠維持。)

　　　*I hope it holds up*. 的意思是「我希望天氣能
夠保持良好。」it 指「天氣」，等於 this weather。
這類的説法有：

　　　*I hope it holds up*.【第一常用】
　　　 I hope it continues.【第二常用】
　　　 ( 我希望天氣能繼續如此。)
　　　 I hope it lasts.【第三常用】
　　　 ( 我希望天氣能持續這樣。)
　　　 【last〔læst〕*v.* 持續】

I hope it keeps up.【第四常用】

（我希望天氣能持續這樣。）

I hope it stays this way.【第五常用】

（我希望天氣能一直如此。）

I hope it stays like this.【第六常用】

（我希望天氣能一直像這樣。）

***keep up*** 保持；維持　　stay〔ste〕*v.* 保持
***this way*** 這樣

6. ***Let's cross our fingers.***

cross〔krɔs〕*v.* 使交叉

***cross one's fingers***　（將中指彎曲
　　重疊在食指上）祈求好運

> 　　美國人祝福人家的時候，常把中指和食指彎
> 曲重疊，來表示「祝你好運。」***Let's cross our***
> ***fingers.*** 在這裡的意思是「希望我們有好運氣。」
> （＝*Let's hope we get lucky.*）

7. ***Let's enjoy it while we can.***

enjoy〔ɪn'dʒɔɪ〕*v.* 享受

　　　這句話在這裡的意思是「在我們能夠的時候，
享受這個好天氣吧。」也有美國人說：Let's enjoy
this weather while we have it.（當我們有這個天
氣的時候，我們要享受它。）

## 【對話練習】

1. A：**How about this weather?**　　　　A：你覺得這個天氣怎麼樣？

　　B：I can't believe it, either.　　　　B：我也無法相信。
　　　It's wonderful!　　　　　　　　　大氣太棒了！
　　　I love it.　　　　　　　　　　　我很喜歡。

2. A：**We really lucked out.**　　　　　A：我們真幸運。

　　B：We sure did.　　　　　　　　　B：我們的確是。
　　　This is a lucky break.　　　　　　真是幸運。
　　　We couldn't ask for better.　　　　再好也不過了。

3. A：**What a beautiful day!**　　　　　A：多麼好的天氣！

　　B：I agree.　　　　　　　　　　　B：我同意。
　　　It's gorgeous.　　　　　　　　　天氣真好。
　　　We couldn't ask for more.　　　　我們無法再要求什麼了。

4. A：**It's not too hot.**　　　　　　　A：不會太熱。

　　B：No, it's not.　　　　　　　　　B：是的，天氣不會太熱。
　　　I'm glad the heat is gone.　　　　我很高興熱天消失了。
　　　The temperature is perfect.　　　　溫度剛剛好。
　　　【heat〔hit〕*n.* 熱
　　　　temperature〔'tɛmprətʃɚ〕*n.* 溫度】

5. A：**It's not too cold.**　　　　　　A：不會太冷。

　　B：Spring is finally here.　　　　　B：春天終於來了。
　　　The weather is perfect.　　　　　天氣非常好。
　　　We should enjoy it while it　　　　在天氣持續這樣的時候，
　　　lasts.　　　　　　　　　　　　我們應該好好享受。

6. A : **It's just right**.

   B : It's perfect.

      It's my kind of weather.

      I love a day like this.

A：天氣剛剛好。

B：太完美了。

   這是我喜歡的天氣。

   我喜歡像這樣的日子。

7. A : **I hope it holds up**.

   B : So do I.

      Think positive.

      I'm sure it will.

     【positive〔'pɑzətɪv〕*adj.* 樂觀的】

A：我希望天氣能保持良好。

B：我也是。

   要樂觀。

   我相信它會持續下去。

8. A : **Let's cross our fingers**.

   B : I already have.

      I hope it works.

      Let's hope for the best.

     【work〔wɜk〕*v.* 有效；起作用

      *hope for the best* 抱持樂觀的

       態度；凡事往好處想】

A：希望我們有好運氣。

B：我已經這樣希望了。

   我希望會有效。

   我們抱持樂觀的態度吧。

9. A : **Let's enjoy it while we can**.

   B : You're right.

      Let's seize the day.

      Let's make the most of it.

     【*seize the day* 把握時機；及時行樂

      *make the most of* 善用】

A：在我們能夠的時候，享受這個好天氣吧。

B：你說得對。

   我們要把握時機。

   我們要善用今天。

# *5. We need to cross.*

| | |
|---|---|
| We need to cross. | 我們需要過馬路。 |
| *Let's* cross the street. | 我們穿越馬路吧。 |
| *Let's* get to the other side. | 我們過馬路到另外一邊吧。 |
| | |
| Heads up. | 注意。 |
| *Look* both ways. | 看看兩個方向的來車。 |
| *Look* before you cross. | 在你過馬路以前要看一看。 |
| | |
| The traffic is dangerous. | 來往的車輛很危險。 |
| It's like a jungle out there. | 交通很危險。 |
| You can never be too careful. | 你要非常小心。 |

\*\* ——————————————

cross〔krɔs〕*v.* 橫越　　***get to***　到達
side〔saɪd〕*n.* 邊　　***heads up***　注意
way〔we〕*n.* 方向
traffic〔'træfɪk〕*n.* 交通；來往的車輛及行人
dangerous〔'dendʒərəs〕*adj.* 危險的
jungle〔'dʒʌŋgḷ〕*n.* 叢林　　***out there***　外面；在那邊
***can never be too***~　再~也不爲過；愈~愈好

## 【背景說明】

　　　當你要和朋友一起穿越馬路的時候，就可以說這九句話。

1. ***We need to cross***.
   cross〔krɔs〕*v.* 橫越；穿越

   　　這句話在這裡的意思是「我們需要過馬路。」
   　美國人常說的有：

   　　***We need to cross***.【第一常用】
   　　We need to cross the street.【第三常用】
   　　（我們必須穿越街道。）
   　　We need to get to the other side.【第六常用】
   　　（我們必須到另一邊。）

   　　We need to get over there.【第四常用】
   　　（我們必須過去那裡。）
   　　We need to go over there.【第五常用】
   　　（我們必須過去那裡。）
   　　We need to cross here.【第二常用】
   　　（我們必須在這裡過馬路。）

We need to cross.

We need to cross here.

BOOK 7

## 2. *Let's cross the street.*

這句話字面的意思是「我們穿越街道吧。」
也就是我們常說的「我們過馬路吧」。美國人常
說的有：

> ***Let's cross the street.*** 【第一常用】
> Let's cross here. 【第一常用】
> （我們在這裡過馬路吧。）
> Let's cross. 【第一常用】
> （我們過馬路吧。）
>
> Let's go across here. 【第二常用】
> （我們在這裡過馬路吧。）
> Let's go to the other side. 【第三常用】
> （我們到另一邊去吧。）
> Let's take the crosswalk. 【第四常用】
> （我們走行人穿越道吧。）
>
> ***go across*** 橫越
> crosswalk〔ˈkrɔsˌwɔk〕*n.* 行人穿越道

## 3. *Let's get to the other side*
*get to* 到達

這句話和上面一句意義相同，字面的意思是
「我們到另外一邊吧。」在這裡表示「我們過馬路
到另外一邊吧。」也可以說成：Let's go to the
other side.

**4. *Heads up*.**

> 這句話的意思是「抬頭。」這句話源自 Keep your heads up. ( 把你們的頭抬起來。) 在軍隊裡面，軍官常和士兵們說：Heads up. ( 抬頭。) 或 Keep your heads up, men. ( 士兵們，把頭抬起來。)【men 在此作「士兵」解】現在用在日常生活中，即使對一個人，也用複數的 Heads up.
>
> 在這一回中，說 "Heads up." ( 頭抬起來。) 是暗示叫你「注意。」( = *Pay attention*. )

**5. *Look both ways*.**

way〔we〕*n.* 方向

> 這句話字面的意思是「看看兩個方向。」引申為「看看兩個方向的來車。」也可以加長為 Look both ways before you cross the street. ( 在你過馬路以前，要看看雙向的來車。)

**6. *Look before you cross*.**

> 這句話的意思是「在你過馬路以前要看一看。」這種說法有：
>
> ***Look before you cross*.**【第一常用】
> **Look first, then walk.**【第四常用】
> ( 先看一看再走。)
> **Look first before you walk.**【第三常用】
> ( 先看一看再走。)【first 可省略】

BOOK 7

Look first before you cross. 【第二常用】

（過馬路之前要先看一看。）

Check out the traffic first. 【第五常用】

（要先看看來往的車輛。）

Make sure the coast is clear. 【第六常用】

（要確定沒有危險。）

***check out*** 檢查　　coast〔kost〕*n.* 海岸

clear〔klɪr〕*adj.* 無阻礙的

***the coast is clear*** 無人阻礙；沒有危險【表示巡

邏隊不在的走私黑話】

7. ***The traffic is dangerous***.

traffic〔'træfɪk〕*n.* 來往的車輛及行人

dangerous〔'dendʒərəs〕*adj.* 危險的

traffic 主要的意思是「交通」，在這裡是指
「來往的車輛」。這句話的意思是「來往的車輛很
危險。」美國人也常說：The traffic is heavy.
（來往的車輛很多。）或 The traffic is not safe.
（來往的車輛不安全。）

8. ***It's like a jungle out there***.

jungle〔'dʒʌŋgl〕*n.* 叢林；雜亂危險的地方；弱肉
強食的地方　　***out there*** 外面；在那裡

這句話的字面意思是「它就像在外面的一個叢林
中。」「叢林」表示「雜亂危險的地方」( *a vicious
area of confusion* )。這句話在這裡引申為「交通
很危險。」英文解釋是：It's dangerous and chaotic.
【chaotic〔ke'ɑtɪk〕*adj.* 混亂的】

　　*out there* 這個片語，在字典上沒有，但是美國人常說，① 表示字面的意思：

> Look at the rain *out there*. (你看外面下雨了。)
> What's going on *out there*? (外面發生什麼事?)
> What's that noise *out there*?
> (外面那個是什麼聲音?)

② 比喻用法：此時可把 out there 看成是 there 的加強語氣。

> *It's like a jungle out there*. (交通很危險。)
> It's dangerous *out there*. (那裡很危險。)
> There are a lot of people *out there* shopping today.
> (今天那裡有很多人在買東西。)

【比較1】

> *It's like a jungle there*. (誤)【語氣太弱，美國人不說】
> *It's like a jungle out there*. 【美國人常說】
> 由於這句話是在強調交通混亂，如果不用 out there 來加強語氣，就奇怪了。
> It's dangerous there. 【一般語氣】
> It's dangerous out there. 【加強語氣】

【比較2】

> It's like a jungle *out there*. 【當你站在路邊時說】
> It's like a jungle *out here*. 【當你在開車時說】
> 上面兩句話意義相同，都表示「交通很危險。」
> 但是說話者所在的位置不同。

9. ***You can never be too careful.***

   ***can never be too~*** 再~也不爲過 ( = *cannot be too~* )

   這句話的意思是「你再怎麼小心也不爲過。」意思就是「你要非常小心。」

   下面都是美國人在過馬路時常說的話：

   ***You can never be too careful.*** 【第一常用】

   = You can't be too careful. 【第一常用】
   ( 你再怎麼小心也不爲過。 )

   You have to be careful. 【第二常用】
   ( 你必須小心。 )
   You have to take care of yourself. 【第二常用】
   ( 你必須保重。 )
   【***take care of*** 照顧】

   Watch your step. 【第四常用】
   ( 要注意你的腳步；要小心。 )
   Be cautious. ( 要小心。 )【第五常用】
   Always be careful. ( 總是要小心。 )【第三常用】

   watch〔watʃ〕 *v.* 注意　　step〔stɛp〕 *n.* 腳步
   ***watch*** *one's* ***step*** 小心腳步；小心
   cautious〔'kɔʃəs〕 *adj.* 小心的

BOOK 7

## 【對話練習】

1. A: **We need to cross**.
   B: That's right.  It's on the
      other side.
      We can cross over there.
      Let's wait for the light.

   A：我們需要過馬路。
   B：沒錯，它在另外一邊。

      我們可以在那裡過馬路。
      我們等紅綠燈吧。

2. A: **Let's cross the street**.
   B: I'm with you.
      Let's go for it.
      After you.

   A：我們過馬路吧。
   B：我同意。
      我們走吧。
      你先請。

3. A: **Let's get to the other side**.
   B: Where shall we cross?
      We need a crosswalk.
      We can cross here.

   A：我們過馬路到另外一邊吧。
   B：我們要在哪裡過馬路？
      我們需要走行人穿越道。
      我們可以在這裡過馬路。

4. A: **Heads up**.
   B: I'm looking.
      I'll be careful.
      Don't worry.

   A：注意。
   B：我正在看。
      我會小心。
      不要擔心。

5. A: **Look both ways**.
   B: That's good advice.
      I will.
      Here comes a break in traffic.

   A：看看兩個方向的來車。
   B：那是個好建議。
      我會的。
      這裡車流剛好中斷可穿越。

【break〔brek〕*n.* 中斷；間歇　 ***a break in traffic*** 車流間歇時間】

6. A : **Look before you cross**.

   B : Let's wait for this car.
   The coast is clear.
   Let's go.

A：在你過馬路以前要看一看。

B：我們等這輛車通過吧。
現在沒有危險。
走吧。

7. A : **The traffic is dangerous**.

   B : People drive fast here.
   We have to watch out.
   Let's be careful.
   【*watch out* 小心】

A：來往的車輛很危險。

B：這裡的人車子開得很快。
我們必須要小心。
我們小心一點吧。

8. A : **It's like a jungle out there**.

   B : It sure is.
   We need to watch our step.
   We have to stay on our toes.
   【toe〔to〕*n.* 腳趾
   *stay on* one's *toes* 保持警覺】

A：交通很危險。

B：的確是。
我們必須要小心。
我們必須保持警覺。

9. A : **You can never be too careful**.

   B : I don't agree.
   Caution has its limits.
   Sometimes you have to take a chance.
   【caution〔ˈkɔʃən〕*n.* 小心；謹慎    *take a chance* 冒險；碰運氣】

A：你要非常小心。

B：我不同意。
小心會有限制。
有時候你必須冒險。

BOOK 7

# 6. *Don't jaywalk*.

| | |
|---|---|
| ***Don't*** jaywalk. | 不要擅自穿越馬路。 |
| ***Don't*** go against the light. | 不要闖紅燈。 |
| You'll get hit by a car. | 你會被車撞到。 |
| | |
| ***Wait*** on the curb. | 在路邊等。 |
| ***Wait*** for the green. | 等綠燈。 |
| Always use the crosswalk. | 一定要使用行人穿越道。 |
| | |
| ***Be*** alert. | 要小心。 |
| ***Be*** careful. | 要小心。 |
| Use your head to stay safe. | 用你的頭腦來保命。 |

** ─────────────────────

jaywalk〔'dʒe͵wɔk〕*v.* ( 不遵守交通規則 ) 擅自穿越馬路
***go against*** 違反
light〔laɪt〕*n.* 交通號誌燈 ( = *traffic light* )
hit〔hɪt〕*v.* 撞　curb〔kɝb〕*n.* ( 人行道旁的 ) 邊欄或邊石
green〔grin〕*n.* 綠色信號燈
crosswalk〔'krɔs͵wɔk〕*n.* 行人穿越道
alert〔ə'lɝt〕*adj.* 留心的；警覺的　head〔hɛd〕*n.* 頭腦
***use one's head*** 運用頭腦思考　stay〔ste〕*v.* 保持

## 【背景説明】

這一回和上一回一樣，都是在過馬路前，跟
朋友説的話，不管他有沒有要擅自穿越馬路，都
可説這些話。

1. ***Don't jaywalk.***

jaywalk〔ˈdʒeˌwɔk〕*v.*（不遵守交通規則）擅自穿越馬路

jaywalk 中的 jay〔dʒe〕，發音和字母 j 相同，
jay 的意思是「鄉巴佬」(*rural person*)。

jaywalk 的字面意思是「鄉
巴佬走路，不懂交通規則」，所
以，***Don't jaywalk.*** 的意思就是
「不要擅自穿越馬路。」

2. ***Don't go against the light.***

**go against** 違背；違反

light〔laɪt〕*n.* 交通燈誌號；指示燈

這句話的字面意思是「不要違背燈號。」引
申爲「不要闖紅燈。」美國人也常説：Don't
cross against the light.（過馬路不要闖紅燈。）

【比較】

***Don't go against the light.***【較常用，美國人喜歡簡化】
Don't go against the red light.【正，常用】

BOOK 7

3. *You'll get hit by a car*.

hit〔hɪt〕v. 撞【三態同形：hit-hit-hit】

這句話的意思是「你會被車撞到。」

下面都是美國人常說的話：

*You'll get hit by a car*.【第一常用】

You could get hit.【第一常用】

（你可能會被撞。）

You might get hit.【第一常用】

（你可能會被撞。）

You'll get hit. （你會被撞。）【第一常用】

You could get hurt.【第二常用】

（你可能會受傷。）

【could 可用 might 代替】

You could get killed.【第三常用】

（你可能會死。）

【could 可用 might 代替。

*get killed* （因意外而）死亡】

4. *Wait on the curb*.

curb〔kɝb〕n. ( 車道與人行道旁的 ) 邊欄或邊石

這句話的意思是「在路邊等。」

也可以說成 Wait on the sidewalk.

（在人行道上等。）

【sidewalk〔'saɪd,wɔk〕n. 人行道】

5. ***Wait for the green***.

green〔grin〕*n.* 綠色信號燈

　　這句話的意思是「等綠燈。」

【比較】　***Wait for the green***.【第一常用】

　　　　= Wait for the light.【第二常用】

　　　　= Wait for the green light.【第三常用】

6. ***Always use the crosswalk***.

always〔'ɔlwez〕*adv.* 總是；一定

crosswalk〔'krɔs,wɔk〕*n.* 行人穿越道

　　這句話的意思是「一定要使用行人穿越道。」

　　也有美國人說成：Always cross at the crosswalk.

　　（過馬路一定要走行人穿越道。）

7. ***Be alert***.

alert〔ə'lɝt〕*adj.* 警覺的；留心的

　　這句話字面的意思是「要有警覺的。」引申為
「要小心。」等於 Be careful.

　　下面都是美國人常說的話：

> ***Be alert***.【第一常用】
>
> = Be careful.（要小心。）【第三常用】
>
> = Stay alert.（要保持警覺。）【第二常用】

= Be on your toes. ( 要機警。)【第六常用】

= Keep your eyes open. ( 要提高警覺。)【第五常用】

= Keep an eye out. ( 要密切注意。)【第四常用】

toe〔to〕*n.* 腳趾　　**on** *one's* **toes** 機警的
**keep** *one's* **eyes open** 提高警覺
**keep an eye out** 密切注意

8. ***Use your head to stay safe.***

head〔hɛd〕*n.* 頭腦
**use** *one's* **head** 運用頭腦　　stay〔ste〕*v.* 保持

　　這句話字面的意思是「用你的頭腦來保持安全。」
引申爲「用你的頭腦來保命。」這是美國人過馬路
時常說的話。

　　也可以只說 Use your head! ( 用你的頭腦！)
也有人說：Always use your head. ( 一定要用你
的頭腦。) 這些句子的含意都是「在你行動以前要
想一想。」( = *Be smart. Think before you act.* )

　　　美國人對熟的朋友或是晚輩，常用 *Use your*
*head*. 如：

　　　You're smart. *Use your head.*
　　　（你很聰明。用你的頭腦。）
　　　*Use your head.* Don't be careless.
　　　（用你的頭腦。不要不小心。）
　　　Take your time. *Use your head.* You
　　　　can do it.
　　　（慢慢做。用你的頭腦。你可以做到。）

## 【對話練習】

1. A：**Don't jaywalk**.

　　B：I never do.
　　　That's a dangerous habit.
　　　I wouldn't think of trying it.
　　　【habit〔ˈhæbɪt〕*n.* 習慣】

　　　　　　　　　　　　　　A：不要擅自穿越馬路。

　　　　　　　　　　　　　　B：我從來不會。
　　　　　　　　　　　　　　　那是個危險的習慣。
　　　　　　　　　　　　　　　我不會想嘗試這麼做。

2. A：**Don't go against the light**.

　　B：Don't worry. I'll wait.
　　　I'll wait for it to change.
　　　It's safer that way.

　　　　　　　　　　　　　　A：不要闖紅燈。

　　　　　　　　　　　　　　B：不要擔心。我會等。
　　　　　　　　　　　　　　　我會等到燈號轉換。
　　　　　　　　　　　　　　　那樣比較安全。

3. A：**You'll get hit by a car**.

　　B：I wouldn't want that.
　　　That would be terrible.
　　　I'll be careful.

　　　　　　　　　　　　　　A：你會被車撞到。

　　　　　　　　　　　　　　B：我不想那樣。
　　　　　　　　　　　　　　　那會很可怕。
　　　　　　　　　　　　　　　我會小心的。

4. A：**Wait on the curb**.

　　B：I always do.
　　　It's the safest place.
　　　It's not smart to take chances.
　　　【smart〔smɑrt〕*adj.* 聰明的
　　　　***take chances*** 冒險】

　　　　　　　　　　　　　　A：在路邊等。

　　　　　　　　　　　　　　B：我都是這麼做。
　　　　　　　　　　　　　　　路邊是最安全的地方。
　　　　　　　　　　　　　　　冒險並不聰明。

5. A：**Wait for the green**.

　　B：I can wait.
　　　There's no rush.
　　　It's not worth taking a risk.
　　　【rush〔rʌʃ〕*n.* 匆忙　***be worth* + *V-ing*** 值得～　***take a risk*** 冒險】

　　　　　　　　　　　　　　A：等綠燈。

　　　　　　　　　　　　　　B：我可以等。
　　　　　　　　　　　　　　　不急。
　　　　　　　　　　　　　　　不值得冒險。

6. A：**Always use the crosswalk**.

　B：I do.
　　It's the safest option.
　　And it's the law.
　　【option ('ɑpʃən ) *n.* 選擇】

A：一定要使用行人穿越道。

B：我會。
　它是最安全的選擇。
　而且法律也這樣規定。

7. A：**Be alert**.

　B：I'll watch out.
　　I'll keep an eye out.
　　I'll pay attention.
　　【*keep an eye out* 密切注意
　　　*pay attention* 注意】

A：要小心。

B：我會小心。
　我會密切注意。
　我會注意。

8. A：**Be careful**.

　B：Thanks, I will.
　　I'll be cautious.
　　You take care, too.
　　【cautious ('kɔʃəs ) *adj.* 小心的；
　　　謹慎的　*take care* 注意；小心】

A：要小心。

B：謝謝，我會的。
　我會小心。
　你也要小心。

9. A：**Use your head to stay safe**.

　B：I'll do my best.
　　I'll watch for trouble.
　　I'll be on guard at all times.
　　【*watch for* 留意
　　　*on guard* 小心；警戒】

A：用你的頭腦來保命。

B：我會盡力。
　我會留意不要惹上麻煩。
　我會一直很小心。

# 7. *Here's a favorite park.*

| | |
|---|---|
| Here's a favorite park. | 這裡是大家所喜愛的公園。 |
| *It's* a popular spot. | 它是一個大家喜歡的地方。 |
| *It's* a super place to unwind. | 這是讓人放鬆的超好地方。 |
| | |
| This park is alive. | 這個公園生氣勃勃。 |
| *It's* full of energy. | 它充滿了活力。 |
| *It's* the place to be. | 它是該去的地方。 |
| | |
| *You can see* families enjoying themselves. | 你可以看到很多家庭玩得很愉快。 |
| *You can see* people exercising. | 你可以看到人們在運動。 |
| Mornings and evenings are best. | 早晨和晚上最好。 |

\*\* ———————————————————

favorite〔'fevərɪt〕*adj.* 特別受喜愛的；最喜愛的
popular〔'pɑpjələ〕*adj.* 受歡迎的
spot〔spɑt〕*n.* 地點；場所
super〔'supə〕*adj.* 極好的；超級的
unwind〔ʌn'waɪnd〕*v.* 放鬆（= *relax*）
alive〔ə'laɪv〕*adj.* 熱鬧的；有活力的；生氣勃勃的
*be full of* 充滿　　energy〔'ɛnədʒɪ〕*n.* 活力
*enjoy oneself* 玩得愉快　　exercise〔'ɛksə‚saɪz〕*v.* 運動

BOOK 7

## 【背景說明】

　　當你看到一個公園，裡面有很多人，你就可以講這九句話。

1. *Here's a favorite park*.

favorite〔ˈfevərɪt〕*adj.* 特別受喜愛的；最喜歡的

　　這句話的意思是「這裡是大家所喜愛的公園。」
( = *Here's a popular park*. )

【比較】下面兩句話意思不同。

　　　*Here's a favorite park*.【常用】
　　　Here's my favorite park.【常用】
　　　（這是我最喜愛的公園。）

2. *It's a popular spot*.

popular〔ˈpɑpjələ〕*adj.* 受歡迎的
spot〔spɑt〕*n.* 地點；場所

　　這句話的意思是「它是一個大家喜歡的地方。」

【比較1】

　　　*It's a popular spot*.【語氣輕鬆】
　　　= It's a popular place.【語氣正式】

【比較2】

　　　*It's a popular spot*.【大家都可以說】
　　　= It's a hot spot.【年輕人較喜歡說】
　　　【hot〔hɑt〕*adj.* 熱門的；受歡迎的】

3. *It's a super place to unwind.*

super〔'supɚ〕 *adj.* 極好的；超級的

unwind〔ʌn'waɪnd〕*v.* 放鬆（= *relax*）

這句話的意思是「這是讓人放鬆的超好地方。」

下面各句意義大致相同，都是美國人常說的話，我們按照使用頻率排列：

① *It's a super place to unwind.*【第一常用】

② It's a great place to relax.【第二常用】
　　（這是個讓人放鬆的好地方。）

③ It's a good place to take a break.【第三常用】
　　（這是個讓人休息的好地方。）

【relax〔rɪ'læks〕*v.* 放鬆　　*take a break* 休息一下】

4. *This park is alive.*

alive〔ə'laɪv〕*adj.* 活著的；有活力的；熱鬧的；生氣勃勃的

alive 的主要意思是「活著的」，當你看到公園裡面有很多人，或很多活動在那裡舉辦，你就可以說：*This park is alive.*（這個公園生氣勃勃。）

如果你看到公園裡沒有人，死氣沈沈，你就可以說：This park is dead.（這個公園死氣沈沈。）或 This park is so boring.（這個公園眞是乏味。）

dead〔dɛd〕*adj.* 無生氣的；無活力的

boring〔'borɪŋ〕*adj.* 無聊的；乏味的

BOOK 7

【比較】下面三句話都常用：

> **This park is alive.**【第一常用】
> = This park is lively.【第二常用】
> （這個公園生氣勃勃。）
> = This park is full of life.【第三常用】
> （這個公園充滿活力。）

lively〔'laɪvlɪ〕*adj.* 有生氣的；活潑的
***full of life*** 充滿活力；很熱鬧

5. ***It's full of energy***.
   ***be full of*** 充滿　　energy〔'ɛnə·dʒɪ〕*n.* 活力

   這句話的意思是「它充滿了活力。」也可說成：
   It's full of action.（它有各種活動。）

6. ***It's the place to be***.

   > 這句話源自 It's the place to be at. 或 It's the
   > place to be in. 意思是「它是該去的地方。」說話時
   > 為了簡潔，而省略介詞。美國人常說：On holidays,
   > home is the place to be.（放假時，該待在家裡。）

7. ***You can see families enjoying themselves***.
   ***enjoy*** *oneself* 玩得愉快（= *have fun* = *have a good time*）

   這句話的意思是「你可以看到很多家庭玩得
   很愉快。」源自 You can see *many* families
   enjoying themselves. 這句話等於 You can
   see families having a good time.

8. *You can see people exercising*.

exercise (ˈɛksɚˌsaɪz) v. 運動

這句話的意思是「你可以看到人們在運動。」
下面各句意思相同：

*You can see people exercising*.【第一常用】
You can see people working out.【第二常用】
【*work out* 在此作「運動」解。】
You can see people doing exercise.【第三常用】
【*do exercise* 運動】

在字典上，take exercise 也作「運動」解，但是美國人不說，只有英國人才說。

9. *Mornings and evenings are best*.

這句話的意思是「早晨和晚上最好。」源自
Mornings and evenings are the best time to
be there. (早晨和晚上去那裡最好。)

下面各句意思相同：

*Mornings and evenings are best*.【第一常用】
Morning and evening are the best times.
(早上和晚上是最好的時間。)【第二常用】
Dawn and dusk are good times.【第三常用】
(黎明和黃昏是很好的時間。)
【dawn (dɔn) *n.* 黎明　　dusk (dʌsk) *n.* 黃昏】

## 【對話練習】

1. A：**Here's a favorite park.**　　　　A：這裡是大家所喜愛的公園。
　　B：It certainly looks popular.　　　　B：它確實看起來很受歡迎。
　　　No wonder.　It's beautiful.　　　　難怪。公園這麼漂亮。
　　　I like it already.　　　　　　　　　我已經喜歡上它了。
　　　【*no wonder* 難怪】

2. A：**It's a popular spot.**　　　　　A：它是一個大家喜歡的地方。
　　B：I can see that.　　　　　　　　B：我看得出來。
　　　It must be a great place.　　　　它一定是個很棒的地方。
　　　What do people come here for?　　爲什麼大家要來這裡？

3. A：**It's a super place to unwind.**　A：這是讓人放鬆的超好地方。
　　B：It looks very relaxing.　　　　B：它看起來讓人覺得很輕鬆。
　　　Peace and quiet is important.　　安詳和寧靜是很重要的。
　　　It's good to have a place to　　　　有個可以放鬆的地方是很
　　　relax.　【peace〔pis〕n. 安詳　　好的。
　　　　quiet〔'kwaɪət〕n. 寧靜】

4. A：**This park is alive.**　　　　　A：這個公園生氣勃勃。
　　B：It certainly looks lively.　　　B：它確實看起來生氣勃勃。
　　　What do people do here?　　　　大家來這裡做什麼？
　　　What's all the excitement　　　　爲什麼大家這麼興奮？
　　　about?

5. A：**It's full of energy.**　　　　A：它充滿了活力。
　　B：It's got a great atmosphere.　B：它的氣氛很好。
　　　It's certainly not dull.　　　　它確實不沉悶。
　　　I like a vibrant place.　　　　　我喜歡有活力的地方。
　　　【atmosphere〔'ætməs,fɪr〕n. 氣氛　dull〔dʌl〕adj. 沈悶的
　　　　vibrant〔'vaɪbrənt〕adj. 充滿活力的】

6. A : **It's the place to be**.

A：它是該去的地方。

   B : It's the best place to hang out.
   The whole world comes here.
   Let's join in. 【*hang out* 閒蕩】

B：它是閒逛最好的地方。
   全世界的人都來到這裡。
   我們一起加入吧。

7. A : **You can see families enjoying themselves**.

A：你可以看到很多家庭玩得很愉快。

   B : Lots of people bring their kids here.
   It's a wholesome place.
   It's a good place for the whole family.
   【wholesome〔'holsəm〕 *adj.* 有益健康的】

B：許多人帶他們的孩子來這裡。
   它是個有益健康的地方。
   對全家人而言，它是個好地方。

8. A : **You can see people exercising**.

A：你可以看到人們在運動。

   B : They're certainly dedicated.
   It's a good way to keep fit.
   That's what we ought to do.
   【dedicated〔'dɛdɪ͵ketɪd〕 *adj.* 專注的
   *ought to* 應該 ( = *should* )】

B：他們確實很專注。
   它是保持健康的好方法。
   那是我們應該要做的。

9. A : **Mornings and evenings are best**.

A：早晨和晚上最好。

   B : That works for me.
   How about tomorrow evening?
   We can meet at the coffee shop.
   【work〔wɝk〕 *v.* 行得通】

B：那很適合我。
   明天晚上如何？
   我們可以在咖啡廳見面。

# 8. *Here's a great market*.

| | |
|---|---|
| Here's a great market. | 這裡有一個很棒的市場。 |
| *It's* pretty famous. | 它非常有名。 |
| *It's* noted for its bargains. | 那裡的東西出名的便宜。 |
| | |
| *You should* haggle. | 你應該討價還價。 |
| *You should* negotiate. | 你應該討價還價。 |
| You must talk the price down. | 你必須殺價。 |
| | |
| The sellers are pros. | 這些人很會賣東西。 |
| *They'll* steal you blind. | 他們要騙你太容易了。 |
| *They'll* rip you off without blinking an eye. | 他們敲你竹槓時，面不改色。 |

**\*\*** ─────────────

market〔'mɑrkɪt〕*n.* 市場　　pretty〔'prɪtɪ〕*adv.* 非常
famous〔'feməs〕*adj.* 有名的　　noted〔'notɪd〕*adj.* 有名的
***be noted for*** 以～有名　　bargain〔'bɑrgɪn〕*n.* 便宜貨
haggle〔'hægḷ〕*v.* 討價還價
negotiate〔nɪ'goʃɪ,et〕*v.* 談判；交涉；討價還價
seller〔'sɛlɚ〕*n.* 銷售者；賣方
pro〔pro〕*n.* 專家（= *expert*）
steal〔stil〕*v.* 偷；不知不覺中取走
blind〔blaɪnd〕*adj.* 瞎的　　*adv.* 盲目地
***rip*** *sb.* ***off*** 敲某人竹槓　　blink〔blɪŋk〕*v.* 眨（眼）

## 【背景説明】

　　當你到了戶外市場,那裡的東西通常是可以討
價還價的,美國不多,但也有,像西雅圖( Seattle )、
紐奧良( New Orleans )等,在亞洲國家就很多了。
到了市場,你就可以和你朋友説這九句話。

1. ***Here's a great market.***
   great〔 gret 〕*adj.* 很棒的
   market〔'mɑrkɪt 〕*n.* 市場

   　　這句話的意思是「這裡有一個很棒的市場。」
   也可説成:This is a great market. ( 這是一個很
   棒的市場。 ) 或 It's a great market. ( 它是一個很
   棒的市場。 )

2. ***It's pretty famous.***
   pretty〔'prɪtɪ 〕*adv.* 非常【pretty 的主要意思是「漂亮的」】
   famous〔'feməs 〕*adj.* 有名的

   　　這句話的意思是「它非常有名。」下面各句意
   思相同:

   　　***It's pretty famous.***【第一常用】
   　　It's well-known. ( 它很有名。 )【第二常用】
   　　It's widely known. ( 它很有名。 )【第五常用】
   　　well-known〔'wɛl'non 〕*adj.* 有名的
   　　widely〔'waɪdlɪ 〕*adv.* 廣泛地

Everybody knows it. 【第四常用】
（大家都知道它。）
Everybody knows about it. 【第三常用】
（大家都知道它。）
Everybody's heard of it. 【第六常用】
（大家都聽說過它。）
【*know about* 知道關於～的事　　*hear of* 聽說】

3. **It's noted for its bargains.**

noted〔'notɪd〕*adj.* 有名的　　***be noted for*** 因～而有名
bargain〔'bɑrgɪn〕*n.* 便宜貨　*v.* 討價還價

　　這句話的字面意思是「它以它的便宜貨而有名。」
也就是「那裡的東西出名的便宜。」

　　下面各句意義相同，我們按照使用頻率排列：

① **It's noted for its bargains.** 【第一常用】
② It's famous for its bargains. 【第二常用】
（那裡的東西出名的便宜。）
③ It's well-known for its bargains. 【第三常用】
（那裡的東西出名的便宜。）
【well-known「有名的」，也可以只用 known。】

④ It's renowned for its bargains.
（那裡的東西出名的便宜。）
⑤ It's celebrated for its bargains.
（那裡的東西出名的便宜。）

renowned〔rɪ'naʊnd〕*adj.* 有名的
celebrated〔'sɛlə,bretɪd〕*adj.* 有名的

【比較】下面三句使用頻率非常接近：

> ***It's noted for its bargains.*** 【第一常用】
> It's noted for its low prices. 【第三常用】
> （那裡的價格出名的低。）
> It's noted for good deals. 【第二常用】
> （那裡的東西出名的便宜。）
> 【deal〔dil〕*n.* 交易　***a good deal*** 便宜貨】

## 4. *You should haggle.*

haggle〔'hægḷ〕*v.* 討價還價（= *bargain*）

這句話的意思是「你應該討價還價。」下面是
美國人常說的話，意思非常接近：

> ***You should haggle.*** 【第一常用】
> You should bargain. 【第二常用】
> （你應該討價還價。）
> You should argue the price. 【第六常用】
> （你應該議價。）
> bargain〔'bɑrgɪn〕*v.* 討價還價
> argue〔'ɑrgjʊ〕*v.* 爭論；辯論
>
> You should try to get a discount. 【第三常用】
> （你應該爭取打折。）
> Try to get it cheaper. 【第四常用】
> （想辦法讓它便宜一點。）
> Try to talk the price down. 【第五常用】
> （想辦法殺價。）
> 【get〔gɛt〕*v.* 獲得；使　discount〔'dɪskaʊnt〕*n.* 折扣】

5. ***You should negotiate.***

negotiate〔nɪˈgoʃɪˌet〕*v.* 談判；交涉；討價還價

　　negotiate 主要的意思是「談判」，在這裡作「討價還價」解，詳見「東華英漢大辭典」p.2224。這句話的意思是「你應該討價還價。」

6. ***You must talk the price down.***

　　這句話字面的意思是「你必須把價錢談低。」引申為「你必須殺價。」在字典上找不到 talk the price down，但是美國人常說，例如：He ***talked the price down*** and got a good deal.
（他殺價後，買到便宜的東西。）

7. ***The sellers are pros.***

seller〔ˈsɛlɚ〕*n.* 銷售者；賣方
pro〔pro〕*n.* 專家（= *expert*）

　　這句話字面的意思是「這些賣東西的人是專家。」也就是「這些人很會賣東西。」也可說成：The sellers are experts.（這些賣東西的人是專家。）
〔ˈɛkspɝts〕*n. pl.* 專家

【比較】pro 是 professional 的省略。
***The sellers are pros.***【較常用】
The sellers are professionals.
【正，較少用】　〔prəˈfɛʃənl̩z〕*n. pl.* 專家

8. ***They'll steal you blind.***

steal〔stil〕*v.* 偷；騙取；不知不覺中取走
blind〔blaɪnd〕*adj.* 瞎的　*adv.* 盲目地；未加思考地

這句話有兩個意思：

① **blind** 當副詞用，作「盲目地；未加思考地」解。

> They'll steal you *blind.*
>
> 這句話字面的意思是「他們會盲目地從你那裡偷東西。」steal 是由 steal from 簡化而來，引申為「他們騙你不眨眼。」也就是「他們沒有良心。」
> ( = *They have no conscience.* )
> 　　　　　　　　〔'kanʃəns〕*n.* 良心

② **blind** 當形容詞用，作「瞎的；看不見的」解。

> They'll steal you *blind.*
>
> 這句話字面的意思是「他們把你當作瞎子來欺騙。」( = *They'll cheat you as easily as stealing from a blind person.* ) 這句話引申為「他們要騙你太容易了。」

在這一回裡的 ***They'll steal you blind.*** 兩個意思都解釋得通。

BOOK 7

9. ***They'll rip you off without blinking an eye.***

*rip* *sb.* *off* 敲某人竹槓

blink 〔 blɪŋk 〕 *v.* 眨（眼）

　　這句話的字面意思是「他們敲你的竹槓而不
眨眼。」引申為「他們敲你竹槓時，面不改色。」

　　***rip* *sb.* *off*** 的被動式是 *sb.* ***get ripped off***
不是 *sb.* *be ripped off*（誤）。

> 美國人常說：
>
> I got ripped off.（我被敲竹槓了。）
> Don't get ripped off.　Be careful.
> （不要被敲竹槓。要小心。）
> The salesman ripped me off.
> （那個售貨員敲了我竹槓。）
> 【salesman 〔ˈselzmən 〕 *n.* 售貨員；推銷員】

　　***without blinking an eye*** 的字面意思是「不
眨眼睛」引申為「面不改色」( with a straight
face ) 或「沒有罪惡感」( without feeling any
guilt )。

## 【對話練習】

1. A : **Here's a great market**.
　 B : I like this place.
　　　It's really big.
　　　It looks so alive.
　　　【alive〔ə'laɪv〕*adj.* 熱鬧的；
　　　　有活力的】

　　　A : 這裡有一個很棒的市場。
　　　B : 我喜歡這個地方。
　　　　　它真的很大。
　　　　　它看起來非常熱鬧。

2. A : **It's pretty famous**.
　 B : I've heard of it.
　　　It's got a good name.
　　　Everyone knows it.
　　　【*have got* 有
　　　　*a good name* 好的名聲】

　　　A : 它非常有名。
　　　B : 我聽說過它。
　　　　　它的名聲很好。
　　　　　每個人都知道它。

3. A : **It's noted for its bargains**.
　 B : Great. I love a good
　　　bargain.
　　　I can't pass one up.
　　　Let's go find some good
　　　deals. 【*pass up* 錯過】

　　　A : 那裡的東西出名的便宜。
　　　B : 太好了，我喜歡好的便宜
　　　　　貨。
　　　　　我不會錯過任何的便宜貨。
　　　　　我們去找一些便宜貨吧。

4. A : **You should haggle**.
　 B : I'll try.
　　　Can you show me how?
　　　I'll follow your lead.
　　　【show〔ʃo〕*v.* 給～看　　*follow one's lead* 以某人為榜樣】

　　　A : 你應該討價還價。
　　　B : 我會試試看。
　　　　　你可以告訴我怎麼做嗎？
　　　　　我會以你為榜樣。

5. A : **You should negotiate**.　　　　　A：你應該討價還價。

　　B : I'll offer a lower price.　　　　　B：我會出較低的價錢。
　　　　I'm willing to compromise.　　　　我願意和對方妥協。
　　　　I'm sure we can reach an　　　　　我確定我們可以達成協
　　　　agreement. 【offer〔'ɔfə〕v. 出（價）　議。
　　　　willing〔'wɪlɪŋ〕adj. 願意的
　　　　compromise〔'kɑmprə͵maɪz〕v. 妥協
　　　　agreement〔ə'grimənt〕n. 協議】

6. A : **You must talk the price down**.　　A：你應該殺價。

　　B : Everything is negotiable.　　　　　B：每樣東西都可以討價還價。
　　　　Nothing is fixed.　　　　　　　　　沒有什麼價格是固定的。
　　　　That's the way to get a deal.　　　那正是買到便宜貨的方法。
　　　　【negotiable〔nɪ'goʃɪəbḷ〕adj. 可協商的
　　　　fixed〔fɪkst〕adj. 固定的】

7. A : **The sellers are pros**.　　　　　A：這些人很會賣東西。

　　B : They bargain well.　　　　　　　B：他們很會討價還價。
　　　　They have lots of experience.　　　他們很有經驗。
　　　　They know what they're doing.　　　他們很清楚自己在做什麼。

8. A : **They'll steal you blind**.　　　　A：他們要騙你太容易了。

　　B : I'll be careful.　　　　　　　　　B：我會小心。
　　　　I don't want to pay too much.　　　我不想付太多錢。
　　　　I don't want to get cheated.　　　　我不想被騙。
　　　　【cheat〔tʃit〕v. 欺騙】

9. A : **They'll rip you off without**　　　A：他們敲你竹槓時，面不改
　　　　**blinking an eye**.　　　　　　　　色。

　　B : No if I can help it.　　　　　　　B：如果我能避免，就不會。
　　　　I'm a seasoned traveler.　　　　　我是個經驗豐富的遊客。
　　　　I know how to handle myself.　　　我知道如何照顧自己。
　　　　【help〔hɛlp〕v. 避免；阻止　　seasoned〔'siznd〕adj. 經驗豐富的】

# 9.  *This store is number one.*

| | |
|---|---|
| This store is number one. | 這家商店最好。 |
| *It's the* top place to shop. | 這裡是買東西最好的地方。 |
| *It's the* hottest store in town. | 它是城裡最受歡迎的店。 |
| | |
| *They have* the best stuff. | 他們有最好的東西。 |
| *They have* the top brands. | 他們有賣最好的品牌。 |
| There's always a sale going on. | 總是有東西在特價出售。 |
| | |
| This store is unbelievable. | 這家店令人難以相信。 |
| *They*'ve got everything you need. | 他們有你所需要的每樣東西。 |
| *They* have it all from A to Z. | 他們什麼都有。 |

**

*number one* 最好的；一流的
top〔tɑp〕*adj.* 最高級的；最優良的
shop〔ʃɑp〕*v.* 在商店購物
hot〔hɑt〕*adj.* 熱門的；受歡迎的    *in town* 在城裡
stuff〔stʌf〕*n.* 東西    brand〔brænd〕*n.* 品牌
sale〔sel〕*n.* 特價；拍賣    *go on* 進行
unbelievable〔͵ʌnbə'livəbl̩〕*adj.* 令人無法相信的
*they've got* 他們有    *from A to Z* 從頭到尾；完全地

## 【背景説明】

當你和朋友逛街，經過一家生意很好的商店，你就可以立刻說這九句話。

1. ***This store is number one.***

   ***number one*** ① *n.* 第一名；第一號
   　　　　　　　　② *adj.* 最好的；頭等的

   > 根據 A Dictionary of American Idioms，number one 當名詞時，可寫成 Number One，當形容詞時，要寫成 number one。

   ***This store is number one.*** 的意思是「這家商店最好。」

   以下都是美國人常說的話：

   > ***This store is number one.***【第一常用】
   > This store is the best.【第二常用】
   > （這家商店最好。）
   > This is the best store.【第三常用】
   > （這是最好的商店。）

   This is the most popular store.【第六常用】
   （這是最受歡迎的商店。）
   This is my favorite store.【第九常用】
   （這是我最喜歡的商店。）
   This store is tops.（這家店最好。）【第四常用】
   【favorite〔'fevərɪt〕*adj.* 最喜歡的
   　tops〔tɑps〕*adj.* 極好的；非常好的】

This place is the best.【第五常用】

（這家店是最好的。）

There is no better store.【第七常用】

（沒有比它更好的店了。）

There's not a better place around.【第八常用】

（沒有比這家更好的店了。）

【around〔ə'raʊnd〕*adv.* 到處】

2. ***It's the top place to shop.***

top〔tɑp〕*n.* 頂端　*adj.* 最高級的；最優良的

shop〔ʃɑp〕*n.* 商店　*v.* 在商店購物；購物；購買

top 主要的意思是「頂端」，在這裡是指「最好
的」( = *the very best* )。這句話的意思是「這裡是買
東西最好的地方。」可能表示「在這裡買東西最划得
來。」也可能表示「這個地方的貨物品質最好。」

【比較 1】

***It's the top place to shop.***【第一常用】

It's the best place to shop.【第二常用】

（在這裡買東西最好。）

It's the very best place to shop.【第四常用】

（在這裡買東西最好。）

It's the most popular place to shop.【第五常用】

（這裡是最受歡迎的購物地點。）

It's the number one place to shop.【第三常用】

（在這裡買東西最好。）

【比較2】

> ***It's the top place to shop.*** 【第一常用】
> = It's the top place to buy things. 【第三常用】
> （在這裡買東西最好。）
> = It's the top place to go shopping. 【第二常用】
> （在這裡是購物的最好地點。）

這句話不可說成：*It's a top place to purchase.*
（誤）因為 shop 是「到商店買東西」，purchase 是
純粹「購買」，這一句話會被人誤以為是去買一個
高級的地方，況且現在美國人極少用 purchase，
而多用 buy。

3. ***It's the hottest store in town.***
hot〔hɑt〕*adj.* 熱的；熱門的；受歡迎的
***in town*** 在城裡

> hottest 的主要意思是「最熱的」，在這裡引
> 申為「最熱門的；目前最受歡迎的」( = *the most
> popular* )、或「最有名的」( = *the most famous* )，
> 或「生意最好的」( = *doing the best business* )。
> in town 的意思是「在城裡」( = *in the city* )。這
> 句話的意思是「它是城裡最受歡迎的店。」

【比較1】

**It's the hottest store in town.**【第二常用】

= It's the hottest store **in the city.**【第四常用】

（它是城裡最受歡迎的店。）

= It's the hottest store **around.**【第一常用】

（它是最受歡迎的店。）

= It's the hottest store **anywhere.**【第三常用】

（它是最受歡迎的店。）

【anywhere (ˈɛnɪˌhwɛr) *adv.* 任何地方；無論何處】

【比較2】

**It's the hottest store in town.**【第一常用】

It's the most popular store in town.【第二常用】

（它是城裡最受歡迎的店。）

It's the busiest store in town.【第四常用】

（它是城裡生意最好的店。）

It's *the* store.（它是最好的店。）【第六常用】

【the 在此應唸成〔ði〕表強調，用斜體字，也是表強調。

這句話源自 It's the very best store.】

It's the place to shop.【第三常用】

（它是購物最好的店。）

【源自 It's the very best place to shop.】

Everyone comes here.【第五常用】

（大家都來這裡。）

BOOK 7

4. **They have the best stuff.**

stuff〔stʌf〕*n.* 東西

這句話的意思是「他們有最好的東西。」

以下都是美國人常說的話：

**They have the best stuff.**【第一常用】

They have the best products.【第二常用】
（他們有最好的產品。）

They have the best merchandise.【第六常用】
（他們有最好的商品。）

product〔'prɑdəkt〕*n.* 產品
merchandise〔'mɝtʃən,daɪz〕*n.* 商品

They have quality products.【第五常用】
（他們有品質好的產品。）

They have quality goods.【第四常用】
（他們有品質好的商品。）

They have the nicest things.【第三常用】
（他們有最好的商品。）

quality〔'kwɑlətɪ〕*adj.* 品質好的
goods〔gʊdz〕*n. pl.* 商品

BOOK 7

5. ***They have the top brands***.
brand〔brænd〕*n.* 品牌【源自 brand name（品牌名稱）】

> 　　這句話的意思是「他們有頂級的品牌。」也可
> 說成：They have the best brands.（他們有賣最
> 好的品牌。）或 They have all the famous
> brands.（他們有賣各種名牌。）

　　看到一家店裡面，什麼名牌都有，你可以說：
All the best brands are here.（這裡有賣所有的名
牌。）這句話也可簡化成：They have the brands.
意思是「他們有名牌在賣。」

6. ***There's always a sale going on***.
sale〔sel〕*n.* 出售；拍賣；廉價出售；特價
***go on*** 進行

　　sale 的主要意思是「出售」，這句話字面的意
思是「總是有銷售在進行中。」但在這裡，「銷售」
是指「廉價出售」，所以，這句話在這裡的意思是
「總是有東西在特價出售。」

下面是美國人常說的話：

> ***There's always a sale going on***.【第一常用】
> There's always something on sale.【第五常用】
> （總是有東西在拍賣。）
> There's always a discount on something.
> （總是有東西在打折。）【第六常用】
> 【***on sale*** 拍賣；特價　　discount〔ˈdɪskaʊnt〕*n.* 折扣】

Something is always on sale. 【第二常用】
（總是有東西在特價。）
They're always having a sale. 【第四常用】
（他們總是在特價。）
You can always get a bargain here. 【第三常用】
（你在這裡總是能買到便宜貨。）
【get〔gɛt〕v. 買　　bargain〔'bɑrgɪn〕n. 便宜貨】

7. ***This store is unbelievable.***

　　unbelievable〔ˌʌnbə'livəbḷ〕*adj.* 令人無法相信的

　　　　這句話的意思是「這家店令人難以相信。」

　　　　下面都是美國人常說的話，我們按照使用頻
　　率排列：

　　　① This store is ***unbelievable***. 【第一常用】
　　　② This store is ***incredible***. 【第二常用】
　　　　（這家店令人難以相信。）
　　　③ This store is ***amazing***. 【第三常用】
　　　　（這家店讓人十分驚訝。）

　　　　incredible〔ɪn'krɛdəbḷ〕*adj.* 令人無法相信的
　　　　amazing〔ə'mezɪŋ〕*adj.* 令人驚訝的

④ This store is *remarkable*.（這家店太棒。）

⑤ This store is *fantastic*.

（這家店眞是太棒了。）

⑥ This store is *too good to be true*.

（這家店好得令人難以相信。）

⑦ This store is *wonderful*.（這家店太棒了。）

remarkable〔rɪˋmɑrkəbḷ〕*adj.* 出色的；卓越的；

令人驚奇的

fantastic〔fænˋtæstɪk〕*adj.* 很棒的

***too good to be true*** 好得令人難以相信

## 8. *They've got everything you need.*

***they've got*** 他們有

這句話美國人講快的時候，就說：They got⋯
很少說 *They have got*⋯。意思是「他們有你所需
要的每樣東西。」下面是美國人常說的話：

***They've got everything you need.***【第一常用】
They have everything you want.【第二常用】
（他們有你所想要的每樣東西。）
They have everything.【第四常用】
（他們什麼都有。）

They've got everything.【第五常用】
（他們什麼都有。）
They've got it all.（他們全部都有。）【第三常用】
They have it all.（他們什麼都有。）【第六常用】

You'll find whatever you need here. 【第七常用】
（你在這裡會找到任何你所需要的東西。）
You can find whatever you want here. 【第八常用】
（你在這裡能找到任何你想要的東西。）
You can get whatever you're looking for here.
（你在這裡能買到任何你要找的東西。）【第九常用】
【get〔gɛt〕v. 買】

No matter what you want, you'll find it here.
（無論你要什麼，在這裡你都能找到。）【第十二常用】
It's a one-stop shopping center. 【第十常用】
（它是個「一次購足」的購物中心。）
This store will have whatever you want.
（這家商店會有你想要的任何東西。）【第十一常用】
【one-stop shopping 一次購足】

9. **They have it all from A to Z.**
   **from A to Z** 從頭到尾；完全地；徹底地

　　這句話的意思是「他們什麼都有。」也可以只
說：They have it all. （他們什麼都有。）而 from
A to Z 是用來加強語氣。

　　美國人常說 from A to Z，這個成語要看句
子的意思，來決定它的意義，主要的意思是「從
頭到尾」。

【例】 They have everything from *A to Z*.

（他們什麼都有。）

They do it all *from A to Z*. （他們什麼都做。）

( = *They do everything*. )

That hotel offers every service

*from A to Z*. （那家旅館提供一切服務。）

She ordered everything on the menu

*from A to Z*. （她菜單上什麼都點了。）

【比喻「她點了很多東西。」; order〔ˋɔrdɚ〕 *v.* 點（菜）

menu〔ˋmɛnju〕 *n.* 菜單】

You know everything about grammar

*from A to Z*. 【grammar〔ˋgræmɚ〕 *n.* 文法】

（你文法非常精通；什麼文法你都懂。）

We publish everything *from A to Z*.

（我們什麼都出版。）【publish〔ˋpʌblɪʃ〕 *v.* 出版】

　　*have it all* 已經成為慣用語，字典上查不到，意
思是「什麼都有」等於 have everything。美國著名
的脫口秀主持人 Oprah Winfrey〔ˋoprɑˋwɪnfrɪ〕，
它的名言是：You can *have it all*.  You just can't
have it all at once.（你可以擁有一切，但是你不可
能突然間什麼都有。）【*all at once* 突然地】

【比較】 *They have it all*. 【正，是慣用句】

　　　　 *They have all*.

　　　　【誤，文法對，美國人不說】

BOOK 7

## 【對話練習】

1. A: **This store is number one**.　　　A: 這家商店最好。
   B: It's the biggest and the best.　　B: 它是最大而且是最好的。
   I love shopping here.　　　　　　　我喜歡在這裡購物。
   It's a great place.　　　　　　　　它是個很棒的地方。

2. A: **It's the top place to shop**.　　A: 這裡是買東西最好的地方。
   B: There's some great stuff here.　B: 這裡有一些很棒的東西。
   Other stores are second-rate.　　其他的商店都是二流的。
   Let's get started.　　　　　　　　我們開始吧。
   【stuff〔stʌf〕*n.* 東西
   　*second-rate* 二流的;次等的】

3. A: **It's the hottest store in town**.　A: 它是城裡最受歡迎的店。
   B: No wonder it's so crowded.　　B: 難怪它如此的擁擠。
   It must have great
   merchandise.　　　　　　　　　　它一定有很棒的商品。
   I can't wait to have a look.　　　我等不及要看一下。
   【*no wonder* 難怪
   　crowded〔'kraʊdɪd〕*adj.* 擁擠的
   　merchandise〔'mɝtʃən,daɪz〕*n.* 商品】

4. A: **They have the best stuff**.　　A: 他們有最好的東西。
   B: I'm looking for the best.　　　B: 我正在尋找最好的。
   Quality is important.　　　　　　品質很重要。
   I won't settle for less.　　　　　我不會勉強接受品質較
   【*settle for* 勉強接受】　　　　　差的。

5. A：**They have the top brands**.

　　B：I only want the best.
　　　Designer goods are worth the price.
　　　That's why they're in fashion.
　　　【designer〔dɪˋzaɪnə〕*n.* 設計師
　　　　*in fashion* 很流行】

A：他們有頂級的品牌。

B：我只要最好的。
　買設計師的商品是值得的。
　那就是爲什麼他們總是很流行的原因。

6. A：**There's always a sale going on**.

　　B：The prices are really low.
　　　I can't believe how cheap it all is.
　　　How can they afford to stay in business?【afford〔əˋford〕*v.* 負擔得起
　　　　*in business* 經商】

A：總是有東西在特價出售。

B：價格眞的很低。
　我不敢相信它全部都這麼便宜。
　他們怎麼能維持營運？

7. A：**This store is unbelievable**.

　　B：I've never seen better.
　　　I love it.
　　　I could live here.

A：這家店令人難以相信。

B：我從來沒看比它更好的。
　我非常喜歡它。
　我簡直可以住在這裡。

8. A：**They've got everything you need**.

　　B：And more.
　　　It's one-stop shopping.
　　　I've got everything on my list.
　　　【list〔lɪst〕*n.* 清單】

A：他們有你所需要的每樣東西。

B：比那樣多。
　它是能一次購足的地方。
　我已經買到清單上的每樣東西了。

9. A：**They have it all from A to Z**.

　　B：Sounds great!
　　　I'm so excited.
　　　I'm sure they have what I'm looking for.

A：他們什麼都有。

B：聽起來很棒！
　我很興奮！
　我確定他們有我想找的東西。

BOOK 7

# 10. Let's hang out.

| | |
|---|---|
| *Let's* hang out. | 我們待在這裡吧。 |
| *Let's* stick around. | 我們待在附近吧。 |
| *Let's* stay here for a while. | 我們在這裡待一會兒吧。 |
| | |
| *We can* relax. | 我們可以放輕鬆。 |
| *We can* chill out. | 我們可以輕鬆一下。 |
| *We can* mellow out. | 我們可以輕鬆一下。 |
| | |
| *Take a* load off. | 坐下來休息一下。 |
| *Take a* little rest. | 休息一會兒。 |
| We can watch the crowd. | 我們可以看人群走來走去。 |

\*\* ────────────────

**hang out** 閒蕩；消磨時間　　**stick around** 逗留；等待
**for a while** 一會兒　　relax〔rɪˈlæks〕v. 放鬆
chill〔tʃɪl〕v. 變冷　　**chill out** 放鬆一下
mellow〔ˈmɛlo〕v. 變柔和　　**mellow out** 放鬆一下
load〔lod〕n. 負擔　　**take a load off** 坐下來休息一下
**take a rest** 休息一下　　crowd〔kraʊd〕n. 人群

## 【背景說明】

　　當和朋友逛街，逛到想要待在一個地方休息
休息的時候，就可以說這些話了。

1. ***Let's hang out.***

hang〔hæŋ〕*v.* 懸掛

***hang out*** 居住；遊蕩；閒蕩；消磨時間

　　雖然 hang out 這個成語已經在 p.560-561 中，有
詳細的說明它的來源和用法，但是由於字典上都寫得
不清楚，所以我們現在再次說明。

① hang out 後面可接地點，而 hang out
　somewhere 的意思是 spend time
　somewhere 或 waste time somewhere。

【例1】 Let's ***hang out*** at McDonald's
　　　 after school.
　　　 （我們放學後在麥當勞消磨一些時間吧。）

【例2】 I like ***hanging out*** at the mall.
　　　 （我喜歡在購物中心打發時間。）
　　　 【mall〔mɔl〕*n.* 購物中心】

【例3】 Come over and ***hang out*** at my house.
　　　 （來我家玩吧。）

　　　 【此時 hang out 等於 spend some time，這句話的意思
　　　 是來我家看電視，或做其他娛樂活動等。】

② hang out 後面加 with 後，可接人，hang out
with someone 等於 spend time with someone
或 waste time with someone。

【例1】 Don't *hang out* with the wrong people.
（不要和爛人在一起浪費時間。）

【例2】 Never *hang out* with smokers.
（絕不要和抽煙的人在一起。）

【例3】 I enjoy *hanging out* with my classmates.
（我喜歡和同學在一起。）

【例4】 My mom told me to *hang out* less and
study more.
（我媽媽告訴我，要少浪費時間，多讀書。）

在這一回中的 *Let's hang out*. 意思是「我們
待在這裡吧。」(= *Let's stay here*.)

2. *Let's stick around.*
stick〔stɪk〕*n.* 棍子 *v.* 刺；貼著；黏住
*stick around* 徘徊；逗留；等待

stick 這個字，當名詞時，主要意思是「棍子」
之類的東西，當動詞時，可當「刺」或「貼著；黏
住」等。

*Let's stick around.* 字面的意思是「我們黏在
周圍吧。」引申為「我們待在附近吧。」你看美國
人說話多幽默，他們講這些話的時候，心裡想的
是「黏著」，看看下面例句：

Don't go away. ***Stick around***.

（不要走開。待在附近。）

Let's ***stick around*** here for an hour.

（我們待在這裡一小時吧。）

***Stick around***. The night is still young.

（待在這裡，不要走開。夜尚未深。）

【young〔jʌŋ〕*adj.*（夜晚）還早的】

　　stick 這個字，由「黏住」引申的，不只是
stick around，還有：

***Stick with*** me, and I'll treat you to a bite.

（如果你和我在一起，不要走，我會請你吃東西。）

【*treat sb. to* ~　請某人吃 ~　bite〔baɪt〕*n.* 食物；小吃；點心】

***Stick to*** it, and you'll succeed.

（如果你堅持下去，你就會成功。）

3. ***Let's stay here for a while***.

while〔hwaɪl〕*n.* 片刻（= *short period of time*）

　　這句話的意思是「我們在這裡待一會兒吧。」也
可以簡化為 ***Let's stay a while***.（我們待一會兒吧。）

　　在這一回裡的前三句話，意義相同，一口氣說
三句，有加強語氣的意思。

Let's hang out.（我們待在這裡吧。）

= Let's stick around.（我們待在附近吧。）

= ***Let's stay here for a while***.

（我們在這裡待一會兒吧。）

**BOOK 7**

4. ***We can relax.***

relax〔rɪ'læks〕*v.* 放鬆

　　　　這句話的意思是「我們可以放輕鬆。」等於
We can take it easy.

5. ***We can chill out.***

chill〔tʃɪl〕*n.* 寒冷　*v.* 變冷　　***chill out*** 放鬆一下

　　　　chill 的主要意思是「變冷」，out 在這裡的意
思是「完全地；徹底地」，像 I am tired out.（我
已經累死了。）

　　　　***chill out*** 的字面意思是「完全變冷」，引申
爲「冷靜下來」（= *calm down*），或「放鬆一下」
（= *relax*）。

當你看到一個人很緊張，你就可以跟他大聲地説：

　　***Chill out.***（冷靜一下。）
　　Calm down. ***Chill out.***
　　　（冷靜下來。冷靜一下。）
　　Take it easy. ***Chill out.***
　　　（放輕鬆。冷靜一下。）

你看到一群人在喧鬧，你就可以説：

　　***Chill out***, guys.（大家冷靜下來。）
　　Let's just ***chill out***.（我們冷靜一下吧。）
　　All right now, people, ***chill out***…
　　　***chill out***.（現在好了，大家安靜…安靜。）
　　【guy〔gaɪ〕*n.* 人；傢伙】

　　上面各句的 chill out 也可簡化成 chill，因為 out 只是用來加強語氣。最後一句可改成：All right now, people, *chill…chill*.

　　在這一回中，*We can chill out*. 的意思是「我們可以放鬆一下。」和上一句 We can relax. 的意義相同。下面三句話使用頻率大致相同：

> *We can chill out*.（我們可以放鬆一下。）
> = We can relax.（我們可以放輕鬆。）
> = We can take it easy.（我們可以放輕鬆。）

## 6. *We can mellow out*.

mellow〔ˈmɛlo〕*adj.*（水果）熟的；（音、色、光）柔和的；（天氣）溫和的　*v.*（水果）變熟；（音、色、光）變柔和；（天氣）變溫和

　　背 mellow 這個字很容易，只要先背 yellow（黃色的），將 y 改成 m 就行了。ow 字尾通常讀 /o/，在字中讀 /aʊ/，只有少數例外。

> 　　mellow 這個字當形容詞，美國人用得並不多，但他們卻常說 *mellow out*，和 chill out 意思相同：
> ① 冷靜下來（ = *calm down* ; *get less angry* ）；
> ② 放鬆一下（ = *take it easy* ）。

　　*We can mellow out*. 字面的意思是「我們可以變得很柔和。」在這裡引申為「我們可以輕鬆一下。」不能只說 *We can mellow*.（誤）

你要常說 *mellow out* 這個成語：

> Calm down. *Mellow out!*
>
> （冷靜下來。輕鬆一下！）
>
> Don't get angry. *Mellow out.*
>
> （不要生氣。冷靜一下。）
>
> *Mellow out*, guys.（大家安靜下來。）
>
> Everybody *mellow out*.（大家安靜。）
>
> 【Everybody 是稱呼語，不是主詞】
>
> Let's *mellow out* for a while.
>
> （我們輕鬆一下吧。）
>
> Let's *mellow out* right here.
>
> （我們在這裡輕鬆輕鬆吧。）

7. *Take a load off.*

   *take off* 卸除；免除；脫掉；起飛

   load〔lod〕*n.* 負擔

   *take a load off* 坐下來休息一下

> *Take a load off.* 的字面意思是「把負擔去除掉。」在這裡的 load 是指「身體的重量」( *body weight* )，「把身體的重量去除掉。」意思就是「坐下來休息一下。」( = *Sit down and rest.* )

下面都是美國人常說的話：

> ***Take a load off****.*【第一常用】
> = Take a load off your feet.【第七常用】
> （坐下來歇歇腳。）

> = Sit down.（坐下。）【第三常用】
> = Sit down and relax.【第二常用】
> （坐下來，放鬆一下。）
> = Sit a while.（坐一會兒。）【第四常用】

> = Take a seat.（坐下。）【第六常用】
> = Have a seat.（坐下。）【第五常用】
> 【*take a seat* 坐下（= *have a seat*）】

8. ***Take a little rest****.*

***take a rest*** 休息一下

> 　　這句話的意思是「休息一會兒。」一般人只會
> 說：Take a rest. 而你會說：

> Take a rest.（休息一下。）
> ***Take a little rest****.*（休息一會兒。）
> Take a short rest.（休息一下。）

> Take a nice rest.（好好休息一下。）
> Take a five-minute rest.（休息五分鐘。）
> Take a half-hour rest.（休息半小時。）

9. ***We can watch the crowd.***

watch〔wɑtʃ〕v. 觀察
crowd〔krɑʊd〕n. 人群

這句話的字面意思是「我們可以看人群。」引
申為「我們可以看人群走來走去。」crowd 後面省
略了 go by（經過）。

看看下面美國人常說的話：

***We can watch the crowd.***【第一常用】
We can watch the crowds.【第二常用】
（我們可以看人群走來走去。）
We can watch the crowds of people.【第五常用】
（我們可以看人群走來走去。）

We can watch people.【第三常用】
（我們可以看人群走來走去。）
We can people watch.【第四常用】
（我們可以看人群走來走去。）
We can watch the crowds go by.【第六常用】
（我們可以看人群走來走去。）

crowd「人群」，用單複數都可以，複數表示
「一群一群的人」。people watch 字典上沒有，將
來可以會變成 people-watch，成為複合動詞，意
思是「觀察人群」。

【對話練習】

1. A：**Let's hang out**.

   B：Why not?
   There's no place we have
   to be.
   We have time to spare.
   【spare〔spεr〕*v.* 騰出（時間）】

    A：我們待在這裡吧。

    B：為什麼不？
      我們不需要去任何地方。

      我們有多餘的時間。

2. A：**Let's stick around**.

   B：Good idea.
   It's comfortable here.
   Something interesting might
   happen.

    A：我們待在附近吧。

    B：好主意。
      這裡很舒服。
      也許會發生有趣的事情。

3. A：**Let's stay here for a while**.

   B：Fine with me.
   It's a good place.
   There's no place I'd rather be.
   【*would rather* 寧願】

    A：我們在這裡待一會兒吧。

    B：沒問題。
      這是個好地方。
      我沒有更想待的地方。

4. A：**We can relax**.

   B：That's a good idea.
   I'd like that.
   This is a relaxing place.

    A：我們可以放輕鬆。

    B：那是個好主意。
      我喜歡那樣。
      這是個可以讓人放鬆的
      地方。

5. A : **We can chill out**.

A：我們可以輕鬆一下。

　B : I could use a rest.
　　　Let's just take it easy.
　　　There's no sense in rushing.
　　　【*could use* 有點想要
　　　　sense〔sɛns〕*n.* 意義
　　　　rush〔rʌʃ〕*v.* 匆忙】

B：我有點想要休息一下。
　我們放輕鬆吧。
　匆匆忙忙沒什麼意義。

6. A : **We can mellow out**.

A：我們可以輕鬆一下。

　B : You're right.
　　　We should enjoy ourselves.
　　　Let's enjoy the moment.

B：你說的對。
　我們應該好好玩一玩。
　讓我們享受這一刻吧。

7. A : **Take a load off**.

A：坐下來休息一下。

　B : That sounds great.
　　　Don't mind if I do.
　　　What a nice spot!
　　　【spot〔spɑt〕*n.* 地點】

B：聽起來很棒。
　如果我這麼做，你不要介意。
　這個地方真好！

8. A : **Take a little rest**.

A：休息一會兒。

　B : Thanks, I need one.
　　　A break will do us good.
　　　We certainly deserve one.
　　　【break〔brek〕*n.* 休息
　　　　*do sb. good* 對某人有益
　　　　deserve〔dɪˈzɝv〕*v.* 應得】

B：謝謝，我需要休息一會兒。
　休息對我們有益。
　我們確實應該休息一下。

9. A : **We can watch the crowd**.

A：我們可以看人群走來走去。

　B : People-watching is my hobby.
　　　People are so interesting.
　　　I could watch them all day.

B：看人群是我的嗜好。
　人群很有趣。
　我可以觀察他們一整天。

# 11. *This city is dynamic*.

| | |
|---|---|
| This city is dynamic. | 這個城市充滿活力。 |
| *It's a* mix of East and West. | 它是東、西方的混合。 |
| *It's a* combination of old and new. | 它是新和舊的結合。 |
| | |
| This city never sleeps. | 這個城市從不睡覺。 |
| *It's* a 24/7 city. | 這個城市是不夜城,全年無休。 |
| *It's* always on the go. | 它總是很忙碌。 |
| | |
| This city has it all. | 這個城市什麼都有。 |
| *To* see it is to like it. | 看到它,你就會喜歡它。 |
| *To* live here is to love it. | 住在這裡,你就會愛上它。 |

**  ————————

dynamic〔daɪ'næmɪk〕*adj.* 動態的;充滿活力的
mix〔mɪks〕*n.* 混合　　East〔ist〕*n.* 東方(各國)
West〔wɛst〕*n.* 西洋;歐美(各國)
combination〔͵kɑmbə'neʃən〕*n.* 結合
old〔old〕*n.* 舊事物　　new〔nju〕*n.* 新事物
*24/7* 唸成 twenty-four seven,指「一星期七天,二十四
　小時不停」,也就是「全年無休」。
*on the go* 很忙碌　　*has it all* 什麼都有

## 【背景説明】

　　當你和朋友在一起逛街，看到三更半夜還車水馬龍，你就可以説這些話了。

1. **This city is dynamic.**

　　dynamic〔daɪ'næmɪk〕*adj.* 動態的；充滿活力的；生氣勃勃的（= *full of energy*）

　　這句話的意思是「這個城市充滿活力。」美國人常説 dynamic 這個字。如果你看到一個女強人，你可以説：She is so dynamic.  She is always on the go.（她真是充滿了活力。她總是非常忙碌。）【*on the go* 很忙碌】

> ***This city is dynamic.***【第一常用】
> = This city is lively.【第五常用】
> 　（這個城市充滿了活力。）
> = This city is full of energy.【第三常用】
> 　（這個城市充滿了活力。）
> 【lively〔'laɪvlɪ〕*adj.* 有活力的】
>
> = This city is full of life.【第二常用】
> 　（這個城市充滿了活力。）
> = This city is very active.【第六常用】
> 　（這個城市非常活躍。）
> = This city moves fast.【第四常用】
> 　（這個城市動得很快。）
> 【active〔'æktɪv〕*adj.* 活躍的　　move〔muv〕*v.* 移動】

BOOK 7

= This city is always on the go.【第七常用】
　（這個城市總是很忙碌。）
= This city is always changing.【第八常用】
　（這個城市總是在改變。）
= This city is changing all the time.【第九常用】
　（這個城市一直在改變。）【*all the time*　一直】

2. *It's a mix of East and West.*
　mix〔mɪks〕*n.* 混合；混合物
　East〔ist〕*n.* 東方（各國）
　West〔wɛst〕*n.* 西洋；歐美（各國）

　　　這句話的意思是「它是東、西方的混合。」美
　國人喜歡簡化，把 mixture 說成 mix，就像把
　mathematics（數學）說成或寫成 math 一樣。句
　中的 East and West 不可寫成 *east and west*（東
　方和西方），因為這裡的 East 是指「東方各國」，
　West 是指「西洋；歐美各國」。這句話也可以說
　成：It's a marriage of East and West.（它是
　東、西方的結合。）【marriage〔'mærɪdʒ〕*n.* 密切的
　結合】或 It's a combination of East and West.
　（它是東、西方的結合。）

　【比較】 *It's a mix of East and West.*【正，通俗】
　　　　 It's a mixture of East and West.
　　　　　　【正式，但美國人少用】

3. **It's a combination of old and new**.

combination〔ˌkɑmbəˈneʃən〕n. 結合

old〔old〕n. 舊事物　　new〔nju〕n. 新事物

　　　這句話的意思是「它是新和舊的結合。」是指
這個城市有新的文化，也有舊的文化；有傳統，
也有現代的思維，也可以說成：It combines the
old with the new. ( 它結合了新和舊。)【combine
〔kəmˈbaɪn〕v. 結合】或 It's a mix of old and new.
( 它是新和舊的混合。) 意思都一樣。

4. **This city never sleeps**.

　　　在大城市裡，像紐約，白天、晚上都很熱鬧，
你就可以說：**This city never sleeps**. ( 這個城市從
不睡覺。) 或 This city never stops. ( 這個城市從
不停止。) 花旗銀行 ( Citibank )
的廣告詞是 THE CITI NEVER
SLEEPS，暗示該銀行永遠不打烊。

5. **It's a 24/7 city**.

　　　24/7 說成：twenty-four seven，意思是
twenty-four hours a day, seven days a week
( 一天二十四小時，一個禮拜七天 )，這句話的意
思是「這個城市是不夜城，全年無休。」

　　　**It's a 24/7 city**. 是年輕人近幾年的流行語，老
一輩的人會說：It's a 24-hour city. ( 它是不夜城。)

BOOK 7

下面都是美國人常說的話：

*It's a 24/7 city.*【第一常用】

This city is on the go 24/7.【第六常用】

（這個城市很忙碌，全年無休。）

This city never shuts down.【第四常用】

（這個城市從不打烊。）

【*shut down* 關閉；打烊】

This city is never closed.【第三常用】

（這個城市從不打烊。）

This city never closes down.【第五常用】

（這個城市從不打烊。）

This city is always open.【第二常用】

（這個城市一直都是開著的。）

【closed〔kozd〕*adj.* 停止營業的

*close down* 歇業；打烊

open〔'opən〕*adj.* 營業中的；開著的】

This city is open night and day.【第八常用】

（這個城市日夜都開著。）

This city is open day and night.【第九常用】

（這個城市日夜都開著。）

This city is open all the time.【第七常用】

（這個城市一直都開著。）

【*night and day* 日夜不停地（= *day and night*）】

BOOK 7

6. ***It's always on the go.***
***on the go*** 不停地活動；很忙碌

　　　　這句話的意思是「它總是很忙碌。」on the go
可指「人」也可指「非人」。我們可以說 She is on
the go.（她很忙碌。）或 ***The city is on the go.***
（這個城市很忙碌。）on the go 的同義成語是 on
the run，但 on the run 卻不能修飾「非人」。

　　【比較】　***It's always on the go.***【正】
　　　　　　***It's always on the run.***【誤】

7. ***The city has it all.***
***have it all*** 什麼都有

　　　　這句話的意思是「這個城市什麼都有。」也可
以說成：The city has everything you need.
（這個城市有你需要的一切東西。）或 This city
is full of things to do.（不管你想做什麼，都可以
在這個城市做。）

8. ***To see it is to like it.***
　　　　這句話的意思是「看到它，你就會喜歡它。」
下面都是美國人常說的話：

> ***To see it is to like it.***【第一常用】
> = Once you see it, you'll like it.【第五常用】
> 　　（一旦你看到它，你就會喜歡它。）
> = If you see it, you'll like it.【第二常用】
> 　　（如果你看到它，你就會喜歡它。）
> 　　【once〔wʌns〕*conj.* 一旦】

BOOK 7

= Once you visit, you'll like it. 【第六常用】

（一旦你去過，你就會喜歡它。）

= If you visit, you'll like it. 【第三常用】

（如果你去過，你就會喜歡它。）

= You'll like it when you see it. 【第四常用】

（當你看到它，你就會喜歡它。）

【visit (ˈvɪzɪt) v. 拜訪】

英文有個諺語是：To see is to believe.（眼見爲信；百聞不如一見。）也可説成：Seeing is believing. 兩者使用頻率相同。但是在這裡，就不一樣了。

【比較】 *To see it is to like it.* 【正】

*Seeing it is liking it.*

【誤，文法對，但美國人不説】

9. *To live here is to love it.*

這句話的意思是「住在這裡，你就會愛上它。」也可説成：If you live here, you'll love it.（如果你住在這裡，你就會愛上它。）也有美國人説：You'd love living here.（你會很喜歡住在這裡。）或 Everyone who lives here loves it.（住在這裡的每一個人，都愛這裡。）

BOOK 7

## 【對話練習】

1. A：**This city is dynamic**.　　　　　A：這個城市充滿活力。

　 B：It's fast-paced.　　　　　　　B：它的步調很快。

　　 I like the atmosphere.　　　　　我喜歡這種氣氛。

　　 I like the hustle and bustle.　　 我喜歡這種忙亂。

　　 【pace〔pes〕*n.* 步調

　　　 ***hustle and bustle*** 擠來擠去；忙亂】

2. A：**It's a mix of East and West**.　A：它是東、西方的混合。

　 B：It's an interesting combination.　B：它是個有趣的結合。

　　 I like the diversity.　　　　　　我喜歡多樣性。

　　 You can find anything here.　　 你可以在這裡找到任

　　 【diversity〔daɪ'vɝsətɪ〕*n.* 多樣性】　何東西。

3. A：**It's a combination of old and**　A：這是新和舊的結合。
　　 **new**.

　 B：I appreciate the old.　　　　　B：我欣賞舊的事物。

　　 I'm fascinated by the new.　　 我對新的事物著迷。

　　 It's a perfect combination.　　 它是個完美的結合。

　　 【appreciate〔ə'priʃɪ,et〕*v.* 欣賞

　　　 fascinate〔'fæsn̩,et〕*v.* 使著迷】

4. A：**This city never sleeps**.　　　A：這個城市從不睡覺。

　 B：It's perfect for night owls.　　 B：對夜貓子來說，這個

　　 There's always something　　　 城市非常的完美。
　　 to do.　　　　　　　　　　　 總是有事情可以做。

　　 It's my kind of place.　　　　 這是個我喜歡的地方。

　　 【owl〔aʊl〕*n.* 貓頭鷹；熬夜的人　***night owl*** 熬夜的人；夜貓子】

5. A：**It's a 24/7 city**.

   B：It never closes.
   That's really convenient.
   It suits me.
   【close〔kloz〕*v.* 關閉；打烊
   　suit〔sut〕*v.* 適合】

A：這個城市是不夜城，全年無休。

B：它從不打烊。
　　那真的很方便。
　　它適合我。

6. A：**It's always on the go**.

   B：We'll never be bored.
   There's a lot to do.
   I hope I can keep up.
   【*keep up* 跟上】

A：它總是很忙碌。

B：我們絕不會覺得無聊。
　　有很多事情可以做。
　　我希望我可以跟上它的腳步。

7. A：**This city has it all**.

   B：That's what I want.
   I can't wait to explore.
   Let's get out there and
   see it.
   【explore〔ɪkˋsplor〕*v.* 探險】

A：這個城市什麼都有。

B：那正是我想要的。
　　我等不及要去探險了。
　　我們出去看看吧。

8. A：**To see it is to like it**.

   B：I like it already.
   I can't wait to see it.
   When do we start?

A：看到它，你就會喜歡它。

B：我已經喜歡上它了。
　　我等不及要看看它。
　　我們什麼時候開始？

9. A：**To live here is to love it**.

   B：There is a lot to love.
   It's a very nice place.
   I can see why you like it
   so much.

A：住在這裡，你就會愛上它。

B：有很多令人喜愛的地方。
　　這是個很好的地方。
　　我可以了解你為什麼會這麼喜
　　歡它。

# 12. *You're a fun person*.

| | |
|---|---|
| *You're* a fun person. | 和你在一起很愉快。 |
| *You're* great to be with. | 和你在一起很棒。 |
| I like being around you. | 我喜歡和你在一起。 |
| | |
| *You're* easygoing. | 你很隨和。 |
| *You're* easy to please. | 你很容易滿意。 |
| You have a nice personality. | 你的個性很好。 |
| | |
| I like your spirit. | 我欣賞你的活力。 |
| *You're* full of life. | 你很有活力。 |
| *You're* always a good time. | 和你在一起總是很愉快。 |

\*\*

fun〔fʌn〕*adj.* 好玩的；有趣的；令人愉快的
great〔gret〕*adj.* 很棒的
around〔əˈraʊnd〕*prep.* 在…周圍
easygoing〔ˈizɪˈgoɪŋ〕*adj.* 脾氣隨和的；隨遇而安的
please〔pliz〕*v.* 取悅；使滿意
personality〔͵pɝsn̩ˈælətɪ〕*n.* 個性
spirit〔ˈspɪrɪt〕*n.* 精神；活力
*be full of* 充滿　　life〔laɪf〕*n.* 活力

BOOK 7

## 【背景説明】

和朋友在一起玩了一天，要道別的時候，該怎麼稱讚他呢？這一回的九句，是最佳的選擇。

1. ***You're a fun person.***

fun 〔 fʌn 〕 *adj.* 好玩的；有趣的；令人愉快的

這句話的意思，並不完全是「你是個有趣的人。」而是「你是個令人愉快的人。」也就是「和你在一起很愉快。」

【比較】 ***You're a fun person.*** ( 你是個令人愉快的人。)

【和你在一起，既有趣又令人愉快。】

You're an interesting person.

( 你是個有趣的人。)

【和你在一起，並不一定很愉快。】

下面是美國人常説的話，我們按照使用頻率排列：

① ***You're a fun person.*** 【第一常用】

② You're really fun. 【第二常用】

( 和你在一起，真的很愉快。)

③ You're fun to be with. 【第三常用】

( 和你在一起很愉快。)

④ It's fun to be with you.

( 和你在一起很愉快。)

⑤ You're a lot of laughs.

( 和你在一起會笑口常開。)

⑥ You're not boring at all.

( 和你在一起一點也不無聊。)

2. **You're great to be with**.

　　great〔 gret 〕*adj.* 很棒的

　　　　這句話的意思是「和你在一起很棒。」這類的話
　　美國人常說的有：

　　　　　**You're great to be with**.【第一常用】
　　　　　It's great being with you.【第三常用】
　　　　　( 和你在一起很棒。)
　　　　　【It's great to be with you. 太正式，美國人少說。】
　　　　　Spending time with you is great.【第四常用】
　　　　　( 和你在一起很棒。)

　　　　　I love being with you.【第五常用】
　　　　　( 我很喜歡和你在一起。)
　　　　　I love spending time with you.【第六常用】
　　　　　( 我很喜歡和你在一起。)
　　　　　I really enjoy your company.【第二常用】
　　　　　( 我真的很喜歡和你在一起。)
　　　　　【company〔'kʌmpənɪ〕*n.* 陪伴】

3. **I like being around you**.

　　around〔 ə'raʊnd 〕*prep.* 在…周圍

　　　　這句話字面的意思是「我喜歡在你周圍。」引申
　　爲「我喜歡和你在一起。」美國人也常說成：I like
　　spending time with you.( 我喜歡和你在一起。)

　　【比較】 ***I like being around you***.【正，常用】
　　　　　 *I like being around with you*.【誤】
　　　　　 I like being with you.【正，常用】
　　　　　 上面各句的 like，都可改成 enjoy。

BOOK 7

4. *You're easygoing.*

easygoing〔'izɪ'goɪŋ〕*adj.* 脾氣隨和的；隨遇而安的

　　這句話字面的意思是「你是隨和的。」也就是我們中文所說的「你很隨和。」或是「你脾氣很好。」也有美國人說：You're easy to get along with.
（你很好相處。）【*get along with* 和～相處】

5. *You're easy to please.*

please〔pliz〕*v.* 取悅；使高興；使喜歡；使滿意

　　這句話字面意思是「你很容易被取悅。」引申為「你很容易滿意。」

　　看到一個人，你隨便講些什麼，他都很興奮，你就可以稱讚他說：You're easily excited.（你很容易興奮。）如果你請一個人吃東西，不管吃什麼，他都很高興、很滿足，你就可以說：*You're easy to please.*（你很容易滿意。）

【比較】 You're easy *to please.*【正】
　　　　*You're easy to be pleased.*
　　　　【誤，不定詞當形容詞或副詞時，通常用主動代替被動。】

6. *You have a nice personality.*

personality 〔,pɝsn̩'ælətɪ〕 *n.* 個性

　　這句話的意思是「你有很好的個性。」也就是「你的個性很好。」

【比較1】

> 中文：你的個性很好。
> 英文：*Your personality is nice.*
> 　　【誤，文法對，美國人不說】
> *You have a nice personality.*【正】

【比較2】

*You have a nice personality.*【第一常用】
You have a great personality.【第二常用】
（你的個性很好。）
You have a good personality.【第六常用】
（你的個性很好。）
【美國人較少用，因為語氣較弱】

You have a wonderful personality.【第三常用】
（你的個性很棒。）
You have a terrific personality.【第五常用】
（你的個性棒極了。）
You have a super personality.【第四常用】
（你的個性超好。）
【terrific〔tə'rɪfɪk〕*adj.* 很棒的】

7. ***I like your spirit.***

spirit〔'spɪrɪt〕*n.* 精神；熱忱；勇氣；活力；氣質

> spirit 的主要意思是「精神」，但卻包含無限多的意思。
>
> 當一個人很熱心幫助你的時候，你可以說：
> You're very enthusiastic. ***I like your***
> ***spirit.***（你很熱心。我欣賞你的熱忱。）
>
> 當一個人很勇敢地做某件事情，你就可以說：
> You're not afraid to try. ***I like your***
> ***spirit.***（你勇於嘗試。我欣賞你的勇氣。）
>
> 當你看到一個人精力充沛，總是不會累，你可以說：
> You're full of energy. ***I like your***
> ***spirit.***（你充滿精力。我欣賞你的活力。）
>
> 在這一回中，***I like your spirit.*** 是指「我欣賞你的活力。」

I like your spirit.

8. *You're full of life.*

　　*be full of* 充滿　　life〔laɪf〕*n.* 生命；活力

　　　這句話的意思是「你充滿了活力。」也就是「你很有活力。」下面各句的意思很接近，我們按照使用頻率排列：

---

① *You're full of life.*【第一常用】
　（你很有活力。）
② You're full of spirit.【第二常用】
　（你很有精神。）
③ You're full of energy.【第三常用】
　（你很有精力。）
　【energy〔'ɛnədʒɪ〕*n.* 精力；活力】

④ You're full of pep.（你很有精力。）
⑤ You're full of vigor.（你很有精力。）
⑥ You're full of vitality.（你很有活力。）
　pep〔pɛp〕*n.* 精力；活力
　vigor〔'vɪgə〕*n.* 精力；活力
　vitality〔vaɪ'tælətɪ〕*n.* 活力

---

9. *You're always a good time.*

---

　　　在所有的中外字典中，都找不到 *You're a good time.* 這一類的句子，但是，美國人常說這句話，字典上沒有的，我們特別詳加說明。

---

BOOK 7

在這裡，a good time 的意思就是 fun，可修飾「人」，也可修飾「非人」。

> **You're always a good time.**
> （和你在一起總是很愉快。）
> Her parties are always **a good time**.
> （她的宴會總是很好玩。）
> Going out with you is **a good time**.
> （和你一起出去很好玩。）
>
> Going abroad is **a good time**.
> （出國很好玩。）
> Disneyland is always **a good time**.
> （迪斯耐樂園總是很好玩。）
> abroad〔ə'brɔd〕*adv.* 到國外
> Disneyland〔'dɪznɪ,lænd〕*n.* 迪斯耐樂園
>
> Eating at the night market is **a good time**.
> （在夜市吃東西很好玩。）
> New Year's Eve is **a good time**.
> （除夕很好玩。）
> Watching that TV show is always
>   **a good time**.
> （看那個電視節目總是很愉快。）
> **night market** 夜市　　**New Year's Eve** 除夕
> show〔ʃo〕*n.* 節目

BOOK 7

## 【對話練習】

1. A: **You're a fun person**.
   B: Thanks. That's nice of you to say.
   I like to enjoy myself.
   I hope you enjoyed yourself, too.

   A: 和你在一起很愉快。
   B: 謝謝。你這麼說，人眞好。
   我喜歡玩得很愉快。
   我希望你也可以玩得很愉快。

2. A: **You're great to be with**.
   B: That's nice to hear.
   Thanks for the compliment.
   I enjoy your company, too.
   【compliment〔'kɑmpləmənt〕*n.* 稱讚】

   A: 和你在一起很棒。
   B: 很高興聽到你這麼說。
   謝謝你的讚美。
   我也很喜歡有你作伴。

3. A: **I like being around you**.
   B: I like hanging out with you, too.
   I like having you around.
   We're well matched.
   【*hang out with sb.* 和某人在一起
   match〔mætʃ〕*v.* 相配

   A: 我喜歡和你在一起。
   B: 我也喜歡和你在一起。
   我喜歡和你在一起。
   我們非常相配。

4. A: **You're easygoing**.
   B: I believe in taking it easy.
   I like a carefree life.
   There's no use in worrying.
   【*believe in* 相信…是好的　　*take it easy* 放輕鬆
   carefree〔'kɛr,fri〕*adj.* 無憂無慮的
   *there's no use in V-ing* ～是沒有用的】

   A: 你很隨和。
   B: 我相信輕鬆一點比較好。
   我喜歡無憂無慮的生活。
   擔心是沒有用的。

5. A : **You're easy to please**.　　　　A：你很容易滿意。

　　B : I enjoy most things.　　　　　B：大部份的事物我都喜歡。
　　　 I don't ask for much.　　　　　　我不會要求太多。
　　　 I'm happy with what I have.　　　我對我所擁有的很滿足。

6. A : **You have a nice personality**.　A：你的個性很好。

　　B : You're too kind.　　　　　　　B：你太過獎了。
　　　 I just enjoy being with　　　　　　我只是喜歡和大家在一起。
　　　 people.
　　　 They make me happy.　　　　　　他們能讓我高興。

7. A : **I like your spirit**.　　　　　A：我欣賞你的活力。

　　B : I like yours, too.　　　　　　　B：我也欣賞你的。
　　　 Attitude is important.　　　　　　態度是重要的。
　　　 A positive outlook helps.　　　　積極的人生觀是有幫助的。
　　　【appreciate〔ə'priʃɪˌet〕v. 欣賞
　　　　 positive〔'pɑzətɪv〕adj.
　　　　　 積極的；樂觀的
　　　　 outlook〔'aʊtˌlʊk〕n. 看法】

8. A : **You're full of life**.　　　　　A：你很有活力。

　　B : I just try to think positive.　　B：我只是試著抱持樂觀的想法。
　　　 I believe anything is　　　　　　我相信任何事都是可能的。
　　　 possible.
　　　 It's the secret to success.　　　　這是成功的秘訣。
　　　【secret〔'sikrɪt〕n. 祕密；祕訣】

9. A : **You're always a good time**.　A：和你在一起總是很愉快。

　　B : Thanks!　　　　　　　　　　　B：謝謝！
　　　 I like to have fun.　　　　　　　我喜歡玩得愉快。
　　　 If it isn't fun, I don't want　　　如果不好玩，我就會不想做
　　　 to do it.　　　　　　　　　　　這件事。

# 一方面學英文，
# 一方面訓練自己的口才

　　「一口氣英語」是精挑細選出來的好句子，你背完之後，不僅英文好，口才也變好了，你會說出有禮貌、體貼、謙虛的話，人人都會喜歡你。

　　我們過去學英文，不知道浪費了多少時間，學了 KK 音標，發音還是不好，因為沒有趁年輕時，模仿外國人的聲音，沒有開口說英文；我們學了文法，文法還是沒學通，文法的規則無限多，例外也無限多，有哪個人真正完全懂文法呢？懂文法就會說英文嗎？有些句子文法對，但是美國人卻不習慣說，自己造句太危險了。

　　傳統的方法，是把學英文當作學問來研究，太辛苦了，美國人由於說的和寫的不一樣，所以他們才需要學文法。如果背了「一口氣背會話」，我們所說的話，都是經過熟背過，**我們知道自己所說的，是正確的、是很好的句子，所以說出來當然有信心，寫起來也有信心。**

　　有了「一口氣背會話」，學英文有了目標，只要一回一回地背下去，就愈來愈會說英文。還不認識字的小孩子，只要跟著 CD 不斷地唸，他就自然能夠背下來。年紀大的人，剛開始背，也許困難，但是會愈背愈快，同時也能遠離煩惱，返老還童。

劉毅

# 「一口氣背會話」經 BOOK 7

唸英文要像唸經一樣，每天大聲唸，從起床到睡覺，唸得比看得快，最後不看也會唸，養成習慣後，你會全身舒爽，你試試看，奇妙無比。

1. ***Let's*** hit the road.
   ***Let's*** get moving.
   ***Let's*** hustle out of here.

   ***Do you*** like to walk?
   ***Do you*** mind walking?
   We'll see more on foot.

   ***I***'m a big walker.
   ***I*** walk to stay in shape.
   Are your shoes suitable for walking?

2. Oops!
   Hold it a second.
   I almost forgot.

   ***I***'m short of cash.
   ***I*** need some bucks.
   ***I*** need to hit an ATM.

   ***You can*** join me.
   ***You can*** wait here.
   It's up to you.

3. Thanks for waiting.
   ***Sorry*** about that.
   ***Sorry*** I took so long.

   The line was long.
   ***It was*** slower than slow.
   ***It was*** the line from hell.

   ***I almost*** lost it.
   ***I almost*** blew a fuse.
   ***I*** was ready to explode.

4. How about this weather?
   We really lucked out.
   What a beautiful day!

   ***It's*** not too hot.
   ***It's*** not too cold.
   ***It's*** just right.

   I hope it holds up.
   ***Let's*** cross our fingers.
   ***Let's*** enjoy it while we can.

5. We need to cross.
   ***Let's*** cross the street.
   ***Let's*** get to the other side.

   Heads up.
   ***Look*** both ways.
   ***Look*** before you cross.

   The traffic is dangerous.
   It's like a jungle out there.
   You can never be too careful.

6. ***Don't*** jaywalk.
   ***Don't*** go against the light.
   You'll get hit by a car.

   ***Wait*** on the curb.
   ***Wait*** for the green.
   Always use the crosswalk.

   ***Be*** alert.
   ***Be*** careful.
   Use your head to stay safe.

7. Here's a favorite park.
   *It's* a popular spot.
   *It's* a super place to unwind.

   This park is alive.
   *It's* full of energy.
   *It's* the place to be.

   *You can see* families enjoying
      themselves.
   *You can see* people exercising.
   Mornings and evenings are best.

8. Here's a great market.
   *It's* pretty famous.
   *It's* noted for its bargains.

   *You should* haggle.
   *You should* negotiate.
   You must talk the price down.

   The sellers are pros.
   *They'll* steal you blind.
   *They'll* rip you off without
      blinking an eye.

9. This store is number one.
   *It's the* top place to shop.
   *It's the* hottest store in town.

   *They have* the best stuff.
   *They have* the top brands.
   There's always a sale going on.

   This store is unbelievable.
   *They*'ve got everything you need.
   *They* have it all from A to Z.

10. *Let's* hang out.
    *Let's* stick around.
    *Let's* stay here for a while.

    *We can* relax.
    *We can* chill out.
    *We can* mellow out.

    *Take a* load off.
    *Take a* little rest.
    We can watch the crowd.

11. This city is dynamic.
    *It's a* mix of East and West.
    *It's a* combination of old and new.

    This city never sleeps.
    *It's* a 24/7 city.
    *It's* always on the go.

    This city has it all.
    *To* see it is to like it.
    *To* live here is to love it.

12. *You're* a fun person.
    *You're* great to be with.
    I like being around you.

    *You're* easygoing.
    *You're* casy to please.
    You have a nice personality.

    I like your spirit.
    *You're* full of life.
    *You're* always a good time.

# BOOK 8 和外國人搭訕

▶8-1 看到一個外國人坐在椅子上，旁邊有空位，你可以說：

> Is this seat taken?
> Is anyone sitting here?

▶8-2 坐在椅子上，可和外國人繼續說：

> How are you?
> How's it going?
> Having a good day?

▶8-3 問旁邊的外國人時間：

> Excuse me, please.
> What time is it?
> Do you have the time?

▶8-4 可以和外國人聊聊天氣：

> What a rotten day!
> What a terrible day!

▶8-5 看到外國人好像需要幫忙，就可說：

> Need any help?
> Need a hand?

▶8-5 問外國人你書中不懂的地方：

> Can I ask a favor?
> Can you spare a minute?
> Can you help me with this?
>
> What does this mean?

▶ 8-7 可以學美國人一樣，讚美別人的服裝：

> I like your shirt!
> That's your color!
> That looks great on you!

▶ 8-8 感覺外國人有點面熟時說：

> You look familiar.
> You got me thinking.
> ⋮

▶ 8-9 想得到一些資訊，就問他：

> Can I ask you a question?
> I need information.
> ⋮

▶ 8-10 想和外國人進一步聊天時說：

> Mind if I join you?
> Care for some company?
> ⋮

▶ 8-11 想問他的身份時，就可說：

> I bet you're a student.
> Where do you study?
> ⋮

▶ 8-12 走在街上，問路怎麼走：

> I'm a little lost.
> I need directions.
> ⋮

# 1. *Is this seat taken?*

| | |
|---|---|
| *Is* this seat taken? | 這個位子有人坐嗎？ |
| *Is* anyone sitting here? | 有沒有人坐這裡？ |
| Mind if I sit down? | 你介不介意我坐在這裡？ |
| | |
| *Is it* OK? | 可以嗎？ |
| *Is it* all right? | 好嗎？ |
| Do you mind? | 你介意嗎？ |
| | |
| What a crowd! | 這麼多人！ |
| This place is packed! | 這個地方很擁擠！ |
| Seats are going fast! | 座位很快就不見了！ |

\*\*
_____

seat〔sit〕*n.* 座位　　*take a seat* 坐下
mind〔maɪnd〕*v.* 介意
*all right* 沒問題的；好的
crowd〔kraʊd〕*n.* 人群
packed〔pækt〕*adj.* 擠滿人的　　go〔go〕*v.* 消失

BOOK 8

## 【背景説明】

　　當你看到一個外國人，旁邊有個空位，你想坐在他旁邊，就可用這九句話，做爲開場白。

### 1. *Is this seat taken?*

seat〔sit〕*n.* 座位　　take〔tek〕*v.* 就（座）

　　take a seat 是「坐下」，take this seat 是「坐這個座位」，它的被動就是 This seat is taken. （這個位子已經被坐了。）變成問句就是：*Is this seat taken?*（這個位子有人坐嗎？）

　　下面都是美國人常説的話：

*Is this seat taken?*【第一常用】

Is this seat free?【第三常用】

（這個位子是空著的嗎？）【free 也可改成 open】

Is this seat available?【第八常用】

（這個位子可以坐嗎？）

free〔fri〕*adj.* 空著的

available〔ə'veləbḷ〕*adj.* 可利用的；可獲得的

Is this seat occupied?【第二常用】

（這個位子有人坐嗎？）

Is this seat reserved?【第六常用】

（這個位子有人保留了嗎？）

Is this seat saved?【第四常用】

（這個位子有人保留了嗎？）

occupied〔'akjə,paɪd〕*adj.* 被占據的

reserve〔rɪ'zɝv〕*v.* 保留　　save〔sev〕*v.* 保留

Is this seat being reserved?【第七常用】

（這個位子有人保留嗎？）

Is this seat being saved?【第五常用】

（這個位子有人保留嗎？）

## 2. *Is anyone sitting here?*

這句話的意思是「有沒有人坐在這裡？」也可以加強語氣說成：Is anyone sitting here in this seat?（有沒有人坐在這個位子？）也可以更有禮貌地說：Can I sit here?（我可以坐在這裡嗎？）

## 3. *Mind if I sit down?*

mind〔maɪnd〕v. 介意；反對

這句話源自：Do you mind if I sit down?
意思是「你介不介意我坐在這裡？」它的回答和一般問句不一樣，因為 mind 是「介意；反對」的意思，不能說 Yes 來表示同意。

【例】 A: *Mind if I sit down?*

（你介不介意我坐在這裡？）

B: Not at all.（一點也不。）【第一常用】

Don't mind at all.【第二常用】

（一點也不介意。）

I don't mind at all.【第三常用】

（我一點也不介意。）

No, it's OK. 【第七常用】
（不介意，沒關係。）
Be my guest. （請便。）【第八常用】
No problem. （沒問題。）【第九常用】

Go ahead. （請便。）【第四常用】
（= *No, go ahead.*）
Go right ahead. （請便。）【第五常用】
（= *No, go right ahead.*）
Sure, go ahead. 【第六常用】
（當然可以，請便。）

　　當美國人回答 "Do you mind～?" 之類的句子時，他們不會回答：*Yes, go ahead.* 或 *Certainly, go ahead.* 但他們回答：Sure, go ahead. 實在找不出原因來，可看成是習慣用法，是各種考題中常出現的答案。

　　下面各句美國人也常說，我們按照使用頻率排列：

① *Mind if I sit down?* 【第一常用】
② Mind if I sit here? 【第二常用】
　　（你介不介意我坐這裡？）
③ Mind if I sit? 【第三常用】
　　（你介不介意我坐下來？）

④ Is it OK to sit here? （可以坐這裡嗎？）
⑤ OK to sit here? （可以坐這裡嗎？）

⑥ Is it all right to sit here? （可以坐這裡嗎？）
⑦ All right to sit here? （可以坐這裡嗎？）

BOOK 8

### 4. *Is it OK?*
　　*Is it all right?*
　　*Do you mind?*

　　　　這三句話的意思是:「可以嗎？好嗎？你介意嗎？」
這三句話可以說是一個萬用會話句型，只要拜託別人
任何事，都可以用得到。

【例1】　Can I borrow your pen?
　　　　（我可以跟你借筆嗎？）
　　　　*Is it OK?*（可以嗎？）
　　　　*Is it all right?*（好嗎？）
　　　　*Do you mind?*（你介意嗎？）

【例2】　Can you lend me some money?
　　　　（你能不能借我一些錢？）
　　　　*Is it OK?*（可以嗎？）
　　　　*Is it all right?*（好嗎？）
　　　　*Do you mind?*（你介意嗎？）

【例3】　Can I use your cell phone?
　　　　（我可不可以用你的手機？）
　　　　*Is it OK?*（可以嗎？）
　　　　*Is it all right?*（好嗎？）
　　　　*Do you mind?*（你介意嗎？）
　　　　【*cell phone* 手機】

【例4】 Can we study together?
　　　　（我們能不能一起讀書？）
　　　　*Is it OK?*（可以嗎？）
　　　　*Is it all right?*（好嗎？）
　　　　*Do you mind?*（你介意嗎？）

【例5】 Can we go to the movies?
　　　　（我們可不可以去看電影？）
　　　　*Is it OK?*（可以嗎？）
　　　　*Is it all right?*（好嗎？）
　　　　*Do you mind?*（你介意嗎？）
　　　　【*go to the movies*　去看電影】

【例6】 I'd like to talk to you.
　　　　（我想要和你談一談。）
　　　　*Is it OK?*（可以嗎？）
　　　　*Is it all right?*（好嗎？）
　　　　*Do you mind?*（你介意嗎？）

【例7】 Can I practice my English with you?
　　　　（我可以跟你練習英文嗎？）
　　　　*Is it OK?*（可以嗎？）
　　　　*Is it all right?*（好嗎？）
　　　　*Do you mind?*（你介意嗎？）

BOOK 8

5. ***What a crowd!***

crowd〔kraud〕*n.* 人群

　　這句話在這裡的意思是「這麼多人！」這是感嘆句（詳見「文法寶典」p.4,148），What + a + 名詞！在美語中，通常把後面的主詞和動詞省略。

　　下面是美國人常說的話：

> ***What a crowd!***【第一常用】
> What a big crowd!（這麼多人！）【第二常用】
> What a big crowd in here!【第六常用】
> （這裡這麼多人！）
>
> There are a lot of people here!【第四常用】
> （這裡人真多！）
> There are a lot of people in here!【第五常用】
> （這裡人真多！）
> What a large group!（這麼多人！）【第三常用】
> 　　〔grup〕*n.* 群；團體
> 【這句話也可以說成：What a big group! 但少說
> 　*What a large crowd!*】

　　中國人說「人山人海」，美國人不說：*People mountain, people sea.*（誤）在台灣，有些美國人聽到太多人這樣說，所以也會開玩笑地跟著說。正確的說法是：What a crowd! 等。

6. ***This place is packed!***

packed〔pækt〕*adj.* 擠滿人的；擁擠的；爆滿的

　　pack 的主要意思是「包裝；捆紮」，這句話字面的意思是「這個地方被捆紮起來了！」引申為「這個地方很擁擠！」現在很多字典已經把 packed 變成純粹的形容詞，意思是「擁擠的；爆滿的」（= *very crowded*），packed 的語氣比 crowded 強烈。

　　下面是美國人常說的話：

> ***This place is packed!***【第一常用】
> This place is really packed!【第四常用】
> （這個地方真的很擁擠！）
> This place is crowded!【第二常用】
> （這個地方很擁擠！）
>
> This place is really crowded!【第五常用】
> （這個地方真的很擁擠！）
> This place is full!【第三常用】
> （這個地方客滿了！）
> This place is wall-to-wall!【第六常用】
> （這個地方人真多！）

full〔fʊl〕*adj.* 客滿的
wall-to-wall〔ˋwɔltəˋwɔl〕*adj.* 把整個地板都蓋住的；大量的

BOOK 8

7. *Seats are going fast!*

go〔go〕*v.* 消失

　　　這句話字面的意思是「座位很快就消失了！」
也就是「座位很快就不見了！」go fast 通常是指
「（時間）很快過去」、「（東西）很快被用完」或
「很快消失」，在不同的句中，有不同的意思。

【例】 My money *is going fast*.
（我的錢很快就要用完了。）
Our vacation time *is going fast*.
（我們的假期很快就要過去了。）
Today *is* really *going fast*.
（今天的時間真的過得很快。）

All items on sale *were going fast*.
（所有的特價品很快就被賣完。）
Many traditional customs *are going fast*.
（許多傳統的習俗很快就會消失。）
The best seats always *go fast*.
（最好的位子總是很快就沒有了。）

item〔'aɪtəm〕*n.* 物品　　***on sale*** 特價
traditional〔trə'dɪʃənl̩〕*adj.* 傳統的
custom〔'kʌstəm〕*n.* 習俗

BOOK 8

**BOOK 8**

## 【對話練習】

1. A：**Is this seat taken?**　　　　A：這個位子有人坐嗎？

　 B：No, it's not.　　　　　　　 B：不，沒有。

　　　 It's not taken.　　　　　　　　沒有人坐。

　　　 No one is sitting here.　　　　沒有人坐這裡。

2. A：**Is anyone sitting here?**　　A：有沒有人坐這裡？

　 B：Nope.　　　　　　　　　　 B：沒有。

　　　 This seat is open.　　　　　　　這個位子是空著的。

　　　 This seat is available.　　　　 這個位子可以坐。

　　　【nope〔nop〕*adv.* 不；不是
　　　　（= *no*）】

3. A：**Mind if I sit down?**　　　 A：你介不介意我坐在這裡？

　 B：Go right ahead.　　　　　　 B：請便。

　　　 I don't mind at all.　　　　　　 我一點也不介意。

　　　 I don't mind a bit.　　　　　　 我一點也不介意。

　　　【*a bit* 一點】

4. A：**Is it OK?**　　　　　　　　 A：可以嗎？

　 B：Sure, it's OK.　　　　　　　 B：當然可以。

　　　 It's all right.　　　　　　　　 沒關係。

　　　 It's fine with me.　　　　　　 我覺得可以。

5. A：**Is it all right?**

　B：Yes, it is.
　　 It's quite all right.
　　 It's all right with me.

A：可以嗎？

B：是的，可以。
　　 眞的可以。
　　 我覺得可以。

6. A：**Do you mind?**

　B：I don't mind at all.
　　 Make yourself at home.
　　 Be my guest.
　　【*make yourself at home*　不要拘束
　　　*be my guest*　請便】

A：你介意嗎？

B：我一點也不介意。
　　 不要拘束。
　　 請便。

7. A：**What a crowd!**

　B：Yes, it is.
　　 It's a huge crowd.
　　 It's always full in here.
　　【huge〔hjudʒ〕*adj.* 巨大的】

A：這麼多人！

B：是的，的確是。
　　 人眞多。
　　 這裡總是會客滿。

8. A：**This place is packed!**

　B：It sure is!
　　 It's really packed.
　　 It's packed like a can of sardines.
　　【can〔kæn〕*n.* 罐頭
　　　sardine〔sɑr'din〕*n.* 沙丁魚】

A：這個地方很擁擠！

B：的確是！
　　 眞的很擁擠。
　　 擠得像沙丁魚罐頭。

9. A：**Seats are going fast!**

　B：They really are.
　　 I can see that.
　　 I only see a few empty seats
　　 left.【left〔lɛft〕*adj.* 剩下的】

A：座位很快就不見了！

B：的確是。
　　 我看得出來。
　　 我看到只剩下幾個空
　　 位。

BOOK 8

# 2. How are you?

| | |
|---|---|
| *How* are you? | 你好嗎？ |
| *How*'s it going? | 情況進展得如何？ |
| Having a good day? | 你今天愉快嗎？ |
| | |
| I haven't seen you before. | 我以前沒看過你。 |
| *Are you* new in town? | 你是不是剛來這裡的？ |
| *Are you* working or visiting here? | 你是在這裡工作，還是來這裡玩？ |
| | |
| *How long* have you been here? | 你來這裡多久了？ |
| *How long* are you staying? | 你要待多久？ |
| Do you like it here? | 你喜不喜歡這裡？ |

**\*\*** ──────────────

go〔go〕*v.* 進展　　new〔nju〕*adj.* 新來的
***in town*** 在城裡；在這裡（ = *here* ）
visit〔'vɪzɪt〕*v.* 遊覽　　stay〔ste〕*v.* 停留

【背景説明】

　　　一般人看到外國人，只會説 How are you?
而你一口氣就可以説這九句話。

1. *How are you?*

　　　這句話有兩個意思：①你好嗎？②你好。
( = *Hi!*〔haɪ〕*int.* 嗨 ) 看到任何人，都可以説這
句話來打招呼，並不一定希望別人回答。

　　【比較】 How 和 are 不可縮寫。
　　　　　　*How are you?*【正】
　　　　　　*How're you?*【誤】

　　　所有打招呼的用語，在「演講式英語會話
總整理」中，有詳細說明。

2. *How's it going?*
go〔go〕*v.* 進展

　　　這句話的意思是「情況進展得如何？」it 是指
everything，所以，也可説成：How's everything
going? ( 一切情況進展得如何？) 有的美國人也
説：How's it going today? ( 今天情況如何？)
或 How's it going with you? ( 你好嗎？)

3. *Having a good day?*

> 這句話源自 Are you having a good day?
> （你今天愉快嗎？）這和 Have a good day.
> （再見。）不同。除非說成 Have a good day?
> （你今天愉快嗎？）( = *Did you have a good day?* )

下面都是美國人常說的話：

*Having a good day?*【第一常用】
You having a good day?【第二常用】
（你今天愉快嗎？）
Are you having a good day?【第三常用】
（你今天愉快嗎？）

How's your day?（你今天好嗎？）【第四常用】
How's your day going?【第五常用】
（你今天好嗎？）
How's your day so far?【第七常用】
（你今天到目前為止還好嗎？）
【*so far* 到目前為止】

You having a good day today?【第八常用】
（你今天愉快嗎？）
Are you having a good day today?【第九常用】
（你今天愉快嗎？）
How's your day today?【第六常用】
（你今天好嗎？）

【第一、第二和第八常用的句子，是美國人常說的話，
但不適合書寫】

4. ***I haven't seen you before****.*

　　這句話的意思是「我以前沒看過你。」下面都
是美國人常說的話：

　　***I haven't seen you before****.*【第一常用】
　　I haven't seen you here before.【第三常用】
　　（我以前沒在這裡看過你。）
　　Haven't seen you before.【第六常用】
　　（以前沒看過你。）

　　I've never seen you before.【第二常用】
　　（我以前從未見過你。）
　　I've never seen you here before.【第四常用】
　　（我以前在這裡從未見過你。）
　　I've never seen you around here before.
　　（我以前從沒在附近見過你。）【第五常用】
　　【***around here*** 附近】

　　如果你看到一位美女，你想和她搭訕，如果你
說：You look very familiar.（妳看起來很面熟。）
她如果回答：No, I don't think so.（不，我不覺
得。）你就很尷尬了。說了 ***I haven't seen you
before****.* 之後，還可以繼續說下去。

5. *Are you new in town?*

new〔nju〕*adj.* 新來的

*in town* 在城裡；在這裡（= *here*）

　　這句話字面的意思是「你是不是新到城裡來的？」引申爲「你是不是剛來這裡的？」美國人説 in town，字面意思是「城裡」，等於中文的「這裡」。

　　從前，美國人住得很分散，彼此很少見面，在一個小鎮上，看到一個陌生人，他們都會很好奇，就會問：*Are you new in town?*（你是不是剛來這裡的？）

　　中國人思想中，很少説「在城裡」，美國人卻常説 *in town*。

【例】 There is a new store *in town*.
　　（在城裡有家新的商店。）
　　He just arrived *in town*.
　　（他剛剛來到這裡。）
　　Is he *in town*?（他是不是在城裡？）
　　【意思是「他是不是沒有出遠門？」】

　　What's going on *in town* this week?
　　（這個禮拜城裡有沒有什麼活動？）
　　What's new *in town*?
　　（城裡有沒有發生什麼新鮮事？；
　　　城裡有沒有什麼消息？）
　　What's playing *in town*?
　　（城裡演什麼電影？）

　　*go on* 發生；進行；舉行
　　play〔ple〕*v.* 上演；放映；播出

下面各句是美國人常説的話，我們按照使用頻率
排列：

① ***Are you new in town?***【第一常用】
② Are you new here?【第二常用】
　　（你是不是剛來這裡的？）
③ Are you new here in town?【第三常用】
　　（你是不是剛來這裡的？）

④ Have you just arrived?
　　（你是不是剛到這裡？）
⑤ Are you a new arrival?
　　（你是不是新來的？）
⑥ May I ask you if you're new here?
　　（請問你是不是剛到這裡？）
　　【arrival〔ə'raɪvl̩〕*n.* 到達之人】

⑦ You look like you're new, are you?
　　（你看起來像是剛到這裡的，是嗎？）
　　【不可説成 aren't you，詳見「文法寶典」p.7】
⑧ Are you from here?
　　（你是不是這裡的人？）
⑨ Have you recently arrived here?
　　（你是最近才到這裡的嗎？）
　　【recently〔'risn̩tlɪ〕*adv.* 最近】

6. *Are you working or visiting here?*

   visit〔'vɪzɪt〕 *v.* 遊覽

   　　這句話的意思是「你是在這裡工作，還是來這
   裡玩？」

   【比較】 *Are you working or visiting here?*【常用】
   　　　　Are you working or just visiting?【常用】
   　　　　（你是來這裡工作，還是只是來玩？）
   　　　　Are you here on business or for
   　　　　　pleasure?
   　　　　（你是來這裡出差，還是來玩？）
   　　　　【少用，太正式，年輕人不會說，但是美國海關
   　　　　　人員喜歡問】
   　　　　*on business* 因公；有事　　*for pleasure* 為了玩樂

7. *How long have you been here?*

   　　這句話的意思是「你來這裡多久了？」這句話
   美國人也常說成：How long have you been in
   town?（你來這裡多久了？）

   【比較】 *How long have you been here?*【正】
   　　　　*How long have you come here?*【誤】
   　　　　【詳見「文法寶典」p.336】

8. *How long are you staying?*

stay〔ste〕*v.* 停留

　　　這句話的意思是「你要待多久？」用現在進行
式表示未來（詳見「文法寶典」p.342）。也可以説成：
How long will you stay? 句意相同。

　　　下面是美國人常説的話：

　　　*How long are you staying?*【第一常用】
　　　How long are you staying for?
　　　（你要待多久？）【第三常用】
　　　How long will you stay?【第二常用】
　　　（你會待多久？）

　　　How long are you staying here?
　　　（你要在這裡待多久？）【第四常用】
　　　How long are you staying here for?
　　　（你要在這裡待多久？）【第六常用】
　　　How long will you stay here?
　　　（你會在這裡待多久？）【第五常用】

　　　How long are you here for?【第七常用】
　　　（你要在這裡多久？）
　　　How long will you be here?
　　　（你會在這裡多久？）【第八常用】
　　　How long will you be here for?
　　　（你會在這裡多久？）【第九常用】

How long are you planning to stay?

（你打算待多久？）【第十一常用】

How long do you plan to stay?

（你打算待多久？）【第十常用】

How long do you think you'll stay?

（你認為你會待多久？）【第十二常用】

### 9. *Do you like it here?*

中國人看到美國人，常喜歡問他：*Do you like here?*（誤）因為 here 是副詞，不能做動詞 like 的受詞。應該說成：*Do you like it here?*（你喜不喜歡這裡？）it 在此籠統地指情況或事情，有時中文可以不譯。

下面是美國人常說的話：

*Do you like it here?*【第一常用】

Do you like everything here?【第四常用】

（你喜歡這裡的一切嗎？）

Do you like living here?【第三常用】

（你喜歡住在這裡嗎？）

Do you like being here?【第二常用】

（你喜歡待在這裡嗎？）

Do you like working here?【第六常用】

（你喜歡在這裡工作嗎？）

Do you like spending time here?【第五常用】

（你喜歡待在這裡嗎？）

【spend〔spɛnd〕v. 度過（時間）】

## 【對話練習】

1. A：**How are you?**

   B：I'm fine.
   Thank you.
   How about you?

2. A：**How's it going?**

   B：Pretty good.
   Things are OK.
   Things are looking good.
   【pretty〔'prɪtɪ〕adv. 相當】

3. A：**Having a good day?**

   B：Yes, I am.
   I really am.
   Thanks for asking.

4. A：**I haven't seen you before.**

   B：I don't know why not.
   I come here a lot.
   I'm here almost every day.
   【*a lot* 常常】

5. A：**Are you new in town?**

   B：No, I'm not new.
   I've been here a while.
   I don't consider myself new.
   【while〔hwaɪl〕n.（一段）時間】

A：你好嗎？

B：我很好。
謝謝。
你呢？

A：情況進展得如何？

B：很好。
一切都還好。
情況看起來不錯。

A：你今天愉快嗎？

B：是的，我很愉快。
我真的很愉快。
謝謝你問我。

A：我以前沒看過你。

B：我不知道為什麼沒有。
我常來這裡。
我幾乎每天都在這裡。

A：你是不是剛來這裡的？

B：不，我不是剛來這裡的。
我來這裡一陣子了。
我不認為我是剛來這裡
的。

BOOK 8

6. A：**Are you working or visiting here?**

   B：I'm employed.
   I'm working part-time now.
   I plan to work full-time soon.
   【employ〔ɪm'plɔɪ〕*v.* 僱用
   part-time〔'pɑrt'taɪm〕*adv.* 兼職地
   full-time〔'fʊl'taɪm〕*adv.* 全職地】

A：你是在這裡工作，還是來這裡玩？

B：我有工作。
   我現在是在兼職。
   我打算不久就做全職。

7. A：**How long have you been here?**

   B：I've been here four months.
   It seems like four weeks!
   It's such an exciting place.

A：你來這裡多久了？

B：我來這裡四個月了。
   感覺好像是四個星期！
   這裡是個令人興奮的地方。

8. A：**How long are you staying?**

   B：I plan to stay one year.
   I might stay for two years.
   It all depends on my job.
   【*depend on* 視～而定】

A：你要待多久？

B：我打算待一年。
   我可能會待兩年。
   全都要視我的工作而定。

9. A：**Do you like it here?**

   B：I sure do.
   It's a great change of pace.
   I wouldn't want to be anywhere else.
   【*a change of pace* 換換口味】

A：你喜不喜歡這裡？

B：我當然喜歡。
   換換口味很好。
   我不會想去任何其他的地方。

BOOK 8

# 3.  *What time is it?*

| | |
|---|---|
| Excuse me, please. | 對不起，拜託。 |
| What time is it? | 現在幾點？ |
| Do you have the time? | 你知不知道現在幾點？ |
| | |
| *I* forgot my watch. | 我忘記戴手錶。 |
| *I*'ve lost track of time. | 我不知道時間。 |
| *I* have no idea what time it is. | 我不知道現在幾點。 |
| | |
| *I* appreciate it. | 我很感激你。 |
| *I* thank you so much. | 我非常感謝你。 |
| You're very kind. | 你真好心。 |

BOOK 8

\*\* ————————

track 〔 træk 〕 *n.* 蹤跡
*lose track of*  失去…的蹤跡；不知道
*have no idea*  不知道
appreciate 〔 ə'priʃɪˌet 〕 *v.* 感激
kind 〔 kaɪnd 〕 *adj.* 親切的；好心的

BOOK 8

## 【背景説明】

　　想要和陌生人說話，問問時間，是一個好方
法。對方如果反應很熱情，你就可以繼續跟他談
下去。

### 1. *Excuse me, please*.

　　美國人習慣，跟別人說話以前，先説：
Excuse me.（對不起。）説 *Excuse me,*
*please*. 則比 Excuse me. 更有禮貌。

　　凡是請求別人做某事前，都可先説：*Excuse*
*me, please*.（對不起，拜託。）如：*Excuse me,*
*please*.  May I ask you a question?（對不起，
拜託。我可以問你一個問題嗎？）美國人也常常
把 please 連接其他的句子，如：

> *Excuse me, please* repcat that.
> （對不起，請重覆說一遍。）
> *Excuse me, please* don't do that.
> （對不起，請不要那樣做。）
> *Excuse me, please* wait a minute.
> （對不起，請等一下。）
> repeat〔rɪ'pit〕*v.* 重覆；重說
> minute〔'mɪnɪt〕*n.* 片刻

2. ***What time is it?***

　　這句話的意思是「現在幾點？」

　　下面都是美國人常說的話：

***What time is it?***【第一常用】

What time is it now?（現在幾點？）【第四常用】

What time is it right now?【第五常用】

（現在幾點？）

Do you know what time it is?【第六常用】

（你知道現在幾點嗎？）

What time is it, please?【第二常用】

（請問現在幾點？）

What's the time?（現在幾點？）【第三常用】

3. ***Do you have the time?***

　　這句話的意思是「你知不知道現在幾點？」

【比較】下面兩句話，一個字不同，整句意義不同：

***Do you have the time?***（= *What time is it?*）

Do you have time?（= *Are you free?*）

（你有時間嗎？）

***Do you have the time?*** 的 time，源自

timepiece（計時器；鐘錶）。

下面是美國人常說的話，我們按照使用頻率排列：

① *Do you have the time?* 【第一常用】

② Do you know the time? 【第二常用】

（你知不知道現在幾點？）

③ Do you by any chance have the time?

（你是不是剛好知道現在幾點？）【第三常用】

【用 by any chance（剛好；碰巧）較客氣】

④ Do you by any chance know the time?

（你是不是剛好知道現在幾點？）

⑤ Can you give me the time?

（你能不能告訴我現在幾點？）

⑥ Can you tell me the time?

（你能不能告訴我現在幾點？）

【give〔gɪv〕v. 告訴】

4. *I forgot my watch*.

這句話的意思是「我忘了戴手錶。」也可以說成：I forgot to wear my watch today. 或 I forgot to put on my watch today. 意思都是「我今天忘了戴手錶。」【wear〔wɛr〕v. 戴（= *put on*）】

5. *I've lost track of time*.

track〔træk〕*n.* 蹤跡

*lose track of* 失去…的蹤跡；不知道；沒有記錄；忘記；
　　與…失去聯繫

BOOK 8

　　　track 的意思是「蹤跡；痕跡；(人、動物的) 足
跡；軌道」，*lose track of* 的字面意思是「失去…的
蹤跡」，可能源自古時候打獵，追蹤動物的足跡，當
獵人找不到獵物的足跡時，他們會說：We've *lost*
*track of* the deer. (我們看不到鹿的足跡了。) 後
來，lose track of 也用到其他方面，如人們找不
到小孩時，就說：I've *lost track of* my kids. (我
不知道小孩子跑哪裡去了。)

　　　*I've lost track of time*. 字面的意思是「我已經
失去時間的蹤跡。」引申為「我不知道時間。」

　　　*lose track of* 在不同的句中，有不同的解釋，例
如你遲到了，你可以說：Sorry, I'm late. *I lost track*
*of* time. (抱歉，我遲到了。我忘了時間。) 此時，lose
track of 就作「忘記」解，依句意，要用過去式。

【比較】
　　　*I've lost track of time*. (我不知道時間。)
　　　( = *Now I don't know the time*. )
　　I lost track of time. (我當時忘了時間。)
　　　( = *I forgot what time it was*. )

lose track of time 這個成語，用現在完成式，表示現
在不知道時間，用過去式，表示過去忘記了時間，如：
The movie was so good. I lost track of time. (電影
太好了，我看得都忘了時間。)

6. **I have no idea what time it is**.
   **have no idea** 不知道

   這句話的意思是「我不知道現在幾點。」源自
   *I have no idea of what time it is.*（爻）將句中的
   of 省略掉。

   【比較1】

   I have no idea <u>what time it is</u>.
   　　　　【名詞子句該用敘述句的形式】
   I have no idea <u>what time is it</u>. 【誤】
   　　　　【名詞子句不能用疑問句的形式】

   【比較2】 下面各句意義相同：

   **I have no idea what time it is**. 【第一常用】
   I don't know what time it is. 【第四常用】
   （我不知道現在幾點。）

   I have no idea of the time. 【第二常用】
   （我不知道現在幾點。）
   I don't know the time. 【第三常用】
   （我不知道現在幾點。）

7. **I appreciate it**.
   appreciate〔ə'priʃɪ,et〕v. 感激

   這句話的意思是「我很感激你。」不可說成
   *I appreciate you.*（我很賞識你。）

8. *I thank you so much*.

這句話的意思是「我非常感謝你。」也可以
只說：Thank you so much.（非常感謝你。）
（= *Thank you very much*.）說 *I thank you so much*. 比較正式，比較有禮貌。

9. *You're very kind*.

kind〔kaɪnd〕*adj*. 親切的；好心的

這句話的意思是「你真好心。」（= *You're very nice*.）

下面都是美國人常說的話：

> *You're very kind*.【第一常用】
> You're so kind.（你真好心。）【第二常用】
> You're kind.（你很好心。）【第四常用】
>
> You're a kind person.【第五常用】
> （你是個好心的人。）
> You're a very kind person.【第六常用】
> （你是個非常好心的人。）
> That's very kind of you.【第三常用】
> （你那麼做真是好心。）
> 【美國人較少說 It's very kind of you.】
>
> 也有美國人說：You're very kindhearted.
> （你非常好心。）【kindhearted〔'kaɪnd'hɑrtɪd〕*adj*.
> 心腸好的】這句話和中國人思想一樣，但並沒有像我
> 們中文說得那麼普遍。

BOOK 8

## 【對話練習】

1. A：**Excuse me, please.**

 B：What is it?

 What do you want?

 What can I do for you?

A：對不起，拜託。

B：什麼事？

 你想要我做什麼？

 我能為你做什麼？

2. A：**What time is it?**

 B：Let me see.

 Let me check my watch.

 It's exactly twelve noon.

 【exactly〔ɪg'zæktlɪ〕*adv.* 正好

 noon〔nun〕*n.* 正午】

A：現在幾點？

B：讓我看看。

 讓我看一下我的手錶。

 正好中午十二點整。

3. A：**Do you have the time?**

 B：I sure do.

 It's one thirty.

 It's actually one thirty-one.

 【actually〔'æktʃʊəlɪ〕*adv.* 事實上】

A：你知不知道現在幾點？

B：我當然知道。

 現在是一點半。

 事實上是一點三十一分。

4. A：**I forgot my watch.**

 B：Don't worry about it.

 I have a watch.

 I can tell you the time.

A：我忘記戴手錶。

B：別擔心。

 我有手錶。

 我可以告訴你現在幾點。

5. A： **I've lost track of time**.

   B： I'm sorry.
   I can't help you.
   I also have no idea.

A：我不知道時間。

B：很抱歉。
我無法幫你。
我也不知道。

6. A： **I have no idea what time it is**.

   B： I can tell you.
   It's nine forty.
   It's twenty to ten.

A：我不知道現在幾點。

B：我可以告訴你。
現在是九點四十分。
差二十分鐘就十點。

7. A： **I appreciate it**.

   B： Don't mention it.
   Don't say another word.
   I'm glad I could help.
   【mention〔'mɛnʃən〕v. 提到
   glad〔glæd〕adj. 高興的】

A：我很感激你。

B：不客氣。
不要再說了。
我很高興能幫上忙。

8. A： **I thank you so much**.

   B： You're very welcome.
   It's my pleasure.
   It's really nothing at all.
   【pleasure〔'plɛʒɚ〕n. 榮幸】

A：我非常感謝你。

B：真的不客氣。
這是我的榮幸。
真的不算什麼。

9. A： **You're very kind**.

   B： Thank you for saying so.
   I'm glad I could help.
   I'm here when you need me.

A：你真好心。

B：謝謝你這麼說。
很高興我能幫上忙。
你需要我的話，我都在
這裡。

# 4. *What a rotten day!*

| | |
|---|---|
| *What a* rotten day! | 好爛的天氣！ |
| *What a* terrible day! | 天氣眞糟糕！ |
| Pretty awful, huh? | 天氣很糟糕，不是嗎？ |
| | |
| *It's* crummy. | 眞糟糕。 |
| *It's* lousy. | 天氣很糟糕。 |
| This really stinks. | 天氣眞的很糟糕。 |
| | |
| *It's* gloomy. | 天氣很陰沈。 |
| *It's* depressing. | 它令人沮喪。 |
| This really gets me down. | 這種天氣眞使我難受。 |

** ─────────────

rotten〔ˈrɑtn̩〕*adj.* 腐爛的；令人討厭的；壞的
terrible〔ˈtɛrəbl̩〕*adj.* 可怕的；很糟糕的
pretty〔ˈprɪtɪ〕*adv.* 非常　　awful〔ˈɔfl̩〕*adj.* 可怕的；糟糕的
crummy〔ˈkrʌmɪ〕*adj.* 無價值的；低劣的；糟糕的
lousy〔ˈlaʊzɪ〕*adj.* 糟糕的
stink〔stɪŋk〕*v.* 發出惡臭；很糟糕
gloomy〔ˈglumɪ〕*adj.* 陰暗的；陰沈的
depressing〔dɪˈprɛsɪŋ〕*adj.* 令人沮喪的
down〔daʊn〕*adj.* 沮喪的　　*get sb. down* 使某人沮喪

【背景説明】

　　　如果你參加美國人的旅行團，認識了新朋友，他們常談論天氣，來避免尷尬。

1. *What a rotten day!*
　rotten 〔'ratn̩〕 *adj.* 腐爛的；令人討厭的；壞的

　　　*rotten* 這個字的主要意思是「腐爛的」，像 *rotten* eggs（腐爛的蛋），*rotten* fruit（腐爛的水果），現在常引用到其他的地方，意思是「壞的；無聊的；糟糕的；令人討厭的」，要看實際情況，或前後文的句意來決定。例如：

> *What a rotten day!*（好爛的天氣！）
> What a *rotten* idea!（好爛的點子！）
> What a *rotten* thing to do!
> （要做這件事眞討厭！）
> （= *What a terrible thing to do!*）
>
> What a *rotten* movie!（好爛的電影！）
> What a *rotten* book!（好爛的書！）
> What a *rotten* headache!（頭好痛！）
> 【headache〔'hɛd,ek〕 *n.* 頭痛】

BOOK 8

He's a *rotten* person.（他是個爛人。）

He's *rotten* to the core.（他爛到底了。）

He's *rotten* through and through.

（他太爛了。）

core〔kɔr〕*n.* 核心

*be rotten to the core* 壞透了

*through and through* 完全地；徹底地

【比較】 *What a rotten day!*【正，常用】

*What a rotten day it is!*

【文法對，但美國人不說】

2. *What a terrible day!*

terrible〔'tɛrəb!〕*adj.* 可怕的；很糟糕的

這句話的意思是「天氣眞糟糕！」下面都是美
國人常説的話：

*What a terrible day!*【第一常用】

What a miserable day!【第四常用】

（天氣眞是令人難受！）

What a horrible day!【第六常用】

（天氣眞是糟透了！）

miserable〔'mɪzərəb!〕*adj.* 令人難受的；令人痛苦的

horrible〔'hɑrəb!〕*adj.* 糟透的

What a lousy day!（天氣眞糟糕！）【第五常用】

What a rotten day!（好爛的天氣！）【第二常用】

What an awful day!（天氣眞糟糕！）【第三常用】

3. ***Pretty awful, huh?***

pretty〔'prɪtɪ〕*adv.* 非常；相當　*adj.* 漂亮的
awful〔'ɔfḷ〕*adj.* 可怕的；糟糕的
huh〔hʌ〕*int.* 哈！哼！；什麼【表示驚奇、輕視或疑問等】

> 這句話是由 It's pretty awful, huh? 省略而
> 來，huh 的中文翻譯要看前後意思來決定：
>
> ***Pretty awful, huh?***（天氣很糟糕，不是嗎？）
> 【huh = don't you agree】
> You're late again, ***huh***?
> （你又遲到了，對不對？）【huh = right】
> ***Huh?*** What did you say?
> （什麼？你說什麼？）【huh = what】
>
> 關於 huh 的用法，可參照 Ronald Harmon 的
> "TALKIN' AMERICAN"。

4. ***It's crummy.***

crummy〔'krʌmɪ〕*adj.* 無價值的；低劣的；糟糕的

> crummy 這個字源自 crumb〔krʌm〕*n.* 麵包屑，
> 通常 mb 在字尾，後面的 b 不發音。crumb 的形容
> 詞是 crumby（滿是麵包屑的），因為是衍生字，
> b 一樣不發音，美國人說成〔'krʌmɪ〕，卻要寫成
> crumby，唸的跟寫的不一樣，於是發明了新字
> ***crummy***。在字典上，這兩個字都是形容詞，但
> 現在美國人極少用 crumby，都用 ***crummy*** 來代替。

麵包屑沒有價值，都被丟掉，所以 *crummy* 引申爲「無價值的；低劣的；糟糕的」。*It's crummy.* 的意思是「眞糟糕。」凡是你對任何東西不滿意，你都可以用這個字。

I'm a *crummy* speller. ( 我常拼錯字。 )
【crummy = bad，speller〔'spɛlɚ〕 *n.* 拼字的人】
She's a *crummy* driver.
( 她車開得很糟糕。 )【crummy = poor】
I have a *crummy* memory.
( 我的記憶力很差。 )【crummy = poor】

My sister has a *crummy* job.
( 我姐姐的工作不好。 )
【crummy = bad，sister 可能是姐姐或妹妹，
　　　美國人分得不那麼清楚】
What a *crummy* idea!
( 這個點子眞糟糕！ )【crummy = bad】
He's in a *crummy* situation.
( 他的情況很糟。 )【crummy = bad】

*crummy* 這個字，美國人常說，你也要常說，說起話來才像美國人。

例如，你看到一家爛餐廳，你可以說：

That's a *crummy* restaurant.

（那是一家爛餐廳。）

Their food tastes *crummy*.

（他們的食物嚐起來很糟糕。）

Their bathrooms are *crummy*.

（他們的廁所很糟糕。）

【bathroom〔'bæθ,rum〕*n.* 廁所】

Their service is *crummy*.

（他們的服務很差。）

The whole place is *crummy*.

（整個餐廳都很糟糕。）

I had a *crummy* time.

（我曾經有過不好的經驗。）

whole〔hol〕*adj.* 整個的
place〔ples〕*n.* 餐廳；地方

BOOK 8

5. **It's lousy**.

lousy〔'lauzɪ〕*adj.* 糟糕的；差勁的；惡劣的；討厭的

> lousy 這個字源自 louse〔laus〕*n.* 蝨子，這個字的形容詞是 lousy，字面的意思是「有蝨子的」，引申為「糟糕的；差勁的；惡劣的；討厭的」，按照實際情況，有無限多的意思，和 crummy 意思很接近。例如：

He did a **lousy** job. ( 他做得很糟糕。)

He did **lousy** on the exam.

( 他考試考得很糟。)

【do 後面可接形容詞，詳見 p.39】

That's a **lousy** song. ( 那首歌難聽死了。)

下面是美國人碰到天氣不好時，常說的話，我們按照使用頻率排列：

① **It's lousy**. ( 天氣很糟糕。)【第一常用】

② It's a lousy day.【第二常用】

( 今天天氣真差勁。)

③ It's lousy out today.【第三常用】

( 今天外面天氣很差。)

④ It's lousy outside.

( 外面天氣很糟糕。)

⑤ The weather is so lousy. ( 天氣很糟糕。)

⑥ This kind of weather is lousy.

( 這種天氣很糟糕。)

6. ***This really stinks.***

stink〔stɪŋk〕*v.* 發出惡臭；非常拙劣；令人討厭；很糟糕

> stink 的主要意思是「發出惡臭」，當你進到了廁所，發覺臭氣沖天，你就可以說：This place stinks.（這裡好臭。）

> *stink* 可引申很多意思，要看實際情況及上下文而定。例如：
> > That movie really *stinks*.
> > （那部電影真的很爛。）
> > Smoking *stinks*.
> > （抽煙不好；抽煙很難聞。）
> > I think the idea *stinks*.
> > （我認為這個點子很爛。）

> *stink* 用在天氣方面，有：
> > ***This really stinks.***（這種天氣真的很糟糕。）
> > This weather really *stinks*.
> > （這種天氣真的很糟糕。）
> > This kind of weather *stinks*.
> > （這種天氣真的很糟糕。）

年輕人喜歡把 ***This really stinks.*** 說成 This really sucks.（這真是令人討厭。）由於 suck〔sʌks〕*v.* 令人討厭；令人不愉快這個字的主要意思是「吸」，有性暗示，所以說這句話比較粗魯。

7. **It's gloomy**.

gloomy〔'glumɪ〕*adj.* 陰暗的；陰沈的；憂鬱的；沮喪的；
　　沒有希望的；悲觀的

　　gloomy 的字面意思是「陰暗的」( = *partially
dark* )，可引申出很多意思，要看上下文而定：

　　　Cheer up!  Don't be so *gloomy*.
　　　（振作起來吧！不要這麼沮喪。）
　　　【*cheer up* 振作起來；gloomy = sad】
　　　You look *gloomy* today.
　　　（你今天看起來很憂鬱。）
　　　【gloomy = depressed】
　　　What *gloomy* news!
　　　（多麼令人沮喪的消息！）
　　　【gloomy = depressing】

　　gloomy 用在天氣上，美國人常説的有：

　　　*It's gloomy*.（天氣很陰沈。）【第一常用】
　　　It's *gloomy* today.【第四常用】
　　　（今天天氣很陰沈。）
　　　It's really *gloomy* today.【第五常用】
　　　（今天天氣真的很陰沈。）

　　　It's *gloomy* out.（外面天氣很陰沈。）【第二常用】
　　　It's *gloomy* out today.【第三常用】
　　　（今天外面天氣很陰沈。）
　　　This kind of day is so *gloomy*.【第六常用】
　　　（這種天氣很陰沈。）
　　　【out〔aut〕*adv.* 在外面】

8. **It's depressing**.

depressing〔dɪˈprɛsɪŋ〕*adj.* 令人沮喪的；沈悶的

depress（使沮喪）是情感動詞，它的用法是：

> It depresses me.（它使我沮喪。）【第三常用】
> = I'm depressed.（我很沮喪。）【第二常用】
> 【人做主詞用被動，但無被動意思】
> = **It's depressing**.（它令人沮喪。）【第一常用】
> 【非人做主詞，用主動或現在分詞】

下面是美國人常說的話，我們按照使用頻率排列：

① **It's depressing**.【第一常用】
　　（它令人沮喪。）

② It's so depressing.【第二常用】
　　（它很令人沮喪。）

③ It's a depressing day.【第三常用】
　　（天氣真令人沮喪。）

④ This weather is depressing.
　　（這種天氣令人沮喪。）

⑤ This weather depresses me.
　　（這種天氣使我沮喪。）

⑥ This is depressing weather.
　　（這是令人沮喪的天氣。）

BOOK 8

9. ***This really gets me down.***

　　down〔daʊn〕*adj.* 沮喪的；情緒低落的

　　***get sb. down*** 使某人沮喪

　　　　這句話的意思是「這種天氣真使我難受。」

　　　　down 作「沮喪的」解，可能源自 down in the
　　dumps，它的字面意思是「垃圾堆的下面」，引申為
　　〔dʌmps〕*n. pl.* 垃圾堆
　　「沮喪的」。例如：

　　　　　I've been ***down in the dumps*** for the
　　　　　last few days.
　　　　= I've been ***down*** for the last few days.
　　　　（最近幾天以來，我的情緒很低落。）
　　　【down = down in the dumps = depressed】

　　　　***get sb. down*** 字面的意思是「使某人沮喪」，
　　也就是「使某人難過」。例如，美國人常勸告別人：

　　　　Don't let bad scores ***get you down***.
　　　　（考壞不要難過。）【score〔skor〕*n.* 分數】
　　　　Don't let the bad day ***get you down***.
　　　　（不要讓壞天氣影響你的情緒。）
　　　　Don't let other people ***get you down***.
　　　　（不要因為別人對你的批評而難過。）

　　　【這句話中的 other people 是暗示「別人的批評、
　　　　嘲笑、不良的行為等」。】

【對話練習】

1. A：**What a rotten day!**　　　　　A：好爛的天氣！

　　B：It sure is.　　　　　　　　　B：的確是。

　　　This weather stinks.　　　　　　這種天氣真糟糕。

　　　This weather is the worst!　　　這種天氣是最糟的！

2. A：**What a terrible day!**　　　　A：天氣真糟糕！

　　B：You're not kidding.　　　　　B：你說的沒錯。

　　　It's a miserable day.　　　　　　天氣真令人難受。

　　　It's an awful day.　　　　　　　天氣真糟糕。

　　　【kid〔kɪd〕v. 開玩笑】

3. A：**Pretty awful**, huh?　　　　　A：天氣很糟糕，不是嗎？

　　B：It really is.　　　　　　　　B：的確是。

　　　It's a horrible day.　　　　　　天氣真糟糕。

　　　I wish I could go back to bed.　　真希望我能回去睡覺。

4. A：**It's crummy.**　　　　　　　A：真糟糕。

　　B：I disagree.　　　　　　　　　B：我不同意。

　　　I don't agree.　　　　　　　　我不同意。

　　　It's not that bad at all.　　　　根本沒那麼糟。

　　　【disagree〔͵dɪsə'gri〕v. 不同意

　　　　　***not…at all*** 一點也不】

BOOK 8

5. A：**It's lousy**.

   B：I know it's bad.
      I know it's not good.
      Complaining won't help.
      【complain〔kəm'plen〕v. 抱怨】

A：天氣很糟糕。

B：我知道天氣很糟。
   我知道天氣不好。
   抱怨也沒用。

6. A：**This really stinks**.

   B：Stop complaining!
      I've heard enough!
      I don't want to hear any more!
      【*not…any more* 不再】

A：天氣眞的很糟糕。

B：不要再抱怨了！
   我聽膩了！
   我不想再聽了！

7. A：**It's gloomy**.

   B：It could be worse.
      It could be a lot worse.
      Gloomy is better than a
      typhoon!
      【typhoon〔taɪ'fun〕n. 颱風】

A：天氣很陰沈。

B：原本還可能更糟。
   原本還可能比這糟很多。
   天氣陰沈總好過有颱
   風！

8. A：**It's depressing**.

   B：I agree.
      I know it is.
      It's a little depressing.

A：它令人沮喪。

B：我同意。
   我知道的確如此。
   它是有點令人沮喪。

9. A：**This really gets me down**.

   B：Well, look at it this way.
      Things could be worse.
      Try to look on the bright side.

A：這種天氣眞使我難受。

B：嗯，這樣看好了。
   情況原本可能更糟。
   要試著看事情的光明面。

# 5.  *Need any help?*

| | |
|---|---|
| *Need* any help? | 需要任何幫助嗎？ |
| *Need* a hand? | 需要幫助嗎？ |
| Can I do anything for you? | 我能為你做些什麼事嗎？ |
| | |
| Any problem? | 有任何問題嗎？ |
| *Anything* wrong? | 有什麼不對勁嗎？ |
| *Anything* I can do? | 有什麼我能做的嗎？ |
| | |
| *I*'d like to help. | 我很願意幫忙。 |
| *I* don't mind a bit. | 我一點也不介意。 |
| *I*'d be happy to help. | 我會很高興幫忙。 |

BOOK 8

\*\*—————————————

hand〔hænd〕*n.* 手；幫助
problem〔'prɑbləm〕*n.* 問題
wrong〔rɔŋ〕*adj.* 不對勁的；有問題的
mind〔maɪnd〕*v.* 介意
*a bit* 一點    *not…a bit* 一點也不

## 【背景説明】

在街上，看到外國人東張西望，找不到路，
都可説這九句話，表示善意。

1. ***Need any help?***

這句話源自 Do you ***need any help***？意思是
「你需要任何幫助嗎？」。

【比較1】***Need any help?***【第一常用】
（需要任何幫助嗎？）
***Need some help?***【第一常用】
（需要一些幫助嗎？）
Need my help?【和認識的人説】
（需要我幫忙嗎？）

Do you need any help?【第二常用】
（你需要任何幫助嗎？）
Do you need some help?【第二常用】
（你需要一些幫助嗎？）
Do you need my help?【第三常用】
（你需要我幫忙嗎？）

【比較2】***Need any help?***【語氣輕鬆】
Do you need any help?【語氣較正式】
May I ask, do you need any help?【最客氣】
（我可以請問，你需要任何幫助嗎？）

## 2. *Need a hand?*

hand〔hænd〕*n.* 手；幫助（尤指「動手幫助」）

　　這句話的意思是「需要幫助嗎？」源自 *Do you need a helping hand?*【少用】【*helping hand* 幫助】

　　*Need a hand?* 主要意思是「需不需要我動手幫助？」現在也用在精神層面的幫助。如：Do you need a hand with your homework?（你需不需要我協助你做家庭作業？）

【比較】 下面五句話意義相同，我們按照使用頻率
　　　　排列：

① *Need a hand?*【第一常用】
② Do you need a hand?【第二常用】
　　（你需要幫助嗎？）

③ Would you like a hand?
　　（你想要人幫助嗎？）
④ How about a hand?
　　（我幫你的忙如何？）
⑤ Can I lend you a hand?
　　（我能幫你嗎？）

*How about*～?　～如何？
*lend sb. a hand* 幫助某人

**BOOK 8**

3. *Can I do anything for you?*

這句話的意思是「我能為你做些什麼事嗎？」
下面各句意義相同，我們按照使用頻率排列：

① Can I do anything?【第一常用】

（我能做什麼事嗎？）

② *Can I do anything for you?*【第二常用】

③ Can I do anything to help?

（我能做什麼事來幫忙嗎？）

④ Can I do anything to help you?

（我能做什麼事來幫忙你嗎？）

⑤ Can I do anything to help you out?

（我做什麼事來幫忙你嗎？）

【*help sb. out* 幫助某人解決困難】

4. *Any problem?*

這句話源自 Is there any problem? 意思是
「有任何問題嗎？」

下面各句意義相同，都是美國人常說的話：

> *Any problem?*【第一常用】
>
> Any problem here?【第二常用】
>
> （這裡有任何問題嗎？）
>
> Is there any problem?（有任何問題嗎？）【第三常用】
>
> Is there any problem here?【第五常用】
>
> （這裡有任何問題嗎？）
>
> Is there a problem?（有問題嗎？）【第四常用】

5. *Anything wrong?*

wrong〔rɔŋ〕*adj.* 不對勁的；有問題的

這句話的意思是「有什麼不對勁嗎？」源自
Is there anything wrong? 或 Is anything wrong?

【比較】　***Anything wrong?***【一般語氣】
Is anything wrong?【稍正式】
Is there anything wrong?【較正式】

如果你看到一個人，身體不舒服，你想提供
幫助，最有禮貌的說法是：Excuse me, *is there
anything wrong*?（對不起，有什麼不對勁嗎？）

6. *Anything I can do?*

這句話的意思是「有什麼我能做的嗎？」源自
Is there *anything I can do*?

【比較】　下面都是美國人常說的話：

***Anything I can do?***【第一常用】
Anything I can do for you?【第三常用】
（有什麼我能為你做的嗎？）
Anything I can do to help?【第二常用】
（有什麼我能幫得上忙的嗎？）

Is there anything I can do?【第四常用】
（有什麼我能做的嗎？）
Is there anything I can do for you?【第六常用】
（有什麼我能為你做的嗎？）
Is there anything I can do to help?【第五常用】
（有什麼我能幫得上忙的嗎？）

7. *I'd like to help*.

這句話的意思是「我很願意幫忙。」(= *I'm willing to help*.)

下面都是美國人常說的話，我們按照使用頻率排列：

① *I'd like to help*.【第一常用】

② I'd like to help you.【第二常用】
（我很願意幫你。）

③ I'd like to help you out.【第三常用】
（我很願意幫你的忙。）

④ I'd like to help you in any way.
（我很願意儘量幫你的忙。）

⑤ I'd like to help you any way I can.
（我很願意儘量幫你的忙。）

⑥ I'd like to help you any way at all.
（我很願意儘量幫你的忙。）

【way〔we〕*n.* 方式；方面　　*at all* 即使】

【比較】*I'd like to help*.【輕鬆，常用】
I would like to help.【較正式，少用】

8. *I don't mind a bit*.

   *a bit*  一點點；少許     *not…a bit*  一點也不

   這句話的意思是「我一點也不介意。」下面都是
美國人常說的話：

   *I don't mind*. ( 我不介意。)【第一常用】

   I don't mind at all. ( 我一點也不介意。)【第二常用】

   I don't mind a bit. ( 我一點也不介意。)【第三常用】

   【mind 是及物和不及物兩用動詞，故上面三句也可
   說成 I don't mind it.  I don't mind it at all.
   I don't mind it a bit.】

9. *I'd be happy to help*.

   這句話的意思是「我會很高興幫忙。」用假設
法表示客氣，If 子句 *If you asked me…*. 放在心
中不說出來。不可說成：*I'll be happy to help*.
因為這是表示未來願意幫忙。

   下面各句意義相同，都是美國人常說的話：

   *I'd be happy to help*. 【第一常用】

   I'm happy to help. ( 我很高興幫忙。)【第一常用】

   I'm very happy to help. 【第一常用】
   ( 我非常高興幫忙。)

   I'd be happy to help you. 【第二常用】
   ( 我會非常高興幫你的忙。)

   I'd be happy to help you out. 【第二常用】
   ( 我會非常高興幫你的忙。)

   I'd be happy to help in any way. 【第三常用】
   ( 我非常高興儘量幫你的忙。)

BOOK 8

## 【對話練習】

1. A : **Need any help?**　　　　　　A：需要任何幫助嗎？

   B : I sure do.　　　　　　　　　B：我的確需要。
   I need help right now.　　　　　我現在需要幫助。
   You came at just the right　　　你來得正是時候。
   time.

2. A : **Need a hand?**　　　　　　　A：需要幫助嗎？

   B : Yes, I do.　　　　　　　　　B：是的，我需要。
   I could use a hand.　　　　　　我有點想要別人幫忙。
   I would like that very　　　　　我非常需要幫忙。
   much.【*could use* 有點想要】

3. A : **Can I do anything for you?**　A：我能為你做些什麼事嗎？

   B : No, thank you.　　　　　　　B：不用，謝謝。
   Everything is OK.　　　　　　一切都還好。
   Everything is under control.　　一切都在控制之下。
   【*under control* 在控制之下】

4. A : **Any problem?**　　　　　　　A：有任何問題嗎？

   B : I'm not sure.　　　　　　　B：我不確定。
   I'm glad you asked.　　　　　我很高興你問我。
   I might need some help.　　　我可能需要一些幫助。

5. A：**Anything wrong?**

B：Nothing is wrong.
Nothing is the matter.
Everything is all right.
【*the matter* 不對勁的
*all right* 沒問題的；好的】

A：有什麼不對勁嗎？

B：沒什麼不對勁。
沒什麼不對勁。
一切都還好。

6. A：**Anything I can do?**

B：Not right now.
I don't need any help.
I want to thank you for asking.

A：有什麼我能做的嗎？

B：現在沒有。
我不需要任何幫助。
我想謝謝你問我。

7. A：**I'd like to help**.

B：I know you would.
That's kind of you.
It's nice of you to offer.
【offer〔ˈɔfɚ〕*v.* 提供】

A：我很願意幫忙。

B：我知道你願意。
你人真好。
你願意提供幫助，你
人真好。

8. A：**I don't mind a bit**.

B：I'm happy to hear that.
I was afraid you'd mind.
I feel much better about it now.

A：我一點也不介意。

B：很高興聽你這麼說。
我很怕你會介意。
現在我覺得好多了。

9. A：**I'd be happy to help**.

B：That would be great!
I can't refuse.
I'd really welcome your help.
【refuse〔rɪˈfjuz〕*v.* 拒絕】

A：我會很高興幫忙。

B：那真是太棒了！
我無法拒絕。
我真的很歡迎你來幫
忙。

# 6. Can I ask a favor?

Can I ask a favor?　　　　　　能不能請你幫個忙？

*Can you* spare a minute?　　　你能不能抽出一點時間？

*Can you* help me with this?　　你能不能幫我做這件事？

*What* does this mean?　　　　這是什麼意思？

*What*'s this about?　　　　　　這是什麼意思？

I can't figure this out.　　　　我不了解這個。

*I* don't want to disturb you.　　我不想要打擾你。

*I* hope I'm not bothering
　you.　　　　　　　　　　　我希望我沒打擾到你。

If you're busy, I understand.　　如果你忙的話，我會了
　　　　　　　　　　　　　　解的。

\*\*

favor〔'fevə〕*n.* 恩惠；幫忙

*ask sb. a favor* 請某人幫忙

spare〔spɛr〕*v.* 抽出（時間）　　minute〔'mɪnɪt〕*n.* 片刻

*help sb. with sth.* 幫助某人做某事

mean〔min〕*v.* 意思是　　*figure out* 了解

disturb〔dɪ'stɜb〕*v.* 打擾　　bother〔'baðə〕*v.* 打擾

## 【背景説明】

當你有什麼不懂的，想請教外國人，你就可以
説這九句話，作爲開場白。

1. ***Can I ask a favor?***
favor〔'fevɚ〕 *n.* 恩惠；幫助；善意的行爲
***ask sb. a favor*** 請某人幫忙（= *ask a favor of sb.*）

這句話源自 Can I ask a favor of you? 意思
是「能不能請你幫個忙？」美國人説話喜歡簡化，
常把後面的 of you 省略。

下面是美國人常説的話：
Can I <u>ask you a favor</u>?【第二常用】
　　　授與動詞　間接受詞　直接受詞
（我能不能請你幫個忙？）
Can I ask a favor of you?【第五常用】
（我能不能請你幫個忙？）
【間接受詞和直接受詞對調，因爲動詞 ask 的關
　係，須加介系詞 of】
***Can I ask a favor?***【簡化的句子】【第一常用】
（我能不能請你幫個忙？）

Can you do <u>me</u> a favor?【第三常用】
　　　　　間接受詞　直接受詞
（你能不能幫我一個忙？）
Can you do a favor for me?【第四常用】
（你能不能幫我一個忙？）
【間接受詞和直接受詞對調，因爲動詞 do 的關
　係，須加介系詞 for】

【比較】 ***Can I ask a favor?*** 【正】
*Can you do a favor?* 【誤】
這句話應該改成：Can you do a favor for me?
或 Can you do me a favor? ( 你可不可以幫我
一個忙？)

2. ***Can you spare a minute?***
spare〔spɛr〕v. 抽出（時間）；讓給

spare 的主要意思是「空閒的；多餘的；備用的」，
像「空閒時間」是 spare time，「備胎」叫作 spare
tire。由於是多餘的或空閒的，所以 spare 當動詞時，
才會有「抽出（時間）；讓給」的意思。

***Can you spare a minute?*** 源自 Can you spare
a minute *of your time?* 字面的意思是「你能不能抽出
一分鐘的時間？」引申為「你能不能抽出一點時間？」

下面是美國人常說的話：

***Can you spare a minute?*** 【第一常用】
Can you spare me a minute? 【第一常用】
（你能不能抽出一點時間給我？）
Can you give me a minute? 【第一常用】
（你能不能給我一點時間？）

Can you spare me a minute of your time?
（你能不能抽出一點時間給我？）【第四常用】
Can you spare a minute of your time?
（你能不能抽出一點時間？）【第三常用】
Can you spare a few minutes? 【第二常用】
（你能不能抽出幾分鐘時間？）

3. *Can you help me with this?*
   *help sb. with sth.* 幫助某人做某事

　　在中文思想中，help 像是授與動詞，後面要接
間接受詞和直接受詞，但是在英文中，help 後的間
接受詞和直接受詞之間，要有 with。(「文法寶典」
p.279、280 中，有這些特殊的動詞。)

【比較1】*Can you help me this?*【誤，中外思想不同】
　　　　*Can you help me with this?*【正】
　　　　Can you help me?【正】

【比較2】下面兩句話意義相同，使用頻率接近：

　　　　*Can you help me with this?*【最常用】
　　　　（你能不能幫我做這件事？）
　= Can you help me out with this?【較常用】
　　　　（你能不能幫個忙，做這件事？）
　　【*help sb. out* 幫某人一個忙】

4. *What does this mean?*
   mean〔min〕*v.* 意思是

　　這句話的意思是「這是什麼意思？」也可以說成：
What is the meaning of this?

　　如果有哪一個字不認識，你可以問外國人：What
does this word mean?（這個字是什麼意思？）如果
哪個表格不會填，你可以問：What does this form
mean?（這個表格是做什麼用的？我看不懂。）
【form〔fɔrm〕*n.* 表格】當別人給你任何一張紙，你不
知道是做什麼用的，你就可以說：What does this
paper mean?（這張紙是做什麼用的？我看不懂。）

### 5. *What's this about?*

這句話字面的意思是「這是關於什麼的？」引申為
「這是什麼意思？」( = *What's the meaning of this?* )

【比較1】 What is this?【一般語氣】
　　　　　（①這是什麼東西？②這是什麼意思？）
　　　　　What is this about?【語氣稍強】
　　　　　（這是什麼意思？）
　　　　　What is this all about?【語氣最強】
　　　　　（這究竟是什麼意思？）

【比較2】 *What's this about?*【語氣輕鬆，較常用】
　　　　　What is this about?【語氣稍強，常用】

### 6. *I can't figure this out.*
*figure out* 了解

這句話的意思是「我不了解這個。」也可以說
成：I can't figure out the meaning of this. ( 我
不了解這個的意思。) 或 I can't figure out what
this means. ( 我不了解這是什麼意思。)

【比較】 *I can't figure this out.*【正】
　　　　I can't *figure out* this word.【正】
　　　　（我不了解這個字的意思。）

figure out 的受詞，如果是代名詞，須放在
figure 和 out 的中間，如果是名詞、名詞片語或
名詞子句，就要放在 figure out 的後面。

7. ***I don't want to disturb you***.

　　disturb〔dɪˈstɜb〕*v.* 打擾

　　　　這句話的意思是「我不想要打擾你。」

　　　【比較1】　disturb 可做及物和不及物兩用動詞：

　　　　　　***I don't want to disturb you***.【較常用】

　　　　　　I don't want to disturb.【常用】

　　　　　　（我不想打擾。）

　　　【比較2】　***I don't want to disturb you***.

　　　　　　　【受高深教育的人喜歡説，如律師、教授、老師等】

　　　　　　I don't wanna disturb you.【一般人喜歡説】

　　　　　　　〔ˈwɑnə〕( = *want to* )

8. ***I hope I'm not bothering you***.

　　bother〔ˈbɑðə〕*v.* 打擾

　　　　這句話的意思是「我希望我沒打擾到你。」也

　　可説成：I don't want to bother you.（我不想打

　　擾你。）也有美國人喜歡説：Am I bothering you?

　　（我有沒有打擾你？）

9. ***If you're busy, I understand***.

　　　　這句話的意思是「如果你忙的話，我會了解。」

　　　【比較】　***If you're busy, I understand***.【較常用】

　　　　　　If you're busy, I'll understand.【常用】

BOOK 8

小心下面錯誤的文法觀念：

```
┌────【錯誤的文法句型】────┐
│                              │
│   If + S. + V.···S. + ⎰ shall ⎱ + V. │
│                        ⎱ will  ⎰     │
│                              │
└──────────────────────────┘
```

　　背了這個公式，你就被束縛了。事實上，這是
「直說法」，主要子句可以有十二種時態，不一定
只是 shall 或 will。(詳見「文法寶典」p.356)

　　下面都是美國人常說的話，主要子句中，都沒
有用 shall 或 will 表示未來：

***If you're busy, I understand.***【第一常用】
If you're busy, I totally understand.【第六常用】
（如果你忙的話，我完全了解。）

If you're busy, it's OK.【第二常用】
（如果你忙的話，沒有關係。）
If you're busy, that's OK.【第三常用】
（如果你忙的話，沒有關係。）

If you're busy, that's no problem.【第四常用】
（如果你忙的話，沒有關係。）
If you're busy, that's no problem at all.
（如果你忙的話，眞的沒有關係。）【第五常用】

If you're busy, no problem.【第四常用】
（如果你忙的話，沒關係。）
If you're busy, don't worry about it.
（如果你忙的話，不必擔心這件事。）【第七常用】

## 【對話練習】

1. A : **Can I ask a favor?**

   B : You sure can.
   You know you can.
   You can ask me anything.

   A：能不能請你幫個忙？

   B：當然可以。
   你知道你可以的。
   你可以要求我做任何事。

2. A : **Can you spare a minute?**

   B : I'm sorry, I can't.
   I'm super busy.
   I'm really in a rush.
   【super〔'supɚ〕*adv.* 十分；非常
   *in a rush* 匆忙】

   A：你能不能抽出一點時間？

   B：很抱歉，我不能。
   我很忙。
   我真的很趕時間。

3. A : **Can you help me with this?**

   B : It would be my pleasure.
   I'd be happy to help.
   I'd love to help you out.
   【pleasure〔'plɛʒɚ〕*n.* 榮幸】

   A：你能不能幫我做這件事？

   B：這會是我的榮幸。
   我很樂意幫忙。
   我很樂意幫你的忙。

4. A : **What does this mean?**

   B : I don't know.
   I have no idea.
   I'll have to look it up.
   【*look up* 查閱】

   A：這是什麼意思？

   B：我不知道。
   我不知道。
   我得查一下。

5. A : **What's this about?**

   B : That's a good question.
   I'm not sure.
   I have to take a good look at it.

   A：這是什麼意思？

   B：那是個好問題。
   我不確定。
   我必須好好看一下。

BOOK 8

6. A : **I can't figure this out**.

  B : We can do it together.
  We can figure it out.
  Two heads are better than
  one.

A：我不了解這個。

B：我們可以一起做。
  我們可以把它弄清楚。
  三個臭皮匠，勝過一個
  諸葛亮。

7. A : **I don't want to disturb you**.

  B : Don't be polite.
  Don't worry about that.
  You're not disturbing me.

A：我不想要打擾你。

B：別客氣。
  別擔心。
  你沒打擾到我。

8. A : **I hope I'm not bothering you**.

  B : No, you're not.
  You're not bothering me.
  You're not bothering me one
  bit. 【*not…one bit* 一點也不
  ( = *not…at all* )】

A：我希望我沒打擾到你。

B：不，你沒有。
  你沒打擾到我。
  你一點都沒打擾到我。

9. A : **If you're busy, I understand**.

  B : No, not at all.
  I've always got time for you.
  Don't be shy about asking
  for my help.
  【shy〔ʃaɪ〕*adj.* 害羞的；不好意思的】

A：如果你忙的話，我會了
  解的。

B：不，一點都不忙。
  我一定會有時間幫你。
  找我幫忙不必不好意思。

# 7.　*I like your shirt!*

| | |
|---|---|
| I like your shirt! | 我喜歡你的襯衫！ |
| *That*'s your color! | 那個顏色最適合你！ |
| *That* looks great on you! | 你穿那件衣服很好看！ |
| | |
| *It*'s a nice style. | 它的款式很好看。 |
| *It* caught my eye. | 它讓我想不看都不行。 |
| *It*'s just what I'm looking for. | 它正是我在找的。 |
| | |
| Where did you get it? | 你在哪裡買的？ |
| When did you buy it? | 你什麼時候買的？ |
| Mind if I ask the price? | 你介意我問價錢嗎？ |

**\*\***————————

shirt〔ʃɜt〕*n.* 襯衫
great〔gret〕*adj.* 極美的；極好的；很棒的
style〔staɪl〕*n.* 風格；款式　　eye〔aɪ〕*n.* 目光；注意
*catch one's eye* 引起某人的注意
get〔gɛt〕*v.* 得到；買　　mind〔maɪnd〕*v.* 介意
price〔praɪs〕*n.* 價格

## 【背景説明】

　　美國人習慣見到他人都會稱讚，除了説 You look great.　You look nice. 之類的話外，還會稱讚對方的衣服，這是美國人的文化。

1. ***I like your shirt!***
   shirt〔ʃɜt〕*n.* 襯衫

　　　這句話的意思是「我喜歡你的襯衫！」美國人有時候會開玩笑説：I want your shirt!（我想要你的襯衫！）並非真正跟你要你身上的襯衫，只是一種稱讚。

> 　　shirt 是所有襯衫的通稱，大部份上半身的衣服，不管男裝或女裝，都可稱作 shirt。
>
> **shirt** ──┬─ dress shirt（有領子、有袖子，並有前開扣子的襯衫）
>
> ├─ sports shirt（有領子的運動衫）〔sports〕*adj.* 運動的
>
> ├─ T-shirt（短袖圓領運動衫）
>
> ├─ blouse〔blaʊs〕*n.* 女用襯衫（= *woman shirt*）
>
> └─ jersey〔'dʒɜzɪ〕*n.* 制服式的運動衫

【比較1】 ***I like your shirt!***【常用】
        I like your T-shirt!【年輕人喜歡説】
        I like your sports shirt!【少用】

        I like your dress shirt!【少用】
        I like your blouse!【少用】
        I like your jersey!【年輕人喜歡説】

美國人還常説：
    I like your outfit!
        〔ˈaʊtˌfɪt〕*n.* 全套服裝
只要身上穿兩件以上的，都可稱作 outfit。

【比較2】
    I like your outfit!
    （我喜歡你的服裝！）
    I like your suit!
      〔sut〕*n.* 西裝；套裝
    （我喜歡你的西裝！）
    I like your dress!（我喜歡妳的洋裝！）
      〔drɛs〕*n.* 洋裝

outfit  suit  dress

suit 是「西裝」，通常男人穿，有些女生也穿 suit，
我們稱作「套裝」；dress 是「（一件式的）洋裝」。

當你稱讚別人，「我喜歡你的衣服！」時，不可
説成：*I like your clothes!* 因為 clothes 是所有衣服
的總稱，我們可以説：She has nice clothes.（她有
好的衣服。）She wears nice clothes.（她穿好的衣
服。）Put your clothes away.（把你的衣服收拾好。）
【*put away* 收拾】Let's go buy some clothes.（我們
去買一些衣服吧。）

【比較】

英文：I like your clothes!

中文：我喜歡你現在穿的衣服！【誤】

我喜歡你所有的衣服！【正】

( = *I like your wardrobe!* )

【wardrobe〔ˈwɔrdˌrob〕 *n.* 全部服裝】

我喜歡你平常穿的衣服！【正】

( = *I like what you usually wear!* )

我喜歡你穿衣服的品味！【正】

( = *I like your taste in clothing!* )

　　凡是男生或女生的外套，只要是非正式，都稱作 jacket〔ˈdʒækɪt〕 *n.* 有袖的短上衣、外套、夾克。正式一點的，就叫作 coat〔kot〕 *n.* 外套，正式或非正式無法區別時，你就可說 jacket 或 coat。

## 2. *That's your color!*

　　這句話字面的意思是「那是你的顏色！」引申為「那個顏色最適合你！」也就是「你穿那個顏色的衣服最好看！」( = *That color makes you look great!* )

【比較】下面兩句話句意不同：

*That's your color!*（那個顏色最適合你！）

【不一定是你喜歡的顏色，但是很適合你】

That's your favorite color!

（那是你最喜歡的顏色！）【不一定穿起來最好看】

BOOK 8

3. ***That looks great on you!***

great〔gret〕*adj.* 極美的；極好的；很棒的

這句話字面的意思是「那件衣服在你身上看起來很好看！」也就是「你穿那件衣服很好看！」on you 的意思是「穿在你身上的時候」( = *when you're wearing it* )。

下面都是美國人常說的話：

***That looks great on you!***【第一常用】
That looks good on you!【第二常用】
（你穿那件衣服很好看！）
That looks cool on you!【第六常用】
（你穿那件衣服很好看！）
【cool〔kul〕*adj.* 酷的；極好的】

That looks fantastic on you!【第四常用】
（你穿那件衣服很好看！）
That looks elegant on you!【第五常用】
（妳穿那件衣服很高雅！）【限對女生說】
That looks so nice on you!【第三常用】
（你穿那件衣服很好看！）

fantastic〔fæn'tæstɪk〕*adj.* 很棒的
elegant〔'ɛləgənt〕*adj.* 高雅的

4. ***It's a nice style.***

nice〔naɪs〕*adj.* 好的

style〔staɪl〕*n.* 風格；款式；樣式

（*= a sort, a type of something*）

　　這句話的字面意思是「它是好的款式。」也就是「它的款式很好看。」這句話也可以說成：That's a nice style. 或和中國人思想相近的 That style is nice.

　　下面都是美國人常說的話：

> ***It's a nice style.***【最常用】
> It's a great style.【最常用】
> （它的款式很好看。）
> It's a wonderful style.【最常用】
> （它的款式很棒。）
>
> It's a fantastic style.【較常用】
> （它的款式很棒。）
> It's a fashionable style.【常用】
> （它的款式很時麾。）
> It's an excellent style.【較常用】
> （它的款式很棒。）
>
> fashionable〔'fæʃənəbḷ〕*adj.* 流行的；時麾的
> excellent〔'ɛkslənt〕*adj.* 極佳的

**BOOK 8**

5. *It caught my eye.*

eye〔aɪ〕*n.* 目光；看；注意

*catch* one's eye   引起某人的注目；引起某人的注意
（=*attract one's attention*）

這句話字面的意思是「它抓到我的目光。」

引申為「它讓我想不看都不行。」

6. *It's just what I'm looking for.*

這句話的意思是「它正是我在找的。」暗示

「它正是我想要買的。」美國人買東西喜歡說：

I'm looking for…，詳見 p.146。

下面都是美國人喜歡說的話：

It's just what I want.【最常用】
（它正是我想要的。）

It's just what I need.【最常用】
（它正是我需要的。）

*It's just what I'm looking for.*【最常用】
（它正是我想要買的。）

It's what I'm looking for.【最常用】
（它是我想要買的。）

It's what I want.【較常用】
（它是我想要的。）

It's what I want to buy.【常用】
（它是我想要買的。）

7. ***Where did you get it?***

get〔gɛt〕*v.* 得到；買

　　　這句話的字面意思是「你在哪裡得到的？」
大部份都暗示「你在哪裡買的？」( = *Where did
you buy it?* ) 也可能暗示「誰給你的？」( = *Who
gave it to you?* )

　　　如果問「你在哪個商店買的？」就可以說：
What store did you get it at? 或 What store
did you buy it at?

8. ***When did you buy it?***

　　　這句話的意思是「你什麼時候買的？」也可以
說成：When did you get it? ( 你什麼時候買的？)
也有美國人說：How long ago did you buy it?
( 你是多久以前買的？)

【比較】　***When did you buy it?***【正】

　　　　　*What time did you buy it?*
　　　　　【誤，文法對，但美國人不說】

　　　美國人問別人「什麼時候買的？」通常是問
「哪一天買的？」，不會問「什麼時間買的？」，
因為 What time 通常是指「今天的什麼時間」
( what time today )。

### 9. *Mind if I ask the price?*

mind〔maɪnd〕v. 介意    price〔praɪs〕n. 價格

　　這句話源自 Do you mind if I ask the price?
（你介意我問價錢嗎？）也可説成：Mind if I ask
you the price?（你介意我問你價錢嗎？）

　　下面都是美國人常説的話：

*Mind if I ask the price?*【較常用】
（你介意我問價錢嗎？）
Mind if I ask how much?【較常用】
（你介意我問多少錢嗎？）
Mind if I ask how much it was?【常用】
（你介意我問這個東西多少錢嗎？）

Mind if I ask the cost?【較常用】
（你介意我問價錢嗎？）
Mind if I ask how much it cost?【常用】
（你介意我問它值多少錢嗎？）
Mind if I ask how much you paid?【常用】
（你介意我問你付了多少錢嗎？）

cost〔kɔst〕n. 價格；費用  v. 值…價錢
pay〔pe〕v. 支付

　　由於美國人不喜歡別人問多少錢，所以問價
錢時，最好用 Mind if～?

BOOK 8

## 【對話練習】

1. A：**I like your shirt!**　　　　　A：我喜歡你的襯衫！

　　B：Thank you.　　　　　　　　B：謝謝。
　　　　It's brand-new.　　　　　　　　它是全新的。
　　　　I just bought it.　　　　　　　　我剛買的。
　　　　【brand-new〔'brænd'nju〕adj. 全新的】

2. A：**That's your color!**　　　　　A：那個顏色最適合你！

　　B：Everyone says that.　　　　　B：大家都那麼說。
　　　　I hear that a lot.　　　　　　　　我常聽人家那麼說。
　　　　I guess it must be true.　　　　　我猜一定是真的。
　　　　【*a lot* 常常】

3. A：**That looks great on you!**　　A：你穿那件衣服很好看！

　　B：Thanks for the compliment.　B：謝謝你的讚美。
　　　　You flatter me.　　　　　　　　你使我受寵若驚。
　　　　You're such a sweet-talker.　　　你的嘴巴真甜。
　　　　【compliment〔'kɑmpləmənt〕n. 稱讚
　　　　flatter〔'flætɚ〕v. 使受寵若驚；奉承
　　　　sweet-talker〔'swit'tɔkɚ〕n. 說甜言
　　　　蜜語的人】

4. A：**It's a nice style.**　　　　　A：它的款式很好看。

　　B：I like it, too.　　　　　　　B：我也很喜歡。
　　　　It's popular right now.　　　　　這種款式現在很受歡迎。
　　　　It's a popular style.　　　　　　它是個受歡迎的款式。

BOOK 8

5. A：**It caught my eye**.

　B：I love to hear that.
　　That makes me feel good.
　　That's music to my ears.
　　【*be music to one's ears* 令某人感覺
　　悅耳】

A：它讓我想不看都不行。

B：聽你這麼說我真高興。
　那讓我感覺很好。
　那讓我覺得很悅耳。

6. A：**It's just what I'm looking for**.

　B：I'm glad you told me.
　　I know where to find it.
　　I can help you get it.

A：它正是我在找的。

B：很高興你告訴我。
　我知道去哪裡買。
　我可以幫你買。

7. A：**Where did you get it?**

　B：It was a gift.
　　It was a present.
　　Someone gave it to me.
　　【gift〔gɪft〕n. 禮物
　　present〔'prɛzn̩t〕n. 禮物】

A：你在哪裡買的？

B：這是禮物。
　這是禮物。
　別人送給我的。

8. A：**When did you buy it?**

　B：I got it last weekend.
　　I bought it last week.
　　I bought it last Saturday afternoon.

A：你什麼時候買的？

B：我上個週末買的。
　我上星期買的。
　我上星期六下午買的。

9. A：**Mind if I ask the price?**

　B：It was three hundred bucks.
　　The guy wanted three-fifty.
　　I managed to talk him down.
　　【buck〔bʌk〕n. 元　*manage to V.* 設法…　*talk sb. down* 殺價】

A：你介意我問價錢嗎？

B：三百元。
　那人想要三百五十元。
　我設法跟他殺價。

BOOK 8

# 8. *You look familiar*.

| | |
|---|---|
| *You* look familiar. | 你看起來很面熟。 |
| *You* got me thinking. | 你讓我想想看。 |
| Have we met before? | 我們以前見過面嗎？ |
| | |
| *I feel like* I know you. | 我覺得我好像認識你。 |
| *I feel like* I've seen you somewhere. | 我覺得我好像在哪裡看過你。 |
| I can't recall your name. | 我想不起你的名字。 |
| | |
| I'm Pat Smith. | 我是派特‧史密斯。 |
| Everyone calls me Pat. | 大家都叫我派特。 |
| May I ask your name? | 能不能請問你叫什麼名字？ |

\*\* ─────────────────

familiar〔fə'mɪljɚ〕 *adj.* 熟悉的
get〔gɛt〕 *v.* 使得　　think〔θɪŋk〕 *v.* 想；思考
meet〔mit〕 *v.* 遇到；與～見面　　*feel like* 覺得好像
somewhere〔'sʌmˌhwɛr〕 *adv.* 在某處
recall〔rɪ'kɔl〕 *v.* 想起

## 【背景説明】

　　當你看到任何俊男、美女，或任何心中喜歡的人，都可以説這九句話去接近他。

1. ***You look familiar.***

familiar〔fəˋmɪljɚ〕*adj.* 熟悉的

　　這句話的字面意思是「你看起來是熟悉的。」引申爲「你看起來很面熟。」( = *Your face looks familiar.* ) 背 familiar 這個字，可先背 family（家庭；家人），家人彼此之間當然是比較「熟悉的」。familiar 字尾是 iar，重音在倒數第二音節上。

　　説 ***You look familiar.*** 的時候，美國人習慣用食指指著對方，食指通常向上；如果直接指著對方，則表示譴責。

***You look familiar.***【第一常用】
You look familiar to me.【第五常用】
（我覺得你看起來很面熟。）

You look so familiar.【第三常用】
（你看起來很面熟。）
You look very familiar.【第二常用】
（你看起來很面熟。）
You really look familiar.【第四常用】
（你真的看起來很面熟。）

BOOK 8

You look like somebody I've met. 【第十常用】
（你看起來像是某個我見過的人。）
【meet〔mit〕v. 認識；見面】
You look like somebody I know. 【第九常用】
（你看起來像是某個我認識的人。）
You look like somebody I've seen before.
（你看起來像是某個我以前看過的人。）
【第十一常用】
【上面三句話，也可只說 You look like somebody.】

I think I know you. 【第十二常用】
（我想我認識你。）
I think I recognize you. 【第十三常用】
（我想我認得你。）
I think I've met you. 【第十四常用】
（我想我見過你。）
【recognize〔'rɛkəɡ,naɪz〕v. 認得】

I feel like I know you, but I'm not sure.
（我覺得我認識你，但我不確定。）
【第八常用】
Your face looks familiar. 【第六常用】
（你的臉看起來很面熟。）
Your face seems familiar. 【第七常用】
（你的臉似乎很面熟。）【seem〔sim〕v. 似乎】

2. ***You got me thinking.***
　get〔gɛt〕v. 使得
　think〔θɪŋk〕v. 想；思考；思索；想到

　　　　這句話是美國人的思想，中國人沒有，美國人常說 You got me～. 或 You made me～. 這句話的意思是「你讓我動腦筋想。」相當於中國人所説的「你讓我想想看。」

　　　　get 這個字，在意義上像是使役動詞，後面可接分詞或形容詞做受詞補語，例如：

　　***You got me*** worried. (你使我擔心。)
　　【由於 worry 是情感動詞，所以用過去分詞 worried】
　　***You got me*** tired out. (你使我累死了。)
　　【tire (使疲倦) 用法和情感動詞相同】
　　***You got me*** so excited. (你使我很興奮。)
　　【excite (使興奮) 是情感動詞】

　　***You got me*** going again.
　　(你使我再次出發；你使我又有精神了。)
　　***You got me*** going crazy. (你使我發瘋。)
　　【***go crazy*** 發瘋】
　　***You got me*** very upset. (你使我很生氣。)
　　【upset〔ʌpˈsɛt〕adj. 不高興的】

【比較1】　You got = You've got
　　　　　***You got me thinking.***
　　　　　　(你讓我想想看。)【通俗，口語，一般人常用】
　　　　　You've got me thinking.
　　　　【白領階級、教授、律師等喜歡説】

【比較2】 *You got me thinking.*【正】
*You made me think.*【文法對，美國人不說】
You made me think about it.【正】
（你讓我思考這件事。）

　　在所有中外字典上，都找不到 *You got me thinking.* 這句話，但是在日常生活中，美國人常說，等於 You got me started thinking.（你讓我開始動腦筋想。）如果加強語氣，可說成：You got me thinking a lot.（你讓我動腦筋拼命想。）

3. *Have we met before?*

meet〔mit〕v. 遇到；與…會面；認識

　　這句話的意思是「我們以前見過面嗎？」。

【比較】 下面各句意思接近，但語氣不同：

Have we met?（我們見過嗎？）【語氣輕鬆】
*Have we met before?*【一般語氣】
（我們以前見過面嗎？）
Have we ever met before?【語氣較強】
（我們以前是不是曾經見過面？）
Have you and I ever met before?【語氣最強】
（你和我以前是不是曾經見過面？）

4. **I feel like I know you**.

　**feel like** 覺得好像（ = *feel as if* )

　　　　這句話的意思是「我覺得我好像認識你。」在
句中，like 是連接詞，相當於 as if。

> 　　在傳統文法上，like 是介系詞，as if 是連接
> 詞，但是現在美國人說 I feel like 比 I feel as
> if 更常用。

　　　　**I feel like I know you**.
　　= I feel as if I know you.
　　（我覺得我好像認識你。）

　　　　**I feel like** wc've met.
　　= I feel as if we've met.
　　（我覺得我們好像見過面。）

　　　　**I feel like** I've seen you before.
　　= I feel as if I've seen you before.
　　（我覺得我好像以前見過你。）

　　　　**I feel like** I'm a child again.
　　= I feel as if I'm a child again.
　　（我覺得我好像回到小時候。）
　　【這句話可簡化為：I feel like a child again.】

　　　　**I feel like** I'm an idiot.
　　= I feel as if I'm an idiot.【idiot〔'ɪdɪət〕*n.* 白痴】
　　（我覺得我好像是白痴。）
　　【這句話可簡化為：I feel like an idiot.】

5. ***I feel like I've seen you somewhere.***
somewhere〔'sʌm,hwɛr〕*adv.* 在某處

　　　　這句話的意思是「我覺得我好像在哪裡看過你。」
也可說成：I think I've seen you somewhere.
（我認爲我在哪裡看過你。）或 It seems like I've
seen you somewhere.（我好像在哪裡看過你。）

6. ***I can't recall your name.***
recall〔rɪ'kɔl〕*v.* 想起

　　　　這句話的意思是「我想不起你的名字。」美
國人也常說：I forgot your name.（我忘記你
的名字。）

　　　下面三句話意義相同：

　　***I can't recall your name.***【第二常用】
　= I can't remember your name.【第一常用】
　　　（我不記得你的名字。）
　= I can't figure out your name.【第三常用】
　　　（我想不出你的名字。）
　　【***figure out*** 想出】

## 7. *I'm Pat Smith*.

　　這句話的意思是「我是派特·史密斯。」Pat 這個名字，男女生都可以用，源自：Patrick〔'pætrɪk〕*n.* 派翠克（男生名），或 Patricia〔pə'trɪʃə〕*n.* 派翠西亞（女生名），含有「出身高貴的」意思，這個名字在愛爾蘭很受歡迎。

　　這句話也可說成：My full name is Pat Smith.（我的全名是派特·史密斯。）My first name is Pat.（我的名字是派特。）My last name is Smith.（我姓史密斯。）【*full name* 全名　*first name* 名字　*last name* 姓（= family name = surname〔'sɝ,nem〕）】

## 8. *Everyone calls me Pat*.

　　這句話的意思是「大家都叫我派特。」也有美國人說：Everyone likes to call me Pat.（大家都喜歡叫我派特。）

下面是美國人常說的話：

*Everyone calls me Pat*.【第三常用】
Just call me Pat.（叫我派特就好。）【第一常用】
You can call me Pat.【第二常用】
（你可以叫我派特。）

Most people call me Pat.【第五常用】
（大部份的人都叫我派特。）
My friends call me Pat.【第四常用】
（我的朋友叫我派特。）
People like to call me Pat.【第六常用】
（大家喜歡叫我派特。）

BOOK 8

BOOK 8

9. *May I ask your name?*

這句話的意思是「能不能請問你叫什麼名字？」

【比較1】　ask 後面，間接受詞常省略。

　　　　*May I ask your name?*【常用】
　　　　= May I ask you your name?【常用】

【比較2】

　　　　What's your name?（你叫什麼名字？）
　　　　【較不禮貌，年輕人之間彼此可以說，但不能跟長輩說】

　　　　May I ask you what your name is?

　　　　（我可以請問你叫什麼名字嗎？）
　　　　【這句話太囉嗦了，文法對，美國不說，是書本英語】

　　　　*May I ask your name?*【既有禮貌又常用】

下面三句話，美國人也常說，使用頻率相同：

　　　　Please tell me your name.
　　　　（請告訴我你的名字。）
　　　　Can you tell me your name?
　　　　（你能不能告訴我你的名字？）
　　　　I'd like to know your name.
　　　　（我想知道你的名字。）

【對話練習】

1. A：**You look familiar**.

   B：So do you.

   　　You do, too.

   　　You look familiar to me.

2. A：**You got me thinking**.

   B：What do you mean?

   　　Why do you say that?

   　　A penny for your thoughts.

3. A：**Have we met before?**

   B：I don't think so.

   　　I don't believe so.

   　　I'm pretty sure the answer
   　　is no.

   　　【pretty (ˊprɪtɪ) *adv.* 相當】

4. A：**I feel like I know you**.

   B：That's strange.

   　　That's a little weird.

   　　I feel the same way, too.

   　　【weird ( wɪrd ) *adj.* 奇怪的】

A：你看起來很面熟。

B：你也是。

　　你也一樣。

　　我覺得你看起來很面熟。

A：你讓我想想看。

B：什麼意思？

　　你為什麼那樣說？

　　告訴我你在想什麼。

A：我們以前見過面嗎？

B：我認為應該沒有。

　　我想應該沒有。

　　我很確定答案是沒有。

A：我覺得我好像認識你。

B：那就奇怪了。

　　那有一點奇怪。

　　我也有同感。

BOOK 8

BOOK 8

5. A：**I feel like I've seen you somewhere**.

  B：Maybe you have.
  I get around a lot.
  I'm here almost every day.

A：我覺得我好像在哪裡看過你。

B：也許你看過我。
  我常到附近。
  我幾乎每天來這裡。

6. A：**I can't recall your name**.

  B：Don't worry about it.
  It's no big deal.
  It happens to everyone.
  【*big deal* 了不起的事
    no 當副詞時，等於 not at all】

A：我想不起你的名字。

B：別擔心。
  沒什麼大不了的。
  ( = *It's not a big deal at all.* )
  這種情況每個人都會有。

7. A：**I'm Pat Smith**.

  B：What a swell name!
  I like your name.
  It's a nice sounding name.
  【swell〔swɛl〕*adj.* 很棒的】

A：我是派特·史密斯。

B：這個名字真棒！
  我喜歡你的名字。
  這個名字很好聽。

8. A：**Everyone calls me Pat**.

  B：OK, Pat.
  My name is William.
  But you can call me Bill.

A：大家都叫我派特。

B：好的，派特。
  我的名字叫威廉。
  不過你可以叫我比爾。

9. A：**May I ask your name?**

  B：My full name is Pat Smith.
  My nickname is Smitty.
  You can call me Pat.
  【nickname〔'nɪkˌnem〕*n.* 綽號】

A：能不能請問你叫什麼名字？

B：我的全名是派特·史密斯。
  我的綽號是 Smitty。
  你可以叫我派特。

# 9.　*Can I ask you a question?*

| | |
|---|---|
| Can I ask you a question? | 我能問你一個問題嗎？ |
| *I* need information. | 我需要一些資訊。 |
| *I* could use some advice. | 我有點想要一些建議。 |
| | |
| I just got here. | 我剛到這裡。 |
| It's my first time. | 這是我的第一次。 |
| I don't know my way around. | 我對這個地方不熟悉。 |
| | |
| *What's* worth a look? | 什麼值得看？ |
| *What's* interesting to see? | 有什麼有趣的東西可以看？ |
| Anything special or famous nearby? | 附近有沒有什麼特別的或有名的東西？ |

\*\* ───────────────

information〔͵ɪnfɚ'meʃən〕*n.* 消息；資訊
*could use* 有點想要　　advice〔əd'vaɪs〕*n.* 忠告；建議
just〔dʒʌst〕*adv.* 剛剛　　get〔gɛt〕*v.* 到達
around〔ə'raʊnd〕*adv.* 在周圍；在附近
*know* one's *way around* 對（某處的）地理很清楚；熟知情況
worth〔wɝθ〕*adj.* 值得的　　look〔lʊk〕*n.* 看
interesting〔'ɪntrɪstɪŋ〕*adj.* 有趣的
famous〔'feməs〕*adj.* 有名的
nearby〔'nɪr'baɪ〕*adv.* 在附近

## 【背景説明】

當你出國旅遊，碰到熱情的外國人，你就可以
説這九句話，請教他哪裡好玩。

### 1. *Can I ask you a question?*

這句話的意思是「我能問你一個問題嗎？」也可
以簡化成：Can I ask a question?（我能問一個問
題嗎？）

【比較】 *Can I ask you a question?*
　　　　【較通俗，説這句話比較自然】
　　　 May I ask you a question?【較禮貌】
　　　　（我可以問你一個問題嗎？）

### 2. *I need information.*

information〔͵ɪnfɚˋmeʃən〕*n.* 消息；情報；資料；資訊

這句話的意思是「我需要一些資訊。」

下面是美國人常説的話，我們按照使用頻率排
列，第一句和第二句的使用頻率非常接近：

① *I need information.*【第一常用】
② I need some information.【第二常用】
　　（我需要一些資訊。）

③ I need to know what's going on.【第三常用】
　　（我需要知道情況如何。）
④ I need to know what's up.
　　（我需要知道情況。）

⑤ I need to know something.
（我需要知道一些事情。）

⑥ I need to know about something.
（我需要知道一些事情。）

⑦ I need to know about this place.
（我需要知道有關這裡的情形。）

⑧ I need to know what's around here.
（我需要知道這附近有什麼。）

3. *I could use some advice*.

*could use* 有點想要

advice〔əd'vaɪs〕*n.* 忠告；勸告；建議

could use 的用法，在所有字典上都沒有，我們在 p.50-51 中，已有說明。could use 在這裡作「有點想要」解。*I could use some advice*. 的意思是「我有點想要一些建議。」用假設法動詞 could use 表示客氣，if 子句放在心中未說出來。這句話不能說成：*I can use some advice*.（誤）

看看下面 *could use* 的例子：

I *could use* a cold drink right now.
（我現在有點想喝杯冷飲。）
I *could use* an umbrella right now.
（我現在有點想要一把雨傘。）
I sure *could use* more money right now.
（我現在真的有點需要更多的錢。）
drink〔drɪŋk〕*n.* 飲料　　*right now* 現在
umbrella〔ʌm'brɛlə〕*n.* 雨傘

She is all alone. She *could use* a friend.
（她單獨一個人。她有點需要朋友。）
He is very unorganized. He *could use*
a secretary.
（他很沒有條理。他可能需要一位祕書。）
He's so busy. He *could use* some help.
（他太忙了。他有點需要一些幫助。）

alone〔ə'lon〕 *adj.* 單獨的
unorganized〔ʌn'ɔrgən,aɪzd〕 *adj.* 無組織的；沒有條理的
secretary〔'sɛkrə,tɛrɪ〕 *n.* 祕書

【比較】 *I could use some advice*.
（我有點想要一些建議。）
【客氣、輕鬆、對陌生人說】
I need some advice.【較直接】
（我需要一些建議。）

4. *I just got here*.

just〔dʒʌst〕 *adv.* 剛剛　　get〔gɛt〕 *v.* 到達

這句話的意思是「我剛到這裡。」句子可以變
長為 I just got here a few days ago.（我幾天前
才剛到這裡。）或 I just got here a few minutes
ago.（我幾分鐘前才剛到這裡。）

【比較】 *I just got here*.【通俗，常用】
*I've just got here*.【文法對，美國人不用】
*I have just got here*.【文法對，美國人不用】

BOOK 8

原則上，I got 源自 I've got 或 I have got，
但是這麼短的句子，加上 have，純粹爲了滿足文
法上的需要，對句意上沒有幫助，所以美國人現在
只說 *I just got here.*（= *I just arrived.*）

5. *It's my first time*.

　　這句話的意思是「這是我的第一次。」也可說
成：It's my first time here.（這是我第一次來這
裡。）也可以加強語氣說成：This is my first
time here.（這是我第一次來這裡。）或 This is
the first time I've been here.（這是我第一次來
這裡。）

6. *I don't know my way around*.
around〔ə'raʊnd〕*adv.* 在周圍；在附近
*know one's way around* 對（某處的）地理很清楚；
　　熟知情況

　　I don't know the way. 的意思是「我不知道
路。」I don't know my way. 意思是「我不知道
我走的路。」*I don't know my way around*. 的
字面意思是「我不知道我在附近走的路。」（= *I
don't know my way around here.*）引申爲「我對
這個地方不熟悉。」也有美國人說：I don't know
the way around. 但並不普遍。

BOOK 8

下面各句意義很接近，都是美國人常說的話，我們按照使用頻率排列：

① *I don't know my way around.*【第一常用】
② I don't know this place.【第二常用】
　　（我對這個地方不熟悉。）
③ I don't know this area.【第三常用】
　　（我對這個地區不熟悉。）
　　【area〔ˈɛrɪə〕*n.* 地區】

④ I don't know this place very well.
　　（我對這個地方不是很熟。）
⑤ I'm not familiar with this area.
　　（我對這個地區不是很熟。）
　　【familiar〔fəˈmɪljɚ〕*adj.* 熟悉的】

## 7. *What's worth a look?*

worth〔wɝθ〕*adj.* 值得的　　look〔lʊk〕*n.* 看

這句話的意思是「什麼是值得看的？」worth 這個字是形容詞，但是可接受詞，如果要接動名詞，就要接主動的、及物動詞，但無受詞。

下面三句話意思相同：

*What's worth a look?*【第一常用】
What's worth taking a look at?【第三常用】
（什麼是值得看的？）
What's worth seeing?【第二常用】
（什麼是值得看的？）
*take a look at*「看一眼」，是及物動詞片語。
*be worth + V-ing* 值得～

8. *What's interesting to see?*
   interesting〔ˈɪntrɪstɪŋ〕 *adj.* 有趣的

　　　這句話的意思是「有什麼有趣的東西可以看？」
也可說成：What's fun to see?（有什麼有趣的東
西可以看？）或 What's exciting to see?（有什
麼好玩的東西可以看？）【fun〔fʌn〕*adj.* 有趣的
exciting〔ɪkˈsaɪtɪŋ〕*adj.* 好玩的；刺激的】也有美國人
說：What's a popular place to see?（大家都喜
歡看什麼地方？）

　　　*What's interesting to see?* 也可以加強語氣
說成：What's interesting to see around here?
（這附近有什麼有趣的東西可以看？）

9. *Anything special or famous nearby?*
   famous〔ˈfeməs〕 *adj.* 有名的
   nearby〔ˈnɪrˈbaɪ〕 *adv.* 在附近

　　　這句話源自 Is there anything special or
famous nearby?（附近有沒有什麼特別的或有名的東西？）
也可說成：Anything special or famous around
here?（在這附近有沒有什麼特別的或有名的東西？）

## 【對話練習】

1. A: **Can I ask you a question?**
   B: Of course you can.
   What is it?
   What can I do for you?

   A: 我能問你一個問題嗎？
   B: 當然可以。
   什麼問題？
   我能為你做什麼？

2. A: **I need information**.
   B: Please tell me more.
   Please be specific.
   What kind of information?
   【specific〔spɪˋsɪfɪk〕adj. 明確的】

   A: 我需要一些資訊。
   B: 請多告訴我一些。
   請明確一點。
   是哪一種資訊？

3. A: **I could use some advice**.
   B: What's the matter?
   Tell me what's up.
   Maybe I can help.

   A: 我有點想要一些建議。
   B: 怎麼了？
   告訴我發生什麼事了。
   也許我能幫得上忙。

4. A: **I just got here**.
   B: Welcome!
   You must be excited.
   You have a lot to see and do.

   A: 我剛到這裡。
   B: 歡迎！
   你一定很興奮吧。
   你有很多可以看、可以做的。

5. A: **It's my first time**.
   B: I remember my first time.
   I remember that feeling.
   The first time is the best.

   A: 這是我的第一次。
   B: 我記得我第一次的情形。
   我記得當時的感覺。
   第一次是最好的。

BOOK 8

6. A: **I don't know my way around.**

  B: I understand.
    I know that feeling.
    Just do the best you can.
    【*do the best* one *can* 盡力】

A：我對這個地方不熟悉。

B：我知道。
　我知道那種感覺。
　只要盡力就好。

7. A: **What's worth a look?**

  B: Let me see.
    I suggest that you go
    downtown.
    I recommend a walk in
    the park.
    【recommend〔ˌrɛkə'mɛnd〕v. 推薦】

A：什麼是值得看的？

B：讓我想想看。
　我建議你去市中心。

　我推薦你去公園散步。

8. A: **What's interesting to see?**

  B: The shopping district is
    interesting. 〔'dɪstrɪkt〕n. 地區
    The university campus is
    very nice. 〔'kæmpəs〕n. 校園
    The City Hall area is a
    must-see.
    〔'mʌst'si〕n. 應該看的東西

A：有什麼有趣的東西可以看？

B：購物區很有趣。

　大學的校園很不錯。

　市政府那一區是非看不可
　的地方。

9. A: **Anything special or famous
    nearby?**

  B: That depends.
    What's your definition of
    special?
    What types of things would
    you like to see?

A：附近有沒有什麼特別的或
　有名的東西？

B：看情況。
　你對特別的定義是什麼？

　你想看哪一類的東西？

BOOK 8

BOOK 8

# 10.　*Mind if I join you?*

| | |
|---|---|
| Mind if I join you? | 介不介意我和你在一起？ |
| Care for some company? | 你要不要人陪？ |
| I don't want to intrude. | 我不想要打擾。 |
| | |
| *I*'m not doing anything. | 我沒有事情做。 |
| *I*'d welcome the conversation. | 我歡迎你和我說話。 |
| It would make my day. | 它會使我今天很高興。 |
| | |
| *Let's* have a chat. | 我們聊聊天吧。 |
| *Let's* shoot the breeze. | 我們聊聊吧。 |
| Ask me anything you like. | 問我任何你喜歡問的事。 |

**　*

join〔dʒɔɪn〕v. 參加；和…在一起　　*care for* 想要；喜歡
company〔'kʌmpənɪ〕n. 公司；陪伴
intrude〔ɪn'trud〕v. 干擾；打擾
welcome〔'wɛlkəm〕v. 歡迎；愉快地接受
*make one's day* 使某人（當日）非常高興
chat〔tʃæt〕n. 聊天　　shoot〔ʃut〕v. 射擊
breeze〔briz〕n. 微風　　*shoot the breeze* 聊天

BOOK 8

## 【背景説明】

在美國，要和美國人聊天太容易了，只要早上到麥當勞或公園，看到那些老人坐在那裡，你就可以説這些話，去和他們一起聊天。

1. *Mind if I join you?*

join〔 dʒɔɪn 〕*v.* 參加；加入；和…在一起；和…一起做同樣的事

中國人看到一個陌生人坐在那裡，通常會説：「我可不可以坐你旁邊？」美國人卻説：*Mind if I join you?* 這句話字面的意思是「介不介意我參加你？」引申爲「介不介意我和你在一起？」暗示「你介不介意我和你聊天？」或「你介不介意我和你做同樣的事？」可以對一個人説，也可以對一群人説。

*Mind if I join you?* 源自 Do you mind if I join you?（你介不介意我和你在一起？）。

【比較1】 Do you mind if I join you?
【較通俗，常用】
Would you mind if I joined you?
【較正式，常用】

【比較2】 上面兩句話簡化後，就成爲下面兩句：

*Mind if I join you?* 【常用】
= Mind if I joined you? 【常用】

BOOK 8

下面都是美國人常說的話：

***Mind if I join you?*** 【第一常用】
Do you mind if I join you? 【第五常用】
（你介不介意我和你在一起？）
Do you mind if I join you for a while?
（你介不介意我和你在一起一會兒？）【第九常用】

Care if I join you? 【第二常用】
（你介不介意我和你在一起？）
Do you care if I join you? 【第六常用】
（你介不介意我和你在一起？）
Do you care if I join you for a while?
（你介不介意我和你在一起一會兒？）【第十常用】

Is it OK to join you? 【第三常用】
（可以和你在一起嗎？）
Is it OK if I join you? 【第七常用】
（我可以和你在一起嗎？）
Is it OK with you if I join you? 【第十一常用】
（我可以和你在一起嗎？）

Would it be OK if I joined you? 【第八常用】
（我可以和你在一起嗎？）
Would you mind if I joined you? 【第四常用】
（你介意我和你在一起嗎？）
Would you mind if I joined you for a while?
（你介意我和你在一起一會兒嗎？）【第十二常用】
【最後三句話是假設法，表示客氣】

2. **Care for some company?**

**care for** 想；要；想要；喜愛；喜歡

company〔ˈkʌmpənɪ〕*n.* 公司；陪伴

> care 的主要意思是「關心；在乎；介意；憂慮」，care for 的字面意思是「為～而關心」，引申為「想要；喜歡」，要看上下文來決定它的意思。在古老的電影中，常看到一位服務生，手上拿著一個托盤，問：*Care for* some tea?（要不要喝些茶？）
>
> 　　*Care for some company?* 這句話源自 Do you care for some company? 字面的意思是「你要不要一些陪伴？」引申為「你要不要人陪？」。

【比較】　**Care for some company?**
（你要不要人陪？）
*Care for my company?*【誤】

> 　　這句話文法對，美國人不說。但他們說：Do you care for my company?（你喜歡我陪你嗎？）。*care for* 在不同的句中，有不同的解釋，在這裡作「喜歡」解。同樣地，Don't you *care for* my company? 字面意思是「你不要我的陪伴嗎？」引申為「你不喜歡我陪你嗎？」。

BOOK 8

下面是美國人常說的話：

***Care for some company?*** 【第一常用】

Do you care for some company? 【第三常用】

（你要不要人陪？）

Would you care for some company?

（你要不要人陪？）【第八常用】

Mind some company? 【第二常用】

（你介意有人陪你嗎？）

Do you mind some company? 【第五常用】

（你介意有人陪嗎？）

Would you mind some company? 【第七常用】

（你介意有人陪嗎？）

Do you mind company? 【第四常用】

（你介意有人陪嗎？）

Do you mind my company? 【第六常用】

（你介意我陪你嗎？）

Mind if you have some company? 【第九常用】

（你介意有人陪嗎？）

3. *I don't want to intrude*.

intrude〔ɪn'trud〕*v.* 干擾；干涉；打擾

　　這句話的意思是「我不想要打擾。」源自 I don't want to intrude on you.（我不想要打擾你。）

【比較】intrude 作「打擾」解時，爲不及物動詞：

*I don't want to intrude*.【常用】
= I don't want to bother you.【最常用】
　（我不想要打擾你。）
= I don't want to disturb you.【較常用】
　（我不想要打擾你。）

【bother〔'bɑðɚ〕*v.* 打擾　disturb〔dɪ'stɝb〕*v.* 打擾】

4. *I'm not doing anything*.

　　這句話字面的意思是「我現在沒有在做任何事。」意思是「我沒有事情做。」( = *I have nothing to do*.) 也可以加強語氣說成：I'm not doing anything right now. 或 I'm not doing anything at the moment. 意思都是「我現在沒事情做。」

美國人也常說：

I'm free.（我有空。）
I'm free at the moment.（我目前有空。）
I'm available.（我有空。）

free〔fri〕*adj.* 空閒的　　*at the moment* 目前
available〔ə'veləbḷ〕*adj.* 有空的

5. *I'd welcome the conversation*.

welcome〔ˈwɛlkəm〕*v.* 歡迎;愉快地接受

　　這句話的字面意思是「我歡迎談話。」也就是「我歡迎你和我說話。」也可説成:I'd welcome a conversation. 句意相同。一定要用 I'd… 或 I would…,因爲説話者並不確定對方是否同意,用假設法助動詞 would 表示客氣,所以,此時不可説成:*I welcome the conversation*.(誤)

【比較1】

　　*I'd welcome the conversation*.【較常用】
　　I would welcome the conversation.【常用】

【比較2】　the conversation 因爲已經指定是「你和我的談話」,所以不須再加 with you。

　　*I'd welcome the conversation*.【正】
　　*I'd welcome the conversation with you*.【誤】
　　I'd welcome a conversation with you.【正】

　　除了上面所説的以外,美國人還常説:

　　　I'd enjoy the conversation.
　　　　(我喜歡和你説話。)
　=I'd enjoy a conversation.
　　　　(我喜歡和你説話。)

　=I'd like to talk with you.
　　　　(我想要和你説話。)
　=I'd like to chat with you.
　　　　(我想要和你聊天。)【chat〔tʃæt〕*v.* 聊天】

6. *It would make my day.*

*make one's day* 使某人（當日）非常高興

這句話的意思是「它會使我今天很高興。」

*It would make my day.* 的含意有：

① It would make me very happy today.
（它會使我今天非常高興。）

② It would be the best thing about today.
（對於今天，它將是最好的事。）

③ It would make me feel like today
was worthwhile.(ˋwɝθˋhwaɪl) *adj.* 值得的；有意義的
（它將使我感覺到今天是有意義的。）

*It would make my day.* 也可説成：Talking
with you would make my day.（和你談話會使
我今天很高興。）

　在美國警匪電影中，往往有這種情節，有一位
警察拿著手槍對準歹徒，他希望歹徒做些反抗，他
就可以一槍把他打死，
警察説："Go for your
gun! Go ahead! *Make
my day.*"（去拿槍吧。去
拿吧！讓我今天爽一爽吧。）

Go for your gun!
Go ahead!
Make my day.

看到朋友，你可以説：

Seeing you always *makes my day.*
（看到你總是讓我非常高興。）

老師可以跟學生説：

> If everyone gets a hundred, it would
> *make my day*.
> （如果大家都考 100，我會很高興。）

美國學生常説：

> A high score would *make my day*.
> （考高分會讓我今天很高興。）

7. *Let's have a chat*.

chat〔tʃæt〕*n*. 聊天

　　這句話的意思是「我們聊聊天吧。」
　　下面是美國人常説的話：

> *Let's have a chat*.【最常用】
> = Let's chat. ( 我們聊聊天吧。)【最常用】
> = Let's have a talk.【較常用】
> 　( 我們談一談吧。)
> = Let's talk. ( 我們談一談吧。)【較常用】
> = Let's have a conversation.【常用】
> 　( 我們説説話吧。)
> = *Let's converse*. ( 誤 )

conversation 的動詞是 converse〔kən'vɝs〕*v.* 談
話，converse 這個字現在在日常生活中很少用，如
果你和美國人説這個字，他們會覺得很奇怪，在報
紙上或許會看到這個字，如：The two leaders
converse about their future cooperation. ( 這兩
個領袖談論有關他們未來的合作。)

想要邀請別人談話，還可以說：

> Care for a chat?（想要聊天嗎？）
> Can we chat?（我們可以聊天嗎？）
> Mind if we chat?（你介意我們聊天嗎？）

8. *Let's shoot the breeze.*

shoot〔ʃut〕*v.* 射擊　　breeze〔briz〕*n.* 微風
*shoot the breeze* 聊天；說大話

> 　　shoot 的主要意思是「射擊」，shoot the breeze
> 字面的意思是「射擊微風」，引申為「聊天」或「說
> 大話」。拿槍射擊，應該是朝向目標射擊才對，對
> 著微風射擊，暗示「無目標地聊天」。這句話的意思
> 是「我們聊聊吧。」
>
> 　　美國一般年輕的男人喜歡說：Let's shoot the
> shit. 字面的意思是「讓我們射大便吧。」引申為
> 「我們聊聊吧。」

【比較】　下面三句話意義相同，都表示「我們聊聊
　　　　　天吧。」

> *Let's shoot the breeze.*【常用，文雅】
> Let's shoot the shit.【最常用，但最粗魯】
> Let's shoot the bull.【粗魯，常用】

美國年輕男孩子喜歡說這句話，bull〔bʊl〕的主要意思
是「公牛」，但在這裡 bull 是源自 bullshit〔'bʊlˌʃɪt〕，
字面的意思是「公牛屎」，就和我們中文說的「狗屎」
一樣，是粗話。

9. *Ask me anything you like.*

這句話的意思是「問我任何你喜歡問的事。」
源自 You can ask me anything you like to
ask. (你可以問我任何你喜歡問的事。)

下面是美國人常說的話,我們按照使用頻率
排列:

① Ask me anything. (問我任何事情。)【第一常用】
② Ask me anything at all.【第二常用】
　（問我任何事情。）
③ *Ask me anything you like.*【第三常用】
　（問我任何你喜歡問的事。）

④ Ask me anything you'd like.【第一常用】
　（問我任何你想問的事。）
⑤ Ask me anything you'd like to know.
　（問我任何你想知道的事。）
⑥ Ask me anything you want to know.
　（問我任何你想知道的事。）

⑦ You can ask me anything.
　（你可以問我任何事。）
⑧ You can always ask me anything.
　（你隨時可以問我任何事。）
⑨ You can ask me anything you like.
　（你可以問我任何你想問的事。）

## 【對話練習】

1. A：**Mind if I join you?**                    A：介不介意我和你在一起？

   B：No, not at all.                            B：不，一點也不。

   　I'd like that very much.                    　我非常想要和你在一起。

   　I'm so glad you asked.                      　很高興你開口問我。


2. A：**Care for some company?**                 A：你要不要人陪？

   B：That would be nice.                        B：好啊。

   　I could use some company.                   　我有點想要人陪。

   　I'm bored here by myself.                    　我自己在這裡很無聊。

   　【bored〔bord〕*adj.* 無聊的

   　　*by oneself* 獨自】


3. A：**I don't want to intrude.**               A：我不想要打擾。

   B：You're not.                               B：你沒有。

   　You wouldn't be.                           　你不會打擾我。

   　You'd be very welcome.                      　我非常歡迎你。


4. A：**I'm not doing anything.**                A：我沒有事情做。

   B：That's good.                              B：很好。

   　Come join me.                              　來和我在一起吧。

   　Come keep me company.                      　來和我作伴吧。

BOOK 8

5. A: **I'd welcome the conversation**.　　A：我歡迎你和我說話。
　 B: So would I.　　　　　　　　　　 B：我也是。
　　 I would, too.　　　　　　　　　　　 我也是。
　　 I'd enjoy a good talk.　　　　　　　 我想好好談一談。

6. A: **It would make my day**.　　　　 A：它會使我今天很高興。
　 B: What a kind thing to say!　　　　 B：你這麼說真好！
　　 I don't deserve it.　　　　　　　　　 我不敢當。
　　 I should be praising you.　　　　　　 應該是我稱讚你。
　　【deserve〔dɪ'zɝv〕v. 應得】

7. A: **Let's have a chat**.　　　　　　 A：我們聊聊天吧。
　 B: All right.　　　　　　　　　　　　 B：好的。
　　 Let's talk for a while.　　　　　　　 我們聊一會兒吧。
　　 Let's catch up on the news.　　　　　 我們來聊聊新聞吧。
　　【*catch up on* 得到關於…的消息】

8. A: **Let's shoot the breeze**.　　　　 A：我們聊聊吧。
　 B: Good idea.　　　　　　　　　　　 B：好主意。
　　 That sounds good to me.　　　　　　 聽起來不錯。
　　 That sounds like a great　　　　　　 聽起來像是個很棒的
　　 idea.　　　　　　　　　　　　　　　 主意。

9. A: **Ask me anything you like**.　　 A：問我任何你喜歡的事。
　 B: Wow!　　　　　　　　　　　　　 B：哇！
　　 Anything at all?　　　　　　　　　　 任何事嗎？
　　 You certainly are brave.　　　　　　 你真的很勇敢。
　　【*at all* 全然　　brave〔brev〕adj. 勇敢的】

# 11. *I bet you're a student*.

| | |
|---|---|
| I bet you're a student. | 我想你一定是個學生吧。 |
| Where do you study? | 你在哪裡讀書？ |
| What grade are you in? | 你是幾年級學生？ |
| | |
| *How*'s your school? | 你的學校怎麼樣？ |
| *How* do you like it? | 你覺得它怎麼樣？ |
| Is it tough or easy? | 它是難讀還是容易讀？ |
| | |
| *Do you* like your teachers? | 你喜不喜歡你的老師？ |
| *Do you* get lots of homework? | 你有沒有很多功課要做？ |
| What's your favorite class? | 你最喜歡上什麼課？ |

** ——————

bet〔bɛt〕*v.* 打賭；確信　　*I bet* 我敢打賭；我確信
grade〔gred〕*n.* 年級　　tough〔tʌf〕*adj.* 困難的
easy〔'izɪ〕*adj.* 容易的；輕鬆的
favorite〔'fevərɪt〕*adj.* 最喜愛的

BOOK 8

## 【背景說明】

　　如果你想和學生用英文聊聊天，就可以這九句
話為開場白。

1. **I bet you're a student.**
　　bet〔 bεt 〕v. 打賭；確信
　　**I bet** 我敢打賭；我有把握；我確信

　　　美國人喜歡賭博，**I bet** 是美國人常說的話，
尤其和陌生人說 **I bet** 之類的話，很幽默，也很
輕鬆。

> 　　**I bet you're a student.** 字面的意思是「我敢
> 打賭你是一個學生。」引申為「我想你一定是個學
> 生吧。」源自 I bet that you're a student, aren't
> you?（我打賭你是個學生，對不對？）所以，在這
> 裡，**I bet** 有「我猜想」的意味，等於 I guess，或
> I'm guessing。在中文中，「我猜想」和「我想…
> 一定」意義相同。

【比較1】　**I bet you're a student.**【較常用】
　　　　　　I bet that you're a student.【常用】

【比較2】　**I bet you're a student.**【通俗，常用】
　　　　　　I'm betting you're a student.
　　　　　　　【加強語氣，常用】

BOOK 8

凡是你要和陌生人開始講話，你都可以用

*I bet* 這個句型：

*I bet* you're a tourist.  You look like
a tourist.

（我想你一定是個觀光客吧。你看起來像個觀光客。）

【tourist〔'tʊrɪst〕*n.* 觀光客】

*I bet* you're from the States.  Your accent
sounds like it.

（我想你一定是美國人吧。你的口音聽起來像。）

【*the States* 美國    accent〔'æksɛnt〕*n.* 口音】

*I bet* you have many boyfriends.
You're very attractive.

（我想妳一定有很多男朋友。妳非常吸引人。）

【attractive〔ə'træktɪv〕*adj.* 吸引人的】

*I bet* you're a good student.  You look
very smart.

（我想你是個好學生。你看起來很聰明。）

【smart〔smɑrt〕*adj.* 聰明的】

*I bet* you're in college.  You look like
a college student.

（我想你一定在讀大學。你看起來像個大學生。）

college〔'kɑlɪdʒ〕是大學、學院、專科的總稱，中國
人把大學生、專科生分得很清楚，美國人則一般通
稱 college student，就像我們中國人過去說「大專
生」一樣。如果你說 university student，則僅限於
「大學生」，美國人少用。

BOOK 8

下面各句意義相同：

**I bet you're a student.**【第一常用】

= I bet that you're a student.【第二常用】

（我想你一定是個學生吧。）

= I'm betting that you're a student.【第五常用】

（我想你一定是個學生吧。）

= I think you're a student.【第六常用】

（我想你是個學生。）

= I guess you're a student.【第四常用】

（我猜你是個學生。）

= You look like a student.【第三常用】

（你看起來像個學生。）

2. **Where do you study?**

這句話的意思是「你在哪裡讀書？」如果禮貌

一點，可以問：May I ask where you study?

（我可以問你在哪裡讀書嗎？）或 Can I ask where

you study?（我能不能問你在哪裡讀書？）

下面都是美國人常說的話：

**Where do you study?**【第一常用】

Where do you go to school?【第二常用】

（你在哪裡上學？）

Where do you attend school?【第三常用】

（你在哪裡上學？）

【attend〔ə'tɛnd〕v. 上（學）】

Which school do you study at?【第七常用】
（你在哪一所學校讀書？）
Which school do you go to?【第八常用】
（你就讀哪一所學校？）
Which school do you attend?【第九常用】
（你就讀哪一所學校？）

What's your school?【第十二常用】
（你的學校是哪一所？）
What's your school's name?【第十一常用】
（你的學校名字是什麼？）
What's the name of your school?【第十常用】
（你的學校名字是什麼？）

What school do you study at?【第四常用】
（你在什麼學校讀書？）
What school do you go to?【第五常用】
（你就讀什麼學校？）
What school do you attend?【第六常用】
（你就讀什麼學校？）

3. ***What grade are you in?***
grade〔gred〕*n.* 年級；等級；分數

　　grade 的主要意思是「等級」，在這裡作「年級」解，這句話源自 What grade are you in at school? 或 What grade are you in in school? 字面的意思是「你在學校裡面是什麼年級？」也就是「你是幾年級學生？」

在美國大部份的州，小學（elementary school）是從一年級到五年級，國中（junior high school）是從六年級到八年級，高中（senior high school，簡稱 high school）是從九年級到十二年級，換句話說，美國人是小學五年，國中三年，高中四年，所以，問：*What grade are you in?* 是問高中以下的所有學生，問大學生，則要問：What year are you in?（你幾年級？）這句話也可問中、小學的學生。

由於美國高中和大學都要唸四年，所以，凡是高一或大一學生，都可稱作 freshman（新鮮人；高一新生；大一新生），高二、大二學生，稱作 sophomore〔'sɑfm̩,or〕，高三、大三學生，稱作 junior〔'dʒunjə〕，高四、大四學生，稱作 senior〔'sinjə〕。

下面都是美國人常説的話：

What year are you?（你唸幾年級？）【第一常用】
What year are you in?（你唸幾年級？）【第三常用】
What year are you in at school?【第六常用】
（你在學校唸幾年級？）

What grade are you?（你是幾年級？）【第一常用】
*What grade are you in?*
（你是幾年級學生？）【第四常用】
What's your grade?（你是幾年級？）【第八常用】

What grade level are you?【第二常用】

（你是幾年級？）

What grade level are you in?【第五常用】

（你唸幾年級？）

What grade level are you in at school?

（你在學校唸幾年級？）【第七常用】

【level〔ˋlɛvl〕*n.* 程度；階級】

### 4. *How's your school?*

這句話的意思是「你的學校怎麼樣？」也有美國人喜歡問：Is it a good school?（是不是好學校？）美國人常喜歡問是新學校或舊學校，因為新學校通常比較好，他們常說：Is it a new school?（是不是新學校？）或 Is it an old school?（是不是舊學校？）

### 5. *How do you like it?*

這句話的意思是「你覺得它怎麼樣？」這句話單獨說，就是：How do you like your school?（你覺得你的學校怎麼樣？）( = *What do you think of your school?* ) 這句話是問喜歡的程度，和 Do you like it?（你喜不喜歡？）不同。

## 6. *Is it tough or easy?*

tough〔tʌf〕*adj.* 困難的;艱苦的
easy〔'izɪ〕*adj.* 容易的;輕鬆的

這句話字面的意思是「它是困難還是容易?」
引申為「它是難讀還是容易讀?」源自 Is it tough
or easy for you? (對你而言,它是難讀還是容易
讀?)不容易讀的學校叫 tough school,容易讀
的學校,叫作 easy school,在 tough school 裡
面,很難得高分,在 easy school 裡面,很容易
得高分。

考完試後,問學生考試難不難,可以説:
Was the exam tough or easy? (考試難還是簡
單?)問同學功課難不難,可以説:Is your
homework tough or easy? (你的功課難還是
簡單?)

## 7. *Do you like your teachers?*

這句話的意思是「你喜不喜歡你的老師?」也
可以問:How are your teachers? (你的老師怎
麼樣?)或 How do you like your teachers?
(你覺得你的老師怎麼樣?)

**8. *Do you get lots of homework?***

　　　　這句話的意思是「你有沒有很多功課要做？」美國人也有家庭作業，但不像我們那麼多，通常一個小時就可以做完。

　　　　下面各句意義相同：

　　　　***Do you get lots of homework?*** 【較常用】
　　= Do you get a lot of homework? 【較常用】

　　= Do you have lots of homework? 【常用】
　　= Do you have a lot of homework? 【常用】

**9. *What's your favorite class?***

favorite〔'fevərɪt 〕*adj.* 最喜愛的

　　　　這句話的意思是「你最喜歡上什麼課？」也可說成：Which class is your favorite class?
（你最喜歡上哪一種課程？）

【比較】　***What's your favorite class?***
　　　　What's your favorite subject?
　　　　（你最喜歡的科目是什麼？）
　　　　【subject〔'sʌbdʒɪkt 〕*n.* 科目】

　　　　通常，你最喜歡上的課，就是你最喜歡的科目，但有時不一樣，例如：

　　　　English is my favorite subject.
　　　　History class is my favorite class,
　　　　because the teacher is fun.
　　　　（英文是我最喜歡的科目。歷史課是我最
　　　　喜歡上的課，因為老師很風趣。）

## 【對話練習】

1. A：**I bet you're a student.**
   B：Good guess!
   You're right!
   How did you know?

   A：我想你一定是個學生吧。
   B：猜得好！
   你猜對了！
   你怎麼知道的？

2. A：**Where do you study?**
   B：I study at Central.
   I'm a student at Central High.
   I go to Central Senior High School.

   A：你在哪裡讀書？
   B：我在中央讀書。
   我是中央高中的學生。
   我就讀中央高中。

3. A：**What grade are you in?**
   B：I'm a freshman.
   I'm in grade nine.
   I'm in the ninth grade.

   A：你是幾年級學生？
   B：我是高一學生。
   我是九年級。
   我是九年級學生。

4. A：**How's your school?**
   B：It's the number one school.
   It's the top school in the city.
   It has an excellent reputation.
   【reputation〔ˌrɛpjəˈteʃən〕*n.* 名聲】

   A：你的學校怎麼樣？
   B：它是最棒的學校。
   它是本市最好的學校。
   它的名聲很好。

5. A：**How do you like it?**
   B：Sometimes I love it.
   Sometimes I hate it.
   It depends on how busy I am.
   【hate〔het〕*v.* 討厭　***depend on*** 視～而定】

   A：你覺得它怎麼樣？
   B：我有時候喜歡它。
   我有時候討厭它。
   要看我有多忙而定。

6. A : **Is it tough or easy?**

A：它是難讀還是容易讀？

B : It's a little of both.
It's both difficult and easy.
That's a hard question to answer.

B：兩者都有一點。
它既難又容易。
這個問題很難回答。

7. A : **Do you like your teachers?**

A：你喜不喜歡你的老師？

B : My teachers are the best.
They're a super bunch.
They make learning fun.
【super〔'supɚ〕*adj.* 超級的；極好的
bunch〔bʌntʃ〕*n.* 一群】

B：我的老師都是最棒的。
他們是一群超好的老師。
他們讓學習的過程變得
很有趣。

8. A : **Do you get lots of homework?**

A：你有沒有很多功課要
做？

B : We get a lot!
We get way too much!
We always have loads of homework.
【*way too much* 太多
*loads of* 很多】

B：我們功課很多！
我們的功課太多了！
我們總是有一大堆功課。

9. A : **What's your favorite class?**

A：你最喜歡上什麼課？

B : I'd have to say history.
It's very interesting to me.
I enjoy learning about the past.

B：我必須說是歷史。
我覺得歷史很有趣。
我喜歡了解過去發生的
事。

# *12. I'm a little lost.*

| | |
|---|---|
| *I*'m a little lost. | 我有點迷路。 |
| *I* need some directions. | 我需要你告訴我一下怎麼走。 |
| Can you set me straight? | 你能不能告訴我正確的路？ |
| | |
| Where's the metro? | 地下鐵在哪裡？ |
| Which way is it? | 它是在哪個方向？ |
| How do I get there from here? | 我如何從這裡到那裡？ |
| | |
| *How* close am I? | 離我有多近？ |
| *How* far away is it? | 它有多遠？ |
| Thank you so much for your time. | 非常感謝你的時間。 |

**\*\*** ─────────────

lost〔lɔst〕*adj.* 迷路的
direction〔də'rɛkʃən〕*n.* 方向；指引
set〔sɛt〕*v.* 使（成某狀態）
straight〔stret〕*adj.* 直的；正確的
***set sb. straight*** 讓某人了解　　metro〔'mɛtro〕*n.* 地下鐵
way〔we〕*n.* 方向　　get〔gɛt〕*v.* 到達
close〔klos〕*adj.* 接近的　***far away*** 遙遠

## 【背景説明】

　　到了美國，問別人路，是認識朋友的方法之一，你最好找一些看起來沒有事情做的人，比較可以得到熱情的回應。

1. *I'm a little lost.*

lose〔luz〕*v.* 失去；迷失；使迷路

lost〔lɔst〕*adj.* 迷路的

> 　　lose 的主要意思是「失去」，lose *oneself* 的意思是「失去自己」，它的被動是 *sb.* be lost「某人迷路了」，由於 lost 這個字用得很普遍，已經成為純粹的形容詞，類似的有：I'm done.（我做完了。）I'm finished.（我做完了。）【詳見 p.318-319】及 I'm packed.（我行李打包好了。）【詳見 p.448-450】。這些在字典上沒有解釋清楚的，我們都有最詳細的説明。

> 【比較】從下面兩句話可以證明，lost 已經成為純粹的形容詞。
>
> I'm very lost.（我眞的迷路了。）
>
> 【正，由於 lost 已經變成純粹形容詞，所以可用 very 修飾】
>
> *I'm much lost.*【誤，過去分詞才能用 much 修飾，所以 lost 不是過去分詞】

　　*I'm a little lost.* 的意思是「我有點迷路了。」
真是奇怪，美國男人不喜歡説自己迷路，覺得迷路
是很難爲情的事，所以通常加上 a little。中國人，
不管男女，迷路的時候，通常會説「我迷路了。」
美國男人卻説 *I'm a little lost.* 之類的話，甚至很
多美國男人連問路都不好意思，寧願開車轉來轉去。

【比較】 ***I'm a little lost.*** 【常用，男女適用】

　　　　I'm lost.（我迷路了。）【美國女人説，男人不説】

　　下面是美國人常説的話，男女都適用：

***I'm a little lost.*** 【第一常用】
I'm a bit lost.（我有點迷路了。）【第三常用】
I'm a little bit lost.（我有點迷路了。）【第二常用】
【***a bit*** 有點（= *a little bit*）】

I think I'm lost.（我想我迷路了。）【第四常用】
It seems like I'm lost.【第六常用】
（我似乎迷路了。）

I might be lost.（我可能迷路了。）【第七常用】
I could be lost.（我可能迷路了。）【第八常用】
I'm pretty sure I'm lost.【第五常用】
（我很確定我迷路了。）

　　下面的話，通常只有美國女生才説，我們按照
使用頻率排列：

① I'm lost.（我迷路了。）【第一常用】
② I'm really lost.（我眞的迷路了。）【第二常用】
③ I'm very lost.（我眞的迷路了。）【第三常用】

④ I'm totally lost. ( 我完全迷路了。)
⑤ I'm completely lost. ( 我完全迷路了。)
⑥ I'm absolutely lost. ( 我真的完全迷路了。)

totally〔'totḷɪ〕 adv. 完全地
completely〔kəm'plitlɪ〕 adv. 完全地
absolutely〔'æbsə‚lutlɪ〕 adv. 絕對地;完全地

## 2. *I need some directions.*

direction〔də'rɛkʃən〕 n. 方向;( pl. )(行路的)指引;說明

　　direction 的主要意思是「方向」,在這裡作「指引」解,要用複數形 directions。

　　這句話字面的意思是「我需要一些指引。」引申為「我需要你告訴我一下怎麼走。」

　　下面都是美國人問路時喜歡說的話,我們按照使用頻率排列:

① I need directions.【第一常用】
　　( 我需要你告訴我怎麼走。)
② *I need some directions.*【第二常用】
③ I need directions, please.【第三常用】
　　( 請你告訴我怎麼走。)

④ Can you give me directions?
　　( 你能告訴我怎麼走嗎?)
⑤ Can you tell me the way?
　　( 你能告訴我怎麼走嗎。)
⑥ Can you direct me on how to get there?
　　( 你能指引我如何到那裡嗎?)
　　【direct〔də'rɛkt〕 v. 指引　　on〔ɑn〕 prep. 關於】

3. *Can you set me straight?*

set〔sɛt〕*v.* 使（成某種狀態）

straight〔stret〕*adj.* 直的；正確的

***set sb. straight***　①糾正某人（＝*correct sb.*）

　　　　　　　　　　②讓某人了解（＝*make sb. understand*）

> 　　*set sb. straight* 的字面意思是「把某人弄直」，引申為「糾正某人」（＝*set sb. right*）。這句話的字面意思是「你能不能糾正我？」在這一回裡，引申為「你能不能告訴我正確的路？」。
>
> 　　*set sb. straight* 這個成語，美國人常說，在不同的句中，有不同的意思，一般字典沒有解釋清楚。
>
> 【例1】　I'm sorry I confused you.
> 　　　　　Let me *set you straight*.
> 　　　　　（我很抱歉，我把你弄糊塗了。
> 　　　　　　讓我向你解釋清楚。）
> 　　　　　【confuse〔kən'fjuz〕*v.* 使困惑
> 　　　　　　set you straight = make you understand】
>
> 【例2】　If I make a mistake, please *set me straight*.（如果我做錯了，請糾正我。）
> 　　　　　【set me straight = correct me】
>
> 【例3】　You can *set me straight* at any time.
> 　　　　　（你可以隨時糾正我。）
> 　　　　　【set me straight = correct me
> 　　　　　　*at any time* 隨時】

## 4. *Where's the metro?*

metro〔'mɛtro〕*n.* 地下鐵 ( = *subway system in the city* )

　　metro 這個字，源自 metropolitan
〔ˌmɛtrə'pɑlətṇ〕*adj.* 大都會的，由於地下鐵是屬
於大都會的產物，所以，美國人把「地下鐵」稱
作 metro。

> 　　*Where's the metro?* 這句話的字面意思是
> 「地下鐵在哪裡？」和中文一樣，往往是問「地
> 下鐵站在哪裡？」( = *Where's the metro station?* )
>
> 　　在大都市裡的捷運系統，不管是在地底下，
> 或在地面上，都可稱作 metro。台灣的捷運叫作
> MRT ( Mass Rapid Transit )，但在美國則稱作
> metro。而 subway（地下鐵）只限於在地底下的
> 捷運。
>
> 　　在台灣的美國人認為，台灣的捷運系統，應
> 該稱作 metro 較合理，比較能夠讓他們了解，稱
> 作「大衆捷運系統」( MRT )，太麻煩，他們往往
> 記不清楚是 MTR 還是 MRT，可見 MRT 不是
> 美國人所說的話。

　　以下是美國人常說的話：

*Where's the metro?* 【第一常用】
Where's the metro station? 【第四常用】
（地下鐵站在哪裡？）
Where's the metro station from here? 【第六常用】
（地下鐵站在哪裡？）

Where's the nearest metro station?【第七常用】
（最近的地下鐵站在哪裡？）
Where's the closest metro station?【第八常用】
（最近的地下鐵站在哪裡？）
Where's the metro from here?【第五常用】
（地下鐵在哪裡？）

I'm looking for the metro.【第一常用】
（我在找地下鐵。）
I want the metro.【第三常用】
（我要找地下鐵。）
I want to get to the metro.【第二常用】
（我想去地下鐵站。）
【*get to* 到達】

　　上面這些話，如果單獨使用時，前面最好加上
Excuse me, sir.（對不起，先生。）或 Excuse me,
ma'am.（對不起，女士。）較有禮貌。
〔 mæm 〕*n.* 女士

5. ***Which way is it?***
way〔 we 〕*n.* 方向

　　這句話的意思是「它是在哪個方向？」( = *Which
direction is it?*) 也可加強為：Which way is it
from here?（從這裡要往哪個方向走？）

BOOK 8

### 6. *How do I get there from here?*

這句話的意思是「我要如何從這裡到那裡？」也可簡化成：How do I get there?（我要如何到那裡？）

【比較】 How do I get there?【一般語氣】

***How do I get there from here?*【加強語氣】**

（我要如何從這裡到那裡？）

Please tell me how I get there from here.（請告訴我如何從這裡到那裡。）【較正式】

前兩句話的 do 都可改成 can，而 get 可改成 go。

### 7. *How close am I?*

close〔klos〕*adj.* 接近的

這句話字面的意思是「我有多接近？」，也就是「離我有多近？」。

下面是美國人常說的話：

***How close am I?*【第一常用】**

How near am I?（離我有多近？）【第二常用】

How close am I to it?（它離我有多近？）【第八常用】

How near am I to it?（它離我有多近？）【第九常用】

Is it close?（它很近嗎？）【第六常用】

Is it near?（它很近嗎？）【第七常用】

Am I near it?（我離它近嗎？）【第四常用】

Am I near or far?（離我近還是遠？）【第五常用】

Am I close?（離我近嗎？）【第三常用】

### 8. *How far away is it?*

這句話的意思是「它有多遠？」也可以簡化為：
How far is it?（它有多遠？）或加長為：How
far away is it from here?（它離這裡有多遠？）
如果問地下鐵站有多遠，可以說：How far is the
metro?（地下鐵站有多遠？）或 How far is the
metro from here?（地下鐵站離這裡有多遠？）

### 9. *Thank you so much for your time.*

這句話的意思是「非常感謝你的時間。」在美
國，別人幫了你的忙，一定要致謝，否則他們會生
氣，他們說不定會說：In this country, you should
say thank you to everyone who helps you.（在
這個國家，你應該對幫助你的人說「謝謝你」。）

別人幫了小忙，你可以只說 Thank you. 幫得
愈多，你就要說得愈長，來表示你的感謝。

Thank you.（謝謝你。）
Thank you so much.（非常謝謝你。）
***Thank you so much for your time.***
（非常感謝你的時間。）

I want to thank you so much for your time.
（我要非常感謝你的時間。）

I really want to thank you a lot for
    giving me so much of your time.
（我真的要非常感謝你給我這麼多的時間。）

## 【對話練習】

1. A：**I'm a little lost**.　　　　　A：我有點迷路了。

　　B：Where are you going?　　　B：你要去哪裡？
　　　　I can tell you how to get　　　　我可以告訴你如何去那裡。
　　　　there.
　　　　I can give you directions.　　　我可以告訴你怎麼走。

2. A：**I need some directions**.　　A：我需要你告訴我一下怎麼走。

　　B：Where to?　　　　　　　　B：你要去哪裡？
　　　　What's your destination?　　　你的目的地是哪裡？
　　　　Tell me where you want　　　　告訴我你想要去哪裡。
　　　　to go.
　　　　【destination〔͵dɛstə'neʃən〕*n.*
　　　　目的地】

3. A：**Can you set me straight?**　A：你能不能告訴我正確的路？

　　B：I'll give it a try.　　　　　B：我會試試看。
　　　　I'll do my best.　　　　　　我會盡力。
　　　　I'll try to set you straight.　　我會儘量告訴你正確的路。
　　　　【*give it a try* 試試看】

4. A：**Where's the metro?**　　　A：地下鐵在哪裡？

　　B：It's very close.　　　　　　B：很近。
　　　　It's not far away.　　　　　　不遠。
　　　　It's just down that way.　　　就在那個方向。
　　　　【down〔daʊn〕*adv.* 向那邊；在那邊】

BOOK 8

5. A : **Which way is it?**

    B : It's down that way.
       It's in that direction.
       Go down that way and
       you'll see it.

A：它是在哪個方向？

B：就在那個方向。
  就在那個方向。
  往那個方向走，你就會
  看到。

6. A : **How do I get there from here?**

    B : Follow the signs.
       Follow this map.
       Just ask people along the way.
       【follow〔ˈfalo〕*v.* 遵循
       sign〔saɪn〕*n.* 標誌；告示
       *along the way* 沿路】

A：我如何從這裡到那裡？

B：照著標示走。
  照著這張地圖走。
  沿路問人就行了。

7. A : **How close am I?**

    B : You're pretty close.
       You're not far at all.
       You're just ten minutes away.

A：離我有多近？

B：離你很近。
  離你一點都不遠。
  只離你十分鐘的路程。

8. A : **How far away is it?**

    B : It's pretty far away.
       It's a long walk from here.
       It's over half an hour away.

A：它有多遠？

B：很遠。
  從這裡走路去很遠。
  離這裡半個多小時的路程。

9. A : **Thank you so much for
     your time.**

    B : Think nothing of it.
       The pleasure is all time.
       I'm glad I could be of service.
       【*be of service* 有用；有幫助】

A：非常感謝你的時間。

B：不要客氣。
  這是我的榮幸。
  我很高興能幫得上忙。

# 「一口氣背會話」經 BOOK 8

唸英文要像唸經一樣，每天大聲唸，從起床到睡覺，唸得比看得快，最後不看也會唸，養成習慣後，你會全身舒爽，你試試看，奇妙無比。

1. *Is* this seat taken?
   *Is* anyone sitting here?
   Mind if I sit down?

   *Is it* OK?
   *Is it* all right?
   Do you mind?

   What a crowd!
   This place is packed!
   Seats are going fast!

2. *How* are you?
   *How's* it going?
   Having a good day?

   I haven't seen you before.
   *Are you* new in town?
   *Are you* working or visiting here?

   *How long* have you been here?
   *How long* are you staying?
   Do you like it here?

3. Excuse me, please.
   What time is it?
   Do you have the time?

   *I* forgot my watch.
   *I've* lost track of time.
   *I* have no idea what time it is.

   *I* appreciate it.
   *I* thank you so much.
   You're very kind.

4. *What a* rotten day!
   *What a* terrible day!
   Pretty awful, huh?

   *It's* crummy.
   *It's* lousy.
   This really stinks.

   *It's* gloomy.
   *It's* depressing.
   This really gets me down.

5. *Need* any help?
   *Need* a hand?
   Can I do anything for you?

   Any problem?
   *Anything* wrong?
   *Anything* I can do?

   *I'd* like to help.
   *I* don't mind a bit.
   *I'd* be happy to help.

6. Can I ask a favor?
   *Can you* spare a minute?
   *Can you* help me with this?

   *What* does this mean?
   *What's* this about?
   I can't figure this out.

   *I* don't want to disturb you.
   *I* hope I'm not bothering you.
   If you're busy, I understand.

7. I like your shirt!
   *That's* your color!
   *That* looks great on you!

   *It's* a nice style.
   *It* caught my eye.
   *It's* just what I'm looking for.

   Where did you get it?
   When did you buy it?
   Mind if I ask the price?

8. *You* look familiar.
   *You* got me thinking.
   Have we met before?

   *I feel like* I know you.
   *I feel like* I've seen you somewhere.
   I can't recall your name.

   I'm Pat Smith.
   Everyone calls me Pat.
   May I ask your name?

9. Can I ask you a question?
   *I* need information.
   *I* could use some advice.

   I just got here.
   It's my first time.
   I don't know my way around.

   *What's* worth a look?
   *What's* interesting to see?
   Anything special or famous nearby?

10. Mind if I join you?
    Care for some company?
    I don't want to intrude.

    *I'm* not doing anything.
    *I'd* welcome the conversation.
    It would make my day.

    *Let's* have a chat.
    *Let's* shoot the breeze.
    Ask me anything you like.

11. I bet you're a student.
    Where do you study?
    What grade are you in?

    *How's* your school?
    *How* do you like it?
    Is it tough or easy?

    *Do you* like your teachers?
    *Do you* get lots of homework?
    What's your favorite class?

12. *I'm* a little lost.
    *I* need directions.
    Can you set me straight?

    Where's the metro?
    Which way is it?
    How do I get there from here?

    *How* close am I?
    *How* far away is it?
    Thank you so much for your time.

# BOOK 9 上班族的一天

▶9-1 早上一進辦公室，看到同事就可說：

Good morning.
How was your night?
Did you sleep well?

▶9-2 當你打電話找人的時候，你就可以說：

I'm calling for Dale.
My name is Chris.
May I speak to him, please?

▶9-3 當公司快要開會的時候，你可以跟同事說：

We have a meeting.
We have to be there.
We can't be late.

▶9-4 當你要加班的時候，就可以說：

I'm working overtime.
I'm staying late.
I have too much to do.

▶9-5 當你要和別人約會時，你就可說：

Let's make an appointment.
Let's set up a time.
We need to get together.

▶9-6 當你要取消和別人的約會，你就可以說：

I have bad news.
I have to cancel.
I can't make it.

▶9-7 當你外出回到辦公室，就可以問你的同事：

Any messages for me?
Any calls to return?
What needs to be done?

▶9-8 當你想要請假，就可以跟主管說：

I have a favor to ask.
I need some time off.
I have something important to do.

▶9-9 當你想要加薪時，就可以說：

Do you have a minute?
Can I speak with you?
Can we have a word in private?

▶9-10 到了公司休息時間，你就可以說：

It's break time.
How about a drink?
How about some coffee or tea?

▶9-11 當你接到電話時，你就可以說：

How may I help you?
How may I direct your call?
What can I do for you?

▶9-12 下班的時候，你就可以跟同事說：

It's quitting-time.
It's time to get off.
It's time to go home.

# 1. How was your night?

| | |
|---|---|
| Good morning. | 早安。 |
| How was your night? | 你昨晚睡得如何？ |
| Did you sleep well? | 你睡得好不好？ |
| | |
| *How's your* schedule? | 你今天有什麼安排？ |
| *How's your* day today? | 你今天忙不忙？ |
| Are you pretty busy? | 你是不是相當忙？ |
| | |
| *I have a* lot to do. | 我有很多事要做。 |
| *I have a* full day. | 我整天都排得滿滿的。 |
| It's gonna be a long day. | 今天將會很忙。 |

BOOK 9

\*\* —————————

schedule〔'skɛdʒul〕 *n.* 時間表；計劃（表）；日程安排
pretty〔'prɪtɪ〕 *adv.* 很；非常；相當
full〔ful〕 *adj.* 排得滿滿的
gonna〔'gɔnə〕（ = *going to*）

## 【背景説明】

一進辦公室，看到同事，就可以説這九句話，和他們打招呼。

1. *Good morning.*

美國人早上見了面，常説：***Good morning.*** （早安。）或 Morning. （早。）也有人説：What a nice morning! （今天早上天氣真好！）或 Nice morning, isn't it? （早上天氣真好，不是嗎？）

下午打招呼，美國人常説：Good afternoon. （午安。）或 Afternoon. （午安。）【較少用】

在中午時間，美國人不説 *Good noon.* （誤）只説：Hi! How are you? （嗨！你好嗎？）之類的話來代替。【hi〔haɪ〕*interj.* 嗨】

2. *How was your night?*

這句話字面的意思是「你晚上如何？」引申爲：① 你昨晚睡得如何？② 你昨晚玩得如何？到底是哪一個意思，要看實際情況而定。如果你昨天晚上出去玩，那就是第二個意思，如果你昨晚沒有什麼特別的活動，那就是第一個意思。

下面都是美國人常說的話：

***How was your night?***（你昨晚過得如何？）
How was your evening?（你昨晚過得如何？）

How was your weekend?（你週末過得如何？）
How was your holiday?（你假期過得如何？）
How was your Sunday?（你星期天過得如何？）

【比較1】

中文：你昨晚過得如何？

英文：***How was your night?***【最常用】
= How was your night last night?【第二常用】
= How was last night?【第三常用】

【比較2】***How was your night?***【較常用】
How was your evening?【較少用】
How was your evening last night?【較少用】

【比較3】

中文：你昨晚睡得如何？

英文：***How was your night?***【最常用】
= How was your sleep?【常用】
= How did you sleep?【較常用】

## 3. *Did you sleep well?*

這句話的意思是「你睡得好不好？」源自：
Did you sleep well last night?（你昨晚睡得好
不好？）很多美國人縮短為：Sleep well last
night?（昨晚睡得好嗎？）

下面是美國人常說的話：

**BOOK 9**

> ***Did you sleep well?*** 【第一常用】
> Did you sleep well last night?【第二常用】
> （你昨晚睡得好不好？）
> Sleep well last night?【第三常用】
> （昨晚睡得好嗎？）
>
> Did you have a good sleep?【第四常用】
> （你睡得好不好？）
> Did you have a good sleep last night?【第七常用】
> （你昨晚睡得好不好？）
> Did you have a good night's sleep?【第五常用】
> （你睡得好嗎？）
>
> Did you get a good night's sleep?【第六常用】
> （你睡得好嗎？）
> Did you have a restful night?【第八常用】
> （你睡得好嗎？）
> 【restful〔'rɛstfəl〕*adj.* 安寧的；平靜的】

**4.** *How's your schedule?*

schedule〔ˈskɛdʒul〕*n.* 時間表；計劃（表）；日程安排

這句話字面的意思是「你的時間表如何？」引申爲「你今天有什麼安排？」( = *How's your schedule for today?* )

美國人做事情，喜歡事先就做安排，所以他們有 work schedule（工作時間表）、bus schedule（公車時刻表）、tour schedule（旅遊計劃）、office schedule（上班時間表）、flight schedule（班機時刻表）等。

BOOK 9

**5.** *How's your day today?*

這句話的意思是「你今天怎麼樣？」暗示「你今天忙不忙？」( = *Are you going to be busy today?* )

下面是美國人常説的話：

*How's your day today?*【第一常用】
How's your day going to be today?【第四常用】
（你今天會怎樣？）
How's your day going to be?【第二常用】
（你今天會怎樣？）

How busy is your day going to be?【第五常用】
（你今天會多忙？）
How busy are you today?（你今天多忙？）【第三常用】
How busy are you going to be today?【第六常用】
（你今天會多忙？）

**6.** *Are you pretty busy?*

pretty〔'prɪtɪ〕*adv.* 很；非常；相當　*adj.* 漂亮的

　　pretty 的主要意思是「漂亮的」，在此是副詞，作「很；非常；相當」解。這句話的意思是「你是不是相當忙？」

　　下面是美國人常說的話：

*Are you pretty busy?*【第一常用】
Are you pretty busy today?
（你今天是不是相當忙？）
【第四常用】
Are you busy today?
（你今天忙嗎？）【第三常用】

Are you very busy?【第二常用】
（你是不是很忙？）
Are you going to be very busy today?【第六常用】
（你今天是不是會很忙？）
Are you going to be busy?【第五常用】
（你今天會忙嗎？）

　　pretty 這個字做副詞，修飾形容詞，表示程度，很常用，如：

It's *pretty* big.（它相當大。）

He's a *pretty* good student.（他是個相當好的學生。）

It was a *pretty* bad movie.（那部電影很難看。）

7. *I have a lot to do.*

　*a lot*　很多；很多東西

　　　　這句話的意思是「我有很多事要做。」也有美
國人說成：I have a lot of work to do.（我有很
多工作要做。）或 I have a lot of things to do.
（我有很多事要做。）

　　【比較】 ***I have a lot to do.*** 【較常用】
　　　　　　= I have lots to do. 【常用】

8. *I have a full day.*

　full〔ful〕*adj.* 滿滿的；排得滿滿的

　　　　這句話源自 I have a full day planned.（我整
天都排得滿滿的。）【常用】美國人也常說：I have a
full schedule today.（我今天的時間都排得滿滿的。）

9. *It's gonna be a long day.*

　gonna〔'ɡɔnə〕（= *going to* ）

　　　　這句話的意思是「今天將會很忙。」a long
day 在這一回中的意思是 a busy day（忙碌的一
天）。可加強語氣說成：It's gonna be a long
day for me.（我今天將會很忙碌。）

　　　　gonna 本來是口語發音拼成的寫法，由於很常
用，現在已經出現在各類字典中。

　　【比較】 ***It's gonna be a long day.*** 【年輕人喜歡說】
　　　　　　It's going to be a long day.
　　　　　　　　【大部份中老年人習慣說】

BOOK 9

## 【對話練習】

1. A : **Good morning**.

   B : Morning!
   How are you?
   Nice day, huh?
   【huh〔hʌ〕*interj.* 哼；哈】

2. A : **How was your night?**

   B : It was very relaxing.
   I stayed at home.
   I just watched a little TV.
   【relaxing〔rɪ'læksɪŋ〕*adj.*
   令人放鬆的】

3. A : **Did you sleep well?**

   B : I slept great!
   I slept like a baby!
   I got a good night's rest.

4. A : **How's your schedule?**

   B : It's pretty good.
   I'm not too busy.
   I have a light schedule
   today.
   【light〔laɪt〕*adj.* 輕鬆的】

A：早安。

B：早！
你好嗎？
天氣不錯，不是嗎？

A：你昨晚過得如何？

B：很輕鬆。
我待在家裡。
我只是看了點電視。

A：你睡得好不好？

B：我睡得很好！
我睡得像個小嬰兒！
我昨晚睡得很好。

A：你今天有什麼安排？

B：我安排得很好。
我不會很忙。
我今天安排得很輕鬆。

5. A : **How's your day today?**

　A：你今天忙不忙？

 　B : It's looking good.

 　　I have a meeting this afternoon.

 　　Other than that, I'm free.

　B：看起來還可以。

　　我今天下午有個會議。

　　除此之外，我都有空。

　　【meeting〔'mitɪŋ〕n. 會議

　　　***other than*** 除了～之外

　　　free〔fri〕adj. 有空的】

6. A : **Are you pretty busy?**

　A：你是不是相當忙？

 　B : I'm not too busy.

 　　Why do you ask?

 　　Do you need any help?

　B：我不會很忙。

　　你為什麼這麼問？

　　你需要幫忙嗎？

7. A : **I have a lot to do.**

　A：我有很多事要做。

 　B : I know you're busy.

 　　I'll leave you alone.

 　　I don't want to bother you.

　B：我知道你很忙。

　　我不會吵你。

　　我不想打擾你。

　　【***leave sb. alone*** 不理會某人

　　　bother〔'baðɚ〕v. 打擾】

8. A : **I have a full day.**

　A：我整天都排得滿滿的。

 　B : You're always busy.

 　　You work too hard.

 　　You're a workaholic!

　B：你總是很忙。

　　你工作太努力了。

　　你是個工作狂！

　　【workaholic〔ˌwɝkə'halɪk〕n. 工作狂】

9. A : **It's gonna be a long day.**

　A：今天會很忙。

 　B : Don't be discouraged.

 　　Don't worry about it.

 　　Just do your best.

　B：別沮喪。

　　別擔心。

　　盡力就好。

　　【discouraged〔dɪs'kɝɪdʒd〕adj. 沮喪的】

# 2. I'm calling for Dale.

| | |
|---|---|
| I'm calling for Dale. | 我要找戴爾。 |
| My name is Chris. | 我的名字是克里斯。 |
| May I speak to him, please? | 請問我可以和他說話嗎？ |
| | |
| *Is he* in? | 他在不在？ |
| *Is he* available? | 他有沒有空？ |
| Is now a good time? | 現在的時間恰不恰當？ |
| | |
| *Can* I leave a message? | 我能不能留個話？ |
| *Can* you take a message? | 你能不能幫我傳個話？ |
| Please tell him to call me back. | 請告訴他回我電話。 |

\*\* ————————————————————

Dale〔del〕*n.* 戴爾；黛爾
Chris〔krɪs〕*n.* 克里斯；克麗絲
in〔ɪn〕*adv.* 在家；在辦公室
available〔ə'veləbḷ〕*adj.* 有空的　　good〔gud〕*adj.* 恰當的
leave〔liv〕*v.* 留下　　message〔'mɛsɪdʒ〕*n.* 訊息；留言
*leave a message* 留個話　　*take a message* 記錄留言
*call sb. back* 回電話給某人

## 【背景説明】

　　你每天都要打電話給別人，背了這九句話，你就可以用英文説了，跟你朋友開個玩笑，讓他以爲外國人打電話找他。

1. ***I'm calling for Dale.***
   Dale〔del〕*n.* 戴爾；黛爾（這個名字，男女通用）

　　這句話字面的意思是「我要打電話給戴爾。」在此引申爲「我要找戴爾。」如果你要找的人是 Dale Smith 的話，這個人你不熟，你就應該説：I'm calling for Mr. Smith.（我要找史密斯先生。）説 Mr. Smith 較有禮貌，但不親切。

　　【比較 1】***I'm calling for Dale.***【最常用】
　　　　　　 ＝ I'm phoning for Dale.【較常用】
　　　　　　 ＝ I'm telephoning for Dale.【常用】
　　　　　　 【phone〔fon〕*v.* 打電話（＝*telephone*）】

　　call 這個字，主要的意思是「叫；喊叫」，在這裡作「打電話」解，是及物和不及物兩用動詞。

　　【比較 2】***I'm calling for Dale.***【較正式】
　　　　　　 I'm calling Dale.【語氣輕鬆】
　　　　　　（我要找戴爾。）

下面都是美國人打電話時常説的話：

*I'm calling for Dale.*

I'd like to talk to Dale.

（我想和戴爾說話。）

I'd like to talk with Dale.

（我想和戴爾說話。）

Could I talk to Dale?

（我可以和戴爾說話嗎？）

Could I talk with Dale?

（我可以和戴爾說話嗎？）

Could I talk to Dale, please?

（請問我可以和戴爾說話嗎？）

上面各句的 talk，都可改成 speak，使用頻率相同。

很多美國人習慣先説 Hi!、Hello!、Good morning.，或 Good afternoon. 之類的話。

Hi!
Hello!
Good morning.
Good afternoon.
⎫
⎬
⎭
*I'm calling for Mr. Smith.*

嗨！
喂！
早安。
午安。
⎫
⎬
⎭
我要找史密斯先生。

2. *My name is Chris.*

Chris〔krɪs〕*n.* 克里斯；克麗絲【這個名字，男女通用，是男生的 Christopher（克里斯多夫）或女生的 Christine（克麗絲汀）的簡稱】

這句話的意思是「我的名字是克里斯。」下面都是美國人打電話時常說的話：

> *My name is Chris.*
> I'm Chris.（我是克里斯。）
> This is Chris.（我是克里斯。）
> This is Chris calling.（我是克里斯。）

如果你的姓名叫做 Chris Jones（克里斯·瓊
〔krɪs〕〔dʒonz〕
斯），姓是 Jones，名字是 Chris，對於不熟的人，較有禮貌的說法是：My name is Mr. Jones.（我姓瓊斯。）

中國人不大習慣說「我的名字是某某先生。」，因為「先生」是尊稱，可是美國人卻說："My name is Mr. Jones." 或 "I'm Mr. Jones." 之類的話。

3. *May I speak to him, please?*

這句話的意思是「請問我可以和他說話嗎？」下面都是美國人常說的話：

> May I speak to him?【第二常用】
> （我可以和他說話嗎？）
> *May I speak to him, please?*【第一常用】
> 【上面兩句中的 speak to，可改成 speak with】

BOOK 9

BOOK 9

May I talk to him?【第四常用】
（我可以和他說話嗎？）
May I talk to him, please?【第三常用】
（請問我可以和他說話嗎？）
【上面兩句中的 talk to，可改成 talk with】

Can you connect me, please?【第七常用】
（可以請你幫我接通嗎？）
Can you connect me to him, please?
（可以請你幫我接給他嗎？）【第六常用】
Please connect me to him.【第五常用】
（請幫我接給他。）
【connect〔kəˋnɛkt〕v. 使接通線路】

Can you put me through?【第八常用】
（你可以幫我接通嗎？）
Can you put me through to his office?【第九常用】
（你可以幫我接到他的辦公室嗎？）
【*put sb. through* 為（打電話者）接通某人】
【最後五句，都是用在辦公室中】

4. *Is he in?*
　in〔ɪn〕*adv.* 在家；在辦公室

　　　這句話的意思是「他在不在？」源自 Is he
inside?（他在不在家？）或 Is he in his office?
（他在不在辦公室？）也有美國人說：Is he there?
（他在不在？）

5. *Is he available?*

available〔ə'veləbḷ〕*adj.* 有空的

這句話在這裡的意思是「他有沒有空？」打電話給別人的時候，要先問對方有沒有空，比較不會太唐突。

下面都是美國人常說的話，我們按照使用頻率排列：

① **Is he available?**【第一常用】

② Is he available to talk?【第二常用】
（他有空說話嗎？）

③ Is he available to talk right now?【第三常用】
（他現在有空說話嗎？）

④ Is he busy?（他忙嗎？）

⑤ Is he busy right now?（他現在忙嗎？）

⑥ Is he too busy to talk right now?
（他現在會不會忙到沒空說話？）

⑦ Is he free?（他有空嗎？）

⑧ Is he free to talk?（他有空說話嗎？）

⑨ Is he free to talk right now?
（他現在是不是有空說話？）
【free〔fri〕*adj.* 有空的】

⑩ Is he able to talk?（他可以說話嗎？）

　　【*be able to* 能夠】【不可只説 *Is he able?*】

⑪ Is he able to talk right now?

　　（他現在可以說話嗎？）

⑫ Is he able to talk with me right now?

　　（他現在能跟我說話嗎？）

6. *Is now a good time?*

good〔gud〕*adj.* 恰當的

　　　　這句話的意思是「現在的時間恰不恰當？」
good time 字面的意思是「好的時間」，引申爲
「恰當的時間」。

下面都是美國人常説的話：

　　　　*Is now a good time?*【第一常用】

　　　　Is now a good time to talk with him?

　　　　（現在和他說話恰不恰當？）【第六常用】

　　　　Is he able to talk with me right now?

　　　　（現在他能不能和我說話？）【第五常用】

　　　　Is now a convenient time?【第二常用】

　　　　（現在方便嗎？）

　　　　Is it convenient right now?【第三常用】

　　　　（現在方便嗎？）

　　　　Is it convenient for him to talk?

　　　　（現在他方便說話嗎？）【第四常用】

7. *Can I leave a message?*

message〔'mɛsɪdʒ〕 *n.* 訊息;留言
***leave a message*** 留個話

　　leave 的主要意思是「離開」,在這裡作「留下」解,像 leave a tip ( 留下小費 ),leave a phone number ( 留下電話號碼 ) 等。

Can I leave
a message?

　　這句話字面的意思是「我能不能留下一個訊息?」引申為「我能不能留個話?」

　　下面都是美國人常說的話,都是打電話的人說的:

　　***Can I leave a message?***【第一常用】
　　Can I leave a message for him?
　　( 我能不能留個話給他?)【第五常用】
　　Can I leave a message for him with you?
　　( 我能不能請你傳個話給他?)【第六常用】

　　Is it OK to leave a message?【第二常用】
　　( 我可以留話嗎?)
　　Is it possible to leave a message?
　　( 我可以留話嗎?)【第四常用】
　　Do you mind if I leave a message?
　　( 你介意我留個話嗎?)【第三常用】

BOOK 9

8. *Can you take a message?*

> take a message 中的 take，是作「記錄」或「接受」解。像 Take some notes for me. ( 替我記一些筆記。) 或 Take a letter for me. ( 幫我寫封信，我唸你寫。) 【*take notes* 記筆記】
>
> ***Can you take a message?*** 的字面意思是「你能不能把我要說的話寫下來 ( 給我要找的人 )？」( = *Can you write down what I say and give it to the person I want to talk to?* ) 這句話引申為「你能不能幫我傳個話？」

BOOK 9

下面都是美國人打電話時常說的話，我們按照使用頻率排列：

① ***Can you take a message?*** 【第一常用】

② Can you take a message, please? 【第三常用】
 ( 能不能請你幫我傳個話？)

③ Can you take a message for me? 【第二常用】
 ( 你能不能幫我傳個話？)

④ Can you give him a message?
 ( 你能不能傳個話給他？)

⑤ Can you give him a message for me?
 ( 你能不能替我傳個話給他？)

⑥ Can I give you a message for him?
 ( 我能不能留個話給他？)

打電話來的人（caller），只能說：

**Can I leave a message?**（我能不能留個話？）
**Can you take a message?**
（你能不能幫我傳個話？）

接到電話的人（receiver），只能說：

Can I take a message?（要我幫你傳話嗎？）
Would you like to leave a message?
（你想不想留個話？）

　　在中文裡面，Can I take a message? 和 Can you leave a message? 都有「要不要留個話？」的意思，所以很容易搞混，唯有背「一口氣背會話」，變成直覺，說起來就不用想了。

　　在各種考試中，常出現這樣的考題，你只要背下打電話的人說：Can I leave a message? 和 Can you take a message? 你就會作答了。

【例1】 選出兩個正確答案。

A：Hello, I'm calling for Mr. Johnson.
B：I'm sorry, he's not in.
A：_____
(A) Can I take a message?
(B) **Can I leave a message?**
(C) **Can you take a message?**
(D) Would you like to leave a message?

　　【答案】(B) (C)

A：喂，我要找強森先生。

B：很抱歉，他不在。

A：＿＿＿＿＿＿＿＿＿＿＿＿

(A) 要不要我幫你傳個話？

(B) 你能不能幫我傳個話？

(C) 我能不能留個話？

(D) 你想不想留個話？

【例2】 選出兩個正確答案。

A：May I speak to Dale, please?

B：I'm sorry.  Dale is not here. ＿＿＿＿＿＿＿

(A) *Can I take a message?*

(B) Can I leave a message?

(C) Can you take a message?

(D) *Would you like to leave a message?*

【答案】(A) (D)

A：請問戴爾在不在？

B：很抱歉，戴爾不在。＿＿＿＿＿＿＿

(A) 要不要我幫你傳個話？

(B) 你能不能幫我傳個話？

(C) 我能不能留個話？

(D) 你想不想留個話？

【補充說明】

　　一般我們在課本上所學到的「打電話給某人」，是 call *sb.* up，但是我們很少聽到美國人說，因為美國人喜歡簡化。

【比較1】

> Can I call you?【正，較常用】
> （我可以打電話給你嗎？）
> = Can I call you up?【正，較少用】

【比較2】 **call** *sb.* **up** 後面加一些字詞，就常用了。

> Can I call you this evening?【正，常用】
> （我今天晚上可以打電話給你嗎？）
> = Can I call you up this evening?
> 【正，常用，有點加強語氣的味道】

9. *Please tell him to call me back.*

      call *sb.* back 的意思是「回某人電話」，也可簡化成 call back「回電話」。

      這句話的意思是「請告訴他回我電話。」也可簡化爲：Please tell him to call back.

下面都是美國人常説的話：

> Tell him to call me.【第五常用】
> （告訴他打電話給我。）
>
> Tell him to call me back.【第六常用】
> （告訴他回我電話。）
>
> *Please tell him to call me back.*【第一常用】
> （請告訴他回我電話。）

Please tell him to call back.【第二常用】
（請告訴他回我電話。）

Please tell him to call me back later.
（請告訴他待會回我電話。）【第七常用】

Please tell him to call me back as soon as
he can.（請告訴他儘快回我電話。）【第九常用】

【later〔'letɚ〕adv. 待會　*as soon as one can* 儘快】

Please tell him to return my call.【第三常用】
（請告訴他回我電話。）

Please have him return my call.
（請叫他回我電話。）【第四常用】

Could you please tell him to call me back?
（能不能請你告訴他回我電話？）【第八常用】

【*return one's call* 回某人電話】

## 【對話練習】

1. A : **I'm calling for Dale.**　　　　　A：我要找戴爾。

　B : Please hang on.　　　　　　　　B：請等一下。

　　　Please hold the line.　　　　　　　請等一下。

　　　I'll connect your call.　　　　　　我幫你接。

　　　【*hang on* （電話）不掛斷

　　　　（ = *hold the line* ）】

2. A : **My name is Chris.**　　　　　　A：我的名字是克里斯。

　B : What's your last name?　　　　　B：你姓什麼？

　　　What's your full name?　　　　　　你的全名是什麼？

　　　How do you spell your　　　　　　你的名字怎麼拼？

　　　name?

　　　【*last name* 姓】

3. A : **May I speak to him, please?**　　A：請問我可以和他說話嗎？

　B : Please wait a moment.　　　　　B：請等一下。

　　　I'll see if he's in.　　　　　　　　我看看他在不在。

　　　I'll be right back.　　　　　　　　我會馬上回來。

4. A : **Is he in?**　　　　　　　　　　A：他在不在。

　B : I'm not sure.　　　　　　　　　B：我不確定。

　　　Let me check and see.　　　　　　我看一下。

　　　Let me go take a look.　　　　　　我去看一看。

　　　【*take a look* 看一看】

BOOK 9

5. A: **Is he available?**

   B: Yes, he is available.
      I'll put your call through.
      I'll connect you right away.

A:他有沒空？

B:是的，他有空。
   我幫你接過去。
   我立刻幫你轉接。

6. A: **Is now a good time?**

   B: Now is a bad time.
      Now is not convenient.
      Please try again later.

A:現在的時間恰不恰當？

B:現在的時間不恰當。
   現在不方便。
   請稍後再試一次。

7. A: **Can I leave a message?**

   B: Of course you can.
      That's a good idea.
      That's the best thing to do.

A:我可以留個話嗎？

B:當然可以。
   那是個好主意。
   那樣做最好。

8. A: **Can you take a message?**

   B: Yes, I can.
      It's my pleasure.
      What's the message?
      【pleasure〔'plɛʒɚ〕*n.* 榮幸】

A:你能不能幫我傳個話？

B:是的，我能。
   這是我的榮幸。
   你要傳什麼話？

9. A: **Please tell him to call me back.**

   B: OK, I will.
      I'll give him the message.
      I promise I'll tell him.

A:請告訴他回我電話。

B:好的，我會的。
   我會傳話給他。
   我保證我會告訴他。

# 3.  *We have a meeting*.

| | |
|---|---|
| *We have* a meeting. | 我們有會要開。 |
| *We have* to be there. | 我們必須到那裡。 |
| We can't be late. | 我們不能遲到。 |
| | |
| *It's* starting soon. | 快要開始了。 |
| *It's* almost time. | 時間差不多了。 |
| We have to hurry. | 我們必須趕快。 |
| | |
| *Let's* leave now. | 我們現在走吧。 |
| *Let's* go together. | 我們一起去吧。 |
| There is no time to lose. | 沒時間可浪費了。 |

\*\*

meeting〔'mitɪŋ〕*n.* 會議
***have a meeting***  開一次會議
late〔let〕*adj.* 遲到的
hurry〔'hɜɪ〕*v.* 趕快    lose〔luz〕*v.* 浪費

## 【背景説明】

　　大部份的美國公司，每天都開會，辦公室有辦公室會議（office meeting），每一組人員也常開會（group meeting），也有全公司一起開會（company meeting）。在快要開會的時候，你就可以跟同事説這九句話了。

1. *We have a meeting.*
   meeting〔'mitɪŋ〕*n.* 會議
   *have a meeting* 開一次會議

We have a meeting.

　　這句話字面的意思是「我們開一次會議。」在此引申為「我們有會要開。」也有美國人説：
There's a meeting today.（今天有會要開。）have a meeting 這個成語和來去動詞一樣，可用現在式、現在進行式和未來式表示未來。

> ***We have a meeting.***【最常用】
> = We're having a meeting.【較常用】
> = We'll have a meeting.【常用】

　　上面三句話中，第一句和第二句使用頻率很接近。

【比較】下面兩句話意思相同：

> **We have a meeting.**【常用，語氣輕鬆】
> = We are holding a meeting.
> 【正，通常是高階層的主管或經理說的話】

【hold〔hold〕v. 舉行】

**We have a meeting.** 這句話，也可以加長為：
We have a meeting at ten in the conference
room.（我們十點在會議室要開會。）

【conference〔'kɑnfərəns〕n. 會議】

## 2. *We have to be there.*

這句話的意思是「我們必須到那裡。」下面都是
美國人常說的話：

**We have to be there.**【第一常用】
We have to be there early.【第四常用】
（我們必須早點到那裡。）
We have to be there on time.【第三常用】
（我們必須準時到那裡。）【on time 準時】

We have to be there before it starts.【第五常用】
（我們必須在它開始之前到那裡。）
We have to be there no matter what.【第六常用】
（無論如何我們都必須到那裡。）
We must be there.【第二常用】
（我們必須到那裡。）

3. *We can't be late*.

late〔let〕*adj.* 遲到的

　　　這句話的意思是「我們不能遲到。」美國人也常說：We can't get there late.（我們不能遲到。）或 We can't be late for it.（我們不能遲到。）或 We can't be late for the meeting.（我們開會不能遲到。）

【比較】下面各句意義相同：

> ***We can't be late*. 【最常用】**
> We shouldn't be late. 【常用】
> （我們不應該遲到。）
> We mustn't be late. 【正，現在少用】
> （我們絕不能遲到。）
> We don't want to be late. 【最常用】
> （我們不要遲到。）

4. *It's starting soon*.

　　　這句話的意思是「快要開始了。」start 是來去動詞，在此用現在進行式，表示不久的未來。【詳見「文法寶典」p.327】

> ***It's starting soon*. 【最常用】**
> = It starts soon. 【較常用】
> = It'll start soon. 【常用】

BOOK 9

【比較】下面各句意義相同：

> *It's starting soon.*【第一常用】
>
> It's about to start.【第二常用】
>
> （快要開始了。）
>
> It's about to begin.【第三常用】
>
> （快要開始了。）
>
> 【*be about to V*. 快要~】

BOOK 9

5. *It's almost time.*

這句話的意思是「時間差不多了。」

【比較1】 It's time.（時間到了。）
*It's almost time.*（時間差不多了。）
It's about time.（時間差不多了。）

【比較2】 *It's almost time.*【正】
*It's almost that time.*【誤】
It's about that time.【正】
（時間差不多了。）

【注意1】 *It's almost time.* 這個句子，可以接不定
詞片語。

It's almost time *to start*.
（差不多要開始了。）
It's almost time *to begin*.
（差不多要開始了。）
It's almost time *to leave*.
（差不多該走了。）

It's almost time *to get going*.

（差不多該走了。）

It's almost time *to go*. （差不多該走了。）

It's almost time *to hit the road*.

（差不多要上路了。）

【*get going* 出發　*hit the road* 出發；上路】

【注意2】 *It's almost time*. 後面也常接「for + 名
詞」，把句子加長。

It's almost time *for lunch*.

（差不多該吃午餐了。）

It's almost time *for the meeting*.

（差不多該開會了。）

It's almost time *for your appointment*.

（你約會的時間差不多到了。）

【appointment〔əˋpɔɪntmənt〕*n.* 約定；約會】

6. *We have to hurry.*

hurry〔'hɝɪ〕v. 趕快（= *hurry up*）

這句話的意思是「我們要趕快。」也可以說成：

We have to hurry up. 也可以加長爲：

> We have to hurry, or we'll be late.
> （我們必須趕快，否則就會遲到了。）
> We have to hurry to get there.
> （我們必須趕快去那裡。）
> We have to hurry to make it on time.
> （我們必須趕快，才能準時到達。）
> 【*make it* 及時到達】

上面三句的 hurry，都可改成 hurry up。

7. *Let's leave now.*

這句話的意思是「我們現在走吧。」下面都是
美國人常説的話：

> *Let's leave now.*【第一常用】
> Let's leave now, OK?【第五常用】
> （我們現在走吧，好嗎？）
> Let's leave, OK?【第四常用】
> （我們走吧，好嗎？）

> Let's go now.（我們現在走吧。）【第二常用】
> Let's get going now.【第三常用】
> （我們現在走吧。）
> Let's get going right now.【第六常用】
> （我們現在走吧。）

BOOK 9

8. *Let's go together*.

這句話的意思是「我們一起走吧。」

下面都是美國人常說的話，我們按照使用頻率排列：

① Let's go. ( 我們走吧。)【第一常用】
② **Let's go together**. 【第二常用】
③ Let's go there together. 【第三常用】
　　( 我們一起去那裡吧。)

④ Let's both go. ( 我們兩個走吧。)
⑤ Let's both go together.
　　( 我們兩個一起走吧。)
⑥ Let's both go there together.
　　( 我們兩個一起去那裡吧。)

⑦ Let's you and I go. ( 你和我走吧。)
⑧ Let's you and I go together.
　　( 你和我一起走吧。)
⑨ Let's you and I go there together.
　　( 你和我一起去那裡吧。)
　　【第九常用，但語氣最強】

BOOK 9

9. *There is no time to lose.*

lose〔luz〕*v.* 失去；浪費

　　lose 的主要意思是「失去」，在這裡作「浪費」
解。這句話的意思是「沒有時間可以浪費了。」

下面都是美國人常説的話，使用頻率幾乎相同：

> **There is no time to lose.**【第三常用】
> There is no time to waste.【第四常用】
> （沒有時間可以浪費了。）
>
> We have no time to lose.【第一常用】
> （我們沒有時間可以浪費了。）
> We have no time to waste.【第二常用】
> （我們沒有時間可以浪費了。）

　　We have no time to lose. 很常用，但因為
在這一回的句子中，有太多的 We 了，所以我們
才用 *There is no time to lose*.

> Let's leave now.
> Let's go together.
> There is no time to lose.

【對話練習】

1. A：**We have a meeting**.

   B：Oh, my God!

   I almost forgot!

   Thanks for reminding me.

   【remind〔rɪ'maɪnd〕v. 提醒】

A：我們有會要開。

B：噢，天啊！

我差點忘了！

謝謝你提醒我。

2. A：**We have to be there**.

   B：I don't believe it.

   You must be kidding!

   Nobody told me that.

   【kid〔kɪd〕v. 開玩笑】

A：我們必須到那裡。

B：我不相信。

你一定是在開玩笑吧！

沒人告訴我那件事。

3. A：**We can't be late**.

   B：Don't worry about me.

   I won't be late.

   I'm never late.

A：我們不能遲到。

B：別擔心我。

我不會遲到。

我從不遲到。

4. A：**It's starting soon**.

   B：What time does it start?

   What time is it now?

   How many minutes do we

   have?

A：快要開始了。

B：什麼時候開始？

現在幾點了？

我們還剩幾分鐘？

5. A: **It's almost time**.

B: I know we have to go.
I know it's almost time.
I'm trying to get ready.

A：時間差不多了。

B：我知道我們必須走了。
我知道時間差不多了。
我正努力要做好準備。

6. A: **We have to hurry**.

B: Please don't say that!
Please don't rush me!
It makes me very nervous.

【rush〔rʌʃ〕v. 催促
nervous〔'nɜvəs〕adj. 緊張的】

A：我們必須趕快。

B：請不要那麼說！
請不要催我！
這讓我很緊張。

BOOK 9

7. A: **Let's leave now**.

B: OK, let's go.
Let's leave right now.
Let's get out of here.

A：我們現在離開吧。

B：好的，我們走吧。
我們現在離開吧。
我們離開這裡吧。

8. A: **Let's go together**.

B: That's a nice offer.
I'd like that.
I'd like to go together.

【offer〔'ɔfə〕n. 提議
*would like* 想要】

A：我們一起去吧。

B：你這個提議真好。
我很想那樣。
我想和你一起去。

9. A: **There's no time to lose**.

B: You're right.
Go ahead.
I'm right behind you.

【*go ahead* (催促對方) 你先請　right〔raɪt〕adv. 就】

A：沒有時間可以浪費了。

B：你說得對。
你先請。
我就在你後面。

# *4. I'm working overtime.*

| | |
|---|---|
| *I'm* working overtime. | 我要加班。 |
| *I'm* staying late. | 我會待得晚一點。 |
| I have too much to do. | 我有太多工作要做。 |
| | |
| *This* work is due. | 這個工作必須要完成。 |
| *This* has to be done. | 這個必須要做完。 |
| The deadline is coming up. | 截止時間就要到了。 |
| | |
| *I*'m behind. | 我落後了。 |
| *I* have to catch up. | 我必須趕上。 |
| *I*'d like to get ahead. | 我要超前。 |

BOOK 9

** ———————————————

overtime〔'ovə,taɪm〕*adv.* 超出時間地;加班地
***work overtime*** 加班　　stay〔ste〕*v.* 停留
late〔let〕*adv.*(比適當時刻)晚　　due〔dju〕*adj.* 到期的
deadline〔'dɛd,laɪn〕*n.* 截止時間;最後期限
behind〔bɪ'haɪnd〕*adv.* 落在後面　　***catch up*** 趕上
***get ahead*** 領先;超前

## 【背景説明】

當公司需要你加班，或你自己想要加班的時候，你就可説這九句話。

1. ***I'm working overtime.***
overtime〔ˈovɚ͵taɪm〕*adv.* 超出時間地；加班地
***work overtime*** 加班

overtime 主要意思是「超出時間地」，是副詞，這句話字面的意思是「我將超出時間地工作。」就是中國人所説的「我要加班。」這裡用現在進行式，代表不久的未來。

overtime 也常被年輕人簡化成 O.T.〔ˈoˈti〕。美國年輕人常説：I'm working O.T.（我要加班。）或 I'm going to work O.T.（我要加班。）

【比較1】

***I'm working overtime.***【常用】
I will work overtime.【少用】

這句話雖然文法對，卻很少人用，除非老板問你，"Will you work overtime?"（你會加班嗎？）你才會回答説："I will work overtime."（我會加班。）

【比較2】 下面兩句話意義相同，但是説話者的心理狀態不同：

***I'm working overtime.***【一般語氣】
I have to work overtime.【有抱怨的含意】
（我必須加班。）

BOOK 9

BOOK 9

2. *I'm staying late.*

stay〔ste〕*v.* 停留
late〔let〕*adv.*（比適當時刻）晚

這句話的字面意思是「我將待得較晚。」就像我們中國人説的「我會待得晚一點。」用現在進行式表示不久的未來。

*I'm staying late.* 只是表示「我會待晚一點。」也許二十分鐘，也許幾個小時。

【比較1】 下面三句話，一句比一句晚：

*I'm staying late.*【未説明待到多晚】
I'm staying late tonight.【待到晚上】
（我今晚要待晚一點。）
I'm staying very late tonight.【待到深夜】
（我今晚要待到很晚。）

【比較2】 下面兩句話意義不同：

I stayed late last night.【通常在某處】
（我昨晚待得很晚。）
I stayed up late last night.【通常在家】
（我昨晚熬夜到很晚。）
【*stay up* 熬夜（= *stay awake*）】

3. *I have too much to do.*

這句話的意思是「我有太多工作要做。」源自：

I have too much work to do.

【比較 1】

**I have too much to do.**【較常用】

I have too many things to do.

（我有太多事要做。）

【常用，較合乎中國人的文化】

【比較 2】

I have much to do.【第一常用】

（我有很多工作要做。）

I have many things to do.【第二常用】

（我有很多事要做。）

**I have too much to do.**【第三常用】

I have lots to do.【第七常用】

（我有很多工作要做。）

I have a lot to do.【第六常用】

（我有很多工作要做。）

I have tons to do.【第八常用】

（我有一大堆工作要做。）

I have so much to do.【第四常用】

（我有很多工作要做。）

I have too many things to do.【第五常用】

（我有太多事要做。）

【tons〔tʌnz〕*n. pl.* 許多；大量】

4. ***This work is due.***

due〔dju〕*adj.* 到期的；預定應到的；應支付的

這句話字面的意思是「這個工作到期了。」在此引申為「這個工作必須要完成。」

*This work is due.*

由於 due 這個字，已經有未來的意思，所以當和動詞連用時，不可用未來式。

【比較】 This work is due.【正】

*This work will be due.*【誤】

due 這個字，一般中國人都不會用，但美國人常說，我們一定要學會。

【例1】 Her baby *is due* next month.

( = *Her baby is expected to be born next month.* )

(她的預產期是下個月。)

【例2】 This project *is due* next week.

( = *This project must be finished next week.* )

(這個計劃必須在下週完成。)

【project〔ˈprɑdʒɛkt〕*n.* 計劃】

【例 3 】 Our book reports *are due* on Friday.
( = *Our book reports must be handed in on Friday.* )【*hand in*  繳交】
( 我們的讀書報告必須在星期五交。)
【美國老師常要求學生去看書，寫讀書心得，美國人稱作 book report 】

【例 4 】 All phone bills *are due* on the fifth of each month.
( = *All phone bills must be paid on the fifth of each month.* )
( 所有的電話費都必須在每個月的五日繳。)
【bill〔bɪl〕*n.* 帳單】

【例 5 】 He's away on a trip.  He's *due* back tomorrow.
( = *...He's expected to be back tomorrow.* )
( 他去旅行了。預定明天回來。)

5. *This has to be done.*

　　這句話的意思是「這個必須要做完。」源自：
This work has to be done. ( 這個工作必須要做完。) 因為上一句 This work is due. 已經有了 work，所以這一句將 work 省略。也可說成 This has to be finished. ( 這個必須要完成。)

如果説英文，老是想到文法，英文永遠説不好。文法只是大致的歸納，並非全部。這句話如果改成未來式，就不是美國人所説的話。This will have to be done.【誤，have to（必須）已有表示未來的意味，所以不能再用未來式】

這句話後面可接時間：

> This has to be done *today*.
> （這個今天必須做完。）
> This has to be done *by tomorrow*.
> （這個必須在明天以前做完。）
>
> This has to be done *tomorrow*.
> （這個必須在明天做完。）
> This has to be done *on Friday*.
> （這必須在星期五做完。）

6. ***The deadline is coming up.***
   deadline〔ˈdɛd͵laɪn〕*n.* 截止時間；最後期限

> come 的主要意思是「來」，come up 有很多意思，要看前後句意來判斷，原則上，up 是用來加強動詞 come 的語氣。

這句話的意思是「截止時間就要到了。」句中的 coming up 等於 coming soon 或 coming quickly。也可説成：The deadline is approaching.（截止時間就要到了。）【approach〔əˈprotʃ〕*v.* 接近】

【比較】 The deadline is *coming*.【一般語氣】
　　　　 The deadline is *coming up*.【語氣較強】

7. ***I'm behind.***

behind〔bɪ'haɪnd〕*adv.* 落在後面　*prep.* 在～之後

> 　　behind 這個字，是副詞和介系詞，因爲沒有
> 同意義的形容詞，所以常代替形容詞做主詞補語。
> 像 She is out.（她出去了。）中的 out，也是副詞
> 代替形容詞，在 is 後面，做主詞補語。（詳見「文
> 法寶典」p.228）

　　***I'm behind.*** 的意思是「我
落後了。」也可以加強語氣說
成：I'm really behind.（我眞
的落後了。）或 I'm very behind.
（我落後很多。）

*I'm behind.*

【比較】***I'm behind.***【behind 是副詞代替形容詞】
　　　　I'm behind schedule.【behind 是介系詞】
　　　　　（我進度落後了。）

　　　　【schedule〔'skɛdʒʊl〕*n.* 時間表
　　　　　***behind schedule*** 進度落後】

　　***I'm behind.*** 也可以加長爲：

　　I'm behind in my work.
　　　（我工作進度落後了。）
　　I'm behind in what I have to do.
　　　（我必須做的事情進度落後了。）

　　　【上面兩句中，behind 後的 in，都可改成 with】

8. *I have to catch up.*

*catch up* 趕上

這句話的意思是「我必須趕上。」也可加長爲
I have to catch up on my work. ( 我必須趕上我
的工作進度。) 或 I have to catch up on my
assignments. ( 我必須趕上我被指派的工作。)
【assignment〔əˈsaɪnmənt〕*n.* 指派的工作】

9. *I'd like to get ahead.*

*get ahead* 走在前面；領先；超前

這句話的意思是「我要超前。」也可説成：
I'd like to get ahead of schedule. ( 我要超前進度。)
【*get ahead of schedule* 超前進度】

美國經理常跟他的屬下説：I want everyone
to get ahead of schedule. ( 我要每個人都超前進度。)

下面都是美國人常説的話，我們按照使用頻率
排列，前三句使用頻率非常接近：

① *I'd like to get ahead.*【第一常用】

② I want to get ahead. ( 我要超前。)【第二常用】

③ I need to get ahead. ( 我必須超前。)【第三常用】

④ I have to get ahead. ( 我必須超前。)

⑤ I should get ahead. ( 我應該超前。)

⑥ I must get ahead. ( 我必須超前。)

## 【對話練習】

1. A：**I'm working overtime**.

   B：You're so dedicated.
   You're a real role model.
   I wish I could be like you.
   【dedicated〔ˈdɛdəˌketɪd〕*adj.*
   投入的　*role mode* 典範】

   A：我要加班。

   B：你真是投入。
   你真是個典範。
   真希望我能像你一樣。

2. A：**I'm staying late**.

   B：Good for you.
   I think I will, too.
   I have lots to do.
   【*Good for you*. 做得好；很好。】

   A：我會待得晚一點。

   B：很好。
   我想我也會。
   我有很多工作要做。

3. A：**I have too much to do**.

   B：I totally understand.
   I know how you feel.
   I've been in the same
   situation.

   A：我有很多工作要做。

   B：我完全了解。
   我知道你的感覺。
   我也是同樣的情況。

4. A：**This work is due**.

   B：What's your deadline?
   When is it due?
   When do you have to
   hand it in?

   A：這個工作必須要完成。

   B：截止時間是什麼時候？
   什麼時候要完成？
   你什麼時候要交？

BOOK 9

BOOK 9

5. A : **This has to be done.**

   B : You're very responsible.
      You're the one for the job.
      I admire that in you!
      【responsible〔rɪ'spɑnsəb!〕
        *adj.* 負責任的】

A：這個必須要做完。

B：你很負責任。
   你最適合做這個工作。
   我眞欣賞你這一點！

6. A : **The deadline is coming up.**

   B : How soon is that?
      How soon is it due?
      What day is it due on?

A：截止時間就要到了。

B：還要多久？
   還有多久就要完成？
   哪一天到期？

7. A : **I'm behind.**

   B : Don't worry.
      It's not as bad as you think.
      You'll get it done.

A：我落後了。

B：不要擔心。
   沒有你想的那麼糟。
   你會把它做完的。

8. A : **I have to catch up.**

   B : I have confidence in you.
      I know you can do it.
      Take it one step at a time.
      【confidence〔'kɑnfədəns〕*n.* 信心
        take〔tek〕*v.* 承擔；承辦】

A：我必須趕上。

B：我對你有信心。
   我知道你做得到。
   一步一步慢慢來。

9. A : **I'd like to get ahead.**

   B : That's a good idea!
      You're so smart!
      You're always planning ahead.

A：我想要超前。

B：那是個好主意！
   你眞聰明！
   你總是會事前先計劃。

# 5. *Let's make an appointment*.

| | |
|---|---|
| *Let's* make an appointment. | 我們約個時間見面吧。 |
| *Let's* set up a time. | 我們安排一個時間吧。 |
| We need to get together. | 我們需要見面。 |

| | |
|---|---|
| *When* can we meet? | 我們什麼時候可以見面？ |
| *When* is it convenient? | 什麼時間方便？ |
| I'll leave it up to you. | 我將留給你決定。 |

| | |
|---|---|
| *How* about tomorrow morning at nine? | 明天早上九點如何？ |
| *How* does that sound? | 你覺得如何？ |
| Do you have anything planned? | 你有沒有任何計劃？ |

BOOK 9

**\*\***

appointment〔ə'pɔɪntmənt〕*n.* 約會；約定
*set up* 安排　　*get together* 見面；會面
*up to* 由…決定的　　sound〔saʊnd〕*v.* 聽起來
planned〔plænd〕*adj.* 計劃好的

BOOK 9

## 【背景説明】

當你想要提議和別人約時間見面的時候，就可以説這九句話。

1. *Let's make an appointment.*

appointment〔 ə'pɔɪntmənt 〕*n.* 約會；約定

這句話的意思是「我們約個時間見面吧。」可加長爲：

Let's make an appointment to meet.
（我們約個時間見面吧。）
Let's make an appointment to get together.
（我們約個時間見面吧。）
【*get together* 會面；見面】

很多中國人弄不清楚 make an appointment 和 make a date 的區別。appointment 比較正式，如和醫生約定時間見面（doctor's appointment），學生家長和學校老師約定見面（school appointment）等。而 date 是指和朋友之間約定見面，往往指男女約會，例如：He made a date with her.（他和她約會了。）They made a date for the movies.（他們約會去看電影了。）【*the movies* 電影院】

2. *Let's set up a time.*

   *set up* 安排 ( = *arrange* )

> 這句話的意思是「我們安排一個時間吧。」set 這個字,在字典中有無限多的意思,大的字典,甚至多達 58 個意思。set up 這個成語,在成語字典中,也有 23 個意思。所以,到底 set up 當什麼解釋呢?要看句子的上下文決定。

**Let's set up a time.** 中的 set up,是 set 的加強語氣。

【比較】 Let's set a time. 【正,常用】
　　　　 *Let's set up a time.* 【正,常用,語氣稍強】

下面是美國人常説的話:

*Let's set up a time.* 【第一常用】

Let's set up a time to meet. 【第二常用】
（我們安排時間見面吧。）

Let's set up a time for us to meet. 【第三常用】
（我們安排時間見面吧。）

Let's set up a time so we can meet. 【第四常用】
（我們安排時間見面吧。）

Let's set up a date. ( 我們約個日期吧。)【第七常用】

Let's set up a time and place to meet.
（我們約個時間、地點見面吧。）【第五常用】

Let's set up a time and place to get together.
（我們約個時間、地點見面吧。）【第六常用】

【date〔det〕*n.* 日期】

BOOK 9

Let's set up an appointment. 【第八常用】

（我們約個時間吧。）

Let's set up a meeting. 【第九常用】

（我們安排一次會面吧；我們安排一次會議吧。）

Let's set up a meeting to discuss this.

（我們安排一次會面來討論這件事吧。）

【meeting（'mitɪŋ）*n.* 會面；會議】【第十常用】

上面各句中的 set up，等於 set。

3. *We need to get together.*

　　*get together* 會面；見面

這句話的意思是「我們需要見面。」可加長為：

We need to get together *and talk*.

（我們需要見面談一談。）

We need to get together *and discuss this*.

（我們需要見面討論這件事情。）

We need to get together *for a meeting*.

（我們需要見面好好談一談。）

4. *When can we meet?*

這句話的意思是「我們什麼時候可以見面？」

美國人也常說：When can we meet each other?

（我們什麼時候可以見面？）如果和一群人在一起時，

就可說：When can we meet together?（我們什麼時

候可以見面？）

***When can we meet?*** 也可以加長爲：

> **When can we meet *to have a talk?***
> （我們什麼時候可以見面談一談？）
> **When can we meet *to talk about things?***
> （我們什麼時候可以見面談事情？）
> **When can we meet *to talk business?***
> （我們何時可以見面好好談一談？）
> 【*talk business* 談正事（= *talk about business*）】

比較有禮貌的説法是：When do you think we can meet?（你認爲我們什麼時候可以見面？）

## 5. *When is it convenient?*

這句話的意思是「什麼時間方便？」有些美國人簡化爲：When is convenient?【不合文法，可當成慣用句處理】

下面是美國人常説的話：

> ***When is it convenient?***【第一常用】
> When is it convenient for you?【第五常用】
> （你什麼時間方便？）
>
> When is it convenient for you to meet?
> （你什麼時間方便見面？）【第十常用】
> When is it convenient for you to meet
>  with me?【第十一常用】
> （你什麼時間方便跟我見面？）

When is a convenient time?【第四常用】
（什麼時間方便？）

When is a convenient time for you?
（你什麼時間方便？）【第九常用】

When is a good time?【第二常用】
（什麼時間恰當？）

When is a good time for you?【第六常用】
（你什麼時間方便？）

【good〔gud〕*adj.* 恰當的】

What's a good time?【第三常用】
（什麼時間恰當？）

What's a good time for you?【第七常用】
（你什麼時間方便？）

What's a convenient time for you?
（你什麼時間方便？）【第八常用】

6. *I'll leave it up to you.*

  *up to* 由…決定的

　　這句話字面的意思是「我
將把它留給你決定。」也就是
「我將留給你決定。」是由 I'll
leave it to you.（我將把它留給你。）和 It's up to
you.（由你決定。）兩句話組合而成的一句話。

也可以加強語氣說成：

> I'll leave the decision up to you.
>
> （我把決定權留給你。）
>
> I'll leave it all up to you.
>
> （全部由你決定。）
>
> I'll leave everything up to you.
>
> （一切由你決定。）

BOOK 9

7. *How about tomorrow morning at nine?*

這句話的意思是「明天早上九點如何？」源自：
How do you feel about tomorrow morning at
nine?（你覺得明天早上九點如何？）

【比較】 以下四句意義相同：

> ***How about tomorrow morning at nine?***
> 【第一常用】
>
> = How do you feel about tomorrow
> morning at nine? 【第三常用】
>
> = What about tomorrow morning at nine?
> 【第二常用】
>
> = What do you think about tomorrow
> morning at nine? 【第四常用】

8. ***How does that sound?***

sound〔saʊnd〕*v.* 聽起來

> 這句話的字面意思是「那個聽起來如何？」，
> 在此引申為「你覺得那個意見如何？」，也就是
> 「你覺得如何？」。
>
> 凡是你提出建議後，就可接著說這句話，如：
>
>> Let's eat early today. ***How does
>> that sound?***
>> （我們今天早點吃。你覺得如何？）
>>
>> Let's invite her to go with us. ***How does
>> that sound?***
>> （我們邀請她一起去。你覺得如何？）
>
> ***How does that sound?*** 也可以加強語氣說成：
> How does that sound to you?（你覺得如何？）
> 或 How does that sound, OK?（你覺得如何？可
> 以嗎？）

9. ***Do you have anything planned?***

planned〔plænd〕*adj.* 計劃好的

> 這句話的意思是「你有沒有任何計劃？」源自：
> ***Do you have anything which is planned?***【書本英
> 文，美國人不說】

下面都是美國人常說的話：

***Do you have anything planned?***【第一常用】

Do you have anything else planned?

（你有沒有任何其他的計劃？）【第四常用】

Do you have anything planned for then?

（你那時候有沒有任何計劃？）【第五常用】

Do you have anything planned for

　　that time?【第六常用】

（你那時候有沒有任何計劃？）

Do you have plans?（你有計劃嗎？）【第八常用】

Do you have any plans?【第七常用】

（你有任何計劃嗎？）

Do you have any other plans?【第三常用】

（你有任何其他的計劃嗎？）

Do you have other plans?【第二常用】

（你有其他的計劃嗎？）

BOOK 9

## 【對話練習】

1. A：**Let's make an appointment.**

   B：I'm glad you said that.
   I agree we should meet.
   We need to get together.

   A：我們約個時間見面吧。

   B：很高興聽你這麼說。
   我同意我們應該見面。
   我們必須見面。

2. A：**Let's set up a time.**

   B：You set the time.
   I'm free all day.
   Any time is fine with
   me.【free〔frɪ〕*adj.* 空閒的】

   A：我們安排一個時間吧。

   B：你安排時間。
   我整天都有空。
   我任何時間都可以。

3. A：**We need to get together.**

   B：We sure do.
   We need to meet.
   We have a lot to discuss.

   A：我們需要見面。

   B：我們當然需要。
   我們需要見面。
   我們有很多事情要討論。

4. A：**When can we meet?**

   B：I can't meet this week.
   I'm busy all week.
   Let's meet next Monday,
   OK?

   A：我們什麼時候可以見面？

   B：我這個禮拜不行。
   我整個禮拜都很忙。
   我們下星期一見面，可以
   嗎？

5. A : **When is convenient?**　　　　　A：什麼時間方便？

   B : Mornings are convenient.　　　　B：早上很方便。
   　　Mornings are the best time.　　　　早上最好。
   　　The earlier the better for me.　　　對我而言，愈早愈好。

6. A : **I'll leave it up to you.**　　　　A：我將留給你決定。

   B : Please don't do that.　　　　　B：請不要這麼做。
   　　Let's both decide.　　　　　　　我們兩個一起決定。
   　　That's the best way.　　　　　　這樣是最好的方式。

7. A : **How about tomorrow**　　　　A：明天早上九點如何？
   　　**morning at nine?**

   B : That's perfect!　　　　　　　B：太完美了！
   　　That's a perfect time!　　　　　那個時間太完美了！
   　　I was hoping you would say　　　我原本也是希望你會
   　　that.【perfect（'pɝfɪkt）*adj.* 完美的】　　這麼說。

8. A : **How does that sound?**　　　A：你覺得如何？

   B : Sounds great!　　　　　　　B：聽起來很棒！
   　　That's a convenient time.　　　　那個時間很方便。
   　　That's a very good time to meet.　那個時間見面很好。

9. A : **Do you have anything planned?**　A：你有沒有任何計劃？

   B : No, I'm free.　　　　　　　B：沒有，我有空。
   　　My time is yours.　　　　　　　我的時間是你的了。
   　　I'm at your disposal.　　　　　我任由你處置。

   　　【disposal（dɪ'spozḷ）*n.* 處置
   　　　*at one's disposal* 隨某人自由處置；由某人隨意支配】

BOOK 9

# 6. *I have to cancel*.

| | |
|---|---|
| *I have* bad news. | 我有壞消息。 |
| *I have* to cancel. | 我必須取消約會。 |
| I can't make it. | 我沒辦法辦到。 |
| | |
| Something has come up. | 有事情發生了。 |
| *Can we* reschedule? | 我們可不可以重新訂時間？ |
| *Can we* meet another time? | 我們能不能另外找一個時間見面？ |
| | |
| *You* tell me. | 由你決定。 |
| *You* pick the time. | 你選擇時間。 |
| I'll work around your schedule. | 我會根據你的時間來安排我的時間。 |

\*\* ────────────────────

news〔njuz〕*n.* 消息　　cancel〔'kænsl̩〕*v.* 取消；取消約會
***make it*** 成功；辦到　　***come up*** 發生
reschedule〔ri'skɛdʒul〕*v.* 重新排定…的時間
meet〔mit〕*v.* 會面；見面　　pick〔pɪk〕*v.* 挑選；選擇
around〔ə'raund〕*prep.* 以…為中心；根據
schedule〔'skɛdʒul〕*n.* 時間表

## 【背景説明】

　　當你突然有事，想改變主意，取消原來約會，你
就可以説這一回的九句話了。

1. ***I have bad news.***
   news〔njuz〕*n.* 消息

I have
bad news.

　　這句話的意思是「我有壞
消息。」news 是抽象名詞，
不可數，而不可數名詞，可用
單位名詞表「數」的觀念，在
字典上，可以查到 a piece of news 表示「一個消
息」，但是，現在美國人已經不使用了。

【比較】　***I have bad news.***【正，常用】
　　　　*I have a piece of bad news.*
　　　　【文法對，古老用法，現在美國人不用】
　　　　*I have a bad news.*【誤】

這句話可以加長：

　　　　***I have bad news.***
　　　　***I have*** some ***bad news.***
　　　　（我有壞消息。）【可以是一個，或一個以上】
　　　　***I have*** some ***bad news*** for you.
　　　　（我有壞消息要告訴你。）

BOOK 9

I'm afraid *I have bad news*.

（我恐怕有壞消息。）

I'm sorry to say *I have bad news*.

（很抱歉，我有壞消息。）

I hate to tell you but *I have bad news*.

（我很遺憾要告訴你，我有壞消息。）

【hate〔het〕v. 遺憾】

2. *I have to cancel*.

cancel〔ˈkænsl̩〕v. 取消；取消約會

　　cancel 是及物和不及物兩用動詞，所以，cancel 後也可接受詞，像 cancel the meeting（取消會議）或 cancel the appointment（取消約會）等。

　　這句話的意思是「我必須取消約會。」下面都是美國人常說的話：

① *I have to cancel*.【第一常用】

② I have to cancel it.（我必須取消它。）【第二常用】

③ I have to cancel the appointment.【第三常用】
　　（我必須取消約會。）

④ I have to call it off.（我必須取消它。）
　　【*call off*（取消）是及物動詞，後面必須接受詞。】

⑤ I have to call off the appointment.
　　（我必須取消約會。）

　　上面第三和第五句中的 the appointment，可改成 our appointment。

3. *I can't make it.*

*make it* 成功；辦到

> 在字典上，make it 有很多意思，凡是達到了預定的目標，都可說是 make it，在不同的句中，有不同的解釋，參照 p.134。*I can't make it.* 的主要意思是「我沒辦法辦到。」這個句子可以加長：
>
> *I can't make it* to the meeting.
> （我沒辦法參加會議。）【句中的 to 可改為 for】
> *I can't make it* to our appointment.
> （我沒辦法赴約。）
> *I can't make it* today.
> （我今天沒辦法做到。）

比較有禮貌的說法是，在句子前加上 I'm sorry 之類的話，例如：

I'm sorry *I can't make it.*
（很抱歉，我沒辦法辦到。）

I'm afraid *I can't make it.*
（我恐怕沒辦法辦到。）

I apologize. *I can't make it.*
（我很抱歉。我沒辦法辦到。）

【apologize〔ə'pɑlə,dʒaɪz〕v. 道歉】

*I can't make it.*

4. *Something has come up.*

*come up* 發生

　　這句話的意思是「有事情發生了。」很多美
國人也說：Something has just come up. 或
Something's just come up. 意思都是「剛好有
事情發生。」此時 just 作「剛好；恰好」解。

　　Something 後面往往會加上修飾語來強調，
例如：

Something *important* has come up.
（有重要的事情發生了。）
Something *urgent* has come up.
（有緊急的事情發生了。）
Something *unexpected* has come up.
（有意想不到的事情發生了。）

urgent〔'ɝdʒənt〕*adj.* 緊急的
unexpected〔,ʌnɪk'spɛktɪd〕*adj.* 出乎意料的；意外的

Something *unavoidable* has come up.
（有不可避免的事情發生了。）
Something *unbelievable* has come up.
（有令人難以置信的事情發生了。）
Something *terrible* has come up.
（有可怕的事情發生了。）

unavoidable〔,ʌnə'vɔɪdəbḷ〕*adj.* 無法避免的
unbelievable〔,ʌnbɪ'livəbḷ〕*adj.* 令人難以置信的

【比較】下面兩句話意思相同：

> ***Something has come up.***【較常用，語氣較輕鬆】
> = Something has happened.【常用，語氣較嚴肅】

5. *Can we reschedule?*

reschedule〔rɪ'skɛdʒʊl〕*v.* 改變…的時間；重訂…的
時間表

　　在所有字典中，reschedule 都是及物動詞，
事實上，reschedule 也可作不及物動詞，將來字
典早晚會改。這句話的意思是「我們可不可以重新
定時間？」

【比較】 下面兩句話意思不完全相同：

> ***Can we reschedule?***【常用，使用範圍較廣】
> Can we reschedule our appointment?
> （我們可不可以改變約會的時間？）【常用】

這個句子可以加長：

> ***Can we reschedule*** for later tonight?
> （我們能不能改約今天晚上較晚的時候？）
> ***Can we reschedule*** for tomorrow?
> （我們能不能改明天？）
> ***Can we reschedule*** for a later date?
> （我們能不能改約比較晚的日期？）
> 【date〔det〕*n.* 日期】

6. *Can we meet another time?*

meet〔mit〕*v.* 見面；會面

　　這句話的意思是「我們能不能另外找一個時間見面？」meet 是及物和不及物兩用動詞，another time 是副詞片語，源自 at another time，和 some other time 意義相同，都表示「另一個時間」。

下面各句意思接近：

　*Can we meet another time?*【第一常用】
　Can we meet at another time?【第三常用】
　（我們能不能另外找一個時間見面？）
　Can we meet some other time?【第二常用】
　（我們能不能另外找一個時間見面？）
　【some other time 也可說成 at some other time】

　Can you meet me at another time?【第十常用】
　（你能不能另外找一個時間和我見面？）
　Can you and I meet at another time?【第十一常用】
　（我們能不能另外找一個時間見面？）
　Can we get together at another time?【第十二常用】
　（我們能不能另外找一個時間碰面？）
　【*get together* 相聚；碰面】

Can we change the time? 【第七常用】

（我們能不能改時間？）

Can we change the meeting time? 【第八常用】

（我們能不能更改見面的時間？）

Can we change the meeting to another time?

（我們能不能改另一個時間見面？）【第九常用】

【meeting (ˈmitɪŋ) *n.* 會面】

How about another time? 【第四常用】

（另一個時間如何？）

How about meeting at another time? 【第五常用】

（另一個時間見面如何？）

Let's meet at another time, OK? 【第六常用】

（我們另外找一個時間見面，好嗎？）

7. *You tell me.*

　　這句話字面的意思是「你告訴我。」引申為「我會聽你的。」（ = *I'll listen to you.* ) 或「由你來決定。」( = *I'll let you decide.* ) 說 *You tell me.* 的時候，*You* 要重讀。

*You tell me.*

這個句子可以加長，此時 You 就不需要重讀：

> *You tell me* what time. 【最常用】
> （你決定什麼時間。）
> *You tell me* what time you prefer. 【常用】
> （告訴我你比較喜歡什麼時間。）
> *You tell me* what time you like. 【較常用】
> （告訴我你喜歡什麼時間。）
> 【prefer〔prɪˈfɝ〕v. 比較喜歡】

上面句子中的 You tell me 都可改成 You can
tell me。

8. *You pick the time.*
pick〔pɪk〕v. 挑選；選擇（= *select*；*choose*）

這句話的意思是「你選擇時間。」

【比較1】 下面三句話意思相同：

> *You pick the time.* 【第一常用】
> You choose the time. 【第二常用】
> You select the time. 【第三常用】
> 【choose〔tʃuz〕v. 選擇 　select〔səˈlɛkt〕v. 挑選】

【比較2】 下面都是美國人常說的話：

> *You pick the time.* 【第一常用】
> You can pick any time. 【第五常用】
> （你可以選擇任何時間。）
> You can pick any time you like. 【第六常用】
> （你可以選擇你想要的任何時間。）

You can pick the time. 【第二常用】

（你可以選擇時間。）

I'll let you pick the time. 【第三常用】

（我會讓你選擇時間。）

I want you to pick the time. 【第四常用】

（我要你選擇時間。）

9. *I'll work around your schedule.*

around〔ə'raʊnd〕*prep.* 以⋯為中心；根據

schedule〔'skɛdʒʊl〕*n.* 時間表

　　work 的主要意思是「工作」，在這裡是及物
動詞，作「安排」解，只是 work 後面省略了 my
schedule。

　　這句話源自：I'll work my schedule around
your schedule. 意思是「我將根據你的時間來安排
我的時間。」句中的 around
作「根據」解。也可說成：
I'll work my schedule
around yours.（我將根據你
的時間來安排我的時間。）

【yours = your schedule】

*I'll work around your schedule.*

【比較】

*I'll work around your schedule.*【正】
*I'll arrange around your schedule.*【誤】

第二句應改成：I'll arrange *my schedule* around
your schedule. 或 I'll arrange *my time* around
your schedule. 因為 *I'll work around your
schedule.* 這句話，已經成為固定用法，大家都已
經習慣簡化。

　　*I'll work around your schedule.* 是非常體貼
的一句話，說這句話顯示你很有教養。

【例】　When are you free? *I'll work around
　　　　your schedule.*

　　　　（你什麼時候有空？我會根據你的時間來
　　　　安排我的時間。）

　　　　【free〔frɪ〕*adj.* 有空的】

　　　　You're so busy. *I can work around
　　　　your schedule.*

　　　　（你那麼忙。我可以根據你的時間來安排
　　　　我的時間。）【*I'll work around*…也可說
　　　　成 I can work around…】

BOOK 9

## 【對話練習】

1. A：**I have bad news**.

   B：Let's hear it.

   　　Just tell me.

   　　Just spit it out.

   　　【*spit it out* 全盤說出；坦白說出】

2. A：**I have to cancel**.

   B：Oh, no!

   　　Oh, that is bad news!

   　　I'm really sorry to hear that.

3. A：**I can't make it**.

   B：What a shame!

   　　What a pity!

   　　I'm very disappointed to hear that.

   　　【*a shame* 遺憾的事

   　　　disappointed (ˌdɪsə'pɔɪntɪd )

   　　　*adj.* 失望的】

4. A：**Something has come up**.

   B：Oh, really?

   　　What has come up?

   　　What has happened?

A：我有壞消息。

B：我們來聽聽看吧。

　　告訴我吧。

　　把它說出來吧。

A：我必須取消約會。

B：噢,真是糟糕!

　　噢,那真是個壞消息!

　　聽到這件事我真的很遺憾。

A：我沒辦法辦到。

B：真可惜!

　　真可惜!

　　聽到這件事我很失望。

A：有事情發生了。

B：噢,真的嗎?

　　發生什麼事了?

　　發生什麼事了?

BOOK 9

5. A : **Can we reschedule?**
   B : You know we can.
   I can reschedule.
   I'll meet you at any time.

A：我們可不可以重新訂時間？
B：你知道我們可以的。
　　我可以重新訂時間。
　　我隨時都可以和你見面。

6. A : **Can we meet another time?**
   B : I don't think so.
   I don't think I can.
   My schedule is really tight.
   【tight〔taɪt〕*adj.* 緊湊的；排滿的】

A：我們能不能另外找一個時間見面？
B：我想不行吧。
　　我不認爲我可以。
　　我的時間眞的排得滿滿的。

7. A : **You tell me.**
   B : Well, let's see.
   I'm free all day Friday.
   I'm free the day after tomorrow, too. 【*let's see* 我想想看】

A：由你決定。
B：嗯，我想想看。
　　我星期五整天有空。
　　我後天也有空。

8. A : **You pick the time.**
   B : OK, I will.
   Let's meet late tomorrow afternoon.
   Let's meet at four-thirty, OK?

A：你選擇時間。
B：好的，我會的。
　　我們明天下午晚一點見面。
　　我們四點半見面，好嗎？

9. A : **I'll work around your schedule.**
   B : That's very kind of you.
   How about 4:30?
   I'm free then.

A：我會根據你的時間來安排我的時間。
B：你人眞好。
　　四點半如何？
　　我那時有空。

# 7. *Any messages for me?*

| | |
|---|---|
| *Any* messages for me? | 有沒有人留話給我？ |
| *Any* calls to return? | 有沒有電話要回？ |
| What needs to be done? | 有什麼需要做的？ |
| | |
| *Could you check* this over? | 你能不能幫我檢查看看？ |
| *Could you check* for mistakes? | 你能不能看看有沒有錯誤？ |
| Proofread this for me. | 幫我校對這個。 |
| | |
| *Please* type this up. | 請把這個打好。 |
| *Please* print out a copy. | 請印一份出來。 |
| I need to fax it right away. | 我需要把它立刻傳眞出去。 |

\*\* ─────────────

message〔'mɛsɪdʒ〕*n.* 訊息；留言　　call〔kɔl〕*n.* 電話
return〔rɪ'tɝn〕*v.* 回（電話）　　*check over* 檢查
proofread〔'pruf,rid〕*v.* 校對　　type〔taɪp〕*v.* 打字
*print out* 印出　　copy〔'kɑpɪ〕*n.* 一份
fax〔fæks〕*v.* 傳眞　　*right away* 立刻

## 【背景説明】

　　你任何時間進了辦公室，都可以問同事：Any messages for me?…等。當你寫完了任何文件或報告，你就可以請你的同事檢查一下有沒有錯，説：Could you check this over?…等。

1. **Any messages for me?**
message〔'mɛsɪdʒ〕*n.* 訊息；留言

　　這句話的意思是「有沒有人留話給我？」源自：Are there any messages for me?【常用】( 有沒有人留話給我？) 或 Do you have any messages for me?【常用】( 有沒有人請你留話給我？)

2. **Any calls to return?**
call〔kɔl〕*n.* 電話　　***return a call*** 回電話

　　call 的主要意思是「呼喊聲；叫聲」，在這裡作「電話」解，等於 phone call。這句話的意思是「有沒有電話要回？」源自：Are there any phone calls for me to return?【有人説】( 我有沒有電話要回？)

　　Any calls *to return*? to return 是不定詞片語當形容詞用，修飾 calls。也有美國人説：Do I have to return any calls?【常用】( 我需不需要回電話？)

下面是美國人常說的話：

*Any calls to return?*【第一常用】

Any calls for me to return?【第二常用】

（我有沒有電話要回？）

Any phone calls for me to return?【第三常用】

（我有沒有電話要回？）

Are there any calls for me?【第五常用】

（有人打電話找我嗎？）

Are there any calls for me to return?【第六常用】

（我有沒有電話要回？）

Do I have any calls to return?【第四常用】

（我有電話要回嗎？）

3. *What needs to be done?*

這句話的意思是「有什麼需要做的？」

下面都是美國人常說的話：

*What needs to be done?*【第一常用】

What needs to get done?【第二常用】

（有什麼需要完成的？）

What needs to be taken care of?【第三常用】

（有什麼需要處理的？）

【done〔dʌn〕*adj.* 完成的　*take care of* 處理】

BOOK 9

BOOK 9

Is there anything that needs to be done?

（有什麼需要做的事嗎？）【第五常用】

Is there something that needs to be done?

（有什麼需要做的事嗎？）【第六常用】

Anything that needs to be done?【第四常用】

（有什麼需要做的事嗎？）

4. *Could you check this over?*

*check over* 核對；檢查（*= examine*；*check it very carefully*）

這句話的意思是「你能不能幫我檢查看看？」

【比較】下面三句話意思相同：

Could you check this?【第一常用】

= *Could you check this over?*

【第二常用，語氣稍強】

= Could you check this out?

【第三常用，語氣稍強】【*check out* 檢查】

check over 源自在你手上的東西，可以翻來覆去地看，所以，拿在手上的東西，才可以用 check over。如果檢查外面的東西，就用 check out。

【比較】 There is a new restaurant.  Let's go

{ 
check it out.【正】【check out 的使用範圍很廣】
*check it over.*【誤】
}

【因為餐廳不是可以放在手上翻來覆去地看的東西】

5. *Could you check for mistakes?*

這句話的意思是「你能不能看看有沒有錯誤？」

下面都是美國人常説的話：

**Could you check for mistakes?**【第一常用】
Could you check this for mistakes?【第二常用】
（你能不能看看這個有沒有錯誤？）
Could you check this for any mistakes?【第三常用】
（你能不能看看這個有沒有錯誤？）

【比較】

中文： 你能不能看看有沒有錯誤？

英文： *Could you check to see mistakes?*【誤】
Could you check to see if there are any
mistakes?【正，常用，to see 可改成 and see】
*Could you check for mistakes?*【正，較常用】

6. *Proofread this for me.*

proofread〔'pruf,rid〕*v.* 校對（ = *read in order to find
errors and mark corrections*）

這句話的意思是「幫我校對這個。」

【比較】 下面兩句意義相同：

**Proofread this for me.**【語氣較正式】
= Check this for me.【語氣較輕鬆】

7. *Please type this up*.

type〔taɪp〕*v.* 打字（用電腦或打字機）

這句話的意思是「請把這個打好。」type 和 type~up 都是指「打字」。這句話可增長爲：Please type this up for me.（請幫我把這個打好。）或 Please type this up when you have time.（當你有時間時，請把這個打好。）

> *Please type this up.*

【比較】 下面兩句意義相同：

> Please type this. 【語氣輕鬆】
>   （請打這個。）
> = Please type this up. 【語氣稍強，較常用】
>   （請把這個打好。）

8. *Please print out a copy*.

print〔prɪnt〕*v.* 印刷　　*print out* （電腦）印出
copy〔'kɑpɪ〕*n.* 一份

這句話的意思是「請印一份出來。」也可說成：Please print a copy.（請印一份。）美國人也常說成：Could you please print out a copy?（能不能請你印一份出來？）

BOOK 9

9. ***I need to fax it right away.***

    fax〔fæks〕*v.* 傳眞    ***right away*** 立刻

這句話的意思是「我需要把它立刻傳眞出去。」
如果你單獨說這句話，就可說成：I need to fax
this right away. ( 我需要把這個立刻傳眞出去。)

下面都是美國人常說的話：

I need to fax it ***right away***. 【第一常用】
I need to fax it ***right now***. 【第三常用】
( 我需要立刻把它傳眞出去。)
I need to fax it ***immediately***. 【第二常用】
( 我需要立刻把它傳眞出去。)
I need to fax it ***as soon as possible***. 【第四常用】
( 我需要儘快把它傳眞出去。)

***right now*** 現在；立刻
immediately〔ɪ'midɪtlɪ〕*adv.* 立刻
***as soon as possible*** 儘快

## 【對話練習】

1. A : **Any messages for me?**      A：有沒有人留話給我？

   B : Yes, you have a message.      B：有，你有一個留言。
       Mr. Smith called for you.         史密斯先生打電話找你。
       He wants you to call him         他要你回他電話。
       back. 〔*call for sb.* 打電話找某人〕

2. A : **Any calls to return?**      A：有沒有電話要回？

   B : Nope.      B：沒有。
       Not right now.         現在沒有。
       Not at the moment.         目前沒有。
       【nope 〔nop〕 *adv.* 不；不是 ( = *no* )
          *at the moment* 目前】

3. A : **What needs to be done?**      A：有什麼需要做的？

   B : You have a report to finish.      B：你有個報告要完成。
       You have some phone         你有一些電話要打。
       calls to make.
       You have a meeting after         你吃完午餐後有個會議
       lunch. 〔*make a call* 打電話〕         要開。

4. A : **Could you check this over?**      A：你能不能幫我檢查看看？

   B : I'd be happy to.      B：我很樂意。
       It's no problem at all.         沒問題。
       It would be my pleasure.         這是我的榮幸。

BOOK 9

5. A：**Could you check for mistakes?**　　A：你能不能看看有沒有錯誤？

　　B：I sure can.　　　　　　　　　　　B：當然可以。

　　　I can look it over.　　　　　　　　　我可以檢查看看。

　　　I'll proofread it for you.　　　　　　我會替你校對。

　　　【*look over* 檢查】

6. A：**Proofread this for me**.　　　　　A：幫我校對這個。

　　B：Yes, sir.　　　　　　　　　　　　B：好的，先生。

　　　I'll do it right now.　　　　　　　　我立刻就做。

　　　I'll do it right away.　　　　　　　　我立刻就做。

7. A：**Please type this up**.　　　　　　A：請把這個打好。

　　B：Sure thing.　　　　　　　　　　　B：當然好。

　　　Do you need this for today?　　　　　你今天就要嗎？

　　　Do you want it single or　　　　　　你要一行一行打，還是隔

　　　double-spaced?　　　　　　　　　行打？

　　　【single（'sɪŋɡḷ）*adj.* 單一的

　　　　*double-spaced* 隔行打的】

8. A：**Please print out a copy**.　　　　A：請印一份出來。

　　B：Just one copy?　　　　　　　　　B：只要一份嗎？

　　　Would you like two or three?　　　　你要不要兩、三份？

　　　Would you like a few more　　　　　你要不要多印幾份，以備

　　　just in case?【*in case* 以防萬一】　不時之需？

9. A：**I need to fax it right away**.　　　A：我需要把它立刻傳真出去。

　　B：I can take care of that for you.　　　B：我可以幫你做。

　　　Where's it going?　　　　　　　　要傳去哪裡？

　　　What's the fax number?　　　　　　傳真號碼是幾號？

　　　【*take care of* 處理】

BOOK 9

# 8. *I need some time off.*

| | |
|---|---|
| *I* have a favor to ask. | 我要請你幫個忙。 |
| *I* need some time off. | 我需要一些時間休息。 |
| *I* have something important to do. | 我有一些重要的事情要做。 |
| | |
| *Can I take a* leave of absence? | 我可不可以請假？ |
| *Can I take a* day off? | 我可不可以請一天假？ |
| Would this Friday be OK? | 這個星期五可以嗎？ |
| | |
| Sorry for the trouble. | 很抱歉造成你的麻煩。 |
| *I*'ll work extra hours next week. | 我下星期會增加工作時間。 |
| *I* promise I'll make it up. | 我保證我會補回來。 |

**\*\*** ─────────────

favor〔'fevɚ〕*n.* 恩惠；幫忙　　off〔ɔf〕*adv.* 不工作；休息
leave〔liv〕*n.* 休假；准許　　absence〔'æbsn̩s〕*n.* 缺席
***take a leave of absence*** 請假【通常是較長時間的假】
***take a day off*** 請一天假　　trouble〔'trʌbl̩〕*n.* 麻煩；打擾
extra〔'ɛkstrə〕*adj.* 額外的　　hours〔aurz〕*n. pl.* 時間
promise〔'prɑmɪs〕*v.* 保證　　***make up*** 補足；彌補；補償

BOOK 9

## 【背景説明】

當你想要向你的主管請假的時候，你就可以説
這九句話，他聽了一定會欣然接受你的請求。

1. ***I have a favor to ask.***

   favor (ˈfevɚ) *n.* 恩惠；幫助；善意的行為

   favor 有很多意思，在字典
上，主要的意思是「恩惠」，但
在會話中，常作「幫忙」解。
這句話的意思是「我要請你幫
個忙。」

I have a
favor to ask.

　　【比較】 下面三句意思相同：

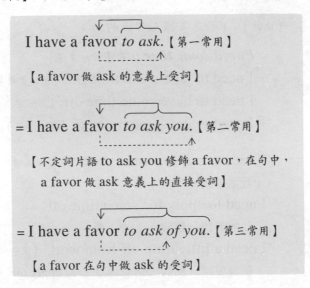

I have a favor *to ask*. 【第一常用】

【a favor 做 ask 的意義上受詞】

= I have a favor *to ask you*. 【第二常用】

【不定詞片語 to ask you 修飾 a favor，在句中，
　a favor 做 ask 意義上的直接受詞】

= I have a favor *to ask of you*. 【第三常用】

【a favor 在句中做 ask 的受詞】

下面三句話，美國人也常說：

> Can I ask a favor?（我能請你幫個忙嗎？）
> = Can I ask you a favor?
> = Can I ask a favor of you?

請別人幫忙的説法太多了，像美國人常説：Do
me a favor.（幫我一個忙。）I need a big favor.
（我需要你幫個大忙。）等，以後陸續會談到。

2. *I need some time off.*

off〔ɔf〕*adv.* 不工作；休息（= *away or free from
regular work*）

這句話的意思是「我需要一些時間休息。」源自：
I need some time off from work.（我需要一些時間
休息，不工作。）

【比較】下面是美國人常説的話：

> *I need some time off.*【第一常用】
> = I need to take some time off.【第二常用】
> = I need to have some time off.【第三常用】
> = I need to get some time off.【第四常用】

> I need to ask for some time off.【第五常用】
> （我需要請一些假。）
> I need to apply for some time off.
> （我需要請一點假。）【第七常用，較正式】
> I need a little time off from work.【第六常用】
> （我需要請一點假，休息休息。）【*apply for* 申請】

3. *I have something important to do*.

下面是美國人常說的話：

　　這句話的意思是「我有一些重要的事情要做。」

I have things to do.【第四常用】
（我有事情要做。）

I have something to do.【第一常用】
（我有事情要做。）

I have some important things to do.
（我有一些重要的事情要做。）【第三常用】

I have something urgent to do.【第五常用】
（我有一些緊急的事情要做。）

*I have something important to do*.【第二常用】

I have something *to do that* just can't wait.
（我有刻不容緩的事情要做。）【第六常用】
【urgent〔ˈɝdʒənt〕*adj.* 迫切的；緊急的】

4. *Can I take a leave of absence?*

leave〔liv〕*v.* 離開　*n.* 離開；休假；准許（= *permission*）
absence〔ˈæbsn̩s〕*n.* 缺席

　　*Can I take a leave of absence?* 的字面意思
是「你可不可以准許我缺席？」引申為「我可不可以
請假？」所以，take a leave of absence 的意思是
「請假」。這句話也可以說成：Can I take some time
off？或 Can I have some time off？都表示「我可
不可以請假？」。

【比較】 ***Can I take a leave of absence?***
【常用，正式，在辦公室説較恰當。】
Can I take a leave?
【常用，較不正式，工廠員工喜歡説，而 take a leave 是 take a leave of absence 的省略。】

5. *Can I take a day off?*

***take a day off*** 請一天假

這句話的意思是「我可不可以請一天假？」也可説成：Can I have a day off？（我可不可以請一天假？）或 Can I have one day off？（我可不可以請一天假？）

比較客氣的説法是：Can you give me a day off？（你能不能給我一天假？）

6. *Would this Friday be OK?*

這句話的意思是「這個星期五可以嗎？」也可以簡化爲：Would Friday be OK？（星期五可以嗎？）或加長爲 Would this Friday be OK with you？（你覺得這個星期五可以嗎？）句中的 OK 都可改成 alright〔ɔl'raɪt〕。

【比較】 ***Would this Friday be OK?***【常用，較禮貌】
Is this Friday OK?【常用，禮貌】
（這個星期五可以嗎？）

7. *Sorry for the trouble.*

trouble〔'trʌbḷ〕*n.* 麻煩；打擾   *v.* 給（某人）添麻煩

這句話源自：*I'm sorry*
*for the trouble it will cause*
*you.*【美國人不說】意思是「很
抱歉造成你的麻煩。」

Sorry for
the trouble.

【比較】下面三句話意思相同：

> *Sorry for the trouble.*【第一常用】
> Sorry for troubling you.【第三常用】
> Sorry to trouble you.【第二常用】

8. *I'll work extra hours next week.*

extra〔'ɛkstrə〕*adj.* 額外的
hours〔aʊrz〕*n. pl.* 時間

這句話的意思是「我下星期會增加工作時間。」
也可說成：I'm willing to work extra hours next
week.（我願意下星期加班。）【willing〔'wɪlɪŋ〕*adj.*
願意的】或 I can work extra hours next week.
（我下星期可以加班。）句中的 extra hours 都可以
改成 extra time 或 more hours 或 more time。

下面都是美國人常說的話：

I'll stay late next week.【第一常用】
（我下星期會待得晚一點；我下星期會加班。）
I'll stay later next week.【第二常用】
（我下星期會待得晚一點。）

stay〔ste〕v. 停留　　late〔let〕adv. 晚
later〔'letɚ〕adv. 較晚

***I'll work extra hours next week.***【第四常用】
I'll put in extra hours next week.【第三常用】
（我下星期會增加工作時間。）

【***put in*** 花費；付出（時間）】

I'll stay at work late next week.【第五常用】
（我下星期會加班。）
I'll stay late at work next week.【第六常用】
（我下星期會加班。）

【***at work*** 在工作場所】

　　I'll stay late next week. 最常用，stay late
作「待得晚一點」( = *stay after normal hours* ) 解，
在辦公室，就是指「加班」( = *stay at work late* )。
這句話的意思是「我下星期會待得晚一點；我下星期
會加班。」美國人也常說成：I'll work late next
week. 使用頻率和句意都相同。由於我們在第九冊
第四回中，已經講過 I'm staying late. 所以，這一
回不選這個句子。

9. ***I promise I'll make it up.***

promise〔'prɑmɪs〕*v.* 保證

***make up***　補足；彌補；補償

　　這句話的意思是「我保證我會補回來。」it 是指「工作」或「時間」。I promise 後面可以加 that，也可以省略，省略時，語氣較輕鬆。

下面各句意思相同，都是美國人常說的話：

　　***I promise I'll make it up.***【第一常用】

　　I promise I'll make up my work.

　　（我保證我會把工作補回來。）【第二常用】

　　I promise I'll make up all my work.

　　（我保證我會把全部的工作補回來。）【第四常用】

　　I promise I'll make up any missed work.

　　（我保證我會把沒做的工作補回來。）【第三常用】

　　【missed〔mɪst〕*adj.* 遺漏的】

【比較】　以下是表示「我保證…」的說法，我們按照
　　　　　使用頻率排列，在實際會話中，可交替使用：

　　① ***I promise***…（我保證…）【第一常用】

　　② I swear…（我發誓…）【第二常用】

　　③ You have my word…【第三常用】

　　　　（我向你保證…）

　　　　【不可說成：*You have my words…*（誤）】

　　【swear〔swɛr〕*v.* 發誓　　word〔wɜd〕*n.* 諾言；保證】

④ I assure you that... ( 我向你保證… )
　　【第四常用，that 可以省略。】

⑤ I guarantee that... ( 我保證… )
　　【第五常用，that 可以省略。】

⑥ I guarantee you that... ( 我向你保證… )
　　【第六常用，that 可以省略。】

assure〔əˈʃur〕v. 向～保證
guarantee〔͵gærənˈti〕v. 保證；向～保證

【例】

$$I \begin{cases} \text{promise} \\ \text{swear} \\ \text{assure you} \\ \text{guarantee} \\ \text{guarantee you} \end{cases} \text{(that) I'll do it.}$$

【劉毅老師的話】

　　背「一口氣背會話」時，中英文一起背，剛開始會不習慣，你可以先聽 CD，模仿美籍播音員的腔調；也可以先背每一回九句英文，背完之後，再加上中文一起背，會記得更清楚。

## 【對話練習】

1. A：**I have a favor to ask.**
   B：Go ahead and ask.
      You can ask me anything.
      You always have a friend
      in me.【*go ahead* 請便
      *have a friend in sb.* 有某人這位朋友】

    A：我要請你幫個忙。
    B：儘管開口。
       你可以請我幫忙任何事。
       你永遠都有我這個朋友。

2. A：**I need some time off.**
   B：What's the reason?
      What's the matter?
      Is everything OK?

    A：我需要一些時間休息。
    B：理由是什麼？
       怎麼了？
       一切都還好吧？

3. A：**I have something important
      to do.**
   B：I understand.
      I know it must be important.
      Go do what you have to do.

    A：我有一些重要的事情要做。
    B：我了解。
       我知道一定是很重要的事。
       去做你必須做的事。

4. A：**Can I take a leave of absence?**
   B：Take a leave!
      You have my permission.
      You can take a leave of absence.

    A：我可以請假嗎？
    B：儘管請假！
       我准許你。
       你可以請假。

5. A：**Can I take a day off ?**
   B：We are too busy.
      We can't do without you.
      I'm sorry I have to say no.
      【*can't do without* 不能沒有】

    A：我可不可以請一天假？
    B：我們太忙了。
       我們不能沒有你。
       很抱歉，我必須要說「不
       行」。

BOOK 9

6. A: **Would this Friday be OK?**　　A：這個星期五可以嗎？

　　B: I don't know right now.　　　B：我現在不知道。
　　　 I can't tell you right now.　　　我現在無法告訴你。
　　　 Please ask me again　　　　　請明天再問我一次。
　　　 tomorrow.

7. A: **Sorry for the trouble.**　　　A：很抱歉造成你的麻煩。

　　B: Don't even mention it.　　　B：千萬別客氣。
　　　 It's my pleasure.　　　　　　這是我的榮幸。
　　　 It's no trouble at all.　　　　一點也不麻煩。

8. A: **I'll work extra hours next**　A：我下星期會增加工作
　　　 **week.**　　　　　　　　　　　時間。

　　B: That's an excellent idea.　　B：那是個好主意。
　　　 That would be great.　　　　那真是太好了。
　　　 That would be very helpful.　那會很有幫助。

　　　【excellent (ˈɛkslənt ) *adj.* 極好的
　　　　helpful (ˈhɛlpfəl ) *adj.* 有幫助的】

9. A: **I promise I'll make it up.**　　A：我保證我會補回來。

　　B: I know you will.　　　　　　B：我知道你會。
　　　 I have confidence in you.　　　我對你有信心。
　　　 I know you can keep up with　我知道你能趕上你的
　　　 your work.　　　　　　　　　工作進度。

　　　【confidence (ˈkɑnfədəns ) *n.* 信心
　　　　***keep up with*** 趕得上；不落後】

# *9. I'd like some feedback.*

| | |
|---|---|
| Do you have a minute? | 你有沒有一點時間？ |
| *Can* I speak with you? | 我可不可以和你說話？ |
| *Can* we have a word in private? | 我們可不可以私下談一談？ |
| | |
| I'd like some feedback. | 我想要一些意見。 |
| *How*'s my performance? | 我的表現如何？ |
| *How* am I doing so far? | 到目前爲止我的表現如何？ |
| | |
| I want to get better. | 我想要變得更好。 |
| *Please* give me some input. | 請給我一些建議。 |
| *Please* tell me what you think. | 請告訴我你的看法如何。 |

** ————————————————

minute〔'mɪnɪt〕*n.* 分鐘；片刻；一會兒

*have a word* 說一兩句話　*in private* 私下地；祕密地

feedback〔'fid,bæk〕*n.* 反應；反饋意見

performance〔pə'fɔrməns〕*n.* 表現

do〔du〕*v.* 表現　*so far* 到目前爲止

input〔'ɪn,pʊt〕*n.* 訊息；評論；建議

## 【背景説明】

在公司上班，也許老板很久沒給你加薪，你就
可以説這九句話來請問他，對你的工作是否滿意。
在美國大學裡，同學也常用這些話，來請問他的教
授，以免被當掉。

BOOK 9

1. *Do you have a minute?*

minute〔'mɪnɪt〕*n.* 分鐘；片刻；一會兒

這句話字面的意思是「你
有沒有一分鐘時間？」在這裡
引申為「你有沒有一點時間？」
也可以簡化為：You have a
minute?（你有一點時間嗎？）
美國人也常説成：Got a
minute?（有一點時間嗎？）這句話也可以加長為：

*Do you have
a minute?*

Do you have a minute *to talk*?

（你有時間談一談嗎？）

Do you have a minute *to talk with me*?

（你有時間和我談一談嗎？）

Do you have a minute *or are you busy*?

（你有時間，還是很忙呢？）

2. *Can I speak with you?*

　　這句話的意思是「我可不可以和你說話？」也
可說成：Can I talk with you?（我可不可以和你
談一談？）

　　　　*Can I speak with you?* 可加長為：

Can I speak with you *right now*?
（我現在可不可以和你說話？）
Can I speak with you *for a minute*?
（我可以跟你說一會兒話嗎？）
Can I speak with you *about something*?
（我可以和你談點事情嗎？）

3. *Can we have a word in private?*
word〔wɝd〕*n.* 談話
*have a word* 說一兩句話（= *have a few words*）
private〔'praɪvɪt〕*adj.* 私下的；私人的
*in private* 祕密地（= *secretly*）；私下地
　（= *not in the presence of other people*）

　　　private 的主要意思是「私下的」，是形容詞，
in private 是「介詞 + 形容詞」所形成的成語（有
些字典因為這個成語，而把 private 當成名詞）。
這句話的意思是「我們可不可以私下談一談？」也可
以說成：Can we have a word alone? 或 Can we
have a few words alone? 意思是「我們可不可以單
獨地談一談？」【alone〔ə'lon〕*adv.* 單獨地】

BOOK 9

這句話也可以說得更禮貌一點：

Do you think we can have a word in private?
（你覺得我們可不可以私下談一談？）
Is it OK if we have a word in private?
（我們私下談談可以嗎？）

4. *I'd like some feedback.*

feedback〔'fid,bæk〕*n.* 反應；反饋的意見

從字根上分析，可知道 feedback 的真正意思，
feed 的主要意思是「餵」或是「給」，feedback 的
字面意思是「給回去」，字典上的主要意思是「回
饋」。事實上，在日常生活中，feedback 常作「（反
應的）意見」解，在 *The American Heritage
Dictionary* 上的解釋是 the return of information
about the result of a process or activity。例如，
At the end of the meeting, the manager asked
for feedback.（在會議結束時，經理問大家的意見。）

*I'd like some feedback.* 的意思是「我想要
一些意見。」

【比較】

中文： 我想要一些意見。
英文： *I'd like some feedback.*【正，常用】
I'd like some opinions.
【正，限跟一群人說】
I'd like your opinions.【正】

下面是美國人常説的話：

> ***I'd like some feedback.***【第一常用】
> I want some feedback.【第二常用】
> （我想要一些意見。）
> I welcome your feedback.【第七常用】
> （我樂於接受你的意見。）
> 【welcome〔'wɛlkəm〕*v.* 樂於接受】
>
> I'd like some feedback from you.
> （我想要你的一些意見。）【第八常用】
> I'd like you to give me some feedback.
> （我想要你給我一些意見。）【第九常用】
> I hope you can give me some feedback.
> （我希望你能給我一些意見。）【第三常用】
>
> Please give me some feedback.
> （請給我一些意見。）【第四常用】
> I hope you can give me some feedback.
> （我希望你可以給我一些意見。）【第六常用】
> Can you give me some feedback?
> （你能給我一些意見嗎？）【第五常用】

5. ***How's my performance?***
performance〔pə'fɔrməns〕*n.* 表現；執行

　　這句話的意思是「我的表現如何？」也可以説成：How's my work performance? 或 How's my job performance? 意思都是「我的工作表現如何？」。

下面都是美國人常說的話：

> ***How's my performance?*** 【第一常用】
> How's my performance so far? 【第二常用】
> （到目前為止我表現得如何？）
> How's my performance lately? 【第三常用】
> （我最近表現得如何？）【lately〔'letlɪ〕 *adv.* 最近】

> How do you feel about my performance?
> （你覺得我的表現如何？）【第六常用】
> What do you think of my performance?
> （你認為我的表現如何？）【第五常用】
> What do you think of my work?
> （你覺得我的工作如何？）【第四常用】

> 【中國人常說 *How do you think of...* （誤），
> 　美國人聽了很難受。】

6. ***How am I doing so far?***

do〔du〕*v.* 表現　　***so far*** 到目前為止

這句話的意思是「到目前為止我的表現如何？」
do 在這裡作「表現」解，是不及物動詞。

下面都是美國人常說的話，我們按照使用頻率
排列：

① How am I doing?（我的表現如何？）【第一常用】
② ***How am I doing so far?*** 【第二常用】
③ How am I doing at my job?【第三常用】
　（我工作上的表現如何？）

④ Am I doing OK?（我表現得好嗎？）

⑤ Am I doing well?（我表現得好嗎？）

⑥ How do you think I'm doing?

（你認為我表現得如何？）

### 7. *I want to get better*.

　　這句話的意思是「我想要變得更好。」get 等於 become，但是美國人較少說 *I want to become better*. 句中的 get better 常用 improve（改進）取代。

I want to get better.

下面都是美國人常說的話：

*I want to get better*.【第一常用】

I want to be better.（我想要變得更好。）【第四常用】

I want to get better and better.【第五常用】

（我想要變得愈來愈好。）

I want to improve.（我想要改進。）【第二常用】

I want to improve myself.【第六常用】

（我想要改進我自己。）

I want to make progress.【第三常用】

（我想要有進步。）

【progress（'prɑgrɛs）*n.* 進步】

BOOK 9

*I want to get better.* 也可加長爲：

I really want to get better.

（我眞的想要變得更好。）

I really want to get better at this.

（我眞的想在這一方面變得更好。）

I really want to get better at doing this.

（我眞的想要更擅長做這個。）

【*be good at* 擅長】

8. *Please give me some input.*

input〔ˈɪnˌpʊt〕*n.* 輸入；訊息；評論

> input 的主要意思是「輸入」，在這裡作「觀點」( = *viewpoint* ) 或「批評；評論」( = *comment* ) 解。( 見 *The American Heritage Dictionary* p.95 )
>
> 這句話字面的意思是「請給我一些批評。」引申爲「請給我一些建議。」等於 Please give me some feedback. ( 請給我一些意見。) 或 Please give me some advice. ( 請給我一些建議。) input 在此可以指「任何的資訊」( = *any kind of information* )。

以下都是美國人常說的話：

*Please give me some input.*【第一常用】

Please give me some input if you can.【第八常用】

（如果可以的話，請你給我一些建議。）

Can you please give me some input?

（能不能請你給我一些建議？）【第七常用】

I'd welcome some input.【第三常用】

（我樂於接受一些建議。）

I'd appreciate some input.【第四常用】

（我會很感激你給我一些建議。）

I invite you to give me some input.

（我請你給我一些建議。）【第九常用】

appreciate〔əˈpriʃɪ‚et〕*v.* 感激

invite〔ɪnˈvaɪt〕*v.* 請求

I could use some input.【第五常用】

（我有點想要一些建議。）

I really need some input.【第六常用】

（我真的需要一些建議。）

I'd like some input.【第二常用】

（我想要一些建議。）

【*could use* 有點想要（詳見「一口氣英語①」p.5-5）】

9. *Please tell me what you think.*

　　這句話的意思是「請告訴我你的看法如何。」也

可以說成：Could you please tell me what you

think?（能不能請你告訴我你的看法是什麼？）或簡化

為：Tell me what you think.（告訴我你的看法。）

BOOK 9

【對話練習】

1. A: **Do you have a minute?**

   B: Sure, I have a minute.
   What's on your mind?
   What do you want to talk
   about?

   A: 你有一點時間嗎？

   B: 當然，我有一點時間。
   你在想什麼？
   你想要談什麼？

2. A: **Can I speak with you?**

   B: Now is not a good time.
   I'm busy at the moment.
   Can we talk in about half
   an hour?
   【*at the moment* 目前】

   A: 我可不可以和你說話？

   B: 現在不是個好時間。
   我目前很忙。
   我們可以半小時後再談
   嗎？

3. A: **Can we have a word in
   private?**

   B: Of course we can.
   Please come into my office.
   Please shut the door
   behind you.
   【shut〔ʃʌt〕v. 關閉】

   A: 我們能不能私下談一談？

   B: 當然可以。
   請進來我的辦公室。
   請隨後把門關上。

4. A: **I'd like some feedback.**

   B: So far, so good.
   You are really improving.
   You are getting better
   every day.

   A: 我想要一些意見。

   B: 到目前為止還好。
   你真的有在進步。
   你每天都變得愈來愈好。

5. A : **How's my performance?**

   B : I'm glad you asked.

   I want to compliment you.

   You are doing outstanding work.

   【compliment (ˈkɑmpləˌmɛnt ) *v.* 稱讚
   outstanding (ˈaʊtˈstændɪŋ ) *adj.* 傑出的】

A：我的表現如何？

B：我很高興你問我。

　　我想稱讚你。

　　你表現得很出色。

6. A : **How am I doing so far?**

   B : You are doing terrific.

   You're an excellent worker.

   Everyone is glad you're here.

   【terrific ( təˈrɪfɪk ) *adj.* 極好的】

A：我到目前為止表現得如何？

B：你表現得很棒。

　　你是個很優秀的員工。

　　大家都很高興你在這裡。

7. A : **I want to get better.**

   B : I know how you feel.

   We all feel the same way.

   We all want to improve.

A：我想要變得更好。

B：我知道你的感覺。

　　我們都有相同的感受。

　　我們都想進步。

8. A : **Please give me some input.**

   B : I did notice a few things.

   Try to relax a little more.

   Try not to be so nervous.

   【notice (ˈnotɪs ) *v.* 注意到
   nervous (ˈnɜvəs ) *adj.* 緊張的】

A：請給我一些建議。

B：我的確注意到一些事。

　　試著再放鬆一點。

　　試著不要太緊張。

9. A : **Please tell me what you think.**

   B : I'll be happy to.

   I'll give you my honest opinion.

   I'll tell you exactly what I think.

   【exactly ( ɪgˈzæktlɪ ) *adv.* 確切地】

A：請告訴我你的看法如何。

B：我很樂意。

　　我會誠實告訴你我的意見。

　　我會把我的想法確實告訴
　　你。

# *10.* *It's break time*.

| | |
|---|---|
| It's break time. | 休息時間到了。 |
| *How about* a drink? | 喝杯飲料如何？ |
| *How about* some coffee or tea? | 喝些咖啡或茶如何？ |
| | |
| *What's* new? | 你好嗎？ |
| *What's* the latest? | 有什麼最新消息？ |
| What have you been up to? | 你最近在忙些什麼？ |
| | |
| *How's your* family? | 你的家人好嗎？ |
| *How's your* workload? | 你的工作有多忙？ |
| Are you handling everything OK? | 你是不是每件事情都處理得很好？ |

**　*　

break〔brek〕*n.* 休息　　***break time*** 休息時間
drink〔drɪŋk〕*n.* 飲料；飲料的一份或一杯
latest〔'letɪst〕*adj.* 最新的　　***be up to*** 忙於
family〔'fæməlɪ〕*n.* 家人
workload〔'wɝk,lod〕*n.* 工作（量）；工作負擔
handle〔'hændl〕*v.* 處理　　OK〔'o'ke〕*adv.* 很好；不錯

## 【背景説明】

　　大部份的美國公司，在早上 10 點左右，都有 15 分鐘的休息時間，12 點到 1 點，是午餐時間，由於他們沒有午睡的習慣，有了 break time（休息時間），他們就不會太勞累。

1. *It's break time.*

   break〔brek〕*n.* 休息

   It's break time.

   > 這句話的意思是「休息時間到了。」break time（休息時間），是兩個字，不像一個字的 lunchtime（午餐時間）、dinnertime（晚餐時間）、summertime（夏季）。

　　目前在字典上，尚無法找到 *breaktime*（誤）這個字，將來說不定會有，因為在網路上已經出現 breaktime，但還是寫成 break time 較多。

下面都是美國人常說的話：

> ***It's break time.***【第一常用】
> It's our break time.【第二常用】
> （我們的休息時間到了。）
> It's time for our break.【第三常用】
> （我們的休息時間到了。）

BOOK 9

It's time to take a break. 【第七常用】

（休息時間到了。）

It's time for our morning break. 【第九常用】

（我們早上的休息時間到了。）

It's time for a break. （休息時間到了。）【第八常用】

Let's go on a break. （我們休息吧。）【第十一常用】

Let's take a break. 【第十常用】

（我們休息一下吧。）

Let's have a break. 【第十二常用】

（我們休息一下吧。）

Time for a break.

（休息時間到了。）【第四常用】

Time to take a break. 【第六常用】

（休息時間到了。）

Time for our break. 【第五常用】

（我們的休息時間到了。）

2. *How about a drink?*

drink〔drɪŋk〕*n.* 飲料；飲料的一杯或一份

這句話的意思是「喝杯飲料如何？」源自 *How do you feel about having a drink with me?*【文法對，美國人不說】美國人把 How about 多說成 How 'bout〔'haʊˌbaʊt〕。【'bout 是 about 的縮寫字】

下面都是美國人常說的話：

> ***How about a drink?*** 【第一常用】
> How about having a drink? 【第五常用】
> （喝杯飲料如何？）
> How about having a drink with me?
> （和我一起喝杯飲料如何？）【第六常用】
> 【have〔hæv〕*v.* 吃；喝】
>
> Would you like a drink? 【第二常用】
> （你想喝杯飲料嗎？）
> Would you like to join me for a drink?
> （你想和我一起喝杯飲料嗎？）【第三常用】
> How about joining me for a drink?
> （和我一起喝杯飲料如何？）【第四常用】

3. *How about some coffee or tea?*

這句話的意思是「喝些咖啡或茶如何？」美國人
也常說成：Would you like some coffee or tea?
（你要不要一些咖啡或茶？）或 Can I get you some
coffee or tea?（要不要我拿些咖啡或茶給你？）

對於熱的咖啡和茶，你只能說：How about
a *cup* of coffee?（來杯咖啡如何？）或 How about
a *cup* of tea?（來杯茶如何？）你不能說：… *a
glass of coffee?*（誤）或 … *a glass of tea?*（誤）

4. ***What's new?***

new〔nju〕*adj.* 新的；新鮮的

中國人見面常説：「你吃飽了沒有？」美國人
則説：What's new?（有什麼新鮮事？）或 What's
happening?（發生什麼事？）或 What's up?（發
生什麼事？）這類的話，都是打招呼
用語。

當美國人説：***What's new?*** 的
時候，並不一定眞正在問你「有什
麼新鮮事？」而是在跟你打招呼。

What's new?

【比較1】

***What's new?***【只是打招呼】

（有什麼新鮮事？；怎麼樣？；你好嗎？）

What's the news?

是眞正在問你「有什麼消息？」「有什麼新聞？」

【比較2】

A: ***What's new?***（有什麼新鮮事？；你好嗎？）

B: Nothing much.（沒什麼。）

【A 和 B 在互相打招呼，通常只是在問個人的情況】

A: What's the news?（有什麼消息嗎？）

B: The boss is going overseas.

（老板要出國了。）

【overseas〔͵ovə'siz〕*adv.* 到海外】

下面是美國人常説的話：

**What's new?**【第一常用】

What's new with you?（你好嗎？）【第二常用】

What's new with you lately?【第六常用】

（你最近好嗎？）【lately〔'letlɪ〕*adv.* 最近】

What's new with you recently?【第九常用】

（你最近好嗎？）

What's new with you these days?

（你最近好嗎？）【第十常用】【*these days* 最近】

What's new in your life?【第七常用】

（你生活過得好嗎？）

What's new? Anything?【第四常用】

（你好嗎？有什麼新鮮事？）

【Anything? 來自 Is there anything new?】

Anything new with you?（你好嗎？）【第五常用】

Anything new in your life?【第八常用】

（你生活過得好嗎？）

Anything new?（你好嗎？）【第三常用】

5. **What's the latest?**

latest〔'letɪst〕*adj.* 最新的

這句話是 What's the latest news? 的省略，
意思是「有什麼最新消息？」由於 the latest 後面
的名詞常省略，很多字典已經把 the latest 看成名
詞，表示「最新發展；最新消息；最新款式」。

BOOK 9

【比較】 ***What's the latest?***
（有什麼最新消息？）【較常用】
What's the news?（有什麼消息？）【常用】

下面都是美國人常說的話：

***What's the latest?***
What's the latest with you?
（你有什麼最新消息？）

What's the latest news?
（有什麼最新消息？）
What's the latest news with you?
（你有什麼最新消息？）

6. *What have you been up to?*

**be up to** 忙於（ = *be doing* ）

　　這句話的字面意思是「你最近在做什麼？」引申為「你最近在忙些什麼？」源自：What have you been up to lately?（常用）這句話的現在式是：What are you up to?（ = *What are you doing?* ）意思是「你現在在做什麼？；你現在在忙些什麼？」

7. *How's your family?*

family〔'fæməlɪ〕*n.* 家人

　　這句話的意思是「你的家人好嗎？」是美國人見到朋友常說的話。他們還常說：

How are your parents?（你的父母好嗎？）

How are your wife and kids?

（你的太太和小孩如何？）【kid〔kɪd〕*n.* 小孩】

How are your brothers and sisters?

（你的兄弟姊妹好嗎？）

下面都是美國人常説的話：

> *How's your family?*

***How's your family?***【第一常用】

How's your family doing?

（你的家人好嗎？）【第三常用】

How's everyone in your family?

（你家裡的每個人都好嗎？）【第五常用】

How's the family?（你的家人好嗎？）【第二常用】

How's the family doing?【第四常用】

（你的家人好嗎？）

How's the family these days?【第六常用】

（你的家人最近好嗎？）

Is your family well?（你的家人好嗎？）【第八常用】

Is everyone in your family doing well?【第九常用】

（你們家的每個人都好嗎？）

How's everything with your family?【第七常用】

（你的家人一切都好嗎？）

well〔wɛl〕*adj.* 健康的；安好的
***do well*** 情況好

BOOK 9

BOOK 9

8. *How's your workload?*

workload〔'wɝk,lod〕*n.* 工作（量）；工作負擔
（= *the amount of work assigned to sb.*）

　　　這句話字面的意思是「你的工作量如何？」引
申為「你的工作有多忙？」（= *How busy are you?*）
美國人也常說：How's your *workload* today?
（你今天的工作有多忙？）如果幾天沒見到同事，
你可以說：How has your *workload* been lately?
（你最近的工作有多忙？）這句話是 How's your
workload? 的完成式，加上 lately 而已。也有美國
人說：Do you have a heavy *workload*?（你的工
作多不多？）（= *Do you have a lot of work to do?*）
【heavy〔'hɛvɪ〕*adj.* 大量的】

9. *Are you handling everything OK?*

handle〔'hændl̩〕*v.* 處理（= *deal with*）；
負責（= *have responsibility for*）
OK〔'o'ke〕*adv.* 很好；不錯

　　　handle 的意思很多，主要是「處理」，這個單
字很好背，只要先背 hand（手），加上 le，就行
了。這句話的意思是「你是不是每件事情都處理得
很好？」美國人常簡化為：Handling everything
OK?（一切都處理得好嗎？）或 You handling
everything OK?（你一切都處理得好嗎？）【省略 Are】
OK 在此是副詞，常用 alright 或 all right 來代替。

## 【對話練習】

1. A：**It's break time.**
   B：That's great!
   That's what I like to hear!
   Break time is finally here!

1. A：休息時間到了。
   B：太棒了！
   那正是我想聽到的！
   休息時間終於到了！

2. A：**How about a drink?**
   B：No, thank you.
   I'm not very thirsty.
   I had a lot to drink earlier.

2. A：喝杯飲料如何？
   B：不用了，謝謝。
   我不是很渴。
   我之前喝了很多飲料了。

3. A：**How about some coffee or tea?**
   B：Sounds good to me!
   I could use a nice drink.
   A cup of tea would hit the spot.
   【*could use* 有點想要
   　*hit the spot* 切合需要】

3. A：喝些咖啡或茶如何？
   B：聽起來不錯！
   我有點想喝杯好喝的飲料。
   一杯茶正好符合我的需要。

4. A：**What's new?**
   B：Nothing much really.
   Nothing much is going on.
   I can't think of anything new.
   【*go on* 進行；發生】

4. A：有什麼新鮮事？
   B：其實沒什麼。
   沒什麼事發生。
   我想不到有什麼新鮮事。

5. A：**What's the latest?**
   B：John got engaged.
   Mary broke up with Ted.
   Our boss is going overseas.
   【engage〔ɪnˋgedʒ〕*v.* 使訂婚　　*break up with sb.* 和某人分手】

5. A：有什麼最新消息？
   B：約翰訂婚了。
   瑪麗和泰德分手了。
   我們的老板要出國了。

BOOK 9

6. A: **What have you been up to?**

   B: Not much, lately.
   Not a heck of a lot.
   Just doing the same old
   things. 【*a heck of a lot* 許多】

   A：你最近在忙些什麼？

   B：最近沒什麼。
   沒什麼事。
   只是做些同樣的事情。

7. A: **How's your family?**

   B: My parents are enjoying
   retirement.
   My siblings are doing great.
   Thanks for asking.
   【siblings (ˈsɪblɪŋz) *n. pl.* 兄弟姊妹】

   A：你的家人好嗎？

   B：我的父母很喜歡退休後的
   生活。
   我的兄弟姊妹都很好。
   謝謝你的關心。

8. A: **How's your workload?**

   B: Sometimes it's heavy.
   Sometimes it's light.
   My workload is always
   changing.
   【heavy (ˈhɛvɪ) *adj.* (工作) 繁重的；
   辛苦的    light ( laɪt ) *adj.* 輕鬆的】

   A：你的工作有多忙？

   B：有時候工作量大。
   有時候工作輕鬆。
   我的工作量一直在改變。

9. A: **Are you handling
   everything OK?**

   B: Oh, sure.
   It's tough, but I can manage.
   Everything will work out
   fine in the end.
   【tough ( tʌf ) *adj.* 困難的    manage (ˈmænɪdʒ ) *v.* 設法應付
   *work out* (順利) 進行】

   A：你是不是每件事情都處理
   得很好？

   B：哦，當然。
   是很困難，但我可以應付。
   每件事到最後都會沒問題
   的。

BOOK 9

# 11.  *How may I help you?*

| | |
|---|---|
| *How may I* help you? | 我可以怎樣幫助你？ |
| *How may I* direct your call? | 你要我幫你轉接給誰？ |
| What can I do for you? | 我能爲你做什麼？ |
| | |
| Please hold. | 請不要掛斷。 |
| *I'll* be right with you. | 我會立刻回來。 |
| *I'll* go check and see. | 我去看一看。 |
| | |
| *He* can't come to the phone. | 他無法來接電話。 |
| *He*'s tied up right now. | 他現在很忙。 |
| Please leave your name | 請留下你的姓名和電話 |
|   and number. | 號碼。 |

BOOK 9

\*\* ─────────────

direct〔dəˈrɛkt〕v. 指引；指導
*direct one's call* 轉接某人的電話
hold〔hold〕v. 握住；持續    right〔raɪt〕adv. 立刻
check〔tʃɛk〕v. 檢查；查看
*come to the phone* 來接電話    *be tied up* 很忙碌
*right now* 現在    leave〔liv〕v. 留下
number〔ˈnʌmbɚ〕n. 號碼；電話號碼

BOOK 9

## 【背景說明】

在辦公室接到電話，禮貌的說法，應該是先報自己的名字，像 Pat speaking.（我是派特。）或公司的名字，像 Learning Publishing Company.（學習出版公司。）如果都不想說，就說：Good morning.（早安。）或 Good afternoon.（午安。）等，最禮貌的說法是：

Thanks for calling.（謝謝你打電話來。）
Learning Publishing Company.
（這裡是學習出版公司。）
This is Pat speaking.（我是派特。）

1. *How may I help you?*

美國人常說：May I help you?（要我爲你效勞嗎？）電話裡面較常用 *How may I help you?* 意思是「我可以怎樣幫助你？」（= *In what way can I help you?*）

下面都是美國人常說的話：

*How may I help you?*【第一常用】
How can I help you?【第二常用】
（我可以怎樣幫助你？）
How can I assist you?【第六常用】
（我可以怎樣幫助你？）【assist〔ə'sɪst〕v. 幫助】

How can I be of service? 【第三常用】
（我可以怎樣爲你效勞？）
How may I serve you? 【第五常用】
（我可以怎樣爲你效勞？）
How may I be of service? 【第四常用】
（我可以怎樣爲你效勞？）
【*be of service* 效勞　　serve〔sɝv〕*v.* 爲（某人）效勞】

BOOK 9

2. *How may I direct your call?*
　direct〔dəˈrɛkt〕*v.* 指引；指導

　　direct 的名詞是 direction（方向），所以，
direct 的主要意思是「指引（到某個方向）」，像
Let me direct you on how to get there.（讓我
指引你如何去那裡。）

　　direct your call 的字面意思是「指引你的電話
（到某個方向）」，引申爲「轉接你的電話（給某人）」。
How may I direct your call? 的字面意思是「我可
以怎樣指引你的電話？」引申爲「你要我幫你轉接給
誰？」（= *Who can I connect you with?*）
　　美國人也常說：

Who would you like to talk to?
（你想找誰說話？）
Who would you like to speak with?
（你想找誰說話？）
What extension are you calling?（你打幾號分機？）
【extension〔ɪkˈstɛnʃən〕*n.* 分機】

3. *What can I do for you?*

這句話的意思是「我能爲你做什麼？」也可說成：
What can I do to help you?（我能幫你做什麼？）

4. *Please hold.*

hold〔hold〕v. 拿住；握住；持續

hold 是及物和不及物兩用動詞，這句話的字面
意思是「請抓住。」源自 Please hold the line.（請
抓住電話線。）引申爲「請不要掛斷。」美國人在電
話中說：Please hold. 或 Hold, please. 意思就是
「請等一下。」

這句話也常加強語氣說成：Please hold the line.
Don't hang up.（請等一等，不要掛斷。）或 Please
hold the line. I'll be right back.（請等一等。我馬
上回來。）

【比較】 下面兩句意思相同，都表示「請不要掛斷。」
　　　*Please hold.*【一般語氣，較常用】
　　　= Please hold on.【語氣稍強，常用】

下面是美國人常說的話：

　　　*Please hold.*【第一常用】
　　　Please hold the line.【第二常用】
　　　（請不要掛斷。）
　　　Please hold the line, OK?【第八常用】
　　　（請不要掛斷，好嗎？）

Hold the line. ( 不要掛斷。)【第十常用】

Hold the line, please. ( 請不要掛斷。)【第四常用】

Hold, please. ( 請不要掛斷。)【第三常用】

Please hold on. ( 請不要掛斷。)【第七常用】

Hold on, please. ( 請不要掛斷。)【第五常用】

Hold the wire. ( 請不要掛斷。)

【第十二常用，英式英語，美國人不用】

【wire〔waɪr〕*n.* 電話線 (= *telephone wire*)】

Don't hang up. ( 不要掛斷。)【第十一常用】

Please wait. ( 請稍等。)【第九常用】

Hang on, please. ( 請不要掛斷。)【第六常用】

【*hang up* 掛斷電話　　*hang on* 不掛斷 ( 電話 )】

5. *I'll be right with you.*

right〔raɪt〕*adv.* 立刻 (= *immediately* = *at once*)

句中的 right 是副詞，表示「立刻」，句意上和 right away 相同。例如，Do it right after lunch. ( 午餐後立刻做這件事。)

*I'll be right with you.* 字面的意思是「我將立刻和你在一起。」在這裡引申為「我會立刻回來。」 (= *I'll be right back.*)

I'll be with you. 和 *I'll be right with you.* 不同，例如，美國人常說：I'll be with you for one week. ( 我將和你在一起一個禮拜。) I'll be with you all weekend. ( 我將整個週末都和你在一起。)

下面是美國人常說的話：

> *I'll be right with you*. 【第二常用】
> I'll be right back. 【第一常用】
> （我會立刻回來。）
> I'll be back in a flash. 【第五常用】
> （我會立刻回來。）【*in a flash* 立刻】

> I'll be back right away. 【第四常用】
> （我會立刻回來。）
> I'll be with you in a minute. 【第三常用】
> （我會立刻回來。）
> I'll be with you in no time at all. 【第六常用】
> （我會立刻回來。）

> 【*right away* 立刻　*in a minute* 立刻　*in no time* 立刻】

6. *I'll go check and see*.

check〔tʃɛk〕*v.* 檢查（= *examine*）；查看（= *take a look*）

　　這句話的字面意思是「我去檢查看看。」引申為
「我去看一看。」也可說成：I'll check and see.
（我去看一看。）或 I'll go and see.（我去看一看。）

【比較】

> *I'll go check and see*. 【正，常用】
> *I'll go to check and see*. 【文法正確，但少用】
> *I'll go and check and see*.
> 【誤，文法正確，但美國人不用，因為兩個 and 太拗口】

下面是美國人常說的話：

I'll check and see.（我去看一看。）【第一常用】

***I'll go check and see.***【第二常用】

I'll go, check and see.（我去看一看。）【第三常用】

I'll go and see.（我去看一看。）【第五常用】

I'll go take a look.（我去看一看。）【第四常用】

I'll go and find out.（我去查清楚。）【第六常用】

【*take a look* 看一看　　*find out* 查明】

I'll check it out and see.（我去看一看。）【第七常用】

I'll check it out for you.【第八常用】

（我替你去看一看。）

I'll check and see if he's in.【第九常用】

（我去看看他在不在。）

【*check out* 查看　　in〔ɪn〕*adj.* 在裡面；在家】

## 7. *He can't come to the phone*

這句話字面的意思是「他沒辦法來到電話這裡。」
引申為「他沒辦法來接電話。」

「come to＋名詞」的類似用法有：

He can't come to the party.

（他沒辦法來參加舞會。）

He can't come to the dinner.（他沒辦法來吃晚餐。）

He can't come to the movies.

（他沒辦法來看電影。）

下面是美國人常説的話：

***He can't come to the phone***. 【第一常用】

He can't answer the phone right now. 【第六常用】

（他現在無法接電話。）

He can't talk on the phone

right now. 【第五常用】

（他現在沒辦法講電話。）

【***answer the phone*** 接電話】

He can't come
to the phone.

He can't take your call.

（他沒辦法接你的電話。）【第三常用】

He can't talk right now. 【第二常用】

（他現在沒辦法講電話。）

He's not free at the moment. 【第四常用】

（他現在沒空。）

***take*** *one's* ***call*** 接某人的電話　　free〔frɪ〕*adj.* 有空的
***at the moment*** 目前

He's unable to come to the phone.

（他無法來接電話。）

He's busy at the moment. 【第七常用】

（他現在在忙。）

He's unavailable at the moment. 【第八常用】

（他現在不在。）

***be unable to V.*** 無法
unavailable〔͵ʌnə'veləbḷ〕*adj.*（人）不在的

8. *He's tied up right now.*

tie〔 taɪ 〕*v.* 綁
**be tied up**　忙得無法分身；非常忙碌（ = *be very busy*）
**right now**　現在；立刻

　　這句話的字面意思是「他現在被綁起來了。」引
申爲「他現在很忙。」也可以有禮貌地說：I'm sorry.
He's tied up right now.（很抱歉，他現在很忙。）

下面都是美國人常說的話：

　　**He's tied up right now.**【第一常用】
　　He's tied up at the moment.【第二常用】
　　（他現在很忙。）
　　He's tied up at this time.【第五常用】
　　（他現在很忙。）【*at this time*　現在】

　　He's busy right now.（他現在很忙。）【第三常用】
　　He can't be disturbed.【第六常用】
　　（他現在不能被打擾。）
　　He's not free at the moment.【第四常用】
　　（他現在沒空。）
　　【disturb〔 dɪ'stɝb 〕*v.* 打擾】

BOOK 9

9. *Please leave your name and number.*

leave〔liv〕*v.* 留下

number〔'nʌmbɚ〕*n.* 號碼；電話號碼

　　這句話的意思是「請留下你的姓名和電話號碼。」這裡的 number 是指 telephone number（電話號碼）。

　　下面都是美國人常說的話：

Please leave a message.

（請留個話。）【第一常用】

Please leave a contact number.【第三常用】

（請留下連絡電話。）

Please leave a number where you can be reached.【第四常用】

（請留下你的連絡電話。）

【contact〔'kɑntækt〕*n.* 連絡　　reach〔ritʃ〕*v.* 連絡】

*Please leave your name and number.*

（請留下你的姓名及電話。）【第二常用】

Please leave your name, number and a message.【第五常用】

（請留下你的姓名、電話及留言。）

Please leave your contact information.

（請留下你的連絡資料。）【第六常用】

【information〔,ɪnfɚ'meʃən〕*n.* 資訊；資料】

美國典型的電話答錄機的錄音是：

We're sorry we're unable to come to the
phone right now. *Please leave your name,
number, and message after the beep.*

（很抱歉，我們現在沒辦法接電話。請在嗶聲後，
留下你的姓名、電話和留言。）

*be unable to V.* 無法～　*come to the phone* 來接電話
*right now* 現在　　message〔'mɛsɪdʒ〕*n.* 訊息；留言
beep〔bip〕*n.* 嗶嗶聲

　　在 1970 年代至 1990 年代，美國人的答錄機的
錄音本來是：We're sorry we're not at home
right now.　Please leave your name.... 後來美
國警察勸告民眾，不要留言說自己不在家，以免
小偷闖空門。

*We're sorry we're unable to come to the
phone right now. Please leave your name,
number, and message after the beep.*

BOOK 9

## 【對話練習】

1. A：**How may I help you?**　　　　　A：我可以怎樣幫助你？

　B：I'm a customer.　　　　　　　　　B：我是個顧客。
　　I'm calling with a complaint.　　　　我打電話來投訴。
　　I'd like to talk to a manager.　　　　我想要找經理。

　　【complaint ( kəm'plent ) *n.* 抱怨】

2. A：**How may I direct your call?**　　A：你要我幫你轉接給誰？

　B：Please connect me to Mr.　　　　　B：請幫我轉接給史密斯先
　　Smith.　Give me extension　　　　　　生。幫我轉分機 102。
　　one-oh-two.
　　Extension one-oh-two, please.　　　　請轉分機 102。

3. A：**What can I do for you?**　　　　A：我能為你做什麼？

　B：I'm calling for Mr. Smith.　　　　　B：我要找史密斯先生。
　　Can you please connect my call?　　　能不能請你幫我轉接？
　　Can you put him on the line?　　　　你能讓他接電話嗎？

　　【connect ( kə'nɛkt ) *v.* 接通】

4. A：**Please hold**.　　　　　　　　　A：請不要掛斷。

　B：All right.　　　　　　　　　　　　B：好的。
　　I'll hold the line.　　　　　　　　　我不會掛斷電話。
　　Please don't forget me.　　　　　　　請不要把我忘了。

5. A：**I'll be right with you**.　　　　　A：我會立刻回來。

　B：Take your time.　　　　　　　　　B：慢慢來。
　　I can wait.　　　　　　　　　　　　我可以等。
　　I'm not going anywhere.　　　　　　我哪裡都不去。

6. A：**I'll check and see.**

   B：I'd appreciate that.
   I'd like that.
   I really have to know.

   【appreciate〔əˈpriʃɪˌet〕*v.* 感激】

A：我去看一看。

B：我很感激。
我希望你那麼做。
我真的必須要知道。

7. A：**He can't come to the phone.**

   B：I'm sorry to hear that.
   I really need to talk to him.
   I have something very
   important to discuss.

A：他無法來接電話。

B：聽你那麼說我很遺憾。
我真的必須找他談話。
我有很重要的事要討論。

8. A：**He's tied up right now.**

   B：When is he available?
   When will he be free?
   When can I talk with him?

   【available〔əˈveləbl〕*adj.* 有空的】

A：他現在很忙。

B：他什麼時候有空？
他什麼時候有空？
我什麼時候可以和他說
話？

9. A：**Please leave your name
   and number.**

   B：I prefer to call back.
   I'd like to try again later.
   What's a good time to
   call?

   【*call back* 再打電話過來　good〔gud〕*adj.* 適合的】

A：請留下你的姓名和電話
號碼。

B：我比較想再打過來。
我想要待會再試試看。
什麼時候打來比較適
合？

# 12. *It's quitting time*.

| | |
|---|---|
| *It's* quitting time. | 下班時間到了。 |
| *It's* time to get off. | 下班時間到了。 |
| *It's* time to go home. | 該回家了。 |
| | |
| Oh, man! | 噢，啊！ |
| *I'm* really tired out. | 我真的累死了。 |
| *I'm* glad this day is over. | 我很高興今天的工作結束了。 |
| | |
| *We* did good. | 我們做得好。 |
| *We* earned our pay. | 我們的錢是辛苦賺來的。 |
| *We* worked our tails off today. | 我們今天很努力工作。 |

\*\* ────────────────────

quitting time〔ˈkwɪtɪŋˈtaɪm〕*n.* 下班時間
***get off*** 離開；下班　　oh〔o〕*interj.* 噢；喔；哎喲
man〔mæn〕*interj.* 啊；呀；喂
***be tired out*** 十分疲勞；筋疲力盡
glad〔glæd〕*adj.* 高興的　　over〔ˈovɚ〕*adv.* 完畢；結束
earn〔ɝn〕*v.* 賺（錢）；（經由努力而）獲得
pay〔pe〕*n.* 薪水；報酬　　tail〔tel〕*n.* 尾巴
***work*** *one's **tail off*** 非常努力工作（= *work very hard*）

## 【背景説明】

這一回的九句，是美國人下班的時候常説的話。

1. *It's quitting time.*
   quit〔kwɪt〕*v.* 停止；停止工作
   quitting time〔'kwɪtɪŋ'taɪm〕*n.* 下班時間

   quit 的主要意思是「停止」，也可以作「停止工作」解。quitting time 的字面意思是「停止工作的時間」，引申爲「下班時間」。*It's quitting time.* 的意思是「下班時間到了。」

   下面都是美國人常説的話：

   > *It's quitting time.*【第一常用】
   > It's time to quit.（下班時間到了。）【第三常用】
   > It's time to quit working.【第五常用】
   > （下班時間到了。）

   > Quitting time.（下班了。）【第二常用】
   > Time to quit.（下班時間到了。）【第四常用】
   > Time to quit working.【第六常用】
   > （下班時間到了。）

   【比較】*It's quitting time.*【常用，較正式】
   　　　　It's quittin' time.【常用，一般工人、
   　　　　年輕人喜歡説，輕鬆，較不正式】

**2. *It's time to get off.***

> ***get off*** 從…下來；下車；離開；下班

　　get off 有很多意思，字面意思是「離開」，在這裡是「下班」。美國人常說：What time do you get off？（你什麼時候下班？）***It's time to get off.*** 的意思是「下班時間到了。」

下面都是美國人常說的話：

> ***It's time to get off.*** 【第一常用】
> It's time to get off work. 【第二常用】
> （下班時間到了。）
>
> It's time to stop work. 【第五常用】
> （該停止工作了。）
> It's time to stop working. 【第六常用】
> （該停止工作了。）
>
> It's time to punch out.
> （該打卡下班了。）【第三常用】
> It's time to clock out. 【第四常用】
> （該打卡下班了。）

> ***punch out*** 打卡下班
> ***clock out*** 打卡下班

3. *It's time to go home.*

這句話字面的意思是「回家的時間到了。」也就是「該回家了。」

下面是美國人常說的話：

Time to go home.（該回家了。）【第二常用】
*It's time to go home.*（該回家了。）【第一常用】
It's time for us to go home.【第六常用】
（我們該回家了。）

Time to go.（該走了。）【第三常用】
Time to leave.（該離開了。）【第四常用】
Time to get out of here.【第五常用】
（該離開這裡了。）

最後三句，可改成 It's time to....。

4. *Oh, man!*

oh〔o〕*interj.* 噢；喔；啊；哎喲
man〔mæn〕*interj.* 啊；呀；喂；嗨；嘿

當你對一件事情表示「驚奇」、「恐懼」、「生氣」，或是「痛苦」，你就可以說 Oh!（噢！）或 Man!（啊！）或 *Oh, man!*（噢，啊！）。

這句話不要和 "Hey, man!"（嘿，老兄！）搞混。"Hey, man!" 是美國人常用的打招呼用語。
【hey〔he〕*interj.* 嘿】

BOOK 9

下面各句話意義相同：

【比較】 ***Oh, man!*** （噢，啊！）【第一常用】

Oh, boy! （噢，哇！）【第三常用】

Oh, God! （噢，天啊！）【第二常用】

Oh, my! （噢，天啊！）【第四常用】

Oh, my goodness! 【第五常用】

（噢，我的天啊！）

boy〔bɔɪ〕*interj.* 咦；哇
goodness〔'gʊdnɪs〕*interj.* 天啊（= *God* ）

除了 ***Oh, man!*** 以外，其他的感嘆詞，如 Wow!
（哇！）、God! （天啊！）、My God! （我的天啊！）、
Ooh! （噢！）等，詳見 p.706-707。

5. *I'm really tired out.*

***be tired out*** 十分疲勞；筋疲力盡（= *be worn out*）

這句話的意思是「我真的累死了。」美國人也常
說成：I'm really worn out. 這兩句話的意思和使用
頻率都相同。

【比較1】 ***I'm really tired out.***

（我真的累死了。）【語氣較強】

I'm really tired. （我真的很累。）【一般語氣】

【比較2】 I'm tired out. （我累死了。）【第二常用】

***I'm really tired out.*** 【第一常用】

（我真的累死了。）

I'm so tired out. （我非常累。）【第三常用】

上面三句的 tired out，都可說成 tired。

6. *I'm glad this day is over*.

glad〔glæd〕*adj.* 高興的　　over〔ˈovɚ〕*adv.* 完畢；結束

這句話的字面意思是「我很高興這一天結束了。」
引申為「我很高興今天的工作結束了。」

在字典上，over 是副詞，少數副詞沒有同義
的形容詞，就用副詞代替形容詞，做主詞補語，
例如：He is *out*.（他出去了。）Is anybody
*home*?（有人在家嗎？）Class is *over*.（下課了。）
句中的 out、home 和 over，都是副詞代替形容
詞。（詳見「文法寶典」p.228）

this day 和 today 意思相同。美國人常喜歡先
說 I'm glad、I'm happy 之類的話，例如：

> *I'm glad* today is over.
> （我很高興今天的工作結束了。）
> *I'm happy* today is over.
> （我很高興今天的工作結束了。）
> *I'm pleased* today is over.
> （我很高興今天的工作結束了。）
> 【pleased〔plizd〕*adj.* 高興的】

> *I'm grateful* today is over.
> （我真慶幸今天的工作結束了。）
> *I'm thankful* today is over.
> （我很高興今天的工作結束了。）
> grateful〔ˈgretfəl〕*adj.* 感激的；慶幸的
> thankful〔ˈθæŋkfəl〕*adj.* 感激的；高興的

BOOK 9

BOOK 9

### 7. *We did good*.

這句話的意思是「我們做得好。」

在文法上，*We did good*. 有兩種說法：

① did 是不完全不及物動詞，相當於 be 動詞，此時，good 是形容詞，做主詞補語。但是，和句意「我們做得好。」不太符合，因為在句意上，「做得好」的「好」，應該是副詞。

② did 是不及物動詞，good 是副詞，合乎句意，但缺點是 good 當副詞有點奇怪，因為一般都是形容詞。

所以，我們勉強把 do 當作 be 動詞看，凡是表示責備或稱讚的時候，do 後面都可以接形容詞做主詞補語，這種說法很多，詳見 p.39-40。

【比較1】 從下面三句話可知道，do 後面可接形容詞或副詞：

*We did **good***. 【正，第一常用】
　　　　形容詞

= We did ***well***. 【正，第二常用】
　　　　副詞

= We did ***fine***. 【正，第三常用，為了配合
　　　　形容詞

這句話，有些字典將 fine 當作副詞看】

有些字典上爲了配合 *We did good.* 硬是把 good 當成副詞來看。美國人常説這句話，但很多教英文的教授，卻不敢講，也不敢寫這句話，他們認爲，We did well. 才正確。

【比較2】 ***We did good.*** 【常用】
= We did a good job. 【常用】
= We did good work. 【常用】
【小心不可説成：...*a good work.* 因爲 work 是不可數名詞。】

8. ***We earned our pay.***

earn〔ɜn〕*v.* 賺（錢）；（經由努力而）獲得
pay〔pe〕*n.* 薪水；報酬

如果不背「一口氣英語」，你很難學會這句話。字面的意思是「我們賺到了我們的薪水。」引申爲「我們的錢是辛苦賺來的。」源自早期工廠是按小時或按日計酬，工人常説：We did good. ***We earned our pay.***（我們做得很好。我們辛苦賺到我們的薪水。）説這兩句話，是用來稱讚自己很努力。美國經理也常稱讚他的職員：You worked hard. ***You really earned your pay.***（你很努力。你的錢眞的是辛苦賺來的。）

You worked hard.
You really earned your pay.

美國軍官常對士兵說：You did a great job today. ***You earned your pay***. ( 你今天表現很好。 你的錢是辛苦賺來的。)

美國主管看到不認真的員工，會說：Work harder! ***Earn your pay!*** ( 工作努力一點！錢應該 是辛苦賺來的！)

現在，不管是藍領或白領階級，都常說 ***We earned our pay***. 這句話。

9. *We worked our tails off today*.
tail〔tel〕*n*. 尾巴
***work*** *one's* ***tail off*** 非常努力工作 ( = *work very hard* )

> 在所有的英漢字典上，都找不到 work *one's* tail off 這個成語，但美國人常說，在 NTC's Dictionary of American Slang 中，可以找到這 個成語。

> 這句話的字面意思是「我們今天工作太努力了， 把尾巴都磨掉了。」( *We worked so hard today that our tails fell off*. ) 引申為「我們今天很努力工作。」

【比較】 下面三句話美國人都常說：

***We worked our tails off today***. 【較文雅，幽默話】
We worked our butts off today. 【較粗魯】
We worked our asses off today.
【最粗魯，但美國人常用】
【butt〔bʌt〕*n*. 屁股　　ass〔æs〕*n*. 屁股】

BOOK 9

　　美國人下了班喜歡説：I worked my tail
off today.（我今天工作很努力。）注意此時 tail
是單數。

　　下面都是美國人常説的話，使用頻率非常
接近：

We really worked hard today.【第一常用】
（我們今天很努力工作。）
We worked like hell today.【第二常用】
（我們今天拼命地工作。）
We worked like crazy today.【第四常用】
（我們今天拼命地工作。）
【*like hell* 拼命地　　*like crazy* 拼命地】

We worked like dogs today.【第五常用】
（我們今天工作得很辛苦。）
***We worked our tails off today.***【第三常用】
（我們今天很努力工作。）
We worked our fingers to the bone today.
（我們今天拼命工作。）【第六常用】
*work like a dog* 拼命工作
*work one's **fingers to the bone*** 拼命工作；不停地工作

We worked our asses off today.【第七常用】
（我們今天很努力工作。）
We worked our butts off today.【第八常用】
（我們今天很努力工作。）

## 【對話練習】

1. A：**It's quitting time**.　　　　　　A：下班時間到了。
   B：Boy, that was fast!　　　　　　B：哇，時間過得眞快！
   　　Time really flies!　　　　　　　時間眞的過得很快！
   　　The afternoon flew right by!　　下午的時間一下子就過去了！
   　　【fly〔flaɪ〕*v.*（時間）飛也似地過去
   　　***fly by***　（時間）飛逝
   　　right〔raɪt〕*adv.* 一直地】

2. A：**It's time to get off**.　　　　　A：下班時間到了。
   B：You are right.　　　　　　　　B：你說的對。
   　　Time is up.　　　　　　　　　　時間到了。
   　　Time to get out of here.　　　　該走了。

3. A：**It's time to go home**　　　　A：該回家了。
   B：No, you are wrong!　　　　　　B：不，你錯了！
   　　We still have five minutes.　　　我們還有五分鐘。
   　　We have five more minutes　　　我們還剩五分鐘。
   　　to go.【***to go*** 剩下的】

4. A：**Oh, man!**　　　　　　　　　A：噢，啊！
   B：What's wrong?　　　　　　　　B：怎麼了？
   　　What's the matter?　　　　　　　怎麼了？
   　　Why did you say that?　　　　　你爲什麼那麼說？

5. A：**I'm really tired out**.　　　　A：我眞的累死了。
   B：You do look tired.　　　　　　B：你眞的看起來很累。
   　　Your eyes look so sleepy.　　　你的眼睛看起來很想睡。
   　　You need to get more rest.　　　你需要多休息。
   　　【sleepy〔'slipɪ〕*adj.* 想睡的】

BOOK 9

6. A : **I'm glad this day is over**     A：我很高興今天的工作結束了。

    B : It was a tough day.     B：今天眞是辛苦。

      I had a difficult time.     我今天很辛苦。

      I'm glad it's over, too.     我也很高興今天的工作

      【tough〔tʌf〕*adj.* 費力的     結束了。

        difficult〔'dɪfə‚kʌlt〕*adj.* 艱難的】

7. A : **We did good**.     A：我們做得好。

    B : I agree with you.     B：我同意你的說法。

      I'm proud of our effort.     我以我們的努力爲榮。

      Our team did great!     我們這個團隊做得很好！

8. A : **We earned our pay**.     A：我們的錢是辛苦賺來的。

    B : We certainly did!     B：當然是！

      We worked super hard!     我們工作超努力的！

      Our boss is lucky to have us!     老板有我們眞是幸運！

      【super〔'supə〕*adv.* 十分；非常】

9. A : **We worked our tails off**
       **today**.     A：我們今天很努力工作。

    B : We sure did.     B：的確是。

      We went above and beyond     我們所做的已超出工作的

      the call of duty.     需要。

      I sure hope somebody     我眞希望有人能注意到！

      appreciates it!

      【*go beyond one's duty* 超出某人的職責範圍

       *the call of duty* 工作的需要     appreciate〔ə'priʃɪ‚et〕*v.* 欣賞；知道】

BOOK 9

# 你會愈背愈快

　　有一位擔任駕駛工作的譚先生，來告訴我們說，「一口氣背會話」改變了他的一生，他說他一天複習 1,000 多句英語，沒有煩惱、不寂寞，每天都非常快樂。

　　有一次，譚先生發覺他的客人想去上廁所，就問了一句："Do you need to use the facilities?"（你需要上廁所嗎？）【「一口氣背會話③」第 11 課】這句話使這位美籍乘客非常震驚，他告訴譚先生的老闆說："Your driver's English impressed me very much."（我很佩服你司機的英文。）有些句子，美國人都認為外國人不會說，如果你說了，就會讓他們很佩服。「一口氣背會話」就充滿了很多這種句子。

　　「一口氣背會話⑨」是每天在辦公室所需要用到的英文，背熟後，你一進辦公室，看到同事，就可以說："Good morning. How was your night? Did you sleep well?" 一般的書，讀者只是看一看，很少人讀完，而「一口氣背會話」，卻要全部背得滾瓜爛熟。**當你一冊接一冊地背下去的時候，你會很有成就感**，你會發現，你的記憶力愈來愈好；你會愈背愈快。

　　「一口氣背會話」中的背景說明，徹底釐清了中外文化的差異，哪些句子美國人常說，哪些句子少說，哪些句子文法對，但美國人不說，都有明確的交代。當你背「一口氣背會話」，背到變成直覺後，再看看「背景說明」，是一種享受。也可以挑選其他你所需要的句子，加以變化。

劉毅

唸英文要像唸經一樣，每天大聲唸，從起床到睡覺，唸得比看得快，最後不看也會唸，養成習慣後，你會全身舒爽，你試試看，奇妙無比。

1. Good morning.
   How was your night?
   Did you sleep well?

   *How's your* schedule?
   *How's your* day today?
   Are you pretty busy?

   *I have a* lot to do.
   *I have a* full day.
   It's gonna be a long day.

2. I'm calling for Dale.
   My name is Chris.
   May I speak to him, please?

   *Is he* in?
   *Is he* available?
   Is now a good time?

   *Can* I leave a message?
   *Can* you take a message?
   Please tell him to call me back.

3. *We have* a meeting.
   *We have* to be there.
   We can't be late.

   *It's* starting soon.
   *It's* almost time.
   We have to hurry.

   *Let's* leave now.
   *Let's* go together.
   There is no time to lose.

4. *I'm* working overtime.
   *I'm* staying late.
   I have too much to do.

   *This* work is due.
   *This* has to be done.
   The deadline is coming up.

   *I*'m behind.
   *I* have to catch up.
   *I*'d like to get ahead.

5. *Let's* make an appointment.
   *Let's* set up a time.
   We need to get together.

   *When* can we meet?
   *When* is it convenient?
   I'll leave it up to you.

   *How* about tomorrow morning at nine?
   *How* does that sound?
   Do you have anything planned?

6. *I have* bad news.
   *I have* to cancel.
   I can't make it.

   Something has come up.
   *Can we* reschedule?
   *Can we* meet another time?

   *You* tell me.
   *You* pick the time.
   I'll work around your schedule.

7. *Any* messages for me?
   *Any* calls to return?
   What needs to be done?

   *Could you check* this over?
   *Could you check* for mistakes?
   Proofread this for me.

   *Please* type this up.
   *Please* print out a copy.
   I need to fax it right away.

8. *I* have a favor to ask.
   *I* need some time off.
   *I* have something important to do.

   *Can I take a* leave of absence?
   *Can I take a* day off ?
   Would this Friday be OK?

   Sorry for the trouble.
   *I* 'll work extra hours next week.
   *I* promise I'll make it up.

9. Do you have a minute?
   *Can* I speak with you?
   *Can* we have a word in private?

   I'd like some feedback.
   *How*'s my performance?
   *How* am I doing so far?

   I want to get better.
   *Please* give me some input.
   *Please* tell me what you think.

10. It's break time.
    *How about* a drink?
    *How about* some coffee or tea?

    *What's* new?
    *What's* the latest?
    What have you been up to?

    *How's your* family?
    *How's your* workload?
    Are you handling everything OK?

11. *How may I* help you?
    *How may I* direct your call?
    What can I do for you?

    Please hold.
    *I'll* be right with you.
    *I'll* go check and see.

    *He* can't come to the phone.
    *He*'s tied up right now.
    Please leave your name and number.

12. *It's* quitting-time.
    *It's* time to get off.
    *It's* time to go home.

    Oh, man!
    *I'm* really tired out.
    *I'm* glad this day is over.

    *We* did good.
    *We* earned our pay.
    *We* worked our tails off today.

# BOOK 10 接待外國賓客

▶10-1 當你想要打電話問你的客人何時到達、坐什麼飛機時，就可說：

> When are you arriving?
> What's the date and time?
> What's your airline and flight number?

▶10-2 當你到達機場，一看到來訪的外國人，你就說：

> Welcome!
> You made it!
> I'm glad you're here.

▶10-3 看到外國客人拿到行李，你就說：

> Let me help.
> Let me carry that.
> I insist.

▶10-4 在汽車裡面，繼續和外國客人說：

> First time here?
> Been here before?
> Have any questions?

▶10-5 聽不懂外國客人講的話時，你就可以說：

> I beg your pardon?
> I didn't catch that.
> What did you say?

▶10-6 當你要帶外國客人去玩，你如果有什麼計劃，就可以說這九句：

> Here's the schedule.
> Take a look.
> See if it's OK.

▶10-7 當你要請外國客人吃飯的時候，你就可以說：

How about a meal?
Let me invite you.
I know some good places.

▶10-8 在餐廳，要點菜的時候，就可以和外國客人說：

Order anything.
Choose what you like.
Don't worry about the price.

▶10-9 看到外國客人身體不舒服，你就可以說：

Are you all right?
Is anything the matter?
Is everything OK?

▶10-10 當你打算帶外國客人出去玩的時候，你就可以說：

What are you doing this weekend?
Have any plans?
Want to meet?

▶10-11 當你想要和外國客人約時間開車去接他時，你就可以說：

Let's start out early tomorrow.
I'll pick you up at seven-thirty.
I'll be there on time.

▶10-12 當你在機場替外國客人送行，要離別時，你就可以說：

I'm sorry you're leaving.
I enjoyed your visit.
I look forward to seeing you
again.

# *1.  When are you arriving?*

| | |
|---|---|
| When are you arriving? | 你什麼時候到達？ |
| **What's** the date and time? | 什麼日期和什麼時間？ |
| **What's** your airline and flight number? | 你搭什麼航空公司，班機號碼是幾號？ |

| | |
|---|---|
| What are your plans? | 你有什麼計劃？ |
| Do you have reservations? | 你有預訂飯店嗎？ |
| Shall I book a room for you? | 要不要我幫你預訂房間？ |

BOOK 10

| | |
|---|---|
| It's fall here. | 現在這裡是秋天。 |
| The weather is getting colder. | 天氣愈來愈冷了。 |
| Please pack some warm clothes. | 請帶一些保暖的衣服。 |

\*\*────────────

arrive〔əˋraɪv〕v. 到達   date〔det〕n. 日期
airline〔ˋɛr͵laɪn〕n. 航空公司   flight〔flaɪt〕n. 班機
number〔ˋnʌmbɚ〕n. 號碼
reservation〔͵rɛzɚˋveʃən〕n. 預訂
shall〔ʃəl〕aux. 要不要～；～好嗎   book〔bʊk〕v. 預訂
fall〔fɔl〕n. 秋天   weather〔ˋwɛðɚ〕n. 天氣
pack〔pæk〕v. 打包   warm〔wɔrm〕adj. 保暖的；暖和的
clothes〔kloz , kloðz〕n. pl. 衣服

## 【背景説明】

當遠方的朋友或客人要來了，最好事先打電話確認抵達時間和班機。此時下面九句話就可派上用場。

1. ***When are you arriving?***
   arrive〔ə'raɪv〕v. 到達

   這句話的意思是「你什麼時候到達？」

   > 來去動詞 arrive（到達）、go（去）、come（來）、leave（離開）、fly（搭飛機前往）等，可以用現在進行式表示「不久的未來」（詳見「文法寶典」p.341）。這句話當然也可以用未來式，説成：When will you arrive?（你將何時抵達？）

   下面是美國人常説的話，我們按照使用頻率排列：

   ① ***When are you arriving?***【第一常用】
   ② When will you arrive?【第二常用】
      （你將何時抵達？）
   ③ When will you be here?【第三常用】
      （你將何時到這裡？）

   ④ What's your arrival date?
      （你到達的日期是什麼時候？）
   ⑤ What date are you arriving?
      （你到達的日期是什麼時候？）
   ⑥ When are you coming?（你什麼時候來？）
   【arrival〔ə'raɪv̩〕adj. 到達的】

## 2. *What's the date and time?*

date〔det〕*n.* 日期

> 這句話的意思是「什麼日期和什麼時間？」很清楚地詢問日期和時間。源自：What's the date and time *of your flight*?（你的班機日期和時間為何？）為了避免重複，time 前面的 the 省略了。背這句話時要注意，大範圍的 date（日期）在前面，小範圍的 time（時間）在後面，就不會弄錯了。

下面都是美國人常說的話：

What's the date of your flight?【第三常用】
（你的班機日期是什麼時候？）
What's your flight time?【第四常用】
（你的班機時間是什麼時候？）
***What's the date and time?***【第一常用】

What date are you flying?【第五常用】
（你搭飛機的日期是什麼時候？）
On what date are you flying?【第六常用】
（你搭飛機的日期是什麼時候？）

What time are you flying?【第七常用】
（你何時搭飛機？）
【不可說 *On what time are*…，可說 At what time…?】
What's your arrival time?（你何時抵達？）【第八常用】
What's your flight information?【第二常用】
（你的飛航情報是什麼？）
【flight information（飛航情報）泛指什麼航空公司、哪個航班、什麼時間出發及抵達等相關資訊】

3. ***What's your airline and flight number?***

airline〔'ɛr,laɪn〕*n.* 航空公司　　flight〔flaɪt〕*n.* 班機

這句話的意思是「你搭什麼航空公司，班機號碼是幾號？」和上一句一樣，背的時候，大範圍的 airline（航空公司）在前面，小範圍的 flight number（班機號碼）在後面，就不會弄錯。

下面都是美國人常說的話，前三句的使用頻率非常接近：

What's your airline?【第二常用】
（你搭什麼航空公司？）
What's your flight number?【第三常用】
（你的班機號碼是幾號？）
***What's your airline and flight number?***【第一常用】

What's the number of your flight?【第七常用】
（你的班機號碼是幾號？）
What's the name of your airline
　and your flight number?【第八常用】
（你搭什麼航空公司，你的班機號碼是幾號？）

What airline are you flying?【第五常用】
（你搭什麼航空公司？）
What airline are you taking?【第四常用】
（你搭什麼航空公司？）
What airline are you coming on?【第六常用】
（你搭什麼航空公司？）
【fly〔flaɪ〕*v.* 搭乘（航空公司的）飛機　take〔tek〕*v.* 搭乘】

### 4. *What are your plans?*

這句話的意思是「你有什麼計劃？」

【比較】 plan 可用單複數，複數的 plans 強調説
話者認爲不只一個計劃。

> *What are your plans?*【較常用】
> （你有什麼計劃？）
> What is your plan?【常用】
> （你有什麼計劃？）

下面都是美國人常説的話，我們按照使用頻率
排列：

① *What are your plans?*【第一常用】

② What are your travel plans?【第二常用】
　（你有什麼旅行計劃？）

③ What do you want to do?【第三常用】
　（你想要做什麼？）【travel〔'trævl〕*n.* 旅行】

④ Have you made any plans?
　（你有做任何計劃嗎？）

⑤ Have you made any arrangements?
　（你有做任何安排嗎？）

⑥ What are your accommodation plans?
　（你有什麼住宿的計劃？）

arrangement〔ə'rendʒmənt〕*n.* 安排
accommodation〔ə,kɑmə'deʃən〕*n.* 住宿

BOOK 10

5. ***Do you have reservations?***

reservation〔͵rɛzəˈveʃən〕*n.* 預約；預訂

> 這句話在這裡的意思是「你有預訂飯店嗎？」
> 源自：Do you have any hotel reservations?
> （你有預訂任何飯店嗎？）美國人也常說：Do
> you have any reservations? 或 Have you made
> any reservations? 美國人常用 reservations 這個
> 複數形式，即使他所表示的意思是單數。這也許是
> 因爲預訂旅館房間的過程不只一次，如先預訂好，
> 還要再確認等，所以，下面兩句話意思相同。
>
> ***Do you have reservations?***【常用】
> = Do you have a reservation?【較常用】

6. ***Shall I book a room for you?***

shall〔ʃəl〕*aux.* 要不要～；～好嗎　book〔buk〕*v.* 預訂

> 　本句中，shall 用於一、三人稱，表示徵求對
> 方的意見，作「要不要～；～好嗎」解。Shall I…?
> = Do you want me to…? 或 Shall he…? = Do you
> want him to…? 這句話的意思是「要不要我幫你預
> 訂個房間？」

下面是美國人常說的話：

***Shall I book a room for you?***
【第一常用，較有禮貌】
Should I book a room for you?【第三常用】
（我該不該替你預訂個房間？）
Can I book a room for you?【第二常用】
（我可以替你預訂個房間嗎？）

7. ***It's fall here.***

fall〔fɔl〕*n.* 秋天 ( = autumn〔'ɔtəm〕)

這句話的意思是「現在這裡是秋天。」源自：
It's the fall season here. 因為秋天也是落葉的時
節 ( It's a time when the leaves *fall*.)，美國人
幽默，就喜歡用 fall，較少用 autumn。約有百
分之七十的美國人用 fall，百分之三十的人用
autumn，而英國人則習慣用 autumn。

讀者可依實際的季節，將句中的 fall 換成
spring ( 春天 )、summer ( 夏天 )，或 winter
( 冬天 )。

8. ***The weather is getting colder***

weather〔'wɛðə〕*n.* 天氣　　get〔gɛt〕*v.* 變得

這句話的意思是「天氣愈來愈冷了。」源自：
The weather here is getting colder. ( 這裡的天氣
愈來愈冷了。) The weather 可以用 It 來取代，變
成：It's getting colder. ( 天氣愈來愈冷了。) 也可
以加強語氣說成：It's getting colder here. ( 這裡
的天氣愈來愈冷了。)

【比較】　「be getting + 形容詞」表示「變得…；
愈來愈…」，後面的形容詞，可用比較級
或原級。

***The weather is getting colder.*** 【語氣稍強】
The weather is getting cold. 【一般語氣】

BOOK 10

讀者可以依季節，套用下面的句子：

春天

**The weather is getting warmer.**
（天氣愈來愈暖和了。）
It's getting warmer here.
（這裡的天氣愈來愈暖和了。）
The temperature is rising.
（溫度正在上升。）

temperature〔'tɛmprətʃɚ〕n. 溫度
rise〔raɪz〕v. 上升

夏天

**The weather is getting hotter.**
（天氣愈來愈熱了。）
It's getting hotter here.
（這裡的天氣愈來愈熱了。）
The temperature is high.（溫度很高。）

秋天

**The weather is getting colder.**
（天氣愈來愈冷了。）
It's getting colder here.
（這裡的天氣愈來愈冷了。）
The temperature is dropping.
（溫度正在下降中。）【drop〔drɑp〕v. 下降】

冬天

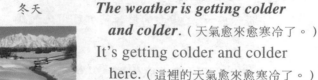

**The weather is getting colder
  and colder.**（天氣愈來愈寒冷了。）
It's getting colder and colder
  here.（這裡的天氣愈來愈寒冷了。）
The temperature is low.（溫度很低。）

9. ***Please pack some warm clothes.***

pack〔pæk〕v. 打包　　warm〔wɔrm〕adj. 保暖的；暖和的
clothes〔kloz , kloðz〕n. pl. 衣服

這句話字面的意思是「請打包一些保暖的衣服。」
引申為「請帶一些保暖的衣服。」( = *Please bring some*
*warm clothes.*) 也有美國人說：Please pack something
warm.（請帶一些保暖的衣服。）或 Don't forget to
bring warm clothes.（不要忘了帶保暖的衣服。）
讀者可依實際的季節，套用下列的句子：

【春夏】

***Please pack some light clothes.***

（請帶一些輕便的衣服。）

Dress light.（穿輕便的衣服。）

Bring shorts and T-shirts.

（帶短褲和 T 恤。）

light〔laɪt〕adj. 輕便的　 adv. 輕裝地
shorts〔ʃɔrts〕n. pl. 短褲　　T-shirt〔'ti,ʃɜt〕n. T 恤

【秋冬】

***Please pack some warm clothes.***

Dress warmly.（穿暖和一點。）

Bring heavy clothes.

（帶厚重的衣服。）

Be prepared for cold weather.

（要為寒冷的天氣做好準備。）

warmly〔'wɔrmlɪ〕adv. 暖和地　　heavy〔'hɛvɪ〕adj. 厚重的
prepared〔prɪ'pɛrd〕adj. 準備好的

## 【對話練習】

1. A：**When are you arriving?**　A：你什麼時候到達？

　 B：I'll be there next week.　B：我下禮拜到那裡。
　　 I'm arriving on Tuesday.　我會在星期二到。
　　 My arrival time is 5 p.m.　我抵達的時間是下午五點。

2. A：**What's the date and time?**　A：什麼日期和什麼時間？

　 B：I'll be arriving on the　B：我將在七號到。
　　 seventh.
　　 That's the 7th of May.　是五月七日。
　　 The time will be five p.m.　時間是下午五點。

3. A：**What's your airline and**　A：你搭什麼航空公司，班機
　　 **flight number?**　　號碼是幾號？

　 B：My airline is Northwest.　B：我搭的是西北航空。
　　 My flight number is 019.　班機號碼是 019。
　　 That's N-W-o-one-nine.　它是 NW019。
　　 【northwest〔͵nɔrθ'wɛst〕*n.* 西北
　　　 o-one-nine 要唸成〔'o'wʌn'naɪ〕】

4. A：**What are your plans?**　A：你有什麼計劃？

　 B：I'm not sure.　B：我不確定。
　　 I haven't decided yet.　我還沒決定。
　　 What do you suggest?　你有什麼建議？
　　 【suggest〔sə'dʒɛst〕*v.* 建議】

5. A : **Do you have reservations?**

   B : No, I don't.

   　　I haven't made any reservations.

   　　Can you help me out?

   　　【*help sb. out* 幫忙某人】

A : 你有預訂飯店嗎？

B : 不，我沒有。

　　我沒預訂任何飯店。

　　你可以幫我嗎？

6. A : **Shall I book a room for you?**

   B : Yes, please do.

   　　That would be wonderful.

   　　That would help me a lot.

A : 要不要我幫你訂個房間？

B : 好，麻煩你。

　　那真是太好了。

　　那幫了我很大的忙。

7. A : **It's fall here**.

   B : Yes, it's such a pretty time.

   　　The colors are fantastic.

   　　It's my favorite time of year.

   　　【fantastic〔fæn'tæstɪk〕*adj.* 很棒的】

A : 現在這裡是秋天。

B : 是啊，是很美的時刻。

　　四周的顏色很漂亮。

　　秋天是我一年當中最喜愛的季節。

8. A : **The weather is getting colder**.

   B : Thanks for telling me.

   　　I'll be prepared.

   　　I don't want to get sick!

A : 天氣愈來愈冷了。

B : 謝謝你告訴我。

　　我會做好準備。

　　我可不想生病！

9. A : **Please pack some warm clothes**.

   B : That's good advice.

   　　I will for sure.

   　　I'll bring a coat.

   　　【advice（建議）為不可數名詞。

   　　*for sure* 一定

   　　coat〔kot〕*n.* 外套；大衣】

A : 請帶一些保暖的衣服。

B : 那是很好的建議。

　　我一定會帶。

　　我會帶一件外套。

BOOK 10

# 2. *You made it!*

| | |
|---|---|
| Welcome! | 歡迎！ |
| You made it! | 你來了！ |
| I'm glad you're here. | 我很高興你來了。 |
| | |
| *I*'m pleased to meet you. | 很高興認識你。 |
| *I*'ve heard so much about you. | 我聽過很多關於你的事。 |
| It's an honor. | 很榮幸認識你。 |
| | |
| *How* was your flight? | 你這趟飛行如何？ |
| *How* are you feeling? | 你現在感覺如何？ |
| What shall we do first? | 你覺得我們應該先做什麼？ |

** ————————————————

welcome〔'wɛlkəm〕*interj.* 歡迎
***make it*** 成功；辦到；做到　　glad〔glæd〕*adj.* 高興的
pleased〔plizd〕*adj.* 高興的
meet〔mit〕*v.* 認識；和～見面　　honor〔'ɑnɚ〕*n.* 光榮的事
flight〔flaɪt〕*n.* 飛行；班機；搭機旅行　　feel〔fil〕*v.* 感覺

## 【背景説明】

到機場接機的時候，見到了客人，就立刻可説
這九句話來寒暄。

1. ***Welcome!***

welcome〔'wɛlkəm〕*interj.* 歡迎

這句話是 I welcome you! 的省略，意思是「歡
迎！」也可加長爲：I welcome you to my country!
（我歡迎你來我國！）或 I welcome you to our city!
（我歡迎你來我們這個城市！）如果不只一個人去接
機，你可説：We welcome you!（我們歡迎你！）

【比較1】

***Welcome!***（歡迎！）【正】

***You welcome!***【誤，Welcome! 不是命令句，
　　所以前面不可加 You。】

【比較2】　下面兩句話意思不同：

***Welcome!***（歡迎！）【見面時説】

You're welcome!（隨時歡迎你！）【再見時説】

這句話有兩個意思：①再見時説，相當於 You're
welcome anytime!（隨時歡迎你！）②當別人向
你道謝的時候，你説：You're welcome! 表示
「不客氣！」

BOOK 10

下面是美國人常說的話：

*Welcome!*（歡迎！）【第一常用】

I welcome you!（我歡迎你！）【第二常用】

Let me welcome you!（我歡迎你！）【第三常用】

You're welcome here!【第六常用】

（歡迎你來到這裡！）

Welcome to my country!【第五常用】

（歡迎你到我國來！）

Greetings and welcome!【第四常用】

（你好，歡迎！）

【greetings（'gritɪŋz）*n. pl.* 問候語，作「你好」解】

2. *You made it!*

   *make it* 成功；辦到；做到

> 這句話字面的意思是「你辦到了！；你成功了！」
> 在這裡引申為「你到了！」相當於 You're here!
> （你來了！）make it 的用法很多，在不同的句中，
> 有不同的意思。【參照 p.272 及 p.575】
>
> 也可加強語氣說成：You finally made it!（你
> 終於到了！）也可以幽默地說：You made it in one
> piece!（你平安到達！）
> 【*in one piece* 未受傷地；安然無恙地】

下面是美國人常說的話：

***You made it!***【第一常用】
I'm glad you made it!【第二常用】
（很高興你來了！）
I'm so glad you made it!【第三常用】
（我很高興你來了！）【so〔so〕*adv.* 非常】

Great! ***You made it!***【第五常用】
（太棒了！你來了！）
Hey! ***You made it!***（嘿！你來了！）【第四常用】
Wonderful! ***You made it!***【第六常用】
（太棒了！你來了！）
【hey〔he〕*interj.* 嘿】

Thank God you made it!【第十一常用】
（謝天謝地，你來了！）
Congratulations! ***You made it!***【第七常用】
（恭喜你！你來了！）
【congratulations〔kən͵grætʃəˈleʃənz〕*n. pl.* 恭喜】

You made it OK!（你平安抵達了！）【第八常用】
You made it safely!（你安全到達了！）【第九常用】
You made it safe and sound!【第十常用】
（你安然無恙地到達了！）

OK〔ˈoˈke〕*adv.* 沒問題地；順利地
safely〔ˈseflɪ〕*adv.* 安全地　　***safe and sound*** 安然無恙

3. ***I'm glad you're here.***

glad〔glæd〕*adj.* 高興的

　　　這句話的意思是「很高興你來了。」也可説成：
I'm glad that you're here. 也可簡化成：Glad
you are here. 也可以加強語氣説成：I'm so glad
you're here.（我很高興你來了。）

4. ***I'm pleased to meet you.***

pleased〔plizd〕*adj.* 高興的
meet〔mit〕*v.* 認識；和～見面

　　　這句話的意思是「我很高興認識你。」也可加
強語氣説成：I'm very pleased to meet you.
（我很高興認識你。）please（使高興）是情感動
詞，人做主詞時，用過去分詞，此時 pleased 已
經轉換成純粹的形容詞，所以可以用 very 來修飾
pleased。在文法上，very 修飾現在分詞，much
修飾過去分詞，由此可知，pleased 在這裡不是過
去分詞，已經變成純粹的形容詞，所以才可以用
very 修飾。

　　　meet 這個字可作「認識」或「和～見面」解。
當和新認識的人初次見面時，通常説：I'm pleased
to meet you.（我很高興認識你。）**再次見面時，就
可説：*I'm pleased to meet you again*.**（我很高興
再次見到你。）此時 meet 當作「和～見面」解。

BOOK 10

　　下面是美國人常說的話，第一句和第二句使用
頻率非常接近：

***I'm pleased to meet you.***【第一常用】
Pleased to meet you.【第二常用】
（很高興認識你。）
I'm very pleased to meet you.【第三常用】
（我很高興認識你。）

I'm very pleased to meet you today.
（我很高興今天能認識你。）【第六常用】
I'm pleased at this chance to meet you.
（我很高興有這個機會認識你。）【第七常用】
I'm pleased to have this opportunity
　　to meet you.【第八常用】
（我很高興有這個機會認識你。）
【opportunity〔͵ɑpɚˋtjunətɪ〕*n.* 機會】

I'm delighted to meet you.【第四常用】
（我很高興認識你。）【delighted〔dɪˋlaɪtɪd〕*adj.* 高興的】
I'm happy to meet you.【第五常用】
（我很高興認識你。）
I'm pleased to make your acquaintance.
（我很高興認識你。）【第九常用】
這句話適用於正式場合，現在美國人較少用，較老一輩
的人才說。
acquaintance〔əˋkwentəns〕*n.* 認識；認識的人
***make one's acquaintance*** 認識某人

BOOK 10

5. *I've heard so much about you.*

　　這句話字面的意思是「我聽過很多關於你的事。」相當於中文的「久仰，久仰。」

　　下面都是美國人常說的話，我們按照使用頻率排列：

① *I've heard so much about you.*【第一常用】

② I've heard a lot about you.【第二常用】
　　（我聽過很多關於你的事。）

③ I've heard many good things about you.
　　（我聽過很多關於你的好話。）【第三常用】

④ I've heard people say so much about you.
　　（我聽過人們說好多關於你的事。）

⑤ People have told me so much about you.
　　（人們告訴我好多關於你的事。）

⑥ You have quite a reputation.
　　（你的名聲相當好。）
　　*quite a*　出眾的；了不起的；非凡的
　　reputation〔ˌrɛpjəˈteʃən〕*n.* 名聲

⑦ Your reputation precedes you.
　　（你的聲名遠播。）

⑧ I've heard so many people praise you.
　　（我聽過很多人稱讚你。）

⑨ You have such a good reputation.
　　（你的名聲很好。）
　　【precede〔prɪˈsid〕*v.* 在…之前　　praise〔prez〕*v.* 稱讚】

6. ***It's an honor.***

honor〔ˈɑnɚ〕*n.* 光榮的事

　　　　這句話的字面意思是「這是件光榮的事。」引申爲「眞榮幸。」源自 It's an honor to meet you. ( 很榮幸認識你。)

下面都是美國人常說的話：

***It's an honor.***【第一常用】
It's a great honor. ( 非常榮幸認識你。)【第四常用】
It's a real honor.【第三常用】
( 眞的很榮幸認識你。)
【real〔ˈriəl〕*adj.* 眞正的】

It's an honor to meet you.【第五常用】
( 很榮幸認識你。)
It's an honor for me to meet you.【第七常用】
( 我很榮幸認識你。)
It's an honor to me to meet you.【第八常用】
( 我很榮幸認識你。)
【用 to me 或 for me 均可】

I'm honored. ( 我很榮幸。)【第二常用】
I'm honored to meet you.【第六常用】
( 我很榮幸認識你。)
I'm honored to be able to meet you.
( 我很榮幸能夠認識你。)【第九常用】
【honored〔ˈɑnɚd〕*adj.* 感到光榮的　　***be able to V.*** 能夠~】

BOOK 10

### 7. *How was your flight?*

flight〔flaɪt〕*n.* 飛行；班機；搭機旅行

　　flight 是 fly 的名詞，在這裡作「搭機旅行」（= *plane trip*）解，也就是整個搭機的過程。這句話的意思是「你這趟飛行如何？」也有美國人說成：How was the flight?（這趟飛行怎樣？）

　　下面都是美國人常說的話，我們按照使用頻率排列：

① *How was your flight?*【第一常用】

② How was your trip?【第二常用】
　　（你旅途還順利嗎？）

③ Did you have a smooth flight?【第三常用】
　　（你這趟飛行還順利嗎？）
　　【smooth〔smuð〕*adj.* 平穩的；順利的】

④ Did you have a good flight?
　　（你這趟飛行還順利嗎？）

⑤ Did you have a good trip?
　　（你的旅途還順利嗎？）

⑥ Did everything go OK?
　　（一切都還順利嗎？）【go〔go〕*v.* 進展】

⑦ Was the flight OK?（這趟飛行還順利嗎？）

⑧ Any problems with your flight?
　　（你這趟飛行有任何問題嗎？）

⑨ Any problems on the flight?
　　（這趟飛行有任何問題嗎？）

BOOK 10

8. ***How are you feeling?***

feel〔fil〕*v.* 感覺

> 　　這句話任何時候，和任何人都可說。當你和朋
> 友沒話說的時候，爲避免尷尬，你就可以說：***How
> are you feeling?*** 來打破僵局，意思是「你現在感
> 覺如何？」在這裡源自 How are you feeling after
> your trip? ( 旅行之後你覺得怎樣？ ) 也有美國人常
> 說成：Are you feeling OK? ( 你覺得還好嗎？ )
> 或 Do you feel OK? ( 你覺得還好吧？ )

【比較】下面兩句話意思相同，使用頻率也相同：

> ***How are you feeling?***【現在進行式，語氣稍強】
> How do you feel?【現在式，一般語氣】
> ( 你覺得如何？ )

BOOK 10

9. ***What shall we do first?***

　　shall 用於第一、三人稱，表徵求對方的意見。
這句話的意思是「你覺得我們應該先做什麼？」
( = *What do you think we should do first?* )

【比較】下面兩句話意思相同：

> ***What shall we do first?***【較禮貌，正式】
> What should we do first?【通俗，較常用】

下面都是美國人常說的話，我們依照使用頻率
排列：

① ***What shall we do first?*** 【第一常用】

② What should we do first? 【第二常用】
（我們應該先做什麼呢？）

③ What would you like to do first? 【第三常用】
（你想先做什麼？）

④ What's the first thing you want to do?
（你想先做的事是什麼？）

⑤ What do you feel like doing first?
（你想先做什麼？）

⑥ What do you want to do first?
（你想先做什麼？）

【*feel like V-ing* 想要～】

What shall we do first?

## 【對話練習】

1. A: **Welcome!**
   B: Thank you.
      It's great to be here.
      It's so nice to see you.

   A：歡迎！
   B：謝謝。
      很高興來到這裡。
      能見到你真好。

2. A: **You made it!**
   B: Yes, I did.
      Thanks for being here.
      Thanks for meeting me.
      【meet〔mit〕v. 迎接】

   A：你來了！
   B：是啊，我來了。
      謝謝你來。
      謝謝你來接我。

3. A: **I'm glad you're here.**
   B: Me too.
      I almost didn't come.
      Now I'm happy that I did.

   A：我很高興你來了。
   B：我也是。
      我差點不能來。
      現在我很高興我來了。

4. A: **I'm pleased to meet you**.
   B: I feel the same way.
      I'm pleased to meet you, too.
      It's a real pleasure.
      【*the same way* 同樣地
         pleasure〔'plɛʒɚ〕n. 高興的事】

   A：我很高興認識你。
   B：我也一樣。
      我也很高興認識你。
      真的很高興。

5. A: **I've heard so much about you**.
   B: I hope it's all good.
      I've heard a lot about your
      company, too.
      You have an excellent
      reputation.
      【excellent〔'ɛksḷənt〕adj. 極好的】

   A：我聽過很多關於你的事。
   B：我希望都是好話。
      我也聽過很多關於你們
      公司的事。
      你們的名聲很好。

BOOK 10

BOOK 10

6. A：**It's an honor**.

   B：You flatter me.
      The honor is all mine.
      I feel honored to meet
      you.【flatter〔'flætɚ〕*v.* 奉承】

A：很榮幸認識你。

B：你太抬舉我了。
     這是我的榮幸。
     我很榮幸認識你。

7. A：**How was your flight?**

   B：It was pretty good.
      It was mostly OK.
      We did have a little bit
      of turbulence, though.

      【mostly〔'mostlɪ〕*adv.* 大多
        turbulence〔'tɝbjələns〕*n.* 亂流
        though〔ðo〕*adv.* 可是；不過】

A：你這趟飛行如何？

B：這趟飛行非常好。
     大致上還算順利。
     不過我們的確遇到了一點
     亂流。

8. A：**How are you feeling?**

   B：I'm a little tired.
      I'm a bit hungry.
      But I'm excited to be
      here.【*a bit* 稍微；有點】

A：你現在感覺如何？

B：我有點累。
     我有點餓。
     但是來到這裡我很興奮。

9. A：**What shall we do first?**

   B：That's a good question.
      I'll let you decide.
      What do you think we
      should do?

A：你覺得我們應該先做什麼？

B：那是個好問題。
     我讓你決定。
     你認為我們應該做什麼？

# *3.  Shall we go now?*

| | |
|---|---|
| Shall we go now? | 我們現在可以走了嗎？ |
| I have a car outside. | 我的車在外面。 |
| Please follow me. | 請跟我走。 |
| | |
| *Let me* help. | 讓我幫你。 |
| *Let me* carry that. | 讓我來拿。 |
| I insist. | 我堅持。 |
| | |
| Here's the car. | 車子在這裡。 |
| Bags go in the trunk. | 行李要放在後車廂。 |
| Hop in. | 上車。 |

**BOOK 10**

\*\* ————————————————————

shall〔ʃəl〕*aux.* 要不要～；～好嗎
outside〔ˈaʊtˈsaɪd〕*adv.* 在外面　　follow〔ˈfɑlo〕*v.* 跟隨
carry〔ˈkærɪ〕*v.* 攜帶；拿；提　　insist〔ɪnˈsɪst〕*v.* 堅持
bag〔bæg〕*n.* 手提袋；行李　　*go in* 被放入
trunk〔trʌŋk〕*n.*（汽車）行李箱；後車廂
hop〔hɑp〕*v.* 跳　　*hop in* 上車

## 【背景説明】

在機場見到客人，就可禮貌地詢問對方，是否已準備要離開，順便幫忙拿行李。練熟了這九句話，相信客人會對你的體貼有禮，留下深刻的印象。

1. ***Shall we go now?***

shall 〔ʃəl〕 *aux.* 要不要～；～好嗎

> shall 用於一、三人稱，表示徵求對方的意見（詳見 p.1136）。***Shall we go now?*** 的意思是「我們現在可以走嗎？」也可以加長説成：Shall we go to my car now?（我們現在可以去坐我的車嗎？）或縮短爲：Shall we go?（我們可以走了嗎？）

下面是美國人常説的話，我們按照使用頻率排列：

① Shall we go?（我們可以走了嗎？）【第一常用】

② ***Shall we go now?***【第二常用】

③ Do you want to go now?【第三常用】
（你想現在走嗎？）

④ Are you ready to go?（你準備好要走了嗎？）

⑤ Are you all set to go?（你準備好要走了嗎？）
【***all set*** 準備好的（= *ready*）】

⑥ Are you all set? ( 你準備好了嗎? )

⑦ Are you ready? ( 你準備好了嗎? )

第六、第七句暗示「你準備好要走了嗎?」也可以簡
化成 All set? ( 準備好了嗎? ) 或 Ready? ( 準備好了
嗎? ) 說的時候,尾音要向上揚。

2. *I have a car outside.*

outside〔'aʊt'saɪd〕 *adv.* 在外面

　　這句話的意思是「我有一輛車在外面。」引申
爲「我的車在外面。」源自: I have a car parked
outside. ( 我有一輛車停在外面。 )

【park〔pɑrk〕 *v.* 停 ( 車 )】

　　下面是美國人常說的話,我們按照使用頻率
排列:

① *I have a car outside.*【第一常用】

② I have a car waiting outside.【第二常用】
　 ( 我的車在外面等。 )

③ I've got a car outside.【第三常用】
　 ( 我有一輛車在外面。 )【*have got* 有】

④ My car is outside. ( 我的車在外面。 )

⑤ My car is right outside.
　 ( 我的車就在外面。 )

⑥ My car is parked outside.
　 ( 我的車停在外面。 )

【right〔raɪt〕 *adv.* 就在 ( =*just* )】

### 3. *Please follow me.*

follow〔'falo〕*v.* 跟隨

　　　這句話字面的意思是「請跟我走。」中文和英文一樣，「跟」並不一定是要你緊跟在我後面，而是含有「和我一起走。」( = *Come with me.* ) 或「我帶你去。」( = *I'll take you there.* ) 的意思。

　　　*Please follow me.* 也可說成：Just follow me. ( 就跟著我走吧。) 或 I want you to follow me. ( 我希望你跟我走。) 或 Follow me, OK? ( 跟著我走，好嗎？)

### 4. *Let me help.*

　　　這句話的意思是「讓我幫你。」可加長為：Let me help you. ( 讓我幫你忙。) 或 Let me help you with that. ( 讓我幫你拿那個。) 講這句話的時候，手要伸出去幫忙拿行李。也有美國人說：Let me help you with your bags. ( 讓我幫你拿行李。)

> *Let me help.*

【bag 在此是指「行李」，參照 p.365-366】

5. ***Let me carry that.***

carry〔'kærɪ〕*v.* 攜帶；提；拿

　　這句話字面的意思是「讓我來拿那樣東西。」也就是「讓我來拿。」。

【比較】下面三句話意思相同，使用頻率也相同：

> ***Let me carry that.***
> = Let me take that.（讓我來拿。）
> = Let me get that.（讓我來拿。）
> 【上面三句話的 that，可改成 it】

　　***Let me carry that.*** 也可說成：Let me carry your bag.（讓我幫你拿行李。）或 Let me carry that bag.（讓我來拿那個行李。）

6. ***I insist.***

insist〔ɪn'sɪst〕*v.* 堅持

　　這句話的意思是「我堅持。」源自：I insist on doing it.（我堅持做這件事。）或 I insist on helping you.（我堅持幫助你。）

> ***I insist.*** 這句話很好用，可以用在句子後面，加強語氣。例如：
>
> You go first. ***I insist.***（你先走。我堅持。）
> Let me pay. ***I insist.***（讓我付錢。我堅持。）
> Let me drive you home. ***I insist.***
> （讓我開車載你回家。我堅持。）
> 【pay〔pe〕*v.* 付錢　***drive sb.*** 開車載某人】

BOOK 10

7. **Here's the car.**

　　這句話的意思是「車子在這裡。」也可說成：
The car is here. 或加強語氣說成：The car is
right here.（車子就在這裡。）

【比較】 下面三句話意思相同，使用頻率也接近：

**Here's the car.**【較禮貌，因為未強調「我的」】
Here's my car.（我的車在這裡。）【一般語氣】
Here's our car.（我們的車在這裡。）【較禮貌】

8. **Bags go in the trunk.**
bag〔bæg〕n. 手提袋；行李
**go in** 被放入【見「東華英漢大辭典」p.1361】
trunk〔trʌŋk〕n.（汽車）行李箱；後車廂

　　這句話太棒了！你不背，就永遠學不會，因為
它是慣用句，字面的意思是「行李被放入後車廂。」
也就是「行李要放在後車廂。」( = *The bags go in the
trunk.* )由於使用太多，而把定冠詞 The 省略，整句
話變成慣用句。

【比較1】 **Bags go in the trunk.**【較常用】
　　　　　The bags go in the trunk.【常用】

【比較2】 **Bags go in the trunk.**【慣用句，省略 The】
　　　　　*Bags should go in the trunk.*
　　　　　【誤，這句話又不是慣用句，The 怎麼能省略呢？】
　　　　　The bags should go in the trunk.【正】
　　　　　（行李該放在後車廂。）【有建議的意思】

也有美國人說 Bags go in the back.（行李放在後面。）有兩個意思，可能是：「行李放在後座（the back seat）。」或「行李放在後車廂（the trunk）。」

「被放入」是 go in，「被放在上面」是 go on，「被放在後面」是 go behind。下面各句中的 The 都不可省略，因為都不是慣用句：

The food *goes in* the fridge.

（食物要放在冰箱裡。）【fridge〔frɪdʒ〕*n.* 冰箱】

The books *go on* that shelf.

（書要放在那個書架上。）【shelf〔ʃɛlf〕*n.* 書架】

The shoes *go behind* the door.

（鞋子要放在門後。）

下面都是美國人常說的話：

*Bags go in the trunk.*【第一常用】

Bags go in the back.【第三常用，是慣用句】

（行李放在後面。）

The bags go in the trunk.【第二常用】

（行李要放在後車廂。）

【back 可能指「後座」或「後車廂」】

Let's put the bags in the trunk.【第六常用】

（我們把行李放在後車廂吧。）

Put the bags in the trunk.【第四常用】

（把行李放在後車廂。）

Put the bags in the back.【第五常用】

（把行李放在後面。）

9. ***Hop in.***

hop〔hɑp〕v. 跳　　***hop in*** 上車

　　***Hop in.*** 的字面意思是「跳進來。」引申為「上車。」意思及用法和 Get in. 相同。(詳見 p.639-640)***Hop in.*** 和 Jump in. 並沒有「趕快上車」的意思。

【比較】

***Hop in.***【幽默用語】
Jump in.【幽默用語】
(上車。)
Get in. (上車。)【一般語氣】

　　叫別人坐到前面，就說：Hop in the front with me. (和我一起坐在前面。) 叫別人坐到後面，就說：Hop in the back. (坐到後面。) 這都是年輕人喜歡說的話。【front〔frʌnt〕n. 前面】

　　對於年長者，較禮貌的說法是：Please get in the front. (請坐在前面。) 或 Please get in the back. (請坐在後面。)

　　當朋友開車載你一個人的時候，你應該坐在前面，千萬不要坐在後座，把朋友當作司機。如果載兩個以上的人時，美國人的習慣是，年紀大的優先 (Age comes first.)；第二順位是女性優先 (Ladies come before gentlemen.)；第三順位是和駕駛人關係密切的優先。例如：朋友開車載一對夫婦，看哪個是他的朋友，哪個就坐前面。

雖然在字典上，hop 的意思是「跳」，中文的
「跳進來。」和英文的 Hop in. 看起來，都有「趕
快上車」的意思，但事實上，現代美語把 Hop in.
只作「上車。」解，並不強調趕快上車。如果你要
叫別人趕快上車，你可以說：

We're pressed for time. *Hop in*.
（我們趕時間。趕快上車。）

*Hop in*. Let's get out of here.
（趕快上車。我們離開這裡吧。）

【*be pressed for time* 趕時間】

*Hop in*.【說這句話語氣須急促，才表示「趕快上車。」】
Quickly, *hop in!*（趕快上車！）
【美國人不說 *Hop in quickly.*（誤）】
Hurry up! *Hop in*.（趕快上車！）

*Hop in*. We're in a hurry.（趕快上車。我們趕時間。）
It's getting late. *Hop in*.（時間很晚了。趕快上車。）
We have to go. *Hop in*.
（我們得走了。趕快上車。）

*Hop in*. 表示上小型車，如小轎車（car）、計
程車（taxi）。如果要上公車（bus）、船（boat）、
飛機（plane）等，就要用 Hop on.。

Here's the bus. *Hop on*.（公車來了。上車吧。）
Please *hop on* the next plane and fly here.
（請搭下一班飛機，飛來這裡。）

## 【對話練習】

1. A：**Shall we go now?**　　　　　　A：我們現在可以走了嗎？
   B：Sounds good to me.　　　　　B：聽起來不錯。
   　　I'm ready.　　　　　　　　　　我準備好了。
   　　Let's go.【sound〔saʊnd〕v. 聽起來】　　我們走吧。

2. A：**I have a car outside.**　　　　　A：我的車在外面。
   B：Wonderful!　　　　　　　　　B：太棒了！
   　　That's convenient.　　　　　　　真方便。
   　　You're very thoughtful.　　　　你真體貼。
   　　【thoughtful〔'θɔtfəl〕adj. 體貼的】

3. A：**Please follow me.**　　　　　　A：請跟我走。
   B：All right.　　　　　　　　　　B：好的。
   　　Lead the way.　　　　　　　　　帶路吧。
   　　I'll follow you.　　　　　　　　我會跟著你。
   　　【lead〔lid〕v. 帶（路）】

4. A：**Let me help.**　　　　　　　　A：讓我幫你。
   B：Thanks.　　　　　　　　　　　B：謝謝。
   　　I appreciate it.　　　　　　　　我很感激。
   　　You're so kind.　　　　　　　你人真好。
   　　【appreciate〔ə'priʃɪ,et〕v. 感激】

5. A：**Let me carry that.**　　　　　　A：讓我來拿。
   B：Thanks, but that's not necessary.　B：謝謝，但是不需要。
   　　It isn't very heavy.　　　　　　不會很重。
   　　I think I can manage it on my　　我想我可以自己處理。
   　　own.

6. A：**I insist**.

   B：OK.

   I won't argue.

   How can I refuse?

   【argue〔'argjʊ〕 *v.* 爭論

   refuse〔rɪ'fjuz〕 *v.* 拒絕】

A：我堅持。

B：好吧。

我不跟你爭。

我怎麼能拒絕呢？

7. A：**Here's the car**.

   B：Nice car.

   It looks good.

   I like it a lot.【*a lot* 非常】

A：車子在這裡。

B：好車。

它看起來不錯。

我很喜歡。

8. A：**Bags go in the trunk**.

   B：Of course.

   That's right.

   I almost forgot.

A：行李要放在後車廂。

B：當然。

你說得沒錯。

我差點忘了。

9. A：**Hop in**.

   B：OK.

   I'm with you.

   Let's hit the road.

   【*be with sb.* 贊成某人

   *hit the road* 上路】

A：上車。

B：好的。

我贊成。

我們上路吧。

BOOK 10

# 4. First time here?

| | |
|---|---|
| First time here? | 第一次來這裡嗎？ |
| Been here before? | 以前來過這裡嗎？ |
| Have any questions? | 有任何問題嗎？ |
| | |
| *Are you* tired at all? | 你累不累啊？ |
| *Are you* hungry or thirsty? | 你餓不餓、渴不渴？ |
| If you need anything, let me know. | 如果你需要什麼東西，要讓我知道。 |
| | |
| How do you like this weather? | 你覺得這個天氣怎麼樣？ |
| *Is it* different? | 有沒有什麼不同？ |
| *Is it* like this back home? | 這裡的天氣和你家鄉的相同嗎？ |

**

here〔hɪr〕*adv.* 到這裡　　been〔bɪn, bin〕*v.* 曾到過
tired〔taɪrd〕*adj.* 疲倦的　　*at all* 絲毫；一點
hungry〔'hʌŋgrɪ〕*adj.* 飢餓的　　thirsty〔'θɝstɪ〕*adj.* 口渴的
let〔lɛt〕*v.* 讓　　weather〔'wɛðɚ〕*n.* 天氣
different〔'dɪfrənt〕*adj.* 不同的
*back home* 在你的家鄉；在你住的地方

## 【背景説明】

　　對於初次見面的朋友，提出一些無關緊要的問題，可避免冷場。這九句話都是美國人常説的。

1. ***First time here?***

here〔hɪr〕*adv.* 到這裡

　　這句話是個省略句，意思是「第一次來這裡嗎？」源自：Is it your ***first time here***?（你第一次來這裡嗎？）或 Is this your ***first time here***?（這是你第一次來這裡嗎？）美國人也常説成：Are you here for the first time?（你第一次來這裡嗎？）【*for the first time*（生平）第一次】比較正式的説法是：Is this your first time to visit here?（這是你第一次來這裡嗎？）

BOOK 10

2. ***Been here before?***

been〔bɪn, bin〕*v.* 曾去過

　　這句話是個省略句，意思是：「以前來過這裡嗎？」源自：Have you ***been here before***?（你以前來過這裡嗎？）也有美國人説成：Have you ever ***been here before***?（你以前曾經來過這裡嗎？）【*have ever been* 曾經去過】

【比較】***Been here?***【誤，句意不完全】
***Been here before?***【正】
Have you ever been here?【正】
（你曾經來過這裡嗎？）
【沒有 before，但有 ever（曾經），句意完全】

### 3. *Have any questions?*

這句話的意思是「有任何問題嗎？」源自：Do
you *have any questions*？（你有任何問題嗎？）這
句話也可簡化成：Any questions?（有任何問題
嗎？）any 後面可接單數或複數名詞，但美國人大多
用複數，像 Any problems?（有問題嗎？）Any
difficulties?（有困難嗎？）如果是不可數名詞，就
只能用單數，如：Any information?（有什麼消息
嗎？）或 Do you have any money?（你有錢嗎？）
【information〔͵ɪnfɚˋmeʃən〕*n.* 消息；情報；資料】

### 4. *Are you tired at all?*

tired〔taɪrd〕*adj.* 疲倦的　　*at all* 絲毫；一點；究竟；到底

這句話在這裡的意思是「你累不累啊？」一般
人不懂 at all 的用法，以爲 at all 只用在 not at all
（一點也不），事實上，at all 在 A Dictionary of
American Idioms（p.14）中説得很清楚，*at all*
在疑問句中，表有各種程度，從小到大，等於 in
any degree，可能指「一點」（a little；a bit）或
是「很多」（a lot），説話者沒有明確表示「很多」
或是「一點」。簡單地説，*at all* 用在疑問句中，有
加強語氣的作用。

*Are you tired at all?* 有下列的涵義：

① Are you really tired?（你是不是眞的很累？）
② Are you very tired?（你是不是非常累？）
③ Are you feeling tired?（你是不是覺得累？）

④　Are you a little tired?（你是不是有點累？）

⑤　Are you tired in any way?

（你有沒有任何方面的疲勞？）

【in any way = in any form，指身體方面，

或精神方面，或情緒方面等】

【比較】 下面兩句話意思接近：

> Are you tired?（你累不累？）【一般語氣】
>
> *Are you tired at all?*【禮貌、親切，語氣稍強】
>
> （你累不累啊？）
>
> 【用 at all，表示即使有一點累，也要告訴我。】

*at all* 可以用在很多句中，以加強語氣，例如：

Are you hungry *at all*?（你餓不餓啊？）

Are you thirsty *at all*?（你口渴嗎？）

Are you busy *at all*?（你忙嗎？）

Are you free *at all*?（你有空嗎？）

Are you nervous *at all*?（你緊張嗎？）

Are you worried *at all*?（你擔心嗎？）

free〔frɪ〕*adj.* 有空的　　nervous〔ˈnɜvəs〕*adj.* 緊張的
worried〔ˈwɜɪd〕*adj.* 擔心的

## 5. *Are you hungry or thirsty?*

hungry〔ˈhʌŋgrɪ〕*adj.* 飢餓的　　thirsty〔ˈθɜstɪ〕*adj.* 口渴的

這句話的意思是「你餓不餓、渴不渴？」也可加

強語氣說成：Are you hungry or thirsty *at all*?

（你有沒有一點餓，或一點渴？）也有美國人說成：

Do you feel hungry or thirsty?（你覺得餓或渴嗎？）

6. **If you need anything, let me know.**
   let〔lɛt〕v. 讓

   　　這句話的意思是「如果你需要什麼東西，要讓我
   知道。」可加強語氣說成：If you need anything,
   just let me know.（如果你需要什麼東西，就要讓我
   知道。）【just〔dʒʌst〕adv. 直接地；就】

   　　也有美國人常說成：Whatever you need, let
   me know.（無論你需要什麼，要讓我知道。）let me
   know 也可以翻譯成「告訴我；通知我」。

7. **How do you like this weather?**
   weather〔'wɛðɚ〕n. 天氣

   　　這句話的意思是「你覺得這個天氣怎麼樣？」
   美國人很喜歡用 How do you like~? 來詢問他
   人的意見，像：How do you like this idea?
   （你覺得這個主意如何？）

   【比較】

   > A：*Do you like this weather?*
   > 　　（你喜歡這個天氣嗎？）
   > B：Yes, I do.（是的，我喜歡。）

   > A：*How do you like this weather?*
   > 　　（你覺得這個天氣怎麼樣？）
   > B：I think it's great.  I like it a lot.
   > 　　（我覺得很好。我很喜歡。）

   　　關於 How do you like this weather? 的同義
   句子，請參照 p.769。

8. *Is it different?*

different〔ˈdɪfrənt〕*adj.* 不同的

這句話的意思是「有沒有什麼不同？」it 在這裡
是指「天氣」。可加長，變成長的句子，來加強語氣。

> *Is it different?*
> Is it different *here*?
> （這裡的天氣有沒有什麼不同？）
> Is it different *here from where you live*?
> （這裡的天氣和你住的地方有沒有什麼不同？）

9. *Is it like this back home?*

back home 在這裡的意思是「在老家；在你
的家鄉」( back in your hometown ) 或「在你住
的地方」( back where you live )。

這句話在這裡的意思是「這裡的天氣像不像
你住的地方？」it 在此指「天氣」，所以也可説
成：Is the weather like this back home?

用敘述句分析這句話較清楚。

It is *like this* <u>back</u> home.
　　　　　　　　副詞　　副詞

like this 是介詞片語，當形容詞用，做主詞補
語。副詞可以修飾動詞、形容詞和副詞本身，在此
副詞 back 修飾地方副詞 home。

　　　back 可以當名詞、形容詞和副詞，當副詞時，表示「在原處；回原處」或「從前」。

例如：　go <u>back</u>（回去）【back 當副詞，作「回原處」解】

<u>Back</u> in my hometown, everyone knows each other.

（在我的家鄉，大家彼此都認識。）

【back 作「在原處」解】

<u>Back</u> in high school, I was very shy.
　副詞　　　　副詞片語

（從前我在高中時，很害羞。）

【back 作「從前」解。　shy〔ʃaɪ〕*adj.* 害羞的】

Back when I was a child, I had no worries at all.

（從前我小時候，一點煩惱都沒有。）

back 作「從前」解。　worry〔'wɝɪ〕*n.* 煩惱
I had no worries at all. = I didn't have a single worry. 句中的 at all 修飾 no，作「絲毫；一點」解。

Back in the good old days, prices were very low.

（在從前好日子的時候，什麼都很便宜。）

【back 作「從前」解。　*good old days* 往日美好的時光】

## 【對話練習】

1. A：**First time here?**

   B：Yes, it is.

   You guessed right.

   How did you know?

   【guess〔gɛs〕*v.* 猜】

   A：第一次來這裡嗎？

   B：是的，是第一次。

   你猜對了。

   你怎麼知道的？

2. A：**Been here before?**

   B：Nope.

   Never.

   This is my first time.

   【nope〔nop〕*adv.* 不；不是（= *no*）】

   A：以前來過這裡嗎？

   B：沒有。

   從來沒有。

   這是我第一次來。

3. A：**Have any questions?**

   B：Yes, I do.

   Thanks for asking.

   I have a lot.

   A：有任何問題嗎？

   B：是的，我有問題。

   謝謝你問我。

   我有好多問題。

4. A：**Are you tired at all?**

   B：Yes, I am.

   I'm a little sleepy.

   It's been a long day.

   sleepy〔'slipɪ〕*adj.* 想睡的

   It's been a long day. 詳見 p.120

   A：你累不累啊？

   B：是的，我累了。

   我有點想睡。

   真是漫長的一天。

BOOK 10

5. A : **Are you hungry or thirsty?**

B : No, not at all.
I'm fine for now.
I'll let you know if I am.
【*not at all* 一點也不　*for now* 目前】

A：你餓不餓、渴不渴？

B：不，一點也不。
我目前還好。
如果我餓或渴的話，
我會讓你知道。

6. A : **If you need anything, let me know**.

B : I sure will.
That's a kind offer.
I appreciate it.
【offer ('ɔfɚ) *n.* 提議
appreciate ( ə'priʃɪ‚et ) *v.* 感激】

A：如果你需要什麼東
西，要讓我知道。

B：我當然會。
那真是體貼的提議。
我很感激。

7. A : **How do you like this weather?**

B : It's very nice.
I like it a lot.
I feel very comfortable.

A：你覺得這個天氣怎麼樣？

B：天氣很好。
我非常喜歡。
我覺得很舒服。

8. A : **Is it different?**

B : Yes, it's a little different.
The temperature here is higher.
It's warmer here.
【temperature ('tɛmprətʃɚ ) *n.* 氣溫】

A：有沒有什麼不同？

B：是的，有點不同。
這裡的氣溫比較高。
這裡的天氣比較暖和。

9. A : **Is it like this back home?**

B : Yes, but it's much colder.
Home is further to the north.
There's already snow on the
ground. 【further ('fɝðɚ ) *adv.* 更遠】

A：這裡的天氣和你家鄉的
相同嗎？

B：是的，不過冷多了。
我的故鄉在更北方。。
地上已經積雪了。

# *5.  I beg your pardon?*

| | |
|---|---|
| *I* beg your pardon? | 對不起，請再說一遍好嗎？ |
| *I* didn't catch that. | 我沒聽懂。 |
| What did you say? | 你說什麼？ |
| | |
| *Could you* repeat that? | 你能不能再說一遍？ |
| *Could you* speak up? | 你可以說大聲一點嗎？ |
| Please speak slowly. | 請說慢一點。 |
| | |
| I don't get it. | 我聽不懂你說的話。 |
| What do you mean? | 你的意思是什麼？ |
| Please explain it to me. | 請解釋給我聽。 |

BOOK 10

\*\*─────────────

beg〔bɛg〕*v.* 請求    pardon〔'pɑrdn̩〕*n.* 原諒
catch〔kætʃ〕*v.* 聽懂    repeat〔rɪ'pit〕*v.* 重複；重說
*speak up* 大聲說    get〔gɛt〕*v.* 了解；聽懂
mean〔min〕*v.* 意思是
explain〔ɪk'splen〕*v.* 解釋；說明

## 【背景説明】

當你聽不懂外國人説的話時，就可運用這九句話中的一兩句。背會這一課，每次聽不懂別人説的話，就可以交替使用。

**BOOK 10**

1. ***I beg your pardon?***

   beg〔bεg〕*v.* 請求　　pardon〔ˋpɑrdn̩〕*n.* 原諒

   I beg your pardon. 的意思是「我請求你原諒。」( = *Please forgive me.* ) 在這裡，***I beg your pardon?*** 有問號，音調往上升，是「請你再說一遍好嗎？」

   下面三句話，美國人也常説，使用頻率接近，尾音要向上揚，都含有「對不起」的意思，我們中國人聽不懂，也會説：「對不起，請再説一遍。」

   Pardon? ( 對不起，請再說一遍好嗎？ )
   Pardon me? ( 對不起，請再說一遍好嗎？ )
   Excuse me? ( 對不起，請再說一遍好嗎？ )

2. ***I didn't catch that.***

   catch〔kætʃ〕*v.* 抓住；聽懂

   這句話字面的意思是「我沒抓住那個東西。」在這裡引申爲「我沒聽懂。」説這句話，有一點幽默的意味，因爲 catch 的主要意思是「抓住」。

下面都是美國人常說的話，我們按照使用頻率排列：

① ***I didn't catch that.*** 【第一常用】
② I didn't catch your meaning.
（我沒聽懂你的意思。）【第二常用】
③ I didn't catch what you said. 【第三常用】
（我沒聽懂你說的話。）

④ I didn't understand what you said.
（我聽不懂你說的話。）
⑤ I don't understand you.
（我聽不懂你說的話。）
⑥ I don't understand what you just said.
（我聽不懂你剛剛說的話。）
【just〔dʒʌst〕*adv.* 剛剛】

⑦ I didn't get what you said.
（我不了解你說的話。）【get〔gɛt〕*v.* 了解】
⑧ I couldn't understand what you said.
（我不能了解你說的話。）
⑨ I didn't hear what you said.
（我沒聽到你說的話。）

3. ***What did you say?***

這句話的意思是「你說什麼？」源自 What did
you just say?（你剛剛說什麼？）也可以加強語氣
說成：What did you just say to me?（你剛剛跟
我說什麼？）

BOOK 10

4. ***Could you repeat that?***

repeat〔rɪ'pit〕*v.* 重複;重說

這句話的意思是「你能不能再說一遍?」
(=*Could you say that again?*) 也有美國人
說成:Please repeat that.(請再說一遍。)或
Please say that again.(請再說一遍。)對熟的
朋友說:Say that again.(再說一遍。)

【比較】 ***Could you repeat that?***【禮貌】
　　　　 Can you repeat that?【一般語氣,常用】

5. ***Could you speak up?***【參照「教師一口氣英語」p.3~4】

***speak up*** ①大聲說　②大膽說

這句話的意思是「你可以說大聲一點嗎?」

下面是美國人常說的話,我們按照使用頻率排列:

① ***Could you speak up?***【第一常用】
② Could you please speak up?
　　(可以請你說大聲一點嗎?)【第二常用】
③ Louder please.(請大聲一點。)【第三常用】
　　【louder〔'laʊdɚ〕*adv.* 較大聲地】

④ Please say it louder.(請說大聲一點。)
⑤ Please speak a little louder.
　　(請說稍微大聲一點。)
⑥ Please talk louder.(請說大聲一點。)

**6. *Please speak slowly*.**

　　這句話的意思是「請說慢一點。」以下是美國人
常說的話，我們按照使用頻率排列：

① ***Please speak slowly*.** 【第一常用】

② Slowly please. (請慢一點。)【第二常用】

③ Speak slowly, please. (請說慢一點。)【第三常用】

④ Please talk slowly. (請說慢一點。)

⑤ Please say it slowly. (請說慢一點。)

⑥ Please speak a little more slowly.

　　(請稍微說慢一點。)

**7. *I don't get it*.**

get〔gɛt〕*v.* 得到；了解；聽懂

　　這句話的字面意思是「我沒有得到它。」在這
裡的意思是「我聽不懂你說的話。」it 在此是指「你
說的話」( what you said )。***I don't get it*.** 是慣用
句，要用現在式，等於 I don't understand. 或 I
don't understand you. (我聽不懂你說的話。)

【比較】

中文：我聽不懂你說的話。

英文：***I don't get it*.** 【正，是慣用句】

　　　***I didn't get it*.** 【誤，慣用句不能改變】

　　　I didn't get that. 【正】

　　　I didn't get what you said. 【正】

8. **What do you mean?**

mean〔min〕v. 意思是

　　在中文裡，如果説「你是什麼意思？」可能有不
滿的語氣，英文是 What are you talking about?
或 What's the meaning of this?

　　但是，**What do you mean?** 則完全沒有這個意
思，應翻成「你的意思是什麼？」也可以加強語氣説
成：What do you mean by that?（你那樣說是什麼
意思？）也有美國人説成：What's your meaning?
（你的意思是什麼？）或 Tell me what you mean.
（告訴我你的意思是什麼。）**What do you mean?**
明明是問過去的事，但爲什麼用現在式呢？因爲它是
慣用句，反倒不能用過去式。

【比較】 **What do you mean?**【正，是慣用句】
　　　　 *What did you mean?*【誤，慣用句不能改變】
　　　　 What did you mean by that?【正】
　　　　（你那麼說是什麼意思？）

9. **Please explain it to me.**

explain〔ɪk'splen〕v. 解釋；說明

　　這句話的意思是「請解釋給我聽。」explain *sth.*
to *sb.* 是「向某人解釋某事」。

【比較1】 explain 不是授與動詞，後面不可直接接
人做受詞：

***Please explain it to me.*** 【正】

*Please explain me it.* 【誤】

【這是中國人的思想，美國人不說。】

【比較2】 當 explain 後的受詞太長時，需要倒裝。

Please explain to me what you're talking
about. 【正】　　　名詞子句做 explain
的受詞

*Please explain what you're talking about
to me.* 【誤，to me 太遠，沒辦法修飾 explain】

Please explain what you're talking about. 【正】

BOOK 10

下面都是美國人常說的話：

Please explain it. (請解釋一下。)【第三常用】

***Please explain it to me.*** 【第一常用】

Please explain it to me in detail. 【第二常用】

(請詳細解釋給我聽。)

【detail (´ditel) *n.* 細節　***in detail*** 詳細地】

Please explain to me what you're talking about.

(請把你在談論的解釋給我聽。)【第六常用】

Please explain what you mean. 【第五常用】

(請解釋你的意思是什麼。)

Please explain what it means. 【第四常用】

(請解釋它是什麼意思。)

## 【對話練習】

1. A：**I beg your pardon?**　　　　A：對不起，請再說一遍好嗎？

   B：What's the matter?　　　　　B：怎麼了？
   
   Don't you understand?　　　　你不了解嗎？
   
   Want me to say it again?　　　要我再說一遍嗎？

2. A：**I didn't catch that.**　　　　A：我沒聽懂。

   B：Which part?　　　　　　　　B：哪個部分？
   
   I'll say it again.　　　　　　我再說一遍。
   
   Listen carefully.　　　　　　聽仔細了。

3. A：**What did you say?**　　　　A：你說什麼？

   B：I was talking about the　　　B：我剛剛在談論天氣。
   weather.
   
   I asked you a question.　　　我問你一個問題。
   
   How do you like this　　　　你覺得這個天氣如何？
   weather?

4. A：**Could you repeat that?**　　A：你能不能再說一遍？

   B：Sure can.　　　　　　　　　B：當然可以。
   
   No problem at all.　　　　　一點問題也沒有。
   
   I'd be happy to.　　　　　　我很樂意。
   
   【 Sure can. = I sure can. 】

5. A : **Could you speak up?**

B : Of course I can.

My voice is too low.

Sorry about that.

【voice〔vɔɪs〕*n.* 聲音

low〔lo〕*adj.* 低的；小的】

A：你可以說大聲一點嗎？

B：當然可以。

我的聲音太小了。

很抱歉。

6. A : **Please speak slowly**.

B : OK, I understand.

I'll slow down.

I'll speak slowly for you.

【*slow down* 減慢；變慢；放慢】

A：請說慢一點。

B：好的，我了解。

我會放慢速度。

我會為你說慢一點。

7. A : **I don't get it**.

B : I'm sorry.

Let me be clearer.

The store was closed.

A：我聽不懂你說的話。

B：很抱歉。

我說得更清楚一點。

商店已經打烊了。

8. A : **What do you mean?**

B : My meaning is simple.

I just want to know how

you feel.

Are you tired, hungry or

thirsty?

A：你的意思是什麼？

B：我的意思很簡單。

我只是想知道你感覺

如何。

你覺得累、餓或渴嗎？

9. A : **Please explain it to me**.

B : Sorry.

I didn't express it well.

I just wanted to make sure

you're OK.

【common〔'kɑmən〕*adj.* 常見的；普通的】

A：請解釋給我聽。

B：抱歉。

我沒有表達得很清楚。

我只是想確定你沒問

題。

# 6. *Here's the schedule.*

| | |
|---|---|
| Here's the schedule. | 這是行程表。 |
| Take a look. | 看一看。 |
| See if it's OK. | 看一看是否可以。 |
| | |
| *I*'d like your opinion. | 我想要你的意見。 |
| *I* want your approval. | 我希望有你的同意。 |
| You can change it if you want. | 如果你想改，就可以改。 |
| | |
| *Let's* discuss it. | 我們一起討論吧。 |
| *Let's* go over it. | 我們檢查一下吧。 |
| I want everything to be clear. | 我想要一切都很清楚。 |

\*\*──────────────

schedule〔'skɛdʒʊl〕*n.* 行程表
***take a look*** 看一看　　if〔ɪf〕*conj.* 是否
***I'd like*** 我想要（= *I would like* = *I want*）
opinion〔ə'pɪnjən〕*n.* 意見　　approval〔ə'pruvḷ〕*n.* 同意
change〔tʃendʒ〕*v.* 改變　　discuss〔dɪ'skʌs〕*v.* 討論
***go over*** 查看；檢查　　clear〔klɪr〕*adj.* 明確的；清楚的

## 【背景説明】

　　帶客人出去參觀或訪問，當你需要把安排好的行程，拿給客人看的時候，就可以説這九句話。

1. ***Here's the schedule.***
   schedule〔ˈskɛdʒʊl〕*n.* 行程表

　　這句話字面的意思是「行程表在這裡。」引申爲「這是行程表。」雖然 ***Here's the schedule.*** 是 The schedule is here. 的倒裝，但兩句話意思不同。

【比較】***Here's the schedule.***（這是行程表。）

　　　　The schedule is here.

　　　　（行程表在這裡。）

BOOK 10

Here's the schedule.

The schedule is here.

　　*Here's the schedule*. 也可說成：Here's your schedule. ( 這是你的行程表。) 或 Here's our schedule. ( 這是我們的行程表。)

　　如果指定是今天的，就說：Here's today's schedule. ( 這是今天的行程表。) 如果指定是這個禮拜的，就可以說成：Here's this week's schedule. ( 這是這個禮拜的行程表。)

2. *Take a look*.
   *take a look*　看一看

　　這句話的意思是「看一看。」可以有禮貌地說成：Please take a look. ( 請看一看。) 或加強語氣說成：Please take a look at it. ( 請看一看它。) 上面各句的 take 都可改成 have。

【比較】下面兩句話意思相同：

*Take a look*.【較常用】
= Have a look.【常用】

3. *See if it's OK*.
   if〔ɪf〕*conj.* 是否

　　這句話的意思是「看一看是否可以。」if 子句在 see, ask, know 之類的字後面，if 等於 whether ( 是否 )，引導名詞子句。

這句話也有美國人說成：See if you agree.（看
看你是否同意。）或 See if everything looks OK.
（看一看是不是一切都可以。）

【比較】 ***See if it's OK.***【常用，通俗】
　　　　＝ See whether it's OK.【少用】

***See if it's OK***. 可以加長為：See if you think
it's OK.（看看你認爲行不行。）或 See if it's OK
with you.（看看你覺得可不可以。）

4. ***I'd like your opinion***.
　***I'd like*** 我想要（＝*I would like*）
opinion〔ə'pɪnjən〕*n.* 意見

　　句中的 I'd like 等於 I want。這句話的意思是
「我想要你的意見。」也有美國人說成：I'd like to
hear your opinion.（我想要聽你的意見。）或 I'd
like to know your opinion.（我想要知道你的意見。）

【比較1】下面兩句話意思相同：

　　　***I'd like your opinion***.【較常用】
　　　＝ I would like your opinion.【常用】

【比較2】

　　　***I'd like your opinion***.【較有禮貌】
　　　＝ I want your opinion.【語氣較嚴肅】

BOOK 10

5. ***I want your approval.***

want 〔 wɑnt 〕 *v.* 希望有；想要
approval 〔 ə'pruvḷ 〕 *n.* 同意

> want 一般作「想要」解，在這裡作「希望有」解。這句話的意思是「我希望有你的同意。」也有美國人說成：I want your OK. ( 我希望有你的同意。)【OK 在此是名詞，作「同意」解】或 I want you to agree. ( 我希望你同意。)

6. ***You can change it if you want.***

change 〔 tʃendʒ 〕 *v.* 改變；變更

> 這句話的意思是「如果你想改，就可以改。」也可說成：You can change it if you like. ( 如果你喜歡，你就可以改。) 或 You can change it if you'd like. ( 如果你想改，就可以改。)
>【you'd like = you want】

> 這句話也可簡化爲：You can change it. ( 你可以更改。) 或 Feel free to change it. ( 你可以隨意更改。)【*feel free to V.* 可以隨意~；可以自由~】

可以加強語氣說成：

I want you to know you can change it if you want.
( 我希望你知道，如果你想改，你就可以改。)
You can change any part if you want.
( 如果你想改，你可以改任何部份。)
It's OK to change any part you want.
( 你想改任何部份都可以。)

**7. *Let's discuss it*.**

discuss〔dɪ'skʌs〕*v.* 討論

　　　　這句話的意思是「我們一起討論吧。」也可加強語氣説成：Let's *you and I* discuss it.（我們兩個人一起討論吧。）【you and I 為 Let's 中的 us 的同位語，在此加強語氣】

　　下面三句話意思相同：

　　　　***Let's discuss it*.【常用，白領階級喜歡説】**
　　　　= Let's talk about it.【較常用】
　　　　= Let's talk it over.【常用】
　　　　【***talk about*** 討論　　***talk*** sth. ***over*** 討論某事】

**8. *Let's go over it*.**

***go over*** 檢查；仔細查看

　　　　go over 的字面意思是「走過；越過；從…上面經過」，引申為很多意思，像「複習」（= *review*）；在這裡，go over 的意思是「檢查」（= *examine*）或「仔細查看」。

　　　　這句話的意思是「我們檢查一下吧。」可加強語氣説成：

　　　　　　Let's go over it together.
　　　　　　（我們一起檢查一下吧。）
　　　　　　Let's go over it carefully.
　　　　　　（我們一起仔細檢查吧。）

BOOK 10

9. ***I want everything to be clear.***

clear〔klɪr〕*adj.* 清楚的；明確的

這句話的意思是「我想要一切都很清楚。」可以簡單說成：Let's make everything clear.（我們把每件事情都弄清楚吧。）

可以加強語氣說成：

$$
\text{I want everything to be }
\begin{cases}
\text{very} \\
\text{perfectly} \\
\text{extremely} \\
\text{totally}
\end{cases}
\text{ clear.}
$$

（我想要每件事情都清清楚楚，明明白白。）

perfectly〔'pɝfɪktlɪ〕*adv.* 完全地；非常
extremely〔ɪk'strimlɪ〕*adv.* 極度地；非常
totally〔'totl̩ɪ〕*adv.* 完全地

美國人也常說：

I want everything to be understood clearly.
（我想要每件事情都被弄清楚。）
I want everything to be completely understood.
（我想要每件事情都完全被了解。）
I don't want any misunderstanding.
（我不想要有任何誤解。）

completely〔kəm'plitlɪ〕*adv.* 完全地
misunderstanding〔,mɪsʌndɚ'stændɪŋ〕*n.* 誤解；誤會

## 【對話練習】

1. A : **Here's the schedule.**　　　　　A：這是行程表。

   B : Thanks a million.　　　　　　　B：真是太感謝了。

   This is useful.　　　　　　　　　　這很有用。

   I've been waiting for this.　　　　　我一直在等這個。

   【Thanks a million.

   　= Thanks very much.】

2. A : **Take a look.**　　　　　　　　A：看一看。

   B : OK, I will.　　　　　　　　　　B：好的，我會的。

   This is very important.　　　　　　這很重要。

   I'll take a quick look.　　　　　　我會很快地看一下。

3. A : **See if it's OK.**　　　　　　　A：看一看是否可以。

   B : All right, I will.　　　　　　　B：好的，我會的。

   I'll have a look.　　　　　　　　　我會看一看。

   I'll see if it's OK.　　　　　　　　我會看看是否可以。

4. A : **I'd like your opinion.**　　　　A：我想要你的意見。

   B : Thanks for asking.　　　　　　B：謝謝你問我。

   I appreciate that.　　　　　　　　我很感激。

   Just give me a minute.　　　　　　請給我一點時間。

   【appreciate〔ə'priʃɪˌet〕*v.* 感激

   　***a minute*** 一會兒時間；片刻】

5. A : **I want your approval.**　　　　A：我希望有你的同意。

   B : It looks fine.　　　　　　　　　B：它看起來很好。

   I approve.　　　　　　　　　　　　我同意。

   You have my OK.　　　　　　　　　我同意你。

   【approve〔ə'pruv〕*v.* 贊成；同意】

6. A : **You can change it if you want**.

B : I don't think we need to.
It looks satisfactory.
We don't have to change a
thing.
【satisfactory (ˌsætɪsˈfæktərɪ ) *adj.*
令人滿意的】

A：如果你想改，就可以改。

B：我不覺得我們需要改。
它看起來很令人滿意。
我們什麼都不必改。

7. A : **Let's discuss it**.

B : Excellent idea.
We should talk it over.
I'm interested in what you
think. 【*talk over* 討論】

A：我們一起討論吧。

B：很棒的主意。
我們應該討論它。
我對你的想法很有興趣。

8. A : **Let's go over it**.

B : Yes, we should review it.
We don't want any confusion.
We want to avoid mistakes.
【review ( rɪˈvju ) *v.* 再檢查
confusion ( kənˈfjuʒən ) *n.* 混淆】

A：我們檢查一下吧。

B：好的，我們應再檢查一下。
我們不想造成任何混淆。
我們要避免錯誤。

9. A : **I want everything to be clear**.

B : I couldn't agree more.
Let's get everything in the
open.
We should be on the same
page.
【open (ˈopən ) *n.* 公開狀態　　*be on the same page* 意見一致；立場相同】

A：我想要一切都很清楚。

B：我非常同意。
我們把一切都公開。

我們應該意見一致。

BOOK 10

# 7. *How about a meal?*

| | |
|---|---|
| How about a meal? | 吃頓飯如何？ |
| Let me invite you. | 我想請你。 |
| I know some good places. | 我知道一些好地方。 |
| | |
| *You'll* like it. | 你會喜歡的。 |
| *You'll* have fun. | 你會很開心。 |
| It'll be a good time. | 那將很愉快。 |
| | |
| Do you have time? | 你有時間嗎？ |
| We won't be gone long. | 我們不會離開很久。 |
| You're welcome to join me. | 歡迎你和我一起去。 |

BOOK 10

\*\*────────────

*How about ~ ?*  ～如何？     meal〔mil〕*n.* 一餐

invite〔ɪn'vaɪt〕*v.* 邀請

*have fun*  玩得愉快；開心；高興

*a good time*  愉快的時光     gone〔gɔn〕*adj.* 離去的

long〔lɔŋ〕*adv.* 長久地；很久地

welcome〔'wɛlkəm〕*adj.* 受歡迎的

join〔dʒɔɪn〕*v.* 參加；加入；和…一起做同樣的事

【背景說明】

你想請客人或朋友吃飯，該怎麼說呢？下面幾句話不僅傳遞邀約的訊息，也表示出你的誠意。

1. *How about a meal?*

*How about~?* ~如何？　　meal〔mil〕*n.* 一餐

這句話的意思是「吃頓飯如何？」源自 *How do you feel about having a meal with me?*【文法對，但美國人不說】我們在 p.1092-1093 中，有詳細説明。美國人也常説成：Let's eat together.（我們一起吃吧。）或 Let's eat a meal together.（我們一起吃頓飯吧。）

下面是美國人常説的話：

*How about a meal?*【第一常用】
How about having a meal?【第二常用】
（吃頓飯如何？）
How about eating a meal?【第四常用】
（吃頓飯如何？）

How about a meal with me?【第六常用】
（和我一起吃頓飯如何？）
How about having a meal with me?【第三常用】
（和我一起吃頓飯如何？）
How about eating a meal with me?【第五常用】
（和我一起吃頓飯如何？）

2. ***Let me invite you***.

invite〔ɪn'vaɪt〕*v.* 邀請

　　這句話字面的意思是「讓我邀請你。」引申為「我想請你。」源自：Please let me invite you to eat.（請讓我請你吃飯。）說 ***Let me invite you***. 就是要付錢請別人吃飯，中文和英文都有這個意思。

下面是美國人常說的話，我們按照使用頻率排列：

***Let me invite you***.【第一常用】

Let me invite you to eat.【第四常用】
（我想請你去吃飯。）

Please let me invite you to eat.【第二常用】
（請讓我請你去吃飯。）

Please let me invite you for a meal.【第三常用】
（請讓我請你去吃飯。）

I want to invite you to eat.【第五常用】
（我想請你去吃飯。）

I want to invite you to a meal.【第七常用】
（我想請你去吃飯。）

I really want to invite you to eat.【第六常用】
（我真的想請你去吃飯。）

---

不想請客，但想和外國人一起吃飯時，可說：

Feel like a meal?（想要吃頓飯嗎？）

Want to go eat together?（要不要一起去吃飯？）

Let's eat together.（我們一起吃飯吧。）

### 3. *I know some good places*.

　　　　這句話的意思是「我知道一些好地方。」源自：
I know some good places to eat.（我知道一些吃飯
的好地方。）美國人也常說：I know some good
spots.（我知道一些好的地點。）或 I know some
good restaurants.（我知道一些好的餐廳。）

【spot〔spɑt〕*n.* 地點】

### 4. *You'll like it*.

　　　　這句話的意思是「你會喜歡它。」引申為「你會
喜歡的。」可以加強語氣說成：

I'm sure you'll like it.（我確信你會喜歡的。）
I promise you'll like it.（我保證你會喜歡的。）
I guarantee you'll like it.（我保證你會喜歡的。）

【promise〔'prɑmɪs〕*v.* 保證　　guarantee〔͵gærən'ti〕*v.* 保證】

### 5. *You'll have fun*.

*have fun* 玩得愉快；開心；高興

　　　　這句話的意思是「你會很開心。」have fun 後
面可以加上動名詞，fun 之後省略了 in，如：

You'll have fun *eating out*.
（出去吃，你會很開心。）
You'll have fun *going out to eat*.
（出去吃，你會很開心。）
You'll have fun *eating something new*.
（吃點新東西，你會很開心。）

美國人最喜歡講下面三句話：

> ***You'll have fun.***【第一常用】
> You'll have a good time.【第二常用】
> （你會很開心。）
> You'll enjoy it.（你會很喜歡的。）【第三常用】
> 【enjoy〔ɪn'dʒɔɪ〕*v.* 喜歡】

## 6. *It'll be a good time.*

　　***a good time*** 愉快的時光

　　　這句話字面的意思是「那將是愉快的時光。」
引申為「那將很愉快。」句中的 It 是指 Eating
with me（和我一起吃東西），所以，也可以說
成：Eating with me will be a good time.（和我
一起吃東西會很愉快。）a good time 可改成 a fun
time 或 a great time。

　　【比較】下面兩句話意義不同：

> ***It'll be a good time.***（那將很愉快。）
> You're a good time.（和你在一起很愉快。）

　　這句話在本書的 p.848 中，有詳細的說明和例句。

## 7. *Do you have time?*

　　　這句話的意思是「你有時間嗎？」（= *Are you
free?*）句中的 time 是抽象名詞，不加冠詞，和
Do you have the time?（你知不知道現在幾點？）
意思完全不同。

邀請別人吃飯，最好先問別人有沒有空，免得被拒絕。

下面三句話是美國人常說的：

***Do you have time?*** 【第一常用】

Do you have any time?

（你有任何時間嗎？）【第二常用】

Do you have any free time?

（你有任何空閒時間嗎？）

【第三常用】【*free time* 空閒時間】

Do you have time?

8. ***We won't be gone long.***

gone〔gɔn〕*adj.* 離去的　　long〔lɔŋ〕*adv.* 長久地；很久地

句中的 gone，已經變成純粹形容詞，作「離去的」解，be gone = be away。因為 go 是不及物動詞，沒有被動，所以由此可證明 gone 不是過去分詞，而是形容詞。

這句話的意思是「我們不會離開很久。」long 可以當形容詞，也可以當副詞，研究 long 是形容詞或副詞太辛苦了，看看這句話的演變就知道了。

下面各句意思相同，都表示「我們不會離開很久。」

We won't be gone for a long time. 【少用】

We won't be gone a long time. 【常用】

We won't be gone for long. 【常用】

***We won't be gone long.*** 【常用】

We won't be long. 【最常用】

美國人也喜歡説：It won't take long.（不會花太久時間。）或 We won't take long.（我們不會花太久時間。）take long 的用法，詳見 p.761。

9. ***You're welcome to join me***.

welcome〔'wɛlkəm〕*v.* 歡迎　*adj.* 受歡迎的

join〔dʒɔɪn〕*v.* 參加；加入；和…在一起；和…一起做同樣的事

這句話字面的意思是「歡迎你加入我。」引申為「歡迎你和我一起去。」也可加強語氣説成：

You're always welcome to join me.

（隨時都歡迎你和我一起去。）

I want you to know you're welcome to
　join me.

（我希望你知道，我歡迎你和我一起去。）

Please know that you're welcome to join me.

（希望你要知道，我是歡迎你和我一起去的。）

也有美國人説：

I invite you to join me.

（我邀請你和我一起去。）

You can join me if you'd like.

（如果你想要的話，你可以和我一起去。）

I'd like to invite you to join me.

（我想邀請你和我一起去。）

## 【對話練習】

1. A：**How about a meal?**

   B：I'd like to, but I can't.
   I'm extremely busy right now.
   How about a rain check?
   【extremely〔ɪk'strimlɪ〕*adv.* 非常地
   *a rain check* 改天】

   A：吃頓飯如何？
   B：我想去，但是不行。
   我現在很忙。
   改天如何？

2. A：**Let me invite you**.

   B：That's kind of you.
   I want to treat you, too.
   Let's go Dutch, OK?
   【*go Dutch* 各付各的】

   A：我想請你。
   B：你人真好。
   我也想請你。
   我們各付各的，好嗎？

3. A：**I know some good places**.

   B：I bet you do.
   I trust your judgment.
   OK, I'll follow you.
   【bet〔bɛt〕*v.* 確信；斷定
   judgment〔'dʒʌdʒmənt〕*n.* 判斷】

   A：我知道一些好地方。
   B：我相信你知道。
   我相信你的判斷。
   好，我跟你走。

4. A：**You'll like it**.

   B：I'm sure I will.
   I'm not picky.
   I'm easy to please.
   【picky〔'pɪkɪ〕*adj.* 愛挑剔的
   please〔pliz〕*v.* 取悅】

   A：你會喜歡的。
   B：我相信我會。
   我不挑剔。
   我很容易被取悅。

5. A：**You'll have fun**.

   B：I know that.
   You don't have to tell me.
   I always have fun with you.

A：你會很開心。

B：我知道。
   你不必跟我說。
   和你在一起，我總是很
   開心。

6. A：**It'll be a good time**.

   B：I know it will.
   You are lots of fun.
   I like doing things with you.
   【*lots of* 大量的；很多的
   fun〔fʌn〕*n.* 樂趣；有趣的人】

A：那將很愉快。

B：我知道會。
   你很有趣。
   我喜歡和你一起做事。

7. A：**Do you have time?**

   B：Of course, I do.
   I have time for you.
   You are important to me.

A：你有時間嗎？

B：我當然有。
   我有時間給你。
   你對我很重要。

8. A：**We won't be gone long**.

   B：I hope not.
   I have a lot of work to do.
   Let's be back in half an hour.

A：我們不會離開很久。

B：希望不會。
   我有很多工作要做。
   我們半小時內回來吧。

9. A：**You're welcome to join me**.

   B：Thanks for the invitation.
   Let me talk it over with my
   wife.
   She may have made plans
   for us.

A：歡迎你和我一起去。

B：謝謝你的邀請。
   讓我跟我太太談一談。

   她可能已經替我們擬定
   別的計劃了。

BOOK 10

# 8. *Order anything*.

| | |
|---|---|
| Order anything. | 隨便點任何東西。 |
| Choose what you like. | 選擇你喜歡的。 |
| Don't worry about the price. | 別擔心價錢。 |
| | |
| This dish is a house favorite. | 這道菜是這個餐廳的招牌菜。 |
| I've had it before. | 我以前吃過。 |
| It's very tasty. | 它很好吃。 |
| | |
| How is it? | 你覺得怎麼樣？ |
| Is it good? | 好不好吃？ |
| Want some more? | 還要再來一些嗎？ |

**BOOK 10**

\*\* ——————————————————

order〔'ɔrdɚ〕*v.* 點（菜）　　choose〔tʃuz〕*v.* 選擇
dish〔dɪʃ〕*n.* 菜餚　　***worry about*** 擔心
price〔praɪs〕*n.* 價錢
favorite〔'fevərɪt〕*n.* 最受喜愛的人或物
***house favorite*** 招牌菜　　have〔hæv〕*v.* 吃；喝
tasty〔'testɪ〕*adj.* 美味的；好吃的

【背景説明】

　　當你請別人吃飯的時候，拿到了菜單，你就可以先説：Order anything. 等六句話，他吃的時候，你可以再問他：How is it? 等三句話。

1. ***Order anything.***
order〔'ɔrdɚ〕v. 點（菜）

　　order 的主要意思是「命令」，在此作「點（菜）」解。這句話的意思是「隨便點任何東西。」引申爲「隨便點，不要客氣。」( = *Order anything. Don't be polite.* )

　　下面都是美國人常説的話：

***Order anything.***【第一常用】
***Order anything*** at all. ( 儘量點。)【第二常用】
【 at all 是加强語氣，詳見 p.4-5 】
***Order anything*** on the menu. 【第六常用】
( 菜單上的任何東西都可以隨便點。)
【 menu〔'mɛnju〕n. 菜單 】

***Order anything*** you like. 【第三常用】
( 隨便點你喜歡的。)
***Order anything*** that you like. 【第七常用】
( 隨便點你喜歡的。)
***Order anything*** you desire. 【第八常用】
( 隨便點你想吃的。)【 desire〔dɪ'zaɪr〕v. 想要 】

You can *order anything*.【第五常用】
（你可以隨便點任何東西。）
Please *order anything*.【第四常用】
（請隨便點任何東西。）
Feel free to *order anything*.【第九常用】
（你可以隨便點。）【*feel free to V*. 可以隨意地～】

2. ***Choose what you like***.
choose〔tʃuz〕v. 選擇

　　這句話的意思是「選擇你喜歡的。」

　　下面是美國人常說的話，我們按照使用頻率排列：

① ***Choose what you like***.【第一常用】
② Choose whatever you like to eat.【第二常用】
　　（選任何你想吃的。）
　　【whatever〔hwɑt'ɛvɚ〕pron. 任何東西】
③ Choose whatever you want.【第三常用】
　　（選任何你想要的。）

④ Select what you like.（選任何你喜歡的。）
⑤ Pick what you like.（選任何你喜歡的。）
⑥ Order what you like.（點任何你喜歡的。）
　【select〔sə'lɛkt〕v. 挑選　　pick〔pɪk〕v. 挑選】

3. ***Don't worry about the price***.

***worry about*** 擔心    price〔praɪs〕*n.* 價錢

　　　　這句話的意思是「別擔心價錢。」其隱含的意思是:「你儘量點,由我付錢。」

下面是美國人常說的話,我們按照使用頻率排列:

① ***Don't worry about the price***.【第一常用】
② Don't even think about the cost.【第二常用】
　（費用的事想都不用想。）
③ Just forget about the price.【第三常用】
　（價錢的事別放在心上。）
　【cost〔kɔst〕*n.* 費用】

④ Don't pay attention to the price.（別管價錢。）
⑤ Don't worry at all about the price.
　（完全不用擔心價錢。）
⑥ Don't worry one single bit about the price.
　（絲毫不用擔心價錢的事。）

***pay attention to*** 注意　***not…at all*** 一點也不
single〔'sɪŋ!〕*adj.* 單一的　bit〔bɪt〕*n.* 一點點
***not one single bit*** 一點也不 ( = *not a bit* = *not at all* )

4. ***This dish is a house favorite***.
dish〔dɪʃ〕*n.* 菜餚
favorite〔'fevərɪt〕*n.* 最受喜愛的人或物
***house favorite*** 招牌菜

　　　house 主要意思是「房子」,在這裡作「餐廳」解,等於 restaurant（見 The American Heritage Dictionary p.851）。

通常 favorite 當形容詞用，作「最喜愛的」解，但在這裡，作「最受喜愛的東西」解，是名詞。favorite 當名詞，用法很多，例如：This meal is my favorite.（這餐飯是我最喜歡的。）或 She is a class favorite.（她是全班最喜歡的同學。）

這句話字面的意思是「這道菜是餐廳最受喜愛的菜。」也就是「這道菜是這個餐廳的招牌菜。」（= *This dish is very popular.*）也有美國人說成：This dish is a customer favorite.（這道菜是顧客最喜歡的。）

【比較】 house favorite 可能是指最好的或最好的之一。注意下面兩句話的冠詞所代表的意思：

This dish is *a* house favorite.
（這道菜是招牌菜。）【招牌菜也許好幾道】
This dish is *the* house favorite.
（這道菜是這家餐廳最好的菜。）

This dish is a house favorite.

**5. *I've had it before*.**

have〔hæv〕*v.* 吃；喝

> have 的主要意思是「有」，在這裡作「吃」解。
> 這句話的意思是「我以前吃過。」( = *I've eaten it*
> *before*. ) 也可說成：I've had this dish before.
> （我以前吃過這道菜。）或 I've ordered it before.
> （我以前點過這道菜。）

**6. *It's very tasty*.**

tasty〔'testɪ〕*adj.* 美味的；好吃的

> 這句話的意思是「它很好吃。」( = *It's very*
> *delicious*. ) 也可以說成：It's a very tasty dish.
> （它是一道很好吃的菜。）稱讚東西好吃，可參
> 照 p.80。

**7. *How is it?***

> 這句話源自：How is it to you?（你覺得怎
> 麼樣？）因為說這句話時還在吃，所以用現在式。
> 吃完飯後，再問的話，就要說：How was it?
> （你覺得怎麼樣？）

下面是美國人常說的話，我們按照使用頻率排列：

① *How is it?*【第一常用】

② How do you like it?（你覺得怎麼樣？）【第二常用】

③ What do you think?（你覺得怎麼樣？）【第三常用】

　【*How* do you think?（誤）是中國人常犯的錯誤，要小心。】

BOOK 10

## 8. *Is it good?*

good 有很多意思，在這裡作「好吃的」解。*Is it good?* 的意思是「好不好吃？」也可說成：Is it a good dish? （這道菜好吃嗎？）或 Does it taste good to you? （你覺得好吃嗎？）也有美國人常說：Do you think it's good? （你認為好吃嗎？）或 Is it OK?  Do you like it? （可以嗎？你喜歡嗎？）

這句話用現在式，因為說的時候還在吃。吃完飯後，就要說：Was it good? （好吃嗎？）

## 9. *Want some more?*

more〔mor〕*adj.* 另外的；多餘的

這句話的意思是「還要再來一些嗎？」源自：Do you want to eat some more? （你想要再多吃一些嗎？）

下面是美國人常說的話，我們按照使用頻率排列：

① *Want some more?* 【第一常用】
② Do you want to eat some more? 【第二常用】
   （你想要再多吃一些嗎？）
③ How about some more? 【第三常用】
   （再來一些怎麼樣？）【*How about~?*  ～怎麼樣？】

④ Would you like some more?
   （你想要再吃一些嗎？）
⑤ Would you care for some more?
   （你想要再吃一些嗎？）
⑥ Can I order you some more?
   （要我為你再點一些嗎？）【*care for*  想要】

## 【對話練習】

1. A：**Order anything**.

   B：Thanks, I will.
   I'm really hungry.
   Let me check out the menu.
   【*check out* 看看】

2. A：**Choose what you like**.

   B：It won't be easy.
   Everything looks delicious.
   I can't make up my mind.
   【*make up one's mind* 下決心】

3. A：**Don't worry about the price**.

   B：You're so generous.
   I appreciate the offer.
   But let's share the bill, OK?
   【generous（'dʒɛnərəs）*adj.* 慷慨的
   appreciate（ə'priʃɪ,et）*v.* 感激
   offer（'ɔfɚ）*n.* 提供】

4. A：**This dish is a house
   favorite**.

   B：It sounds very tasty.
   It must be quite special.
   I think I'll follow the crowd.
   【*follow the crowd* 跟隨大家；
   跟大家一樣】

A：隨便點任何東西。

B：謝謝，我會的。
我真的好餓。
我來看看菜單。

A：選擇你喜歡的。

B：那不容易。
每樣看起來都很好吃。
我沒辦法決定。

A：別擔心價錢。

B：你真慷慨。
你的心意我很感激。
但是，讓我們一起分
擔費用，好嗎？

A：這道菜是這個餐廳的
招牌菜。

B：聽起來好像很好吃。
它一定很特別。
我想我要跟大家一樣。

5. A: **I've had it before**.

B: Was it delicious?

Do you recommend it?

Do you want to try it again?

【recommend〔ˌrɛkə'mɛnd〕v. 推薦

try〔traɪ〕v. 嘗試；試吃】

A: 我以前吃過。

B: 好吃嗎？

你推薦嗎？

你想再吃一次嗎？

6. A: **It's very tasty**.

B: Then I'll have to try it.

I'm going to order it.

I hope it's not too expensive.

A: 它很好吃。

B: 那麼，我就必須嚐嚐看。

我會點這道菜。

我希望不會太貴。

7. A: **How is it?**

B: It's yummy.

It has two different flavors.

It tastes both sweet and sour.

【yummy〔'jʌmɪ〕adj. 好吃的

flavor〔'flevɚ〕n. 味道

sour〔saʊr〕adj. 酸的】

A: 你覺得怎麼樣？

B: 很好吃。

它有兩種不同的味道。

它嚐起來又甜又酸。

8. A: **Is it good?**

B: It's exceptional.

In my opinion, it's perfect.

I give it two thumbs up.

【exceptional〔ɪk'sɛpʃənḷ〕adj. 極好的

thumb〔θʌm〕n. 拇指】

A: 好不好吃？

B: 很棒。

我認爲很完美。

我對它翹起兩手的大拇

指，表示讚賞。

9. A: **Want some more?**

B: Want? Yes.

Need? No.

I think I've had enough.

A: 還要再來一些嗎？

B: 想要？是的。

需要？並不。

我想我已經吃飽了。

# 9.  *Are you all right?*

| | |
|---|---|
| Are you all right? | 你沒問題吧？ |
| *Is* anything the matter? | 有什麼不對勁的嗎？ |
| *Is* everything OK? | 一切都還可以吧？ |
| | |
| *You* look a little pale. | 你的臉色有點蒼白。 |
| *You* must be exhausted. | 你一定是累壞了。 |
| I bet you're tired. | 我想你一定是累了。 |
| | |
| Can I get you anything? | 我能為你拿任何東西嗎？ |
| Want to take some medicine? | 要吃點藥嗎？ |
| Do you want me to take you to the doctor? | 你要不要我帶你去看醫生？ |

BOOK 10

** ——————————————

*all right* 沒問題的    *the matter* 不對勁的

pale〔pel〕*adj.* 蒼白的

exhausted〔ɪgˈzɔstɪd〕*adj.* 筋疲力盡的

bet〔bɛt〕*v.* 打賭    *I bet* 我敢說；我相信；我認為；我想

tired〔taɪrd〕*adj.* 疲倦的    get〔gɛt〕*v.* 去拿來

take〔tek〕*v.* 吃（藥）    medicine〔ˈmɛdəsn̩〕*n.* 藥

## 【背景説明】

　　看到你身邊的人，臉上露出疲憊，或是感覺有些不對勁時，就可以說這些話來表示關切。

1. *Are you all right?*
   *all right* 沒問題的

　　看到認識或不認識的人，身體不舒服，都可說：*Are you all right?* 意思是「你沒問題吧？」或簡化說成：You all right? ( 你還好吧？ )【尾音向上揚】

【比較1】下面兩句的 all right 和 alright 發音相同，寫法不同：

> *Are you all right?*【正式】
> Are you alright?【非正式】
> 【alright 等於 all right，但較不正式，多見於漫畫、廣告中】

【比較2】下面兩句話意思相同：

> *Are you all right?*【較常用】
> Are you feeling all right?【常用，語氣較強】
> ( 你感覺還好嗎？ )

【比較3】下面兩句話意思相同：

> 　*Are you all right?*【較常用】
> = Are you OK? ( 你還好吧？ )【較輕鬆】

## 2. *Is anything the matter?*

*the matter* 不對勁的 ( = *wrong* )

matter 主要的意思是「事務」，是名詞，the matter 合在一起，卻是一個形容詞片語，等於 wrong ( 不對勁的 )，在牛津字典中，當作成語來看，be the matter = be wrong，後面常和 with 連用，所以，這句話可加強爲：Is there anything the matter with you? ( 你有什麼不對勁的嗎？)

*Is there anything the matter?* 主要的意思是「有什麼不對勁的嗎？」( = *Is there anything wrong?* )

下面各句意思相同：

*Is anything the matter?*【第二常用】
= Is there anything the matter?【第五常用】

= Is anything wrong?【第一常用】
= Is there anything wrong?【第四常用】

= Is anything bothering you?【第三常用】
= Is there anything bothering you?【第六常用】
【bother〔'baðɚ〕v. 困擾】

## 3. *Is everything OK?*

這句話的意思是「一切都還可以吧？」和 Is everything all right?句意相同，也可以加強語氣說成：Is everything OK with you? ( 你一切還好吧？) 或 Is everything going OK? ( 一切進行得順利吧？) OK 可用 all right 來代替，句意相同。【go〔go〕v. 進行】

BOOK 10

【比較】

> ***Is everything OK?***【正】
>
> ***Is anything OK?***【誤】
>
> 這句話文法對，句意錯，因為不能說「是不是任何東西都還好？」。

4. ***You look a little pale***.

pale〔pel〕*adj.* 蒼白的

　　這句話的字面意思是「你看起來有點蒼白。」引申為「你的臉色有點蒼白。」

【比較】下面兩句話意思相同：

> ***You look a little pale.***【美國人思想】
>
> = Your face looks a little pale.
>
> 【中國人思想和美國人的思想】

下面是美國人常說的話：

> ***You look a little pale.***【第一常用】
>
> You look a little sick.【第二常用】
>
> （你看起來臉色有點蒼白。）
>
> You look a little under the weather.【第三常用】
>
> （你看起來有點不舒服。）
>
> Your face looks a little white.【第四常用】
>
> （你的臉色看起來有點蒼白。）

> sick〔sɪk〕*adj.* （臉色）蒼白的
>
> ***under the weather*** 身體不適的
>
> white〔hwaɪt〕*adj.* （臉色）蒼白的

當一個人看起來不對勁，有很多種說法，美國人天天使用，你不學不行：

You look { tired. / haggard. / spent. }　　你看起來 { 很疲倦。 / 很憔悴。 / 筋疲力盡。 }

haggard〔'hægəd〕 *adj.* 憔悴的

spent〔spɛnt〕 *adj.* 筋疲力盡的

You look { pale. / awful. / wasted. }　　你看起來 { 臉色蒼白。 / 糟透了。 / 好憔悴。 }

awful〔'ɔful〕 *adj.* 可怕的；很糟的

wasted〔'westɪd〕 *adj.* 落魄的；憔悴的

You look { sleepy. / drowsy. / sluggish. }　　你看起來 { 睡眼惺忪。 / 很睏的樣子。 / 很遲鈍。 }

sleepy〔'slipɪ〕 *adj.* 想睡的　　drowsy〔'drauzɪ〕 *adj.* 昏昏欲睡的

sluggish〔'slʌgɪʃ〕 *adj.* 呆滯的；行動遲緩的

You look { wiped out. / burned out. / worn-out. }　　你看起來 { 筋疲力盡。 / 好疲倦。 / 筋疲力盡。 }

***wiped out*** 筋疲力盡的

***burned out*** 很疲倦的；筋疲力盡的

worn-out〔'wɔrn'aut〕 *adj.* 筋疲力盡的【當形容詞時，不可寫成 *worn out*】

BOOK 10

　　***wiped out*** 本來意思是「被擦掉；被抹掉」，可引申為「被徹底毀滅、謀殺」。當一個人精力都被毀滅掉了，表示他「筋疲力盡」( = *exhausted* )。

　　***burned out*** 原指「被燒完了；燃料用盡」，當你的精力都被燒完了，表示你「很疲倦」( = *tired* ; *exhausted* )。

　　worn-out 源自「穿破的；用壞的」，因為過度使用，而用壞、用盡了精力和體力，表示「筋疲力盡的」( = *tired out* ; *weary* )。

$$You \begin{cases} \text{don't look right.} \\ \text{don't look well.} \\ \text{don't look yourself.} \end{cases} \quad 你看起來 \begin{cases} 不對勁。 \\ 不太好。 \\ 不對勁。 \end{cases}$$

　　You don't look yourself. 是由 You don't look your *normal* self. 簡化而來。你看來不是平常的自己，表示「你看起來不對勁。」也可說成：You look under the weather. (你看起來不太舒服。)

$$You \ look \ like \begin{cases} \text{hell.} \\ \text{death warmed over.} \\ \text{you're in low spirits.} \end{cases}$$

$$你看起來 \begin{cases} 糟透了。 \\ 像行屍走肉。 \\ 情緒低落。 \end{cases}$$

***warm over*** 重新加熱　　***be in low spirits*** 情緒低落

You look like death warmed over. 形容人已經死了，但又被加了一點溫，想讓他活過來，表示「你看起來很可怕。」

You look $\left\{\begin{array}{l}\text{like a zombie.}\\\text{like a ghost.}\end{array}\right\}$

你看起來 $\left\{\begin{array}{l}\text{像僵屍。}\\\text{像鬼一樣。}\end{array}\right\}$

zombie〔'zɑmbɪ〕*n.* 僵屍　　ghost〔gost〕*n.* 鬼

美國人的習慣是，早上一見面，看到你精神好，一定會說 You look wonderful. 等。看到你很疲倦的樣子，他也會說 You look like a zombie today. 講不好的，沒什麼惡意，只是開坑笑。自己感覺精神不好，也可以問對方：Do I look like a zombie today？

BOOK 10

5. ***You must be exhausted.***

exhausted〔ɪg'zɔstɪd〕*adj.* 筋疲力盡的

這句話的意思是「你一定是累壞了。」可以用 really 來加強語氣，説成：You really must be exhausted.（你眞的一定是累壞了。）really 也可以放在 be 之前，或 exhausted 之前。

***You must be exhausted.*** 中的 exhausted，可用 very tired，或 worn-out 等同義形容詞取代，可參照第 4 句的背景説明。

## 6. *I bet you're tired*.

bet〔bɛt〕v. 打賭　*I bet* 我敢說；我相信；我認為；我想
tired〔taɪrd〕adj. 疲倦的

美國人喜歡幽默，常在他們的語言中表現。I
bet 的主要意思是「我敢打賭」，在這裡引申為「我
敢說；我確信；我認為；我想」。這句話的意思是
「我想你一定是累了。」( = *I think you're tired.* )

美國人常在句子前加上 I bet、I guess 或 I
imagine 來改變語氣。

【比較】下面四句話意思非常接近：

*I bet you're tired.* 【語氣最強】
I guess you're tired. 【一般語氣】
（我想你一定是累了。）
I imagine you're tired. 【一般語氣】
（我想你一定是累了。）
I think you're tired. 【語氣第二強】
（我想你一定是累了。）

I guess 的意思是「我猜想；我認為」，I
imagine 的意思是「我想像；我猜想；我認為」。

## 7. *Can I get you anything?*

get〔gɛt〕v. 去拿來

在字典上，get 有無限多的意思，每一本字典不
盡相同。在這裡，get 作「去拿來」或「拿來」解。
這句話的意思是「我能為你拿任何東西嗎？」( = *Can
I bring you anything?* )

美國人也常說：Is there anything I can get you?（有沒有任何東西是我可以拿給你的？）或簡化爲：Anything I can get you?（有任何我能爲你拿的東西嗎？）***Can I get you anything?*** 也可說成 Can I get you something?（我能爲你拿什麼東西嗎？）

## 8. *Want to take some medicine?*

take〔tek〕*v.* 吃（藥）　　medicine〔ˈmɛdəsn̩〕*n.* 藥

> 這句話的意思是「要吃點藥嗎？」源自：Do you want to take some medicine?（你要吃點藥嗎？）「吃藥」不能說 *eat medicine*（誤）或 *drink medicine*（誤），無論吃藥丸或喝藥水，一定要用 take。

***Want to take some medicine?*** 可簡化爲：Want some medicine?（要吃點藥嗎？）或 Need some medicine?（需要一些藥嗎？）

## 9. *Do you want me to take you to the doctor?*

這句話源自…to the doctor's office? 而 doctor's office 的意思是「醫生的診所」，所以，這句話的意思是「你要不要我帶你去醫生的診所？」也就是「你要不要我帶你去看醫生？」英文中，「去看醫生」的慣用語有：go to the doctor's office，go to the doctor's，或 go to see a doctor，或省略 see，變成 go to a doctor。所以，這句話也可說成：Do you want me to take you to a doctor?

BOOK 10

## 【對話練習】

1. A：**Are you all right?**　　　　　　　A：你沒問題吧？
   B：Actually, no, I am not.　　　　　　B：事實上，我並不好。
   　　I don't feel too good.　　　　　　　我覺得不太好。
   　　I'm under the weather today.　　　　我今天不太舒服。
   　　【actually (ˈæktʃʊəlɪ ) adv. 事實上】

2. A：**Is anything the matter?**　　　　　A：有什麼不對勁的嗎？
   B：No, nothing is the matter.　　　　　B：沒有，沒什麼不對勁的。
   　　I'm perfectly fine.　　　　　　　　我很好。
   　　Everything is A-OK.　　　　　　　一切都很好。
   　　【perfectly (ˈpɝfɪktlɪ ) adv. 非常
   　　A-OK (ˈeˌoˈke ) adj. 沒問題的】

3. A：**Is everything OK?**　　　　　　　A：一切都還可以吧？
   B：Yes, everything is fine.　　　　　　B：是啊，一切都很好。
   　　Thanks for asking.　　　　　　　　謝謝你問我。
   　　Thank you for your concern.　　　　謝謝你的關心。
   　　【concern ( kənˈsɝn ) n. 關心】

4. A：**You look a little pale.**　　　　　A：你的臉色有點蒼白。
   B：Do I really?　　　　　　　　　　　B：我眞的會嗎？
   　　It's because I'm tired.　　　　　　那是因爲我累了。
   　　I didn't sleep well last night.　　　我昨天晚上沒睡好。

5. A：**You must be exhausted.**　　　　　A：你一定是累壞了。
   B：Yes, I'm pretty beat.　　　　　　　B：是啊，我好累。
   　　It's been a long day.　　　　　　　眞是漫長的一天。
   　　I really feel burned-out.　　　　　我的確感到筋疲力盡。
   　　【pretty (ˈprɪtɪ ) adv. 非常　　beat ( bit ) adj. 很累的 ( = *very tired* )】

6. A：**I bet you're tired**.

　 B：I sure am.

　　 I'm beat.

　　 I'm ready for bed.

A：我想你一定是累了。

B：我當然是。

　 我累壞了。

　 我很想睡。

7. A：**Can I get you anything?**

　 B：Yes, if you don't mind.

　　 I'd like some fresh juice.

　　 Can we stop and buy
　　 some?

　　【mind〔maɪnd〕v. 介意
　　　 fresh〔frɛʃ〕adj. 新鮮的】

A：我能爲你拿任何東西嗎？

B：好的，如果你不介意的話。

　 我想要一些新鮮果汁。

　 我們可以停下來買一
　 些嗎？

8. A：**Want to take some
　　 medicine?**

　 B：No, thank you.

　　 Thanks anyway.

　　 I really don't need it.

　　【anyway〔'ɛnɪ,we〕adv. 無論如何】

A：要吃點藥嗎？

B：不用了，謝謝你。

　 無論如何，還是要謝謝你。

　 我眞的不需要。

9. A：**Do you want me to take
　　 you to the doctor?**

　 B：Yes, I'd like that.

　　 That sounds great.

　　 It's just what I need.

A：你要不要我帶你去看
　 醫生？

B：好的，我想去看。

　 那聽起來不錯。

　 那正是我所需要的。

BOOK 10

# 10. *Have any plans?*

| | |
|---|---|
| What are you doing this weekend? | 這個週末你打算做什麼？ |
| Have any plans? | 有任何計劃嗎？ |
| Want to meet? | 想要見面聚一聚嗎？ |
| | |
| I have some free time. | 我有一些空閒時間。 |
| *Want to* go sightseeing? | 想要去觀光嗎？ |
| *Want to* do something fun? | 想做一些好玩的事嗎？ |
| | |
| Let me be your guide. | 讓我當你的導遊。 |
| *What* are your interests? | 你的興趣是什麼？ |
| *What* do you want to do? | 你想要做什麼？ |

\*\* ─────────────

weekend〔'wik,ɛnd〕*n.* 週末

plan〔plæn〕*n.* 計劃　　meet〔mit〕*v.* 見面

free〔fri〕*adj.* 空閒的；有空的　　*free time* 空閒時間

sightsee〔'saɪt,si〕*v.* 觀光【sightseeing 在此是動名詞】

fun〔fʌn〕*adj.* 好玩的；有趣的

guide〔gaɪd〕*n.* 導遊　　interest〔'ɪntrɪst〕*n.* 興趣

## 【背景説明】

到了週末，如果你想要邀請你的客人或朋友出去玩，你就可以説這九句話，來展現你的誠意。

1. ***What are you doing this weekend?***
   weekend〔'wik'ɛnd〕*n.* 週末

   這句話的意思是「這個週末你打算做什麼？」this 和時間名詞連用，就變成副詞片語，像 this morning（今天早上），this week（這個禮拜），所以前面不需要加介系詞。【詳見「文法寶典」p.100】

   【比較 1】
   時間名詞前有 this，that，last，next 等字修飾時，成爲副詞性受詞，前面不可加介系詞。

   ***What are you doing this weekend?***【正】
   *What are you doing for this weekend?*【誤】

   【比較 2】下面三句話意思相同：

   ***What are you doing this weekend?***
   【正，常用】

   = What will you do this weekend?
   【正，太正式，不常用】

   = What are you going to do this weekend?
   【正，常用】

BOOK 10

*What are you doing this weekend?* 中的
this weekend，可用 for the weekend 來代替，
即 What are you doing *for the weekend*？（這
個週末你打算做什麼？）也可用 this Saturday
and Sunday 來代替 this weekend，即 What
are you doing *this Saturday and Sunday*？（這
個禮拜六、禮拜天你打算做什麼？）

可用 What's going on 或 What's up 來代
替 What are you doing，即 *What's going on*
this weekend? 或 *What's up* this weekend?
意思都相同，都表示「你這個週末有什麼計劃？」
What's up? 和 What's going on? 的用法可參
照 p.6-7。

2. *Have any plans?*
plan〔plæn〕*n.* 計劃

這句話的意思是「有任何計劃嗎？」源自：Do
you have any plans?（你有任何計劃嗎？）

下面都是美國人常説的話：

*Have any plans?*【第三常用】
Do you have any plans?【第二常用】
（你有任何計劃嗎？）
Do you have plans?【第一常用】
（你有計劃嗎？）

Do you have anything planned?【第四常用】

（你有任何計劃嗎？）

Have you planned anything yet?【第五常用】

（你已經有任何計劃了嗎？）

I'd like to know if you have any plans.

（我想知道你是不是有任何計劃。）【第六常用】

【plan〔plæn〕*v.* 計劃　　yet〔jɛt〕*adv.* 已經】

3. ***Want to meet?***

meet〔mit〕*v.*（約好）見面

　　meet 可以當及物和不及物動詞，主要的意思是「見面」，在這裡的意思是「見面聚一聚」，等於 get together。***Want to meet?*** 的意思是「要不要見面聚一聚？」源自：Do you want to meet?（你要不要見面聚一聚？）和中國人的思想「要不要見面？」不謀而合。

　　如果要請別人吃飯，就可以說：Want to meet for dinner?（要不要一起吃頓飯？）或 Let's meet for dinner.（我們一起吃頓飯吧。）

　　下面都是美國人常說的話，意思大致相同：

***Want to meet?***【第二常用】

Want to get together?（想要聚一聚嗎？）【第四常用】

Want to do something together?【第五常用】

（想要一起去做些事嗎？）

Want to spend some time together?【第六常用】
（想要一起花些時間聚一聚嗎？）
Do you want to get together?【第三常用】
（你想聚一聚嗎？）
Do you want to meet me?【第一常用】
（你想和我約個時間見面嗎？）

4. ***I have some free time.***

free〔fri〕*adj.* 空閒的；有空的　　***free time*** 空閒時間

　　這句話的意思是「我有一些空閒時間。」可以簡
化為：I have free time.（我有空閒時間。）或 I'm
free.（我有空。）或 I'm available.（我有空。）也
可加強語氣說成：I'm totally free.（我完全有空。）
【available〔ə'veləbḷ〕*adj.* 有空的　totally〔'totḷɪ〕*adv.* 完全地】

也可加上確定時間：

I have some free time
- now（現在）.
- right now（就在現在）.
- tonight（今天晚上）.
- this afternoon（今天下午）.
- tomorrow（明天）.
- this weekend（這個週末）.
- on Saturday（星期六）.

　　***I have some free time.*** 也可說成：I'm not
doing anything.（我沒有什麼事可以做。）或 I
have nothing to do.（我沒事做。）這些句子都表
示自己有空。

## 5. *Want to go sightseeing?*

sightsee〔ˈsaɪtˌsi〕*v.* 觀光

> 　　這句話的意思是「想要去觀光嗎？」源自：Do you want to go sightseeing?（你想要去觀光嗎？）go 的後面若是接休閒娛樂、體育運動類的動詞，則該動詞須以動名詞(V-ing)呈現，如：go swimming（去游泳）、go shopping（去購物）、go hiking（去健行）、go sightseeing（去觀光）等。

下面都是美國人常說的話，我們按照使用頻率排列：

① *Want to go sightseeing?*【第一常用】

② Want to do some sightseeing?【第二常用】
（想去觀光嗎？）
【*do some sightseeing* 去觀光（= *go sightseeing*）】

③ Want to sightsee?（想去觀光嗎？）【第三常用】

④ Want to sightsee with me?
（想和我一起去觀光嗎？）

⑤ Want to see the sights?（想去看看風景名勝嗎？）

⑥ Want to go to some interesting places?
（想去一些有趣的地方嗎？）

*the sights* 風景名勝
interesting〔ˈɪntrɪstɪŋ〕*adj.* 有趣的

BOOK 10

6. **Want to do something fun?**

fun〔fʌn〕*adj.* 好玩的；有趣的

這句話的意思是「想做一些好玩的事嗎？」源自：Do you want to do something fun?（你想做一些好玩的事嗎？）美國人也常説：Want to have some fun?（想做一些好玩的事嗎？）或 Would you like to do something fun?（你想做一些好玩的事嗎？）

7. **Let me be your guide.**

guide〔gaɪd〕*n.* 導遊

這句話的意思是「讓我做你的導遊。」問美國人需不需要導遊，也可以説：Would you like a guide?（你要不要導遊？）或 Would you like me to be your guide?（要不要我當你的導遊？）

下面都是美國人常説的話，意思大致相同：

**Let me be your guide.**【第三常用】
Let me be your tour guide.【第五常用】
（讓我當你的導遊。）
Let me guide you around.【第四常用】
（讓我帶你四處遊覽。）

***tour guide*** 導遊　guide〔gaɪd〕*v.* 引導
around〔ə'raʊnd〕*adv.* 到處；四處
***guide*** sb. ***around*** 帶某人四處遊覽

Let me show you around.【第一常用】
（讓我帶你四處遊覽。）
Let me take you around.【第二常用】
（讓我帶你四處遊覽。）
I'd like to be your tour guide.【第七常用】
（我想當你的導遊。）
【*show sb. around* 帶某人四處遊覽（=*take sb. around*）】

I want to be your guide.【第六常用】
（我想要當你的導遊。）
I volunteer to be your guide.【第九常用】
（我自願當你的導遊。）
Let me act as your tour guide.【第八常用】
（讓我擔任你的導遊。）
【volunteer〔͵vɑlən'tɪr〕*v.* 自願　*act as* 擔任】

8. ***What are your interests?***
interest〔'ɪntrɪst〕*n.* 興趣；愛好；喜好

　　這句話的意思是「你的興趣是什麼？」interest
作「興趣；愛好；喜好」解時，多用複數形。下面
都是美國人常說的話，我們按照使用頻率排列：

① ***What are your interests?***【第一常用】
② What are you interested in?【第二常用】
　（你對什麼有興趣？）
③ What are you interested in seeing?【第三常用】
　（你對參觀什麼有興趣？）
【*be interested in*~　對~有興趣】

④ What would you like to see? ( 你想參觀什麼？ )

⑤ What is interesting to you?

　　( 你對什麼有興趣？ )

⑥ What kind of things would you like to see?

　　( 你想看哪一類的事物？ )

【interesting〔'ɪntrɪstɪŋ〕*adj.* 有趣的；引起興趣的】

　　當對方陷入沈思，無法回答你的問題時，你可

以給他一些提示：

Do you like historical, cultural, scenic or

　　shopping areas? ***What are your interests?***

( 你喜歡歷史的、文化的、風景優美的，或可購

　　物的地方嗎？你的興趣是什麼？ )

historical〔hɪs'tɔrɪkḷ〕*adj.* 歷史的
cultural〔'kʌltʃərəl〕*adj.* 文化的
scenic〔'sinɪk〕*adj.* 風景優美的
shopping〔'ʃɑpɪŋ〕*adj.* 購物用的

9. ***What do you want to do?***

　　這句話的意思是「你想要做什麼？」下面三句話

意思相同，都很常用：

***What do you want to do?*** 【第一常用】

= What would you like to do? 【第二常用】

= What do you feel like doing? 【第三常用】

【***feel like V-ing*** 想要～】

## 【對話練習】

1. A : **What are you doing this weekend?**

   B : I haven't decided.
   I haven't made any plans.
   Do you have any good ideas?

   A：這個週末你打算做什麼？

   B：我還沒決定。
   我還沒擬定任何計劃。
   你有什麼好主意嗎？

2. A : **Have any plans?**

   B : Nothing definite yet.
   I don't have any plans.
   I welcome any suggestions.
   【definite (ˈdɛfənɪt ) adj. 確定的
   suggestion ( səgˈdʒɛstʃən ) n. 建議】

   A：有任何計劃嗎？

   B：還沒確定。
   我沒有任何計劃。
   我欣然接受任何建議。

3. A : **Want to meet?**

   B : That's an excellent idea.
   Let's spend time together.
   Let's meet and have some fun.
   【excellent (ˈɛkslənt ) adj. 極好的】

   A：想要見面聚一聚嗎？

   B：那是個很棒的主意。
   我們聚一下吧。
   讓我們見個面聚一聚，
   做些好玩的事吧。

4. A : **I have some free time.**

   B : What a coincidence!
   So do I.
   Let's do something together.
   【coincidence ( koˈɪnsədəns ) n. 巧合】

   A：我有一些空閒時間。

   B：真巧！
   我也是。
   我們一起做些事吧。

5. A : **Want to go sightseeing?**

   B : Of course, I'd love to.
   Let's tour around.
   Let's see all the famous
   places. 【tour ( tur ) v. 旅行】

   A：想要去觀光嗎？

   B：當然，我很樂意。
   我們去四處遊覽吧。
   我們去參觀所有的名勝吧。

BOOK 10

6. A : **Want to do something fun?**　　A：想做一些好玩的事嗎？

　　B : You bet I do.　　　　　　　　　B：我當然要。
　　　　Let's have some fun.　　　　　　我們一起去玩吧。
　　　　Let's go have a good time.　　　我們去玩個痛快吧。

　　　　【*you bet* 當然；一定】

7. A : **Let me be your guide.**　　　　A：讓我當你的導遊。

　　B : That's fine with me.　　　　　　B：可以啊。
　　　　I can't refuse.　　　　　　　　　我不能拒絕。
　　　　You can be my tour guide.　　　你可以當我的導遊。

8. A : **What are your interests?**　　　A：你的興趣是什麼？

　　B : I like traveling around.　　　　B：我喜歡到處旅行。
　　　　I like to visit scenic spots.　　我喜歡遊覽風景區。
　　　　I enjoy hiking and
　　　　photography.　　　　　　　　　我喜歡健行和攝影。

　　　　【hike〔haɪk〕v. 健行
　　　　　photography〔fə'tɑgrəfɪ〕n. 攝影】

9. A : **What do you want to do?**　　　A：你想要做什麼？

　　B : Let's see the famous　　　　　　B：我們去參觀著名的旅
　　　　attractions.　　　　　　　　　　　遊勝地。
　　　　Then, let's tour the　　　　　　　然後，我們再遊覽市
　　　　downtown area.　　　　　　　　　中心。
　　　　I'd also like to visit a　　　　　我也想去參觀博物館。
　　　　museum.

　　　　【attraction〔ə'trækʃən〕n. 吸引人之物；旅遊勝地】

# 11. *Let's start out early tomorrow*.

| | |
|---|---|
| Let's start out early tomorrow. | 我們明天早點出發。 |
| *I'll* pick you up at seven-thirty. | 我會在七點半開車去接你。 |
| *I'll* be there on time. | 我會準時到那裡。 |
| | |
| Please meet me out front. | 請在門口和我見面。 |
| *I'll* be waiting in the car. | 我會在車子裡面等你。 |
| *I'll* keep driving around if I can't park. | 如果我沒辦法停車的話，我就會不停地繞圈子。 |
| | |
| Don't eat anything before. | 你先不要吃任何東西。 |
| I'll take you for a good breakfast. | 我將帶你去吃一頓豐盛的早餐。 |
| Your batteries will be fully charged. | 你將會充滿活力。 |

BOOK 10

\*\* ————————————————————

*start out* 動身；出發　　*pick sb. up* 開車接某人
*on time* 準時　　meet〔mit〕*v.* 和…見面
*out front* 在門外　　*keep + V-ing* 一直…；不停地…
around〔ə'raʊnd〕*adv.* 兜著圈子
park〔pɑrk〕*v.* 停車　　battery〔'bætərɪ〕*n.* 電池
fully〔'fʊlɪ〕*adv.* 完全地　　charge〔tʃɑrdʒ〕*v.* 使充電

## 【背景説明】

　　　　當你打算開車去接外國人的時候,就可以說這
九句話了。

1. *Let's **start out** early tomorrow*.
　　start〔start〕v. 開始;動身　　***start out*** 動身;出發;啓程

　　　　這句話的意思是「我們明天早點出發。」由於
start 本身也有「動身;出發」的意思,所以,也
可以說成:***Let's start early tomorrow***. 兩句話的
意思完全相同。

　　　　下面都是美國人常説的話:

　　　Let's start early tomorrow.【第一常用】
　　　( 我們明天早點出發。 )
　　　***Let's start out early tomorrow***.【第二常用】
　　　Let's start off early tomorrow.【第三常用】
　　　( 我們明天早點出發。 )
　　　【***start off*** 出發 ( = *start out* = *start* )】

　　　Let's get started early tomorrow.【第四常用】
　　　( 我們明天早點出發。 )
　　　Let's get an early start tomorrow.【第五常用】
　　　( 我們明天早點出發。 )
　　　【***get started*** 開始;出發　　start〔start〕n. 開始;出發】

　　　Let's get out early tomorrow.【第九常用】
　　　( 我們明天早點出去。 )
　　　Let's get going early tomorrow.【第六常用】
　　　( 我們明天早點走吧。 )
　　　【***get going*** 動身;走吧 ( = *get moving* )】

Let's leave early tomorrow.【第七常用】

（我們明天早點出發。）

Let's hit the road early tomorrow.【第八常用】

（我們明天早點上路。）【*hit the road*　上路】

I suggest we start early tomorrow.【第十常用】

（我建議我們明天早點出發。）

I suggest we leave early tomorrow.【第十一常用】

（我建議我們明天早點出發。）

2. *I'll pick you up at seven-thirty.*

*pick sb. up*　開車接某人

BOOK 10

　　pick 的意思是「挑選；選擇」，pick up 的主要意思是「撿走；拿起」，pick up 在字典上有十九個意思，到底是什麼意思，要看句子的上下文來決定。pick *sb.* up 字面的意思是「把某人撿起來」，引申爲「開車接某人」。從這個成語，我們可以看出，美國人語言的幽默。

　　這句話的意思是「我會在七點半開車去接你。」當然是指在七點半到那裡接他，並非在七點半才從家裡出發。如果在七點半左右要去接他，你就可以說：I'll pick you up around seven-thirty.（我會在七點半左右開車去接你。）如果強調七點半準時，你就可以說：I'll pick you up at seven-thirty sharp.（我會在七點半準時開車去接你。）

【sharp〔ʃɑrp〕*adv.*（時間）準；正】

3. ***I'll be there on time.***
   ***on time*** 準時

> 　　這句話的字面意思是「我會準時到那裡。」
> 一般在學校，老師通常跟學生説：Don't be late.
> （不要遲到。）但是，跟朋友約會，叫別人不要遲
> 到，是很不禮貌的。所以，美國人通常會説：***I'll***
> ***be there on time.*** 暗示對方也要準時，不要遲到，
> 不要讓你等他。你看，説話真是一種藝術，講得
> 好聽，人人喜歡。

　　下面都是美國人常説的話，都是在暗示對方不
要遲到，我們按照使用頻率排列：

① I'll be on time.（我會準時。）【第一常用】
② ***I'll be there on time.***【第二常用】
③ I'll be there on time for sure.【第三常用】
　　（我一定會準時到那裡。）【***for sure*** 一定】

④ I won't be late.（我不會遲到。）
⑤ I won't keep you waiting.（我不會讓你等。）
⑥ I'll be punctual.（我會準時。）
　　【punctual（ˈpʌŋktʃʊəl）*adj.* 準時的】

4. ***Please meet me out front.***

meet〔mit〕*v.* 和…見面　　***out front*** 在門外

> 　　中國人說的「門口」並不是 *the mouth of the outside door*（誤），而是 out in front of the door（在門的前面的外面），簡化說成 out front（在門外），即我們說的「在門口」。這句話的意思是「請在門口和我見面。」

　　　　也有美國人說成：

Please meet me *outside the front door.*

（請在門口和我見面。）【第一常用】【outside 是介系詞】

Please meet me outside in front of the door.

（請在門口和我見面。）【第二常用】【outside 是副詞】

Please meet me out in front of the door.

（請在門口和我見面。）【第三常用】

【front〔frʌnt〕*adj.* 前面的　*n.* 前面　***in front of*** 在～前面】

　　　***out front*** 可以指所有建築物的門口：

out front　　　　　out front　　　　　　out front

獨棟房屋的門口　　　大廈的門口　　　　飯店的門口
( out in front of　　( out in front of　　( out in front of
　the house )　　　　the building )　　　　the hotel )

BOOK 10

5. ***I'll be waiting in the car.***

這句話在這裡的意思是「我會在車子裡面等你。」
( = *I'll be waiting for you in the car.* ) 句中的 in
the car 也可以說成 in my car。

下面三句意思相同，都是美國人常說的話：

I'll wait in my car.【一般語氣】
***I'll be waiting in my car.***【語氣稍強】
I'll be there waiting for you in my car.
【語氣最強】

6. ***I'll keep driving around if I can't park.***
***keep + V-ing*** 一直…；不停地…
around〔ə'raund〕*adv.* 兜著圈子　　park〔park〕*v.* 停車

這句話的意思是「如果我沒辦法停車的話，我
就會不停地繞圈子。」keep driving 是「不停地開
車」，也可說成 continue driving（持續地開車）。

整句話加強語氣的說法是：

I'll keep driving around and around if I can't
find a place to park.（如果我找不到地方停車，
我就會不停地一個圈子一個圈子繞。）

I'll keep driving around and around the block,
waiting for you if I can't find a place to park.
（如果我找不到地方停車，我就會不停地繞著街道兜
圈子等你。）

也有美國人說：I'll keep driving around the block.（我會繞著街區不停地開。）

【block〔blɑk〕*n.* 街區（四條街道中間的區域）】

***I'll keep driving around if I can't park.*** 句中的 park，主要意思是「公園」，在這裡當動詞用，作「停車」解，可當及物和不及物兩用動詞。所以，這句話也可說成：…if I can't park my car.

park 作「停車」解時，是指停車的期間，你可以離開你的車子；而 stop 則是指「暫時停下來」，人在車子裡。

例如：

I'll ***stop*** at the curb and wait for you.
（我將在路邊停下來等你。）

I ***stopped*** and waited, but you never showed up.
（我停下來等你，但你一直都沒出現。）

【curb〔kɝb〕*n.* 路的邊石、邊欄　***show up*** 出現】

【比較】park 和 stop 不同：

I can't park.（我沒辦法找到停車的地方。）
（ = *I can't find a place to stop.*）
I can't stop.（我無法停下來。）

**BOOK 10**

7. ***Don't eat anything before***.

這句話源自：Don't eat anything before
*I get there*.（在我到之前，不要吃任何東西。）意思
是「你先不要吃任何東西。」

下面三句話意思相同：

Don't eat anything *before*.【第一常用】
= Don't eat anything *beforehand*.【第二常用】
= Don't eat anything *in advance*.【第三常用】
【eat 也可以當不及物動詞，anything 可省略】
beforehand〔bɪˈforˌhænd〕*adv.* 事先
*in advance* 事先

8. ***I'll take you for a good breakfast***.

這句話的意思是「我將帶你去吃一頓豐盛的
早餐。」而「豐盛的早餐」說法有：① a good
breakfast；② a nice breakfast；③ a great
breakfast；④ a big breakfast。

也有美國人說：I'll take you out for a good
breakfast.（我將帶你到外頭吃一頓豐盛的早餐。）
或 I want to take you out for a good breakfast.
（我想要帶你到外頭吃一頓豐盛的早餐。）

注意，後面接地點，才要用 to，如：I'll *take*
you *to* a nice restaurant.（我將帶你到一家好的餐
廳。）

9. ***Your batteries will be fully charged***.

battery〔'bætərɪ〕*n.* 電池
fully〔'fʊlɪ〕*adv.* 完全地
charge〔tʃɑrdʒ〕*v.* 使充電

　　這句話的意思是「你的電池將被完全地充電。」
引申爲「你將會充滿活力。」也可以加強語氣說成：
Your batteries will be fully charged up. 這種比
喻用法，美國人常說，但在所有的字典中，都找不
到，所以我們要詳加說明：

　　A long weekend can charge your batteries.
　　（長週末將會使你有充份休息，恢復體力。）

　　【由於美國土地很大，爲了方便旅行，通常把星期一
　　　和週六、週日連在一起，變成三天假期，稱爲 long
　　　weekend（長週末）。】

　　The foot massage really charged my batteries.
　　（腳底按摩眞的使我有精神。）

　　【massage〔mə'sɑʒ〕*n.* 按摩】

　　也可用 recharge〔ri'tʃɑrdʒ〕*v.* 給…再充電，
來代替 charge，說成：Your batteries will be
fully recharged.（你會再次充滿活力。）

　　batteries 爲什麼一定要用複數呢？可能是源
自於一個電池能量不夠。

BOOK 10

## 【對話練習】

1. A：**Let's start out early tomorrow**.
   B：I totally agree.
   That's a great idea.
   We can avoid the rush hour
   traffic. 【*rush hour* 交通尖峰時間】

   A：我們明天早點出發。
   B：我完全同意。
   那是個好主意。
   我們可以避開交通尖峰
   時間。

2. A：**I'll pick you up at seven-thirty**.
   B：That's a perfect time.
   I'll be waiting for you.
   Don't worry; I won't be late.

   A：我會在七點半去接你。
   B：那個時間正好。
   我會等你。
   別擔心；我不會遲到的。

3. A：**I'll be there on time**.
   B：I'd appreciate that.
   I won't be late, either.
   I hate it when people are late.
   【appreciate〔ə'priʃɪ,et〕*v.* 感激】

   A：我會準時到那裡。
   B：我很感激。
   我也不會遲到。
   我討厭有人遲到。

4. A：**Please meet me out front**.
   B：Sure thing, OK.
   I'll wait outside the door.
   I'll be on the sidewalk next
   to the curb. 【*sure thing* 當然
   sidewalk〔'saɪd,wɔk〕*n.* 人行道】

   A：請在門口和我見面。
   B：當然，沒問題。
   我會在門口等。
   我會在路邊的人行道
   上等你。

5. A：**I'll be waiting in the car**.
   B：You won't need to.
   I'll be there early.
   I won't make you wait for me.

   A：我會在車子裡面等你。
   B：你不需要等。
   我會很早就去那裡。
   我不會讓你等我。

6. A : **I'll keep driving around if I can't park**.

 B : Don't worry about parking. I'll be there when you arrive. I'll be ready to leave with you.

A：如果我無法停車，我就會不停地繞圈子。

B：別擔心停車的問題。你到的時候我就會在那裡。我會準備好跟你一起離開。

7. A : **Don't eat anything before**.

 B : That's good advice. I won't spoil my appetite. I won't eat anything without you. 【spoil〔spɔɪl〕*v.* 破壞 appetite〔'æpə,taɪt〕*n.* 食慾】

A：你先不要吃任何東西。

B：那是很好的建議。我不會破壞食慾。我不會不等你就自己先吃東西。

8. A : **I'll take you for a good breakfast**.

 B : I can't wait. That sounds so great! There's nothing that I'd like better.

A：我將帶你去吃一頓豐盛的早餐。

B：我等不及了。聽起來眞棒！我最喜歡的就是這個。

9. A : **Your batteries will be fully charged**.

 B : Good, since they're just about to die. I need a little break. It will be nice to put my feet up.

A：你將會充滿活力。

B：好，因爲我差不多快沒電了。我需要休息一下。能休息一下很好。

【***put one's feet up*** （把腳放在高處）放鬆休息】

BOOK 10

# 12. *I'm sorry you're leaving*.

| | |
|---|---|
| *I*'m sorry you're leaving. | 我很遺憾你要離開了。 |
| *I* enjoyed your visit. | 和你在一起的這段時間很愉快。 |
| *I* look forward to seeing you again. | 我盼望能再見到你。 |
| Come back anytime. | 請隨時回來。 |
| *You*'re always welcome. | 隨時歡迎你。 |
| *You* have an open invitation. | 隨時歡迎你。 |
| *Have* a safe trip. | 希望你旅途平安。 |
| *Have* a nice flight. | 祝你飛行順利。 |
| Take care returning home. | 回家路上要小心。 |

\*\* ——————————

sorry〔ˈsɔrɪ〕*adj.* 遺憾的　　enjoy〔ɪnˈdʒɔɪ〕*v.* 喜歡；享受
visit〔ˈvɪzɪt〕*n.* 拜訪；逗留；作客　　***look forward to*** 盼望；期待
anytime〔ˈɛnɪˌtaɪm〕*adv.* 在任何時候；隨時
welcome〔ˈwɛlkəm〕*adj.* 受歡迎的
open〔ˈopən〕*adj.* 沒有時間限制的
invitation〔ˌɪnvəˈteʃən〕*n.* 邀請函
safe〔sef〕*adj.* 安全的　　flight〔flaɪt〕*n.* 飛行
***take care*** 注意；小心　　return〔rɪˈtɜn〕*v.* 返回

## 【背景説明】

當你的朋友即將離開，送他到機場的時候，你就可以説這九句話，來表達你心中的依依不捨與祝福。

1. ***I'm sorry you're leaving.***

sorry〔ˈsɔrɪ〕*adj.* 抱歉的；遺憾的

sorry 的主要意思是「抱歉的」，在這裡作「遺憾的；難過的；可惜的」解。這句話的意思是「我很遺憾你要離開了。」美國人常簡化為：Sorry

I'm sorry you're leaving.

you're leaving. 也有美國人説：I'm sorry you have to leave. (我很遺憾，你必須走了。) 或 I'm sorry to see you leave. (看到你要走了，我很難過。)

【比較1】

> ***I'm sorry you're leaving.*** 【較常用，語氣輕鬆】
> I'm sorry that you're leaving. 【常用，較正式】

【比較2】

> ***I'm sorry you're leaving.***
> 【來去動詞 leave 用現在進行式，表「不久的未來」】
> *I'm sorry you will leave.*
> 【誤，文法對，美國人不説】

I'm sorry 可以用其他的片語來取代，例如：

> *I feel bad that* you're leaving.
> （你要離開了，我覺得很遺憾。）
> *I'm sad that* you're leaving.
> （你要離開了，眞令人難過。）
> *It is sad that* you're leaving.
> （你要離開了，我很難過。）
> 【bad〔bæd〕*adj.* 遺憾的　　sad〔sæd〕*adj.* 悲傷的】

> *It's a pity that* you're leaving.
> （你要離開了，眞是可惜。）
> *It's a shame that* you're leaving.
> （你要離開了，眞是可惜。）
> *What a shame that* you're leaving.
> （你要離開了，眞是可惜。）
> 【pity〔'pɪtɪ〕*n.* 可惜的事　　shame〔ʃem〕*n.* 可惜的事】

上面各句中的 that 均可省略，省略後，語氣較輕鬆。

2. *I enjoyed your visit.*

enjoy〔ɪn'dʒɔɪ〕*v.* 享受；喜歡
visit〔'vɪzɪt〕*n.* 拜訪；逗留；作客

這句話的字面意思是「我享受你的拜訪。」在這
裡引申爲「和你在一起的這段時間很愉快。」可以加
強語氣說成：I really enjoyed your visit.（和你在
一起的這段時間，我眞的很愉快。）或 I enjoyed your
visit here with me very much.（和你在一起的這段
期間，我眞的很愉快。）

下面各句意思相同：

　　　　***I enjoyed your visit.*** 【第一常用】

　　= I enjoyed your stay here. 【第五常用】

　　　（你留在這裡的期間，我很愉快。）

　　= I enjoyed your company. 【第三常用】

　　　（我很高興有你的陪伴。）

　　stay〔ste〕*n.* 停留期間
　　company〔'kʌmpənɪ〕*n.* 陪伴

　　= I enjoyed being with you. 【第二常用】

　　　（我很喜歡和你在一起。）

　　= I enjoyed having you visit. 【第四常用】

　　　（和你在一起的這段期間，我很愉快。）

　　這句話不可說成：*I enjoyed having your visit.*
　　（誤）因為 have 是使役動詞，加受詞後，須接原
　　形動詞，做受詞補語，否則句意不完全。

## 3. *I look forward to seeing you again.*

*look forward to* 盼望；期待

　　　這句話的意思是「我盼望能再見到你。」也就
　　是「我希望能再見到你。」( = *I hope to see you
　　again.* ) 句中的 look forward to 的 to 是介系詞，
　　後面要接動名詞。美國人也常說成：I'm looking
　　forward to seeing you again. 兩者使用頻率相
　　同，句意也相同。

4. **Come back anytime**.

anytime〔͵ɛnɪ'taɪm〕*adv.* 在任何時候；隨時

這句話字面的意思是「在任何時候回來。」引申為「請隨時回來。」可以更有禮貌地説：Please come back anytime. ( 請隨時回來。) 或加強語氣説成：I invite you to come back anytime you have the chance. ( 只要你一有機會,我邀請你隨時回來。)

**anytime** 是一個字,是副詞,等於 at any time ( 在任何時候 ),分開來的 **any time** 是名詞片語。

下面都是美國人常説的話,句意大致相同：

**Come back anytime.**【第一常用】

Come back and visit anytime.【第四常用】
( 請隨時回來拜訪我們。)

Come back and see us anytime.【第二常用】
( 請隨時回來看我們。)

Come back **anytime you wish**.【第六常用】
( 你願意的話,請隨時回來。)
【anytime 在此是連接詞】

You can come back anytime you like.
( 你喜歡的話,可以隨時回來。)【第三常用】

Please come back again anytime you can.
( 請隨時回來。)【第五常用】

【wish〔wɪʃ〕*v.* 希望；想要  like〔laɪk〕*v.* 喜歡；想要】

5. ***You're always welcome***.

welcome〔'wɛlkəm〕 *adj.* 受歡迎的

這句話的字面意思是「你總是受歡迎的。」引
申為「隨時歡迎你。」可加長為：

You're always welcome to visit us.
（隨時歡迎你來拜訪我們。）

下面都是美國人常說的話：

You're welcome anytime.【第三常用】
（隨時歡迎你。）

***You're always welcome***.【第一常用】
（隨時歡迎你。）

You're welcome here with us.【第四常用】
（我們隨時歡迎你來這裡。）

You're welcome here anytime.【第二常用】
（這裡隨時歡迎你。）

Our door is always open for you.【第五常用】
（我們的大門總是為你而開。）

We'll always welcome you with open arms.
（我們總是張開雙臂歡迎你。）【第六常用】

【***with open arms*** 張開著雙臂；熱烈地（歡迎）】

BOOK 10

6. ***You have an open invitation.***

open〔'opən〕*adj.* 沒有時間限制的

invitation〔͵ɪnvə'teʃən〕*n.* 邀請函

> 　　這句話字面的意思是「你有一張沒有使用期限的邀請函。」引申為「隨時歡迎你。」open 的主要意思是「開著的；打開的；開放的」，在這裡作「沒有使用期限的」解，an open ticket 是「沒有使用期限的車票」，所以，an open invitation 就是「沒有使用期限的邀請函」。實際上並沒有這種邀請函，只是一種隨時歡迎對方來訪的說法。

下面各句意思相同，都表示「隨時歡迎你。」

　　***You have an open invitation.*** 【第六常用】

　= You're welcome anytime. 【第一常用】

　　（隨時歡迎你。）

　= You can visit anytime. 【第三常用】

　　（你可以隨時來這裡。）

　= You're always welcome. 【第二常用】

　　（隨時歡迎你。）

　= Our door is always open to you. 【第五常用】

　　（我們的大門總是為你而開。）【to 也可改成 for】

　= Come visit anytime. 【第四常用】

　　（你可以隨時來拜訪我們。）

　　【come 後面省略 and 或 to】

BOOK 10

## 7. *Have a safe trip*.

safe〔sef〕*adj.* 安全的      trip〔trɪp〕*n.* 旅行

　　這句話源自：I hope you have a safe trip. 意思是「我希望你有一個安全的旅行。」也就是「希望你旅途平安。」也可以幽默地說：Arrive in one piece. ( 祝你平安到達。)【*in one piece*「安然無恙地」，in one piece 的用法，參照 p.649-650】

## 8. *Have a nice flight*.

flight〔flaɪt〕*n.* 飛行

　　這句話的字面意思是「有一個好的飛行。」引申為「祝你飛行順利。」源自：I hope you have a nice flight. ( 我希望你飛行順利。)

下面都是美國人常說的話，我們按照使用頻率排列：

① *Have a nice flight*.【第一常用】
② Have a good flight.【第二常用】
　( 祝你飛行順利。)
③ Have a smooth flight.【第三常用】
　( 祝你飛行順利。)
　【smooth〔smuð〕*adj.* 順利的】

④ Have a safe flight. ( 祝你飛行平安。)
⑤ Have a pleasant flight. ( 祝你飛行愉快。)
⑥ I hope you have a nice flight.
　( 我希望你飛行順利。)

BOOK 10

9. **Take care returning home.**

**take care** 注意；小心　　return〔rɪ'tɝn〕 v. 返回

這句話源自：Take care of yourself while you're returning home. 意思是「在你回家的時候要照顧你自己。」所以，***Take care returning home.*** 的意思就是「回家路上要小心。」

下面各句意思相同，我們按照使用頻率排列：

① ***Take care returning home.***【第一常用】
② Take care of yourself returning home.
（回家路上要小心。）【第二常用】
③ Take care going home.【第三常用】
（回家路上要小心。）

④ Be careful returning home.
（回家路上要小心。）
⑤ Have a safe trip home.
（祝你一路平安到家。）
⑥ Get home safely.（祝你平安到家。）

⑦ Be careful on your way home.
（回家路上小心。）
⑧ Arrive home safely.（祝你平安到家。）
⑨ Please take care of yourself on your trip home.（回家路上請保重。）

## 【對話練習】

1. A：**I'm sorry you're leaving**.

   B：I'm sad to leave, too.
   I just hate to go.
   I really enjoyed this place.
   【hate〔het〕*v.* 不願意；討厭
   just〔dʒʌst〕*adv.* 真地；實在是】

   A：我很遺憾你要離開了。

   B：要離開我也很難過。
   我真不想走。
   我真的很喜歡這個地方。

2. A：**I enjoyed your visit**.

   B：Thank you for saying that.
   I had a wonderful time here.
   I appreciate everything you
   did for me.
   【appreciate〔ə'prɪʃɪ,et〕*v.* 感激】

   A：和你在一起的這段時間
   很愉快。

   B：謝謝你這麼說。
   我在這裡很愉快。
   感謝你為我所做的一切。

3. A：**I look forward to seeing
   you again**.

   B：We'll meet again for sure.
   I'm looking forward to it.
   Let's meet often in the
   future. [*for sure* 一定]

   A：我盼望能再見到你。

   B：我們一定會再見面的。
   我很期待。
   我們以後常常見面吧。

4. A：**Come back anytime**.

   B：I promise I will be back.
   I'll return again soon.
   I'll visit as often as I can.
   【promise〔'prɑmɪs〕*v.* 保證；答應】

   A：請隨時回來。

   B：我保證我會回來。
   我很快就會再回來。
   我會儘可能常來拜訪，

BOOK 10

BOOK 10

5. A : **You're always welcome**.　　　　A：隨時歡迎你。

　　B : That's kind of you to say.　　　B：你這麼說，眞是好人。

　　　　Your words touch my heart.　　　你的話讓我很感動。

　　　　I appreciate your hospitality　　我非常感謝你的熱情

　　　　so much.

　　【*touch one's heart* 感動某人

　　　　hospitality〔,hɑspɪˈtælətɪ〕*n.* 熱情款待】

6. A : **You have an open invitation**.　　A：隨時歡迎你。

　　B : Thanks!　　　　　　　　　　　B：謝謝！

　　　　I'm sure you'll see me soon.　　我相信你很快就會看到我。

　　　　I'm itching to come back.　　　我很想回來。

　　【itch〔ɪtʃ〕*v.* 很想】

7. A : **Have a safe trip**.　　　　　　A：希望你旅途平安。

　　B : Thank you, I will.　　　　　　B：謝謝你，我會的。

　　　　Don't worry about me.　　　　別爲我擔心。

　　　　I always travel safely.　　　　我總是旅途平安。

8. A : **Have a nice flight**.　　　　　A：祝你飛行順利。

　　B : I always do.　　　　　　　　　B：我一直都是。

　　　　I'm a good air traveler.　　　　我是個很棒的空中旅行家。

　　　　I'm very comfortable on　　　　在飛機上我很自在。

　　　　planes.

9. A : **Take care returning home**.　　A：回家路上要小心。

　　B : I promise I'll be careful.　　　B：我保證我會很小心。

　　　　I appreciate your concern.　　　感謝你的關心。

　　　　You take care of yourself,　　　你自己也要保重。

　　　　too.【concern〔kənˈsɜn〕*n.* 關心】

# 「一口氣背會話」經 BOOK 10

唸英文要像唸經一樣，每天大聲唸，從起床到睡覺，唸得比看得快，最後不看也會唸，養成習慣後，你會全身舒爽，你試試看，奇妙無比。

1. When are you arriving?
   *What's* the date and time?
   *What's* your airline and flight
      number?

   What are your plans?
   Do you have reservations?
   Shall I book a room for you?

   It's fall here.
   The weather is getting colder.
   Please pack some warm clothes.

2. Welcome!
   You made it!
   I'm glad you're here.

   *I*'m pleased to meet you.
   *I*'ve heard so much about you.
   It's an honor.

   *How* was your flight?
   *How* are you feeling?
   What shall we do first?

3. Shall we go now?
   I have a car outside.
   Please follow me.

   *Let me* help.
   *Let me* carry that.
   I insist.

   Here's the car.
   Bags go in the trunk.
   Hop in.

4. First time here?
   Been here before?
   Have any questions?

   *Are you* tired at all?
   *Are you* hungry or thirsty?
   If you need anything, let me know.

   How do you like this weather?
   *Is it* different?
   *Is it* like this back home?

5. *I* beg your pardon?
   *I* didn't catch that.
   What did you say?

   *Could you* repeat that?
   *Could you* speak up?
   Please speak slowly.

   I don't get it.
   What do you mean?
   Please explain it to me.

6. Here's the schedule.
   Take a look.
   See if it's OK.

   *I*'d like your opinion.
   *I* want your approval.
   You can change it if you want.

   *Let's* discuss it.
   *Let's* go over it.
   I want everything to be clear.

7. How about a meal?
   Let me invite you.
   I know some good places.

   *You'll* like it.
   *You'll* have fun.
   It'll be a good time.

   Do you have time?
   We won't be gone long.
   You're welcome to join me.

8. Order anything.
   Choose what you like.
   Don't worry about the price.

   This dish is a house favorite.
   I've had it before.
   It's very tasty.

   How is it?
   Is it good?
   Want some more?

9. Are you all right?
   *Is* anything the matter?
   *Is* everything OK?

   *You* look a little pale.
   *You* must be exhausted.
   I bet you're tired.

   Can I get you anything?
   Want to take some medicine?
   Do you want me to take you to
      the doctor?

10. What are you doing this weekend?
    Have any plans?
    Want to meet?

    I have some free time.
    *Want to* go sightseeing?
    *Want to* do something fun?

    Let me be your guide.
    *What* are your interests?
    *What* do you want to do?

11. Let's start out early tomorrow.
    *I'll* pick you up at seven-thirty.
    *I'll* be there on time.

    Please meet me out front.
    *I'll* be waiting in the car.
    *I'll* keep driving around if I can't
       park.

    Don't eat anything before.
    I'll take you for a good breakfast.
    Your batteries will be fully charged.

12. *I*'m sorry you're leaving.
    *I* enjoyed your visit.
    *I* look forward to seeing you again.

    Come back anytime.
    *You*'re always welcome.
    *You* have an open invitation.

    *Have a* safe trip.
    *Have a* nice flight.
    Take care returning home.

# BOOK 11　當一個好客人 ★

▶11-1　當你想去朋友家拜訪時，就可以打電話跟他說：

> Hey, it's me.
> How the heck are you?
> It's been a while.

▶11-2　當你一進朋友家的時候，就說：

> My, your home is gorgeous.
> It looks so inviting.
> It feels warm and friendly.

▶11-3　進到客廳後，坐在沙發上，就可說：

> I like the decoration.
> It's very stylish.
> It has a comfortable feel.

▶11-4　看到朋友的傢俱，就可說：

> Your furniture is lovely.
> Every piece is attractive.
> It really makes the room.

▶11-5　當你一走進廚房，就可說：

> Your kitchen is modern.
> You have more shelves and cabinets.
> It's much nicer than mine.

▶11-6　快要吃飯時，看到主人忙裡忙外，就可以說：

> Put me to work.
> Give me something to do.
> If you don't let me help, I'll feel guilty.

▶ 11-7　坐在餐桌吃飯時，你就可以說：

This smells marvelous.
The aroma is incredible.
It looks too good to eat.

▶ 11-8　看到主人可愛的小baby，就可說：

What a cute baby!
What a little angel!
What an adorable child!

▶ 11-9　看到主人的小孩，就可說：

You have a great kid.
He looks like you.
He looks intelligent and bright.

▶ 11-10　看到主人家的狗，就可說：

What a great-looking dog!
What a perfect companion!
Is it a he or she?

▶ 11-11　看到主人有這麼好的家庭，就可說：

Look at you.
You have it all.
You've got everything.

▶ 11-12　要告別時，在門口，你就可說：

You are a wonderful host.
Thanks for your hospitality.
Thanks for having me over.

# *1. Hey, it's me.*

| | |
|---|---|
| Hey, it's me. | 嘿，是我。 |
| How the heck are you? | 你究竟怎樣？ |
| It's been a while. | 自從我們上次見面以來，<br>已經很久了。 |
| | |
| *I*'m coming to your area. | 我要到你家附近。 |
| *I*'ll be in your neck of the woods. | 我將去你那邊。 |
| *I*'m anxious to see you. | 我急於想見你。 |
| | |
| Can I come over? | 我能不能順便拜訪你？ |
| Are you up for a visitor? | 方便去拜訪你嗎？ |
| We can catch up on things. | 我們可以聊聊近況。 |

BOOK 11

**\*\*** ──────────────

hey〔he〕*interj.* 嘿；喂；啊    heck〔hɛk〕*n.* hell 的委婉語
*the heck* 究竟；到底    while〔hwaɪl〕*n.* 一會兒；一段時間
area〔'ɛrɪə〕*n.* 地區；地方    neck〔nɛk〕*n.* 脖子；狹長地帶
*neck of the woods* 地帶；地段；附近地區
anxious〔'æŋkʃəs〕*adj.* 渴望的    *come over* 順便拜訪
*catch up on* 得到關於…的消息；趕完（應完成的工作）

## 【背景説明】

　　當你想要到外國人家裡作客，你就可以打電話給他，説這九句好聽的話。

1. *Hey, it's me.*

　　hey〔he〕*interj.* 嘿；喂；啊

> 　　hey 主要用在引起別人注意或打招呼，在這裡是打招呼，相當於 hi〔haɪ〕或 hello〔həˈlo〕，可翻成「嘿」或「喂」。
>
> 　　打招呼常用的有：① Hey!（嘿！）② Hi!（嗨！）③ Hello!（哈囉！）④ What's up?（怎麼樣啊？）⑤ How are you?（你好嗎？）
>
> 　　這句話的意思是「嘿，是我。」不能説成：*Hey, it's I.*（誤）
>
> 　　也可加上對方的姓名，説成：Hey, Pat, it's me.（嘿，派特，是我。）也可以加長爲：Hey, it's me calling from Taiwan.（嘿，是我，我從台灣打電話來。）
>
> 對常打電話給他的人，可説：
> > *Hey, it's me again.*（嘿，又是我。）
> > *Hey, it's just me.*（嘿，就是我。）

對很久沒打電話給他的人，就可說：

**Hey**, *it's me*. Are you surprised?

（嘿，是我。你驚訝嗎？）

**Hey**, *it's me*. Can you believe it?

（嘿，是我。你相信嗎？）

禮貌一點的話，就可以說：

**Hey**, *it's me*. How are you?

（嘿，是我。你好嗎？）

下面是美國人常說的話：

**Hey**, *it's me*. 【最常用】

Hey, this is me. （嘿，這是我。）【第三常用】

Hey, it's me calling. 【第二常用】

（嘿，這是我打電話給你。）

【比較】 Hey, it's me calling. 【正】

*Hey*, *it's my calling*. 【誤】

**BOOK 11**

2. **How the heck are you?**

heck〔hεk〕*n.* hell 的委婉語

**the heck** 究竟；到底（= *in the heck*）

這句話的意思是「你究竟怎樣？」（= *How in the heck are you?*）美國人喜歡用 **the heck**（究竟；到底）來加強疑問句的語氣，如 What **the heck** do you have?（你究竟有什麼？）或 Where **the heck** are you going?（你究竟要去哪裡？）

【比較1】

***How the heck are you?***

【語氣委婉，男女都可用】

How the hell are you?

【語氣粗魯，只有男生用】

【***the hell*** 究竟 ( = *in hell* )】

How the heck are you?

在字典上，能找到 ***the hell*** 和 ***in hell***，但是沒有 in the hell，不過美國人常說：How in the hell are you? ( 你究竟怎樣？) ***the heck*** 可說成 ***in the heck***，不可說成 *in heck* ( 誤 )。

【比較2】 下面是美國人對熟的朋友常說的話，句意相同，我們按照使用頻率排列：

① ***How the heck are you?*** 【第一常用】

② How ***in the world*** are you? 【第二常用】
（你究竟怎樣？）

③ How ***on earth*** are you? 【第三常用】
（你究竟怎樣？）

【***in the world*** 究竟；到底 ( = *on earth* )】

④ How ***in Heaven's name*** are you?
（你究竟怎樣？）

⑤ How ***in God's name*** are you?
（你究竟怎樣？）

⑥ How ***in the name of God*** are you?
（你究竟怎樣？）

【***in Heaven's name*** 究竟 ( = *in God's name* = *in the name of God* )】

3. *It's been a while.*

while〔hwaɪl〕*n.* 一會兒；一段時間

> while 可表「短時間」，也可表示「長時間」，如
> 果要區分，就可説 a short while 或 a long while，

例如：

I arrived here *a short while* ago.
（我不久前才到這裡。）

I haven't seen her for *a long while*.
（我已經很久沒見過她了。）

　　*It's been a while.* 字面的意思是「已經有一段
時間了。」在這裡引申爲「已經很久了。」( = *It's
been a long time.* ) 源自：It's been a while since
we last saw each other. ( 自從我們上次見面以來，
已經很久了。)【last〔læst〕*adv.* 上一次】*It's been a
while*. 也可以加強語氣説成：It's been quite a
while. ( 已經好久了。)

【比較】 下面兩句意思相同：

　　　　*It's been a while.* 【較常用】

　　= It has been a while. 【常用，強調】

　　下面各句意思相同，我們按照使用頻率排列，
第一句和第二句使用頻率非常接近：

① *It's been a while.* 【第一常用】

② It's been a long time. ( 已經很久了。)【第二常用】

③ It's been too long. ( 已經太久了。)【第三常用】

【It's been a long time. 在本書的 p.494-495 有説明。】

BOOK 11

④ A long time has passed.

（已經過了很長的時間了。）

⑤ A lot of time has passed.

（已經過了很久了。）

⑥ Much time has passed.

（已經過了很久了。）

【pass〔pæs〕v. 經過】

4. *I'm coming to your area.*

area〔'ɛrɪə〕n. 地區；地方

原則上，come 是「來」，go 是「去」，但是，有時必須用 come 代替 go，表示親切，例如：

I'll come to see you.（我會去看你。）

Mom, I'm coming home.【小孩打電話常說】

（媽，我要回家了。）

I'm coming soon.（我很快就來了。）

所以，*I'm coming to your area.* 的意思是「我要到你家附近。」your area 相當於 your neighborhood（你家附近）。

【neighborhood〔'nebɚ͵hʊd〕n. 鄰近地區】

【比較1】

*I'm coming to your area.*【正】

*I'm going to your area.*【誤，文法對，不親切，

　　既然到別人那裡去，就要表示出你的情感。】

【比較 2 】

I'm going to be in your area.【正】

（我要到你家附近。）

*I'm coming to be in your area.*【誤】

**be going to + V.** 即將~

【比較 3 】 下面兩句話都正確：

I'm coming to your school.【正，較有感情】

（我要到你的學校。）

I'm going to your school.【正，一般語氣】

（我要去你的學校。）

【比較 4 】 下面兩句話意思不同：

I'm coming to your area.

（我要到你家附近。）

I'm coming to your place.

（我要去你家。）【 your place = your home 】

【比較 5 】 「來去動詞」的現在進行式、未來式，和
未來進行式，都可表未來。

*I'm coming to your area.*

【來去動詞 come，用現在進行式，表「不久的未來」，
表示「即將要去」。】

I'll come to your area.

（我將去你家附近。）【沒有說明何時要去】

I'll be coming to your area.

（我要到你家附近。）

【未來進行式可表「預定的未來」。】

BOOK 11

5. *I'll be in your neck of the woods.*

neck〔nɛk〕*n.* 脖子；狹長地帶

*neck of the woods* 地帶；地段；附近地區

> neck 主要意思是「脖子」，常引申爲像脖子一樣的「狹長地帶」，或「地帶」。*neck of the woods* 原指「森林中的居住地區」，因爲從前人們多住在森林中，在此引申爲「地帶；附近地區」。*in your neck of the woods* 字面的意思是「在你森林中居住的地區」，引申爲「在你那一帶」( = *in your area* )。這句話的意思是「我將去你那邊。」

【比較】 下面各句意思相同，我們按照使用頻率排列，前三句使用頻率非常接近：

① *I'll be in your neck of the woods.*
【親切、友善、幽默】【第一常用】

② I'll be in your area.【第二常用】
（我將去你家附近。）

③ I'll be in your neighborhood.【第三常用】
（我將去你家附近。）

④ I'll be in your region.
（我將去你家附近。）

⑤ I'll be in your part of town.
（我將去你家附近。）

⑥ I'll be in your section of town.
（我將去你家附近。）

region〔ˈridʒən〕*n.* 地方；地帶　　town〔taʊn〕*n.* 城市；城鎮
section〔ˈsɛkʃən〕*n.* 區域；地區

⑦ I'll be in the region near you.

（我將去你家附近。）

⑧ I'll be in the area near your house.

（我將去你家附近。）

6. *I'm anxious to see you*.

anxious〔'æŋkʃəs〕*adj.* 渴望的；急著要

這句話的意思是「我急於想見你。」可以加強語氣說成：I'm very anxious to see you.（我非常想見你。）句中 anxious 也可改成 eager〔'igɚ〕*adj.* 渴望的；極想，說成：I'm eager to see you. 兩句意思相同。

美國人也常說：I can't wait to see you.（我迫不及待想見你。）或 I really want to see you.（我真想見你。）

7. *Can I come over?*

*come over* 順便拜訪

*come over* 有很多意思，字面的意思是「從遠方過來」，在此作「順便拜訪」解，在字典上的英文解釋是 pay a casual visit。

這句話的意思是「我能不能順便拜訪你？」可以加強語氣說成：Can I *come over* and visit you?（我能不能順便去拜訪你？）【and 連接兩個同義的單字或片語，有加強語氣的作用。】

也有美國人説成：Mind if I *come over*?（你介不介意我順道拜訪你？）

【比較】 下面兩句話意思完全不同：

> **Can I come over?**（我可不可以順便拜訪你？）
>
> Can I come?（我可不可以和你一起去？）
>
> （= *Can I come with you?*）

> **Can I come over?** 當然也可説成：Can I visit you?（我能不能去拜訪你？）或 Can we meet?（我們能不能見面？）

## 8. *Are you up for a visitor?*

在所有中外字典中，都查不到 be up for *sb.* 的成語，只有 *feel up to V-ing*「想要～」（= *feel like V-ing*），但是，*Are you up for a visitor?* 常用，我們一定要詳加研究。

① *be up for* 接名詞，意思是「想要～」，如：

*Are you up for* a bite?（你要不要吃點東西？）
（= *Do you feel like a bite?*）

*Are you up for* a movie tonight?
（你今晚想看電影嗎？）

*Are you up for* a pizza?（你想不想吃披薩？）

*Are you up for* a walk tonight?
（你今晚想不想散步？）

② *be up to* 常接動名詞，意思是「想要～」如：

> *Are you up to* meeting me tonight?
>　（你今晚想不想和我見面？）
>
> *Are you up to* going out after dinner?
>　（你想不想吃完晚餐後出去？）
>
> *Are you up to* going jogging with me?
>　（你想不想和我一起去慢跑？）
>　【jog〔dʒɑg〕*v.* 慢跑】

　　有時 be up to 後面也可接名詞，像 Are you up to it?（你願意嗎？）（= *Are you up for it?*）我們可以把此種情況當成例外。

---

### *Are you up for a visitor?*

源自：Are you feeling up for a visitor? 句中的 up 是形容詞，作「高興的；心情好的」（= *happy*）解。看到外國人精神好，你可以說：You look like  *you're feeling up* today.（你今天看起來心情很好。）相反地，看到一個人垂頭喪氣，你可以說：You look sad. *Are you feeling down?*（你看起來很傷心。你是不是心情不好？）

　　*Are you up for a visitor?* 字面的意思是「你是不是有心情見一個訪客？」（= *Are you feeling up to seeing a visitor?*）在這裡引申為「方便去拜訪你嗎？」通常 *be up for* 後面接名詞，be up to 後面接動名詞，兩者意思相同，都表示「想要～」或「願意～」等。

Are you up for a visitor?

美國人常説：I'm up for the challenge. 或
I'm feeling up for the challenge. 意思是「我準
備好接受挑戰。」(= I'm ready for the challenge.)
在此 up 作「準備好的」(= prepared ; ready) 解，
由此我們可以看出，up 可以引申出很多意思，完
全看句中的意思決定，通常是正面的。

*Are you up for a visitor?* 有三個含意：

① Are you willing to have a visitor?
（你願不願意有人去拜訪你？）

② Are you in the mood for a visitor?
（你想不想要有人去拜訪你？）

③ Are you feeling well enough for a visitor?
（你是不是有好心情，可以接受別人拜訪？）

所以，*Are you up for a visitor?* 也可説成：
Are you up to having a visitor?

9. *We can catch up on things.*

*catch up on* 在字典上有兩個主要的意思，一個
是「得到關於…的消息」(= *learn the news of*…)，
像：Let's *catch up on* each other's news. （我們
互相交換消息吧。）另一個是「趕完（應完成的工
作）」，像：I have to *catch up on* my work. （我必
須趕完我的工作。）可參照 p.1032。

*We can catch up on things*. 可能源自：We can catch up on all the things that have happened since we last met.（我們可以談談自從上次見面以來，所發生的事情。）所以，這句話的意思是「**我們可以聊聊近況。**」美國人也常簡化成：*We can catch up*.（我們可以聊聊。）（= *We can have a conversation*.）

下面各句意思相同，都是美國人常說的話，我們按照使用頻率排列：

① *We can catch up on things*.【第一常用】

② We can catch up on everything.【第二常用】
（我們可以聊聊近況。）

③ We can catch up on all the news.【第三常用】
（我們可以聊聊近況。）【news〔njuz〕*n.* 消息；近況】

④ We can catch up on the latest news.
（我們可以聊聊近況。）

⑤ We can catch up on what we've been doing.（我們可以聊聊近況。）

⑥ We can tell each other what we've been doing.（我們可以聊聊近況。）
【latest〔'letɪst〕*adj.* 最新的】

⑦ We can catch up on what's been going on.
（我們可以聊聊最近發生的事。）

⑧ This is a chance for us to catch up on things.（這是我們可以聊聊近況的機會。）
【*go on* 發生】

BOOK 11

## 【對話練習】

1. A：**Hey, it's me.**

　 B：What a surprise!
　　 Thank you for calling.
　　 It's great to hear your voice.

2. A：**How the heck are you?**

　 B：Things have been great.
　　 Things couldn't be better.
　　 I have no complaints.
　　【complaint〔kəm'plent〕*n.* 抱怨】

3. A：**It's been a while.**

　 B：It's been ages.
　　 It's been way too long.
　　 When did we last get
　　 together?
　　【ages〔edʒz〕*n. pl.* 長時間
　　 way〔we〕*adv.* 太
　　 ***get together*** 聚在一起】

4. A：**I'm coming to your area.**

　 B：That's fantastic.
　　 That's wonderful news.
　　 I'm so happy to hear that.
　　【fantastic〔fæn'tæstɪk〕*adj.* 很棒的】

A：嘿，是我。

B：真是令人驚訝！
　 謝謝你打電話來。
　 聽到你的聲音真棒。

A：你究竟怎樣？

B：情況不錯。
　 再好也不過了。
　 我沒什麼好抱怨的。

A：自從我們上次見面以來，
　 已經很久了。

B：已經很久了。
　 已經太久了。
　 我們上次聚在一起是什
　 麼時候？

A：我要到你家附近。

B：太棒了。
　 這消息真棒。
　 很高興聽到這件事。

5. A : **I'll be in your neck of the woods**.
    B : Let's meet for sure.
       We must get together.
       We can't miss this chance.
       【*for sure* 一定　　miss〔mɪs〕*v.* 錯過】

A : 我將去你那邊。
B : 我們一定要見面。
    我們一定要聚一聚。
    我們不能錯過這次機會。

6. A : **I'm anxious to see you**.
    B : I feel the same way.
       I couldn't agree more.
       That's exactly how I feel.
       【exactly〔ɪg'zæktlɪ〕*adv.* 正是】

A : 我急於想見你。
B : 我也有同樣的感覺。
    我非常同意。
    那正是我的感覺。

7. A : **Can I come over?**
    B : Not right now.
       It's not a good time.
       Maybe later.

A : 我能不能順便拜訪你？
B : 現在不要。
    現在不是個好時機。
    也許待會可以。

8. A : **Are you up for a visitor?**
    B : I love to have visitors.
       I like to entertain.
       Please visit me anytime.
       【entertain〔͵ɛntɚ'ten〕*v.* 招待；娛樂】

A : 方便去拜訪你嗎？
B : 我喜歡有人拜訪我。
    我喜歡招待客人。
    請隨時來拜訪我。

9. A : **We can catch up on things**.
    B : Yes, let's catch up.
       We can have a long talk.
       We can have a nice chat.
       【talk〔tɔk〕*n.* 談話　　chat〔tʃæt〕*n.* 聊天】

A : 我們可以聊聊近況。
B : 是啊，我們來聊聊。
    我們可以聊很久。
    我們可以好好聊一聊。

BOOK 11

# 2. Can I have a tour?

| | |
|---|---|
| My, your home is gorgeous. | 哎呀，你家好美啊。 |
| *It* looks so inviting. | 它看起來非常吸引人。 |
| *It* feels warm and friendly. | 它使人感覺旣溫暖又親切。 |
| | |
| It's very charming. | 它非常迷人。 |
| I'd love to see more. | 我很想要多看一點。 |
| Can I have a tour? | 我能不能參觀一下？ |
| | |
| *It's* a nice neighborhood. | 它在好的地段。 |
| *It's* peaceful and quiet. | 這裡非常安靜。 |
| How did you find this place? | 你是怎麼找到這個地方的？ |

\*\* ──────────────

my〔maɪ〕*interj.*【表示驚訝】哎喲；哎呀
gorgeous〔'gɔrdʒəs〕*adj.* 華麗的；極美的
inviting〔ɪn'vaɪtɪŋ〕*adj.* 吸引人的
feel〔fil〕*v.* 使人感覺　　warm〔wɔrm〕*adj.* 溫暖的
friendly〔'frɛndlɪ〕*adj.* 友善的；親切的
charming〔'tʃɑrmɪŋ〕*adj.* 迷人的；吸引人的
tour〔tʊr〕*n.* 參觀
neighborhood〔'nebɚ،hʊd〕*n.* 鄰近地區；地段
peaceful〔'pisfəl〕*adj.* 平靜的　　quiet〔'kwaɪət〕*adj.* 安靜的

## 【背景説明】

　　進了外國朋友的家，你就可以說這九句話，來稱讚他的家。這一回可以和第三冊第九回連起來使用。

1. ***My, your home is gorgeous.***
my〔maɪ〕*interj.*【表示驚訝】哎喲；哎呀
gorgeous〔ˈgɔrdʒəs〕*adj.* 華麗的；極美的；極好的

> 　　my 的主要意思是「我的」，但在這裡是感嘆詞，源自 My goodness!（天啊！）意思是「哎喲；哎呀」，和 wow〔waʊ〕*interj.* 哇啊，意思相近。所有重要的感嘆詞，在 p.706-707 都有説明。

　　在字典上，gorgeous 的主要意思是「豪華的；華麗的」，但在日常生活中，gorgeous 的主要意思是「很漂亮的」（= *very beautiful*），「很可愛的」（= *very lovely*），「很迷人的」（= *very attractive*）。

　　gorgeous 這個字很好用，你每天都應該說，從早上一起床你就可以說：

What a ***gorgeous*** day!（今天天氣真好！）
　（= *What a beautiful day!*）

　　gorgeous 通常用於稱讚女性，當你一看到了美女，就可跟你同伴說：

She is ***gorgeous***.（她很漂亮。）
　（= *She is a gorgeous girl.*）

BOOK 11

看到你的女性朋友衣服穿得很漂亮，你可以說：

Your dress is *gorgeous*.

（妳的衣服好漂亮。）

看到你的朋友戴了很炫的手

錶，你可以說：

That's a *gorgeous* watch.

（那支錶很漂亮。）

看到了美女穿了很好的鞋子，你就可以說：

Those shoes look *gorgeous* on you.

（妳穿的鞋子很好看。）

　　*My, your home is gorgeous*. 的意思是「哎呀，你家好美啊。」美國人也常說成：Oh, your home is gorgeous. （噢，你家好漂亮。）或 Wow, your home is gorgeous. （哇啊，你家好漂亮。）*Your home is gorgeous*. 也常說成：You have a gorgeous home. （你家好漂亮。）可加強語氣說成：You really have a gorgeous home. （你家真是漂亮。）

下面各句意思接近，都是美國人常說的話：

*Your home is gorgeous*. 【第三常用】

（你家很漂亮。）

Your home is beautiful. 【第一常用】

（你家很漂亮。）

Your home is lovely. 【第二常用】

（你家很漂亮。）

【lovely〔ˈlʌvlɪ〕adj. 可愛的；漂亮的】

Your home is wonderful.【第六常用】

（你家真是太棒了。）

Your home is marvelous.【第九常用】

（你家真是太棒了。）

Your home is fantastic.【第七常用】

（你家真是太棒了。）

marvelous（'marvḷəs）adj. 很棒的
fantastic（fæn'tæstɪk）adj. 很棒的

Your home is very attractive.【第四常用】

（你家非常吸引人。）

Your home is magnificent.【第八常用】

（你家真是太棒了。）

Your home is very elegant.【第五常用】

（你家非常高雅。）

attractive（ə'træktɪv）adj. 吸引人的
magnificent（mæg'nɪfəsṇt）adj. 很棒的
elegant（'ɛləgənt）adj. 高雅的

## 2. *It looks so inviting.*

so（so）adv. 非常
inviting（ɪn'vaɪtɪŋ）adj. 吸引人的；迷人的；有魅力的

> invite 的主要意思是「邀請」，但事物當主詞時，invite 作「引誘；誘惑」解，它的現在分詞 inviting 已經變成純粹的形容詞，常作「吸引人的」（= *attractive* ），「有魅力的」（= *tempting* ）解。

> *It looks so inviting*. 意思是「它看起來非常吸引人。」也有美國人説成：It looks very inviting. 或 It looks so attractive. 意思都相同。單獨説這句話，就要説成：Your home looks so inviting. ( 你家看起來非常吸引人。)

3. *It feels warm and friendly*.

feel〔fil〕*v.* 使人感覺　warm〔wɔrm〕*adj.* 溫暖的
friendly〔'frɛndlɪ〕*adj.* 友善的；親切的

　　句中 feel 的主要意思是「感覺」，一般人只會用人當主詞，像 I feel good today. ( 我今天感覺很好。) 但是，事物當主詞，作「使人感覺」或「摸上去，手感覺」解，很常用，我們非學會不可。例如：

It *feels* cold outside.
( 外面很冷。)

It *feels* good to be on vacation.
( 渡假的感覺眞好。)

This sunshine *feels* good.
( 這陽光使人感覺眞好。)

> *It feels good to be on vacation.*

This cool breeze *feels* great.
( 這涼爽的微風使人感覺眞好。)

It *feels* wonderful to be out of school.
( 不上學的感覺眞好。)

It *feels* so nice to sleep late on Sundays.
( 星期天晚起的感覺眞好。)

【breeze〔briz〕*n.* 微風　late〔let〕*adv.* 晚　*sleep late* 晚起】

This cloth *feels* soft.

（這塊布摸起來很柔軟。）

This new shirt *feels* itchy.

（這件新襯衫穿起來很癢。）

My shoes *feel* too tight.（我的鞋子很緊。）

cloth〔klɔθ〕*n.* 布　　itchy〔ˈɪtʃɪ〕*adj.* 發癢的

tight〔taɪt〕*adj.* 緊的

*It feels warm and friendly.* 的意思是「它使人感覺既溫暖又親切。」(=*It makes me feel warm and friendly.*) 單獨說一句話，就要說成：Your home feels warm and friendly.（你的家使人感覺既溫暖又親切。）

4. *It's very charming.*

charming〔ˈtʃɑrmɪŋ〕*adj.* 迷人的；吸引人的；有魅力的

BOOK 11

這句話的意思是「它非常迷人。」也可說成：It's so charming. 或加強語氣說成：It's very charming here.（這裡非常迷人。）或 It's a very charming place.（這個地方很有魅力。）

在房子裡的任何東西，都可以用 *charming* 來形容。看到牆壁上的畫，就可以說：What a *charming* picture!（多麼吸引人的畫！）看到花瓶，就可以說：That's a charming vase.（那個花瓶真好看。）【vase〔ves〕*n.* 花瓶】

看到沙發前面的茶几，
美國人稱作 coffee table，
就可以說：That's a
*charming* coffee table.
（那個茶几很好看。）

coffee table

*charming* 這個字，美國人常用，中國人不習
慣使用。由於它是一個稱讚的字，我們都應該常
說。看到美女，你可以一口氣稱讚三句，都用到
charming：

You're a *charming* girl.
（妳是一個迷人的女孩。）

You are a
charming girl.

You have a *charming*
personality.
（妳有吸引人的性格。）

Your style is very *charming*.
（妳的氣質很吸引人。）

personality〔‚pɜsn̩'æləti〕 *n.* 性格
style〔staɪl〕 *n.* 風格

看到美好的事物，你可以說：

Your house is so *charming*.（你的房子很迷人。）
Your furniture is very *charming*.
（你的傢俱非常迷人。）
The way you've decorated is *charming*.
（你的裝潢很迷人。）

furniture〔'fɜnɪtʃɚ〕 *n.* 傢俱
decorate〔'dɛkə‚ret〕 *v.* 裝飾；裝潢

What a *charming* outfit! ( 你的穿著很迷人！)

Your shoes are *charming*. ( 你的鞋子很迷人。)

Your handbag is *charming*.

( 你的手提包很迷人。)

outfit〔ˋaʊtˌfɪt〕*n.* 服裝　　handbag〔ˋhændˌbæg〕*n.* 手提包

5. *I'd love to see more*.

love〔lʌv〕*v.* 喜歡；願意；很想

　　這句話源自：I would love to see more *if you don't mind*. ( 如果你不介意的話，我很想多看一點。) 假設法中，也可以有直說法的 if 子句，但不能説成：*... if you didn't mind.* ( 誤)，否則句意就不合理。

　　*I'd love to see mor*e. 意思是「我很想要多看一點。」美國人常用 love 來加強 like 的語氣，作「喜歡；願意；很想」解。more 在此是代名詞，表「更多的東西」。

這句話可加長爲：

I'd love to see some more *of your house*.

( 我很想多看看你的房子。)

I'd love to see more *of the bedrooms and the closets*. ( 我很想多看看你的臥室和衣櫥。)

【bedroom〔ˋbɛdˌrum〕*n.* 臥室　　closet〔ˋklɑzɪt〕*n.* 衣櫥】

BOOK 11

【比較】 I'd love to 和 I'd like to 意思相同，語
氣不同。

**I'd love to see more.**【語氣較強】
= I really want to see more.
（我很想要多看一點；我真的想要多看一點。）

**I'd like to see more.**【一般語氣】
= I want to see more.
（我想要多看一點。）

6. **Can I have a tour?**

tour〔tur〕*n.* 旅行；觀光；參觀

tour 的主要意思是
「旅行」，但在這裡是作
「參觀」解。這句話的意
思是「我能不能參觀一
下？」源自：Can I have
a tour of your house?

Can I have a tour?

（我能不能參觀你的房子？）美國人也常説：

Can you give me a tour?
（你能不能帶我參觀一下？）
Can you give me a tour of your house?
（你能不能讓我參觀你的房子？）
Can you show me around?
（你能不能帶我到處參觀一下？）
【*show sb. around* 帶某人參觀】

7. **It's a nice neighborhood.**

neighborhood〔'nebə,hʊd〕*n.* 鄰近地區；地段；地區

　　這句話是一個省略句，源自：**It's in a nice neighborhood.** 意思是「它在好的地段。」nice neighborhood 是指「鄰居好」( neighbors are good )，也指「地段好」( good location )。

　　美國人也常說：I like your neighborhood. ( 我喜歡你這個地段。) 或 Your neighborhood is very nice. ( 你這個地段很好。)

【比較1】 下面兩句話意思相同，使用頻率也相同：

　　**It's a nice neighborhood.**【正，慣用句】

　　It's in a nice neighborhood.【正】

　　( 它在好的地段。)

【比較2】 **It's a nice neighborhood.** 是慣用句，
　　　　　不能更改：

　　**Your house is a nice neighborhood.**【誤】

　　【你的房子不等於 a nice neighborhood】

　　Your house is in a nice neighborhood.【正】

　　( 你的房子在好的地段。)

It's a nice neighborhood.

8. ***It's peaceful and quiet.***

peaceful〔'pisfəl〕*adj.* 和平的;平靜的
quiet〔'kwaɪət〕*adj.* 安靜的

　　quiet 純粹指「安靜的」,peaceful 的基本意思
是「和平的」,在這裡是指「平靜的;寧靜的;安寧
的」。英文常用同義的形容詞來加強語氣。這句話
的意思是:「這裡非常安靜。」也可以加強語氣說
成:It's so peaceful and quiet. 或 It's very
peaceful and quiet. 意思都是「這裡非常安靜。」
可加長為:It's peaceful and quiet around here.
(這附近非常安靜。)

9. ***How did you find this place?***

　　這句話的意思是「你是怎麼找到這個地方的?」
也可說成:How did you ***discover*** this place?(你
是怎麼發現這個地方的?)可加強語氣說成:How
did you find this ***wonderful*** place?(你是怎麼找
到這麼棒的地方的?)

　　禮貌一點的說法是:***May I ask***, "How did
you find this place?"(可不可以請問,你是如何
找到這個地方的?)( = ***May I ask how you found
this place?***)或 Please tell me how you found
this place.(請告訴我,你是怎麼找到這個地方的。)

【對話練習】

1. A: **My, your home is gorgeous**.　　　　A：哎呀，你家好美啊。

　B: Thank you for saying that.　　　　　B：謝謝你這麼說。

　　We like it, too.　　　　　　　　　　　我們也很喜歡。

　　We worked hard to make it　　　　　　我們很努力要把它弄

　　nice.　　　　　　　　　　　　　　　得很好。

2. A: **It looks so inviting**.　　　　　　A：它看起來非常吸引人。

　B: I hope you're right.　　　　　　　　B：我希望你說的對。

　　I hope that's true.　　　　　　　　　我希望那是真的。

　　I'm happy to hear that.　　　　　　　我很高興聽到這句話。

3. A: **It feels warm and friendly**.　　　A：它使人感覺既溫暖又

　B: That was our goal.　　　　　　　　　　親切。

　　That was our objective.　　　　　　B：那是我們的目標。

　　That's what we wanted to　　　　　　那是我們的目標。

　　achieve.　　　　　　　　　　　　　那是我們想要達成的。

　　【objective〔əb'dʒɛktɪv〕*n.* 目標

　　achieve〔ə'tʃiv〕*v.* 達到】

4. A: **It's very charming**.　　　　　　　A：它非常迷人。

　B: I was just about to say that.　　　　B：我剛剛正要這麼說。

　　It's such a delightful surprise.　　這真令人驚喜。

　　I never would have guessed.　　　　我真是想不到。

BOOK 11

5. A : **I'd love to see more**.　　　　A : 我很想要多看一點。

　 B : OK, follow me.　　　　　　　 B : 好的，跟我來。
　　 Let me show you around.　　　　 讓我帶你四處參觀。
　　 Let me give you a tour.　　　　　讓我帶你參觀。

　　【 follow〔'falo〕v. 跟隨
　　　 **show** *sb.* **around** 帶某人參觀】

6. A : **Can I have a tour?**　　　　 A : 我能不能參觀一下？

　 B : Of course you can.　　　　　 B : 當然可以。
　　 I'll give you one right away.　　 我立刻帶你參觀。
　　 Your wish is my command.　　　 我聽你的。

　　【 wish〔wɪʃ〕n. 願望
　　　 command〔kə'mænd〕n. 命令】

7. A : **It's a nice neighborhood**.　　A : 它在好的地段。

　 B : Yes, the location is good.　　　 B : 是的，地段很好。
　　 Location is so important.　　　　 地段很重要。
　　 Location means everything.　　　 地段是最重要的。

　　【 *mean everything* 是最重要的】

8. A : **It's peaceful and quiet**.　　　A : 這裡非常安靜。

　 B : That's how we like it.　　　　 B : 那就是我們喜歡它的原因。
　　 We like it that way.　　　　　　 我們喜歡這樣。
　　 We hope it never changes.　　　 我們希望永遠不會變。

　　【 *that way* 那樣子】

9. A : **How did you find this place?**　A : 你是怎麼找到這個地方的？

　 B : A friend helped us.　　　　　 B : 朋友幫的忙。
　　 A friend told us about it.　　　　有個朋友告訴我們的。
　　 It's all because of our friend.　　都是因為朋友的緣故。

# *3.  I like the decoration*.

| | |
|---|---|
| I like the decoration. | 我喜歡這種裝潢。 |
| *It*'s very stylish. | 它非常有格調。 |
| *It* has a comfortable feel. | 它給我舒適的感覺。 |
| | |
| The lighting is just right. | 燈光剛好。 |
| All the colors flow well. | 所有的顏色都很搭配。 |
| It creates a relaxed atmosphere. | 它創造了一個溫暖而輕鬆的氣氛。 |
| | |
| *You have* a good eye. | 你很有眼光。 |
| *You have* good taste. | 你有好的品味。 |
| I should hire you to do my house. | 我應該雇用你來裝潢我的房子。 |

BOOK 11

\*\* ――――――――――――――――――――

decoration〔͵dɛkəˈreʃən〕*n.* 裝飾；裝潢
stylish〔ˈstaɪlɪʃ〕*adj.* 有格調的；有氣派的
feel〔fil〕*n.* 感覺　　lighting〔ˈlaɪtɪŋ〕*n.* 照明；光線
*just right* 剛好　　flow〔flo〕*v.* 流動；流暢；順利進行
create〔krɪˈet〕*v.* 創造　　relaxed〔rɪˈlækst〕*adj.* 輕鬆的
atmosphere〔ˈætməs͵fɪr〕*n.* 大氣；氣氛
eye〔aɪ〕*n.* 鑑別力；眼光　　taste〔test〕*n.* 品味；鑑賞力
hire〔haɪr〕*v.* 雇用　　do〔du〕*v.* 裝潢；佈置

## 【背景説明】

　　根據美國人的習慣，到了別人家做客，不講話，別人會覺得奇怪。稱讚的話，説愈多愈好，如此，主人和客人就不會尷尬了。

1. ***I like the decoration.***

decoration〔,dɛkə'reʃən〕*n.* 裝飾；裝潢

　　這句話的意思是「我喜歡這種裝潢。」( = *I like this kind of decoration.* ) decoration 作「裝潢」解時，是抽象名詞，不可數，不能用複數形式，但是，作「裝飾品」解時，是可數名詞。

【比較1】　下面兩句話意思不同：

***I like the decoration.*** ( 我喜歡這種裝潢。)
I like your decorations. ( 我喜歡你的裝飾品。)

【比較2】

***I like the decoration.***【正，常用】
*I like your decoration.*
【誤，句意不清楚，可能表示某一個裝飾品。】
˘ like your style of decoration. 【正】
( 我喜歡你的裝潢風格。)

***I like the decoration.*** 可以加強語氣説成：I like the decoration of this place. ( 我喜歡這裡的裝潢。) 或 I like the decoration in this room.
( 我喜歡這個房間的裝潢。)

## 2. *It's very stylish.*

stylish〔'staɪlɪʃ〕*adj.*　有格調的；有風度的；有氣派的

　　　為了 stylish 這個字，查遍所有中外的字典，在大部份字典上，都作「流行的；時髦的；新式的；漂亮的；高級的」解，這些意思無論用哪一個，都沒辦法完全表達出這個字的本義。幸虧，在「牛津高階雙解字典」中，有了最恰當的翻譯，stylish 作「有格調的」解，才最正確。因為 stylish 這個字，來自 style（格調；風度；氣派）。

　　　*It's very stylish.* 這句話，翻成「它很流行。」也不完全，翻成「它很時髦。」也不完全，最正確的翻譯應該是「**它非常有格調。**」*stylish* 這個字很好用，美國人也常說，例如：

The decoration is *stylish*.（裝潢很有格調。）
The furniture is *stylish*.（傢俱很有格調。）
She is a *stylish* girl.
　（她是個很有格調的女孩。）

*You're a stylish dresser.*

Your outfit is *stylish*.
　（你的服裝非常有格調。）
Your haircut looks *stylish*.
　（你剪的頭髮看起來很有格調。）
You're a *stylish* dresser.（你很會穿衣服。）

outfit〔'aʊt,fɪt〕*n.* 服裝　　haircut〔'hɛr,kʌt〕*n.* 理髮；髮型
dresser〔'drɛsə〕*n.* 穿衣者

Your watch looks very *stylish*.

（你的錶看起來很有格調。）

That's a *stylish* shirt you're wearing.

（你穿的襯衫很有格調。）

Your car looks very *stylish*.

（你的車子看起來很有格調。）

3. *It has a comfortable feel*.

comfortable〔ˈkʌmfətəbḷ〕*adj.* 令人感到舒適的

feel〔fil〕*n.* 氣氛；（物體給人的）感覺

  *feel* 的主要意思是「感覺」，當動詞用；當名詞時，作「（物體給人的）感覺」解，一定要用「非人」當主詞；若用人當主詞，就要用 feeling（感覺），像：I have a comfortable feeling about your decision.（對於你的決定，我感覺很好。）

  *It has a comfortable feel*. 的意思是「它給我舒適的感覺。」( = *It makes me feel comfortable*. )

【比較】*feel* 當名詞時，和 *feeling* 不同：

The room has a comfortable *feel*.【正】

（這房間給人舒適的感覺。）

*The room has a comfortable feeling*.【誤】

The room gives me a comfortable *feeling*.

（這房間使我感覺很舒服。）【正】

4. ***The lighting is just right.***

lighting〔'laɪtɪŋ〕*n.* 照明；照明設備；光線

***just right*** 剛好

　　light 是指單一光源（one light source），
lighting 是指光的亮度（level of light），白天是
光線，晚上是燈光。

　　這句話的意思是「燈光剛好。」可以加強語氣
說成：The lighting in here is just right.（這裡
的燈光剛好。）或 The lighting in this room is
just right.（這房間的燈光剛好。）

這句話可以改成三句：

　　The lighting is not too dark.

　　（光線不會太暗。）

　　It's not too bright.（不會太亮。）

　　It's just right.（剛好。）

　　【dark〔dɑrk〕*adj.* 暗的　　bright〔braɪt〕*adj.* 明亮的】

5. ***All the colors flow well.***

flow〔flo〕*v.* 流動；流暢；順利進行

　　在所有字典上，找不到 ***flow well*** 的成語，但
是美國人常說。***flow well*** 字面的意思是「流得很
順」，引申為「相稱；協調」( = *go well* ; *match
well* )。

這句話引申的意思是「所有的顏色都很搭配。」可以加長為：All the colors in this room flow well together. （在這個房間裡，所有的顏色都非常搭配。）也可說成：*Every color flows well*. （每個顏色都很搭配。）

下面各句意思相同，都是美國人常說的話，我們按照使用頻率排列：

① *All the colors flow well*. 【第一常用】

② All the colors go well. 【第二常用】
   （所有的顏色都很搭配。）

③ All the colors match well. 【第三常用】
   （所有的顏色都很配。）

【go〔go〕v. 適合；相配　match〔mætʃ〕v. 相配】

④ All the colors look good together.
   （所有的顏色配在一起都很好看。）

⑤ All the colors fit nicely together.
   （所有的顏色配在一起很適合。）

⑥ All the colors complement each other.
   （所有的顏色彼此都很相配。）

fit〔fɪt〕v. 適合；配合
nicely〔'naɪslɪ〕adv. 恰好地；精確地
*fit nicely* 恰恰合適
complement〔'kɑmplə,mɛnt〕v. 補充；與…相配

6. *It creates a relaxed atmosphere.*

create〔krɪ'et〕*v.* 創造

relaxed〔rɪ'lækst〕*adj.* 輕鬆的

atmosphere〔'ætməsˌfɪr〕*n.* 大氣；氣氛

　　　relaxed 是純粹的形容詞，和 tired（疲倦的）
一樣，不可寫成 *relax*（誤），因為 relax 是動詞，
作「放鬆；休息」解，像 You work too hard.
You should relax more.（你工作太辛苦了。你應
該多休息。）【參照 p.309-310】

　　　這句話的意思是「它創造了一個輕鬆的氣氛。」
可以加長為：It creates a relaxed atmosphere
in here.（它在這裡創造了一個
輕鬆的氣氛。）也有美國人說
成：It creates a warm
atmosphere. 或 It creates a
cozy atmosphere.（它創造了
一個溫馨的氣氛。）

【cozy〔'kozɪ〕*adj.* 溫暖而舒適的】

7. *You have a good eye.*

eye〔aɪ〕*n.* 眼睛；觀察力；鑑別力；眼光

　　　eye 的主要意思是「眼睛」，an eye 常指「鑑
別力；眼光」，如：You have an eye for beauty.
（你有審美的眼光。）*You have a good eye.* 的意
思是「你很有眼光。」

BOOK 11

這句話可以加長為：You have a good eye for decoration. (你很有裝潢的眼光。) 或 You have a good eye for decorating things. (你對於裝潢東西很有眼光。)

如果你看到你的朋友，帶了一個很漂亮的女朋友，你可以跟他說：You have a good eye for women. (你選女朋友很有眼光。) (= *You have a good eye for selecting women.*)

*You have a good eye for women.*

8. **You have good taste.**

taste 〔 test 〕 *n.* 品味；鑑賞力

這句話的意思是「你有好的品味。」可以加強語氣說：You have excellent taste. (你很有品味。) 可加長為：You have good taste in decoration. (你對裝潢很有品味。)

taste 作「味道；愛好」解時，是可數名詞，如：Honey has a sweet taste. (蜂蜜有甜味。) 但作「品味；鑑賞力」解時，是不可數名詞。

【比較】 **You have good taste.** 【正】
　　　　 *You have a good taste.* 【誤】

9. ***I should hire you to do my house.***

hire〔haɪr〕*v.* 雇用     do〔du〕*v.* 裝潢；佈置

　　句中的 do 很特別，在這裡作「裝潢」解，等
於 decorate。這句話的意思是「我應該雇用你來
裝潢我的房子。」這樣說，有幽默的味道。

　　這句話可以加長為：I should hire you to do
some work at my house.（我應該雇用你來替我裝
潢一下房子。）也可以變成兩句：You're so good.
I should hire you to do my house.（你真行。我
應該雇用你來裝潢我的房子。）

也有美國人說成：

I want to hire you to do my house.
（我想要雇用你來裝潢我的房子。）
I want you to do my house.
（我要你來裝潢我的房子。）
I should get you to decorate my house.
（我應該找你裝潢我的房子。）

You'd be the best person to do my house.
（你會是裝潢我房子的最佳人選。）
You'd be the best choice to do my house.
（你會是裝潢我房子的最佳人選。）
You'd be the best one to do my house.
（你會是裝潢我房子的最佳人選。）
〔the best one = the best person〕

BOOK 11

## 【對話練習】

1. A : **I like the decoration**.
   B : I'm fond of it, too.
   It's very special.
   It's very unique. 【*be fond of* 喜歡
       unique〔ju'nik〕*adj.* 獨特的】

    A：我喜歡這種裝潢。
    B：我也喜歡。
      它非常特別。
      它非常獨特。

2. A : **It's very stylish**.
   B : Everyone says that.
   Everyone says the same thing.
   I guess it must be true.

    A：它非常有格調。
    B：大家都這麼說。
      大家都說一樣的話。
      我猜一定是眞的。

3. A : **It has a comfortable feel**.
   B : I know what you mean.
   It's very well-made.
   They put a lot of care into it.
   【well-made *adj.* 作工考究的
       care〔kɛr〕*n.* 用心；注意】

    A：他給我舒適的感覺。
    B：我知道你的意思。
      它的作工很考究。
      他們很用心。

4. A : **The lighting is just right**.
   B : I'm glad you think so.
   Before, it was too dark in here.
   Now, we've added two lights.
   【add〔æd〕*v.* 增加】

    A：燈光剛好。
    B：很高興你這麼認爲。
      以前這裡太暗了。
      現在我們加了兩盞燈。

5. A : **All the colors flow well**.
   B : They do blend nicely.
   They complement each other.
   They go together well.
   【blend〔blɛnd〕*v.* 協調　　*go together* 相配；協調】

    A：所有的顏色都很搭配。
    B：的確非常協調。
      顏色都能互補。
      顏色都非常協調。

BOOK 11

6. A : **It creates a relaxed atmosphere**.

A：它創造了一個輕鬆的氣氛。

B : It is relaxing.
It's very comfortable.
It makes me feel at ease.

B：它很令人放鬆。
它很舒適。
它令我覺得很自在。

【relaxing〔rɪ'læksɪŋ〕*adj.* 令人放鬆的　*at ease* 舒適；自在】

7. A : **You have a good eye**.

A：你很有眼光。

B : You flatter me.
I don't deserve it.
I don't deserve such praise.

B：你過獎了。
我不敢當。
你這樣稱讚我，眞是不敢當。

8. A : **You have good taste**.

A：你有好的品味。

B : I can't take all the credit.
I didn't do it alone.
I had some help from others.

B：不能全都算是我的功勞。
這不是我一個人做的。
我有找別人幫忙。

【credit〔'krɛdɪt〕*v.* 功勞
alone〔ə'lon〕*adv.* 獨自地】

9. A : **I should hire you to do my house**.

A：我應該雇用你來裝潢我的房子。

B : Are you joking?
Was that a joke?
Don't be ridiculous.

B：你在開玩笑嗎？
你剛剛是在說笑吧。
別開玩笑了。

【joke〔dʒok〕*v.* 開玩笑　*n.* 玩笑　　ridiculous〔rɪ'dɪkjələs〕*adj.* 可笑的】

BOOK 11

# 4. *Your furniture is lovely.*

| | |
|---|---|
| Your furniture is lovely. | 你的傢俱很漂亮。 |
| Every piece is attractive. | 每一件都吸引人。 |
| It really makes the room. | 它真的造就了這個房間。 |
| | |
| That's a fabulous table. | 那張桌子很棒。 |
| Those chairs look fantastic. | 那些椅子看起來很棒。 |
| What type of wood is that? | 那是哪一種木頭？ |
| | |
| This couch feels great. | 這個沙發給人的感覺真棒。 |
| I like the material. | 我喜歡這個材料。 |
| The fabric is so soft and | 這個布料非常柔軟而且 |
|   smooth. | 光滑。 |

\*\* ——————————————————

furniture〔'fɜnɪtʃə〕*n.* 傢俱
lovely〔'lʌvlɪ〕*adj.* 可愛的；漂亮的　　piece〔pis〕*n.* 一件
attractive〔ə'træktɪv〕*adj.* 吸引人的
fabulous〔'fæbjələs〕*adj.* 很棒的；極好的
fantastic〔fæn'tæstɪk〕*adj.* 極好的；很棒的
type〔taɪp〕*n.* 類型；種類　　wood〔wʊd〕*n.* 木材；木頭
couch〔kaʊtʃ〕*n.* (長)沙發　　material〔mə'tɪrɪəl〕*n.* 材料
fabric〔'fæbrɪk〕*n.* 織物；織品；布料
soft〔sɔft〕*adj.* 柔軟的　　smooth〔smuð〕*adj.* 平滑的；光滑的

## 【背景説明】

　　在美國已婚的女人，通常都非常重視傢俱，因為傢俱代表女主人的品味。到人家家裡作客，一定要多稱讚傢俱。

1. ***Your furniture is lovely.***
furniture〔ˈfɝnɪtʃɚ〕 *n.* 傢俱
lovely〔ˈlʌvlɪ〕 *adj.* 可愛的；美麗的；漂亮的

> 　　句中 *lovely* 的主要意思是「可愛的」，但也常作「美麗的；漂亮的」解，如：a *lovely* flower（一朵美麗的花）、a *lovely* sight（美麗的風景）。看到一個女生穿得很漂亮，你就可以說：That's a *lovely* dress you're wearing.（妳穿的衣服真漂亮。）

　　***Your furniture is lovely.*** 的意思是「你的傢俱很漂亮。」可以加強語氣說成：Every piece of your furniture is lovely.（你每一件傢俱都很漂亮。）

*Your furniture is lovely.*

或 All your furniture is lovely.（你所有的傢俱都很漂亮。）也可以用 so 或 very，來加強 lovely 的語氣，說成：

　　　　Your furniture is so lovely.
　　= Your furniture is very lovely.
　　　　（你的傢俱很漂亮。）

lovely 可用 beautiful 等字來取代：

Your furniture is beautiful. ( 你的傢俱很漂亮。)
Your furniture is very attractive.
( 你的傢俱很吸引人。)
Your furniture is charming. ( 你的傢俱很吸引人。)
【charming〔'tʃɑrmɪŋ〕*adj.* 吸引人的】

Your furniture is very nice. ( 你的傢俱很好。)
Your furniture is elegant. ( 你的傢俱很高雅。)
Your furniture is good-looking. ( 你的傢俱很好看。)
【elegant〔'ɛləgənt〕*adj.* 高雅的】

2. *Every piece is attractive.*
piece〔pis〕*n.* 一個；一件
attractive〔ə'træktɪv〕*adj.* 吸引人的

這句話的意思是「每一件都吸引人。」源自：
Every piece of your furniture is attractive. ( 你
每一件傢俱都很吸引人。) 可以加強語氣說成：
Every single piece is very attractive. ( 每一件
都非常吸引人。) 句中的 attractive 可用下列的字
來取代：lovely ( 漂亮的 )、beautiful ( 美麗的 )、
charming ( 吸引人的 )、good-looking ( 好看的 )、
nice-looking ( 好看的 )、gorgeous ( 非常漂亮的 )、
pretty ( 漂亮的 )，如：

Every piece is good-looking. ( 每一件都好看。)
Every piece is gorgeous. ( 每一件都很好看。)
【gorgeous〔'gɔrdʒəs〕*adj.* 華麗的；非常漂亮的】

*Every piece is attractive*. 可以加長爲：

Every piece *in this room* is so attractive.

（這個房間的每一件傢俱都很吸引人。）

Every piece *in your house* is attractive.

（你房子裡面的每一件傢俱都很吸引人。）

Every piece *you have* is attractive.

（你的每一件傢俱都很吸引人。）

3. *It really makes the room*.

make 的主要意思是「製造」，在此作「造就」
解。這句話的意思是「它眞的造就了這個房間。」
可以簡化成：It makes the room.（它造就了這個
房間。）也可以加長爲：It really makes the room
perfect.（它眞的使這個房間看起來很完美。）或 It
really makes the room look so nice.（它眞的使
這個房間看起來很好。）

make 作「造就」解的例子：

You *make* my day.

（你造就了我這一天；你使我快樂。）

Clothes *make* the man.

（衣服造就了人；人要衣裝，佛要金裝。）

What you do *makes* you.

（你的所做所爲，造就了你。）

（ = *What you do makes who you are*. ）

BOOK 11

4. ***That's a fabulous table***.

fabulous〔ˈfæbjələs〕*adj.* 很棒的；極好的
（= *marvelous* = *wonderful*）

　　這句話字面的意思是「那是一張很棒的桌子。」
也就是「那張桌子很棒。」前面可加上 Wow!（哇
啊！）或 Boy!（哇啊！）或 My!（哎啊！）等感
嘆詞，像：Boy! That's a fabulous table.（哇
啊！那張桌子很棒。）可加強語氣說成：That's a
really fabulous table.（那張桌子真的很棒。）

　　除了有抽屜的桌子，叫 desk（書桌）以外，其
他的桌子都可稱作 table。可特別指明在沙發前的桌
子，叫 coffee table（茶几），沙發兩旁的桌子，叫
end table，我們也稱之為「茶几」，餐桌叫 dinner
table。很多美國人早餐都喜歡在廚房的桌子上吃，
叫 kitchen table（廚房餐桌），所以這句話也可說成：

***That's a fabulous***
{
coffee table.
end table.
dinner table.
kitchen table.
}

稱讚永遠不嫌多，看到了客廳漂亮的燈，也可以說：
***That's a fabulous*** lamp.（那個燈很棒。）
【lamp〔læmp〕*n.* 燈】

看到了地毯，就可以說：
***That's a fabulous*** carpet.（地毯很棒。）
【carpet〔ˈkɑrpɪt〕*n.* 地毯】

看到了小塊地毯，就說：

***That's a fabulous*** rug.（那塊地毯很棒。）

【rug〔rʌg〕*n.* 小地毯】

看到牆上的畫，就說：

***That's a fabulous*** painting.

（那幅畫很棒。）

【用顏料畫的畫，叫
painting。畫的通稱，
則是 picture。】

看到花瓶，也可以稱讚：

***That's a fabulous*** vase.

（那個花瓶很棒。）

【vase〔ves〕*n.* 花瓶】

## 5. ***Those chairs look fantastic.***

fantastic〔fæn'tæstɪk〕*adj.* 極好的；很棒的

　　這句話的意思是「那些椅子看起來很棒。」可
分成兩句，說成：I like those chairs. They look
fantastic.（我喜歡那些椅子。它們看起來很棒。）

　　為了接上一句 ***That's a fabulous table.***，可
以加上 too 或 also，說成：Those chairs look
fantastic, too. 或 Those chairs also look
fantastic. 意思都是「那些椅子看起來也很棒。」

下面都是美國人常說的話，意思大致相同：

***Those chairs look fantastic*.【第一常用】**

Those chairs look marvelous.【第六常用】

（那些椅子看起來很棒。）

Those chairs look superb.【第八常用】

（那些椅子看起來很棒。）

marvelous (ˈmɑrvḷəs ) *adj.* 很棒的
superb ( suˈpɝb ) *adj.* 極好的

Those chairs look wonderful.【第三常用】

（那些椅子看起來很棒。）

Those chairs look great.【第二常用】

（那些椅子看起來很棒。）

Those chairs look awesome.【第五常用】

（那些椅子看起來很棒。）

【awesome (ˈɔsəm ) *adj.* 很棒的】

Those chairs look tremendous.【第七常用】

（那些椅子看起來很棒。）

Those chairs look so nice.【第四常用】

（那些椅子看起來很好看。）

Those chairs look elegant.【第九常用】

（那些椅子看起來很高雅。）

【tremendous ( trɪˈmɛndəs ) *adj.* 極好的】

　　英文當中的形容詞相當豐富，我們要經常交替
使用，今天說 fantastic，明天要說 marvelous，
這樣說起話來才生動。

6. *What type of wood is that?*

type〔taɪp〕*n.* 類型；種類

wood〔wʊd〕*n.* 木材；木頭

　　這句話的意思是「那是哪一種木頭？」type 可用 kind 來代替，說成：What kind of wood is that? 句中的 that 可用 it 來代替，說成：What type of wood is it?（它是哪一種木頭？）

　　你需要知道一些木頭的名稱，否則別人回答，你會聽不懂。美國人製作傢俱，認為最貴的木頭是 mahogany〔məˈhɑgənɪ〕*n.* 紅木，第二貴的是 cherry〔ˈtʃɛrɪ〕*n.* 櫻桃木，其他比較值錢的就是 oak〔ok〕*n.* 橡木，walnut〔ˈwɔlnət〕*n.* 胡桃木、chestnut〔ˈtʃɛsnət〕*n.* 栗木、pine〔paɪn〕*n.* 松木。

mahogany　　cherry　　oak

walnut　　chestnut　　pine

【例】 A: *What type of wood is that?*

　　　 B: It's mahogany.（是紅木。）

　　　　 It's made of mahogany.

　　　　（是紅木做的。）【*be made of* 由～製成】

7. ***This couch feels great.***

feel〔fil〕*v.* 使人感覺 couch〔kaʊtʃ〕*n.* (長)沙發

美國人將沙發分為「長
沙發」(couch)和單人沙發
(armchair)。couch 也可
稱作 sofa〔'sofə〕*n.* 沙發，
單人沙發 armchair 也可稱
作 sofa chair。中國人不管
是 couch 或 armchair，都
稱作「沙發」。

couch

armchair

couch〔kaʊtʃ〕這個字，很多人會唸成 coach
〔kotʃ〕*n.* 教練，我們只要知道，原則上 ou 一律讀
/aʊ/，只有少數幾個讀 /o/ 的字為例外，像 shoulder
〔'joldə〕*n.* 肩膀，doughnut〔'donət〕*n.* 甜甜圈等。

***This couch feels great.*** 的意思是「這個沙發
給人的感覺真棒。」【feel 以「非人」做主詞的用法，參
照第二回】也可說成：Your couch feels great.（你
的沙發給人的感覺真棒。）可以加強語氣說成：This
couch feels so great.（這個沙發給人的感覺真好。）

下面都是美國人常說的話：

***This couch feels great.***【第二常用】
This couch feels nice.【第四常用】
　（這個沙發給人的感覺很好。）
This couch feels good.【第三常用】
　（這個沙發給人的感覺很好。）

This couch feels comfortable.【第一常用】
（這個沙發使人覺得很舒服。）
This couch feels soft.【第五常用】
（這個沙發使人覺得很柔軟。）
This couch feels spongy.【第六常用】
（這個沙發使人覺得很有彈性。）

soft〔sɔft〕*adj.* 柔軟的
spongy〔'spʌndʒɪ〕*adj.* 鬆軟有彈性的

以上各句都可用 so 加強語氣，說成 so great，
so nice，so good 等。

8. ***I like the material***.
material〔mə'tɪrɪəl〕*n.* 材料；原料

　　這句話的意思是「我喜歡這個材料。」the 可改
成 this，說成：I like this material.（我喜歡這種
材料。）可以加長為：I like how the material
feels.（我喜歡這個材料給人的感覺。）

也有美國人說：

The material is attractive.（這個材料很吸引人。）
The material looks nice.（這個材料看起來很好。）
The material feels nice.（這個材料摸起來很好。）

　　做沙發的材料通常有三種：① cloth（布）、
② leather（皮革）、③ vinyl〔'vaɪnɪl〕*n.* 樹脂塑膠
（即「塑膠皮；人造皮革」）。

BOOK 11

9. ***The fabric is so soft and smooth.***

fabric〔'fæbrɪk〕*n.* 織物;織品;布料

soft〔sɔft〕*adj.* 柔軟的　　smooth〔smuð〕*adj.* 光滑的

在所有字典上,fabric 都沒有寫清楚,在 The American Heritage Dictionary 上說,fabric 是特別被編織的布(a cloth produced especially by knitting or weaving)。其實,fabric 就是比較厚一點的布料,多用於沙發、地毯和窗簾上。

fabric

cloth

***The fabric is so soft and smooth.*** 的意思是「這個布料非常柔軟而且光滑。」

這句話也可說成:The fabric feels so soft and smooth.(這個布料摸起來非常柔軟而且光滑。)【feel〔fil〕*v.* 摸起來有…感覺;使人覺得】也可加長為:The fabric of this couch is so soft and smooth.(這個沙發的布料非常柔軟而且光滑。)也可以簡化為:The fabric is very nice.(這個布料很好。)或 The fabric feels great.(這個布料摸起來很棒。)

也有美國人說:

The couch feels so soft and smooth.

(這個沙發使人感覺非常柔軟而且光滑。)

The material feels so soft and smooth.

(這個布料摸起來非常柔軟而且光滑。)

## 【對話練習】

1. A：**Your furniture is lovely**.　　A：你的傢俱很漂亮。

　　B：Thank you for saying so.　　B：謝謝你這麼說。
　　　I value your opinion.　　　　我很重視你的意見。
　　　Your compliment means　　　你的稱讚意義重大。
　　　a lot.【value〔'vælju〕v. 重視
　　　compliment〔'kɑmpləmənt〕
　　　n. 稱讚】

2. A：**Every piece is attractive**.　　A：每一件都吸引人。

　　B：I like each piece, too.　　B：我也喜歡每一件。
　　　Each piece is special.　　　每一件都很特別。
　　　Each piece is very unique.　　每一件都非常獨特。
　　　【unique〔ju'nik〕adj. 獨特的】

3. A：**It really makes the room**.　　A：它真的造就了這個房間。

　　B：That's a nice compliment.　　B：那是很好的稱讚。
　　　I think you are right.　　　我認為你說得對。
　　　The furniture is very nice.　　傢俱很不錯。

4. A：**That's a fabulous table**.　　A：那張桌子很棒。

　　B：I'm glad you think so.　　B：很高興你這麼認為。
　　　I really like it, too.　　　我也真的很喜歡。
　　　It's one of my favorites.　　它是我最喜愛的傢俱
　　　【favorite〔'fevərɪt〕n. 最喜愛的　　之一。
　　　人或物】

BOOK 11

5. A : **Those chairs are fantastic**.
　 B : Do you really like them?
　　 I painted them myself.
　　 I take great pride in them.
　　【paint〔pent〕v. 油漆
　　　*take pride in* 以…為榮】

　 A：那些椅子看起來很棒。
　 B：你真的喜歡嗎？
　　　我自己上的油漆。
　　　我非常引以為榮。

6. A : **What type of wood is that?**
　 B : It's California Maple.
　　 The grain is very tight.
　　 Wood of this quality is very
　　 expensive.【maple〔'mepḷ〕n.
　　 楓樹；楓木　grain〔gren〕n. 木紋
　　 tight〔taɪt〕adj. 質地密實的】

　 A：那是哪一種木頭？
　 B：它是加州楓木。
　　　它的木紋非常細。
　　　這種品質的木材非常貴。

7. A : **This couch feels great**.
　 B : I know it does.
　　 It's softer than a bed.
　　 I enjoy it every day.
　　【enjoy〔ɪn'dʒɔɪ〕v. 享受；喜歡】

　 A：這個沙發給人的感覺真棒。
　 B：我知道它很棒。
　　　它比床還要柔軟。
　　　我每天都享用它。

8. A : **I like the material**.
　 B : It is excellent material.
　　 It's very expensive.
　　 It's imported from Italy.
　　【import〔ɪm'port〕v. 進口】

　 A：我喜歡這個材料。
　 B：這是很好的材料。
　　　它非常昂貴。
　　　它是從義大利進口的。

9. A : **The fabric is so soft and
　　 smooth**.
　 B : That's why I bought it.
　　 It feels so wonderful.
　　 It feels soft like silk.
　　【feel〔fil〕v. 使人感覺；摸起來　silk〔sɪlk〕n. 絲】

　 A：這個布料非常柔軟而且
　　　光滑。
　 B：那就是我會買它的原因。
　　　它摸起來很棒。
　　　它摸起來像絲一樣柔軟。

BOOK 11

# 5. Complimenting Different Rooms

| | |
|---|---|
| Your kitchen is modern. | 你的廚房很現代化。 |
| You have more shelves and cabinets. | 你有比較多的架子和櫥櫃。 |
| It's much nicer than mine. | 它比我的好很多。 |
| | |
| *Your* bedrooms are cozy. | 你的臥室很溫馨。 |
| *Your* closets are roomy. | 你的衣櫥很大。 |
| The carpet is thick and plush. | 地毯又厚又豪華。 |
| | |
| The living room is my favorite. | 客廳是我最喜愛的。 |
| It's the highlight of the house. | 它是這個房子最好的部份。 |
| Thank you for showing me around. | 謝謝你帶我參觀。 |

BOOK 11

**

modern〔'mɑdən〕adj. 現代化的   shelf〔ʃɛlf〕n. 架子
cabinet〔'kæbənɪt〕n. 櫥櫃   nice〔naɪs〕adj. 好的
bedroom〔'bɛd͵rum〕n. 臥室   cozy〔'kozɪ〕adj. 溫暖而舒適的
closet〔'klɑzɪt〕n. 衣櫥；衣櫃   roomy〔'rumɪ〕adj. 寬敞的
carpet〔'kɑrpɪt〕n. 地毯   thick〔θɪk〕adj. 厚的
plush〔plʌʃ〕adj. 豪華的   favorite〔'fevərɪt〕n. 最喜歡的人或物
highlight〔'haɪ͵laɪt〕n. 最重要的部份；最好的部份
*show sb. around* 帶某人參觀

## 【背景說明】

　　　　拜訪你的外國朋友的時候，通常他會帶你
去參觀各個房間，說了下面九句話，你就會更
受歡迎。

1. ***Your kitchen is modern.***
   modern〔'madən〕*adj.* 現代化的

　　　　這句話的意思是「你的廚房很現代化。」可加
　長為：

　　Wow, ***your kitchen is modern.***
　　（哇啊，你的廚房很現代化。）
　　Your kitchen is very modern.
　　（你的廚房非常現代化。）
　　Everything in your kitchen is modern.
　　（你廚房的每樣東西都很現代化。）

　美國人也常說：

　　What a modern kitchen!（多麼現代化的廚房！）
　　You have a modern kitchen.
　　（你有現代化的廚房。）
　　This kitchen is really modern.
　　（這個廚房真的很現代化。）

　　　　說完 ***Your kitchen is modern.*** 可以再加上一
　句：You have a lot of modern things.（你有很多
現代化的東西。）

2. ***You have more shelves and cabinets.***

shelf〔ʃɛlf〕*n.* 架子

cabinet〔'kæbənɪt〕*n.* 櫥櫃

　　這句話的意思是「你有比較多的架子和櫥櫃。」源自：You have more shelves and cabinets *than I do.*（你的架子和櫥櫃比我多。）也可說成：Your kitchen has more shelves and cabinets than mine.（你的廚房的架子和櫥櫃比我的廚房多。）也有美國人說：Your kitchen has more places to put things.（你的廚房有比較多的地方放東西。）

shelves

cabinets

3. ***It's much nicer than mine.***

nice〔naɪs〕*adj.* 好的

　　這句話的意思是「它比我的好很多。」也可以說得更清楚一點：Your kitchen is much nicer than mine.（你的廚房比我的好很多。）可簡單說成：It's nicer than mine.（它比我的好。）美國人也常說：It's better than mine.（它比我的好。）或 It's much better than mine.（它比我的好很多。）

BOOK 11

4. *Your bedrooms are cozy*.

bedroom〔'bɛd,rum〕 *n.* 臥室

cozy〔'kozɪ〕 *adj.* 溫暖而舒適的 ( = *warm and comfortable* )【cozy 是美式的拼法，英國人拼成 cosy。】

　　這句話的意思是「你的臥室很溫馨。」也可説成：You have cozy bedrooms. ( 你有溫馨的臥室。) 也可加長爲：I think your bedrooms are very cozy. ( 我認爲你的臥室很溫馨。)

　　下面是美國人常説的話，我們按照使用頻率排列：

① *Your bedrooms are cozy*.【第一常用】

② Your bedrooms look cozy.【第二常用】
　　( 你的臥室看起來很溫馨。)

③ Your bedrooms feel cozy.【第三常用】
　　( 你的臥室使人感覺很溫馨。)

【feel〔fil〕 *v.* 使人覺得】

④ Your bedrooms are comfortable.
　　( 你的臥室很舒適。)

⑤ Your bedrooms look comfortable.
　　( 你的臥室看起來很舒適。)

⑥ Your bedrooms seem so cozy.
　　( 你的臥室似乎很溫馨。)

seem〔sim〕 *v.* 似乎
comfortable〔'kʌmfɚtəbl̩〕 *adj.* 舒適的

⑦　Your bedrooms are warm.

（你的臥室很溫暖。）

⑧　Your bedrooms seem warm.

（你的臥室似乎很溫暖。）

⑨　Your bedrooms feel warm.

（你的臥室使人覺得很溫暖。）

【warm〔wɔrm〕*adj.* 溫暖的】

5. ***Your closets are roomy.***

closet〔'klɑzɪt〕*n.* 衣櫥；衣櫃

roomy〔'rumɪ〕*adj.* 寬敞的；有很多空間的

（= *having plenty of space*）

　　這句話字面的意思是「你的衣櫥有很多空間。」
引申為「你的衣櫥很大。」（= *Your closets are big.*）
closet 這個字背不下來，只要背 close + t 即可。

美國人也常說：

Your closets are spacious.

（你的衣櫥空間很大。）

Your closets are large.

（你的衣櫥很大。）

Your closets are huge.

（你的衣櫥非常大。）

walk-in closet

spacious〔'speʃəs〕*adj.* 寬敞的

huge〔hjudʒ〕*adj.* 巨大的

　　closet 有兩種，一種是傳統的衣櫥，另一種是開
放式的，可以走進去的衣櫥，稱作 ***walk-in closet***。

凡是形容很大的空間，都可用 *roomy*，例如：

American houses are *roomy*.

（美國的房子空間很大。）

First-class seats are more *roomy*.

（頭等艙的座位的空間比較大。）

A good living room should be *roomy*.

（好的客廳應該空間很大。）

first-class〔'fɜst'klæs〕*adj.* 頭等艙的

***living room*** 客廳

6. ***The carpet is thick and plush*.**

carpet〔'kɑrpɪt〕*n.* 地毯　　thick〔θɪk〕*adj.* 厚的

plush〔plʌʃ〕*n.* 絲絨（天鵝絨的一種）

*adj.* 絲絨製的；豪華的

句中的 plush 的主要意思是「絲絨」，在牛津字典上的解釋是 a kind of silk or cotton cloth with a soft nap（一種帶有軟絨毛的絲或棉布）【nap〔næp〕*n.*（絨布上面的）細毛】，但是，plush 在此是形容詞，引申為「豪華的」。

carpet

***The carpet is thick and plush*.** 的意思是「地毯又厚又豪華。」句中的 carpet 也可換作 carpeting〔'kɑrpɪtɪŋ〕*n.* 地毯（總稱），兩者使用頻率相同。也可說成：Your carpet is thick and plush.（你的地毯又厚又豪華。）

【比較 1】下面兩句話意思相同，使用頻率也相同：

***The carpet is thick and plush.*** 【正】

The carpeting is thick and plush. 【正】

【比較 2】carpeting 代表一個或多個地毯（a carpet or carpets），沒有複數形式。

All the carpets are thick and plush. 【正】
（所有的地毯都又厚又豪華。）

All the carpeting is thick and plush. 【正】
（所有的地毯都又厚又豪華。）

*All the carpetings are thick and plush.* 【誤】

美國人也常說：

The carpets are beautiful.（地毯很漂亮。）
Your carpets are beautiful.（你的地毯很漂亮。）

The carpeting is luxurious.（地毯很豪華。）
The carpeting is gorgeous.（地毯很漂亮。）

luxurious〔lʌk'ʒʊrɪəs〕*adj.* 豪華的
gorgeous〔'gɔrdʒəs〕*adj.* 非常漂亮的

Your carpets look lovely.
（你的地毯看起來很漂亮。）

Your carpets are so soft and thick.
（你的地毯又厚又柔軟。）

Your carpets look and feel wonderful.
（你的地毯看起來、摸起來都很棒。）

lovely〔'lʌvlɪ〕*adj.* 可愛的；漂亮的
feel〔fil〕*v.* 感覺起來；摸起來

7. ***The living room is my favorite.***

***living room*** 客廳

favorite〔'fevərɪt〕*n.* 最喜愛的人或物

這句話的意思是「客廳是我最喜愛的。」美國人也常說：I like the living room the most.（我最喜歡客廳。）或 I think the living room is the best.（我認為客廳最好。）

living room

8. ***It's the highlight of the house.***

highlight〔'haɪ,laɪt〕*n.* 最明亮的部份；最重要的部份

highlight 的字面意思是「在畫或照片中最明亮的部份」，可引申出無限多的意思，像在新聞中最重要的部份，在節目中最精彩的部份等，在英文報紙的標題中常見到，如 Business Highlights（商務要點）。

## BUSINESS HIGHLIGHTS

### Hotel Royal Hsinchu welcomes Academia Sinica President Yuan T. Lee

Hotel Royal Hsinchu was recently pleased to welcome Academia Sinica President Yuan T. Lee and academics, who stayed at the Hotel Royal

Hsinchu for a two-day annual academic conference. Pictured here is Academia Sinica President Yuan T. Lee (left) warmly greeted by the hotel's General Manager Joachim Heineke.

Hotel Royal Hsinchu has 208 superior and deluxe rooms as well as 15 executive suites. Each room is equipped with a facsimile machine, free hi-speed Internet access, electrical outlet for computers, DVD player, LCD monitor and Digital TV system. Reservation or information for Hotel Royal Hsinchu can be obtained by calling for 886-3-563-1265. Hotel Royal Hsinchu is accessible on the Internet at www.royal-hsinchu.com.tw.

*It's the highlight of the house.* 的意思是「它是這個房子最好的部份。」( = *It's the best part of the house.* ) 可加長爲：In my opinion, it's the highlight of the house. ( 依我看，它是這個房子最好的部份。) 或縮短爲：It's the highlight. ( 它是最好的部份。)【*in one's opinion* 依某人之見】

即使主人所住的不是獨棟的房屋 ( house )，你也可說 *It's the highlight of the house.* 用 house 是習慣用法。也可把 the house 改成 your home，說成：It's the highlight of your home. ( 它是你家最好的部份。)

9. *Thank you for showing me around.*
*show sb. around* 帶某人參觀

這句話的意思是「謝謝你帶我參觀。」可以輕鬆地說：Thanks for showing me around. ( 謝謝你帶我參觀。) 也可加強語氣說成：Thank you very much for showing me around the house. ( 非常謝謝你帶我參觀整個房子。)

美國人也喜歡說：

Thanks for the tour. ( 謝謝你帶我參觀。)
Thanks for showing me your home.
( 謝謝你讓我參觀你的家。)
Thanks for letting me see your house.
( 謝謝你讓我看你的房子。)
【tour〔tʊr〕*n.* 參觀　show〔ʃo〕*v.* 給~看】

BOOK 11

## 【對話練習】

1. A：**Your kitchen is modern**.

   B：We just remodeled it.
   We renovated it last month.
   It cost us a lot of money.

   【remodel〔ri'mɑdḷ〕*v.* 修改；改建
   renovate〔'rɛnə,vet〕*v.* 整修】

   A：你的廚房很現代化。

   B：我們剛剛才改建。
   我們上個月整修過。
   花了我們很多錢。

2. A：**You have more shelves and cabinets**.

   B：That's the way we planned it.
   We wanted more storage space.
   We needed the extra space.

   【storage〔'storɪdʒ〕*n.* 儲藏
   extra〔'ɛkstrə〕*adj.* 額外的】

   A：你有比較多的架子和櫥櫃。

   B：那是我們的計畫。
   我們想要 有更多儲藏空間。
   我們需要額外的空間。

3. A：**It's much nicer than mine**.

   B：I wouldn't say that.
   It's just a different style.
   Yours is very nice.

   A：它比我的好很多。

   B：我不會這麼說。
   只是風格不同。
   你的是很好的。

4. A：**Your bedrooms are cozy**.

   B：That's important to us.
   We spend a lot of time there.
   Bedrooms should be comfortable.

   A：你的臥室很溫馨。

   B：那對我們很重要。
   我們有很多時間都在那裡。
   臥室應該要很舒服。

BOOK 11

5. A : **Your closets are roomy**.

   B : We like them that way.

      We like walk-in closets.

      We even put mirrors in them.

   【*walk-in closet* 大得可供人進入的
衣櫃　　mirror〔'mɪrə〕 *n.* 鏡子】

A：你的衣櫥很大。

B：我們喜歡這樣。

我們喜歡大得可供人進入的衣櫃。

我們甚至在裡面放鏡子。

6. A : **The carpet is thick and plush**.

   B : That's because it's brand-new.

      We just bought it.

      We purchased it two weeks ago. 【brand-new〔'brænd'nju〕 *adj.* 全新的　　purchase〔'pɝtʃəs〕 *v.* 購買】

A：地毯又厚又豪華。

B：那是因為它是全新的。

我們剛買的。

我們兩個星期前買的。

7. A : **The living room is my favorite**.

   B : It's my favorite, too.

      It has everything I like.

      It's almost perfect to me.

   【perfect〔'pɝfɪkt〕 *adj.* 完美的】

A：客廳是我最喜愛的。

B：它也是我最喜愛的。

它有我喜歡的一切。

它對我而言幾乎是完美的。

8. A : **It's the highlight of the house**.

   B : I'm glad you think so.

      I like to hear that.

      That's the way we planned it.

   【glad〔glæd〕 *adj.* 高興的】

A：它是這個房子最好的部份。

B：很高興你這麼認為。

我喜歡聽你這麼說。

你就是我們原本的計畫。

9. A : **Thank you for showing me around**.

   B : Don't say thanks.

      It was my pleasure.

      You are much too polite.

   【pleasure〔'plɛʒə〕 *n.* 榮幸】

A：謝謝你帶我參觀。

B：不用謝我。

這是我的榮幸。

你太客氣了。

BOOK 11

# 6. *Put me to work*.

| | |
|---|---|
| Put me to work. | 讓我工作。 |
| Give me something to do. | 給我一點事情做。 |
| If you don't let me help, | 如果你不讓我幫忙，我會 |
|   I'll feel guilty. | 覺得有罪惡感。 |
| | |
| Let me set the table. | 讓我來擺餐具。 |
| *Where* are the plates? | 盤子在哪裡？ |
| *Where* do you keep your | 你的餐具放在哪裡？ |
|   silverware? | |
| | |
| You made the meal. | 你做了飯。 |
| *I'll* clear the table. | 我來收拾桌子。 |
| *I'll* do the dishes. | 我來洗碗盤。 |

**＊＊**────────────

put〔put〕v. 使做某事　　guilty〔'gɪltɪ〕adj. 有罪惡感的；內疚的
*set the table* 擺好餐具，準備開飯　　plate〔plet〕n. 盤子
silverware〔'sɪlvɚ‚wɛr〕n. 銀製餐具；銀白色金屬餐具
make〔mek〕v. 做（飯）；烹煮　　meal〔mil〕n. 一餐
clear〔klɪr〕v. 清理；收拾　　*clear the table* 收拾桌子
do〔du〕v. 使清潔；洗滌　　dish〔dɪʃ〕n. 盤子
*the dishes* 餐桌用杯盤類　　*do the dishes* 洗碗盤

## 【背景說明】

　　在客廳裡，看到主人忙著擺餐具，準備吃飯，如果你坐著不動，就太失禮了。此時，你應該站起來，走向餐廳，說這九句話。

1. ***Put me to work.***

put〔 put 〕*v.* 使從事；使做某事

　　這句話的意思是「讓我工作。」源自：You can put me to work. ( 你可以讓我工作。) 或 I want you to put me to work. ( 我希望你讓我工作。)

　　美國人也常說：Let me do something. ( 讓我做點事。) 或 Let me be useful. ( 讓我幫忙。)

【useful〔'jusfəl 〕*adj.* 有用的；能幫上忙的】

Put me to work. 後面可加分詞片語，如：

*Put me to work.*

Put me to work ***doing something useful***.
( 讓我做一些有用的事情。)
Put me to work ***preparing the meal***.
( 讓我準備餐點。)
Put me to work ***cleaning the kitchen***.
( 讓我清理廚房。)

BOOK 11

2. *Give me something to do*.

　　　　這句話的意思是「給我一點事情做。」源自：
I want you to give me something to do. ( 我希
望你給我一點事情做。)

下面是美國人常說的話：

　　*Give me something to do*. 【第四常用】
　　Give me some work to do. 【第三常用】
　　( 給我一些工作做。)
　　Give me something helpful to do. 【第六常用】
　　( 給我做點事來幫你的忙。)
　　【helpful (ˈhɛlpfəl) *adj.* 有幫助的】

　　Give me something useful to do. 【第五常用】
　　( 給我做點事來幫忙。)
　　Give me a job. ( 給我一個工作。)【第一常用】
　　Give me some work. ( 給我一些工作。)【第二常用】

　　Tell me what to do. ( 告訴我要做什麼。)【第七常用】
　　Tell me what I can do. 【第八常用】
　　( 告訴我能做什麼。)
　　Tell me how I can help. 【第九常用】
　　( 告訴我要如何幫忙。)

　　I want to work. ( 我想要工作。)【第十常用】
　　I want to be useful. ( 我想要幫忙。)【第十一常用】
　　I want to do something. 【第十二常用】
　　( 我想要做點事。)

3. *If you don't let me help, I'll feel guilty.*
　 guilty〔'gɪltɪ〕*adj.* 有罪惡感的；內疚的

　　　　這句話的意思是「如果你不讓我幫忙，我會覺得
有罪惡感。」由於前面已經說了：Put me to work.
Give me something to do. 所以，這句話在此可簡
化為：If you don't, I'll feel guilty. ( 如果你不這
麼做，我就會感到內疚。) 也可說成：If you don't
let me do something, I'll feel guilty. ( 如果你不
讓我做點事，我會有罪惡感。)

　　下面都是美國人常說的話：

　　　I'll feel guilty. ( 我會覺得有罪惡感。)【第一常用】
　　　I'll feel bad. ( 我會覺得難過。)【第二常用】
　　　I'll feel sorry. ( 我會覺得遺憾。)【第三常用】
　　　【sorry〔'sɔrɪ〕*adj.* 遺憾的】

　　　I'll feel regretful. ( 我會覺得遺憾。)【第六常用】
　　　I'll feel uncomfortable. 【第五常用】
　　　( 我會覺得不舒服。)
　　　I'll feel a little ashamed. 【第四常用】
　　　( 我會覺得有點羞愧。)
　　　regretful〔rɪ'grɛtfəl〕*adj.* 遺憾的
　　　ashamed〔ə'ʃemd〕*adj.* 感到羞愧的

　　　I'll feel embarrassed. ( 我會覺得尷尬。)
　　　I'll feel like I'm not helping out.
　　　( 我會覺得沒幫上忙。)
　　　embarrassed〔ɪm'bærəst〕*adj.* 尷尬的
　　　*help out* 幫忙

4. **Let me set the table**.

**set the table** 擺好餐具，準備開飯
（＝*prepare the table for the meal*）

這句話的意思是「讓我來擺餐具。」也有美國
人説：Let me help set the table. （讓我幫忙擺餐
具。）或 Let me help you set the table. （讓我幫
你擺餐具。）

> 在字典上，「擺好餐具，準備開飯」的説法有
> **set the table**，lay the table，和 spread the
> table。但是，美國人大多只説 **set the table**，目
> 前還沒有聽到美國人説其他兩個。

5. **Where are the plates?**

plate〔plet〕*n.* 盤子

> 中國人的主要餐具是「碗」（bowl），美國人的
> 主要餐具是「盤子」（plate）。這句話的意思是「盤
> 子在哪裡？」中國人習慣説「碗在哪裡？」而美國人
> 喜歡説「盤子在哪裡？」。

下面都是美國人常説的話：

**Where are the plates?**

【第一常用】

Where are your plates?

（你的盤子在哪裡？）【第二常用】

Where are the plates?

Where can I find the plates?【第五常用】

（我在哪裡可以找到盤子？）

Where can I find your plates?【第六常用】

（我在哪裡可以找到你的盤子？）

Where do you keep the plates?【第三常用】

（你的盤子放在哪裡？）

Where do you put the plates?【第四常用】

（你的盤子放在哪裡？）

Where do you store the plates?【第七常用】

（你的盤子放在哪裡？）

【keep〔kip〕v. 保存　store〔stor〕v. 儲存】

Where do you keep your plates?【第八常用】

（你的盤子放在哪裡？）

Where do you store your plates?【第九常用】

（你的盤子放在哪裡？）

Where do you put your plates?【第十常用】

（你的盤子放在哪裡？）

BOOK 11

6. ***Where do you keep your silverware?***

keep〔kip〕v. 保存

silverware〔'sɪlvɚ‚wɛr〕n. 銀製餐具；銀白色金屬餐具

中國人主要用筷子（chopsticks）和湯匙
（spoon），美國人用刀（knife）、叉（fork）、湯匙
（spoon），統稱為 ***silverware***（銀白色金屬餐具）。

　　*silverware* 是由兩個字組成，silver 是「銀」，ware 是「物品；器皿」，如 kitchenware（廚房用具）、glassware（玻璃製品）等。*silverware* 字面意思是「銀製的用具」，由於從前有錢人都是用銀製成的餐具，到今天，雖然不是銀製的餐具，也把「餐具」稱為 *silverware*。

silverware

　　*Where do you keep your silverware?* 的意思是「你的餐具放在哪裡？」也可說成：Where is your *silverware*?（你的餐具在哪裡？）或 Where do you put your *silverware*?（你的餐具放在哪裡？）Where do you store your *silverware*?（你的餐具放在哪裡？）句中的 your *silverware* 可改成 the *silverware*。【store〔stor〕*v.* 儲存】

【比較】

中文：你的餐具放哪裡？

英文：***Where do you keep your silverware?*** 【較常用】

　　　Where do you keep your knives, forks and spoons?【正，有人說，不常用】

knife〔naɪf〕*n.* 刀子　　fork〔fɔrk〕*n.* 叉子
spoon〔spun〕*n.* 湯匙

7. ***You made the meal.***

make〔mek〕*v.* 做（飯）；烹煮
meal〔mil〕*n.* 一餐；一餐份的食物

　　***make the meal*** 意思是「做飯」，一定要加定
冠詞 the，但是 make breakfast（做早餐）、make
lunch（做午餐）、make dinner（做晚餐），都不加
冠詞 the（詳見「文法寶典」p.222）。

　　***You made the meal.*** 的意思是「你做了飯。」
如果強調你一個人煮的時候，就可說成：You
made the meal without help.（你沒有人幫助，
自己做飯。）或 You made the meal by yourself.
（你獨力自己煮飯。）【*by oneself* 獨自；獨力；靠自己】
可更加強語氣說成：***You made the meal all by
yourself.***（你全靠自己煮飯。）

下面都是美國人常說的話，句意相同：

***You made the meal.***【第一常用】
You did the meal.（你做了飯。）【第四常用】
You did the cooking.（你做了飯。）【第三常用】
〔did the cooking = cooked〕

You cooked the meal.【第二常用】
You prepared the meal.【第五常用】
You got the meal ready.【第六常用】

prepare〔prɪ'pɛr〕*v.* 準備；烹調（餐食等）
***get~ready*** 把~準備好

BOOK 11

BOOK 11

8. *I'll clear the table.*

clear〔klɪr〕*v.* 清理；收拾
*clear the table* 收拾桌子（*= take everything off the table*）

　　這句話的意思是「我來收拾桌子。」可以加強
語氣說成：I'll clear off the table.（我來收拾桌
子。）【*clear off* 清理（*= clear*）】也有美國人說成：
I want to clear the table.（我想要清理桌子。）
或 Let me clear the table.（讓我來清理桌子。）

【比較】下面兩句意思不同：

> *I'll clear the table.*（我來收拾桌子。）
> 【這句話是指把桌上的東西拿走，恢復原狀。
> clear = clear off】
>
> I'll clean the table.（我來把桌子弄乾淨。）
> 【這句話是指把桌子擦乾淨，也許還包括把桌上的東西移走。
> clean = clean off】

9. *I'll do the dishes.*

do〔du〕*v.* 使清潔；洗滌
dish〔dɪʃ〕*n.* 盤；碟
*the dishes* 餐桌用杯盤類
　　【包含 plate（盤子）、cup
　　（杯子）、bowl（碗）和 saucer（碟子）等】

the dishes

> 　　*I'll do the dishes.* 的意思是「我來洗碗盤。」事
> 實上，不只洗盤子，還包含一些餐具（silverware），
> 就像我們中國人說：「我來洗碗。」不只是洗碗，也洗
> 盤子、筷子等。

這句話美國人也常說成：

　　I'll wash the dishes.（我來洗碗盤。）
　　I'll clean the dishes.（我來洗碗盤。）
　　I'll take care of the dishes.
　　（我來打理碗盤。）
　　【*take care of* 照顧；處理】

　　do 的基本意思是「做」，當「使清潔；清洗」解時，用法很多，但一般字典很少說明，我們一定要徹底搞清楚。

　　***I'll do the dishes*.**（我來洗碗盤。）
　　I'll *do* the bathroom.（我來清洗浴室。）
　　I'll *do* the windows.（我來擦窗戶。）
　　【bathroom〔'bæθ,rum〕*n.* 浴室】

　　I'll *do* the floor.（我來擦地板。）
　　I'll *do* the laundry.（我來洗衣服。）
　　I'll *do* the living room.（我來掃客廳。）
　　【laundry〔'lɔndrɪ〕*n.* 送洗的衣物】

　　I'll *do* the garbage.（我來把垃圾倒掉。）
　　I'll *do* the table.（我來清潔桌子。）
　　I'll *do* the bed.（我來整理床鋪。）
　　garbage〔'gɑrbɪdʒ〕*n.* 垃圾
　　***do the bed*** 整理床鋪（= *make the bed*）

BOOK 11

## 【對話練習】

1. A: **Put me to work**.　　　　A：讓我工作。
   B: Absolutely not.　　　　　B：絕對不行。
   I'll allow no such thing.　　我不允許這種事。
   I want you to sit and relax.　我要你坐好，放輕鬆。
   【absolutely (ˈæbsəlutlɪ) *adv.* 絕對】

2. A: **Give me something to do**.　A：給我一點事情做。
   B: Thank you for asking.　　　B：謝謝你的請求。
   I couldn't do that.　　　　　我不能這麼做。
   You are here as my guest.　　你來這裡是我的客人。
   【guest (gɛst) *n.* 客人】

3. A: **If you don't let me help,**　A：如果你不讓我幫忙，
   **I'll feel guilty**.　　　　　我會覺得有罪惡感。
   B: OK, you win.　　　　　　B：好吧，你贏了。
   You can help set the table.　你可以幫忙擺餐具。
   Everything is in the kitchen.　所有的東西都在廚房裡。

4. A: **Let me set the table**.　　A：讓我來擺餐具。
   B: That would be a big help.　B：那會幫我很大的忙。
   The silverware is in this drawer.　餐具在這個抽屜裡。
   The dishes are up in the　　盤子在上面的櫥櫃裡。
   cabinet.【drawer (ˈdrɔr) *n.* 抽屜】

5. A: **Where are the plates?**　　A：盤子在哪裡？
   B: They're in the cabinet.　　B：在櫥櫃裡。
   They're behind the bowls.　　在碗的後面。
   Look in the back corner.　　看一下後面的角落。
   【bowl (bol) *n.* 碗　corner (ˈkɔrnɚ) *n.* 角落】

6. A： **Where do you keep your silverware?**

　　B： It's in that drawer.

　　　　It's next to the dishwasher.

　　　　All our silverware is there.

　　　　【dishwasher (ˈdɪʃˌwɑʃɚ ) *n.* 洗碗機】

A：你的餐具放在哪裡？

B：在那個抽屜裡。

　　在洗碗機旁邊。

　　我們所有的餐具都在那裡。

7. A： **You made the meal**.

　　B： Well, I did have some help.

　　　　You cut the onions and made the sauce.

　　　　I can't take all the credit.

　　　　【onion (ˈʌnjən ) *n.* 洋蔥

　　　　sauce ( sɔs ) *n.* 醬汁

　　　　credit (ˈkrɛdɪt ) *n.* 功勞】

A：你做了飯。

B：嗯，我的確有人幫忙。

　　你切洋蔥和做醬汁。

　　我不能搶走所有的功勞。

8. A： **I'll clear the table**.

　　B： How kind of you to offer!

　　　　That would be terrific.

　　　　That would help me a lot.

　　　　【offer (ˈɔfɚ ) *v.* 提供；提議】

A：我來收拾桌子。

B：你願意這樣真是太好了！

　　那真是太棒了。

　　那會幫我很多忙。

9. A： **I'll do the dishes**.

　　B： Really?

　　　　Are you sure you don't mind?

　　　　I can't believe it!

　　　　【mind ( maɪnd ) *v.* 介意】

A：我來洗盤子。

B：真的嗎？

　　你真的不介意？

　　我真不敢相信！

# 7. *This smells marvelous*.

| | |
|---|---|
| This smells marvelous. | 這個聞起來很香。 |
| The aroma is incredible. | 味道聞起來太香了。 |
| It looks too good to eat. | 它太好了，我捨不得吃。 |
| | |
| Every bite is delightful. | 每一口都好吃。 |
| I've never had better. | 我從來沒吃過更好的。 |
| This really takes the cake. | 這個真的是最好的。 |
| | |
| *My* hat's off to you. | 我對你表示敬意。 |
| *My* compliments to the chef. | 我向主廚致意。 |
| What's the recipe? | 怎麼做的？ |

\*\* ───────────────

smell〔smɛl〕*v.* 聞起來
marvelous〔'mɑrvḷəs〕*adj.* 令人驚嘆的；很棒的
aroma〔ə'romə〕*n.* 芳香；香氣
incredible〔ɪn'krɛdəbḷ〕*adj.* 令人難以置信的
bite〔baɪt〕*n.* （咬的）一口
delightful〔dɪ'laɪtfəl〕*adj.* 令人愉快的（= *enjoyable*）
have〔hæv〕*v.* 吃；喝　　*take the cake* 得第一名；成為最好的
compliment〔'kɑmpləmənt〕*n.* 稱讚；(*pl.*) 問候；致意
chef〔ʃɛf〕*n.* 主廚　　recipe〔'rɛsəpɪ〕*n.* 烹飪法；食譜

## 【背景説明】

當你看到主人，準備了滿桌豐盛的佳餚，熱
情地款待你，你總該説幾句好聽的話吧！

1. ***This smells marvelous.***
   smell〔smɛl〕*v.* 聞起來
   marvelous〔'mɑrvḷəs〕*adj.* 令人驚嘆的；很棒的

   這句話字面的意思是「這個聞起來很棒。」引申
   爲「這個聞起來很香。」可以更清楚地説：

   > This dish smells marvelous.
   > （這道菜聞起來很香。）
   > This meal smells marvelous.
   > （這餐飯聞起來很香。）
   > This food smells marvelous.
   > （這個食物聞起來很香。）
   > 【dish〔dɪʃ〕*n.* 菜餚　meal〔mil〕*n.* 一餐】

   美國人常説的還有：

   > This smells so good.
   > （這個聞起來眞好。）
   > This dish smells great.
   > （這道菜聞起來很棒。）
   > This meal smells fantastic.
   > （這餐飯聞起來眞棒。）
   > 【fantastic〔fæn'tæstɪk〕*adj.* 很棒的】

BOOK 11

可以加強語氣說成：

It all smells marvelous.
（全都聞起來很香。）
Everything here smells marvelous.
（這裡每樣東西都聞起來很香。）
Every dish smells marvelous.
（每道菜都聞起來很香。）

*This smells marvelous.*
中的 marvelous，可用
delicious 等取代，意思都是
「它聞起來很香。」

*This smells marvelous.*

This smells
- delicious（好吃的）.
- wonderful（很棒的）.
- fantastic（很棒的）.
- incredible（不可思議的）.
- tasty（好吃的）.
- sensational（很棒的）.
- mouth-watering（令人垂涎的）.
- scrumptious（很好吃的）.
- out of this world（很棒的）.

fantastic〔fæn'tæstɪk〕*adj.* 很棒的
tasty〔'testɪ〕*adj.* 好吃的
sensational〔sɛn'seʃənḷ〕*adj.* 很棒的
scrumptious〔'skrʌmpʃəs〕*adj.* 很好吃的
*out of this world* 很棒的

2. *The aroma is incredible*.

aroma〔ə'romə〕*n.* 芳香；香氣（= *nice smell*）
incredible〔ɪn'krɛdəbḷ〕*adj.* 令人難以置信的

　　這句話字面的意思是「這香氣是令人難以置信的。」也就是「味道聞起來太香了。」可以加強語氣說成：The aroma is really incredible.（味道眞的太香了。）或 The aroma in here is really incredible.（這裡的味道眞的太香了。）

下面都是美國人常說的話：

*The aroma is incredible*.【第一常用】
The aroma is excellent.【第四常用】
（味道聞起來太香了。）
The aroma is superb.【第五常用】
（味道聞起來太棒了。）

excellent〔'ɛksḷənt〕*adj.* 優秀的；極好的
superb〔su'pɝb〕*adj.* 極好的

BOOK 11

The aroma is wonderful.【第三常用】
（味道聞起來太棒了。）
The aroma is great.【第二常用】
（味道聞起來太香了。）
The aroma is amazing.【第六常用】
（味道聞起來太棒了。）

【amazing〔ə'mezɪŋ〕*adj.* 令人驚奇的】

3. ***It looks too good to eat.***

原則上，too…to～表示「太…而不能～」，不定詞 to～是表示否定的結果，修飾前面的副詞 too。too…to～成雙成對出現，所以在文書上，稱作「相關修飾詞」。

但是在這裡，It looks too good to eat. 如果翻成「它太好了，不能吃。」就不合理了。所以，此句可看成是一種例外，意思是「它太好了，我捨不得吃。」事實上卻是很想吃，是一種極度的恭維話。

【比較】

> ***It looks too good to eat.*** 【特殊含意】
> ( = *It looks so good, I'm afraid to eat it.* )
>
> It looks too bad to eat. 【一般用法】
> ( 它看起來太糟糕了，我不想吃。)
> ( = *It looks so bad, I don't want to eat it.* )

美國人喜歡用 too…to～來恭維，to 後面並不表示真正的否定，而是表示客套，像 You're too good to be true. ( 你好到令人難以置信。) 或 It looks too nice to use. ( 它看起來太好了，捨不得用。) 到底 too…to～中的不定詞片語，表示否定還是肯定，完全要看句意來決定。

## 4. *Every bite is delightful.*

bite〔baɪt〕*n.* (咬的)一口
delightful〔dɪ'laɪtfəl〕*adj.* 令人愉快的 ( = *enjoyable* )

　　這句話字面的意思是「每一口都是令人愉快的。」
引申爲「每一口都好吃。」可以加強語氣說成：
Every single bite is delightful. (每一口都很好
吃。) 或 Every bite is delightful to eat. (每一
口吃起來都很好吃。)【single〔'sɪŋgl〕*adj.* 單一的】

下面都是美國人常說的話：

> *Every bite is delightful.*【第三常用】
> Every bite is delicious.【第一常用】
> 　(每一口都好吃。)
> Every bite tastes great.【第二常用】
> 　(每一口嚐起來都很棒。)
> 　【taste〔test〕*v.* 嚐起來】
>
> Every bite is enjoyable.【第五常用】
> 　(每一口都好吃。)
> Every bite is fantastic.【第四常用】
> 　(每一口都很棒。)
> Every bite is pleasing.【第六常用】
> 　(每一口都好吃。)
> enjoyable〔ɪn'dʒɔɪəbl̩〕*adj.* 令人愉快的
> pleasing〔'plizɪŋ〕*adj.* 令人愉快的

5. *I've never had better.*

have〔hæv〕*v.* 吃；喝

這句話在這裡的意思是「我從來沒吃過更好的。」
源自：I've never had anything better than this.
（我從來沒吃過比這個更好的。）可加強語氣說成：
I've never had a better meal in my life.（我這輩
子從沒吃過比這個更好的一餐。）【meal〔mil〕*n.* 一餐】
用最高級時，就不能用 never，要用 ever，說成：
This is the best meal that I've ever had.（這是我
曾經吃過最好的一餐。）【ever = at any time】

【在本書的 p.1207 中，有提到 I've had it before.（我以前
吃過。）兩回可以混合使用。】

6. *This really takes the cake.*

*take the cake* 得第一名（= *take the first prize*）；
成為最好的（= *be the best*）

take the cake 這個成語，源自在美國社區、學
校或教堂，為了募款，他們常販賣摸彩券，第一特
獎通常是一個大蛋糕。

*This really takes the cake.* 的意思是「這個
真的是第一名；這個真的是最好的。」也可以說成：
This certainly takes the cake.（這當然是最好的。）
如果哪一道菜特別好吃，你可以說：This dish
really takes the cake.（這道菜真的是最好的。）

美國人也常説：This is the best. 或 This is the finest. 意思都是「這是最好的。」

你可常用 *take the cake* 來稱讚人：

Your neat writing *takes the cake*.
（你寫得最整齊。）

This buffet *takes the cake*. It's all delicious.
（這個自助餐最好。全部都好吃。）

This glass of fruit juice really *takes the cake*.（這杯果汁最好喝。）

neat〔nit〕*adj.* 整齊的　writing〔'raɪtɪŋ〕*n.* 書寫；筆跡
buffet〔bu'fe, bʌ'fe〕*n.* （歐式）自助餐
juice〔dʒus〕*n.* 果汁

*take the cake* 也可以用來諷刺人，看到人太會花錢，你可以説：

Your careless spending *takes the cake*.
（你亂花錢第一名。）
【careless〔'kɛrlɪs〕*adj.* 粗心的】

看到人常遲到，你可以説：

Your always being late *takes the cake*.
（你最會遲到。）【late〔let〕*adj.* 遲到的】

看到一個粗魯的人，可以背後説他：

His rude behavior *takes the cake*.
（他最粗魯。）【rude〔rud〕*adj.* 粗魯的】

BOOK 11

7. *My hat's off to you.*

> 　　在所有中外字典上，都找不到這句話的成語，但是美國人常說，我們一定要詳加研究。*My hat's off to you.* 的字面意思是「我對著你把帽子脫下。」引申爲「我向你表示敬意。」也就是「我向你致敬。」説這句話時，有幽默的味道。沒有戴帽子時，可假裝做脱帽的動作。

下面三句意思相同，都表示「我向你致敬。」

**My hat's off to you.**【第一常用】

= My hat goes off to you.【第二常用】

= I take my hat off to you.【第三常用】

【第二句和第一句一樣，字典上沒有，但美國人常説。
take *one's* hat off to *sb.* 向某人表示敬意（= *take off one's hat to sb.*）】

【比較】**My hat's off to you.**【常用】

*My hat is off to you.*

【正，少用，有點像書寫英語】

*My hat's off to you.* 這句話每天都用得到，例如：

You did an excellent job. *My hat's off to you.*（你做得很好。我向你致敬。）

Congratulations on winning! *My hat's off to you.*（恭喜你贏了。我向你致敬。）

You scored 100 on the test. *My hat's off to you.*

（你考試考 100 分。我向你致敬。）

excellent〔'ɛkslənt〕*adj.* 極好的
congratulations〔kən͵grætʃə'leʃənz〕*n. pl.* 恭喜
score〔skor〕*v.* 得（分）

對別人的稱讚，除了說 *My hat's off to you.* 以外，美國人還常說：Great job.（做得好。）You are excellent.（你很棒。）You did a super job.（你做得很好。）等。

8. *My compliments to the chef.*
compliment〔'kampləmənt〕*n.* 稱讚；(*pl.*) 問候；致意（= *greetings*）    chef〔ʃɛf〕*n.* 主廚

這句話的意思是「我向主廚致意。」源自 Please give my compliments to the chef.（請代我向主廚致意。）compliment 表「稱讚」時，有單、複數形式。當表示「問候」時，卻一定要用複數的形式。在這裡，是表示尊敬的問候，也就是「致意」，所以，一定要用複數形式。

【比較】 *My compliments to the chef.* 【正】
*My compliment to the chef.* 【誤】

　　有些名詞一定要用複數形式，如 wishes（祝賀），compliments（問候），regards（問候），congratulations（恭喜）等【詳見「文法寶典」p.84】。

　　美國人在吃飯的時候，不管食物好不好，他們都會在餐桌上，對女主人說：*My compliments to the chef.* 或說 My compliments to you.（我對你表示敬意。）和上一句 My hat's off to you. 相同。

你還可以接著說：

I enjoyed your meal very much.
（我很喜歡你做的飯。）
I love your cooking.
（我愛吃你煮的東西。）
You could be a professional chef.
（你能夠成爲一個專業的主廚。）

enjoy〔ɪnˈdʒɔɪ〕*v.* 喜歡
cooking〔ˈkʊkɪŋ〕*n.* 烹調；飯菜
professional〔prəˈfɛʃənḷ〕*adj.* 專業的

You're an excellent cook.（你眞會做飯。）
You cook a delicious meal.（你做的飯很好吃。）
You really know how to cook.（你眞會做飯。）

【cook〔kʊk〕*n.* 廚師　*v.* 烹調】

【比較】 *My compliments to the chef.*

這是幽默話，到外國人家作客時，對煮飯的女主人說，稱 chef 是恭維，就像我們說的「大廚子」。

Please give my compliments to the chef. 這句話通常是在餐廳跟服務生說，服務生就會將你的訊息，轉達給主廚，很可能主廚就會過來向你致謝。在這個時候，你就可以說：*My compliments to the chef.* 或 My compliments to you.（我向你致意。）

到餐廳裡，常稱讚菜好吃，主廚即使不出來，也會偷看是哪個客人在稱讚他。以後只要你來了，廚師對你的菜就會更加用心，選的材料也會是最好的。

BOOK 11

9. *What's the recipe?*

recipe〔ˈrɛsəpɪ〕 *n.* 烹飪法；食譜；調製法
 ( = *a set of directions with a list of ingredients for making food* )

這句話字面的意思是「烹飪法是什麼？」引申爲「怎麼做的？」可以客氣一點說：May I ask, "What's the recipe?"（我可以問「怎麼做的」嗎？）或 Do you mind if I ask, "What's the recipe?"（你介意我問「是怎麼做的」嗎？）
 ( = *Do you mind if I ask what the recipe is?* )

下面是美國人常說的話：

***What's the recipe?*** 【第一常用】
What's the recipe for this? 【第二常用】
（這是怎麼做的？）
Please tell me the recipe. 【第七常用】
（請告訴我是怎麼做的。）

How do you make this? 【第四常用】
（這是怎麼做的？）
How did you make this? 【第五常用】
（這是怎麼做的？）
How did you prepare this? 【第六常用】
（這是怎麼做的？）
【prepare〔prɪ'pɛr〕v. 烹調（食物）】

I'd like to know the recipe. 【第八常用】
（我想知道是怎麼做的。）
I'd love to know how to make this. 【第九常用】
（我想知道這是怎麼做的。）
What's your recipe for this? 【第三常用】
（這是怎麼做的？）

***I'd like to V.*** 我想要～（= *I want to V.*）
***I'd love to V.*** 我很想要～

「一口氣背會話」背熟了之後，自然可以在腦海中形
成不同的組合。像這一回，就可以和第一冊的第八課
一起使用。

BOOK 11

## 【對話練習】

1. A：**This smells marvelous**.
   B：I hope you like it.
     I hope it tastes good.
     I made it especially for you.

A：這個聞起來很香。
B：我希望你會喜歡。
  我希望它很好吃。
  這是我特地為你做的。

2. A：**The aroma is incredible**.
   B：I'm glad it smells nice.
     I put seasonings in it.
     I added herbs and spices.
     【seasoning〔'siznɪŋ〕*n.* 調味料
     herb〔hɝb, ɝb〕*n.* 藥草；香草
     spice〔spaɪs〕*n.* 香料】

A：味道聞起來太香了。
B：我很高興它聞起來很香。
  我放了調味料在裡面。
  我加了香草和香料。

3. A：**It looks too good to eat**.
   B：Don't say things like that.
     Don't make me feel guilty.
     I want to enjoy every bite.
     【guilty〔'gɪltɪ〕*adj.* 有罪惡感的】

A：它太好了，我不敢吃。
B：別那麼說。
  不要讓我有罪惡感。
  我想要享用每一口食物。

4. A：**Every bite is delightful**.
   B：I'm so glad you think so.
     It pleases me to hear that.
     It makes all the effort
     worthwhile.
     【please〔pliz〕*v.* 取悅；使高興
     worthwhile〔'wɝθ'hwaɪl〕*adj.* 值得的】

A：每一口都好吃。
B：很高興你這麼認為。
  我很高興聽你這麼說。
  它使所有的努力都很
  值得。

BOOK 11

5. A：**I've never had better**.
   B：I don't believe you.
   You're just saying that.
   You're just being polite.
   【polite〔pə'laɪt〕*adj.* 有禮貌的】

A：我從來沒吃過更好的。
B：我不相信你說的話。
   你只是說說而已。
   你只是客套而已。

6. A：**This really takes the cake**.
   B：Thank you so much.
   I feel relieved.
   I was afraid you wouldn't
   like it.【relieved〔rɪ'livd〕*adj.*
   放心的；鬆了一口氣的】

A：這個眞的是最好的。
B：非常謝謝你。
   我覺得鬆了一口氣。
   我還怕你會不喜歡。

7. A：**My hat's off to you**.
   B：I don't know what to say.
   I seldom hear such praise.
   It sure feels good.
   【praise〔prez〕*n.* 稱讚】

A：我對你表示敬意。
B：我不知道該怎麼說。
   我很少聽到這樣的讚美。
   感覺的確很棒。

8. A：**My compliments to the chef**.
   B：I'll let him know that you
   are pleased.
   He'll be happy to hear that
   you enjoyed it.
   Would you like to meet him?

A：我向主廚致意。
B：我會讓他知道你很高興。
   聽到你很喜歡，他會很高興。
   你想和他見面嗎？

9. A：**What's the recipe?**
   B：It's very simple.
   It's right here in this book.
   Let me write it down for you.

A：怎麼做的？
B：很簡單。
   做法就在這本書裡。
   我寫下來給你吧。

# 8. *What a cute baby!*

| | |
|---|---|
| ***What*** a cute baby! | 多麼可愛的小孩！ |
| ***What*** a little angel! | 多麼可愛的小天使！ |
| ***What*** an adorable child! | 多麼討人喜歡的孩子！ |
| | |
| ***How*** old is your baby? | 你的小孩多大了？ |
| ***How*** many months? | 幾個月大？ |
| Is it a boy or a girl? | 它是男孩還是女孩？ |
| | |
| Hi there, sweetie. | 嗨，小可愛。 |
| How about a smile? | 笑一個怎麼樣？ |
| Can I hold him? | 我可不可以抱他？ |

BOOK 11

\*\* ────────────────────

cute〔kjut〕*adj.* 可愛的　　angel〔'endʒəl〕*n.* 天使
adorable〔ə'dorəb!〕*adj.* 可愛的
***hi there***　【招呼語】嗨；你（們）好
sweetie〔'switɪ〕*n.* 心愛的人；親愛的人
***How about ~ ?***　~如何？　　smile〔smaɪl〕*n.* 微笑
hold〔hold〕*v.* 抓住；抱著

## 【背景説明】

不管在任何地方，只要看到可愛的小嬰兒，
都可説這九句話來給他媽媽聽。

1. ***What a cute baby!***

cute〔kjut〕*adj.* 可愛的

「What＋a＋名詞！」是感嘆句，這句話的意
思是「多麼可愛的小孩！」可以加上感嘆詞，説成：
Wow! What a cute baby!（哇啊！多麼可愛的小
孩！）或 Oh my! What a cute baby!（哎呀！多
麼可愛的小孩！）【*Oh my!* 哎呀！】

***What a cute baby!*** 也可以加長爲：What a
cute baby you have!（你的小孩眞可愛！）站得
稍微遠一點時，就可以説：What a cute baby
you have there!（你那個小孩眞可愛！）

除了 ***What a cute baby!*** 以外，美國人還常
説：What a pretty baby!（多麼漂亮的小孩！）
或 What a beautiful baby!（多麼漂亮的小孩！）
可用敘述句説成：

Your baby is cute.（你的小孩很可愛。）

Your baby is so cute.（你的小孩非常可愛。）

Your baby is really cute.（你的小孩眞可愛。）

2. ***What a little angel!***

angel〔'endʒəl〕*n.* 天使

這句話的意思是「多麼可愛的小天使！」如果確定這個小孩是男生，就可以說：What a little prince!（多麼可愛的小王子！）如果是女生，就可以說：What a little princess!（多麼可愛的小公主！）

【prince〔prɪns〕*n.* 王子　princess〔'prɪnsɪs〕*n.* 公主】

***What a little angel!*** 可以簡化成：What an angel!（多麼可愛的天使！）也可以加長爲：What a cute little angel!（多麼可愛的小天使！）

3. ***What an adorable child!***

adorable〔ə'dorəbl̩〕*adj.* 可愛的

這句話的意思是「多麼討人喜歡的孩子！」可加長爲：What an adorable child you have!（你的小孩眞討人喜歡！）美國人也常說：

What a dear child!（多麼可愛的小孩！）

What a precious child!（多麼可愛的小孩！）

What a darling child!（多麼可愛的小孩！）

dear〔dɪr〕*adj.* 親愛的；可愛的
precious〔'prɛʃəs〕*adj.* 珍貴的；可愛的
darling〔'dɑrlɪŋ〕*adj.* 可愛的

可用敘述句說成：

> ***Your child is adorable.*** 【第一常用】
> Your child is charming. 【第五常用】
> （你的小孩真可愛。）
> Your little one is adorable. 【第二常用】
> （你的小孩很可愛。）
>
> 【charming〔'tʃɑrmɪŋ〕*adj.* 迷人的；可愛的
> ***little one*** 小孩；小傢伙】
>
> You have an adorable child. 【第三常用】
> （你的小孩真可愛。）
> You have a darling child. 【第四常用】
> （你的小孩真可愛。）
> You have a delightful child. 【第六常用】
> （你的小孩真可愛。）
>
> 【delightful〔dɪ'laɪtfəl〕*adj.* 令人高興的；可愛的】

### 4. *How old is your baby?*

這句話的意思是「你的小孩多大了？」也可說成：How old is your baby now? （你的小孩現在多大了？）可以禮貌地說成：May I ask, "How old is your baby?" （我可不可以請問你：「你的小孩多大了？」）（ = *May I ask how old your baby is?* ）或 I'd like to know how old your baby is. （我想知道你的小孩多大了。）

如果知道是男孩，就可以說：How old is he? （他多大了？）如果是女孩，就說：How old is she? （她多大了？）

### 5. *How many months?*

　　這句話的意思是「幾個月大？」源自：How many months old is your baby?（你的小孩有幾個月大？）可禮貌地問：Please tell me how many months old your baby is.（請告訴我，你的小孩幾個月大了。）

### 6. *Is it a boy or a girl?*

　　這句話的意思是「它是男孩還是女孩？」可說成：Is your baby a boy or a girl?（你的小孩是男生還是女生？）或 Is your child a boy or a girl?（你的小孩是男生還是女生？）也有美國人說：Is it a he or she?（它是男生還是女生？）

【he〔hi〕*n.* 男性　she〔ʃi〕*n.* 女性】

### 7. *Hi there, sweetie.*

*hi there* 【招呼語】嗨；你（們）好
sweetie〔'switɪ〕*n.* 心愛的人；親愛的人

　　一般美國人打招呼，通常會說 Hi!（嗨！）加強語氣，就說成：*Hi there!*（嗨，你好！）句中的 there 沒有意思，純粹加強語氣。類似的還有：

　　Hello *there*!（哈囉，你好！）
　　Hey *there*!（嘿，你好！）

BOOK 11

What's up *there*?

（怎麼樣啊？；你好嗎？）

What's new *there*?

（有什麼新鮮事嗎？；你好嗎？）

What's happening *there*?

（發生什麼事啊？；你好嗎？）

What's up there?

How's it going *there*?（你好嗎？）

How are you doing *there*?（你好嗎？）

　　你碰到外國人，你跟他說 Hi! 他沒什麼感覺，如果你跟他說 Hi there! 他就會覺得你這個中國人英文怎麼這麼好，很了不起。

　　sweetie 源自 sweetheart〔'swit,hart〕，意思都是「親愛的人；可愛的人；心愛的人」。*Hi there, sweetie.* 在這裡的意思是「嗨，小可愛。」這句話可加長為：*Hi there, sweetie.*  How are you?（嗨，小可愛。你好嗎？）或 *Hi there, sweetie.* You're so beautiful.（嗨，小可愛。你好漂亮啊。）

　　*sweetie* 可用 honey，sugar，beautiful，handsome 等取代。beautiful 可修飾男孩或女孩，像 What a beautiful boy! 但 handsome 只能修飾男孩。

　　下面各句意思相同，都是美國人常説的話，適
合男孩或女孩：

**Hi there, sweetie.**【第一常用】

= Hi there, honey. ( 嗨，心肝寶貝。)【第四常用】

= Hi there, sugar. ( 嗨，親愛的。)【第五常用】

honey〔'hʌnɪ〕*n.* 愛人；心肝寶貝
sugar〔'ʃʊgɚ〕*n.* 親愛的

= Hi there, angel. ( 嗨，小天使。)【第二常用】

= Hi there, darling. ( 嗨，小可愛。)【第三常用】

= Hi there, sweetheart.【第六常用】

　　( 嗨，親愛的。)

darling〔'dɑrlɪŋ〕*n.* 可愛的人；親愛的人
sweetheart〔'swit,hɑrt〕*n.* 愛人

## 8. *How about a smile?*

**How about~?**　~如何？　　smile〔smaɪl〕*n.* 微笑

　　這句話的意思是「笑一個怎麼樣？」可以加長
爲：How about giving me a smile? ( 對我笑一
個怎麼樣？) 或 How about showing me a smile?
( 笑一個給我看好嗎？)【show〔ʃo〕*v.* 給~看】也可
以簡單地説：

Smile. ( 笑一個。)

Show me a smile. ( 笑一個給我看。)

Give me a smile. ( 笑一個給我看。)

BOOK 11

如果小孩子還不笑，你可以再補上三句：

I want a smile. ( 我想要看到一個笑容。 )

I want to see you smile.

( 我想看到你笑。 )【smile 是原形動詞】

I want to see your smile. ( 我想看你的笑容。 )

9. *Can I hold him?*

hold〔hold〕v. 抓住；抱著

hold 的主要意思是「抓住」，在此作「抱著」解。*Can I hold him?* 的意思是「我可不可以抱他？」也可說成：

May I hold him? ( 我可以抱他嗎？ )

Do you mind if I hold him? ( 你介意我抱他嗎？ )

Is it OK to hold him? ( 可以抱他嗎？ )

( = *Is it OK if I hold him?* )

hold〔hold〕v. 抱住和 hug〔hʌg〕v. 擁抱不同，hold 是較長時間的擁抱，hug 則是短暫時間的擁抱。如美國人見面或道別時，會互相擁抱 ( hug )。

You *hug* your grandma. ( 你擁抱你的祖母。 )

You *hold* your lover. ( 你抱著你的愛人。 )

【grandma〔'grændmɑ〕*n.* 祖母；外婆】

You hug your grandma.　　　You hold your lover.

## 【對話練習】

1. A: **What a cute baby!**

   B: Yes, she is cute.
   She has beautiful eyes.
   She has a wonderful smile.

A: 多麼可愛的小孩！

B: 是的，她很可愛。
   她的眼睛很漂亮。
   她笑起來很好看。

2. A: **What a little angel!**

   B: Their baby is an angel.
   She is so sweet and cuddly.
   She has a happy little giggle.

   【sweet〔swit〕*adj.* 可愛的
   cuddly〔'kʌdlɪ〕*adj.* 極可愛的
   giggle〔'gɪgl̩〕*n.* 吃吃笑；咯咯笑】

A: 多麼可愛的小天使！

B: 他們的小孩是個天使。
   她非常可愛。
   她會快樂地小小聲咯
   咯笑。

3. A: **What an adorable child!**

   B: Yes, he is darling.
   He has cute chubby
   cheeks.
   He has soft, lovely skin.

   【darling〔'dɑrlɪŋ〕*adj.* 很漂亮的
   chubby〔'tʃʌbɪ〕*adj.* 圓胖的
   cheek〔tʃik〕*n.* 臉頰】

A: 多麼討人喜歡的孩子！

B: 是的，他很可愛。
   他有可愛而且圓胖的
   臉頰。
   他有柔軟可愛的皮膚。

4. A: **How old is your baby?**

   B: He's eight months old.
   He'll be nine months next
   week.
   He's really growing fast.

A: 你的小孩多大了？

B: 他八個月大。
   他下星期就九個月了。

   他真的長得很快。

BOOK 11

5. A : **How many months?**

　　B : Going on seven.
　　　　A little over half a year.
　　　　She was born in January.

6. A : **Is it a boy or a girl?**

　　B : Can't you tell?
　　　　She's wearing pink.
　　　　She's got a bow in her hair.
　　　　【tell〔tɛl〕*v.* 知道
　　　　　bow〔bo〕*n.* 蝴蝶結】

7. A : **Hi there, sweetie.**

　　B : Please don't get too close.
　　　　Please don't touch her face.
　　　　She is shy of strangers.
　　　　【*be shy of* 見到⋯就害羞
　　　　　stranger〔'strendʒɚ〕*n.* 陌生人】

8. A : **How about a smile?**

　　B : She loves to smile.
　　　　She laughs all the time.
　　　　Just make a silly face and
　　　　you'll see. 【*make a face* 做鬼臉
　　　　　silly〔'sɪlɪ〕*adj.* 愚蠢的；可笑的】

9. A : **Can I hold him?**

　　B : Sorry, you can't.
　　　　He's a sensitive boy.
　　　　Strangers often make him cry.

A：幾個月大？

B：快七個月了。
　　六個多月。
　　她是一月生的。

A：它是男孩還是女孩？

B：你看不出來嗎？
　　她穿粉紅色的。
　　她頭髮上有蝴蝶結。

A：嗨，小可愛。

B：請不要靠太近。
　　請不要摸她的臉。
　　她見到陌生人就害羞。

A：笑一個怎麼樣？

B：她很喜歡笑。
　　她老是笑個不停。
　　只要做個可笑的鬼臉，
　　你就看得到啦。

A：我可不可以抱他？

B：抱歉，不行。
　　他是個敏感的小孩。
　　陌生人常會把他弄哭。

BOOK 11

# *9.　You have a great kid*.

| | |
|---|---|
| You have a great kid. | 你的小孩很棒。 |
| *He looks* like you. | 他看起來像你。 |
| *He looks* intelligent and bright. | 他看起來非常聰明。 |
| | |
| *He*'s very polite. | 他很有禮貌。 |
| *He* acts mature for his age. | 以他的年齡來說，他的舉止很成熟。 |
| | |
| You've raised him well. | 你把他教得很好。 |
| | |
| Kids are a handful. | 小孩真麻煩。 |
| Your child turned out swell. | 你的小孩變得很好。 |
| You must be a good parent. | 你一定是個好的父（母）親。 |

BOOK 11

** ────────────

kid〔kɪd〕*n.* 小孩　　intelligent〔ɪn'tɛlədʒənt〕*adj.* 聰明的
bright〔braɪt〕*adj.* 聰明的　　polite〔pə'laɪt〕*adj.* 有禮貌的
act〔ækt〕*v.* 舉止　　mature〔mə'tʃʊr, mə'tjʊr〕*adj.* 成熟的
raise〔rez〕*v.* 養育；教養
handful〔'hænd,fʊl〕*n.* 難控制的人或物；麻煩的事
*turn out* 結果變成　　swell〔swɛl〕*adj.* 極好的；出色的
must〔mʌst〕*aux.* 一定　　parent〔'pɛrənt, 'pærənt〕*n.* 父；母

## 【背景説明】

　　　當你看到外國朋友的小孩，很懂禮貌，又守規矩，就可以跟你的朋友説這九句話，來稱讚他。

1. ***You have a great kid.***
　　great〔gret〕*adj.* 很棒的　　　kid〔kɪd〕*n.* 小孩

　　　這句話字面的意思是「你有很棒的小孩。」也就是「你的小孩很棒。」等於 Your kid is great. 可加強語氣説成：You have a really great kid.（你的小孩眞的很棒。）或加上 I think，説成：I think you have a great kid.（我認爲你的小孩很棒。）

　　great 可用 nice，super 等字代替，如：

> ***You have a great kid.***【第一常用】
> You have a nice kid.【第一常用】
> （你的小孩很好。）
> You have a super kid.【第四常用】
> （你的小孩很棒。）【super〔'supɚ〕*adj.* 極好的】
>
> You have a wonderful kid.【第二常用】
> （你的小孩很棒。）
> You have a terrific kid.【第三常用】
> （你的小孩很棒。）
> You have a fantastic kid.【第六常用】
> （你的小孩很棒。）
> terrific〔tə'rɪfɪk〕*adj.* 很棒的
> fantastic〔fæn'tæstɪk〕*adj.* 很棒的

BOOK 11

kid 可用 son，daughter，child 代替，説成：

You have a great son. ( 你的兒子很棒。 )

You have a great daughter.

( 你的女兒很棒。 )

You have a great child. ( 你的小孩很棒。 )

【比較】 下面兩句話意思相同：

> ***You have a great kid.*** 【較常用，美國人文化】
> = Your kid is great. 【常用，和中國人思想相同】

## 2. *He looks like you.*

這句話的意思是「他看起來像你。」可以加強
語氣説成：He looks just like you. ( 他看起來就
像你。 ) 或 He looks very much like you. ( 他看
起來非常像你。 ) 或 He looks a lot like you. ( 他
看起來非常像你。 )

*He looks like you.* 也可説成：

He resembles you. ( 他長得像你。 )

He reminds me of you. ( 他使我想到你。 )

He looks like a mini you.

( 他看起來像小型的你。 )

resemble〔rɪˈzɛmbļ〕*v.* 長得像
remind〔rɪˈmaɪnd〕*v.* 使想起
mini〔ˈmɪnɪ〕*adj.* 小型的

*He looks like you.*

He has your characteristics. ( 他有你的特性。)

He has your features. ( 他有你的特徵。)

He has your nose and mouth.

( 他有你的鼻子和嘴巴；他的鼻子和嘴巴和你很像。)

characteristic〔ˌkærɪktə'rɪstɪk〕 *n.* 特性
feature〔'fitʃə〕 *n.* 特性

3. ***He looks intelligent and bright.***

intelligent〔ɪn'tɛlədʒənt〕 *adj.* 聰明的
bright〔braɪt〕 *adj.* 聰明的

　　這句話的意思是「他看起來非常聰明。」and 連接兩個同義的形容詞，有加強語氣的作用。可加強語氣說成：He looks like he is very intelligent and bright. ( 他看起來非常聰明。)

【比較1】 ***intelligent and bright*** 是美國人的習慣用法，不可說成：*bright and intelligent*。

***He looks intelligent and bright.***【正】
*He looks bright and intelligent.*
【誤，文法對，美國人不習慣說】

【比較2】 clever 和 smart 也常成對出現，但順序可互換：

　　He looks smart and clever. 【正，常用】
= He looks clever and smart. 【正，常用】
　　( 他看起來非常聰明。)

【smart〔smɑrt〕 *adj.* 聰明的　　clever〔'klɛvə〕 *adj.* 聰明的】

美國人也常說：

> He looks smart.（他看起來聰明。）
>
> He looks very smart.（他看起來很聰明。）
>
> He looks like a smart kid.
>
> （他看起來像是個聰明的小孩。）

上面三句的 smart 可用 clever 或 sharp〔ʃɑrp〕*adj.* 聰明的 取代。

4. *He's very polite*.

polite〔pə'laɪt〕*adj.* 有禮貌的

這句話的意思是「他很有禮貌。」美國人也常 說成：He's a very polite kid. 或 He's a very polite child. 意思都相同。

【比較】 下面兩句話意思相同：

> *He's very polite*.【較常用】
>
> He is very polite.【常用，語氣稍強】

5. *He acts mature for his age*.

act〔ækt〕*v.* 舉止（= *behave*）；表現（= *appear to be*）

mature〔mə'tʃʊr, mə'tjʊr〕*adj.* 成熟的

在本句中的 act，就像 be 動詞一樣，後須接形 容詞做主詞補語。這句話的意思是「以他的年齡來 說，他的舉止很成熟。」美國人也常說成：He is mature for his age.（以他的年齡來說，他很成熟。）

「act + 形容詞」的例子：

He *acts* polite. ( 他很有禮貌。)

He *acts* well-behaved. ( 他很守規矩。)

He *acts* spoiled. ( 他像是被寵壞了。)

well-behaved (ˈwɛlbɪˈhevd ) *adj.* 行為端正的；守規矩的
spoiled ( spɔɪld ) *adj.* 被寵壞的

*He acts mature for his age.* 也可說成：He's
very mature for his age. ( 以他的年齡來說，他很
成熟。) 或 He seems very mature for his age.
( 以他的年齡來說，他似乎非常成熟。)

【比較】 在「KK音標發音字典」中，mature 有三
種發音。

① mature ( məˈtʃʊr )【此種發音，在「KK音標
發音字典」中沒有，但有些英漢字典有，一般美國
人喜歡說】

② mature ( məˈtjʊr )【受過高等教育的人喜歡
說，如醫生、律師、教授等】

下面都是美國人常說的話：

He acts so mature.【第一常用】

( 他的舉止很成熟。)

He acts so mature for his age.【第三常用】

( 以他的年齡來說，他的舉止很成熟。)

*He acts mature for his age.*【第二常用】

He acts adultlike. ( 他的舉止像大人。)【第七常用】

He acts like an adult. 【第六常用】

( 他的舉止像大人。)

He acts grown-up. 【第五常用】

( 他的舉止像大人。)

adultlike〔 ə'dʌlt,laɪk 〕*adj.* 像大人的

adult〔 ə'dʌlt 〕*n.* 成人；大人

grown-up〔'gron,ʌp 〕*adj.* 成熟的

He acts older. ( 他的舉止比較成熟。)【第四常用】

He acts older than his age. 【第九常用】

( 他的舉止比實際年齡成熟。)

He acts ahead of his age. 【第八常用】

( 他的舉止超過他的年紀。)【*ahead of* 超越】

6. *You've raised him well.*

raise〔 rez 〕*v.* 養育；教養

You've raised him well.

這句話字面的意思是「你
把他養育得很好。」也就是
「你把他教得很好。」

下面都是美國人常說的話：

*You've raised him well.*【第一常用】

You've raised your child well. 【第四常用】

( 你把你的小孩教得很好。)

You are raising him well. 【第二常用】

( 你把他教得很好。)

BOOK 11

You are doing a good job of raising him.

（你把他教得很好。）【第五常用】

You are bringing your child up well.

（你把你的小孩教得很好。）【第六常用】

You've done a good job raising him.

（你把他教得很好。）【第二常用】

【*bring up* 養育；教養】

7. *Kids are a handful.*

handful〔'hænd,ful〕*n.* 難控制的人或物（= *a person or thing that is difficult to control*）；麻煩的事

handful 這個字，看起來像形容詞，卻是一個名詞，主要意思是「一把」，如 a *handful* of candies（一把糖果），但在這裡，*handful* 作「難控制的人」解，不要和 handy（便利的）搞混。

【比較】下面兩句話意思完全不同：

*Kids are a handful.*（小孩眞麻煩。）
Kids are helpful.（小孩能幫得上忙。）

在一般字典上，*handful* 只作「一把；少數；少量」解，但在 Webster's Dictionary（p.882）中，清楚地說明，*handful* 可表示「一點；少數；少量」，也可表示「很多」（= *plenty*），要看前後句意來決定。

【比較】

　　I have *a whole handful of* things to do.

　　（我有很多事要做。）

　　【a whole handful of = a lot of】

　　I only have *a handful of* things to do.

　　（我只有一些事要做。）【a handful of = a few】

　　　所以，*handful* 還表示「手
上滿滿的東西」，源自 hands are
full。你手上有很多東西，你就
可以說：

　　My hands are full.

　　（我手上有很多東西；我很忙碌。）

　　I have a hand *full of things to do*.

　　（我有很多事要做。）

　　I have a handful of things to do.

　　（我有很多事要做。）

**講那麼多，只有一個重點：**

handful（手上滿滿的東西）轉變爲 handful（難管的
人或物）。

　　*Kids are a handful.* 的意思是「小孩是難管的
人。」也就是「小孩眞難管。」或「小孩眞麻煩。」
可加長爲：

I know *kids are a handful*.

（我知道小孩眞難管。）

I've heard *kids are a handful*.

（我聽說小孩眞難管。）

Raising kids can be a handful.

（養育小孩可能很麻煩。）

【比較】 動詞和主詞一致，和補語無關：

*Kids are a handful*.【正】

*Kids are handfuls*.【誤】

*Kids are handful*.【誤】

handful 作「難控制的人或物」解時，永遠用
單數，而且加上冠詞，説成 *a handful*。而且
handful 不能當形容詞用。

*a handful* 很常用，你想用的話，每天都用得到，如：

Life is *a handful*.（生活眞麻煩。）

Learning a new job can be *a handful*.

（學一個新工作可能很麻煩。）

His wife is really *a handful*.

（他的老婆眞麻煩。）

My dad's boss is *a real handful*.

（我爸爸的老板很難纏。）

Working two jobs can be *a handful*.

（做兩件工作眞不容易。）

A crying baby can be *a real handful*.

（小孩哭起來眞麻煩。）

8. ***Your child turned out swell.***

***turn out*** 結果變成（= *come to be*）

swell〔swɛl〕*adj.* 極好的；一流的；出色的

　　這句話的意思是「你的小孩變得很好。」源自：
Your child turned out to be swell. 句中 turned
out 後面的 to be 可省略，也可保留。

　　　swell 這個字，在文章中很少見，但美國人常
說。如：

What a *swell* day!（今天天氣眞好！）

My uncle is a *swell* guy.  He always
　　gives me money.

（我的叔叔眞棒。他總是給我錢。）

We had a *swell* time last night.

（我們咋天晚上玩得很愉快。）

guy〔gaɪ〕*n.* 傢伙；人
***have a swell time*** 玩得很愉快（= *have a great time*）

【比較】　turn out 不能用現在式：

***Your child turned out swell.***【正，常用】

Your child has turned out swell.【正，常用】

***Your child turns out swell.***【誤】

　　turn out 的意思是「結果變成」，是「瞬間動詞」，已
經完成的事情，就要用「現在完成式」，已經過去的
事情，就要用「過去式」，如果用「現在式」，就表示
「咋天變成，今天變成，明天也變成」，因爲「現在式」表
示「不變的事實」，所以 turn out 用現在式不合乎句意。

BOOK 11

下面都是美國人常說的話：

**Your child turned out swell.**【第三常用】
Your child turned out great.【第一常用】
（你的小孩變得很好。）
Your child turned out so well.【第二常用】
（你的小孩變得很好。）

Your child turned out just fine.【第四常用】
（你的小孩變得不錯。）
Your kid turned out perfect.【第五常用】
（你的小孩變得很完美。）
Your son turned out so well.【第六常用】
（你的兒子變得很棒。）

just〔dʒʌst〕*adv.* 很；非常
perfect〔'pɜfɪkt〕*adj.* 完美的】

9. **You must be a good parent.**
   must〔mʌst〕*aux.* 一定
   parent〔'pɛrənt,'pærənt〕*n.* 父；母

   這句話的意思是「你一定是個好的父（母）親。」
   到底是父親還是母親，要看當時所說的對象而定。
   parent 是指「父親」或「母親」一個人，parents
   是指「父母親」，是兩個人。當然你也可以說：You
   must be a good father. （你一定是個好父親。）或
   You must be a good mother. （你一定是個好母親。）

***You must be a good parent.*** 可以加長爲：

I think you must be a good parent.

（我想你一定是個好的父（母）親。）

You surely must be a good parent.

（你一定是個好的父（母）親。）

Judging from your child, you must be a
good parent.

（從你的小孩看來，你一定是個好的父（母）親。）

【***judging from***   由～看來】

前面也可加一個句子，說成：

Your child is so polite. ***You must be a
good parent***.

（你的小孩很有禮貌。你一定是個好的父（母）親。）

Your kid looks so neat and clean. ***You must
be a good parent***.

（你的小孩看起來非常整齊清潔。你一定是個好
的父（母）親。）

Your daughter seems so sweet. ***You must be
a good parent***.

（你的女兒看起來很可愛。你一定是個好的父（母）親。）

neat〔nit〕*adj.* 整齊的；整潔的
***neat and clean*** 整齊清潔【和中國人的想法相同】
seem〔sim〕*v.* 似乎    sweet〔swit〕*adj.* 可愛的

BOOK 11

## 【對話練習】

1. A：**You have a great kid**.　　　A：你的小孩很棒。
   B：Do you really think so?　　　B：你眞的這麼認爲嗎？
   Sometimes I'm not so sure.　　　有時候我不是很確定。
   Sometimes he's a handful.　　　有時候他很難管。

2. A：**He looks like you**.　　　A：他看起來像你。
   B：Many people tell me that.　　　B：很多人跟我這麼說。
   Many say he looks like me.　　　很多人說他看起來像我。
   I hear that a lot.　　　我常聽人這麼說。
   【*a lot* 常常】

3. A：**He looks intelligent and**
   **bright**.　　　A：他看起來非常聰明。
   B：I hope he is smart.　　　B：我希望他很聰明。
   Sometimes he's careless.　　　他有時很粗心。
   Sometimes he's also lazy.　　　有時他也很懶惰。
   【careless（'kɛrlɪs）*adj.* 粗心的
   lazy（'lezɪ）*adj.* 懶惰的】

4. A：**He's very polite**.　　　A：他很有禮貌。
   B：That's what I like to hear.　　　B：那是我喜歡聽到的話。
   That's my favorite
   compliment.　　　那是我最喜歡的稱讚。

   Good manners are most　　　對我而言，有禮貌很
   important to me.　　　重要。
   【compliment（'kɑmpləmənt）*n.* 稱讚
   manners（'mænɚz）*n. pl.* 禮貌】

5. A: **He acts mature for his age**.

   B: I have to agree with you there.

   　　He does act quite grown-up.

   　　He often talks like an adult.

   　　【adult〔ə'dʌlt〕*n.* 成人】

A: 以他的年齡來說，他的
　　舉止很成熟。

B: 這一點我必須同意你。
　　他的舉止很成熟。
　　他講話常常很像大人。

6. A: **You've raised him well**.

   B: His father and I are blessed.

   　　He was such a good child.

   　　We never had trouble with him.

   　　【blessed〔blɛst〕*adj.* 幸福的；幸運的
   　　　trouble〔'trʌbḷ〕*n.* 煩惱】

A: 你把他教得很好。

B: 他的爸爸和我很幸運。
　　他是個好孩子。
　　我們從來都不用煩惱他。

7. A: **Kids are a handful**.

   B: Today's kids are demanding.

   　　They need constant attention.

   　　Raising them can be exhausting.

   　　【demanding〔dɪ'mændɪŋ〕*adj.* 要求
   　　　多的　constant〔'kɑnstənt〕*adj.* 不斷的
   　　　exhausting〔ɪg'zɔstɪŋ〕*adj.* 令人
   　　　筋疲力盡的；累人的】

A: 小孩眞麻煩。

B: 現在的小孩要求很多。
　　需要不斷地注意他們。
　　養育小孩可能是很累人的。

8. A: **Your child turned out swell**.

   B: Thanks for the kind words.

   　　My parents helped a lot.

   　　My mom and dad deserve credit.

   　　【deserve〔dɪ'zɝv〕*v.* 應得
   　　　credit〔'krɛdɪt〕*n.* 功勞】

A: 你的小孩變得很好。

B: 謝謝你說這麼好聽的話。
　　我的父母幫我很多忙。
　　應該都是我爸媽的功勞。

9. A: **You must be a good parent**.

   B: I always try my best.

   　　Sometimes I fall short.

   　　Sometimes I'm far from perfect.

   　　【*fall short* 達不到標準或要求　*far from* 一點也不】

A: 你一定是個好父(母)親。

B: 我總是盡力而爲。
　　有時我達不到標準。
　　有時我一點都不完美。

BOOK 11

# 10. What a great-looking dog!

| | |
|---|---|
| **What a** great-looking dog! | 多麼漂亮的狗！ |
| **What a** perfect companion! | 多麼好的同伴！ |
| Is it a he or she? | 牠是公的還是母的？ |
| | |
| **What**'s his name? | 牠的名字是什麼？ |
| **What** breed is he? | 牠是什麼品種？ |
| Can he do any tricks? | 牠會不會表演任何把戲？ |
| | |
| Come here, fella. | 過來吧，狗狗。 |
| Don't be afraid. | 不要害怕。 |
| I won't hurt you. | 我不會傷害你。 |

BOOK 11

**　**

great-looking〔'gret'lʊkɪŋ〕*adj.* 漂亮的

perfect〔'pɝfɪkt〕*adj.* 完美的

companion〔kəm'pænjən〕*n.* 同伴；夥伴

he〔hi〕*n.* 男性；雄性動物　　she〔ʃi〕*n.* 女性；雌性動物

breed〔brid〕*n.* 品種　　trick〔trɪk〕*n.* 把戲

***do tricks*** 表演把戲　　fella〔'fɛlə〕*n.* 夥伴；小伙子

afraid〔ə'fred〕*adj.* 害怕的　　hurt〔hɝt〕*v.* 傷害

## 【背景説明】

　　不管在外國人家，或是在公園，只要看到狗，
你就可以說下面九句好聽的話。

1. ***What a great-looking dog!***
   great-looking〔ˈgretˈlʊkɪŋ〕*adj.* 漂亮的

   　　「形容詞 + 現在分詞」可以形成「複合形容
   詞」。凡是兩個字以上所形成的形容詞，就稱作
   「複合形容詞」【詳見「文法寶典」p.450】。

   > 　　在字典上，只能找到 good-looking（漂亮的），
   > 但是 great-looking 和 nice-looking 美國人也常
   > 說，和 good-looking 意思都相同，只是語氣稍重。

   　　***What a great-looking dog!*** 的意思是「多麼漂
   亮的狗！」可以加長為：My! What a great-looking
   dog!（哎呀！多麼漂亮的狗！）或 What a great-
   looking dog you have!（你的狗真漂亮！）

   其他稱讚狗的說法有：

   You have a great-looking dog.
   （你的狗真漂亮。）
   That's a great-looking dog.
   （你的狗真漂亮。）
   Your dog looks great.（你的狗真漂亮。）

**BOOK 11**

看到一個美女帶了一隻狗，你想去追這個女生的時候，你就可以說：

**What a great-looking dog!**
（多麼漂亮的狗！）
I envy you.（我羨慕妳。）
I wish I could take him home.
（我希望我可以帶牠回家。）

在美國，特別是在城市，很多單身男女，會帶狗在公園散步，他們隱藏的目的，是想有機會結交朋友。上面三句說了不夠，可再說三句：

He looks well taken care of.
（牠看起來被照顧得很好。）
He looks smart.（牠看起來很聰明。）
He has lots of energy.（牠精力充沛。）

*take care of* 照顧　smart〔smɑrt〕*adj.* 聰明的
energy〔'ɛnədʒɪ〕*n.* 精力；活力

下面是美國人常說的話：

**What a great-looking dog!**【第一常用】
What a good-looking dog!【第三常用】
（多麼漂亮的狗！）
What a nice-looking dog!【第二常用】
（多麼漂亮的狗！）

What a beautiful-looking dog!【第五常用】
（多麼漂亮的狗！）
What a wonderful-looking dog!【第六常用】
（多麼漂亮的狗！）
What a cute-looking dog!【第四常用】
（多麼可愛的狗！）

What a great dog!（多麼棒的狗！）【第九常用】
What a beautiful dog!【第七常用】
（多麼漂亮的狗！）
What a cute dog!（多麼可愛的狗！）【第十一常用】
【cute〔kjut〕*adj.* 可愛的】

What an attractive dog!【第十二常用】
（多麼吸引人的狗！）
What a pretty dog!（多麼漂亮的狗！）【第八常用】
What a nice dog!（多麼好的狗！）【第十常用】
attractive〔ə'træktɪv〕*adj.* 吸引人的
pretty〔'prɪtɪ〕*adj.* 漂亮的

BOOK 11

2. ***What a perfect companion!***
perfect〔'pɜfɪkt〕*adj.* 完美的
companion〔kəm'pænjən〕*n.* 同伴；夥伴

　　這句話的意思是「多麼好的同伴！」也可說
成：What a nice companion! 或 What a great
companion! 意思都相同。也可以說成：He looks
like a perfect companion.（牠看起來像是個好的
夥伴。）

3. **Is it a he or she?**

he〔hi〕*n.* 男性；雄性動物　　she〔ʃi〕*n.* 女性；雌性動物

　　這句話的意思是「牠是公的還是母的？」也可以
說成：Is your dog a he or she?（你的狗是公的還
是母的？）

　　下面各句意思相同，我們按照使用頻率排列，
前三句使用頻率非常接近：

① **Is it a he or she?**【第一常用】
② Is it a boy or girl?（牠是公的還是母的？）【第二常用】
③ Is it a male or female?【第三常用】
　　（牠是公的還是母的？）
【male〔mel〕*n.* 雄性動物　　female〔'fimel〕*n.* 雌性動物】

④ What sex is it?（牠是公的還是母的？）
⑤ Which sex is it?（牠是公的還是母的？）
⑥ What's its gender?（牠是公的還是母的？）
【sex〔sɛks〕*n.* 性別　　gender〔'dʒɛndɚ〕*n.* 性別】

4. **What's his name?**

　　這句話的意思是「牠的名字是什麼？」也可說
成：What's your dog's name? 或 What do you
call your dog? 意思都是「你的狗叫什麼名字？」

【比較】

**What's his name?**【知道狗是公的，或不知道時用】
What's its name?【不知狗是公或母的時候用】
What's her name?【知道狗是母的時候用】

5. ***What breed is he?***

breed〔brid〕*n.* 品種

　　　　這句話的意思是「牠是什麼品種？」也可說成：
What's his breed?（牠是什麼品種？）或 What
kind of dog is he?（牠是哪一種狗？）或 What
type of dog is he?（牠是哪一種狗？）

【kind〔kaɪnd〕*n.* 種類　　type〔taɪp〕*n.* 類型】

　　狗的種類很多，最常見的有：

beagle
〔'bigl〕*n.*
畢爾格獵犬

Dalmatian
〔dæl'meʃən〕*n.*
大麥町犬

collie
〔'kalɪ〕*n.*
柯利狗

chihuahua
〔tʃɪ'wawa〕*n.*
吉娃娃

Labrador
〔'læbrə,dɔr〕*n.*
拉不拉多獵犬

poodle
〔'pudl〕*n.*
貴賓狗

6. ***Can he do any tricks?***

trick〔trɪk〕*n.* 把戲　　***do tricks*** 表演把戲

　　　　這句話的意思是「牠會不會表演任何把戲？」也
可說成：Can your dog do any tricks?（你的狗能
不能表演任何把戲？）或 Can your dog do some
tricks?（你的狗能不能表演一些把戲？）

BOOK 11

下面都是類似的說法：

***Can he do any tricks?***

Does he know any tricks? ( 牠會不會任何把戲？ )

Can he perform any tricks?

（牠會不會表演任何把戲？）【perform〔pɚ'fɔrm〕v. 表演】

What can he do? ( 牠會做什麼？ )

Can he do anything? ( 牠會做什麼？ )

Can he do anything special? ( 牠會不會做什麼特別的事？ )

你可以詢問對方，狗會不會表演下列的把戲：

Can he sit? ( 牠會坐下嗎？ )

Can he shake hands? ( 牠會握手嗎？ )【***shake hands*** 握手】

Can he roll over? ( 牠會翻滾嗎？ )

Can he play dead? ( 牠會裝死嗎？ )

【roll〔rol〕v. 滾動  ***roll over*** 翻滾  ***play dead*** 裝死】

Can he catch a ball? ( 牠會接球嗎？ )

Can he catch a frisbee? ( 牠會接飛盤嗎？ )

Can he fetch an object? ( 牠會不會去把東西拿回來？ )

catch〔kætʃ〕v. 接（球）  frisbee〔'frɪzbi〕n. 飛盤
fetch〔fɛtʃ〕v. 去拿  object〔'ɑbdʒɪkt〕n. 東西；物體

sit        shake hands    catch a ball    catch a frisbee

BOOK 11

7. *Come here*, *fella*.

fella〔ˈfɛlə〕*n*. 夥伴；小伙子

> *fella* 源自 fellow〔ˈfɛlo〕*n*. 傢伙；夥伴。fella 在一般字典中都沒有，只有大字典才找得到，但美國人常用，可用於人，也可用於狗。你可以跟別人說：My uncle is a nice fella.（我叔叔是個好人。）此時 fella 等於 guy〔gaɪ〕*n*. 人。

*Come here*, *fella*. 字面的意思是「過來吧，小伙子。」在此的意思是「過來吧，狗狗。」美國是狗的天堂，很多美國人把狗當自己的孩子，他們對狗的稱呼，比照他們的小孩子。作稱呼用時，面對面不能稱對方為 fella。

【比較1】 *Come here*, *fella*.
　　　　　【正，常用】
　　　　　*Come here*, *fellow*.
　　　　　【誤，文法對，太正式，美國人不用】

【比較2】 *Come here*, *fella*.
　　　　　【只可對寵物說】
　　　　　Come here, boy.
　　　　　【可對人及寵物說】

*Come here, fella.*

下面都是美國人對狗常説的話：

> *Come here*, *fella*.【第二常用】
>
> Come here, *boy*.【只能對公狗説】【第一常用】
>
> （過來，狗狗。）
>
> Come here, *girl*.【只能對母狗説】【第一常用】
>
> （過來，狗狗。）
>
> Come here, *handsome*.【第四常用】
>
> （過來，狗狗。）【只能對公狗説】
>
> Come here, *beautiful*.【第三常用】
>
> （過來，狗狗。）
>
> Come here, *cutie*.（過來，小可愛。）【第五常用】

8. *Don't be afraid.*

   afraid〔ə'fred〕*adj.* 害怕的

   這句話的意思是「不要害怕。」也可以加強語
   氣，説成：Don't be afraid of me.（不要怕我。）

   下面都是美國人常説的話，我們按照使用頻率排列：

   ① *Don't be afraid.*【第一常用】
   ② Don't be scared.（不要害怕。）【第二常用】
   ③ Don't be frightened.【第三常用】
   （不要害怕。）

   scared〔skɛrd〕*adj.* 害怕的
   frightened〔'fraɪtn̩d〕*adj.* 害怕的

④ Don't worry. ( 不要擔心。 )

⑤ There's no need to worry.

( 不需要擔心。 )

⑥ There's nothing to worry about.

( 沒什麼好擔心的。 )

【worry〔'wɜɪ〕v. 擔心　*worry about* 擔心】

⑦ Don't be nervous.

( 不要緊張。 )

⑧ Don't be shy. ( 不要害羞。 )

⑨ Don't be timid. ( 不要害羞。 )

nervous〔'nɜvəs〕adj. 緊張的　shy〔ʃaɪ〕adj. 害羞的
timid〔'tɪmɪd〕adj. 膽小的；害羞的

9. *I won't hurt you.*

hurt〔hɜt〕v. 傷害

這句話的意思是「我不會傷害你。」也可說成：
I'm not going to hurt you. ( 我不會傷害你。 ) 可
以加強語氣說成：I promise I won't hurt you.
( 我保證不會傷害你。 ) 或 Don't worry. I won't
hurt you. ( 別擔心。我不會傷害你。 )

對狗說完 *I won't hurt you*. 後，可再加上兩
句：You won't get hurt. ( 你不會受傷。 ) I'm
your friend. ( 我是你的朋友。 )【*get hurt* 受傷】

BOOK 11

下面都是美國人常說的話：

***I won't hurt you.*** 【第一常用】

I won't harm you. 【第二常用】

（我不會傷害你。）

I'm not going to hurt you. 【第六常用】

（我不會傷害你。）【harm〔hɑrm〕v. 傷害】

No one will hurt you. 【第四常用】

（沒有人會傷害你。）

No one is going to hurt you. 【第五常用】

（沒有人會傷害你。）

You have nothing to be afraid of. 【第九常用】

（你沒什麼好怕的。）【*be afraid of* 害怕】

I won't do anything bad. 【第三常用】

（我不會做任何壞事。）

I'm your friend. 【第七常用】

（我是你的朋友。）

I want to be your friend. 【第八常用】

（我想做你的朋友。）

I only want to pat your head. 【第十常用】

（我只想拍拍你的頭。）

I just want to scratch your back. 【第十一常用】

（我只想抓抓你的背。）

I just want to scratch your neck. 【第十二常用】

（我只想抓抓你的脖子。）

【pat〔pæt〕v. 輕拍　　scratch〔skrætʃ〕v. 抓；搔】

## 【對話練習】

1. A: **What a great-looking dog!**

   B: He just had a bath.
      I just brushed his hair.
      You're seeing him at his best.
      【*have a bath* 洗澡
      brush〔brʌʃ〕*v.* 刷　hair〔hɛr〕*n.* 毛
      *at one's best* 處於最佳狀態】

   A: 多麼漂亮的狗！

   B: 牠剛剛洗完澡。
      我剛剛刷了牠的毛。
      你看到的是牠的最佳
      狀態。

2. A: **What a perfect companion!**

   B: He's a great friend.
      He's a wonderful walking
      partner.
      He's excellent company.
      【partner〔'pɑrtnɚ〕*n.* 夥伴
      company〔'kʌmpənɪ〕*n.* 同伴】

   A: 多麼好的同伴！

   B: 牠是個很棒的朋友。
      牠是個很適合一起散
      步的同伴。
      牠是個很棒的同伴。

3. A: **Is it a he or a she?**

   B: It's a girl.
      She's two years old.
      Her name is Snuggles.

   A: 牠是公的還是母的？

   B: 是母的。
      牠兩歲大。
      牠的名字叫 Snuggles。

4. A: **What's his name?**

   B: His name is Rover.
      He likes to wander.
      That's what rover means.
      【rover〔'rovɚ〕*n.* 流浪者
      wander〔'wɑndɚ〕*v.* 流浪；遊蕩】

   A: 牠的名字是什麼？

   B: 牠的名字叫 Rover。
      牠喜歡流浪。
      那就是 rover 這個字
      的意思。

BOOK 11

5. A：**What breed is he?**

   B：He's a half-breed.
   His father is a collie.
   His mother is a Labrador.
   【half-breed (ˈhæfˈbrid ) *n.* 雜種狗】

A：牠是什麼品種？

B：牠是雜種狗。
的爸爸是柯利狗。
牠的媽媽是拉不拉多獵犬。

6. A：**Can he do any tricks?**

   B：He can sit on command.
   He can shake hands, too.
   He also loves to fetch sticks.
   【command ( kəˈmænd ) *n.* 命令
   ***shake hands*** 握手
   stick ( stɪk ) *n.* 棍子】

A：牠會不會表演任何把戲？

B：牠會聽命令坐下。
牠也會握手。
牠也喜歡去拿棍子回來。

7. A：**Come here, fella.**

   B：Try clapping your hands.
   Try whistling to him.
   He'll come right to you then.
   【clap ( klæp ) *v.* 拍（手）
   whistle (ˈhwɪsḷ ) *v.* 吹口哨
   right ( raɪt ) *adv.* 直接地】

A：過來吧，狗狗。

B：拍手試試看。
對牠吹口哨試試看。
那牠就會直接到你面前。

8. A：**Don't be afraid.**

   B：He's a little shy.
   Try kneeling down.
   Hold your hands out and he'll
   come. 【kneel ( nil ) *v.* 屈膝；跪下
   ***hold out*** 伸出】

A：不要害怕。

B：牠有一點害羞。
跪下來試試看。
把你的手伸出來，牠就會
過來了。

9. A：**I won't hurt you.**

   B：He knows you won't.
   You are with me.
   He knows you are my friend.

A：我不會傷害你。

B：牠知道你不會。
你是和我一起的。
牠知道你是我的朋友。

# *11. I admire you.*

| | |
|---|---|
| Look at you. | 你看看。 |
| *You* have it all. | 你什麼都有。 |
| *You*'ve got everything. | 你什麼都有了。 |
| | |
| *You have* a terrific home. | 你的家很棒。 |
| *You have* an excellent job. | 你有很好的工作。 |
| You're really moving up. | 你真的步步高升。 |
| | |
| *I* admire you. | 我欽佩你。 |
| *I* envy you. | 我羨慕你。 |
| *I* wish I were you. | 我希望我是你。 |

**

*look at* 看　　*have it all* 什麼都有

*you've got* 你有（= *you have*）

terrific〔təˋrɪfɪk〕*adj.* 很棒的

excellent〔ˋɛkslənt〕*adj.* 極好的　　*move up* 晉升；前進

admire〔ədˋmaɪr〕*v.* 欽佩；讚賞；羨慕

envy〔ˋɛnvɪ〕*v.* 羨慕；嫉妒　　wish〔wɪʃ〕*v.* 希望

## 【背景説明】

稱讚別人是美德，稱讚的話，説愈多愈好。這九句話既幽默，又好聽，你應該常對你的朋友説。

1. ***Look at you.***

   ***look at*** 看；注意看

   > 這句話是慣用句，源自：Look at yourself. 字面的意思是「看看你自己。」引申為「你看看。」或「看看你。」可以作為開場白，來加強你要説的話。***Look at you.*** 是和朋友幽默的説法，例如：
   >
   > ***Look at you.*** Wow, you look fantastic.
   > （你看看。哇啊，你看起來真棒。）
   > ***Look at you.*** You look so tired today.
   > （你看看。你今天看起來很疲倦。）
   > ***Look at you.*** Your new hairstyle looks
   >   wonderful.
   > （你看看。你的新髮型看起來很棒。）

   fantastic〔fæn'tæstɪk〕*adj.* 很棒的
   tired〔taɪrd〕*adj.* 疲倦的　hairstyle〔'hɛr,staɪl〕*n.* 髮型
   wonderful〔'wʌndəfəl〕*adj.* 很棒的

*Look at you.*
*Your new hairstyle looks*
  *wonderful.*

***Look at you***. You're doing so great.
　I'm so proud of you.
（看看你。你表現得真好。我非常以你爲榮。）

***Look at you***. You're working so hard.
　I'm worried about your health.
（你看看。你這麼努力。我很擔心你的健康。）

***Look at you***. You look thinner. You've
　lost weight.
（你看看。你看起來瘦了。你的體重減輕了。）

great〔gret〕*adv.* 很棒地　　***be proud of*** 以～爲榮
hard〔hɑrd〕*adv.* 努力地　　***be worried about*** 擔心
thin〔θɪn〕*adj.* 瘦的　　lose〔luz〕*v.* 減輕
weight〔wet〕*n.* 體重

***Look at you***. 前面可加上感嘆詞：

***Hey***, look at you!（嘿，看看你！）【第一常用】

***Wow***, look at you!（哇啊，看看你！）【第二常用】

***My***, look at you!（哇，看看你！）【第三常用】

hey〔he〕*interj.* 嘿　　wow〔waʊ〕*interj.* 哇啊
my〔maɪ〕*interj.* 啊；哇

BOOK 11

【比較】下面三句話意思相同：

***Look at you***.【語氣最輕鬆，較常用】

Look at yourself.（看看自己。）【語氣輕鬆，較常用】

Take a look at yourself.【語氣較嚴肅，常用】

　（看看你自己。）【***take a look at*** 看一看】

2. ***You have it all.***

***have it all*** 什麼都有

> 　在所有中外字典中，都找不到 ***it all*** 的成語，但美國人常說，所以我們一定要詳加研究。***it all*** 的意思是「一切」( *everything* )，等於 all important things in life ( 所有人生中重要的事物 )，像良好的健康 ( *good health* )，好的家庭 ( *nice family* )、好的工作 ( *nice job* )、好的房子 ( *nice house* )、有錢 ( *wealthy* )、長得好看 ( *good-looking* ) 等。

　美國人常鼓勵小孩說：Be honest, work hard and you can ***have it all***. ( 誠實、努力，你就會什麼都有。)

　***You have it all***. 的意思是「你什麼都有。」等於 You have everything. 或 You've got everything. 可以委婉地說：

　　I think ***you have it all***.

　　( 我想你什麼都有了。)

　　It looks like ***you have it all***.

　　( 好像你什麼都有了。)

　　It seems like ***you have it all***.

　　( 似乎你什麼都有了。)

　　【look〔luk〕*v.* 看起來　　seem〔sim〕*v.* 似乎】

*You have it all*. 可加強語氣説成：*You have it all* from A to Z. ( 你每樣東西都有。)

【*from A to Z* 從頭到尾；完全地，詳見 p.818-819】

下面都是加強語氣的説法：

You really *have it all*.

( 你眞的什麼都有了。)

You certainly *have it all*.

( 你的確什麼都有了。)

You're someone who *has it all*.

( 你是個什麼都有的人。)

【certainly〔ˈsɝtn̩lɪ〕*adv.* 當然；無疑地】

3. *You've got everything*.

*you've got* 你有 ( = *you have* )

美國人習慣把 You have it all. 和 *You've got everything*. 連在一起説，有加強語氣的作用。

*You've got everything*. 的意思是「你什麼都有了。」和 You have it all. 的意思相同。也可説成：You have everything. ( 你什麼都有了。) 可加強語氣説成：You've got everything you need. ( 你有所需要的一切。)

【比較】 *You've got everything*.【較常用】
*You have got everything*.【正，較少用】

美國人常對朋友說：

　　You're lucky. **_You've got everything_**.
　　（你真幸運。你什麼都有了。）
　　Congratulations! **_You've got everything_**.
　　（恭喜！你什麼都有了。）
　　I'm happy for you. **_You've got everything_**.
　　（我真為你高興。你什麼都有了。）
　　【congratulations〔kən͵grætʃə'leʃənz〕*n. pl.* 恭喜】

4. **_You have a terrific home_**.
　　terrific〔tə'rɪfɪk〕*adj.* 很棒的

> 　　這句話的意思是「你有一個很棒的家。」也就
> 是「你的家很棒。」( = *Your home is terrific*. ) 句
> 中的 terrific 可用 beautiful（美麗的）、wonderful
> （很棒的）、marvelous（很棒的）、awesome
> 〔'ɔsəm〕（很棒的）來取代。

【比較】下面兩句話意思不完全相同：

　　**_You have a terrific home_**.【可對任何人說】
　　（你有很棒的家。）
　　You have a terrific house.
　　（你有很棒的房子。）【只能對住在獨棟房子的人說】

下面三句意思相同：

　　　　You **_have_** a terrific home.【第一常用】
　　= You **_own_** a terrific home.【第三常用】
　　= You'**_ve got_** a terrific home.【第二常用】
　　　　【own〔on〕*v.* 擁有】

BOOK 11

5. ***You have an excellent job.***

excellent〔ˈɛksl̩ənt〕*adj.* 極好的

這句話的意思是「你有很好的工作。」也就是「你的工作很棒。」( = *Your job is excellent.* ) 可以加強語氣説成：You really have an excellent job. ( 你的工作眞的很棒。) 也可以加長爲：I think you have an excellent job. ( 我覺得你的工作很棒。) 或 In my opinion, you have an excellent job. ( 依我看，你有很好的工作。)

【*in one's opinion* 依某人之見】

也可以説成：

　　You have an excellent career.
　　( 你有很好的事業。)
　　【career〔kəˈrɪr〕*n.* 職業；一生的事業】
　　You have an excellent occupation.
　　( 你有很好的工作。)
　　【occupation〔ˌɑkjəˈpeʃən〕*n.* 工作；職業】

下面都是美國人常説的話：

　　You have a nice job. 【第二常用】
　　( 你的工作很不錯。)
　　You have a good job. 【第一常用】
　　( 你的工作很好。)
　　***You have an excellent job.*** 【第四常用】
　　( 你的工作很棒。)

BOOK 11

You have a great job. 【第三常用】
（你的工作很棒。）
You have a fine job. 【第六常用】
（你的工作很好。）
You have a super job. 【第五常用】
（你的工作很棒。）
【fine〔faɪn〕*adj.* 好的　super〔'supɚ〕*adj.* 極好的】

You have a marvelous job. 【第七常用】
（你的工作很棒。）
You have an outstanding job. 【第八常用】
（你的工作很棒。）
You have a first-rate job. 【第九常用】
（你的工作很好。）

marvelous〔'mɑrvḷəs〕*adj.* 很棒的
outstanding〔'aʊt'stændɪŋ〕*adj.* 傑出的
first-rate〔'fɝst'ret〕*adj.* 第一流的；很好的

6. ***You're really moving up***.
***move up*** 晉升；前進

　　在所有字典中，都沒有把 ***move up*** 解釋清楚，只有 Straight from the Horse's Mouth 字典中，找到這個成語，有這個成語的起源。move up 源自 move up the ladder（爬上樓梯），即「步步高升」。***move up*** 也可說成 ***move up in the world***，意思是「步步高升」或「邁向成功」( = *advance and become successful* )。

*You're really moving up*. 的意思是「你真的步步高升。」可以加強語氣説成：*You're really moving up in the world*. (你真的在一步一步向前邁進。) 或 You're really moving up the ladder. (你真的在步步高升。)

*You're really moving up the ladder.*

【ladder〔'lædɚ〕*n.* 梯子；發跡的途徑】

　　當你看到一個人，買了新房子，或升了官，你就可以説：You're moving up. 或 *You're really moving up*.

下面各句意思相同：

*You're moving up*.【第一常用】
（你正在步步高升。）
You're making progress.【第六常用】
（你正在進步中。）
You're becoming successful.【第三常用】
（你愈來愈成功。）
【progress〔'prɑgrɛs〕*n.* 進步　*make progress* 進步】

You're moving forward.【第二常用】
（你不斷在往前進。）
You're advancing. (你一直在往前進。)【第五常用】
You're rising up. (你正在向上提升。)【第四常用】

move〔muv〕*v.* 移動；前進　forward〔'fɔrwɚd〕*adv.* 往前
advance〔əd'væns〕*v.* 前進　*rise up* 上升

BOOK 11

You're moving up the ladder.【第八常用】

（你正在步步高升。）

You're moving up in the world.【第七常用】

（你正在步步高升。）

You're rising up the ladder.【第九常用】

（你正在步步高升。）

7. **I admire you.**

admire〔əd'maɪr〕*v.* 欽佩；讚賞；羨慕

這句話的意思是「我欽佩你。」可以加強語氣說成：

I really admire you.（我真佩服你。）【第一常用】

I greatly admire you.【第五常用】

（我非常佩服你。）

I truly admire you.【第四常用】

（我真的很佩服你。）

greatly〔'gretlɪ〕*adv.* 大大地；非常地
truly〔'trulɪ〕*adv.* 真正地

I admire you greatly.【第六常用】

（我非常佩服你。）

I admire you a lot.（我非常佩服你。）【第二常用】

I admire you very much.【第三常用】

（我非常佩服你。）【*a lot* 非常】

8. ***I envy you***.

envy〔'ɛnvɪ〕*v.* 羨慕；嫉妒

　　　　這句話的意思是「我羨慕你。」或「我嫉妒你。」和朋友講這句話，並不是真正羨慕或嫉妒，只是一種幽默的稱讚。可以前後各加一句話來加強語氣：I admire you. ***I envy you***. I'm jealous of you.（我欽佩你。我羨慕你。我嫉妒你。）

　　看到你的朋友過好日子，你就可以說：

> You're so lucky. ***I envy you***.
> （你真幸運。我羨慕你。）
> You have such a nice life. ***I envy you***.
> （你過得很好。我很羨慕你。）
> You're always so happy. ***I envy you***.
> （你總是那麼高興。我很羨慕你。）

　　美國年輕人的夢想是：擁有一棟好的房子（a nice house）、一份好的工作（a nice job）、一個漂亮的太太（a beautiful wife）、一部高級汽車（a nice car）。

　　當你看到你的朋友什麼都有的時候，你就可以開玩笑地說：

> You have it all. ***I envy you***.
> （你什麼都有。我真羨慕你。）

BOOK 11

9. ***I wish I were you***.

wish〔wɪʃ〕*v.* 希望

　　這句話的意思是「我希望我是你。」美國人也常
說成：I wish I were in your shoes. ( 我希望我是
你。)【*be in one's shoes*　處於某人立場】或 I wish I
were just like you. ( 我希望我就是和你一樣。)

　　在文法上，I wish 後面要用假設法，be 動詞用
were，但是現代口語中也常用 was 來代替。

【比較1】

　　***I wish I were you***.【正，常用】

　　*I wish I was you*.【文法錯，但美國人常說】

【比較2】　下面兩句話意思有些不同，請注意中文
　　　　　翻譯：

　　***I wish I were you***. ( 我希望我是你。)

　　I wish I could be you. ( 我希望我**能夠**是你。)

　　在這一回九句中，因為已經有了 You're really
moving up. ( 你真的在步步高升。) 所以在這裡，
就不再重覆 really 了。但是，如果只說這一回的最
後三句，就可用 really 加強語氣，即：

　　I admire you. ( 我欽佩你。)

　　I envy you. ( 我羨慕你。)

　　***I really wish I were you***. ( 我真希望我是你。)

## 【對話練習】

1. A：**Look at you.**

   B：What's the matter?
      What about me?
      Did I do something wrong?
      【*What about ~?*　~如何？】

   A：你看看。

   B：怎麼了？
      我怎麼樣？
      我有做錯什麼嗎？

2. A：**You have it all.**

   B：You must be kidding.
      You can't be talking about me.
      I don't have everything.

   A：你什麼都有。

   B：你一定在開玩笑吧。
      你說的不可能是我。
      我並非什麼都有。

3. A：**You've got everything.**

   B：How nice of you to say so!
      But really, looks are
      deceiving.
      I've got problems, too.
      【deceiving〔dɪˈsivɪŋ〕*adj.* 欺騙的】

   A：你什麼都有了。

   B：你這麼說人真好！
      但事實上，外表是會
      騙人的。
      我也有一些問題。

4. A：**You have a terrific home.**

   B：Thanks, I like it, too.
      I'm lucky to have this house.
      This truly is my dream house.
      【dream〔drim〕*adj.* 理想的；夢想的】

   A：你的家很棒。

   B：謝謝，我也很喜歡。
      擁有這棟房子我很幸運。
      這真是我夢想中的房子。

BOOK 11

5. A : **You have an excellent job**.
   B : I have to admit, I love it.
   It's both challenging and
   interesting.
   It's a satisfying occupation.
   【challenging (ˈtʃælɪndʒɪŋ ) *adj.*
   有挑戰性的】

A：你有很好的工作。
B：我必須承認，我很愛這
　　份工作。
　　它既有挑戰性又有趣。
　　它是個令人滿意的工作。

6. A : **You're really moving up**.
   B : I wish that were true.
   My responsibilities are
   always increasing.
   I wish my salary were, too!
   【responsibility ( rɪˌspɑnsəˈbɪlətɪ )
   *n.* 責任　salary (ˈsælərɪ ) *n.* 薪水】

A：你真的步步高升。
B：我希望那是真的。
　　我的責任不斷在增加。

　　我希望我的薪水也是！

7. A : **I admire you**.
   B : What a nice thing to say!
   You truly flatter me.
   I admire you very much, too.
   【flatter (ˈflætɚ ) *v.* 恭維】

A：我欽佩你。
B：你這麼說真好！
　　你真的太過獎了。
　　我也很欽佩你。

8. A : **I envy you**
   B : Don't envy me.
   There is nothing to envy.
   I'm just a normal person.
   【normal (ˈnɔrml̩ ) *adj.* 普通的】

A：我羨慕你。
B：不要羨慕我。
　　沒什麼好羨慕的。
　　我只是個普通人。

9. A : **I wish I were you**.
   B : Be careful what you wish for.
   My life has many difficulties.
   You are lucky you're not me.
   【*wish for* 希望；想要】

A：我希望我是你。
B：許願要小心。
　　我的人生遭遇很多困難。
　　你不是我，所以你很
　　幸運。

# 12.　*You are a wonderful host*.

| | |
|---|---|
| You are a wonderful host. | 你很好客。 |
| *Thanks for* your hospitality. | 謝謝你的款待。 |
| *Thanks for* having me over. | 謝謝你邀請我來。 |
| | |
| Now you owe me a visit. | 現在你要記得，要來我家玩。 |
| Next time, it's my turn. | 下一次輪到我了。 |
| I want to repay your kindness. | 我想要報答你親切的招待。 |
| | |
| It's been real. | 眞是愉快。 |
| *I* had a ball. | 我玩得很愉快。 |
| *I*'ll be seeing you. | 我會再見到你。 |

BOOK 11

**\*\*** ———————————————

wonderful〔'wʌndɚfəl〕*adj.* 很棒的　　host〔host〕*n.* 主人
hospitality〔,hɑspɪ'tælətɪ〕*n.* 款待；熱情招待；好客
*have sb. over* 請某人到家裡來作客
owe〔o〕*v.* 欠　　visit〔'vɪzɪt〕*n.* 拜訪；作客
turn〔tɝn〕*n.* 輪值；輪班　　repay〔rɪ'pe〕*v.* 報答
kindness〔'kaɪndnɪs〕*n.* 親切；親切的行爲；親切的態度
real〔'riəl〕*adj.* 眞正的　　ball〔bɔl〕*n.* 愉快的時刻

## 【背景説明】

在向主人告別的時候，總要説幾句感謝的話吧！下面九句話，是費了九牛二虎之力，才挑選出來，美國人喜歡聽的話。

1. ***You are a wonderful host.***
   wonderful〔'wʌndɚfəl〕*adj.* 很棒的
   host〔hɔst〕*n.*（招待客人的）主人

   這句話字面的意思是「你是很棒的主人。」引申爲「你很好客。」可跟男主人説，也可跟女主人説。如果男女主人都在，可以説：You guys are wonderful hosts.（你們真好客。）

   【guy〔gaɪ〕*n.* 人；傢伙
   ***you guys*** 你們】

> ***You guys are***
> ***wonderful hosts.***

也可加強語氣説：

   You guys are grcat.（你們很棒。）
   You are wonderful hosts.（你們很好客。）
   You are a wonderful host and hostess.
   （你們這對夫婦很好客。）
   【hostess〔'hostɪs〕*n.* 女主人】

【比較】

### *You are a wonderful host.*

【在朋友家，可對男主人或女主人説】

You are a wonderful hostess. 【只可對女主人説】

【hostess〔'hostɪs〕*n.* 女主人】

2. ***Thanks for your hospitality.***

hospitality〔ˌhɑspɪ'tælətɪ〕*n.* 款待；熱情招待；好客

　　這句話的意思是「謝謝你的款待。」可以加強
語氣説成：

Thank you for your generous hospitality.

（謝謝你慷慨的款待。）

I appreciate your hospitality.

（我很感激你的款待。）

I want to thank you for your hospitality.

（我要謝謝你的熱情招待。）

generous〔'dʒɛnərəs〕*adj.* 慷慨的
appreciate〔ə'priʃɪˌet〕*v.* 感激

> ***hospitality*** 這個字很好背，由於 hospital（醫
> 院）這個字，從前是指「旅客招待所」，背這個字，
> 只要記住，hospital + ity 即可。它的形容詞是
> hospitable〔'hɑspɪtəbļ〕*adj.* 好客的；熱情招待的。

　　美國人也常説：Thanks for your kindness.
（謝謝你的親切招待。）【kindness〔'kaɪndnɪs〕*n.* 親切的
態度】或 Thank you for your generosity.（謝謝你
的慷慨招待。）【generosity〔ˌdʒɛnə'rɑsətɪ〕*n.* 慷慨的行爲】

3. ***Thanks for having me over.***

over〔'ovɚ〕*adv.* 從一邊到另一邊；到家裡

***have sb. over*** 請某人到家裡來作客（= *have a visitor*）

　　這句話字面的意思是「謝謝你讓我過來。」引
申爲「謝謝你邀請我來。」（= *Thanks for inviting
me.*）

下面各句意思相同，都是美國人常説的話：

Thanks for having me.【第一常用】
（謝謝你邀請我來。）

***Thanks for having me over.***【第二常用】

Thanks for letting me visit.【第四常用】
（謝謝你讓我來拜訪。）

Thanks for letting me come over.【第三常用】
（謝謝你讓我來。）

let〔lɛt〕*v.* 讓　　visit〔'vɪzɪt〕*v.* 拜訪

***come over*** 過來

Thanks for allowing me to visit.【第五常用】
（謝謝你讓我來拜訪。）

Thanks for inviting me.【第六常用】
（謝謝你邀請我。）

Thanks for inviting me over.【第七常用】
（謝謝你邀請我來。）

【allow〔ə'laʊ〕*v.* 允許；讓　　invite〔ɪn'vaɪt〕*v.* 邀請】

4. *Now you owe me a visit*.

owe〔o〕*v.* 欠　　visit〔'vɪzɪt〕*n.* 拜訪；作客

這句話字面的意思是「現在你欠我一次拜訪。」
引申為「現在你要記得，要來我家玩。」

美國人也常說成：

You now owe me a visit.
（你現在要記得，要來我家玩。）
Now you must visit me.
（現在你一定要來我家玩了。）
Now you have to visit me.
（現在你必須來我家玩了。）

可以加強語氣說成：Now, to be fair, you owe
me a visit.（為了公平起見，你現在要記住，要來我
家玩。）或 Now it's you who owe me a visit.
（現在是你要記住，要來我家玩。）

5. *Next time, it's my turn*.

turn〔tɝn〕*n.* 輪值；輪班

這句話的意思是「下一次輪到我了。」源自
Next time, it's my turn to be the host.（下一次
輪到我請你來我家作客。）也有美國人說成：Next
time, let me have the opportunity.（下一次讓我
有機會請你。）【opportunity〔ˌɑpɚ'tjunətɪ〕*n.* 機會】

【比較】It's my turn. 可看成慣用句，常用現在式
　　　　代替未來。

*Next time, it's my turn*.【正，美國人較常說】
Next time, it'll be my turn.【正，由於太長，美國人較少說】

6. ***I want to repay your kindness.***

repay〔rɪ'pe〕v. 報答

kindness〔'kaɪndnɪs〕n. 親切；親切的行為；親切的態度

　　　kindness 在不同的句中，有不同解釋，完全要看上下文來決定，它的主要意思是「好心；好意」，在這裡是指「親切的招待」( = *kind treatment* )。

　　　這句話的意思是「我想要報答你的親切的招待。」美國人也常說：

I want to repay your hospitality.
（我想要回報你的款待。）

I want to repay your generosity.
（我想要回報你的慷慨招待。）

I want to repay your wonderful treatment.
（我想要回報你這麼好的招待。）

【treatment〔'tritmənt〕n. 對待】

7. ***It's been real.***

real〔'riəl〕adj. 真正的

　　　這句話是固定用法，是慣用句，字面的意思是「它是真的。」引申為「太高興啦。」或「真是愉快。」源自：***It's been a real good time.*** ( = *I had a great time.* )【real〔'riəl〕adv. 真正地】

　　　***It's been real.*** 在美國非常普遍，其他英語系國家的人，像英國人或加拿大人，未必熟悉 ***It's been real.***

a good time 的意思是 fun，可修飾「人」，也可修飾「非人」，在 p.849 中，有詳細的說明。

---

***It's been real.*** 後面可加現在分詞片語，來加長。

| | |
|---|---|
| ***It's been real*** （真高興） | visiting you. （拜訪你。） |
| | being with you today. （今天和你在一起。） |
| | hanging out with you. （和你在一起。） |
| | going out with you. （和你一起出去。） |
| | seeing you. （看到你。） |
| | talking with you. （和你交談。） |
| | being here today. （今天來到這裡。） |

下面都是美國人常說的話：

***It's been real.*** 【第一常用】

It's been really fun. （真是好玩。）【第六常用】

It's been really great. （真是太棒了。）【第七常用】

【fun〔fʌn〕*adj.* 有趣的　*n.* 有趣的事】

It's been really great seeing you. 【第十常用】

（見到你真是太棒了。）

It's been really great visiting you. 【第十一常用】

（來拜訪你真是太棒了。）

It's been really great being here today. 【第十二常用】

（今天能來這裡真是太棒了。）

It's been really unforgettable.【第十四常用】
（眞是令人難忘。）
It's been really special.（眞是特別。）【第十三常用】
It's been a real pleasure.（眞是太愉快了。）【第十五常用】

unforgettable〔͵ʌnfɚˈgɛtəbḷ〕*adj.* 令人難忘的
pleasure〔ˈplɛʒɚ〕*n.* 快樂的事；高興的事

It's been a good time.（眞的很愉快。）【第五常用】
It's been really wonderful.（眞是太棒了。）【第九常用】
It's been really great.（眞是太棒了。）【第八常用】

It's been fun.（眞是好玩。）【第二常用】
It's been great.（眞是太棒了。）【第三常用】
It's been wonderful.（眞是太棒了。）【第四常用】

8. *I had a ball.*

ball〔bɔl〕*n.* 球；舞會；愉快的時刻

> 　　從前，美國人把正式的舞會，稱作 ball，通常
> 在舞會中，會玩得很愉快。have a ball 字面的意
> 思是「有舞會」，現在通常引申為「玩得很愉快」
> （= *have a very good time*）。
>
> 　　*I had a ball.* 的意思是「我玩得很愉快。」可
> 以加長為：I had a ball with you.（我和你在一起
> 玩得很愉快。）或 I had a ball today.（我今天玩得
> 很愉快。）可再加長為：I had a ball with you
> and your family today at your house.（我今天在
> 你家，和你及你的家人玩得很愉快。）

***I had a ball.*** 後可加分詞片語：

I had a ball ***being with you***.

（我和你在一起玩得很愉快。）

I had a ball ***being here***.（我在這裡很愉快。）

I had a ball ***visiting you***.

（來拜訪你，我玩得很愉快。）

I had a ball ***spending time with you***.

（我和你在一起過得很愉快。）

【spend〔spɛnd〕*v.* 花（時間）；度過（時間）】

下面各句意思接近，都是美國人常說的話：

***I had a ball.***【第一常用】

I had a blast.（我玩得很愉快。）【第二常用】

【blast〔blæst〕*n.* 歡樂；滿足】

I had a good time.（我玩得很愉快。）【第三常用】

I had a great time.（我玩得很愉快。）【第四常用】

I had a super time.（我玩得很愉快。）【第七常用】

【***have a good time*** 玩得愉快　super〔'supɚ〕*adj.* 極好的】

I had a nice time.（我玩得很愉快。）【第五常用】

I had a wonderful time.【第六常用】

（我玩得很愉快。）

I had a fantastic time.【第八常用】

（我玩得很愉快。）

【fantastic〔fæn'tæstɪk〕*adj.* 很棒的】

BOOK 11

I had a marvelous time.【第十常用】
（我玩得很愉快。）
I had a remarkable time.【第十一常用】
（我玩得很愉快。）
I had a terrific time.【第九常用】
（我玩得很愉快。）

marvelous〔'marvḷəs〕*adj.* 很棒的
remarkable〔rɪ'markəbḷ〕*adj.* 非凡的；卓越的
terrific〔tə'rɪfɪk〕*adj.* 很棒的

### 9. *I'll be seeing you.*

> 和別人告別，最簡單的說法就是 See you.（再見。）稍正式一點，就說：I'll see you.（我會見到你。）最有感情的說法是 *I'll be seeing you.*（我會再見到你。）用「未來進行式」表示「未來預定的動作」（詳見「文法寶典」p.348）。

這句話也可以加長為：

*I'll be seeing you* again.（我會再見到你。）
*I'll be seeing you* soon.（我會很快見到你。）

I hope *I'll be seeing you* again soon.
（我希望我很快就會再見到你。）
I hope *I'll be seeing you* real soon.
（我希望我很快就會再見到你。）

　和別人告別的時候，冷冷地只說 Good-bye.
沒有感情，應該說些好聽的話，並作出依依不捨的
表情，才像是有教養又體貼的人。

## 【對話練習】

1. A: **You are a wonderful host**.

   B: I don't feel like a host.
   You're such a wonderful
   friend.
   It's easy to treat you nice.
   【treat〔trit〕v. 對待
   nice〔naɪs〕adv. 很好地】

A：你很好客。

B：我覺得自己不像個主人。
你是個很棒的朋友。

要對你好很容易。

2. A: **Thanks for your hospitality**.

   B: Thank you for coming over.
   I enjoyed seeing you.
   Your visit made my day.
   【*make one's day* 使某人非常高興】

A：謝謝你的款待。

B：謝謝你過來。
我很高興見到你。
你來拜訪使我非常高興。

3. A: **Thanks for having me over**.

   B: The pleasure was all mine.
   I can't wait to do it again.
   You're welcome in my
   home at any time.

A：謝謝你邀請我來。

B：這是我的榮幸。
我等不及再邀你一次。
隨時歡迎你來我家。

4. A: **Now you owe me a visit**.

   B: I promise I'll visit.
   I'll call on you real soon.
   I'll try to visit you next
   month. 【real〔'rɪəl〕adv. 眞地】

A：現在你要記得，要來我
家玩。

B：我保證會來拜訪。
我很快就會拜訪你。
我會試著下個月來拜
訪你。

BOOK 11

5. A: **Next time, it's my turn**.

   B: I won't argue with you.
Next time, it's your turn.
Next time, I'll visit you.
【argue ('ɑrgjʊ) *v.* 爭論】

A：下一次輪到我了。

B：我不會跟你爭。
下一次，輪到你了。
下一次，我會去拜訪你。

6. A: **I want to repay your kindness**.

   B: Don't talk such nonsense.
We are special friends.
Nobody has to repay
anybody.
【nonsense ('nɑnsɛns) *n.* 胡說八道】

A：我想要報答你親切的款待。

B：不要胡說。
我們是交情特別的朋友。
沒有人必須要報答任何人。

7. A: **It's been real**.

   B: Yes, it sure has.
It's been a really great time.
It's been terrific talking
with you.

A：眞是愉快。

B：是的，的確是。
的確玩得很愉快。
和你談話很愉快。

8. A: **I had a ball**.

   B: We both had a ball.
I enjoyed every minute, too.
It felt great to catch up on
everything.

A：我玩得很愉快。

B：我們兩個都玩得很愉快。
我也是每一分鐘都很愉快。
聊聊近況的感覺很棒。

9. A: **I'll be seeing you**.

   B: Yes, hopefully very soon.
Let's stay in touch.
Let's meet and visit more
frequently.
【touch ( tʌtʃ ) *n.* 連絡】

A：我會再見到你。

B：是啊，希望很快就能見到。
我們保持聯絡吧。
我們要更常見面和拜訪
對方。

# 「一口氣背會話」經 BOOK 11

唸英文要像唸經一樣，每天大聲唸，從起床到睡覺，唸得比看得快，最後不看也會唸，養成習慣後，你會全身舒爽，你試試看，奇妙無比。

1. Hey, it's me.
   How the heck are you?
   It's been a while.

   *I*'m coming to your area.
   *I*'ll be in your neck of the woods.
   *I*'m anxious to see you.

   Can I come over?
   Are you up for a visitor?
   We can catch up on things.

2. My, your home is gorgeous.
   *It* looks so inviting.
   *It* feels warm and friendly.

   It's very charming.
   I'd love to see more.
   Can I have a tour?

   *It's* a nice neighborhood.
   *It's* peaceful and quiet.
   How did you find this place?

3. I like the decoration.
   *It*'s very stylish.
   *It* has a comfortable feel.

   The lighting is just right.
   All the colors flow well.
   It creates a relaxed atmosphere.

   *You have* a good eye.
   *You have* good taste.
   I should hire you to do my house.

4. Your furniture is lovely.
   Every piece is attractive.
   It really makes the room.

   That's a fabulous table.
   Those chairs look fantastic.
   What type of wood is that?

   This couch feels great.
   I like the material.
   The fabric is so soft and smooth.

5. Your kitchen is modern.
   You have more shelves and cabinets.
   It's much nicer than mine.

   *Your* bedrooms are cozy.
   *Your* closets are roomy.
   The carpet is thick and plush.

   The living room is my favorite.
   It's the highlight of the house.
   Thank you for showing me around.

6. Put me to work.
   Give me something to do.
   If you don't let me help, I'll feel guilty.

   Let me set the table.
   *Where* are the plates?
   *Where* do you keep your silverware?

   You made the meal.
   *I'll* clear the table.
   *I'll* do the dishes.

7. This smells marvelous.
   The aroma is incredible.
   It looks too good to eat.

   Every bite is delightful.
   I've never had better.
   This really takes the cake.

   *My* hat's off to you.
   *My* compliments to the chef.
   What's the recipe?

8. *What* a cute baby!
   *What* a little angel!
   *What* an adorable child!

   *How* old is your baby?
   *How* many months?
   Is it a boy or a girl?

   Hi there, sweetie.
   How about a smile?
   Can I hold him?

9. You have a great kid.
   *He looks* like you.
   *He looks* intelligent and bright.

   *He's* very polite.
   *He* acts mature for his age.
   You've raised him well.

   Kids are a handful.
   Your child turned out swell.
   You must be a good parent.

10. *What a* great-looking dog!
    *What a* perfect companion!
    Is it a he or she?

    *What's* his name?
    *What* breed is he?
    Can he do any tricks?

    Come here, fella.
    Don't be afraid.
    I won't hurt you.

11. Look at you.
    *You* have it all.
    *You've* got everything.

    *You have* a terrific home.
    *You have* an excellent job.
    You're really moving up.

    *I* admire you.
    *I* envy you.
    *I* wish I were you.

12. You are a wonderful host.
    *Thanks for* your hospitality.
    *Thanks for* having me over.

    Now you owe me a visit.
    Next time, it's my turn.
    I want to repay your kindness.

    It's been real.
    *I* had a ball.
    *I'll* be seeing you.

# BOOK 12 當一個好主人

▶12-1 打電話給你的朋友，邀請他來你家作客，你可說：

Come visit me.
Pay me a visit.
Call on me anytime.

▶12-2 朋友一進你家門，你就可說：

Come on in.
Step right inside.
Here is a pair of slippers.

▶12-3 當朋友一坐下來，你就可說：

My home is your home.
Help yourself to anything.
There's lots of stuff in the fridge.

▶12-4 可和朋友談論天氣，避免尷尬：

What a scorcher!
It's boiling outside.
It's hotter than hell.

▶12-5 可和訪客談論近況，說：

So, tell me your news.
How have you been?
Have you been keeping busy?

▶12-6 當看見你的朋友，因為你說的話而不高興的時候，就可說：

Don't get me wrong.
Don't get the wrong idea.
I don't want you to misunderstand.

▶12-7 當你介紹你的太太給客人時，就可以說：

> I'd like you to meet my wife.
> She's my better half.
> She's the brains of the family.

▶12-8 當你邀請客人留下來吃飯時，就可說：

> Please stay for dinner.
> Do me the honor.
> Let's break bread together.

▶12-9 當大家一起吃飯時，你想敬酒，就可說：

> Let me make a toast.
> Let's have a drink together.
> Here's to a fantastic future.

▶12-10 當你要請大家一起照相時，你就可說：

> Let's take a snapshot.
> Let's get a photo together.
> It'll be a nice memory.

▶12-11 當你的客人要走的時候，你就可說：

> Don't leave yet.
> Don't go so soon.
> Stay and talk some more.

▶12-12 餐會完了，送客的時候，你可說：

> Thanks for coming.
> Thanks for being my guest.
> It was nice seeing you.

# *1. Come visit me.*

| | |
|---|---|
| Come visit me. | 來我這裡玩。 |
| Pay me a visit. | 來我這裡玩。 |
| Call on me anytime. | 隨時來我這裡玩。 |
| | |
| *Drop* in whenever. | 隨時來我這裡玩。 |
| *Drop* by when you can. | 你有空就來玩。 |
| Feel free to stop by. | 不要客氣，來坐坐。 |
| | |
| I'm inviting you now. | 我現在邀請你。 |
| My door is always open. | 我永遠歡迎你。 |
| Don't keep me waiting too long. | 不要讓我等太久。 |

BOOK 12

**\*\***

visit〔ˈvɪzɪt〕*v.* 拜訪；遊覽；到 ( 某人家 ) 作客
*pay sb. a visit* 拜訪某人 ( = *visit* )　　*call on* 拜訪
anytime〔ˈɛnɪˌtaɪm〕*adv.* 隨時　　*drop in* 順道拜訪
whenever〔hwɛnˈɛvɚ〕*adv.* 無論何時
*drop by* 順道拜訪　　*feel free to V.* 請自由地…
*stop by* 順道拜訪　　invite〔ɪnˈvaɪt〕*v.* 邀請

## 【背景説明】

當你想要邀請朋友到你家作客的時候，你就可以用電話，或當面説這九句話。

1. ***Come visit me.***
   visit〔ˈvɪzɪt〕*v.* 拜訪；遊覽；在（某人家）作客

> 這句話源自：Come to visit me. 意思是「來我這裡玩。」句中的 visit 主要的意思是「拜訪」，例如：Can I visit you next week?（我可不可以下禮拜去拜訪你？）但是，***Come visit me.*** 如果翻成：「來拜訪我。」就比較不妥，因爲不禮貌。應該翻成：「來看我。」
> （= *Come see me.*）
> 或「來我這裡玩。」
> （= *Come to my place and have some fun.*）

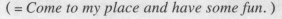

***Come visit me.*** 可加長爲：Come visit me at my house.（來我家玩。）或 Come over and visit me anytime.（隨時過來我這裡玩。）【*come over* 過來】

【比較】下面三句話意思相同：

> ***Come visit me.***【最常用】
> = Come to visit me.【較少用】
> = Come and visit me.【常用】

come 或 go 作命令句或有命令語氣時，可接原形
動詞。【詳見「文法寶典」p.419】

下面都是美國人常說的話：

***Come visit me.*** 【第一常用】

Come visit me anytime. 【第四常用】
（隨時來我這裡玩。）

Come visit me sometime. 【第五常用】
（找個時間來我這裡玩。）

【sometime〔'sʌm,taɪm〕*adv.* 某時】

Come and visit me.（來我這裡玩。）【第二常用】

Come over and visit me. 【第三常用】
（過來我這裡玩。）

I want you to come visit me. 【第六常用】
（我要你來我這裡玩。）

2. ***Pay me a visit.***

visit〔'vɪzɪt〕*n.* 拜訪

***pay sb. a visit*** 拜訪某人

（ = *visit sb.* ）

*Pay me a visit.*

這句話字面的意思是「來拜訪我。」也就是「來
我這裡玩。」可以有禮貌地說：Please pay me a
visit.（請來我這裡玩。）也可以加長爲：I want
you to pay me a visit.（我希望你來我這裡玩。）
【want 在此作「希望」解】或 Come pay me a visit
anytime.（隨時來我這裡玩。）

【比較】下面兩句話意思相同：

> ***Pay me a visit.***【常用】
>
> = Pay a visit to me.【較少用】

3. ***Call on me anytime.***

***call on*** 拜訪 ( = *visit* )

anytime〔'ɛnɪ,taɪm〕*adv.* 隨時 ( = *at any time* )

這句話字面的意思是「隨時來拜訪我。」也就是「隨時來我這裡玩。」可以加長為：You're welcome to call on me anytime. ( 歡迎你隨時來我這裡玩。 ) 或 I want you to call on me anytime you like. ( 我希望你隨時來我這裡玩。 )

【比較1】下面兩句話意思完全不同：

> ***Call on me anytime.*** ( 隨時來我這裡玩。 )
>
> ( = *Visit me anytime.* )
>
> Call me anytime. ( 隨時打電話給我。 )
>
> ( = *Phone me anytime.* )

【比較2】下面三句意思相同：

> ***Call on me anytime.***【最常用、最常寫】
>
> = Call on me any time.【常用、常寫，any time 是名詞片語，表時間，前面介詞可省略】
>
> = Call on me at any time.【少用】

當美國人說 ***Call on me anytime.*** 的時候，並非真正希望你隨時到他家玩，這只是禮貌的應酬話。**到人家家拜訪，應該要事先打電話才對。**

4. ***Drop in whenever***.

***drop in***　順道拜訪（= *pay a casual visit*）

whenever〔hwɛnˋɛvɚ〕*adv.* 無論何時；不管什麼時候

　　　drop 的主要意思是「落下；掉下」，***drop in*** 的字面意思是「掉進」，引申為「順道拜訪」或「偶然拜訪」，說這個成語的時候，有幽默的味道。不一定掉得進去啊，有的時候掉到旁邊，所以就有 ***drop by***、***drop over***、***drop around*** 的成語，都表示「順道拜訪」。

　　　這句話源自：Drop in *on me* whenever *you want to*.（無論何時你想要的時候，都可順道來拜訪我。）***Drop in whenever***. 字面的意思是「無論何時掉進來。」引申為「隨時來我這裡玩。」含有不要特意來看我的意思。在此句中，whenever 已經變成副詞，作「無論何時」解。

【比較1】下面五句意思相同，第一句和第二句使用頻率接近：

***Drop in whenever***.
　　【第一常用】

= Drop by whenever.
　　【第二常用】

= Drop over whenever.
　　【第三常用】

= Drop around whenever.【第四常用】

= Drop round whenever.【第五常用】

【比較2】 這些成語接人時，只能用 ***drop in on sb.***，
因爲 *drop by*、*drop over*、*drop around*
沒掉進去，怎麼
能接 *on sb.* 呢？

Drop in on me whenever.
（隨時來我這裡玩。）
【正，常用】
*Drop by on me whenever.* 【誤】

5. ***Drop by when you can.***
   ***drop by*** 順道拜訪

　　這句話的字面意思是「當你能夠的時候，就掉到
旁邊來一下吧。」引申爲「你儘可能來玩。」或「你有
空就來玩。」美國人也常說成：Drop by whenever
you can.（你儘可能來玩。）可加長爲：I want you
to drop by when you can.（我希望你儘可能來玩。）
或 Drop by when you can find the time.（你有空
時，就來玩。）也有人說：Drop by my house when
you can.（你儘可能來我家玩。）或 Drop by and
see me when you can.（你儘可能來看我。）

下面都是美國人常說的話：

Drop by whenever.（隨時來玩。）【第二常用】
***Drop by when you can.*** 【第一常用】
Drop by when you're able. 【第六常用】
　（你儘可能來玩。）【able〔'ebḷ〕*adj.* 能夠的】

When you are free, drop by. 【第三常用】

（你有空時，就來玩。）【free〔fri〕*adj.* 有空的】

When you have time, drop by. 【第四常用】

（你有時間時，就來玩。）

When you're not doing anything, drop by.

（當你沒事做的時候，就來玩。）【第五常用】

6. *Feel free to stop by*.

*feel free to V*. 請自由地…

*stop by* 順道拜訪（= *stop in*）

　　這句話字面的意思是「感覺自由停在旁邊。」引申為「不要客氣，來坐坐。」從這句話中，你可體會到，美國人語言中充滿著幽默。stop by 的字面意思是「停在旁邊」，stop in 的字面意思是「停在裡面」，這兩個成語都引申為「順道拜訪」，使用頻率相同，所以，當然可說成：Feel free to stop in.（不要客氣，來坐坐。）

*Feel free to stop by*. 可加長為：

Please feel free to stop by anytime.

（請不要客氣，隨時來坐坐。）

Feel free to stop by and visit me.

（不要客氣，順道來我這裡玩。）

【用相同意思的 stop by 和 visit 在一起，有加強語氣的作用】

I want you to feel free to stop by whenever you'd like.

（我希望你不要客氣，隨時想來就來玩。）

BOOK 12

【比較】下面三句話意思相同，使用頻率也相同。

> ***Feel free to stop by**.*
> = Feel free to drop by.
> = Feel free to drop in.

美國人常説 feel free to，表示沒有限制，意思是「不要客氣；不要猶豫；不要想太多」，後面接原形動詞：

Please ***feel free to*** stay for dinner.

（請不要客氣，留下來吃晚餐。）

Please ***feel free to*** order anything you like.

（請不要客氣，點任何你喜歡的東西。）

***Feel free to*** ask me anything you want.

（不要客氣，問我任何你想問的問題。）

【order〔ˈɔrdɚ〕*v.* 點（菜）　feel free to + 原形動詞，
是一個常用句型，詳見 p.642】

7. ***I'm inviting you now***.

invite〔ɪnˈvaɪt〕*v.* 邀請

這句話的意思是「我現在邀請你。」可以改成被動，説成：You're being invited now.（你現在被邀請。）可幽默地説：I'm now officially inviting you.（我現在正式地邀請你。）或 You're now being officially invited.（你現在已經正式被邀請了。）

【officially〔əˈfɪʃəlɪ〕*adv.* 正式地】

也可以加強語氣説成：

I'm inviting you right now.（我現在邀請你。）

I'm officially inviting you right now.

（我現在正式邀請你。）【幽默話】

I'm inviting you now, so you know you're
　welcome.【幽默話】

（我現在邀請你，所以你知道，你是受歡迎的。）

【*right now*　現在】

下面是美國人常説的話：

***I'm inviting you now.***【第一常用】

Now you're invited.【第二常用】

（現在你已經被邀請了。）

Now you're being invited.【第三常用】

（現在你被邀請了。）

Now you have my invitation.【第五常用】

（現在我邀請你。）

Now you have an invitation.【第六常用】

（現在你被邀請了。）

Now you've got an invite.【第四常用】

（現在你被邀請了。）

invitation〔ˌɪnvəˈteʃən〕*n.* 邀請
invite〔ˈɪnvaɪt〕*n.* 邀請（= *invitation*）

注意 invite 當名詞時，重音在第一音節上，本來就有
invitation 這個名詞，爲什麼要用 invite 呢？因爲
invite 是比較非正式、幽默的説法。

BOOK 12

8. *My door is always open.*

　　這句話的意思是「我的門總是開的。」比喻「我永遠歡迎你。」可以加強語氣說成：My door is always open to you.（我的門總是為你而開。）句中的 to you

可說成 for you；My door 也可視情況說成 Our door。在 p.1250 中，曾經講過 You have an open invitation.（隨時歡迎你。）和本句意思相同。

下面是美國人常說的話：

***My door is always open.*** 【第一常用】
I always like to see you. 【第六常用】
（我總是很高興見到你。）

You're always invited. 【第二常用】
（我隨時歡迎你。）
You're always invited to visit. 【第三常用】
（我隨時歡迎你來玩。）

You're always welcome to visit my house.
（隨時歡迎你來我家玩。）【第五常用】
You're always welcome in my home.
（隨時歡迎你來我家。）【第四常用】

BOOK 12

9. *Don't keep me waiting too long.*

keep〔kip〕*v.* 使…維持（某種狀態）

　　這句話的意思是「不要讓我等太久。」可以加長

為：I hope you don't keep me waiting too long.

（我希望你不要讓我等
太久。）或 Make sure
you don't keep me
waiting too long.（你
一定不要讓我等太久。）

*Don't keep me waiting too long.*

【*make sure* 弄清楚；弄確實；確定（= *make certain*）】

下面都是美國人常說的話，我們按照使用頻率排列：

① *Don't keep me waiting too long.*【第一常用】

② Don't make me wait too long.【第二常用】
　　（不要讓我等太久。）
　　【make 是使役動詞，接受詞後，須接原形動詞】

③ Don't make me wait too long for you
　　to visit.【第三常用】
　　（不要讓我等你來玩等太久。）

④ Don't make me wait too long for your
　　visit.（不要讓我等你來玩等太久。）

⑤ Don't keep me waiting too long for you
　　to visit.（不要讓我等你來玩等太久。）

⑥ Don't keep me waiting too long for
　　your visit.（不要讓我等你來玩等太久。）

## 【對話練習】

1. A：**Come visit me**.
   B：I'll visit for sure.
   I accept your invitation.
   I'll visit as soon as I can.
   【*for sure* 必定
   *as soon as one can* 儘快】

   A：來我這裡玩。
   B：我一定會去拜訪。
   我接受你的邀請。
   我會儘快去拜訪。

2. A：**Pay me a visit**.
   B：Thanks for the invitation.
   I'd love to visit you.
   I'm just afraid you are too busy.

   A：來我這裡玩。
   B：謝謝你的邀請。
   我很樂意去拜訪你。
   我只是怕你太忙了。

3. A：**Call on me anytime**.
   B：Tell me when you're free.
   Tell me when is a good time.
   I don't want to disturb you.
   【disturb〔dɪ'stɝb〕*v.* 打擾】

   A：隨時來我這裡玩。
   B：我來之前會打電話。
   我不想打擾你。
   那樣你就會等我。

4. A：**Drop in whenever**.
   B：I'll call before I come.
   I wouldn't want to impose.
   That way you'll be expecting
   me.【impose〔ɪm'poz〕*v.* 打擾；麻煩
   expect〔ɪk'spɛkt〕*v.* 等待；期盼】

   A：隨時來我這裡玩。
   B：我來之前會打電話。
   我不想太麻煩你。
   那樣你就不用一直等
   我了。

5. A：**Drop by when you can**.
   B：You know I will.
   I'd like that very much.
   I'll drop by sometime next
   month.

   A：你有空就來玩。
   B：你知道我會的。
   我很想那樣。
   我下個月會找時間順
   道去拜訪。

6. A： **Feel free to stop by**.

 B： Don't worry; I will.
 I appreciate your offer.
 I'll stop by sometime soon.
 【appreciate〔əˈpriʃɪˌet〕*v.* 感激
 　offer〔ˈɔfɚ〕*n.* 提議】

A：不要客氣，來坐坐。

B：別擔心；我會的。
 我很感激你的提議。
 我很快就會找時間順
 道去拜訪。

7. A： **I'm inviting you now**.

 B： I know you are.
 I know your offer is sincere.
 Thank you so very much.
 【sincere〔sɪnˈsɪr〕*adj.* 眞誠的】

A：我現在邀請你。

B：我知道你是。
 我知道你的提議是眞
 誠的。
 非常謝謝你。

8. A： **My door is always open**.

 B： I know it is.
 You are such a friendly person.
 You are the most hospitable
 person I know.
 【friendly〔ˈfrɛndlɪ〕*adj.* 友善的
 　hospitable〔ˈhɑspɪtəbḷ〕*adj.* 好客的】

A：我永遠歡迎你。

B：我知道你是。
 你是個很友善的人。
 你是我所認識的人當
 中，最好客的。

9. A： **Don't keep me waiting too
 long**.

 B： I promise to visit soon.
 I'll call you in a few weeks.
 It won't be long till we meet
 again.

A：不要讓我等太久。

B：我保證很快就去拜訪。
 我再過幾個星期就會打
 電話給你。
 我們不久就會再次見
 面。

BOOK 12

# *2. Come on in.*

| | |
|---|---|
| Come on in. | 趕快進來。 |
| Step right inside. | 趕快進來。 |
| Here is a pair of slippers. | 這裡有一雙拖鞋。 |
| | |
| Have a seat. | 坐下來。 |
| Sit down and relax. | 坐下來休息休息。 |
| Make yourself at home. | 不要客氣。 |
| | |
| You got here OK. | 你順利到達這裡了。 |
| How was the traffic? | 交通狀況如何？ |
| Any trouble finding this | 找這個地方有沒有任何 |
|   place? | 困難？ |

**

step〔stɛp〕v. 行走；踩；踏　　right〔raɪt〕adv. 立刻；趕快
inside〔'ɪn'saɪd〕adv. 往裡面　　*a pair of* 一雙
slippers〔'slɪpəz〕n. pl. 拖鞋　　*have a seat* 坐下
relax〔rɪ'læks〕v. 放鬆；休息
*make oneself at home* （像在家裡一樣）不拘束；覺得自在
OK〔'o'ke〕adv. 沒問題地；順利地
traffic〔'træfɪk〕n. 交通（量）
trouble〔'trʌbḷ〕n. 麻煩；困難

## 【背景説明】

　　　當你的客人一進門，你就可以説這九句話，表示你歡迎他。

1. ***Come on in.***

　　　這句話的意思是「趕快進來。」源自 Come in.
（進來。）on 有加強語氣的作用。【詳見「教師一口氣英語」p.6–11 】

【比較】Come in. ( 進來。)【一般語氣】
　　　　***Come on in.*** ( 趕快進來。)【加強語氣】
　　　　Come over. ( 過來。)【一般語氣】
　　　　Come on over. ( 趕快過來。)【加強語氣】

　　　***Come on in.*** 可以有禮貌地説成：Please come on in. ( 請趕快進來。)

下面都是美國人常説的話：

Come on in.

　　Come in. 【第一常用】
　　( 進來。)
　　***Come on in.*** 【第二常用】

　　Come inside. ( 進來。)【第三常用】
　　Come on inside. ( 趕快進來。)【第四常用】

　　Welcome. ( 歡迎。)【第六常用】
　　Come right in. ( 趕快進來。)【第五常用】
　　【right〔raɪt〕*adv.* 立刻；趕快】

2. ***Step right inside***.

step〔stɛp〕*v.* 行走;踩;踏
right〔raɪt〕*adv.* 立刻;趕快
inside〔'ɪn'saɪd〕*adv.* 在裡面;往裡面

　　這句話字面的意思是「趕快走進裡面。」也就是「趕快進來。」right 是副詞,在這裡是作「趕快」解,用於加強 step inside 的語氣。step inside 和 step in 意思相同,都是表示「進來」。

　　***Step right inside***. 可以加長為:Please step right inside. (請趕快進來。) 也可以變成兩句來加長,成為:Don't be polite. Please step right inside. (不要客氣。請趕快進來。) 【polite〔pə'laɪt〕*adj.* 客氣的】或 Don't stand at the door. ***Step right inside***. (不要站在門口。趕快進來。)

下面各句意思相同:

Step inside. (進來。)【第一常用】
Come inside. (進來。)【第二常用】
Walk inside. (進來。)【第五常用】

Step on inside. (趕快進來。)【第七常用】
Come on inside. (趕快進來。)【第八常用】
Walk on inside. (趕快進來。)【第九常用】

***Step right inside***. (趕快進來。)【第三常用】
Come right inside. (趕快進來。)【第四常用】
Walk right inside. (趕快進來。)【第六常用】

BOOK 12

3. *Here is a pair of slippers.*

    *a pair of* 一雙　slippers〔ˈslɪpɚz〕*n. pl.* 拖鞋

　　　　這句話的意思是「這裡有一雙拖鞋。」可以加長
爲：Here is a pair of slippers for you to put on.
（這裡有一雙拖鞋要給你穿。）【*put on* 穿上】由於拖
鞋是兩隻，就要用 a pair of。類似的有：a pair of
pants（一條褲子）、a pair of socks（一雙短襪）、
a pair of sneakers（一雙運動鞋）、a pair of gloves
（一副手套）。美國人也常說

成：Here are some slippers.

（這裡有一些拖鞋。）【可能

一雙或多雙拖鞋】或 Please

put on a pair of slippers.

（請穿上一雙拖鞋。）

slippers

　　　　從前，美國人家裡面都是可以穿鞋進去的，現在
有些高級的家庭，也流行要穿拖鞋。如果你不想叫
別人脫鞋，就可以說：Don't take off your shoes.
（不要脫鞋。）( = *Don't take your shoes off.* ) 或
You don't have to take off your shoes.（你不需要
脫鞋。）【*take off* 脫掉】

【比較】 pair 指不可分離，成爲一對時，爲單數。
　　　　【詳見「文馨最新英漢辭典」p.1005】

　　　*Here is a pair of slippers.*【正】
　　　*Here are a pair of slippers.*【誤】

BOOK 12

4. ***Have a seat***.

***have a seat*** 坐下

　　這句話的意思是「坐下來。」可以有禮貌地説：Please have a seat. ( 請坐。 ) 可以加長爲：Have a seat on the couch. ( 坐在沙發上。 ) 或 Have a seat over there. ( 坐在那裡。 )

【couch〔kautʃ〕*n.* 長沙發】

　　在字典上，***Have a seat***. 和 Take a seat. 都表示「坐下。」但是，Take a seat. 語氣嚴肅，有命令的味道，通常在軍隊裡使用，或老師在教室叫學生坐下，而 ***Have a seat***. 就親切多了。

下面的成語意思相同：

$\left\{\begin{array}{l}\end{array}\right.$ ***have a seat*** 【第二常用】
= take a seat 【第三常用】

$\left\{\begin{array}{l}\end{array}\right.$ = seat *oneself* 【第七常用】
= be seated 【第四常用】

$\left\{\begin{array}{l}\end{array}\right.$ = take *one's* seat 【第六常用】
= take a load off 【第五常用】
= sit down 坐下 【第一常用】

load〔lod〕*n.* 重擔

***take a load off*** 坐下；休息

5. *Sit down and relax*.

relax〔rɪˋlæks〕*v.* 放鬆；休息

這句話字面的意思是「坐下來並且休息一下。」也就是我們中國人常說的「坐下來休息休息。」可以有禮貌地說：Please sit down and relax.（請坐下來休息一下。）也可加長爲：I want you to sit down and relax.（我希望你坐下來休息休息。）

sit down

【比較】

Sit down.（坐下。）
Sit up.（坐直。）
【詳見「教師一口氣英語」p.8–10】

sit up

下面都是美國人常說的話：

*Sit down and relax*.【第一常用】
Sit down and take it easy.【第二常用】
（坐下來，放輕鬆。）【*take it easy* 放輕鬆】
Sit down and take a load off.【第三常用】
（坐下來休息一下。）

Have a seat and take it easy.【第五常用】
（坐下來，放輕鬆。）
Have a seat and be comfortable.【第六常用】
（坐下來，不要客氣。）
Please sit and be comfortable.【第四常用】
（請坐，不要客氣。）
【comfortable〔ˋkʌmfﾈtəbḷ〕*adj.* 舒服的；自在的】

6. *Make yourself at home.*

   *make* *oneself* *at home* （像在家裡一樣）不拘束；覺得自在

   　　這句話字面的意思是「使你自己像在自己家一樣
   舒服。」( = *Make yourself comfortable, as if you
   were in your own home.* ) 引申爲「不要客氣。」
   ( = *Make yourself comfortable.* ) 可加強語氣說
   成：Make yourself right at home. ( 千萬不要客
   氣。) 【right〔 raɪt〕*adv.* 完全地】或 Make yourself
   feel at home. ( 不要感到拘束。)

   　　*at home* 的主要意思是「在家」，常引申爲：
   ① 在國內 ② 舒適 ③ 精通。「在家」當然「舒適」，
   對家裡的事物一定「精通」。

   下面都是美國人常說的話，我們按照使用頻率排列：

   ① *Make yourself at home.*【第一常用】

   ② Make yourself comfortable.【第二常用】
   　 ( 不要客氣。)

   ③ Please don't be polite.【第三常用】
   　 ( 請不要客氣。)

   ④ Do whatever you want. ( 想做什麼就做什麼。)
   　 【polite〔 pəˈlaɪt〕*adj.* 有禮貌的；客氣的】

   ⑤ Help yourself to anything.
   　 ( 想要什麼自己拿。)

   ⑥ Let me know if there's anything that you
   　 need. ( 如果你需要任何東西，要讓我知道。)
   　 【*help* *oneself* *to* 自行取用】

7. *You got here OK*.

OK〔'o'ke〕*adv.* 沒問題地;順利地

> 　　這句話的意思是「你順利到達這裡了。」You got here. 的意思是「你來了。」OK 是副詞,作「順利地」解。美國人也常說:You made it OK. (你順利到達了。)【參照p.1144-1145】

You got here OK.

*You got here OK*. 可加長為:

I'm glad *you got here OK*.
（很高興你順利到達這裡了。）【第一常用】
Thank God *you got here OK*.【第三常用】
（謝天謝地,你順利到達這裡了。）
I'm happy that *you got here OK*.【第二常用】
（很高興你順利到達這裡了。）

> 　　*You got here OK*. 不是問句,重讀在 got。如果變成問句,就要說成:You get here OK? (你來這裡順利嗎?) ( =*Did you get here OK?* )

8. *How was the traffic?*

traffic〔'træfɪk〕*n.* 交通（量）

> 　　traffic 除了作「交通」解外,還表示「交通流量」,在這裡指「交通狀況」。這句話的意思是「交通狀況如何?」可以加長為:How was the traffic on your way here? (你來這裡的路上,交通狀況如何?) 或 How was the traffic out there today? (今天外面的交通狀況如何?)【*out there* 的主要意思是「外面;在那裡」,參照 p.781,在此是指 on the roads (在路上)。】

【比較 1】 traffic 前面加不加 the，一般外國人分辨不出來：

**How was the traffic?**【正】

（暗示「你來的路上交通狀況如何？」）

How was traffic?（交通狀況如何？）【正】

【比較 2】 有指定時，traffic 之前就要加 the：

How was the traffic on your way here?【正】

*How was traffic on your way here?*【誤】

9. **Any trouble finding this place?**

trouble〔ˊtrʌblʲ〕 n. 麻煩；困難

　　這句話的意思是「找這個地方有沒有任何困難？」源自：Did you have any trouble finding this place?（你找這個地方有沒有任何困難？）句中的 this place 可代換為 my home（我的家）或 my address（我的地址）。【address〔əˊdrɛs〕 n. 地址】

　　美國人也常問：Did you get lost?（你有沒有迷路？）或 Was it easy to get here?（到這裡容不容易？）【lost〔lɔst〕 adj. 迷路的】

　　當 have 作「有」解時，後接情感名詞，後面往往省略 in，加動名詞。【詳見「文法寶典」p.444】

Did you have $\begin{cases} \text{any trouble} \\ \text{any problem} \\ \text{any difficulty} \\ \text{a hard time} \end{cases}$ (in) finding this place?

（你找這個地方有沒有任何困難？）

## 【對話練習】

1. A: **Come on in**.
   B: All right.
      Thank you.
      How are you?

   A：趕快進來。
   B：好的。
      謝謝。
      你好嗎？

2. A: **Step right inside**.
   B: OK.
      What about my shoes?
      Should I take off my shoes?

   A：趕快進來。
   B：好的。
      我的鞋怎麼辦？
      我該脫鞋嗎？

3. A: **Here is a pair of slippers**.
   B: Thank you very much.
      These feel great.
      They are very comfortable.
      【feel〔fil〕v. 使人感覺】

   A：這裡有一雙拖鞋。
   B：非常謝謝你。
      這雙拖鞋感覺很棒。
      它們非常舒服。

4. A: **Have a seat**.
   B: Thanks.
      You have a lovely office.
      I can see you have good taste.
      【lovely〔ˈlʌvlɪ〕adj. 美麗的；可愛的】

   A：坐下來。
   B：謝謝。
      你的辦公室很漂亮。
      看得出來你品味很好。

5. A: **Sit down and relax**.
   B: OK, I will.
      I like this room.
      It feels very comfortable.

   A：坐下來休息休息。
   B：好的，我會的。
      我喜歡這個房間。
      它使人覺得很舒服。

BOOK 12

6. A : **Make yourself at home**.　　　　A：不要客氣。

　　B : Thank you, I will.　　　　　　　B：謝謝你，我會的。
　　　　You're so kind.　　　　　　　　　　你人眞好。
　　　　I'll make myself at home.　　　　　我會讓自己不要太拘束。

7. A : **You got here OK**.　　　　　　A：你順利到達這裡了。

　　B : Yes, I did.　　　　　　　　　　　B：是的，我是。
　　　　It was easy.　　　　　　　　　　　那很容易。
　　　　It wasn't hard to find.　　　　　　不難找。
　　　　【hard〔hɑrd〕*adj.* 困難的】

8. A : **How was the traffic?**　　　　A：交通狀況如何？

　　B : Traffic was light.　　　　　　　B：交通流量不大。
　　　　There were no delays.　　　　　　沒有延誤。
　　　　The roads were not that bad.　　　路況沒有那麼差。
　　　　【light〔laɪt〕*adj.* (程度或數量)不大的
　　　　　delay〔dɪ'le〕*n.* 延誤】

9. A : **Any trouble finding this**　　A：找這個地方有沒有任何
　　　　**place?**　　　　　　　　　　　　困難？

　　B : Your directions were excellent.　B：你給的指引很清楚。
　　　　It was no trouble at all.　　　　　一點也不困難。
　　　　I had no trouble finding this　　　我找這個地方一點也不
　　　　place.　　　　　　　　　　　　　困難。
　　　　【directions〔də'rɛkʃənz〕*n. pl.* 指引
　　　　　excellent〔'ɛksḷənt〕*adj.* 極好的】

# *3.  My home is your home.*

| | |
|---|---|
| My home is your home. | 我的家就是你家。 |
| Help yourself to anything. | 自己拿任何東西。 |
| There's lots of stuff in the fridge. | 在冰箱裡有很多東西。 |
| It's a little messy. | 我家有點亂。 |
| Please don't mind the clutter. | 請不要介意凌亂。 |
| We're pretty informal around here. | 我們這裡非常隨便。 |
| Wanna use the bathroom? | 想不想要用廁所？ |
| It's just down the hall. | 它就在走道那一邊。 |
| The switch is next to the door. | 開關在門的旁邊。 |

\*\*

***help** oneself to* 自己取用　　***lots of*** 很多
stuff〔stʌf〕*n.* 東西　　fridge〔frɪdʒ〕*n.* 電冰箱
messy〔'mɛsɪ〕*adj.* 凌亂的　　mind〔maɪnd〕*v.* 介意
clutter〔'klʌtə〕*n.* 凌亂；雜亂　　pretty〔'prɪtɪ〕*adv.* 相當；非常
informal〔ɪn'fɔrml̩〕*adj.* 不正式的；隨便的
wanna〔'wɑnə〕*v.* 想要　　bathroom〔'bæθˌrum〕*n.* 廁所
down〔daʊn〕*prep.* 在…那一邊　　hall〔hɔl〕*n.* 走廊；走道
switch〔swɪtʃ〕*n.* 開關　　***next to*** 在…旁邊

BOOK 12

## 【背景説明】

　　　外國客人到你家作客，爲了使他能夠輕鬆
自在，你就可以説下面這些話，使你的客人覺
得很温馨。

1. ***My home is your home.***

　　　這句話的意思是「我的家就是你家。」源自：I
want you to pretend that my home is your home.
（我想要你假裝我的家就是你家。）***My home is
your home.*** 也可説成：My place is your place. 或
My house is your house. 意思都相同。可加長爲：
Hey, my home is your
home. ( 嘿，我的家就是
你家。)【hey〔he〕interj. 嘿】
或 Now, my home is
your home. ( 現在，我
的家就是你家。)

My home is your home.

下面是美國人常説的話，我們按照使用頻率排列：

① ***My home is your home.*** 【第一常用】
② Make yourself at home. 【第二常用】
　　( 不要拘束。)
③ Please feel at home. 【第三常用】
　　( 請不要拘束。)

***make*** *oneself* ***at home*** 不拘束　　***feel at home*** 覺得自在

④ Make believe you're at home.
（假裝像在你家一樣。）

⑤ Make believe you live here.
（假裝像是你住在這裡一樣。）

【*make believe* 假裝（ = *pretend* ）】

⑥ Please think of my home as your home.
（請把我家當作是你家。）

⑦ Please regard my home as your home.
（請把我家當作是你家。）

*think of* A *as* B   認為 A 是 B     regard〔 rɪ'gɑrd 〕*v.* 認為
*regard* A *as* B   認為 A 是 B（ = *think of* A *as* B ）

## 2. *Help yourself to anything.*

*help* oneself *to*   自己取用

這句話字面的意思是「幫助自己拿任何東西。」
引申為「自己拿任何東西。」如果你想叫客人可以
隨意看電視等，你就可以說：Help yourself to
anything in the house.（你可以隨意使用房子裡的
任何東西。）如果你想叫客人拿冰箱裡的東西吃，
你就可以說：Help yourself to anything in the
fridge.（冰箱裡的東西你可以隨便拿。）
【fridge〔 frɪdʒ 〕*n.* 電冰箱】

可以加強語氣說成：Help yourself to anything
you feel like.（你想拿什麼就拿什麼。）或 Don't
be polite. Just help yourself to anything.（不要
客氣。想拿什麼，就拿什麼。）
【*feel like* 想要    polite〔 pə'laɪt 〕*adj.* 客氣的】

下面都是美國人常說的話：

**Help yourself to anything.**【第一常用】
Help yourself to whatever you see.【第四常用】
（你看見的任何東西都可以拿。）
Help yourself to whatever you like.【第五常用】
（你想拿什麼就拿。）

Feel free to help yourself to anything.
（請自由地拿任何東西。）【第六常用】
You're welcome to help yourself to anything.
（歡迎你自己拿任何東西。）【第七常用】
【*feel free to V.* 請自由地…】

You can have anything you'd like.【第三常用】
（你可以拿任何想拿的東西。）
You're welcome to anything.【第二常用】
（歡迎你用任何東西。）【*be welcome to* 可隨意使用】

3. **There's lots of stuff in the fridge.**
   **lots of** 很多　　stuff〔stʌf〕*n.* 東西
   fridge〔frɪdʒ〕*n.* 電冰箱（= *refrigerator*）

> 　　這句話的意思是「在冰箱裡有很多東西。」
> （= *There're lots of things in the fridge.*）美國人習
> 慣說 fridge，極少說 refrigerator〔rɪˈfrɪdʒəˌretə〕
> *n.* 電冰箱。可加長為：**There's lots of stuff in the**
> **fridge.** Go see if there's anything you like.（冰
> 箱裡有很多東西。去看看是否有任何你喜歡的。）

stuff 這個字作「東西；物品」解時，是不可數名詞，它的用法詳見 p.629-630。可加強語氣說成：There is lots of stuff you can eat or drink in the fridge.（冰箱裡有很多東西，你可以吃或喝。）

下面是美國人常說的話：

The fridge is full.（冰箱是滿的。）【第一常用】
The fridge is packed.【第二常用】
（冰箱裝滿了東西。）
The fridge is loaded.【第三常用】
（冰箱裝滿了東西。）

full〔fʊl〕adj. 滿的　　packed〔pækt〕adj. 擠得滿滿的
loaded〔'lodɪd〕adj. 裝滿東西的

Go take a look in the fridge.【第八常用】
（去看看冰箱裡面。）
Check out the fridge.（看看冰箱。）【第七常用】
Have something from the fridge.【第九常用】
（去冰箱拿點東西。）

take a look 看一看　　check out 查看
have〔hæv〕v. 拿到

*There's lots of stuff in the fridge.*【第四常用】
（冰箱裡有很多東西。）
There're many things in the fridge.【第五常用】
（冰箱裡有很多東西。）
We have lots of things in the fridge.【第六常用】
（我們冰箱裡有很多東西。）

BOOK 12

### 4. *It's a little messy*.

messy〔'mɛsɪ〕*adj.* 凌亂的 ( = *disorderly* )；髒的 ( = *dirty* )

　　這句話的意思是「這裡有點亂。」在這裡可指「我家有點亂。」( = *My place is a little messy.* ) 在句中，It 是指 My place (我的家)。外國人和中國人一樣，無論家裡多麼整齊，當客人到自己家，都會謙虛地說「我家有點亂。」可以加長為：

It's a little messy in here today.
（今天這裡有點亂。)【*in here* 在這裡面】
I'm afraid it's a little messy right now.
（現在我恐怕這裡有點亂。)【*right now* 現在】
I'm sorry it's a little messy.
（我很抱歉，這裡有點亂。）

下面是美國人常說的話：

*It's a little messy.*【第一常用】
It's a bit messy. ( 有點亂。)【第三常用】
It's kind of messy. ( 有點亂。)【第二常用】
【*a bit* 有一點　*kind of* 有一點】

It's a little untidy. ( 有點不整齊。)【第八常用】
It's a little dirty. ( 有點髒。)【第四常用】
【untidy〔ʌn'taɪdɪ〕*adj.* 不整潔的；雜亂的】

It's not very neat. ( 不是非常整潔。)【第七常用】
It's not so clean. ( 不是很乾淨。)【第六常用】
It's not very clean. ( 不是非常乾淨。)【第五常用】
【neat〔nit〕*adj.* 整潔的　so〔so〕*adv.* 非常】

BOOK 12

5. ***Please don't mind the clutter.***

mind〔maɪnd〕*v.* 介意

clutter〔'klʌtɚ〕*n.* 凌亂；雜亂；亂七八糟（＝*mess*）

mess 和 clutter 意思相同，因爲上一句已經用了 messy，所以這句話才用 clutter，而不用 mess。***Please don't mind the clutter.*** 的意思是「請不要介意凌亂。」可加強語氣說成：Please don't mind all the clutter.（請不要介意到處亂七八糟。）（＝*Please don't mind the clutter around here.*）

在考試中常見到的 at sixes and sevens（亂七八糟），現在美國人幾乎已經不再使用了。

下面都是美國人常說的話：

***Don't mind the clutter.***（不要介意凌亂。）【第二常用】

Don't mind the mess.【第一常用】
（不要介意亂七八糟。）

Never mind the clutter.【第四常用】
（絕不要介意凌亂。）

Never mind the mess.【第三常用】
（絕不要介意亂七八糟。）

I hope you don't mind the mess.【第五常用】
（我希望你不會介意亂七八糟。）

I hope you don't care about the clutter.
（我希望你不會介意凌亂。）【第六常用】【*care about* 在意】

6. **We're pretty informal around here.**

pretty〔'prɪtɪ〕*adv.* 相當；非常
informal〔ɪn'fɔrml̩〕*adj.* 非正式的；不拘禮節的；隨便的

> pretty 的主要意思是「漂亮的」，在這裡當副詞，作「相當」解 ( = *rather ; very* )。informal 的主要意思是「非正式的」，在這裡作「隨便的」解 ( = *casual* )【詳見「朗文當代高級辭典」p.783】。around here 字面的意思是「在這裡附近」，在此是加強 here 的語氣。

**We're pretty informal around here.** 的意思是「我們這裡非常隨便。」( = *We're pretty casual around here.* )

7. **Wanna use the bathroom?**

wanna〔'wɑnə〕*v.* 想要 ( = *want to* )
bathroom〔'bæθ,rum〕*n.* 廁所

wanna 已經成為正式的單字，在字典上都可以找到，它是 want to 的縮寫。這句話的意思是「想不想要用廁所？」( = *Want to use the bathroom?* ) 源自：Do you want to use the bathroom? ( 你想不想要用廁所？ )( = *Do you wanna use the bathroom?* )

bathroom

【比較】 下面三句話意思相同：

> ***Wanna use the bathroom?*** 【較口語】
> = Want to use the bathroom? 【語氣普通】
> = Do you want to use the bathroom? 【較正式】

　　「廁所」的説法很多，主要的有：bathroom【無論在家裡或是公共場所都可用】、restroom〔'rɛst,rum〕【公共場所的廁所】、toilet〔'tɔɪlɪt〕【在英國、歐洲的廁所，美國人不用】（詳見 p.331-333）。

8. ***It's just down the hall.***
　　down〔daʊn〕*prep.* 沿著；在…那一邊
　　hall〔hɔl〕*n.* 大廳；走廊；走道

> 　　just 的主要意思是「只是」（= *only*），在這裡作「就」解。down 的主要意思是「在下面」，在這裡作「在…那一邊」解（= *away from the present place*）。句中 hall 的主要意思是「大廳」，在這裡作「走道」解（= *narrow walkway*）。
>
> 　　***It's just down the hall.*** 的意思是「它就在走道那一邊。」
>
> It's just down the hall.
>
> 【比較】 ***It's just down the hall.*** 【語氣稍強】
> 　　　　It's down the hall. 【一般語氣】
> 　　　　（它在走道那一邊。）

BOOK 12

可能源自地圖，「北」在上面，「南」在下面，所以，向北方走，用 up；向南方走，用 down。事實上，現在不管東南西北，大多數人都用 down，較少人用 up。

【比較】下面兩句話意思相同：

**It's just down the hall.**【約 70% 的人說】
It's just up the hall.【約 30% 的人說】

要學會 *down* 作「在…那一邊」解的用法：

Let's walk *down* to the park for some
　　exercise.
（讓我們走到公園**那邊**，做些運動。）

I think there's an ATM *down* that way.
（我想**在那邊**有一台自動提款機。）

The World Trade Center is three blocks
　　*down* the street.
（世界貿易中心**要過**三條街。）

*ATM* 自動提款機（= *automated-teller machine*）
block〔blɑk〕*n.* 街區

**It's just down the hall.** 可以加長為：

It's just down the hall on the left.
（它就在走道的左邊。）
（= *It's just down the hall on the left side.*）
【left〔lɛft〕*n.* 左邊　*adj.* 左邊的】

9. ***The switch is next to the door***.

switch〔swɪtʃ〕*n.* 開關    ***next to*** 在…旁邊

　　這句話的意思是「開關在門的旁邊。」switch 也可説成 light switch（電燈開關），如果強調開關在裡面，就可説成：The switch is inside next to the door.（開關在裡面，門的旁邊。）

【inside〔'ɪn'saɪd〕*adv.* 在裡面】

　　如果強調開關在外面，就要説：The switch is outside next to the door.（開關在外面，門的旁邊。）

【outside〔'aʊt'saɪd〕*adv.* 在外面】

switch

　　***The switch is next to the door***. 可加長爲：You'll find the switch next to the door.（你將發現開關在門的旁邊。）或 The switch is on the wall next to the door.（開關在門旁邊的牆上。）美國人也常説：You'll see the switch next to the door.（你將看到開關在門的旁邊。）雖然現在的 switch 是要用按的（press），但是「打開開關。」應該説成：Turn on the switch. 不能説成：*Press the switch*.【誤】只能説：Press the button.（按按鈕。）

　　switch 這個字很好背，你只要記住 s + witch（巫婆），如果 witch 你背不下來，你只要記住 w + itch（癢）即可。用已會的單字來背新的字，很容易。

## 【對話練習】

1. A：**My home is your home**.　　　　A：我的家就是你家。
   B：You're so kind.　　　　　　　　B：你人真好。
   　　That's a nice thing to say.　　　　你這麼說真好。
   　　I really appreciate your　　　　　我真的很感激你的慇懃
   　　hospitality.　　　　　　　　　　款待。
   　　【appreciate〔ə'priʃɪ,et〕v. 感激
   　　hospitality〔,hɑspɪ'tælətɪ〕n.
   　　好客；慇懃款待】

2. A：**Help yourself to anything**.　　　A：自己拿任何東西。
   B：OK, I will.　　　　　　　　　　B：好的，我會。
   　　Thank you so much.　　　　　　　非常謝謝你。
   　　You are too kind.　　　　　　　　你人真是太好了。

3. A：**There's lots of stuff in the**　　A：在冰箱裡有很多東西。
   　　**fridge**.
   B：I'm not hungry.　　　　　　　　B：我不餓。
   　　Thank you anyway.　　　　　　　還是要謝謝你。
   　　I think I'll wait till later.　　　　我想我要等晚一點。
   　　【anyway〔'ɛnɪ,we〕adv. 反正；
   　　無論如何】

4. A：**It's a little messy**.　　　　　　A：我家有點亂。
   B：You must be kidding.　　　　　　B：你一定是在開玩笑。
   　　Your place looks great.　　　　　你家看起來很棒。
   　　It's much cleaner than mine.　　　比我家乾淨很多。
   　　【kid〔kɪd〕v. 開玩笑】

5. A: **Please don't mind the clutter**.　　　A：請不要介意凌亂。

　　B: What are you talking about?　　　　　B：你在說什麼？

　　　There is no clutter here.　　　　　　　這裡並不亂。

　　　Everything looks so nice.　　　　　　　一切看起來都很好。

6. A: **We're pretty informal around here**.　A：我們這裡非常隨便。

　　B: I can see that.　　　　　　　　　　　B：我看得出來。

　　　I like the casual approach.　　　　　　我喜歡隨意的態度。

　　　There's no reason to be so formal.　　　沒有理由很正式。

　　　【casual (ˈkæʒʊəl ) *adj.* 隨便的
　　　　approach ( əˈprotʃ ) *n.* 方法；態度】

7. A: **Wanna use the bathroom?**　　　　　A：想不想要用廁所？

　　B: Yes, I would.　　　　　　　　　　　B：是的，我要。

　　　I'd like to wash my hands.　　　　　　我想上廁所。

　　　Thank you for reminding me.　　　　　謝謝你提醒我。

　　　【*wash one's hands* 上廁所
　　　　remind ( rɪˈmaɪnd ) *v.* 提醒】

8. A: **It's just down the hall**.　　　　　　A：它就在走道那一邊。

　　B: Which door is it?　　　　　　　　　B：哪一個門？

　　　Is it on the right or the left?　　　　　是在右邊或左邊？

　　　Where is the light switch?　　　　　　電燈開關在哪裡？

　　　【right ( raɪt ) *n.* 右邊
　　　　left ( lɛft ) *n.* 左邊】

9. A: **The switch is next to the door**.　　A：開關在門的旁邊。

　　B: I found it.　　　　　　　　　　　　B：我找到了。

　　　I see it.　　　　　　　　　　　　　　我看到了。

　　　I'll be out in a minute.　　　　　　　我馬上出來。

　　　【*in a minute* 立刻】

BOOK 12

# *4. What a scorcher!*

| | |
|---|---|
| What a scorcher! | 好熱的天氣！ |
| *It's* boiling outside. | 外面天氣很熱。 |
| *It's* hotter than hell. | 眞是熱死人了。 |
| | |
| This weather is so humid. | 這個天氣非常潮濕。 |
| *It's* so sticky. | 天氣非常悶熱。 |
| *It* makes me sweat like crazy. | 它使我流很多汗。 |
| | |
| I don't mind dry heat. | 我不在乎乾熱的天氣。 |
| It's the humidity I can't | 我沒辦法忍受潮濕的 |
|   stand. | 天氣。 |
| The air is so damp and wet. | 空氣非常潮濕。 |

\*\* ──────────────

scorcher〔'skɔrtʃɚ〕*n.* 大熱天
boiling〔'bɔɪlɪŋ〕*adj.* 沸騰的；極熱的
hell〔hɛl〕*n.* 地獄　　humid〔'hjumɪd〕*adj.* 潮濕的
sticky〔'stɪkɪ〕*adj.* 黏的；悶熱的　　sweat〔swɛt〕*v.* 流汗
*like crazy* 瘋狂地；拼命地　　mind〔maɪnd〕*v.* 介意；在乎
heat〔hit〕*n.* 熱　　humidity〔hju'mɪdətɪ〕*n.* 潮濕
stand〔stænd〕*v.* 忍受　　damp〔dæmp〕*adj.* 潮濕的

## 【背景説明】

　　美國人見面寒暄，爲了避免僵局，喜歡談論天氣，我們在第七冊第四課裡，談過好的天氣，在第八冊第四課，説過壞天氣，這一課，我們將學怎麼説炎熱的天氣。以後談到天氣，你就有精彩的話説了。

1. ***What a scorcher!***

scorcher〔ˈskɔrtʃɚ〕*n.* 大熱天（ = *very hot day* ）

　　***scorcher*** 這個字，源自 scorch〔skɔrtʃ〕*v.* 把…燒焦，這個字和 score〔skor〕*v.* 得分 接近，只要記得：在大熱天唸書時，唸到焦頭爛額，就會得分了。

　　***What a scorcher!*** 的意思是「好熱的天氣啊！」前面可以加上感嘆詞 wow〔waʊ〕*interj.* 哇 説成：

Wow! What a scorcher!（哇！好熱的天氣啊！）

也可加長爲：

What a real scorcher!（天氣眞的好熱！）

What a scorcher it is outside today!
（今天外面天氣好熱！）

It's a real scorcher outside today, isn't it?
（今天外面天氣眞的好熱，對不對？）

【real〔ˈriəl〕*adj.* 眞正的】

BOOK 12

下面都是美國人常說的話：

> ***What a scorcher!*** 【第一常用】
> What a hot day! (好熱的天氣！)【第二常用】

> It's really hot. (天氣眞的很熱。)【第四常用】
> It's hot as hell. (天氣非常熱。)【第三常用】
> 【***as hell*** 很；非常】

> It's scorching hot. (天氣非常熱。)【第五常用】
> It's boiling hot. (天氣很熱。)【第六常用】

> scorching 和 boiling 是少數現在分詞可以當副
> 詞用的單字，詳見「文法寶典」p.455。這兩個字
> 在此加深形容詞的程度，相當於「極度；非常；
> 很」的意思。

2. ***It's boiling outside.***

boiling〔'bɔɪlɪŋ〕*adj.* 沸騰的；極熱的；炎熱的

> 這句話字面的意思是「天氣在外面已經沸騰了。」
> 引申爲「外面天氣很熱。」(= *The weather is boiling
> outside*.) 這句話源自：It's boiling hot outside
> today. (今天外面天氣很熱。) boiling hot 可當成
> 一個成語，意思是「酷熱的」，也可以把 boiling 當
> 成副詞，作「很」解。如果人在外面，就可省略
> outside，說成：It's boiling. (天氣很熱。) (= *It's
> very hot.*) ***It's boiling outside.*** 也可加長爲：It's
> really boiling outside today. (今天外面眞的很熱。)

下面是美國人常説的話：

***It's boiling outside.*【第一常用】**

It's boiling hot outside.【第二常用】
（外面天氣很熱。）

It feels boiling hot outside.【第五常用】
（外面天氣使人覺得很熱。）

It feels like it's boiling hot outside.【第六常用】
（外面天氣使人覺得非常熱。）

【feel〔fil〕v. 使人感覺】

The air feels boiling hot.【第三常用】
（空氣使人覺得非常熱。）

It feels like I'm being cooked.【第四常用】
（天氣使我覺得好像快被煮熟了。）

3. ***It's hotter than hell.***

hell〔hɛl〕n. 地獄

　　這句話字面的意思是「天氣比地獄還熱。」引申
爲「眞是熱死人了。」( = *The weather is hotter than hell.* ) 也可説成：It's hot as hell. 或 It's as hot as hell. 它們的意思相同，使用頻率也接近。

　　***It's hotter than hell.*** 可以加長爲：It is hotter than hell outside today.（今天外面的天氣眞是熱死人了。）

BOOK 12

4. *This weather is so humid.*

humid〔'hjumɪd〕*adj.* 潮濕的

　　　這句話的意思是「這個天氣非常潮濕。」(= *The weather is very humid.*) 可加長為：This weather *we're having outside today* is so humid. ( 今天外面的天氣非常潮濕。) 或 The weather is so humid *it's hard for me to handle.* ( 這個天氣太潮濕，我很難忍受。)【句中 humid 後省略 that，詳見「文法寶典」p.516。　handle〔'hændl̩〕*v.* 處理；對付】

　　　下面是美國人常説的話，第二常用和第三常用的使用頻率非常接近：

*This weather is so humid.* 【第一常用】

This type of weather is so humid. 【第二常用】
( 這樣的天氣非常潮濕。)
【type〔taɪp〕*n.* 類型】

This kind of weather is so humid. 【第三常用】
( 這種天氣非常潮濕。)
This weather is unbelievably humid.
( 這個天氣潮濕得令人難以置信。)【第五常用】
This weather is awfully humid. 【第四常用】
( 這個天氣潮濕得不得了。)

【unbelievably〔ˌʌnbə'livəblɪ〕*adv.* 令人難以置信地
　awfully〔'ɔflɪ〕在口語中常作「非常；極為；…得不得了」解。】

5. ***It's so sticky***.

sticky〔'stɪkɪ〕*adj.* 黏的;悶熱的

so〔so〕*adv.* 非常

　　sticky 主要的意思是「黏的」或「黏黏的」,但形容天氣的時候,作「悶熱的;濕熱的」解(= *warm and humid*)。***It's so sticky***. 的意思是「天氣非常悶熱。」(= *The weather is so sticky*.)

　　可以加長爲:It's so sticky today, isn't it?(今天天氣很悶熱,對不對?)美國人也常說:What a sticky day!(好悶熱的天氣!)或 The weather feels so sticky.(天氣使人感覺非常悶熱。)

【feel 在此作「使人感覺」解,詳見 p.1278-1279】

6. ***It makes me sweat like crazy***.

sweat〔swɛt〕*v.* 流汗

***like crazy*** 瘋狂地;拼命地(= *like mad*)

　　crazy 主要的意思是「瘋狂的」,雖然在 The American Heritage Dictionary 字典上有當名詞用,作「瘋子;怪人」(= *one who is or appears insane*)解,但美國人幾乎不用。我們可以把 ***like crazy*** 當成「介詞＋形容詞」的成語來背,類似的有:at large(逍遙法外),in short(簡言之),in general(一般而言),in vain(徒勞無功),for certain(必定),for sure(必定)。【詳見「文法寶典」p.193】

BOOK 12

*It makes me sweat like crazy.* 字面的意思是
「它使我拼命流汗。」引申爲「它使我流很多汗。」
( = *It makes me sweat a lot.* ) 可以加長爲：I don't
like this kind of
weather because it
makes me sweat
like crazy. ( 我不喜
歡這樣的天氣，因爲
它使我流很多汗。)

It makes me sweat
like crazy.

> 美國人很喜歡説 *like crazy*，例如：
>
> You study English *like crazy*.
> ( 你拼命學英文。)
> You work *like crazy*. ( 你拼命工作。)
> It's raining *like crazy*. ( 雨下得很大。)

7. *I don't mind dry heat.*

mind〔maɪnd〕*v.* 介意；在乎
dry〔draɪ〕*adj.* 乾的　　heat〔hit〕*n.* 熱

　　這句話的意思是「我不在乎乾熱的天氣。」可加
強語氣説成：I don't mind dry heat at all. ( 我一點
都不在乎乾熱的天氣。) 【*not…at all* 一點也不…】*dry
heat* 可説成 *a dry heat*，兩者意思相同。加上 the，
則表示「指定」，例如：I don't mind *the dry heat*
today. ( 我不在乎今天這樣乾熱的天氣。)

美國人也常說成：I don't mind a dry heat.
（我不在乎乾熱的天氣。）或 A dry heat doesn't
bother me at all.（乾熱的天氣完全不會使我難受。）
( = *I don't mind the dry heat.* )【bother〔'baðɚ〕*v.*
困擾；使苦惱】

　　在美國大陸的西南方，像亞利桑那州、南加
州、內華達州，都屬於這種乾熱的天氣，天氣雖
然熱，但人們不容易流汗。但在東南方，像佛羅
里達州、路易斯安那州及密西西比州等，則屬於
濕熱的天氣，讓人一動就是一身汗。

8. ***It's the humidity I can't stand.***
humidity〔hju'mɪdətɪ〕*n.* 濕氣；潮濕
stand〔stænd〕*v.* 站；忍受

　　這句話的意思是「我沒辦法忍受潮濕的天氣。」
( = *It's the humidity that I can't stand.* ) 美國人喜
歡說 ***I can't stand it.*** 意思是「我無法忍受。」

下面都是美國人常說的話：

　　***I can't stand it.***【第一常用】
　　（我無法忍受。）
　　I can't take it.【第二常用】
　　（我無法忍受。）
　　I can't tolerate it.【第三常用】
　　（我無法忍耐。）
　　【tolerate〔'tɑlə,ret〕*v.* 容忍；忍耐】

It really upsets me. 【第七常用】
（真的氣死我了。）
It bothers me a lot. （煩死我了。）【第六常用】
It drives me crazy. （它使我發瘋。）【第八常用】
upset〔ʌp'sɛt〕v. 使生氣　　bother〔'bɑðɚ〕v. 使煩惱
*drive sb. crazy* 使某人發瘋

I hate it. （我不喜歡；我討厭。）【第四常用】
I really dislike it. 【第五常用】
（我真的不喜歡。）【hate〔het〕v. 討厭】

9. *The air is so damp and wet.*
damp〔dæmp〕adj. 潮濕的；有濕氣的

damp 和 wet 都是作「潮濕的」解，用 and 連
接兩個意思相同的字，有加強語氣的作用。

*The air is so damp and wet.* 的意思是「空氣
非常潮濕。」（= *The air is very wet.*）可以加長為：
The air outside today is so damp and wet. （今天
外面的空氣非常潮濕。）美
國人也常說成：The air is
so humid. （空氣非常潮
濕。）或 There's so much
moisture in the air. （空氣
中的濕氣很重。）

【moisture〔'mɔɪstʃɚ〕n. 濕氣；水份】

## 【對話練習】

1. A：**What a scorcher!**　　　　A：好熱的天氣啊！

   B：You're not kidding.　　　　B：你說得沒錯。
   　　This heat is awful!　　　　　眞是熱得嚇人！
   　　I'm not going outside　　　　我今天不出門了。
   　　today.

   【kid〔kɪd〕*v.* 開玩笑
   　awful〔'ɔfʊl〕*adj.* 可怕的】

2. A：**It's boiling outside.**　　A：外面天氣很熱。

   B：It really is.　　　　　　　B：的確是。
   　　It's too hot to go out.　　　太熱了，不適合出去。
   　　This heat is dangerous.　　這麼熱很危險。

3. A：**It's hotter than hell.**　　A：眞是熱死人了。

   B：I totally agree.　　　　　　B：我完全同意。
   　　It feels like hell outside.　　外面使人覺得像是地獄。
   　　This must be the hottest　　這一定是一年中最熱的
   　　day of the year.　　　　　　一天。

4. A：**This weather is so humid.**　A：這個天氣非常潮濕。

   B：It is very wet.　　　　　　　B：天氣非常潮濕。
   　　It is very damp outside　　　今天外面天氣非常潮濕。
   　　today.
   　　There's a lot of moisture　　空氣中濕氣很重。
   　　in the air.

BOOK 12

5. A : **It's so sticky**.
 B : It is very sticky.
 I hate this kind of weather.
 It makes my clothes stick to
 my skin. 〔skin〔skɪn〕*n.* 皮膚〕

A：天氣非常悶熱。
B：天氣很悶熱。
 我討厭這種天氣。
 它讓我的衣服黏在皮
 膚上。

6. A : **It makes me sweat like crazy**.
 B : It does the same to me.
 I sweat like crazy, too.
 I have to shower three times
 a day. 〔shower〔'ʃaʊɚ〕*v.* 淋浴〕

A：它使我流很多汗。
B：我也是。
 我也流很多汗。
 我一天得沖三次澡。

7. A : **I don't mind dry heat**.
 B : All heat is the same to me.
 I can't stand being hot.
 I'd much rather be cold.
 〔stand〔stænd〕*v.* 忍受〕

A：我不在乎乾熱的天氣。
B：所有的熱對我而言都
 一樣。
 我無法忍受熱。
 我實在寧願冷。

8. A : **It's the humidity I can't stand**.
 B : I couldn't agree with you
 more.
 Humid weather is the worst.
 It's the most uncomfortable.

A：我沒辦法忍受潮濕的
 天氣。
B：我非常同意你。
 潮濕的天氣是最糟的。
 它是最不舒服的。

9. A : **The air is so damp and wet**.
 B : It really is.
 I wish it would rain.
 That would cool things off.
 〔*cool~off* 使~變涼〕

A：空氣非常潮濕。
B：的確是。
 我希望會下雨。
 那樣會比較涼爽。

# **5.** *So, tell me your news.*

| | |
|---|---|
| So, tell me your news. | 哦，告訴我你的近況。 |
| How have you been? | 你好嗎？ |
| Have you been keeping busy? | 你是不是一直很忙？ |
| | |
| *Are you* working hard these days? | 你最近有沒有努力啊？ |
| *Are you* staying out of trouble? | 你是不是平安？ |
| Do you like what you're doing? | 你是不是喜歡做你正在做的事？ |
| | |
| I want to hear everything. | 我想要聽到所有的事。 |
| *Don't* skip a thing. | 不要跳過任何一件事。 |
| *Don't* leave anything out. | 不要遺漏任何事。 |

BOOK 12

** ——————————

so〔so〕*adv.* 哦    news〔njuz〕*n.* 新消息；新情況
keep〔kip〕*v.* 保持；持續    *work hard* 努力
*these days* 最近    *stay out of* 遠離
trouble〔'trʌbl̩〕*n.* 麻煩    skip〔skɪp〕*v.* 跳過；略過
*leave out* 遺漏；省略

## 【背景説明】

　　　當你有客人來看你，爲了表示熱情，你説的話愈多，就愈表示重視他的到來。

1. *So, tell me your news.*

so〔so〕*adv.* 哦　　news〔njuz〕*n.* 新消息；新情況

> 　　so 可當連接詞，連接前面的句子，放在句首，作「那麼」解，也可當副詞，作「哦」解，沒有什麼意思，跟 well 相同。so 也可當感嘆詞，表示「驚奇」，作「啊」解。news 的主要意思是「新聞」，但在這裡作「新消息」、「新情況」解。這句話的意思是「哦，告訴我你的近況。」

So, tell me your news.

【比較】下面兩句話意思不同：

　　Tell me your news.
　　　（告訴我你的近況。）
　　Tell me the news.
　　　（①告訴我新聞。②告訴我你的近況。）

> 　　中國人不太會，也不敢用 so，其實只要把 so 當作語助詞，可以加在任何句子前面，不表示什麼意思。例如：
>
> 　　*So*, how are you feeling?
> 　　　（哦，你現在感覺如何？）
> 　　*So*, are you hungry?（哦，你餓不餓？）
> 　　*So*, how long can you stay?
> 　　　（哦，你可以待多久？）【stay〔ste〕*v.* 停留】

*So*, what shall we do?

（哦，你覺得我們要怎麼做？）

*So*, what time is it?（哦，現在幾點？）

*So*, what are your plans?（哦，你有什麼計劃？）

【比較】下面三句話意思相同，說起來相同，但寫法不同：

So tell me your news.【so 是連接詞，連接前面說過的話】

（那麼，告訴我你的近況。）

（= *Then tell me your news.*）

*So*, *tell me your news*.【so 是副詞，作「哦」解】

（哦，告訴我你的近況。）

（= *Well, tell me your news.*）

So! Tell me your news.【so 是感嘆詞，作「啊」解】

（啊！告訴我你的近況。）

下面都是美國人常說的話：

*Tell me your news*.【第一常用】

Tell me about what you've been up to lately.

（告訴我你最近都在做什麼。）【第七常用】

Tell me the news.（告訴我你的新情況。）【第二常用】

【*be up to* 正在做　lately（'letlɪ）*adv.* 最近】

What's the news?（最近情況如何？）【第四常用】

What's your news?【第五常用】

（你最近的情況如何？）

What's new with you?（你最近好嗎？）【第六常用】

BOOK 12

What's new?（你好嗎？）【第三常用】

Anything new in your life?【第八常用】

（你生活中有沒有什麼新鮮事？）

Anything new going on in your life?

( = *Is there anything new going on in your life?*)

（你生活中有沒有發生什麼新鮮事？）【第九常用】

【*go on* 發生】

### 2. *How have you been?*

這句話的意思是「你好嗎？」是 How are you?
（你好嗎？）的完成式型態。也可加強語氣說成：

How have you been
（你最近好嗎？）
$\begin{cases} \text{recently?【第二常用】} \\ \text{lately?【第一常用】} \\ \text{these days?【第三常用】} \end{cases}$

【recently (ˈrisn̩tlɪ) *adv.* 最近　*these days* 最近】

*How have you been?* 可以簡化成：How've
you been? 或加長為：I'd like to know "*How
have you been?*"（我
想知道，「你近來好
嗎？」）如果幾個月沒
見，你就可以說：How
have you been these
past months?（你最近
這幾個月好嗎？）【past ( pæst ) *adj.* 過去的；剛過去的】

*How have you been?*

### 3. *Have you been keeping busy?*

keep〔kip〕*v.* 保持；持續

　　　　這句話字面的意思是「你是不是一直在保持忙碌？」引申為「你是不是一直很忙？」可加長為：Have you been keeping busy lately?（你最近是不是一直很忙？）也可以用現在進行式，說成：Are you keeping busy?（你是不是一直很忙？）也可簡化為：Have you been busy?（你是不是一直很忙？）可以加強語氣說成：Have you been keeping yourself busy?（你是不是一直使自己很忙呢？）

　　　　根據美國人的文化，每天使自己保持忙碌是好事。

*Have you been keeping busy?* 包含四個意思：

　① Have you been working hard?
　　　（你有沒有一直很努力？）

　② Have you been making progress?
　　　（你有沒有一直在進步？）
　　　【progress〔'prɑgrɛs〕*n.* 進步】

　③ Have you been doing good work?
　　　（你有沒有一直表現得很好？）
　　　【*do good work* 表現得很好】

　④ Have you been doing lots of work?
　　　（你有沒有一直做很多事？）

BOOK 12

4. ***Are you working hard these days?***

   ***work hard*** 努力　　***these days*** 最近

　　　這句話字面的意思是「你這些天來有沒有努力啊？」引申爲「你最近有沒有努力啊？」通常是同輩的朋友之間寒暄的話，不適合和你的老師或老板説。可加強語氣説成：Are you working very hard these days?（你最近有沒有非常努力啊？）美國人常簡化爲：

> Are you working hard?
> （你有沒有努力啊？）
> You working hard?（你有沒有努力啊？）
> Working hard?（努力嗎？）

也可用完成式形式，説成：

> Have you been working hard these days?
> （你最近有沒有一直很努力啊？）

---

　　　***these days*** 源自 these past days（過去這幾天），可翻成「這些天」或「最近」（= *recently* ; *lately* ）。字典上不容易找到 these days 這個成語，但美國人常用，例如：

> How's everything *these days*?
> （**最近**情況如何？）
> How are you *these days*?（你**最近**好嗎？）
> Are you busy *these days*?（你**最近**忙嗎？）

What's new *these days*?

（**最近**有沒有什麼新消息？）

Are you exercising at all *these days*?

（你**最近**有沒有運動一下？）

Are you doing anything new *these days*?

（你**最近**有沒有做什麼新的事情？）

【*at all* 絲毫；一點；究竟；到底　at all 的用法，詳見 p.1168-1169】

## 5. *Are you staying out of trouble?*

*stay out of* 遠離　　trouble〔ˈtrʌbl̩〕*n.* 麻煩

這句話字面的意思是「你是不是遠離麻煩？」*stay out of* 的意思是「遠離」（= *keep away from* ），可引申為「你是不是平安？」，這是美國人常見的寒暄話，有幽默的味道。他們也常用完成進行式，說成：Have you been staying out of trouble?（你是不是一直平安？）更常簡化為：Been staying out of trouble?（一直平安嗎？）或 Been keeping out of trouble?（一直平安嗎？）【*keep out of* 遠離】

下面都是美國人常說的話：

*Are you staying out of trouble?*【第一常用】

Are you keeping out of trouble?【第三常用】

（你是不是平安？）

Are you keeping your nose clean?【第五常用】

（你是不是平安？）

【*keep one's nose clean* 使自己不捲入麻煩】

BOOK 12

Are you avoiding trouble?【第六常用】
（你是不是平安？）
Are you behaving yourself?【第二常用】
（你是不是守規矩？）【句中的 yourself 可省略】
Are you doing OK?（你還好吧？）【第四常用】

avoid〔ə'vɔɪd〕v. 避免　*behave oneself* 守規矩
do〔du〕v. 做；表現；進展

### 6. *Do you like what you're doing?*

這句話的意思是「你是不是喜歡做你正在做的事？」( = *Do you like doing what you're doing?* )
可加長為：Do you like doing what you're doing every day?（你是不是喜歡做你每天做的事？）也可加強語氣說成：Do you love what you're doing?（你是不是非常喜歡你正在做的事？）

Do you like what you're doing?

美國人碰到朋友，常喜歡說：

Do you like your job?（你喜不喜歡你的工作？）
Are you happy?（你快樂嗎？）
Are you happy with your job?
（你滿意你的工作嗎？）【*be happy with* 對～滿意】

這和我們中國人的習慣不同，因為他們非常重視：
Do what you love. Love what you do.（做你愛做的事。愛你做的事。）

7. *I want to hear everything.*

這句話的意思是「我想要聽到所有的事。」hear 是及物和不及物兩用動詞,所以可説成:I want to hear about everything. 意思相同。也可加長爲: I want to hear everything about what you've been doing.(我想要聽到你正在做的每一件事。)

【比較】下面兩句話意思接近:

*I want to hear everything.*【較常用,語氣較強】
(我想要聽到所有的事。)
I want to listen to everything.【常用,一般語氣】
(我想要聽所有的事。)
【*listen to* 是「聽」,hear 是「聽到」。】

下面是美國人常說的話:

*I want to hear everything.*【第一常用】
Tell me everything.【第四常用】
(告訴我所有的事。)
I want you to tell me everything.【第二常用】
(我希望你告訴我所有的事。)

I want to know all your news.【第三常用】
(我想知道你所有的近況。)
Tell me all the details.【第五常用】
(告訴我所有的細節。)
Tell me everything that has happened to you.
(告訴我所有發生在你身上的事。)【第六常用】
【detail〔'ditel〕*n.* 細節】

BOOK 12

I'm anxious to hear your news. 【第七常用】

（我很渴望聽到你的近況。）

I'm eager to hear what you say. 【第九常用】

（我很渴望聽到你說的話。）

I'm looking forward to hearing what you say.

（我很期待聽到你說的話。）【第八常用】

anxious 〔'æŋkʃəs 〕 *adj.* 渴望的

eager 〔'igə 〕 *adj.* 渴望的　　*look forward to* 期待

8. *Don't skip a thing.*

skip 〔 skɪp 〕 *v.* 跳過；略過

這句話的意思是「不要跳過任何一件事。」

（＝*Don't skip anything.*）skip 的主要意思是「跳過」，是及物和不及物兩用動詞，在這裡，skip 等於 skip over，所以，也可說成：*Don't skip over a thing.* 兩句話意思相同。

*Don't skip a thing.*

可以加強語氣説成：

Don't skip over a single thing. （每一件事都不要跳過。）

【single 〔'sɪŋḷ 〕 *adj.* 單一的；一個的】

也有美國人説：Don't skip a single detail.

（不要跳過任何細節。）

9. *Don't leave anything out*.

*leave out*　遺漏；省略（= *omit*）

　　　這句話的意思是「不要遺漏任何事。」可以加長

爲：Please don't leave anything out of your

news.（請不要遺漏你的任何近況。）或 Please don't

leave anything out from what you're about to

tell me.（請不要遺漏任何你要告訴我的事。）

【*be about to V*. 正要～】

下面是美國人常說的話：

*Don't leave anything out*.【第一常用】

Don't leave out anything.【第二常用】

（不要遺漏任何事。）

Don't skip anything.【第三常用】

（不要省略任何事。）

Don't hold anything back.【第七常用】

（不要保留任何事。）

Don't hold back anything.【第八常用】

（不要保留任何事。）【*hold back*　保留】

Don't forget to tell me anything.【第四常用】

（不要忘記告訴我所有的事。）

I want to know everything.【第五常用】

（我想知道所有的事。）

I want to know every single thing.【第六常用】

（我想要知道每一件事。）

【對話練習】

1. A：**So, tell me your news.**　　　　　A：哦，告訴我你的近況。

　 B：I have a new job.　　　　　　　　B：我有了新工作。
　　　I found a new girlfriend.　　　　　　我交了新的女朋友。
　　　I moved into a new apartment.　　　我搬到新的公寓。
　　　【move〔muv〕v. 搬家】

2. A：**How have you been?**　　　　　　A：你好嗎？

　 B：I have been fine.　　　　　　　　　B：我一直很好。
　　　Things have been going very　　　　　情況一直很順利。
　　　well.
　　　I can't complain.　　　　　　　　　我沒什麼好抱怨的。
　　　【go〔go〕v. 進展
　　　　complain〔kəm'plen〕v. 抱怨】

3. A：**Have you been keeping busy?**　　A：你是不是一直很忙？

　 B：Yes and no.　　　　　　　　　　　B：有時是，有時不是。
　　　I have and I haven't.　　　　　　　　我有時忙，有時不忙。
　　　But I really can't complain.　　　　　但我實在是沒什麼好
　　　　　　　　　　　　　　　　　　　抱怨的。

4. A：**Are you working hard these**　　　A：你最近有沒有努力
　　　**days?**　　　　　　　　　　　　　啊？

　 B：I sure am.　　　　　　　　　　　　B：我當然有。
　　　I've been working my tail off.　　　　我很拼命工作。
　　　I'm trying to get a promotion.　　　　我想獲得升遷。
　　　【*work one's tail off* 拼命工作
　　　　promotion〔prə'moʃən〕n. 升遷】

5. A : **Are you staying out of trouble?**　A：你是不是平安？

　　B : Of course I am.　　　　　　　　B：當然是。

　　　　I wouldn't do anything foolish.　　我不會做任何愚蠢的事。

　　　　I wouldn't do anything to cause　　我不會做任何會惹麻煩

　　　　trouble.【cause〔kɔz〕v. 引起】　　的事。

6. A : **Do you like what you're doing?**　A：你是不是喜歡做你正在

　　　　　　　　　　　　　　　　　　　　做的事？

　　B : I like my job a lot.　　　　　　B：我很喜歡我的工作。

　　　　It's very interesting.　　　　　它很有趣。

　　　　Every day offers a new　　　　　每天都有新的挑戰。

　　　　challenge.【offer〔'ɔfɚ〕v. 提供

　　　　　challenge〔'tʃælɪndʒ〕n. 挑戰】

7. A : **I want to hear everything**.　　A：我想要聽到所有的事。

　　B : I'll do my best.　　　　　　　　B：我會盡力。

　　　　I'll try to remember everything.　我會試著想起每一件事。

　　　　I know you love to hear the　　　我知道你喜歡聽新消息。

　　　　news.【*do one's best* 盡力】

8. A : **Don't skip a thing.**　　　　A：不要跳過任何一件事。

　　B : I promise I won't.　　　　　　　B：我保證不會。

　　　　I'll tell you everything.　　　　我會告訴你一切。

　　　　I'll tell you every detail.　　　我會把每個細節告訴你。

9. A : **Don't leave anything out**.　　A：不要遺漏任何事。

　　B : You are so curious.　　　　　　　B：你太好奇了。

　　　　Why are you so curious?　　　　　你爲什麼這麼好奇？

　　　　Do you feel bored with your　　　你對自己的生活感到厭

　　　　life?　　　　　　　　　　　　　倦嗎？

　　【curious〔'kjʊrɪəs〕*adj.* 好奇的　　bored〔bord〕*adj.* 厭倦的】

BOOK 12

# 6. *Don't get me wrong*.

| | |
|---|---|
| *Don't get* me wrong. | 不要誤會我。 |
| *Don't get* the wrong idea. | 不要會錯意。 |
| I don't want you to misunderstand. | 我不想要你誤解我。 |
| | |
| *Don't* get mad. | 不要生氣。 |
| *Don't* take it seriously. | 不要太認真。 |
| I didn't mean anything by it. | 我這麼說沒什麼意思。 |
| | |
| *I was just* kidding. | 我只是在開玩笑。 |
| *I was just* joking around. | 我只是在開玩笑。 |
| You know that's my style. | 你知道那是我的作風。 |

\*\*

---

*get sb. **wrong*** 誤解某人
misunderstand〔ˌmɪsʌndə'stænd〕*v.* 誤解；誤會
mad〔mæd〕*adj.* 生氣的
seriously〔'sɪrɪəslɪ〕*adv.* 認真地；嚴肅地
*take~seriously* 把~看得很認真
mean〔min〕*v.* 意思是　　kid〔kɪd〕*v.* 開玩笑
joke〔dʒok〕*v.* 開玩笑　　*joke around* 開玩笑
style〔staɪl〕*n.* 風格；作風

【背景説明】

　　和外國人交往，常常由於文化不同，會引起誤會，有了這九句話説，你就安全了。

1. ***Don't get me wrong.***

　　***get sb. wrong*** 誤解某人（ = *misunderstand sb.* ）

　　　　這句話的意思是「不要誤會我。」句中的 get 作「了解」解，像 Do you get it?（你了不了解？）wrong 是副詞，作「錯誤地」解，像 You've spelled the word wrong.（你把這個字拼錯了。）或 You guessed wrong.（你猜錯了。）句中的 wrong 都是副詞。

　　【比較】 美國人很少用 wrongly：

　　　　***Don't get me wrong.***【正】
　　　　*Don't get me wrongly.*
　　　　【誤，wrongly 字典上有，文法對，美國人不説】

下面是美國人常説的話，我們按照使用頻率排列：

① ***Don't get me wrong.***【第一常用】
② Don't get the wrong idea. 【第二常用】
　　（不要會錯意。）
③ Don't misunderstand me. 【第三常用】
　　（不要誤會我。）

【misunderstand〔ˌmɪsʌndɚˈstænd〕*v.* 誤會】

BOOK 12

④ Don't take it the wrong way. ( 不要誤會。 )

( = *Don't take it in the wrong way.* )

【在 way 前，介系詞 in 常省略】

⑤ Don't take what I said the wrong way.

( 不要誤會我說的話。 )

⑥ Don't misinterpret what I'm saying.

( 不要誤解我說的話。 )

***take~the wrong way*** 誤會～
misinterpret〔,mɪsɪn'tɝprɪt〕*v.* 誤解

## 2. ***Don't get the wrong idea.***

這句話字面的意思是「不要得到錯誤的念頭。」

引申為「不要會錯意。」可以加長為：Don't get

the wrong idea about it. ( 不要對那件事會錯意。 )

或 Don't get the wrong idea about what I said.

( 不要對我所說的話會錯

意。 )可加強語氣說成：

I don't want you to

get the wrong idea.

( 我不想要你會錯意。 )

*Don't get the wrong idea.*

下面是美國人常說的話：

***Don't get the wrong idea.*** 【第一常用】

Don't get the wrong meaning. 【第六常用】

( 不要會錯意。 )

Don't mistake my meaning. 【第五常用】

( 不要誤會我的意思。 )

meaning〔'minɪŋ〕*n.* 意思
mistake〔mə'stek〕*v.* 弄錯；誤解

Don't misunderstand.【第二常用】
（不要誤會。）
Don't misunderstand me.【第三常用】
（不要誤會我。）
Don't misunderstand what I said.【第四常用】
（不要誤會我說的話。）

3. ***I don't want you to misunderstand me***.

misunderstand〔͵mɪsʌndɚˈstænd〕*v.* 誤解；誤會

　　這句話的意思是「我不想要你誤解我。」由於
misunderstand 是及物和不及物兩用動詞，所以
me 可以省略，說成：I don't want you to
misunderstand.（我不想要你誤會。）可以加強語
氣說成：I *really* don't want you to misunderstand
me.（我真的不想讓你誤會我。）可以加長為：Let
me explain myself because I don't want you
to misunderstand me.（讓我來為我自己解釋，因
為我不想要你誤解我。）【*explain oneself* 為自己的立
場作解釋；說明自己的心意】可以簡化為：Don't
misunderstand me.（不要誤解我。）或 Don't
misunderstand.（不要誤會。）

下面三句話意思相同，使用頻率接近：

　***Don't get me wrong***.【第一常用】
　= Don't get the wrong idea.【第二常用】
　= Don't misunderstand me.【第三常用】

4. ***Don't get mad.***

mad〔mæd〕*adj.* 生氣的

這句話的意思是「不要生氣。」( = *Don't be mad.* ) 句中的 get 相當於 be 動詞。可以加長為：

Don't get mad at me. ( 不要對我生氣。)
Don't get mad about it. ( 不要對這件事情生氣。)
Don't get mad about what I said.
( 不要對我所說的話生氣。)

Please don't get mad. ( 請不要生氣。)
Don't get mad now, OK?
( 現在不要生氣，好嗎？)【OK〔'o'ke〕*adv.* 好】
There is no reason to get mad now.
( 現在沒有理由生氣。)【reason〔'rizn̩〕*n.* 理由】

下面都是美國人常說的話：

***Don't get mad.***【第一常用】
= Don't get angry. ( 不要生氣。)【第二常用】
= Don't get upset. ( 不要不高興。)【第三常用】
【upset〔ʌp'sɛt〕*adj.* 不高興的】

= Don't get irritated. ( 不要生氣。)【第五常用】
= Don't get pissed off. ( 不要生氣。)【第六常用】
= Don't take offense. ( 不要生氣。)【第四常用】

irritated〔'ɪrə,tetɪd〕*adj.* 被激怒的；生氣的
***piss off*** 使生氣　　***get pissed off*** 生氣
說 Don't get pissed off. 時要小心，只適合對親密的朋友說，因為 piss 是「小便」的意思，說起來有些不雅。
offense〔ə'fɛns〕*n.* 冒犯；生氣　　***take offense*** 生氣

5. ***Don't take it seriously.***

seriously〔ˈsɪrɪəslɪ〕*adv.* 認眞地；嚴肅地

***take ~ seriously*** 把～看得很認眞

句中的 take 作「接受或相信」解 ( = *accept or believe* )。***Don't take it seriously.*** 的字面意思是「不要認眞地接受它。」引申爲「不要太認眞。」( = *Don't take it too seriously.* )

可加長爲：Now, don't take it so seriously. ( 現在，不要太認眞。) 或 Please don't take it so seriously. ( 請不要把它看得太認眞。)

Don't take it seriously.

美國人也常說：Don't take it as the truth. ( 不要把它當眞。) 或 Don't take what I said seriously. ( 不要把我所說的話看得太認眞。)【truth〔truθ〕*n.* 事實】

6. ***I didn't mean anything by it.***

mean〔min〕*v.* 意思是　　by〔baɪ〕*prep.* 憑藉；靠；用

這句話的意思是「我這麼說沒什麼意思。」源自：I didn't mean anything bad by saying it. ( 我這麼說沒什麼壞的意思。) 可簡化爲：I didn't mean anything. ( 我沒什麼意思。)

說完 ***I didn't mean anything by it.*** 後，可接著說：

I was just saying for fun. ( 我只是說了好玩。)

I just said it for no reason at all.

( 我那樣說沒什麼理由。)【*for fun* 爲了好玩】

BOOK 12

也可以再接著説：

> I wasn't trying to hurt you.
> （我並不想要讓你難過。）
> I just said it without thinking.
> （我想都沒想就說了。）
> 【hurt〔hɜt〕v. 傷害；使傷心】

7. ***I was just kidding.***

kid〔kɪd〕v. 開玩笑　n. 小孩

這句話的意思是「我只是在開玩笑。」( = *I was only kidding.* ) 可以加長爲：I was just kidding when I said that.（我那樣說只是在開玩笑。）或 I was just kidding with you.（我只是在跟你開玩笑。）

I was just kidding.

美國人也常説：I was just kidding around.（我只是在開玩笑。）或 I was just kidding around with you.（我只是在和你開開玩笑。）

【***kid around*** 開玩笑 ( = *kid* )】句中的 kidding 可以改成 joking 或 fooling，用法相同，後面都可接 around，成爲：I was just joking around with you. 或 I was just fooling around with you. 意思相同。【fool〔ful〕v. 開玩笑 ( = *fool around* )】

下面是美國人常説的話：

> ***I was just kidding.*** 【第一常用】
> ＝ I was just joking.【第二常用】
> 　（我只是在開玩笑。）
> ＝ I was just fooling.【第五常用】
> 　（我只是在開玩笑。）
>
> ＝ I was just kidding around.【第三常用】
> 　（我只是在開開玩笑。）
> ＝ I was just joking around.【第四常用】
> 　（我只是在開開玩笑。）
> ＝ I was just fooling around.【第六常用】
> 　（我只是在開開玩笑。）

上面各句中的 just 可改成 only，用 only 來做
比較時，使用頻率相同。

8. ***I was just joking around.***

joke〔dʒok〕*v.* 開玩笑
***joke around*** 開玩笑

I was just
joking around.

這句話的意思是「我
只是在開開玩笑。」可簡化
爲：I was just joking.
（我只是在開玩笑。）或
I was just joking around by what I said.（我說的
話只是開開玩笑。）可參照上一句 I was just kidding.
的背景説明。

BOOK 12

9. ***You know that's my style***.
style〔staɪl〕*n.* 風格；作風

　　　這句話的意思是「你知道那是我的作風。」
（= *You know that that's my style.*）可加長為：
As my friend, you know that's my style. ( 你是
我的朋友，你知道我的作風。) 可加強語氣說成：
As my friend, you understand and know that's
my style. ( 你是我的朋友，你明白也知道那是我的
作風。) 也可只用 just 來加強，說成：You know
that's ***just*** my style. ( 你知道那就是我的風格。)

下面都是美國人常說的話：

***You know that's my style***. 【第一常用】
You know that's my way. 【第五常用】
( 你知道那是我的作風。)【way〔we〕*n.* 作風】
You know that's my personality. 【第六常用】
( 你知道那是我的個性。)
【personality〔ˌpɝsn̩'ælətɪ〕*n.* 個性；性格】

You know that's the way I am. 【第二常用】
( 你知道我就是那個樣子。)【way〔we〕*n.* 樣子】
You know that's how I am. 【第三常用】
( 你知道我就是那個樣子。)
You know that's what I'm like. 【第四常用】
( 你知道我就是那個樣子。)

　　　在有些文法書上看到的：*You know that's the
way how I am.* 中的 the way how 是古老用法，現
在已經不用了，詳見「文法寶典」p.244。

BOOK 12

## 【對話練習】

1. A : **Don't get me wrong**.

　B : Why shouldn't I?
　　　I heard what you said.
　　　I don't like what you said
　　　at all.

A：不要誤會我。

B：我為什麼不應該？
　　我聽到你說的話了。
　　我一點都不喜歡你說
　　的。

2. A : **Don't get the wrong idea**.

　B : I'll try not to.
　　　Please explain what you
　　　meant.
　　　What you said confused me.
　　　【confuse〔kən'fjuz〕*v.* 使困惑】

A：不要會錯意。

B：我會試著不要。
　　請解釋你的意思。

　　你說的話讓我很困惑。

3. A : **I don't want you to
　　　misunderstand**.

　B : I think your meaning is clear.
　　　I see your point.
　　　I understand.
　　　【see〔si〕*v.* 知道；了解
　　　　point〔pɔɪnt〕*n.* 要點；主要含意】

A：我不希望你誤會。

B：我想你的意思很清楚。
　　我知道你的意思了。
　　我了解。

4. A : **Don't get mad**.

　B : I'm not upset.
　　　I'm not mad at all.
　　　Think nothing of it.
　　　【upset〔ʌp'sɛt〕*adj.* 不高興的】

A：不要生氣。

B：我沒有不高興。
　　我一點都沒生氣。
　　沒關係；不要介意。

BOOK 12

5. A：**Don't take it seriously**.　　　A：不要太認眞。

B：I'm sorry, but I do.　　　　　B：很抱歉，但我就是會。

Your remark was rude.　　　你說的話很粗魯。

It wasn't polite.　　　　　很不禮貌。

【remark〔rɪ'mark〕*n.* 話；評論

rude〔rud〕*adj.* 粗魯的；無禮的】

6. A：**I didn't mean anything by it**.　　A：我這麼說沒什麼意思。

B：I know that you didn't.　　　B：我知道你沒有。

I wasn't offended.　　　　我沒生氣。

Don't worry about what you　不用擔心你說的話。

said.

【offended〔ə'fɛndɪd〕*adj.* 生氣的】

7. A：**I was just kidding**.　　　　A：我只是在開玩笑。

B：I know you were.　　　　B：我知道你是。

I'm not angry at all.　　　我一點都沒生氣。

Don't worry about it, OK?　別擔心，好嗎？

8. A：**I was joking around**.　　　A：我只是在開開玩笑。

B：You joke too much.　　　B：你玩笑開得太過火了。

You are too silly.　　　　你太愚蠢了。

Sometimes people don't like　有時候大家不喜歡那

that.【silly〔'sɪlɪ〕*adj.* 愚蠢的】　樣。

9. A：**You know that's my style**.　　A：你知道那是我的作風。

B：I know you very well.　　　B：我很了解你。

We've been friends a long time.　我們當朋友很久了。

I understand and I forgive　我了解，而且我會原

you.【forgive〔fɚ'gɪv〕*v.* 原諒】　諒你。

# 7. *I'd like you to meet my wife*.

| | |
|---|---|
| I'd like you to meet my wife. | 我想要你認識我的太太。 |
| *She's* my better half. | 她是我的賢內助。 |
| *She's* the brains of the family. | 她是家裡的老大。 |
| | |
| *She* runs the house. | 她管理這個家。 |
| *She's* an exceptional cook. | 她很會煮飯。 |
| I'd be lost without her. | 如果沒有她，我不知道該怎麼辦。 |
| | |
| *She's* a jack-of-all-trades. | 她什麼都會。 |
| *She's* an angel in disguise. | 她像一個天使。 |
| I couldn't ask for more. | 我不能要求更多了。 |

\*\* ————————————————

meet〔mit〕*v.* 認識；和⋯見面
***better half*** 賢內助；妻子；丈夫
brains〔brenz〕*n.* 聰明的人；領導者；中心人物
run〔rʌn〕*v.* 管理    exceptional〔ɪkˈsɛpʃənḷ〕*adj.* 傑出的
cook〔kʊk〕*n.* 廚師    lost〔lɔst〕*adj.* 不知所措的
jack-of-all-trades〔ˌdʒækəvˈɔlˌtredz〕*n.* 萬能先生；萬事通
angel〔ˈendʒəl〕*n.* 天使
disguise〔dɪsˈgaɪz〕*n.* 偽裝    ***ask for*** 要求

BOOK 12

## 【背景説明】

　　當你要介紹你的太太的時候，你就可以説下面九句既幽默又讚美的話。

1. ***I'd like you to meet my wife.***
   ***I'd like*** 我想要（ = *I want* ）
   meet〔 mit 〕*v.* 認識；和⋯見面

   　　meet 有「和⋯見面」和「認識」的意思，在這裡是作「認識」解。這句話的意思是「我想要你認識我的太太。」( = *I want you to meet my wife.* ) 不可説成：*I'd like you to see my wife.* （誤，句意不合理，介紹別人，不能説去「看」別人）可説成：I'd like to introduce my wife to you.（我想向你介紹我的太太。）【句中的 to you 可省略】也可説成：I'd like to introduce you to my wife.（我想把你介紹給我的太太。）

2. ***She's my better half.***
   ***better half*** 太座；先生；夥伴
   ( = *one's wife and occasionally one's husband or partner* )

   　　這句話源自：She's the better half of our team.（她是我們這個團隊較好的一半。）***She's my better half.*** 的字面意思是「她是我較好的一半。」引申爲「她是我的賢內助。」( = *She's my wife.* ) 説 better half 有幽默、恭維的語氣，表示「比我好」( better than me )，就像我們中文恭維太太時，説成「太座」、「賢內助」。

兩個人在一起，關係很密切，即使沒有結婚的女朋友，你也可以說：***She's my better half.*** ( 她是我的好女朋友。) 美國的太太介紹她丈夫的時候，有時也幽默地說：He's my better half. ( 他是我的先生。)

*He's my better half.*

*She's my better half.*

***She's my better half.*** 可加強語氣說成：She's definitely my better half. ( 她的確是我的賢內助。) ( = *She's my better half for sure.* ) 可加長為：I can't deny it. ***She's my better half.*** ( 我不能否認。她是我的賢內助。)【definitely (ˈdɛfənɪtlɪ ) *adv.* 確實地 deny ( dɪˈnaɪ ) *v.* 否認】

感覺上，better half 是複合名詞，好像要寫成 *better-half* ( 誤 )。事實上，查遍所有的字典，better half 中，都沒有連字號。

下面是美國人對太太常說的恭維話，我們按照使用頻率排列：

① ***She's my better half.*** 【第一常用】

② She's better than I am. ( 她比我好。)【第二常用】

③ She's a better person than me. 【第三常用】 ( 她比我好。)

④ She is more capable than I am. 【第四常用】 ( 她比我能幹。)【capable (ˈkepəbḷ ) *adj.* 能幹的】

BOOK 12

3. ***She's the brains of the family.***

brains〔brenz〕*n.* 聰明的人；領導者；中心人物

　　　brain 的主要意思是「頭腦」，brains 的主要意思是「智慧；腦筋」，也可指「聰明的人」或「領導者；中心人物」( person in charge )。

***She's the brains of the family.*** 的意思是「她是家裡的老大。」brains 在此是單數名詞，但也可當複數用，如：My wife and daughter are the

brains of the family. ( 我老婆和女兒主管這個家。)

　　***She's the brains of the family.*** 也可說成：She's the brains around here. ( 她在這裡是老大。) 或 She's the brains in this house. ( 她負責管理這個家。) 如果她是公司的領導人物，就可說成：She's the brains of the company. ( 她是公司的領導人物。)

【比較】 brain 和 brains 不同：

She is a brain. ( 她很聰明。)
( = *She is a smart person.* )
【brain〔bren〕*n.* 頭腦好的人】

She is the brains.
① 她最聰明。( = *She is the smartest person.* )
② 她是領導人物。( = *She is the leader.* )

4. ***She runs the house***.

run〔rʌn〕*v.* 經營；管理

　　這句話的意思是「她管理這個家。」( = *She manages the house.* ) 可加長爲：She is the one who runs the house. ( 她是管理這個家的人。) 可加強語氣説成：She runs the house very well. ( 她把這個家管理得很好。)

　　美國人也常説成：She's in charge around here. ( 這裡由她管理。) 或 She takes care of everything at home. ( 家裡面一切由她打理。) 也可幽默地説：She's the leader of the house. ( 她是一家之主。)【***be in charge*** 負責管理 ***take care of*** 處理　leader〔'lidɚ〕*n.* 領導者】

5. ***She's an exceptional cook***.

exceptional〔ɪk'sɛpʃən̩〕*adj.* 例外的；傑出的
cook〔kʊk〕*n.* 廚師

　　exceptional 的主要意思是「例外的」，在這裡作「非常好的」解 ( = *excellent* )。這句話字面的意思是「她是個非常好的廚師。」( = *She's an excellent cook.* ) 可引申爲「她很會煮飯。」( = *She can really cook.* )

cook 和 cooker 不同，cook 可當動詞，作「煮飯」解，也可當名詞，作「廚子；廚師」解；cooker 的主要意思是「烹飪器具」，雖然在 The American Heritage Dictionary 中，cooker 可當「廚師」解，但是，日常生活中，美國人都不說。你如果說：*She's an exceptional cooker.*（誤）別人會笑死，因爲 cooker 是煮飯用的東西，像「壓力鍋」叫作 pressure cooker，「電鍋」叫作 rice cooker。

cook　　　cooker

下面是美國人常說的話：

***She's an exceptional cook.*** 【第六常用】
She's an excellent cook. 【第一常用】
　（她很會煮飯。）
She's an outstanding cook. 【第五常用】
　（她很會煮飯。）

excellent〔'ɛkslənt〕*adj.* 極好的
outstanding〔'aʊt'stændɪŋ〕*adj.* 傑出的

She's a wonderful cook. 【第二常用】
　（她很會煮飯。）
She's a marvelous cook. 【第四常用】
　（她很會煮飯。）
She's a very good cook. 【第三常用】
　（她很會煮飯。）

wonderful〔'wʌndəfəl〕*adj.* 很棒的
marvelous〔'mɑrvləs〕*adj.* 很棒的

6. ***I'd be lost without her***.

lost〔lɔst〕*adj.* 遺失的；不知所措的（= *confused*）

　　lost 本來是 lose 的過去分詞，在這裡已經變成純粹的形容詞，作「不知所措的」解。這句話的意思是「如果沒有她，我不知道該怎麼辦。」（= *Without her, I'd be lost.*）可加長為：I would really be lost without her help.（如果沒有她的幫助，我真的不知道該怎麼辦。）

　　下面是美國人常說的話，我們按照使用頻率排列：

① ***I'd be lost without her***.【第一常用】

② I'd be helpless without her.【第二常用】
　　（如果沒有他，我就不知道該怎麼辦。）
　　【helpless〔'hɛlplɪs〕*adj.* 茫然不知所措的】

③ I wouldn't know what to do without her.
　　（沒有她，我就不知道該怎麼辦。）【第三常用】

④ I'd be in big trouble without her.
　　（如果沒有她，我就有大麻煩了。）

⑤ I couldn't live without her.
　　（如果沒有她，我就活不下去了。）

7. ***She's a jack-of-all-trades***.

jack-of-all-trades〔͵dʒækəv'ɔl͵tredz〕*n.* 萬能先生；萬事通

　　jack-of-all-trades 來自諺語：A Jack of all trades is master of none.（萬能先生無一精通；樣樣通，樣樣鬆。）【Jack 原是美國人常用的名字，在此指「一般人」。trade 在此指「技藝」。*be master of* 精通】

jack of all trades 這個成語，由於使用很頻繁，在大部份新的字典中，已經變成複合名詞，寫成：jack-of-all-trades，其實有沒有連字號都可以，在 A Dictionary of American Idioms p.217 中，就沒有連字號。

jack-of-all-trades 可用在正面的稱讚或反面的諷刺，在這裡是正面的。*She's a jack-of-all-trades.* 的意思是「她什麼都會。」( = *She can do many things.* ) 暗示「她很能幹。」( = *She's very capable.* )

【capable〔'kepəbl〕 *adj.* 有能力的；能幹的】

8. *She's an angel in disguise.*

angel〔'endʒəl〕 *n.* 天使

disguise〔dɪs'gaɪz〕 *n.* 偽裝　　*in disguise* 偽裝的

這句話字面的意思是「她是偽裝的天使。」

an angel *in disguise* ( 偽裝的天使 )，外表是人，其實為天使，就像我們說的「仙女下凡」，在此引申為「她像是個天使。」( = *She's like an angel.* ) 美國人也常說：She's like an angel in disguise. ( 她像是天使下凡。) 或 She's as nice as an angel. ( 她和天使一樣好。) 相反地，「人面獸心」就是 a devil in disguise，男女都可以用。

有個諺語：A blessing in disguise. ( = *It's a blessing in disguise.* ) 字面的意思是「偽裝的幸福；外表似不幸，其實為幸福。」引申為「因禍得福。」句中的 in disguise 和這句話的 in disguise 用法相同，都當形容詞片語。

9. *I couldn't ask for more.*
   *ask for* 要求

這句話的意思是「我不能要求更多了。」可以加長為：I'm totally satisfied. I couldn't ask for more. ( 我非常滿足。我不能要求更多了。) 或 I'm content. I couldn't ask for more. ( 我很滿足。我不能要求更多了。)【content〔kən'tɛnt〕*adj.* 滿足的】

【比較】 下面兩句話時態不同：

　　*I couldn't ask for more.*【表「現在」】
　　I couldn't have asked for more.【表「過去」】
　　( 我已經不能再要求更多了。)

例如：

　　She's perfect for me. *I couldn't ask*
　　　*for more.*【現在式】
　　( 她對我來說太完美了。我不能要求更多了。)
　　【perfect〔'pɝfɪkt〕*adj.* 完美的】

　　I ate so much food. *I couldn't have*
　　　*asked for more.*【過去式】
　　( 我吃太多食物了。我已經不能再要求更多了。)

BOOK 12

## 【對話練習】

1. A：**I'd like you to meet my wife**.

  B：I'd love to meet her, too.
   We've never met before.
   I've heard so many nice
   things about her.

  A：我想要你認識我的太太。

  B：我也很樂意認識他。
   我們以前從未見過面。
   我聽過好多對她的讚美。

2. A：**She's my better half**.

  B：Most women are.
   Men are so lucky.
   Men would be lost without
   women.

  A：她是我的賢內助。

  B：太多數女人都是。
   男人眞幸運。
   男人如果沒有女人，就不
   知道該怎麼辦。

3. A：**She's the brains of the
   family**.

  B：She must be smart.
   She married a great guy.
   She has to be very intelligent.

   【smart〔smɑrt〕*adj.* 聰明的
    guy〔gaɪ〕*n.* 人；傢伙】

  A：她是家裡的老人。

  B：她一定很聰明。
   她嫁給了一個很棒的人。
   她一定非常聰明。

4. A：**She runs the house**.

  B：I bet she's great.
   She must be very organized.
   She must be a good manager.

   【bet〔bɛt〕*v.* 打賭；想
    organized〔'ɔrgənˌaɪzd〕*adj.* 有組織的；有條理的
    manager〔'mænɪdʒɚ〕*n.* 經理；管家務者】

  A：她管理這個家。

  B：我想她一定很棒。
   她一定是個很有條理的人。
   她一定很會管理家務。

5. A : **She's an exceptional cook**.

   B : Wow!  You're lucky.
   I'm envious of you.
   I love delicious food.
   【envious (ˈɛnvɪəs ) *adj.* 羨慕的】

A：她很會煮飯。

B：哇啊！你真幸運。
   我羨慕你。
   我很喜歡美食。

6. A : **I'd be lost without her**.

   B : That's a nice compliment.
   What a sweet thing to say.
   She's lucky to have you, too.
   【compliment (ˈkɑmpləmənt ) *n.* 稱讚
   sweet ( swit ) *adj.* 討人喜歡的】

A：如果沒有她，我不知
   道該怎麼辦。

B：那是很好的讚美。
   這麼說真是貼心。
   她也很幸運能擁有你。

7. A : **She's a jack-of-all-trades**.

   B : I'm really quite impressed.
   She's a real problem-solver.
   Is there anything she can't do?
   【impressed ( ɪmˈprɛst ) *adj.* 印象深刻的】

A：她什麼都會。

B：我真的印象很深刻。
   她真會解決問題。
   有什麼她不會的事嗎？

8. A : **She's an angel in disguise**.

   B : You should tell her that.
   You should tell her every day.
   That's a beautiful compliment.
   【beautiful (ˈbjutəfəl ) *adj.* 很好的】

A：她像是個天使。

B：你應該告訴她這句話。
   你應該每天都跟她說。
   那是很好的讚美。

9. A : **I couldn't ask for more**.

   B : I think you're right.
   You have everything.
   You don't need anything more.

A：我不能要求更多了。

B：我想你說得對。
   你擁有了一切。
   你不再需要任何東西了。

BOOK 12

# 8. *Please stay for dinner*.

| | |
|---|---|
| Please stay for dinner. | 請留下來吃晚餐。 |
| Do me the honor. | 給我面子。 |
| Let's break bread together. | 我們一起吃飯吧。 |
| | |
| You have no choice. | 你沒有選擇的餘地。 |
| *I won't* let you go. | 我不會讓你走。 |
| *I won't* take no for an answer. | 我一定要你答應。 |
| | |
| Don't make me beg. | 不要讓我求你。 |
| Do it for me. | 幫我一個忙吧。 |
| It would mean a lot to me. | 這件事會對我很重要。 |

BOOK 12

**\*\***

stay〔ste〕*v.* 停留　　do〔du〕*v.* 給予

honor〔'ɑnɚ〕*n.* 榮譽；榮幸　　bread〔brɛd〕*n.* 麵包

*break bread* 一起吃飯　　choice〔tʃɔɪs〕*n.* 選擇

take〔tek〕*v.* 接受　　beg〔bɛg〕*v.* 請求；懇求

mean〔min〕*v.* 意思是；有某種重要性

*mean a lot* 非常重要

## 【背景説明】

當客人到你家，想要留他吃晚餐，就可説下面九句話。根據美國人的習慣，大部份的美國人，都會邀請下午來的客人一起吃晚餐。有時候即使心裡不希望他們留下來，也會説一些客套話，表示禮貌。

1. ***Please stay for dinner***.
   stay〔ste〕v. 停留

   這句話的意思是「請留下來吃晚餐。」可以加長爲：Please stay for dinner with us. (請留下來和我們一起吃晚餐。) 或 Please stay with us for dinner tonight. (請今天晚上留下來和我們一起吃晚餐。) 如果是午餐，就要説：Please stay for lunch. (請留下來吃午餐。) 在聖誕節、感恩節、復活節或新年時，雖然中午吃飯，也稱作 dinner。

   可以加強語氣説成：You must stay for dinner. (你必須留下來吃晚餐。) 或 You have to stay for dinner. (你必須留下來吃晚餐。)

下面是美國人常說的話：

Stay for dinner.【第二常用】
（留下來吃晚餐。）
*Please stay for dinner*.【第一常用】
Please stay here for dinner.【第三常用】
（請留在這裡吃晚餐。）

Have dinner with us.【第五常用】
（和我們一起吃晚餐。）
Stay and eat with us.【第四常用】
（留下來和我們一起吃飯。）
【eat〔it〕*v.* 吃東西；吃飯】

Please eat with us.【第六常用】
（請和我們一起吃飯。）
Please remain for dinner.【第七常用】
（請留下來吃晚餐。）
【remain〔rɪ'men〕*v.* 停留】

2. *Do me the honor.*

do〔du〕*v.* 給予　　honor〔'ɑnɚ〕*n.* 榮譽；榮幸

在句中，do 是授與動詞，作「給」解（= *give*），
類似的有：Do me the favor.（幫我這個忙。）
【*do sb. a favor* 幫某人的忙】

*Do me the honor.*
　間受　直接受詞

honor 的主要意思是「榮譽」，在此作「面子」解【見「東華英漢大辭典」p.1547】。***Do me the honor.*** 的意思是「給我面子。」加直接受詞時，就成為：Do the honor to me. 意思相同。【詳見「文法寶典」p.278】在美國，只有在一群人面前，才說：Don't make me lose face. (不要讓我丟臉；給我面子。) 不能說：*Give me the face.*【誤】

***Do me the honor.*** 在這裡可加長為：Please do me the honor of staying for dinner. (請你賞光留下來吃晚餐。) 或 Please do me the honor of eating with us. (請你給我面子，和我們一起吃飯。)

下面是美國人常說的話：

***Do me the honor.***【第一常用】
Give me the honor.
(給我面子。)【第二常用】
Allow me the honor.
(給我面子。)【第五常用】
【allow〔ə'laʊ〕v. 給與】

It would be an honor.【第三常用】
(這樣我會很榮幸。)
I would consider it an honor.【第四常用】
(我會認為這是個榮幸。)
It would make me feel honored.【第六常用】
(這會讓我覺得很光榮。)

honor〔'ɑnɚ〕n. 光榮；榮幸　　consider〔kən'sɪdɚ〕v. 認為
honored〔'ɑnɚd〕adj. 光榮的

BOOK 12

3. **Let's break bread together.**
   bread〔brɛd〕*n.* 麵包
   **break bread** 一起吃飯（= *eat together* ）

Let's break bread together.

這句話字面的意思是「我們一起折斷麵包吧。」
引申為「我們一起吃飯吧。」
break bread 源自從前朋友
在一起吃飯，會把長麵包
折斷，讓大家一起享用。和
美國人講這句話，他一定會
大笑，因為這麼道地的話，
很少中國人會說。

**Let's break bread together.** 可簡化成：Let's
break bread. 意思相同。美國人也常說：I'd like
to break bread with you.（我想和你一起吃飯。）

下面都是美國人常說的話：

Let's break bread.（我們一起吃飯吧。）【第二常用】
**Let's break bread together.**【第一常用】

Let's share a meal.（我們一起吃飯吧。）【第六常用】
Let's have a meal together.【第五常用】
（我們一起吃飯吧。）
share〔ʃɛr〕*v.* 分享　meal〔mil〕*n.* 一餐
have〔hæv〕*v.* 吃

Let's eat together.（我們一起吃飯吧。）【第三常用】
Let's you and I eat together.【第四常用】
（我們兩個一起吃飯吧。）
【you and I 是同位語，加強 Let's 中的 us 的語氣】

4. ***You have no choice***.

choice〔tʃɔɪs〕*n.* 選擇

這句話的意思是「你沒有選擇的餘地。」( = *You don't have a choice*.) 可加長為: You have no choice in the matter. ( 這件事你沒有選擇的餘地。) 【matter〔'mætɚ〕*n.* 事情】或 I'm sorry, but you have no choice. ( 很抱歉,你沒有選擇的餘地。)

你也可以開玩笑地說: You can't say no. ( 你不能說「不」。) 或 You can't refuse. ( 你不能拒絕。) 【refuse〔rɪ'fjuz〕*v.* 拒絕】

下面是美國人常說的話:

***You have no choice***. 【第一常用】
You have no alternative. 【第四常用】
( 你沒有選擇的餘地。)
【alternative〔ɔl'tɜnətɪv〕*n.* ( 另外 ) 可採用的方法;
   另一個選擇】

You only have one choice. 【第二常用】
( 你只有一個選擇。)
You can only choose this. 【第六常用】
( 你只能選擇這個。)【choose〔tʃuz〕*v.* 選擇】

There's no other choice. 【第三常用】
( 沒有別的選擇。)
There's no other alternative. 【第五常用】
( 沒有別的選擇。)

BOOK 12

5. ***I won't let you go***.

這句話的意思是「我不會讓你走。」(= *I'm not going to let you go.*) 可以加長為:I won't let you go until you eat with us. (在你和我們吃飯以前,我不會讓你走。) 或 I won't let you go without eating with us. (不和我們一起吃飯,我就不讓你走。)

I won't let you go.

【比較】 ***I won't let you go***. 【較常用】
= I will not let you go. 【常用】

下面是美國人常說的話:

***I won't let you go***. 【第一常用】
I won't let you leave. 【第二常用】
( 我不會讓你離開。)

You can't go. (你不能走。)【第三常用】
You're not free to go. 【第六常用】
( 你沒有走的自由。)【free〔frɪ〕*adj.* 自由的】

I'm going to hold you here. 【第四常用】
( 我要把你留在這裡。)
I'm going to keep you here. 【第五常用】
( 我要把你留在這裡。)
【hold〔hold〕*v.* 把…留在~　keep〔kip〕*v.* 使停留】

6. ***I won't take no for an answer.***
   take〔 tek 〕*v.* 接受（＝*accept*）

   　　這句話字面的意思是「我不會接受『不』作爲回答。」（＝*I won't accept no for an answer.*）引申爲「我一定要你答應。」，美國人也常説：I'm not going to let you say no.（我不會讓你說「不」。）或 I don't want to hear you say no.（我不想聽到你説「不」。）也有美國人説：I won't let you say no.（我不會讓你説「不」。）I won't allow you to say no.（我不允許你説「不」。）或 You can't say no.（你不能説「不」。）【allow〔 ə'laʊ 〕*v.* 允許】

7. ***Don't make me beg.***
   beg〔 bɛg 〕*v.* 請求；懇求

   　　這句話是幽默的話，意思是「不要讓我求你。」也可説成：Don't make me beg you. 意思相同，因爲 beg 是及物和不及物兩用動詞。可以加長爲：Don't make me have to beg you.（不要讓我必須求你。）最幽默的説法是：***Please don't make me get down on my knees and beg you.***（請不要讓我跪下來求你。）
   （＝*Please don't make me kneel down and beg you.*）
   knee〔 ni 〕*n.* 膝蓋　　***get down on*** *one's* ***knees*** 跪在地上
   kneel〔 nil 〕*v.* 跪下；跪著　　***kneel down*** 跪下

   　　***Don't make me beg.*** 中的 make 可改成 force，説成：Don't force me to beg.（不要強迫我求你。）
   【force〔 fors 〕*v.* 強迫】

8. **Do it for me**.

> 這句話的主要意思是「為我做吧。」在這裡引申為
> 「幫我一個忙吧。」( = *Do it as a favor to me.* ) 可加
> 長為：I want you to do it for me. ( 我要你幫我一個
> 忙。)

下面是美國人常說的話：

**Do it for me**. 【第一常用】
Do it for a good friend. 【第三常用】
　( 為了一個好朋友而做吧。)
Do it for our friendship. 【第四常用】
　( 為了我們的友誼而做吧。)【friendship〔'frɛndʃɪp〕n. 友誼】

Do it as a favor to me. 【第二常用】
　( 做這件事吧，算是幫我一個忙。)
Do it to make me happy. 【第六常用】
　( 為了使我高興而做吧。)
Do it because we're friends. 【第五常用】
　( 做吧，因為我們是朋友。)【favor〔'fevɚ〕n. 恩惠；幫忙】

9. **It would mean a lot to me**.
mean〔min〕v. 意思是；有某種重要性
**mean a lot** 非常重要

> 這句話的意思是「這件事會對我很重要。」源自：*If
> you agreed*, it would mean a lot to me. ( 如果你同
> 意，這件事會對我很重要。) 可加強語氣說成：It would
> really mean a lot to me. ( 這件事真的會對我很重要。)
> 可以把 to me 放在前面，說成：To me, it would
> mean a lot. ( 對我來說，這件事會很重要。)

## 【對話練習】

1. A：**Please stay for dinner**.

    B：I would love to.

    I would like that a lot.

    Thank you for the invite.

    【*a lot* 非常

    　invite〔ˈɪnvaɪt〕*n.* 邀請】

A：請留下來吃晚餐。

B：我很樂意。

我很樂意那麼做。

謝謝你的邀請。

2. A：**Do me the honor**.

    B：You flatter me.

    It's my honor, not yours.

    I really mean it.

    【flatter〔ˈflætɚ〕*v.* 奉承；恭維】

A：給我面子。

B：你太過獎了。

這是我的榮幸，而不是你的。

我是說真的。

3. A：**Let's break bread together**.

    B：That sounds great.

    That's a wonderful idea.

    Let's have a nice meal

    together.

A：我們一起吃飯吧。

B：聽起來很棒。

真是個好主意。

我們一起好好吃頓飯吧。

4. A：**You have no choice**.

    B：What can I say?

    You don't have to force me.

    It would be my pleasure.

    【pleasure〔ˈplɛʒɚ〕*n.* 榮幸】

A：你沒有選擇的餘地。

B：我能說什麼呢？

你不必強迫我。

這是我的榮幸。

BOOK 12

5. A：**I won't let you go**.

B：You are crazy.
You're so funny.
I guess I have no choice.
【guess〔gɛs〕*v.* 猜想
funny〔'fʌnɪ〕*adj.* 好笑的】

A：我不會讓你走。

B：你瘋啦。
你很好笑。
我想我是沒有選擇的
餘地。

6. A：**I won't take no for an answer**.

B：I won't say no.
I can't say no.
Your offer is too nice to
refuse.【offer〔'ɔfə〕*n.* 提議】

A：我一定要你答應。

B：我不會說「不」。
我不能說「不」。
你的提議好到令人無
法拒絕。

7. A：**Don't make me beg**.

B：Don't be silly.
You don't have to beg.
You know I will agree.
【silly〔'sɪlɪ〕*adj.* 愚蠢的】

A：不要讓我求你。

B：別傻了。
你不需要求我。
你知道我會同意的。

8. A：**Do it for me**.

B：Why should I?
What have you ever done
for me?
You can do it yourself.

A：幫我一個忙吧。

B：我為什麼應該幫忙？
你曾為我做過什麼
嗎？
你自己可以做。

9. A：**It would mean a lot to me**.

B：I feel the same way.
It means a lot to me, too.
It's important to me.

A：這件事會對我很重要。

B：我有同感。
它也對我很重要。
它對我很重要。

# 9. *Let me make a toast.*

| | |
|---|---|
| *Let* me make a toast. | 讓我來敬酒吧。 |
| *Let*'s have a drink together. | 我們一起喝一杯吧。 |
| Here's to a fantastic future! | 爲了美好的未來乾杯！ |
| | |
| *May you* always be happy! | 祝你永遠快樂！ |
| *May you* always be lucky! | 祝你永遠幸運！ |
| *May you* live to be a hundred! | 祝你活到一百歲！ |
| | |
| Cheers! | 乾杯！ |
| Bottoms up! | 乾杯！ |
| Down the hatch! | 乾杯！ |

\*\* ──────────────

toast〔tost〕*n.* 乾杯；敬酒
*have a drink* 喝一杯（尤指酒）
*Here's to⋯!*【敬酒時説】爲⋯乾杯！；祝⋯快樂、健康！
fantastic〔fæn'tæstɪk〕*adj.* 極好的
future〔'fjutʃɚ〕*n.* 未來　　may〔me〕*v.* 但願⋯；祝⋯
happy〔'hæpɪ〕*adj.* 快樂的；幸福的
lucky〔'lʌkɪ〕*adj.* 幸運的　　cheers〔tʃɪrz〕*interj.* 乾杯
bottom〔'batəm〕*n.* 底　　*Bottoms up!* 乾杯！
hatch〔hætʃ〕*n.*（船的）艙口（蓋）
*Down the hatch!* 乾杯！

BOOK 12

## 【背景説明】

　　美國人和中國人一樣，吃飯時有敬酒的習慣，特別是快吃完飯前。有了下面九句話，你就會被人認爲是説英文高手了。

1. ***Let me make a toast.***

toast〔tost〕*n.* 乾杯；敬酒

　　toast 的主要意思是「吐司」，在這裡作「乾杯；敬酒」解。

　　***make a toast***（乾杯；舉杯祝賀）【第一常用】
　= give a toast 【第三常用】
　= propose a toast 【第二常用】
　= offer a toast 【第四常用】
　【propose〔prə'poz〕*v.* 提議　offer〔'ɔfɚ〕*v.* 提供；提議】

　　中國人説「乾杯」，不一定乾杯；但是美國人説 make a toast 等，也並不是要把酒喝完，而是隨意。

　　***Let me make a toast.*** 的意思是「讓我來敬酒吧。」可加長爲：Please let me make a toast to you.（請讓我來敬你。）【句中的 to you 可説成 for you】

Let me make a toast.

BOOK 12

下面都是美國人常説的話：

***Let me make a toast.*** 【第三常用】

Allow me to make a toast. 【第四常用】

（讓我來敬酒。）【allow〔əˋlaʊ〕v. 允許；讓】

I'd like to make a toast.（我想要敬酒。）【第一常用】

I want to make a toast.（我想要敬酒。）【第二常用】

【比較】下面兩句話意思不同：

***Let me make a toast.*** 【一個人向他人敬酒】

（讓我來敬酒吧。）

Let's make a toast. 【建議大家一起乾杯】

（= *Let's make a toast together.*）

（我們一起乾杯吧。）

2. ***Let's have a drink together.***

***have a drink*** 喝一杯

　　have a drink 是「喝一杯」，可能指酒，也可能指任何飲料。這句話的意思是「我們一起喝一杯吧。」可簡化爲：Let's drink together.（我們一起喝吧。）可加強語氣説成：Let's you and I have a drink together.（讓我們兩個一起喝一杯吧。）（= *Let's the two of us have a drink together.*）

【比較】下面兩句話意思不同：

***Let's have a drink together.*** 【在餐桌上説的】

Let's get a drink together. 【提議到外面喝一杯】

（= *Let's go somewhere to get a drink together.*）

（我們一起去喝一杯吧。）

下面是美國人常說的話，我們按照使用頻率排列：

① ***Let's have a drink together.*** 【第一常用】

② **Let's share a drink together.** 【第二常用】
（我們一起喝一杯吧。）【share〔ʃɛr〕 *v.* 分享】

③ **Let's raise our glasses together.**
（我們一起乾杯吧。）

④ **Let's raise our glasses in friendship.**
（我們友好地乾杯吧。）

raise〔rez〕 *v.* 舉起
***raise*** *one's* ***glass*** 舉杯；乾杯
friendship〔'frɛndʃɪp〕 *n.* 友誼；友好
***in friendship*** 友好地；親熱地

3. ***Here's to a fantastic future!***
***Here's to…!*** （敬酒時說）為…乾杯！；祝…快樂、健康！
fantastic〔fæn'tæstɪk〕 *adj.* 極好的
future〔'fjutʃɚ〕 *n.* 未來

　　這句話源自：Here's a drink to a fantastic future for all of us!（這杯酒要祝我們大家有極好的未來！）

　　***Here's to a fantastic future!*** 的意思是「為了美好的未來乾杯！」(= ***Here's to a wonderful future!*** ) 句中的 fantastic 可用 excellent〔'ɛkslənt〕 *adj.* 極好的、great（很棒的）、marvelous〔'mɑrvləs〕 *adj.* 很棒的，和 tremendous〔trɪ'mɛndəs〕 *adj.* 極好的 等字取代。

如果只對一個人，你可以說：Here's to a
fantastic future for both of us!（祝我們兩人有美
好的未來！）如果對兩個以上的人敬酒，就要說成：
Here's to a fantastic future for everyone here!
（祝在場的每一個人都有美好的未來！）【for everyone
here 可說成 for all of us here】

下面三句話，是美國人敬酒時喜歡說著玩的順口溜：

> Here's to you and here's to me.
> I hope we never disagree.
> But if we do, the hell with you and
> here's to me.

（敬你，也敬我。我希望我們兩個人永遠
　不會意見不合。但是如果我們意見不合
　時，我才不管你，我敬我自己。）

disagree〔ˌdɪsə'gri〕*v.* 意見不合
***the hell with you*** 我才不管你
（= *I don't care about you*）【詳見 "Talkin' American"】

4. ***May you always be happy!***

may〔me〕*aux.* 但願…；祝…
happy〔'hæpɪ〕*adj.* 快樂的；幸福的

「May＋主詞＋原形動詞！」形成「祈願句」。
***May you always be happy!*** 的意思是「祝你永遠快
樂！」（= *May you have happiness!*）可簡化為：
May you be happy!（祝你快樂！）
【happiness〔'hæpɪnɪs〕*n.* 快樂；幸福】

BOOK 12

可加長爲：May you always be happy in the future!（祝你未來永遠幸福!）或 May you always be happy, healthy, and wealthy!（祝你永遠快樂、健康，又富有!）

May you always be happy!

【healthy〔'hɛlθɪ〕*adj.* 健康的　wealthy〔'wɛlθɪ〕*adj.* 有錢的】

5. ***May you always be lucky!***
lucky〔'lʌkɪ〕*adj.* 幸運的

這句話的意思是「祝你永遠幸運!」（= *May you always have good luck!*）可加長爲：May you always be lucky all your life!（祝你一生永遠幸運!）

【all your life（你一輩子）是副詞片語，不可說成：*in all your life*】美國人也常說成：I wish you good luck forever.（我祝你永遠幸運。）【wish 作「祝福」解時，是授與動詞。　forever〔fə'ɛvə〕*adv.* 永久地】

6. ***May you live to be a hundred!***

這句話的意思是「祝你活到一百歲!」（= *I hope you live to be a hundred!*）a hundred 可以說成 one hundred、a hundred years old，或 one hundred years old。

在餐桌上，美國人流行的開玩笑的敬酒話是：May you be in heaven a half an hour before the devil knows you're dead.（祝你在魔鬼知道你死掉以前，已經在天堂待半小時了。）

【heaven〔'hɛvən〕*n.* 天堂　devil〔'dɛvl〕*n.* 魔鬼】

7. *Cheers!*

cheers〔tʃɪrz〕*interj.* 乾杯

　　　cheer 的主要意思是「使高興」，在這裡是感嘆詞，作「乾杯」解時，要用複數形。因為喝酒會使你感到高興 ( *Drink will make you feel cheerful.* )。這句話可加長為：*Cheers,* drink up! ( 乾杯，喝完！) 或 Let's drink, *cheers!* ( 我們喝酒吧，乾杯！) cheers 做感嘆詞時，可當作插入語。

8. *Bottoms up!*

bottom〔'batəm〕*n.* 底　　*Bottoms up!* 乾杯！

　　　這句話的字面意思是「底在上面！」引申為「乾杯！」此時的「乾杯」，是真正的喝完。美國人通常喝啤酒，杯子較大，並不像中國人一樣，喝完以後，會把杯底朝上 ( turn the glass upside down )，表示喝完。*Bottoms up!* 可加長為：Come on, bottoms up! ( 趕快，乾杯！)( = *Come on.  Bottoms up!* )

【come on ( 趕快 ) 在句中可當作插入語】

下面都是美國人敬酒時常說的話：

　　　*Bottoms up!*【第一常用】
　　　Drink up!【第二常用】
　　　　( 喝完！；乾杯！)
　　　【*drink up* 喝完】

BOOK 12

Drink it all!（全部喝完！；乾杯！）【第三常用】
Drink it all up!（全部喝光！；乾杯！）【第八常用】

Drink every bit!【第六常用】
（每一滴都喝完！；乾杯！）
Drink every drop!【第五常用】
（每一滴都喝完！；乾杯！）
Drink the whole thing!【第九常用】
（把全部都喝完！；乾杯！）

bit〔bɪt〕*n.* 少量　drop〔drɑp〕*n.* 滴
***the whole thing*** 全部

Finish it all!（全部喝完！；乾杯！）【第四常用】
Don't leave a drop!【第七常用】
（要一滴都不剩！；乾杯！）
【finish〔ˈfɪnɪʃ〕*v.* 喝光　leave〔liv〕*v.* 留下】

9. ***Down the hatch!***
hatch〔hætʃ〕*n.*（船的）艙口（蓋）
***Down the hatch!*** 乾杯！

hatch 的主要意思是「（船的）艙口」或「艙口蓋」。當船隻航行，遇到暴風雨的時候，就要把通往船艙的艙口蓋關起來，通常船員會大喊：Close the hatch!（把艙口蓋關起來！）以免雨往下流進船艙（*to prevent the rain from going down the hatch*）。天氣好的時候，就會把艙口蓋（hatch）打開。

boat hatch

　　美國人説話很幽默，把嘴巴、喉嚨比喻成 hatch，嘴巴像是「艙口」，喉嚨像是「樓梯」，***Down the hatch!*** 的意思是「乾杯!」、「喝完!」但是，美國人喝酒時，不説：*Down the mouth!*（誤）或 *Down the throat!*（誤）

　　美國人習慣把 Cheers!　Bottoms up! 和 ***Down the hatch!*** 一起説，就像我們中國人所説的：「乾杯!乾杯!乾杯!」他們也常説：Here's to you. ***Down the hatch!***（敬你。乾杯!）或 Here's to us. ***Down the hatch!***（敬我們大家。乾杯!）

下面也是美國人敬酒時常説的話：

May you always be healthy, wealthy and wise.

（祝你永遠健康、富有，而且聰明。）

I wish you all the best.

（我祝你萬事如意。）【詳見 p.168-169】

I wish you great happiness.（我祝你非常幸福。）

【wise〔waɪz〕*adj.* 聰明的】

May God bless you always.

（願上帝永遠保佑你。）

May God bless you each and every day.

（願上帝每一天都保佑你。）

bless〔blɛs〕*v.* 祝福；保佑
always〔ˈɔlwez〕*adv.* 永遠地
***each and every*** 每一個

BOOK 12

## 【對話練習】

1. A：**Let me make a toast.**　　　　　A：讓我來敬酒吧。
   B：Go right ahead.　　　　　　　　　B：請便。
   　　I am all for it.　　　　　　　　　　我完全贊成。
   　　Let's do it.　　　　　　　　　　　我們敬酒吧。
   　　【for〔fɔr〕*prep.* 贊成】

2. A：**Let's have a drink together.**　　A：我們一起喝一杯吧。
   B：That's a great idea.　　　　　　　B：眞是個好主意。
   　　Let's drink together.　　　　　　　我們一起喝吧。
   　　What shall we drink to?　　　　　我們該爲什麼而乾杯？
   　　【*drink to* 爲…而乾杯】

3. A：**Here's to a fantastic future!**　　A：爲了美好的未來乾杯！
   B：Good choice.　　　　　　　　　　B：好的選擇。
   　　Let's have a happy future.　　　　讓我們擁有幸福的未來吧。
   　　Let's drink to our future　　　　讓我們爲未來的成功而乾
   　　success.　　　　　　　　　　　　杯吧。

4. A：**May you always be happy!**　　A：祝你永遠快樂！
   B：The same to you.　　　　　　　　B：也同樣祝福你。
   　　I hope you're always　　　　　　我希望你永遠快樂。
   　　happy.
   　　I hope God always blesses　　　我希望上帝永遠保佑你。
   　　you.

5. A : **May you always be lucky!**

   B : That's what I need.

      I need lots of luck.

      I appreciate your wish.

      【luck〔lʌk〕*n.* 運氣

         appreciate〔ə'priʃɪˌet〕*v.* 感激

         wish〔wɪʃ〕*n.* 願望；祈求的事】

A：祝你永遠幸運！

B：那正是我需要的。

   我需要很多運氣。

   我感激你的祝福。

6. A : **May you live to be a hundred!**

   B : And may all your dreams
      come true.

      It's been an honor to be in
      your presence.

      You are a gentleman and a
      scholar.

      【*in one's presence* 有某人出席】

A：祝你活到一百歲！

B：那就祝你所有的夢想
   都能實現。

   你肯出席，我眞的很
   榮幸。

   你是個紳士，也是個
   學者。

7. A : **Cheers!**

   B : Cheers to you, too.

      God bless you.

      Have a happy life.

A：乾杯！

B：你也乾杯。

   願上帝保佑你。

   祝你擁有幸福的生活。

8. A : **Bottoms up!**

   B : No problem.

      I'll drink it all.

      I'm drinking to honor you.

      【honor〔'ɑnɚ〕*v.* 向～表示敬意】

A：乾杯！

B：沒問題。

   我會把它全部喝完。

   我喝酒向你表示敬意。

9. A : **Down the hatch!**

   B : OK, here I go.

      Here's to you.

      Drink every single drop.

      【single〔'sɪŋgl〕*adj.* 單一的】

A：乾杯！

B：好的，我乾了。

   敬你。

   要把每一滴都喝完。

BOOK 12

# 10. *Let's take a snapshot*.

| | |
|---|---|
| *Let's* take a snapshot. | 我們照張相吧。 |
| *Let's* get a photo together. | 我們一起照張相吧。 |
| It'll be a nice memory. | 它將會是美好的回憶。 |
| | |
| Could you please take our picture? | 能不能請你替我們照張相？ |
| My camera is easy to operate. | 我的相機容易操作。 |
| Just press this button. | 只要按這個按鈕。 |
| | |
| Hold still. | 不要動。 |
| Strike a pose. | 擺出一個姿勢。 |
| Smile and say cheese. | 微笑，並且說 cheese。 |

\*\* ————————————

snapshot〔'snæp,ʃɑt〕*n.* 快照；照片
photo〔'foto〕*n.* 相片　　memory〔'mɛmərɪ〕*n.* 記憶；回憶
*take one's picture* 替某人照相
camera〔'kæmərə〕*n.* 照相機　　operate〔'ɑpə,ret〕*v.* 操作
press〔prɛs〕*v.* 按；壓　　button〔'bʌtṇ〕*n.* 按鈕
hold〔hold〕*v.* 維持　　still〔stɪl〕*adj.* 靜止的；不動的
strike〔straɪk〕*v.* 擺出　　pose〔poz〕*n.* 姿勢
cheese〔tʃiz〕*n.* 起司　　*say cheese* 說 cheese；笑一個

## 【背景説明】

　　無論在室内或户外，要和別人一起照相的時候，就可以使用這九句話。

1. ***Let's take a snapshot.***
　snapshot〔'snæpˌʃɑt〕*n.* 快照；照片（= *photograph*）

> 　　在 1970 年代，即可拍相機（instamatic camera）非常流行，只要一照，照片就「立刻」（in a snap）可以出來。snap 本來的意思是「捏手指發出劈啦聲」，當叫別人快一點時，就可說 Snap to it!（趕快！）【詳見「教師一口氣英語」p.8–7】shot 的主要意思是「射擊」，在這裡是指「照相」。snapshot 字面的意思是「趕快射擊」，在 1970 到 80 年代，引申爲「快照」（instant picture）。現在由於使用很頻繁，直接可以當成「照片」解。

　　***Let's take a snapshot.*** 的意思就是「我們照張相吧。」（= *Let's take a picture.*）可加強語氣説成：Let's you and I take a snapshot together.（我們兩個人一起照張相吧。）***Let's take a snapshot.*** 可簡化爲：Let's take a shot.

Let's take a snapshot.

（我們照張相吧。）【比較常用】

下面都是美國人常説的話：

Let's take a picture. 【第一常用】
（我們照張相吧。）
Let's take a photo. 【photo = photograph】
（我們照張相吧。）【第四常用】
*Let's take a snapshot.* 【第七常用】
【*take a picture* 拍照（= *take a photo*）】

Let's get a picture. （我們照張相吧。）【第二常用】
Let's get a photo. （我們照張相吧。）【第五常用】
Let's get a snapshot. （我們照張相吧。）【第八常用】

How about a picture? （照張相如何？）【第三常用】
How about a photo? （照張相如何？）【第六常用】
How about a snapshot? （照張相如何？）【第九常用】

2. *Let's get a photo together.*
photo〔'foto〕*n.* 相片（= *photograph*）

　　這句話的意思是「我們一起照張相。」（= *Let's
get a picture together.*）如果很多人一起照，可加
強語氣說成：Let's get a photo of us all together.
（我們全部一起照張相吧。）如果強調「我們兩個」，
就可說：Let's get a photo of the two of us
together. （我們兩個人一起照張相吧。）或 Let's
you and I get a photo together. （我們兩個人一起
照張相吧。）

「照相」的成語很多，常用的如下：

┌ take a picture【第一常用】          ┌ get a shot【第十常用】
= take a snapshot【第九常用】        = get a picture【第二常用】
└ = take a photograph【第八常用】    └ = get a photo【第五常用】

┌ = have a picture【第三常用】       ┌ = get a photograph【第六常用】
└ = have a picture taken           └ = get a picture taken

　　　【第四常用】                        　　　【第七常用】

【shot〔ʃɑt〕*n.* 攝影；照片　shot 和 snapshot 通用，photo 和
　　photograph 通用，但 shot 和 photo 都比較常用。】

## 3. *It'll be a nice memory.*

memory〔'mɛmərɪ〕*n.* 記憶；回憶

　　　　這句話的字面意思是「它將會是美好的回憶。」
It 在此指「照片」( The photo )，所以，在此可引申
爲「照片將會是美好的回憶。」( = *The photo will be
a nice memory.* )

　　　　It'll 由於是 It will 的縮寫，所以很多人唸成
( 一 ㄠˊ )，應該唸成〔'ɪtl̩〕才對，這個唸法和
little〔'lɪtl̩〕的字尾發音相同。凡是在字音下面有
一點，是表示可把前面的 /ə/ 省略或保留，所以，
〔'ɪtl̩〕也可寫成〔'ɪtəl〕。

　　　　可加強語氣説成：It will be a very nice
memory.（它將會是非常美好的回憶。）可加長爲：
It will be a nice memory for us to keep.（它將會
是我們能夠保存的美好回憶。）或 It will be a nice
future memory.（它將會是未來美好的回憶。）
　　【future〔'fjutʃɚ〕*adj.* 未來的】

BOOK 12

4. ***Could you please take our picture?***
***take one's picture*** 替某人照相

　　這句話的意思是「能不能請你替我們照張相？」
也可說成：Would you please take our picture?
（你願不願意替我們照張相？）或 Would you mind
taking our picture, please? （你介不介意幫我們照
張相，好嗎？）【mind〔maɪnd〕*v.* 介意】比較禮貌的
説法是：Excuse me, but could you please take
our picture? （對不起，能不能請你替我們照張相？）
【I'm sorry 或 Excuse me 後面常接 but，此時 but 沒有意
思，不用翻。】

　　take our picture 也
可説成：take a picture
for us，成爲：Could
you please take a
picture for us? （能不
能請你替我們照張相？）

【比較】

> 用 could 是假設法，表示説話者認爲不該問，所
> 以比較有禮貌。
>
> ***Could you please take our picture?*** 【較有禮貌】
> Can you please take our picture? 【一般語氣】
> （能不能請你替我們照張相？）

5. ***My camera is easy to operate.***

camera〔'kæmərə〕*n.* 照相機
operate〔'ɑpə,ret〕*v.* 操作

　　這句話的意思是「我的相機容易操作。」可加長
為：Don't worry.  My camera is very easy to
operate.（別擔心。我的相機非常容易操作。）或
It's no problem.  My camera is easy to operate.
（沒問題。我的相機容易操作。）

下面是美國人常説的話：

***My camera is easy to operate.***【第一常用】
This camera is easy to operate.【第五常用】
（這台相機容易操作。）
My camera is easy to use.【第二常用】
（我的相機容易使用。）

My camera is simple to use.【第三常用】
（我的相機容易使用。）
This camera is simple to use.【第六常用】
（這台相機容易使用。）
My camera is simple to operate.【第四常用】
（我的相機容易操作。）
【simple〔'sɪmpḷ〕*adj.* 簡單的；容易的】

Anyone can operate this camera.【第七常用】
（任何人都會操作這台相機。）
Anyone can use this camera.【第八常用】
（任何人都會使用這台相機。）

BOOK 12

6. ***Just press this button****.*

press〔prɛs〕*v.* 壓;按　　button〔'bʌtn̩〕*n.* 按鈕

　　　這句話的意思是「只要按這個按鈕。」(= *Only press this button.*) 可以加強語氣説成:Just press this button down. (只要按下這個按鈕。) 或 Just press this button right here. (只要在這裡按這個按鈕。) 可加長爲:All you have to do is just press this button. (你所要做的只是按這個按鈕。) 或 Just press this button to take a picture. (只要按這個按鈕照相。)

*button*

7. ***Hold still****.*

hold〔hold〕*v.* 繼續保持;維持
still〔stɪl〕*adj.* 靜止的;不動的

　　　hold 的主要意思是「抓住」,在此作「維持;保持」解。still 的主要意思是「仍然」,在此作「靜止的」解。這句話字面的意思是「保持靜止。」引申爲「不要動。」(= *Don't move.*) 可以客氣地説:Please hold still. (請不要動。) 可加強語氣説成:Hold perfectly still. (完全不要動。)
【perfectly〔'pɝfɪktlɪ〕*adv.* 完全地 (= *completely*)】可以加長爲:Hold still while I take this picture. (我照相時不要動。) 或 Hold still for the picture. (不要動,才照得好。)

下面是美國人常說的話：

**Hold still.**【第一常用】

Be still.（不要動。）【第五常用】

Freeze.（不准動。）【第三常用】

【freeze〔friz〕*v.* 呆立不動】

Freeze!

Don't move.（不要動。）【第二常用】

Don't move a muscle.【第四常用】

（完全不要動。）

Don't make any movements.【第六常用】

（不要動。）

move〔muv〕*v.* 移動；使移動
muscle（'mʌsḷ）*n.* 肌肉
**not move a muscle** 一動也不動
movement（'muvmənt）*n.* 動作；移動
**make a movement** 動了一下

8. **Strike a pose.**

strike〔straɪk〕*v.* 裝出；擺出
pose〔poz〕*n.* 姿勢　*v.* 擺姿勢

　　strike 的主要意思是「打擊」，在此作「擺出」解。
**Strike a pose.** 的意思是「擺出一個姿勢。」由於 pose
也可以當動詞，作「擺姿勢」解，所以，這句話也可
說成：Pose.（擺個姿勢。）美國人也常說：Strike a
pose now.（現在擺個姿勢。）( = *Pose now.*）當對方
擺好姿勢，就可以說：Hold that pose.（保持那個姿
勢。）【hold〔hold〕*v.* 使保持】

BOOK 12

【比較】 自己造句很危險：

> ***Strike a pose.*** ( 擺個姿勢。)【正】
>
> *Make a pose.* 【誤，中式英文】
>
> *Do a pose.* 【誤，中式英文】
>
> *Put a pose.* 【誤，中式英文】

美國人在照相時，常擺的姿勢有下面五種：

① 照相者說： Smile. ( 微笑。)

　　　　　　 Give a smile. ( 笑一個。)

　　　　　　 Give me a smile. ( 給我笑一個。)

② 照相者說：

　　 Put your arms around each other.

　　 ( 把手臂放在彼此的肩上。)

　　 Put your arms on each other's shoulders.

　　 ( 把手臂放在彼此的肩膀上。)

　　 【shoulder〔'ʃoldə〕 *n.* 肩膀】

③ 照相者說： Give a thumbs-up.  One hand.

（比個豎起大拇指的手勢。用一隻手。）

Give a thumbs-up.  Both hands.

（比個豎起大拇指的手勢。用兩隻手）

thumb〔θʌm〕*n.* 大拇指

thumbs-up〔'θʌmz͵ʌp〕*n.* ( 表示贊成或滿意的 ) 翹拇指

④ 照相者說： Give the peace sign.

（做出一個象徵和平的手勢。）

Peace. ( 比象徵和平的手勢。)

Make the peace sign.

（做出象徵和平的手勢。）

Show the peace sign.

（做出象徵和平的手勢。）

sign〔saɪn〕*n.* 手勢　 peace〔pis〕*n.* 和平
show〔ʃo〕*v.* 表現；露出

BOOK 12

⑤ 照相者説：

Give a number one sign.
（比一個豎起食指的手勢。）
Give me a number one sign.
（給我一個豎起食指的手勢。）

　　美國人不習慣用兩隻手的食指比 number one
的手勢。豎起大拇指（thumbs-up）是表示高興
（happy）、情況很好（Things are great.）。豎起
食指則是表示「第一名」，這和中國文化不同。

9. ***Smile and say cheese.***
　　cheese〔tʃiz〕*n.* 起司　　***say cheese*** 説 cheese；笑一個

> 　　這句話的意思是「微笑，並且説 cheese。」美國
> 人照相時，喜歡説 Smile.（微笑。）或 Say cheese.
> （説 cheese；笑一個。）因爲説 cheese 的時候，嘴
> 巴會咧開，像笑一樣。

　　這句話可加長爲：It's time to smile and say
cheese.（該是微笑，説 cheese 的時候了。）或 Don't
forget to smile and say cheese.（不要忘了微笑，
並且説 cheese。）這句話也可以倒過來，説成：Say
cheese and smile.（説 cheese，並微笑。）

## 【對話練習】

1.  A : **Let's take a snapshot**.

    B : That's a super idea.

    Let's do it right now.

    Let's get everyone together.

    【super〔ˈsupɚ〕*adj.* 極好的】

    A : 我們照張相吧。

    B : 眞是個很棒的主意。

    我們現在就照吧。

    我們叫大家聚在一起吧。

2.  A : **Let's get a photo together**.

    B : I would like that a lot.

    That would be very nice.

    That would be something to

    remember today by.

    A : 我們一起照張相吧。

    B : 我很樂意。

    那樣很好。

    那樣就能有東西可以記

    住今天了。

3.  A : **It'll be a nice memory**.

    B : I totally agree.

    Pictures are nice memories.

    One picture is worth a

    thousand words.

    【worth〔wɝθ〕*adj.* 値…的】

    A : 它將是好的回憶。

    B : 我完全同意。

    照片是很好的回憶。

    一張照片值一千個字；

    千言不如一畫。

4.  A : **Could you please take our
    picture?**

    B : Sure thing.

    Just tell me how.

    How do I use this?

    A : 能不能請你替我們照張

    相？

    B : 當然可以。

    只要告訴我怎麼照。

    我要如何使用這個？

**BOOK 12**

5. A：**My camera is easy to operate**.　　A：我的相機容易操作。

　B：It's so small.　　　　　　　　B：它很小。

　　It looks complicated.　　　　　　它看起來很複雜。

　　Which button do I press?　　　　我要按哪個按鈕？

　【complicated (ˈkɑmpləˌketɪd ) *adj.*
　　複雜的】

6. A：**Just press this button**.　　　　A：只要按這個按鈕。

　B：And then what?　　　　　　　　B：然後呢？

　　Is that all there is?　　　　　　就那樣？

　　I can't believe it's so simple.　　我真不敢相信就這麼
　　　　　　　　　　　　　　　　　　簡單。

7. A：**Hold still**.　　　　　　　　　A：不要動。

　B：Is this OK?　　　　　　　　　　B：這樣可以嗎？

　　Are we all in the picture?　　　　我們都有拍進去嗎？

　　Do we need to move closer?　　　我們需要更靠近嗎？

8. A：**Strike a pose**.　　　　　　　A：擺出一個姿勢。

　B：Formal or informal?　　　　　　B：正式或非正式的？

　　Let's just be natural.　　　　　　我們自然就好。

　　Let's just relax and smile.　　　　我們就放輕鬆，並且
　　　　　　　　　　　　　　　　　　微笑吧。

　【formal (ˈfɔrml̩ ) *adj.* 正式的
　　informal ( ɪnˈfɔrml̩ ) *adj.* 非正式的】

9. A：**Smile and say cheese**.　　　　A：微笑，並且說 cheese。

　B：Give us a one, two, three.　　　B：要跟我們說一、二、三。

　　We don't want to be surprised.　我們不要覺得驚訝。

　　We are ready.　　　　　　　　　我們準備好了。

# 11. *Don't leave yet*.

| | |
|---|---|
| ***Don't*** leave yet. | 現在不要離開。 |
| ***Don't*** go so soon. | 不要這麼早走。 |
| Stay and talk some more. | 留下來再多聊一些。 |
| | |
| What's ***the*** rush? | 急什麼？ |
| Why ***the*** hurry? | 爲什麼要這麼匆忙？ |
| Where's ***the*** fire? | 急什麼？ |
| | |
| It's ***still*** early. | 時間還早。 |
| The night is ***still*** young. | 天色還不是很晚。 |
| You've got lots of time. | 你有很多時間。 |

**

yet〔jɛt〕*adv.* 現在　　soon〔sun〕*adv.* 早；快
stay〔ste〕*v.* 停留　　rush〔rʌʃ〕*n.* 匆忙
hurry〔'hɝɪ〕*n.* 匆忙　　fire〔faɪr〕*n.* 火災
young〔jʌŋ〕*adj.* 尚早的
***you've got*** 你有（= *you have*）　　***lots of*** 很多

## 【背景説明】

當你的朋友要離開，你想留他多待一會兒，就可以説下面九句話。

1. ***Don't leave yet.***

yet〔jɛt〕*adv.* 現在

> yet 的主要意思，用在否定句中，作「尚（未）」解，在這裡，yet 是副詞，作「現在」解（= *now*；*at this time*；*for the present*）。此種用法很多，例如：
>
> Are you through *yet*?（你現在做完了嗎？）
> ( = *Are you through now?* )
> 【through〔θru〕*adj.* 完成的；結束的】
> I'm not sure I can go *yet*.
> ( = *I'm not sure I can go now.* )
> （我不確定我現在可以走。）
>
> Don't eat *yet*.（現在不要吃。）
> ( = *Don't eat now.* )
> Don't sing *yet*.（現在不要唱歌。）
> ( = *Don't sing now.* )

***Don't leave yet.*** 這句話的意思是「現在不要離開。」( = *Don't leave now.* ) 可加強語氣説成：Don't leave just yet.（現在不要離開。）( = *Don't leave just now.* )【*just yet* 現在 ( = *just now* )】或 I don't want you to leave yet.（我不想要你現在離開。）

leave 也可當及物動詞，説成：Don't leave me yet.（現在不要離開我。）或 Don't leave us yet.（現在不要離開我們。）美國人也常説：Don't go yet.（現在不要走。）(= *Don't go now.*) 或 Don't go just yet.（現在不要走。）(= *Don't go just now.*) 有些人喜歡説：You can't leave yet.（你現在不能走。）(= *You can't leave now.*)

## 2. *Don't go so soon.*

soon〔sun〕*adv.* 早；快

這句話的意思是「不要這麼早走。」soon 可以作「快」或「早」解，在這裡作「早」解。可加長爲：You don't have to go so soon.（你不需要這麼早走。）或 I hope you don't go so soon.（我希望你不要這麼早走。）叫別人不要走，也可以只説：Don't go.（不要走。）或加上一句，説成：It's early.  Don't go.（時間還早。不要走。）叫別人不要那麼早回家，可説成：Don't go home so soon.（不要那麼早回家。）(= *Don't go home so early.*)

## 3. *Stay and talk some more.*

這句話的意思是「留下來，再多聊一些。」可以加長爲：Stay here and talk some more with me.（留在這裡，和我多聊一些。）可以簡化成：Stay and talk.（留下來聊天。）或 Stay and talk with me.（留下來和我聊天。）也可加強語氣説成：Don't go.  You can stay and talk some more.（不要走。你可以留下來多聊聊。）【stay〔ste〕*v.* 停留】

talk 可用 chat 來代替，說成：Stay and chat some more. ( 留下來多聊一些。)【chat〔tʃæt〕v. 聊天】

下面是美國人常說的話：

***Don't go so soon.***【第二常用】
Don't leave so soon.【第一常用】
( 不要這麼早離開。)

Don't go so early.【第四常用】
( 不要這麼早走。)
Don't leave so early.【第三常用】
( 不要這麼早離開。)

You don't need to go so soon.【第六常用】
( 你不需要這麼早走。)
You don't need to leave so soon.【第五常用】
( 你不需要這麼早離開。)

4. ***What's the rush?***
rush〔rʌʃ〕n. 匆忙；急迫

這句話的意思是「急什麼？」可以加強語氣說成：What's the big rush? ( 怎麼這麼急？) 或 What's the reason for the rush? ( 為什麼這麼急？)【reason〔'rizn〕n. 理由】the rush 可以說成 your rush，成為：What's your rush? ( 你急什麼？)

美國人也常說：Why are you in a rush? ( 你為什麼匆匆忙忙？) 或 Why are you in such a rush? ( 你為什麼這麼急？)【*in a rush* 匆忙】

5. ***Why the hurry?***

hurry〔'hɜɪ〕*n.* 匆忙；急忙

　　　　這句話的意思是「爲什麼要這麼匆忙？」是慣用句，源自：***Why*** do you feel ***the*** need to be in such a ***hurry***?（爲什麼你覺得有必要這麼匆忙？）我們可以把「Why + the + 名詞？」翻成「爲什麼要～？」例如：Why the gift?（爲什麼要送我禮物？）源自：***Why*** do you feel ***the*** need to give me a ***gift***?（爲什麼你覺得有必要送我禮物？）Why the angry look?（爲什麼你看起來那麼生氣？）源自：***Why*** do you feel ***the*** need to give such an ***angry look***?（爲什麼你覺得有必要看起那麼生氣？）

【look〔luk〕*n.* 臉色；樣子　give〔gɪv〕*v.* 做；顯示出】

　　***Why the hurry?*** 可以加強語氣說成：Why the big hurry?（爲什麼要那麼匆忙？）或 Tell me why the big hurry.（告訴我爲什麼要那麼匆忙。）

下面各句意思相同，使用頻率很接近：

　***Why the hurry?***【第四常用】

= What's the hurry?（急什麼？）【第二常用】

= Why the rush?（爲什麼那麼匆忙？）【第三常用】

= What's the rush?（急什麼？）【第一常用】

= Why are you in a hurry?【第六常用】
　（你爲什麼匆匆忙忙？）

= Why are you in a rush?【第五常用】
　（你爲什麼匆匆忙忙？）

BOOK 12

6. **Where's the fire?**

fire〔faɪr〕*n.* 火災

> 　　這句話字面的意思是「哪裡有火災?」是修辭疑
> 問句,此時肯定的疑問句等於否定的敘述句【詳見
> 「文法寶典」p.4】。
>
> **Where's the fire?**
>
> (哪裡有火
> 災?)引
> 申的意思是「沒有火
> 災。」( = *There's no*
> *fire.* )再引申為「沒有
>
> 緊急的事件。」( = *There's no emergency.* )
> 【emergency〔ɪˈmɝdʒənsɪ〕*n.* 緊急情況】也就是「沒有
> 理由那麼急。」( = *There's no reason to be in a*
> *hurry.* )因此,**Where's the fire?** 可翻成「急什
> 麼?」( = *What's the hurry?* )這是美國人常喜歡
> 說的幽默話,一般字典上找不到,只有在 "Talkin'
> American" p.359 中有。

Where's the fire?

7. **It's still early.**

　　It 指「時間」,這句話的意思是「時間還早。」
( = *The time is still early.* )可加強語氣說成:
It's still very early. (時間還非常早。)可加長
為:It's still early right now. (現在時間還早。)
【*right now* 現在】或 I think it's still early. (我認
為時間還早。)也有美國人說:

　　　　　It's early. (時間還早。)
　　　　　It's too early. (時間還太早。)
　　　　　It's not late. (時間還不晚。)

8. *The night is still young.*

young〔jʌŋ〕*adj.* 尚早的

　　young 的主要意思是「年輕的」，在這裡是指「尚早的」。這句話的意思是「夜尚未深。」也就是「天色還不是很晚。」(= *It is still early in the evening.*) 也可只說：The night is young. (還不晚。) 美國人不說：*The night is old.* (誤) 如果已經很晚，美國人習慣說：It's late in the evening. (已經很晚了。) 字典上常看到的 The night is yet young. (夜尚未深。) 美國人較少說。

9. *You've got lots of time.*

*you've got* 你有 (= *you have*)　　*lots of* 很多

　　這句話的意思是「你有很多時間。」(= *You have lots of time.*) 可簡化為：You have time. (你有時間。) 可加強語氣說成：You've still got lots of time. (你仍然有很多時間。) 可加長為：You've got lots of time left. (你還剩下很多時間。) (= *You have more time left.*)【left〔lɛft〕*adj.* 剩下的】

【比較】下面三句話意思相同：

　　　You've got *lots of* time.【第一常用】

　　= You've got *a lot of* time.【第三常用】

　　= You've got *plenty of* time.【第二常用】

　　　【*plenty of* 很多】

## 【對話練習】

1. A：**Don't leave yet.**

    B：I must go.
    It's getting late.
    I have no choice.
    【choice〔tʃɔɪs〕*n.* 選擇】

    A：不要現在走。

    B：我必須走。
    時間很晚了。
    我沒有選擇的餘地。

2. A：**Don't go so soon.**

    B：I'm afraid I have to.
    I have no more time.
    I have something else to do.

    A：不要這麼早走。

    B：恐怕我必須早走。
    我沒時間了。
    我還有別的事情要做。

3. A：**Stay and talk some more.**

    B：Just ten more minutes.
    Then I have to go.
    I'm sorry, but I can't stay.

    A：留下來，再多聊一些。

    B：只能再十分鐘。
    然後我就必須走了。
    很抱歉，我不能留下來。

4. A：**What's the rush?**

    B：I have a lot to do.
    My time is limited.
    I'm afraid I won't finish
    everything.
    【limited〔ˈlɪmɪtɪd〕*adj.* 有限的】

    A：急什麼？

    B：我有很多事要做。
    我的時間有限。
    我怕沒把所有的事做完。

5. A : **Why the hurry?**

   B : It's getting late.

   I can't be late.

   I have to be there on time.

   【*on time* 準時】

6. A : **Where's the fire?**

   B : I have a meeting to attend.

   It's a business appointment.

   It's very important for my

   company. 【attend〔ə'tɛnd〕*v.* 參加

   appointment〔ə'pɔɪntmənt〕*n.* 約會】

7. A : **It's still early**.

   B : It is early.

   I still have to go.

   I'll stay later next time.

   【*next time* 下一次】

8. A : **The night is still young**.

   B : It's still early.

   We have plenty of time.

   Let's have fun.

9. A : **You've got lots of time**.

   B : Don't say that, please.

   You are tempting me.

   I really must be going.

   【tempt〔tɛmpt〕*v.* 誘惑】

A : 爲什麼要這麼匆忙？

B : 時間很晚了。

我不能遲到。

我必須準時去那裡。

A : 急什麼？

B : 我有會議要參加。

那是商務約會。

那對我的公司非常

重要。

A : 時間還早。

B : 是很早。

我還是必須走。

下次我會留晚一點。

A : 天色還不是很晚。

B : 時間還早。

我們有很多時間。

我們好好玩吧。

A : 你有很多時間。

B : 請別那麼說。

你是在誘惑我。

我眞的必須走了。

BOOK 12

# 12. *Thanks for coming*.

| | |
|---|---|
| ***Thanks for*** coming. | 謝謝光臨。 |
| ***Thanks for*** being my guest. | 謝謝你來作客。 |
| It was nice seeing you. | 看到你眞好。 |
| | |
| It's been delightful. | 我們在一起一直很愉快。 |
| *I* enjoyed every minute. | 我每一分鐘都快樂。 |
| *I* hate to see you go. | 我眞不願意看你走。 |
| | |
| Let's meet more often. | 我們要更常見面吧。 |
| Don't be a stranger. | 不要不連絡。 |
| Stay healthy, happy, and safe. | 希望你保持健康、快樂，和平安。 |

**

guest〔gɛst〕 *n.* 客人
delightful〔dɪ'laɪtfəl〕 *adj.* 愉快的；令人高興的
enjoy〔ɪn'dʒɔɪ〕 *v.* 喜歡；享受
hate〔het〕 *adj.* 眞不願意
stranger〔'strendʒɚ〕 *n.* 陌生人　　stay〔ste〕 *v.* 保持
healthy〔'hɛlθɪ〕 *adj.* 健康的　　safe〔sef〕 *adj.* 安全的

【背景説明】

　　當你的客人要走，或你在餐廳請客吃飯後，做主人的你，站在門口，該和客人說什麼呢？

1. ***Thanks for coming***.

　　這句話的意思是「謝謝光臨。」( = *Thank you for coming.* ) 可加長為：
Thanks so much for coming today. ( 非常謝謝你今天的光臨。) 或
Thanks so much for

coming here to see me. ( 非常謝謝你來這裡看我。)

　　如果純請別人吃飯，就可説：Thanks so much for coming here for dinner. ( 非常謝謝你來這裡吃晚餐。)

2. ***Thanks for being my guest***.
guest〔gɛst〕*n.* 客人

　　這句話的意思是「謝謝你來作客。」可加長為：
Thanks for being my guest here today. ( 謝謝你今天來這裡作客。) 或 I want to say thanks for being my guest today. ( 我想謝謝你今天來做客。)
be my guest 字面的意思是「做我的客人」，還有「我請客」的意思。【詳見 p.519-520】

BOOK 12

3. **It was nice seeing you.**

  這句話的意思是「看到你眞好。」常簡化爲：
Nice seeing you. (看到你眞好。) 可加長爲：It
was so nice seeing you here today. (今天在這
裡看到你眞好。) 原則上，在開始見到朋友的時
候，可說：**It's nice to see you.** (見到你眞好。)
(=*Nice to see you.*) 和朋友告別時，可說：**It
was nice seeing you.** (看到你眞好。)

4. **It's been delightful.**

  delightful〔dɪ'laɪtfəl〕*adj.* 愉快的；令人高興的

  這句話字面的意思是「它一直是令人愉快的。」
It 在此是指「我們在一起的時間」(The time we
spend together)〔spend〔spɛnd〕*v.* 渡過〕，所以，引
申的意思是「我們在一起一直很愉快。」可簡化爲「一
直很愉快。」或「很愉快。」加強語氣時，可說成：It
has been delightful. 意思相同。delightful 可換成
great (很棒的)、wonderful (很棒的)、marvelous
〔'mɑrvləs〕*adj.* 很棒的、fantastic〔fæn'tæstɪk〕*adj.*
很棒的 或 tremendous〔trɪ'mɛndəs〕*adj.* 很棒的。

*It's been delightful.* 可説成：

It's been a delightful
- experience.
- time.
- memory.
- day.

這是很愉快的
- 經驗。
- 時間。
- 回憶。
- 日子。

【memory〔'mɛmərɪ〕*n.* 回憶；記憶】

*It's been delightful.* 可加長爲：It's been delightful seeing you today.（今天看到你很愉快。）或 It's been delightful getting together with you.（和你聚會很愉快。）【*get together* 聚會】

*It's been delightful.* 在這裡不能説成：*It's delightful.* 因爲「現在式」在這裡是表示「現在正在」；表示「從過去到現在」，要用「完成式」形式。但是可用 It was delightful. 因爲説話者認爲，拜訪已經結束，強調在一起的期間，我們過得很愉快。

---

【比較】下面兩句話用法不同：

It's delightful.（很愉快。）
　【「現在式」在此表示「現在正在」，因爲 be 動詞沒有進行式，不可説成：*It's being delightful.*（誤）】

*It's been delightful.*（一直很愉快。）
　【「現在完成式」，表示「已經完成」】

BOOK 12

【例1】　A：How do you like your job?

　　　　　　　（你覺得你的工作怎麼樣？）

　　　　　B：It's delightful.（很愉快。）

　　　　【*How do you like*～? 你喜不喜歡～?；你覺得～如何?】

【例2】　A：How's your job so far?

　　　　　　　（你的工作到目前為止如何？）

　　　　　B：*It's been delightful.*（一直很愉快。）

　　　　【*so far* 到目前為止】

5. *I enjoyed every minute.*

enjoy〔ɪn'dʒɔɪ〕v. 享受；喜歡

　　　　這句話字面的意思是「我享受了每一分鐘。」
引申為「我每一分鐘都快樂。」可加長為：I really
enjoyed every minute with you here today.
（我真的喜歡今天在這裡和你共渡的每一分鐘。）

【比較】*I enjoyed every minute.*【正】

　　　　*I liked every minute.*【誤】

　　　　【這是中式英文，時間應是「享受」（enjoy）的，
　　　　而不是「喜歡」（like）的】

美國人喜歡用 *enjoy*，像：

I *enjoy* being with you.（我喜歡和你在一起。）

I *enjoy* talking with you.（我喜歡和你談話。）

I *enjoy* spending time with you.

　　　　（我喜歡和你在一起。）

BOOK 12

6. ***I hate to see you go.***

hate〔het〕*v.* 恨；真不願意

> 美國人用 hate 很普遍，但常不表示真的恨，我
> 們在 p.341-342 中，有詳細的說明。***I hate to see you***
> ***go.*** 的意思是「我真不願意看你走。」可以加強語氣
> 說成：I really hate to see you go home so soon.
> （我真的不願意看到你這麼早回家。）美國人也常說
> 成：I hate to see you
> leave. （我真不願意看你
> 離開。）或 I don't want
> you to go. （我不想讓你
> 走。）（= *I don't want you*
> *to leave.* )

I don't want you to go.

7. ***Don't be a stranger.***

stranger〔'strendʒɚ〕*n.* 陌生人

> 這句話字面的意思是「不要成為一個陌生人。」
> 引申為「不要變成不認識我。」（= *Don't become like*
> *a stranger to me.* ）或「不要不連絡。」（= *Keep in*
> *touch.* ）【*keep in touch* 保持連絡】

***Don't be a stranger.*** 可加長為：Don't be a
stranger and disappear. （不要消失不連絡。）或
Keep in touch with me. ***Don't be a stranger.***
（要跟我保持連絡。不要不連絡。）
【disappear〔ˌdɪsə'pɪr〕*v.* 消失】

BOOK 12

下面是美國人再見的時候常說的話：

**Don't be a stranger.**【第一常用】

Don't forget to keep in touch.【第六常用】

（不要忘記要保持連絡。）

Don't forget to call me.【第五常用】

（不要忘記要打電話給我。）

Keep in touch. （要保持連絡。）【第二常用】

Contact me often.【第三常用】

（要常跟我連絡。）

Drop me a line.【第四常用】

（要寄--封短信給我。）

*Don't be a stranger.*

contact〔'kɑntækt〕*v.* 和…連絡

line〔lain〕*n.* 短信

**drop** *sb.* **a line** 寄給某人一封短信

### 8. *Let's meet more often.*

这句話的意思是「我們要更常見面吧。」more
often 是 often 的比較級，表示「更常」。可加長爲：
Let's meet more often in the future. （我們以後要
更常見面吧。）或 Let's try to meet more often. （我
們儘量更常見面吧。）可簡化爲：Let's meet often.

（我們常見面吧。）或 Let's meet *more*. （我們要更
常見面吧。）在此 more 是 a lot（常常）的比較級。
美國人也說：Let's meet a lot. （我們常見面吧。）
雖然在字典上，often 的比較級也寫成 *oftener*，但美
國人極少用。

下面是美國人常說的話：

> ***Let's meet more often.*** 【第一常用】
>
> Let's get together more often. 【第三常用】
>
> （我們要更常聚在一起。）
>
> Let's e-mail each other more often. 【第五常用】
>
> （我們要更常互相寄電子郵件。）
>
> ***get together*** 聚在一起
> e-mail〔'i,mel〕*v.* 寄電子郵件給～（= *email*）

> We should meet more often. 【第二常用】
>
> （我們應該更常見面。）
>
> I hope we can meet more often. 【第四常用】
>
> （我希望我們可以更常見面。）

9. ***Stay healthy, happy and safe.***

stay〔ste〕*v.* 保持　　healthy〔'hɛlθɪ〕*adj.* 健康的
safe〔sef〕*adj.* 安全的

　　這句話是命令句，命令句除了表達命令以外，有時還可表示「希望」【詳見「文法寶典」p.358】。

　　***Stay healthy, happy, and safe.*** 在這裡的意思是「希望你保持健康、快樂，和平安。」（= *I hope you stay healthy, happy, and safe.* ）可加長為：Until we meet again, stay healthy, happy, and safe.（在我們下次見面以前，你都要保持健康、快樂和平安。）【until〔ən'tɪl〕*conj.* 到…為止（一直）】

【比較】 stay 可改成 keep 或 remain：

***Stay healthy, happy, and safe.*** 【第一常用】
= Keep healthy, happy, and safe. 【第二常用】
= Remain healthy, happy, and safe. 【第三常用】
【remain〔rɪ'men〕*v.* 保持】

下面都是美國人道別時常說的話：

***Stay healthy, happy, and safe.*** 【第一常用】
I wish you health, happiness, and safety.
（我祝你健康、快樂，和平安。）【第七常用】
【wish 作「祝福」解，是授與動詞】

May you stay healthy, happy, and safe.
（祝你保持健康、快樂，和平安。）【第二常用】
May your life be healthy, happy,
　　and safe. 【第三常用】
（祝你的生活健康、快樂，和平安。）

I hope everything goes well for you. 【第六常用】
（我希望你一切順利。）
I hope you stay healthy and well. 【第四常用】
（我希望你保持健康及順利。）
I hope you stay safe and sound. 【第五常用】
（我希望你一直安然無恙。）

***go well*** 順利　　well〔wɛl〕*adj.* 圓滿的；順利的
***safe and sound*** 安然無恙

## 【對話練習】

1. A：**Thanks for coming**.

　 B：Thank you for having me.
　　 I enjoyed it so much.
　　 I hope I can come again.
　　 【*have sb.* 邀請某人過來】

　　　A：謝謝光臨。

　　　B：謝謝你邀請我來。
　　　　 我非常喜歡這次的聚會。
　　　　 我希望能再來。

2. A：**Thanks for being my guest**.

　 B：It was my pleasure.
　　 You are a great host.
　　 Please be my guest next
　　 time. 【pleasure〔'plɛʒɚ〕*n.* 榮幸
　　　 host〔hɔst〕*n.* 主人】

　　　A：謝謝你來作客。

　　　B：這是我的榮幸。
　　　　 你是個很棒的主人。
　　　　 請下次來當我的客人。

3. A：**It was nice seeing you**.

　 B：Yes, it was such a lovely
　　 night.
　　 It was great to get together.
　　 Let's do it again soon.
　　 【lovely〔'lʌvlɪ〕*adj.* 愉快的】

　　　A：看到你真好。

　　　B：是啊，今天晚上真是愉
　　　　 快。
　　　　 能聚在一起真棒。
　　　　 我們儘快再聚一下吧。

4. A：**It's been delightful**.

　 B：The pleasure was all mine.
　　 Thank you for a lovely time.
　　 I'm eternally grateful.
　　 【eternally〔ɪ'tɜnlɪ〕*adv.* 永遠地
　　　 grateful〔'gretfəl〕*adj.* 感激的】

　　　A：我們在一起一直很愉快。

　　　B：這是我的榮幸。
　　　　 謝謝你讓我覺得很愉快。
　　　　 我會永遠心存感激。

BOOK 12

5. A : **I enjoyed every minute**.

   B : I had fun, too.
   It was a super time.
   You are the reason why.
   【*have fun* 玩得愉快
   super〔'supɚ〕*adj.* 很棒的】

A：我每一分鐘都快樂。

B：我也玩得很愉快。
這段時間眞棒。
都是因爲你的緣故。

6. A : **I hate to see you go**.

   B : I hate to go.
   I wish I could stay.
   I really enjoy being with
   you.

A：我眞不願意看你走。

B：我眞不願意走。
我眞希望可以留下來。
我眞的很喜歡和你在
一起。

7. A : **Let's meet more often**.

   B : Let's meet regularly.
   What do you say?
   When are you free to visit me?
   【regularly〔'rɛgjələlɪ〕*adv.* 定期地】

A：我們要更常見面吧。

B：我們定期見面吧。
你覺得如何？
你何時有空可以來我
這裡玩？

8. A : **Don't be a stranger**.

   B : Don't worry, I won't.
   I'll keep in touch.
   I promise to call you soon.

A：不要不連絡。

B：別擔心，我不會的。
我會保持連絡。
我保證很快就會打給你。

9. A : **Stay healthy, happy, and
   safe**.

   B : I wish the same for you.
   Take care in everything you do.
   May God bless you every day.
   【*take care* 小心】

A：希望你保持健康、快
樂，和平安。

B：我希望你也一樣。
做任何事都要小心。
願上帝每天都保佑你。

BOOK 12

# 「一口氣背會話」經 BOOK 12

唸英文要像唸經一樣，每天大聲唸，從起床到睡覺，唸得比看得快，最後不看也會唸，養成習慣後，你會全身舒爽，你試試看，奇妙無比。

1. Come visit me.
   Pay me a visit.
   Call on me anytime.

   *Drop* in whenever.
   *Drop* by when you can.
   Feel free to stop by.

   I'm inviting you now.
   My door is always open.
   Don't keep me waiting too long.

2. Come on in.
   Step right inside.
   Here is a pair of slippers.

   Have a seat.
   Sit down and relax.
   Make yourself at home.

   You got here OK.
   How was the traffic?
   Any trouble finding this place?

3. My home is your home.
   Help yourself to anything.
   There's lots of stuff in the fridge.

   It's a little messy.
   Please don't mind the clutter.
   We're pretty informal around here.

   Wanna use the bathroom?
   It's just down the hall.
   The switch is next to the door.

4. What a scorcher!
   *It's* boiling outside.
   *It's* hotter than hell.

   This weather is so humid.
   *It's* so sticky.
   *It* makes me sweat like crazy.

   I don't mind dry heat.
   It's the humidity I can't stand.
   The air is so damp and wet.

5. So, tell me your news.
   How have you been?
   Have you been keeping busy?

   *Are you* working hard these days?
   *Are you* staying out of trouble?
   Do you like what you're doing?

   I want to hear everything.
   *Don't* skip a thing.
   *Don't* leave anything out.

6. *Don't get* me wrong.
   *Don't get* the wrong idea.
   I don't want you to misunderstand.

   *Don't* get mad.
   *Don't* take it seriously.
   I didn't mean anything by it.

   *I was just* kidding.
   *I was just* joking around.
   You know that's my style.

7. I'd like you to meet my wife.
*She's* my better half.
*She's* the brains of the family.

*She* runs the house.
*She*'s an exceptional cook.
I'd be lost without her.

*She's* a jack-of-all-trades.
*She's* an angel in disguise.
I couldn't ask for more.

8. Please stay for dinner.
Do me the honor.
Let's break bread together.

You have no choice.
*I won't* let you go.
*I won't* take no for an answer.

Don't make me beg.
Do it for me.
It would mean a lot to me.

9. *Let* me make a toast.
*Let*'s have a drink together.
Here's to a fantastic future!

*May you* always be happy!
*May you* always be lucky!
*May you* live to be a hundred!

Cheers!
Bottoms up!
Down the hatch!

10. *Let's* take a snapshot.
*Let's* get a photo together.
It'll be a nice memory.

Could you please take our picture?
My camera is easy to operate.
Just press this button.

Hold still.
Strike a pose.
Smile and say cheese.

11. *Don't* leave yet.
*Don't* go so soon.
Stay and talk some more.

What's *the* rush?
Why *the* hurry?
Where's *the* fire?

It's *still* early.
The night is *still* young.
You've got lots of time.

12. *Thanks for* coming.
*Thanks for* being my guest.
It was nice seeing you.

It's been delightful.
*I* enjoyed every minute.
*I* hate to see you go.

Let's meet more often.
Don't be a stranger.
Stay healthy, happy, and safe.

剛開始背「一口氣背會話」，也許困難一點。只要堅持下去，一旦學會背快的技巧，就能一冊接一冊地背下去。每一冊108句中英文背到兩分鐘之內，就變成直覺，終生不會忘記，唯有不忘記，才能不斷地累積。

# 美國口語精華 1,296 句索引

※ 每一句話都可以主動對外國人説。

索
引

索引

索
引

索
引

索引

索引

索
引

索
引

本書由「一口氣英語⑦～⑫」合訂而成。
強調中英文一起背，改書名爲「一口氣背
會話下集⑦～⑫」。

## 一口氣背會話下集 ⑦～⑫
## The One Breath English Collection

書＋CD一片 售價：580元

| | |
|---|---|
| 主　　　編／劉　毅 | |
| 發　行　所／學習出版有限公司 | ☎ (02) 2704-5525 |
| 郵 撥 帳 號／05127272 學習出版社帳戶 | |
| 登　記　證／局版台業 2179 號 | |
| 印　刷　所／裕强彩色印刷有限公司 | |
| 台 北 門 市／台北市許昌街 17 號 6F | ☎ (02) 2331-4060 |
| 台灣總經銷／紅螞蟻圖書有限公司 | ☎ (02) 2795-3656 |
| 本公司網址　www.learnbook.com.tw | |
| 電 子 郵 件　learnbook@learnbook.com.tw | |

2020 年 7 月 1 日新修訂 ( 本書改編自「一口氣英語⑦～⑫」)

ISBN 978-986-231-142-4

# 編者的話

親愛的讀者：

　　現在學英文非常簡單，用「手機」就可以學了。我50多年教學的精華，都會在「快手」中播放，歡迎大家模仿我。在課堂上，教我「快手」上的作品，馬上變成名師，學生會愈來愈多，也歡迎在線上模仿我，期待青出於藍而勝於藍！用我研發的教材，最安全，經過層層的校對。一定要學從美國人嘴巴裡說出來的話，且自己每天也能脫口而出。

　　學會話的方法是：一口氣說出三句話，我們要背就背最好的，例如：「由你決定。」最好的三句英文是：You're the boss. 字面的意思是「你是老闆。」You call the shots. （你發號施令，我開槍射擊。）Your wish is my command. （你的希望就是你的我的命令。）當你一口氣說這三句幽默的話，任何人都會佩服你。我花費了好幾年的功夫，才把這三句話累積在一起，人人愛聽！

　　英文不使用，就會忘記！「使用、使用、再使用」，教自己「背過」、「使用過的」句子，有靈魂、有魅力，是上網教學的最高境界！網路上，有網路紅人亂造句子，亂說一通，太可怕了！期待他盡快撤下來。人最怕「吃錯藥」、「學錯東西」。

# 「英文順口溜」一口氣說三句，特別好聽

「快手」和「抖音」是大陸的兩個大平台，有80多萬中外英文老師在發表作品，我每天上午和下午各發表一次。如果「作品」不被人接受，馬上就會被淘汰。

以前，我從來沒有想到，會有這個機會，把我50多年來上課的精華，在手機上發表。過去大家用文法自行造句、自行寫文章，太可怕了！我們問過100多位英文老師：「這裡是哪裡？」大家都翻成：Where is here?（誤）應該是：Where am I? 或 Where are we? 才對。同樣地，「我喜歡這裡。」不能說成 I like here.（誤）要說：I like it here. 才正確。這種例子不勝枚舉！結論：背極短句最安全。

我們發明「英文順口溜」，一口氣說三句，創造了優美的語言，說出來特別好聽。說一句話沒有感情，一口氣說：I like it here. I love it here. This is my kind of place.（我喜歡這裡。我愛這裡。這是我喜歡的地方。）三句話綁在一起，隨口就可說出，多麼令人感到溫暖啊！

今天鍾藏政董事長傳來好消息，我在「抖音」上的粉絲已經超過20萬人了。感謝「小芝」充當攝影師，感謝「北京101名師工廠」讓我一輩子的心血，能夠發光發亮，「劉毅英文」全體的努力當然功不可沒。我們一定要持續努力，來感謝大家的支持。

# 讓我們幫助你成為說英文高手

　　「英文順口溜」即將出版！一切以「記憶」和「實用性」為最優先。以三句為一組，一開口，就是三句話，說出來非常熱情，有溫度。

　　例如：你已經會說："Thank you." 「英文順口溜」教你："Thank you. I appreciate it. I owe you."（謝謝你。我很感謝。我虧欠你。）我們不只在學英文，還在學「口才」，每天說好聽的話，人見人愛。

　　又如："It's my treat. It's on me. Let me pay."（我請客。我請客。讓我來付錢。）學英文不忘發揚中國人好客的文化。一般人道歉時，只會說："I'm sorry." 背了「英文順口溜」，你會說："I'm sorry. I apologize. It's my fault."（對不起。我道歉。是我的錯。）先從三句開始，會愈說愈多，你還可以加上三句："I was wrong. You are right. Please forgive me."（我錯了。你是對的。請原諒我。）

　　「英文順口溜」先在「快手」和「抖音」上教，大家可以在「手機」上免費學。我受益很多，期待分享給所有人！

掃描下載快手APP

# 下載「快手」及「抖音」，免費學「英文順口溜」

　　原來，「說一口流利的英語」是最漂亮的衣服、成功的象徵（a sign of success），苦練出來的英文最美。（The most beautiful English is learned through hard work.）

　　現在，用我們新發明的「英文順口溜」，靠手機APP「快手」就可以輕鬆背好，一口氣說出來，很有信心。例如，一般美國人再見時多說："Bye!" 我們會說："See you soon. See you around. Have a good one."（待會見。回頭見。祝你有美好的一天。）中文要改變語言不容易，但是利用學英文的機會訓練口才，變成體貼、熱情、感恩的人，只要背我們研發的「英文順口溜」，一定可以做到！

　　說話是一種藝術，需要認真學習，說話代表你的「修養、教育、人品」。叫別人不要遲到，不要說："Don't be late. Don't make me wait."（不要遲到。不要讓我等。）可以說：I'll be there on time. On the dot. On the nose.（我會準時到。會準時。非常準時。）成功的人，說話更要客氣、有禮貌，不能讓你身邊的人有壓力。

劉毅